# FIORENZO

## SEBASTIAN NOTHWELL

# CONTENTS

Cover illustration by Jan of Thistle Arts Studio.
Cover design by Kelley of Sleepy Fox Studio.

Thank you to Emma, Felix, Rachel, Sierra, and Zéphyr
for their support and encouragement in making this book possible.

# CONTENT WARNINGS

- vague allusions to past CSA
- the CSA will never be made more explicit than these vague allusions
- references to SA
- the SA itself occurs off-page
- however, the lead-up to the SA and the aftermath of the SA occur on the page
- graphic gore, including...
- hunting scenes, including animals being hurt and/or dying
- fight scenes, some ending in death
- surgeries, some traumatic to the awake patient
- hand mutilation
- genital mutilation
- wound aftercare
- death of parents (past, referenced)
- plague/pandemic (past, referenced)

## HISTORICAL ACCURACY AND OTHER NOTES

While the realm of Halcyon is loosely inspired by the history and culture of the Venetian Republic, there are a multitude of marked and deliberate differences. The most glaring of these are as follows...

- a wildly different religion;
- different attitudes towards gender and sexuality;
- simplified currency;
- a different system of government;
- borrowing of artistic tradition, costume, and cuisine from other parts of the Italic Peninsula and elsewhere on the continent;
- certain liberties taken with geography;
- certain other liberties taken with the art and science of fencing;
- still more liberties taken with the timeline of Western medical science;
- extreme liberties taken with the history of dance;
- the alleged historical poison cantarella has no definitive modern real-world equivalent and if it did it probably wouldn't resemble the poison as used in this story;
- and finally, there may be dragons.

To the author's best knowledge there is no real-world human intersex condition that resembles the creative anatomy appearing in this novel. The fictional character(s) who have this creative anatomy are not intersex. Out of respect for real intersex people the author would prefer these fictional characters not be referred to as intersex in reviews, discussions, or recommendations.

# CHAPTER ONE

C rowds flooded the streets and canals surrounding the dry-docked ship. This, despite the icy winter wind that threatened to spill snow into the lagoon surrounding the city. The paper lanterns strung from windowsill to windowsill across every street, canal, and alleyway defied the evening's darkness. Likewise the music of fiddles, lutes, pipes, tambourines, and raucous human voices defied any gloom. It was the final night of Saturnalia, and the people of Halcyon intended to make the most of it—Fiore among them.

Fiore, a young man of twenty summers, leaned against the railing on the upper deck of the *Kingfisher*, which he called his home. The ship had run aground about a century earlier. Captain Corelli, lacking the funds to make it seaworthy again, had left it ashore and turned it into a tavern. She had willed it to her daughter, also called Corelli, who in turn willed it to her daughter, the third Corelli, who generously let a chamber below-decks to Fiore by the week for his lodging and trade alike.

Tonight, Fiore wore a mask—most holy days in the city required at least a token mask—but his was a mere black-paper domino that covered a slender two inches or so around his eyes and little else. To cover anything more wouldn't serve his purpose.

His clothes didn't cover much, either. He had his breeches and hose, of course. Above the waist, however, he'd untied his shirt-collar's laces so the deep plunging neck opened to expose the dark hair over his bronzed chest. He didn't have the brawn of some fellows, but his small and slender frame still had a particular appeal to a certain sort of gentleman whom he hoped to attract tonight. The scarlet sash around his waist removed any doubts about his trade.

Despite his lack of cloak, the winter wind hardly seemed to touch him. The sheer crush of bodies drinking, dancing, and flirting on the deck created a bonfire's worth of warmth. Fiore had counted himself amongst their number for most of the evening. However, most of the gentlemen on deck seemed more inclined towards his feminine cohorts.

And so he'd made his way to the railing for a breath of fresh air.

The view below proved just as exuberant as the celebration aboard the dry-docked ship. Boats crowded the canal like a pod of playful porpoises, hardly able to slide past each other, each carrying as many masked revelers as it could hold. The narrow fondamenta surrounding the ship itself likewise teemed with a multitude of costumes in a full prism's worth of color.

The clear night sky, the fullness of the moon, the festive lanterns, and the ever-lit aediculae on every bridge and corner combined to set the whole city aglow. It afforded Fiore a marvelous view—

Except for one particular sliver which remained in perpetual shadow.

Shadows flitted all throughout the crowd, for one could hardly have light without casting shade. But this singular shadow remained rooted to one spot. At first Fiore didn't realize why his gaze kept returning over and again to this anomaly. When his mind caught up to his eyes, however, he leaned out and squinted down for a better look at the queer phenomenon.

And realized it was not a shadow at all, but a human figure.

They stood well above the crowd swirling past them. They wore the costume of the bauta: tricorn hat, waistcoat, breeches and hose; the tabarro cloak and zendale hood; and finally the bauta mask itself, with its distinctive prominent beak obscuring everything from nose to throat. Unlike the traditional bauta, however, this particular shadow had everything in black—including the mask itself.

From this distance Fiore couldn't pick out the eyes in the black mask.

Nevertheless he met the mysterious gaze and, when he felt certain he held the bauta's attention, granted them a winning smile and a resplendent bow, arising to toss his hand carelessly over his head as he invoked, "Io Saturnalia!"

Several anonymous voices returned the cheer from the crowds both below and above. The bauta did not. They continued staring up at Fiore in silence for another moment.

Then they dropt their gaze and headed towards the ship's starboard gangplank.

Fiore watched their progress in eagerness. He hadn't really expected his proposition to work from such a distance and towards so mysterious a figure. Whoever they were, they moved with astonishing grace for someone of their stature. Not too drunk yet, if at all, which boded well for Fiore's purpose. He wearied of gentlemen who drank themselves out of performance and then blamed him for their inability to raise their masts.

Soon the bauta had surmounted the ladder and plunged into the crowded deck, whereafter Fiore beheld a particular tricorn hat bobbing well above the rest. The tide of bodies parted as the hat sailed forth, revealing in short order the full costume standing before Fiore.

Or rather, looming over him, for the figure stood at least a head taller on a long, lean, lithe frame.

With scarcely an arm's length between them, Fiore had a better look at their garb. He beheld the same hat, cloak, hood, and mask as before, but now they'd drawn near enough for him to realize the exquisite make and quality of these articles. The mask not of paper but of gleaming leather; the silken hood trimmed in black lace; the cloak's wool of so fine a weave that it seemed almost as shining smooth as the satin lining it. It matched the silver-buttoned waistcoat in black satin rather than wool. Modest sprigs of lace at the cuffs and throat of the white linen shirt beneath provided the only spots of light in an otherwise pure black costume. Black silk stockings clung to well-turned calves, and the satin breeches belied supple thighs. All this Fiore glimpsed as the figure swept their cloak aside to grant him a bow. Their commanding presence and the evident expense of their costume bespoke an aristocrat—yet, Fiore noted, not one too proud to grant courtesy to a courtesan.

"Good evening," a deep voice rumbled up from the mask's depths.

"Good evening," Fiore replied in kind. And then, because it was only polite to enquire, added, "My lord...?"

The bauta—evidently a gentleman—gave a slow and solemn nod.

"I've a room below-decks, if you have coin." Fiore found it best to state his intentions at the outset to prevent any misunderstanding, red sash or no.

The gentleman appeared in no way off-put by this revelation, though admittedly Fiore could perceive little beneath cloak, hood, and mask. "Lead on."

Fiore smiled and offered the gentleman his arm.

And after a moment's hesitation—whether reluctant, shy, or simply astonished at a courtesan's audacity, Fiore couldn't say—the bauta accepted, winding his arm through the crook of Fiore's. His touch, even through both their sleeves, surprised and delighted Fiore with its warmth.

The crowd parted before the pair of them as it'd done for the bauta alone. Fiore led the way across the deck, through the dancers and drinkers, past the bar built into the forecastle to the hatch behind it, and, with a nod to Corelli so she knew he was going below and with whom, down into the belly of the ship.

The captain's daughter had gutted the ship's hold when it became not just a tavern but an inn and brothel. A dry-docked ship, after all, required far less cargo space; just enough to store a few dozen wine-casks would suffice, as opposed to the hundreds of barrels of hard-tack, salt-cod, and fresh water a crew of sailors would need on a years-long voyage, plus whatever goods they intended to transport to or from Halcyon. Thus the floors of the living quarters had dropped down several feet and more rooms put in below them. This meant Fiore could walk quite comfortably below-decks. Even one so tall as the bauta need only duck beneath beams rather than crouch all the way through.

Likewise, unlike the sailors of old, Fiore had an entire cabin to himself, rather than sharing a berth with two-score other sailors all crammed in head-to-foot and stacked three high.

Fiore took more than a little pride in his cabin. The scarlet curtains in the porthole window—as broad in diameter as the span of Fiore's arms and well below the water-line, as if there remained any hopes that the *Kingfisher* could ever return to sea—precisely matched his own scarlet sash. Deck prisms set into its ceiling, original to the ship, gave ample light by day. By night, he had hanging lanterns scavenged from scuttled gondole, their angles softened by curling brass laurel leaves. His own sketches adorned the walls; peculiar corners of Halcyon beneath bridges and behind staircases, alongside figures and portraits of strangers and bed-fellows.

The cabin's most prominent feature was the bed, for reasons beyond even Fiore's profession. He'd cobbled it together out of the remnants of a whaleboat snapped in half by leviathan's jaws and deemed beyond repair, fit only for scrap. While he couldn't make it seaworthy again, he could remove what remained of its keel and all the planks of its hull below the water-line and use them to fill in the jagged gaps until he had what seemed like the prow of a whaleboat sailing through the floorboards and out of his wall into the center of his room. A dozen or so cross-beams sufficed to support a mattress he'd sewn into its peculiar shape.

Fiore could glean little of what the bauta thought of this chamber at first glance. But even beneath the mask and cloak, something in the gentleman's stance as he strode in at Fiore's invitation, how he turned his head to look about at all its features, and the way he laid a reverent hand on the bed's gunwales and slid his fingers up towards its prow, made Fiore think he was at least somewhat impressed.

"Now," Fiore said, shutting the door behind them with a soft thud. "How would you like me?"

They couldn't kiss if the gentleman wished to keep his mask, but he might have Fiore on his knees before him or bent over to take him from behind. Some gentlemen—more than most folks might expect and much more in line with Fiore's own preferences—wished to have Fiore inside them, and perhaps this gentleman would prove of that sort.

The gentleman hesitated. "I'm afraid you may find it strange."

Fiore doubted he would. He had a whole sea-chest of treasures ready for gentlemen who wanted him to bind, gag, switch, or flog them. To the particular gentleman standing before him tonight, he said, "Try me."

Again the gentleman hesitated. "I would like to watch you."

Fiore raised his brows. "Watch me as I...?"

"Pleasure yourself."

Easily enough done. And, as Fiore had predicted, far less strange than the gentleman supposed. He smiled. "As you wish."

A hard swallow travelled down the gentleman's slender throat.

If Fiore had read the gentleman correctly, he seemed the sort who enjoyed a bit of a tease. To that end, Fiore withdrew out of arms' reach and set his fingers to work unwinding the scarlet sash from around his waist. Some fellows liked to keep the sash as a token. Fiore charged more for that; about double the cost of its replacement. Tonight he folded it over his arms, letting the scarlet fabric flow smoothly over the back of his hands, before laying it aside across the bow of his bed for the gentleman to peruse as he wished.

The gentleman spared the sash a lingering glance. Then his dark gaze flicked back to meet Fiore's own.

Fiore bit back a knowing smirk. His fingertips fell to the buttons fastening the knees of his breeches. Then they arose to address the fall-front. This was the part that seemed to draw the interest of most fellows, and the bauta proved no exception. Fewer buttons than the waistcoat, though Fiore found a way to draw them out almost as long.

The breeches joined the sash on the bed. Their loss offered a mere glimpse of his prize before the hem of his shirt fell into place like a demure linen curtain.

Fiore bent to unfasten the garters of his hose in a manner which he knew elongated his whole frame. Some gentlemen liked to claim these as souvenirs as well, and again, Fiore felt willing enough to let them, for a price. The bauta made no mention of it, though if his hungry gaze were anything to go by, he felt sorely tempted. And if Fiore's fingertips did rather more caressing of his own calves than necessity demanded, the gentleman didn't seem to mind in the least.

Garters and hose tossed together on the bed. And at long last he drew his shirt over his head, hiding the gentleman from his view for a mere instant.

When he threw the shirt aside and met the bauta's gaze again, the sheer intensity of the longing in the stare behind the mask seemed ready to devour him.

6

A grin stole over Fiore's face. He had the gentleman in the palm of his hand, without laying a single finger on him.

Still smiling, Fiore performed a quick turn for the gentleman. Not half so elegant as a ballerino before the opera, perhaps, but graceful nonetheless and offering what he'd been told was a magnificent view. Though he had no looking-glass of his own, many of the fellows who hired him had declaimed the beauty of his behind. Several—for Fiore worked with many artists, some as a courtesan and still more as a model —had rendered it in pencil, ink, paint, or sculpture. He wasn't vain enough to ask to keep any of the resulting artworks, but he did appreciate the opportunity to see himself from another angle.

"Does this meet with your approval, signore?" Fiore asked, tossing a coy glance over his shoulder.

While Fiore couldn't see anything of the gentleman's face beyond the dark and compelling eyes, he saw plain how the whole shadowed frame had gone rigid, and it was with a certain hoarse quality that the gentleman replied, "Indeed."

Which Fiore found rather more inspiring than he'd anticipated.

And so, without further ado, he crept onto his bed and knelt atop the counterpane to face the gentleman at the prow.

Fiore smoothed his palms over the tops of his thighs as he settled into his performing posture. There was something about the bauta's evident desire for him that provoked an answering desire within him—perhaps a touch of narcissism on his own part, but so be it. Either way it meant that as he trailed his fingertips down the center of his own bare chest and over his navel through the soft nest of hair surrounding his cock, he was already at half-mast.

The gentleman's hand clenched on the prow. The long and elegant fingers within his black glove attracted Fiore's notice. He imagined how their silken grasp would feel around his prick. Another time, perhaps.

For tonight he had only his own hands.

A few slow strokes sufficed to bring him to a full stand beneath the bauta's compelling gaze. Fiore wondered if the gentleman would remark on his scars. The worst of them remained hidden by the nest of dark hair surrounding his stone-purse. The one which sliced up the left side of the mast to split his foreskin, however, refused to be hidden.

7

The gentleman's gaze lingered on the scar. Or perhaps he merely appreciated Fiore's proud stand. Regardless, he said nothing of either; just clenched and unclenched his hands against the boat's prow. Though Fiore noted a hitch in the gentleman's breath as he gave his cock a swift jerk.

Remarkable restraint, particularly when contrasted against Fiore's own wanton display. For Fiore knew what he liked. And better still, he knew how to perform.

Fiore bit his lip as he smeared the first few drops of seed across the head of his prick with the pad of his thumb. His stomach rippled as he thrust his hips up to meet his own fist. He let his throat unleash the moans the gentleman reined in. His free hand roamed wildly, smoothing over the tops of his trembling thighs and flying up to feel the pulse fluttering in his collar. And throughout all this, Fiore looked up to meet the bauta's masked gaze, then back down at himself, his lashes fluttering with each glance.

The gentleman said nothing. Nor moved, save to clench those strong hands against the wood. But his breathing grew ragged, musical to Fiore's ears, and each catch in his throat made Fiore's cock twitch.

Something about the gentleman's seething desire paired with his impeccable restraint—the thought of the lustful tides surging just behind the flood-wall of his mask—stirred Fiore's imagination. His fist moved faster and faster of its own accord. He envisioned what it might be like to lift the mask from the face and kiss whatever lips lay beneath. To slip his hands beneath the tabarro cloak and delve into the silken breeches to grasp what surely by now must be an iron rod to rival his own. To cross their blades until sparks flew behind both their eyes. To bend the gentleman's great height over the boat's bow and fuck him into oblivion.

And then his cock pulsed in his fist, and torrents of seed spilled over his knuckles as waves of pleasure wracked his body. Instinct bid him curl in on himself, all muscles tautly convulsed. But that would block the splendid view the gentleman had paid for. So instead he fell back against his mattress and let the last burst of his seed spray across his own chest.

The gloved hands clenched again. But this time the whole frame stiffened, and a choked-off gasp echoed from beneath the mask. Unless

Fiore very much mistook the matter, it seemed the gentleman had spent likewise—and all without a single touch.

Satisfaction with both his own pleasure and with a job well done sent a slow smile creeping over Fiore's lips. He raised his seed-spattered hand to his mouth to lick it clean.

The gentleman's eyes widened behind the mask's shadows.

Fiore swept up the seed from his heaving chest with his thumb and sucked it off for good measure.

A low sigh escaped the gentleman.

"Was that to your liking, signore?" Fiore murmured, breathless.

In a haggard and harrowed voice, the gentleman replied, "Quite."

Fiore grinned.

The gentleman released his drowning hold on the bowsprit at last. A steadying breath trembled though his long frame. Then he bowed and strode from the chamber, pausing just long enough to set down a few coins on Fiore's nightstand. The door thudded shut behind him.

Fiore listened to the heels clicking away down the corridor with more than professional interest. When they ceased, he roused himself from his ecstatic stupor and rolled over to his nightstand to inspect his earnings.

His set price for a solo performance was one silver ducat.

The bauta had left six gold zecchini.

Fiore stared at the coins as his mind executed rapid calculations. There was his room and board for the next few months, certainly. He'd set aside half against whatever infirmity might befall him, but even so, he'd still have enough to indulge in several small luxuries. More chalk, charcoal, and drawing paper. Proper pencils, perhaps. A new zibaldone bound in leather. He could almost taste the Crooked Anchor's chocolate even now. His head lightly spun with the windfall, as if he'd already drunk too much of it. He went to his window. A breath of fresh air only increased his giddy thrill.

Still, he retained the presence of mind to enact the proper rite.

He didn't bother untying the strings of his domino mask. It slipped off over his head with ease. Its paper construction felt light as a fallen leaf in his hands. He gave it a fond brush of his fingertips, almost wishing he could keep it as a memento of what had proved a strange but no less delightful evening.

Then he flung out his arm and cast it into the canal to join its brethren in tonight's final sacrifice to Saturn.

"Io Saturnalia," he murmured with another stolen smile.

$\sim$

Enzo had done worse things on impulse.

He'd never hired a courtesan before. On the whole he considered the experience much less sordid than others had led him to believe. Indeed, as he departed the berth, he felt more light-hearted than he had in many months. Not even the sight of Carlotta awaiting him above the hatch could sour his good mood.

Not that he blamed Carlotta in the least. She was merely doing her duty, as implied by the livery she wore—black woolen waistcoat, frock-coat, and breeches, with the embroidered crest in black thread over the waistcoat's left breast the only hint to her loyalties, and this further hidden by the frock coat's lapel. Nor did she seem to blame him for his indulgence, for the look she cast down on him from the top of the ladder appeared mild verging on indifferent. This quickly became a look she cast up at him as he ascended, for he towered over her on even ground, as he towered over most people. She fell into step behind him as he passed her. He set a course not toward the bar or the whirling dance but instead carved a path through the crowd to the gangplank leading off the ship altogether and to the gondola waiting below.

His family's gondola fleet were all shellacked a uniform shade of gleaming beetle-black which gave off the merest glinting hint of the entwined serpent carvings running down their lengths. His own particular gondola awaited him tonight, marked out by its gondolier, Ippolito, rather than by any peculiarity of its own appearance. Carlotta held the felze's heavy woolen drape open for him to enter, then followed him in. Once they'd both settled onto opposite ends of the black-leather-upholstered interior—he facing the fore of the gondola, and she facing the aft—she rapped her knuckles against the black walnut ribs overhead, and Ippolito smoothly slid the craft out to join the current of the canal. Carlotta cast her dispassionate gaze out through the latticework window. Enzo did the same on the opposing side, though his thoughts turned inward rather than toward the city still cavorting in the throes of Saturnalia's final hours.

Carlotta would of course ensure that Lucrezia heard all about Enzo's little adventure. Enzo didn't mind. Again, it was only her duty, and besides, he'd done nothing that his eldest sister or any other member of his family might disapprove of. He'd remained masked, given no one his name, and gone on his way as quietly as he'd arrived.

Most importantly, he'd carried no sword, nor had he started—or finished—any other sort of fight.

And the long, silent, lonesome gondola voyage back to his family's palazzo provided him with ample opportunity for reflection on the evening's unexpected delights.

Lucrezia had permitted him to wander the city throughout Saturnalia, with Carlotta's accompaniment. On the first night, Carlotta had stuck to him like his own shadow, following so close in his footsteps that if he spun he could never see her. By the third night, however, after he'd made it plain through his actions as well as his words that he had no intention of shaking her off his tail, she relaxed her pursuit, following a few steps or sometimes even entire yards behind him. He grew accustomed to her presence, to the point where, if he passed a certain corner and glanced over his shoulder to find her gone, he halted his own progress and waited for her to catch him up. He didn't have any particular destination, after all, or any schedule to meet. His only desire was wandering; the simple relief of going out and stretching his legs amidst novel sights and sounds after so many months spent indoors staring at the same walls and knowing only the company of family and staff. The city in the throes of Saturnalia held enough exuberance by proxy that he didn't feel the need to over-indulge himself in drink or dance or danger. Each night he betook himself to a different island and explored corners he hadn't beheld since childhood—and most not even then.

By the final night of Saturnalia, Carlotta trusted him enough that she didn't even follow him on foot, but rather took him at his word that he would keep to the canals and instead shadowed him by standing aboard his gondola alongside Ippolito and trailing through the waters behind him.

Yet as Enzo had rounded the infamous dry-docked ship and stared up at the wild throng on deck, he'd found himself arrested by the particular sight of the most beautiful man he'd ever beheld.

Even at a distance, the perfection of the masculine figure had shone plain to Enzo's eyes. The lean frame balanced against the deck-railing on lithe arms, the drapery of the pale linen shirt limned in moonlight belying the subtle musculature beneath. The scarlet sash foretold both the fellow's profession and the slender bend of his waist. Between the balusters stood a pair of legs as well-formed as if they'd been turned on the same lathe, one extended and the other cocked at the knee to throw the whole form into a casual contrapposto pose. Though the courtesan stood almost a full head shorter than most of the crowd surrounding him, he carried himself with the confidence of a man thrice his size—like an alley cat amongst hunting hounds, master of its own domain and bowing to none.

Then their eyes had met. And when the courtesan cast down the season's greeting, how could Enzo do otherwise but answer the call?

With a sidelong glance at the gondola to make sure Carlotta marked his intent and destination, he'd strode to the gangplank and began his ascent.

Finding the courtesan in the crowd felt like discovering a garnet amidst gravel. Distance, Enzo realized as he drew up to the man, had done his appearance no justice. Standing over him, he could perceive not just the beauty of his body but the delicate details of his face. The eyes, of course, commanded Enzo's notice first and foremost. They'd called to him from fathoms above and to look into them struck his very soul. Enormous, as dark as Enzo's own garb, creating deep wellsprings that nevertheless held a soft warmth which, with a glance, could spark into a blaze of passion. The face surrounding them proved likewise compelling; full lips which demanded devouring, a noble nose which came to a sharp point, cheekbones carved from marble, a jawline which begged for fingertips to stroke its well-honed edge to the tapered tip of the chin. Nonetheless for all these sharply-drawn divisions, the effect of the whole remained subtle, small, and delicate, like the thousand minute cuts in a gemstone crafting ethereal brilliance.

Amidst all this, Enzo almost forgot to greet him.

Nevertheless, the courtesan smiled in his reply.

Then, in what felt like two shakes of a sail, Enzo found himself taken below-decks.

The courtesan conducted his trade in a matter-of-fact manner that one might consider perfunctory and indifferent, were it not for the ease and charm with which he addressed Enzo. Any lingering hesitations on Enzo's part, the courtesan gently laid aside, and even Enzo's own bizarre request did not dissuade him.

And oh, how splendidly he had fulfilled that request.

The surrender of the sash alone sufficed to raise Enzo to half-mast. The sidelong glances between each garment—a fluttering lash here, a bite of the lip there—spoke almost as loud as Enzo's own pulse pounding in his ears. *I know you want this, and I know how best to give it to you.*

When all at last gave way, Enzo beheld splendor well worth the wait. The lithe, lean, slender, and supple form, thoroughly bronzed by the sun, seemed the work of a sculptor's chisel rather than nature's hand.

The courtesan had spun, giving Enzo a much-appreciated glimpse of the perfect peach of his ass, then mounted the bed. The beauty of his body didn't cease there, for his cock had a graceful upward curve with its pleasing girth tapering towards the tip. The only flaw—and Enzo hesitated to deem it a flaw, for it added significant interest for him—was the scar running from the root up through foreskin like a lightning strike parallel to underside vein. Enzo wished he might have traced it with his tongue, mask be damned.

Still more enticing than even this, however, was the courtesan's gaze. The fleeting, fluttering, ferocious glances that stopped Enzo's heart every time they met his eyes. And then, to see them forced shut as those perfect lips fell open and the lithe back arched in ecstasy to unleash a magnificent spray of seafoam which would've done Neptune himself proud.

Enzo had spent without a touch and felt not a drop of shame for it.

The mere recollection of this evening's encounter would satisfy him not just for tonight but for many nights after. Even so, he had half a mind to return to the *Kingfisher* the very next moment he could slip away.

# CHAPTER TWO

"You're headed out early," Corelli observed as Fiore came up on deck one morning a fortnight or so after Saturnalia.

Fiore cast his gaze to the heavens. "It's afternoon."

"Not by much."

"By enough." He'd calculated his chosen hour of emergence based on when the day would feel warmest. Winter would linger for some months yet.

To that end, Fiore noted how Corelli's gaze lingered on his scarlet woolen half-cape. She said nothing about it, which he knew from experience meant she felt satisfied it would keep him warm enough to wander the fogged streets. While she made no pretense of motherly or even matronly feeling towards him, she did have a vested pecuniary interest in keeping him alive and well, which he appreciated. She kept an eye on whoever he took down into his berth and tracked his comings and goings alone or with strangers. To do less would endanger one of the more popular attractions her tavern had to offer.

Corelli resumed swabbing the deck. "Where're you off to?"

"The Crooked Anchor," Fiore replied. "Then down to Artemisia's."

"Again?" drawled a familiar voice from behind him.

Fiore turned to find Serafina, his fellow courtesan, emerging from the hatch. She'd wrapped herself in her scarlet silk robe patterned with dark blue swallows.

"You'll hardly find a wealthy patron in a sculptor's studio," Serafina continued, sailing past him towards the bar. It wasn't open this early in the day. That had never stopped her.

"Artemisia deals exclusively with wealthy patrons," Fiore countered.

"Yes," Serafina conceded. She dipped an arm beneath the bar and emerged with a glass, which she filled from one of the tapped wine-barrels stacked high against the outer wall of what had once been the captain's quarters. "But are they there to patronize her or to patronize you?"

Fiore tamped down his rising impatience. He'd modelled for Artemisia's work many times. Some of her best pieces showed off his finest features. More than a few had entered her studio and beheld a marble Bacchus or Mercury so beautiful they could hardly bear it—and turned to find that very same creature standing before them in the flesh. Granted, none of them had remained with Fiore for more than a few months, but the strategy had worked thus far, and Fiore hoped it might secure him a more permanent patronage in the near future.

Of course, Serafina already knew all that. But because it wasn't *her* strategy, she gave it little credence.

"You might try the opera," said Serafina. "Filled to bursting with nobles, aristocrats, patricians. All devouring drama of the highest degree for hours at a stretch, only to be disgorged onto the streets with enflamed and unrealized passions. Easy pickings. I could show you around, if you'd like."

Fiore kept his smile pinned in place even as his veins flooded with dread. The opera. Always the damned opera. Serafina liked to tell everyone she'd almost been an opera singer. She sang sometimes in the tavern. By Fiore's estimation, she sang well enough but not operatically. He would know. He preferred non-operatic singing himself, for reasons he didn't care to divulge to her or anyone else. "Are you suggesting Artemisia's work doesn't enflame the passions?"

"In her studio, the passions are enflamed by something they may purchase from her direct," Serafina retorted. "Whereas at the opera, their passions are enflamed by the unattainable—until you arrive to show them precisely how they may attain it."

If Serafina thought the objects of opera-induced passions remained unattainable, she had some serious misconceptions about the enterprise. Her own line of work had far more in common with that of a prized prima donna off the stage, whether in the wings, in the dressing room, or in the refined apartments of a noble patron.

Perhaps Corelli noted the rising tension between her tenants, for she interceded. "The dueling Duke of Drakehaven has returned to the city. They say he fancies lads like yourself. Perhaps you'll find him out at the opera."

"Perhaps," Fiore conceded.

Serafina smiled as she sipped her wine. "Go on, then. Just be sure to come back and tell me what you've found."

Fiore forced himself to mirror her smile and descended, at long last, down the rope-ladder off the port bow of the ship.

The worst part of it was, as his simmering sour mood drove him onward, he knew Serafina was right. By the numbers alone—hundreds of wealthy knobs crowded the theater district every night, compared to perhaps a half-dozen potential clients dropping into Artemisia's studio in the course of a full day. Only a fool would bet on the latter over the former. And Fiore hadn't survived this long by being a fool.

He did, however, attribute much of his survival to going nowhere near the theater district.

Perhaps, he thought as his steps drew ever nearer to the center of the city and the gleaming dome of the temple to Bellenos rising high over the piazza, he could make an exception. Just for today. He could go to an opera house—not inside it, of course, but just linger outside around intermission. And when he inevitably came home empty-handed he could shut Serafina up once and for all. Or at least for another fortnight or so.

And thus, though every instinct screamed for him to continue on southward out of the square towards Artemisia's studio, his steps turned northward towards the theatre district.

His nerves increased as he went along, though he kept a placid smile on for everyone he passed by. Said nerves reached a fever pitch when at last he alighted in the theatrical piazza and settled himself into leaning against one of the marble plinths at the base of Teatro Novissimo's sweeping front staircase. Faint echoes of the music within reached his ears, though whether he imagined them or no he couldn't say for certain. They unnerved him nonetheless. He told himself his fears were unwarranted. Even if they caught him now, it wouldn't do them any good. His voice was already ruined.

"Pardon me."

Fiore whirled toward the sudden speech, half-expecting to see the chirurgeon with knife in hand.

The figure who'd spoken did wear a mask. But not the glass-eyed, bird-beaked mask of the chirurgeon. Instead, the black bauta stood before him. The self-same lithe gentleman who had watched Fiore pleasure himself, now gazing down at Fiore with enquiring and enchanting eyes.

The voice—a deep, sonorous burr which Fiore recognized when combined with the familiar figure and no longer lost in the labyrinth of horrible recollections—continued. "I believe we are acquainted."

Sheer relief had already brought a smile to Fiore's lips. The understatement made him grin. "Intimately."

The eyes beneath the mask smiled likewise.

"Do you enjoy the opera?" Fiore asked, affecting a tone of indifference.

The gentleman hesitated. "May I be honest with you?"

A rare commodity from folk of the gentleman's apparent rank. Fiore wondered if he would actually receive it. "Of course."

"I do not."

Fiore expressed his astonishment at both the candor and the content of the gentleman's answer in a blink. "And yet you attend."

"I was asked to provide an escort."

A wry smile tugged at the corner of Fiore's mouth. "And you abandoned your charge."

The gentleman scoffed. "They don't require an escort. They just want me out of the palazzo."

Fiore raised his brows at this revelation; or rather, he supposed, this confirmation of his prior suspicions.

"The impresario is probably glad to see me go," the gentleman continued. "Now the audience will aim their glasses at the stage rather than our box."

Not just a resident of a palazzo, but one who could afford a box at the opera. Fiore withheld a low whistle. "Do you attract much notice?"

The gentleman shot him a glance. At first Fiore feared he'd overstepped in his sarcasm, but then the eyes lit up with another smile, and a low chuckle emerged from beneath the mask. "Some."

Whether an innate courage or a mere desperation to be anywhere else drove him to speak on, Fiore couldn't say, but his mouth opened again regardless. "Shall we venture off somewhere we might attract less notice?"

Astonished delight gleamed in the dark eyes behind the mask. "Let's. Only—" he added, hesitating again with a glance toward the opera house. "I ought to tell my companions of my intent to abandon them."

"Of course." It seemed the gentleman had a touch more sense of honor than Fiore gave him credit for.

The gentleman bowed and returned to the opera house. He took the entrance stairs two at a time; whether for speed or to show off his long, lithe legs with their splendid calves, Fiore couldn't say.

Several minutes passed as Fiore waited for the gentlemen to re-emerge. He spent the time casting winning glances at passersby, particularly those wearing sumptuous slashed velvets and those whose hands glittered with rings. Some nodded, some smiled, but none took him up on his implicit offer.

"Shall we be off?"

Fiore flinched just as he had before—the looming opera houses keeping him ever on edge—but smiled when he turned to find the gentleman had returned as promised.

"We shall." Fiore offered his arm.

The gentleman hesitated. Belatedly, Fiore recalled how the gentleman had preferred to look rather than touch at their last meeting. Perhaps he had an aversion to touch of all sorts. Or perhaps he had some wound which troubled him.

But before Fiore could do or say anything to smooth the matter over, the gentleman seemed to steel his nerve by drawing himself up and, with a soft smile in his masked eyes, slipped his arm through the crook of Fiore's. His tentative touch held a warmth like sunshine.

"What may I call you?" the gentleman asked.

"Fiore. And you?"

The gentleman blinked. Evidently he hadn't expected to hear his own enquiry echoed back at him. Yet all the same, he replied, "My friends call me Enzo."

Which might be short for Vincenzo or Lorenzo or Innocenzo or anything, really. The gentleman had answered Fiore without giving him any real information—and yet, whilst at the same time giving him permission to indulge in an intimacy. "Are we friends, then?"

"I'd like us to be so, at the very least." Enzo's words carried a note of cautious hope.

Fiore found it charming despite himself. "As would I. Where shall we go?"

Enzo shrugged. "I know not. I'm newly returned to the city, after many years' absence."

"What drew you away?" Fiore asked before he could think better of it.

"The plague. When I was a boy. The threat of its return kept me away until time came for me to attend university. And now..." Enzo gave an expressive twirl of his wrist.

Rather the inverse of Fiore's own history. "If I may speak on the city's behalf, we're delighted to have you returned."

The eyes beneath the mask crinkled in a smile. "All this to say you doubtless know Halcyon better than myself. Where would you suggest?"

"I know of a charming and accommodating bathhouse."

Fiore couldn't see what sort of look appeared on Enzo's face under his mask, but he did notice how his whole posture stiffened, the arm entwined through his own tightening in his grip as the shoulders tensed up. Not one for the bathhouse, then. He supposed he ought to have foreseen such modesty from a gentleman who wore a bauta even outside of festival days.

"Or," Fiore added, "perhaps a coffeehouse would better suit our purposes."

Enzo's tension eased. "Lead on."

Fiore gladly led him down and away from the wretched opera house. His heart lightened with every step they took out of the theatre district. They caught eyes as they went. While the sight of a bauta mask sailing through the crowd was by no means an uncommon occurrence in Halcyon, a black bauta remained unusual. And, Fiore supposed, the disparity in height between himself and Enzo must appear comical. He smiled to think on it.

The coffeehouse, called the Crooked Anchor, lay south-east of the theatre district, just north of the painters' and sculptors' guildhalls. This made it a convenient and popular watering-hole for the artistic set. Despite the name, its signage showed no anchor, crooked or otherwise, but rather a generation or so ago one of the owners had something like a ship's bow built over the entrance, made from a rowboat with a false prow added on its front and painted a gleaming white to match the marble edifice, with seafoam-green trim to catch the eye. Within, amidst the customary bar, benches, and booths of the interior were seafoam-green walls and ceiling adorned with sprigs and effusions of sprawling gold gilding, like the sun's own rays beaming forth from every corner. Some of the gilt had chipped, true enough, and the effect rather dwindled as the eye descended the walls to the point within reach of the tables, for at this pseudo-water-line the drawing began, years of artistic customers taking their creativity out on their surroundings. Most were done in red chalk, this being the most charming yet contrasting shade against the pale blue-green, which gave the whole chamber a rather sunset-like effect. Fiore saw some familiar faces scribbling even now, leaning back in their chairs with coffee cups in one hand and the other scrawling the beginnings of some splendid nudes.

Fiore gave Enzo a moment to take it all in before he suggested, "Shall we?"

Enzo required no further prompting to stride up to the bar and procure two coffees. This done, Fiore led him through the crowd to the back door, beyond which lay a patio filled with tables and chairs that offered a charming view on the corner of two intersecting canals.

Some fellow regulars recognized Fiore along the way and acknowledged him with nods. More turned to look at the black bauta sweeping through them. But Fiore was used to attracting interest with his own appearance, and if Enzo didn't mind the stares, then neither did he. Besides, most returned to their own matters after a glance or two. In an establishment replete with artistic temperaments, a dark masked figure hardly warranted any focus. Particularly when contrasted against the vivid wrapping-gowns several of the patrons wore. A far cry from a theatre-full of audience members gawking through their opera glasses.

Yet as they stepped out into the sunshine, Enzo paused.

"Something wrong?" Fiore asked.

"No," Enzo replied. "Something familiar. Is this where you come to sketch?"

Fiore blinked.

A bashful smile reached the eyes beneath the mask. "The ones in your room are your own handiwork, no?"

"They are," Fiore admitted, still a touch stunned. Most gentlemen didn't notice the artwork adorning his walls.

Enzo gestured to the canal, with gondole and sandoli drifting past, the lanterns gently swaying in the archways of the storehouses across the way, and an aedicula—venerating Bellenos and beseeching his protection over this particular corner of the city—set into the wall beside a bridge replete with wisteria vines. "You've captured it well."

A smile wound its way up Fiore's cheek.

He led Enzo to his favorite corner table. Enzo remained standing whilst Fiore slid onto his customary chair, then set his coffee before him, only seating himself after Fiore had settled. A perfect gentleman, Fiore observed.

Fiore further noted how Enzo chose to arrange his statuesque frame. While he laid it out to its full and considerable extent as he took his place in the chair across from Fiore, not so much as one slender finger at the end of his long arm entered Fiore's sphere. Not even his legs, stretched as they were beneath the table before crossing delicately at the ankle, intruded upon the space Fiore already occupied.

Which left it up to Fiore to intrude upon Enzo's sphere by stretching out his own legs and laying the exterior of his own right foot against the interior of Enzo's left.

Enzo went stiff again for a moment—at which Fiore prepared to retreat—but then relaxed still further than he had before, and contentment warmed his masked eyes.

"Come here often?" Enzo asked, his smile evident in his sonorous voice.

Fiore smiled likewise into his coffee. "I suppose the sketches gave me away."

Enzo took a sip. The coffee cup appeared miniature in his strong yet elegant hands. It vanished altogether beneath the jutting chin of his mask, returning in the wake of the long swallow that travelled magnificently down his throat. "The two trades seem rather entwined."

"Brewing and drawing?" The wry half-smile returned to tug at the corner of Fiore's mouth. "Or drawing and whoring?"

Enzo blinked. "Both, I suppose. Did you pick up one through the other? Or is that too bold to ask?"

"None too bold in the least," Fiore assured him. "And yes. I modeled and more for a particular painter. He wished to pay me in portraits. Alas I proved not quite so vain as he'd hoped."

Enzo's laugh choked in his coffee.

Fiore hid his smile behind his own cup. "Since he had no coin, I demanded payment in materials. Reams of paper, red chalk, black ink. He taught me a little, as well."

"Does he still?" Enzo enquired.

Fiore studied him. From another man, the question might come with a tinge—or more—of jealousy. But Enzo sounded merely curious. Earnest, almost. "No. He acquired a wealthy patron inland. He does well there, from what I've heard."

Enzo raised his cup in salute to the artist's success.

"And you?" Fiore asked. "What do you do when you're not suffering an opera?"

The low chuckle rumbling up from Enzo's throat sang through Fiore's heart-strings. "Fencing. And," Enzo added, in a more bashful tone, "I draw a little as well."

A wry smile crept up Fiore's cheek. "Do you, now?"

"A little," Enzo said again.

"And what do you draw? Coffeehouses? Canals?" Fiore's smile broadened. "Gondoliers?"

A hard swallow rippled beneath the shadow of a beard just beginning to cast itself over Enzo's throat. Fiore wanted to kiss bruises onto it.

"Perhaps," Enzo admitted. "I haven't been in the city long enough to begin. Mostly I draw flora and fauna. And... some more unusual subjects."

Nudes, of course. Fiore couldn't cease smiling. To have the noble, dashing, striking figure of the mysterious bauta-clad Enzo bashfully confess to doing just *a little* art of his own, yet remain too shy to admit to drawing the sort of thing Fiore had posed for more oft than he cared to count. No wonder he'd noticed Fiore's drawings, having done his own. Charming beyond compare. Intoxicating, almost. Fiore couldn't wait to unfurl the tight-wound rosebud of secrets into full bloom. And, furthermore, to peel away the petals of cape and mask to reveal what delicacies lay beneath.

Aloud, Fiore replied, "I adore unusual subjects."

Another smile lit up Enzo's dark eyes.

～

Enzo spent the entire encounter yearning to kiss him.

From the moment of their unexpected reunion outside the opera house; to hearing his name for the first time, Fiore, and what a curious coincidence that was, and how delightfully it danced on Enzo's tongue; to the suggestion of a bathhouse, to which Enzo could of course never acquiesce but nonetheless appreciated, the thought of Fiore's bare skin glowing beneath the sheen of steam and sweat; to the intoxicating sensation of Fiore's arm twined through his to lead him, ever so gently, to the coffeehouse; to watch that magnificent masculine gem pulse with every swallow of his slender swanlike throat, and how his shirt collar slid towards his shoulder as he gestured, revealing the delicate curve of his clavicle; and to discover through their conversation that they held more in common than mere lust—not that Enzo objected to satisfying lust, but for one who'd left all his friends behind at university, he had great appreciation for a deeper connexion.

And yet despite their growing bond, the bauta mask still stood between them.

The true beauty of the bauta's design, in Enzo's opinion, was its practicality. It hid the wearer's identity from view altogether, while the broad beak allowed one to eat, drink, and speak freely. He'd worn it daily for almost a year now, ever since Lucrezia had withdrawn him from university, and found it perfectly comfortable. Reassuring, even, to know he'd not be judged by his appearance.

Today, however, he had discovered its singular flaw.

One might eat, drink, and speak beneath the bauta mask—but one could not kiss.

Enzo felt as if it would drive him mad.

A kiss should've been the reward for all Fiore had done. More than kisses. Fiore deserved a king's ransom. The offer of the bathhouse had sorely tempted Enzo, but to disrobe altogether in public tended to raise questions from strangers which he'd rather not answer. And while he held great desire for Fiore, he wasn't quite so foolish as to believe he could trust him with all his secrets at only their second meeting.

"Do you have anywhere to be?" Fiore asked suddenly.

Enzo, who'd quite lost himself in gazing at the perfect lips just out of his reach, blinked. "Pardon?"

"The opera must be over by now. Do your charges require your escort home?"

A laugh escaped Enzo. Giovanna and Antonio hardly required his escort. And he no longer required theirs, for Carlotta had kept up with him ever since he left the opera house. At first he thought he'd left her behind, not seeing her shadow in the crowd outside Teatro Novissimo nor along the streets—though, of course, Fiore had captivated him from the start and left him hardly any notice for anything or anyone else. But he did retain the presence of mind to glance around the coffeehouse as they entered and keep a weather eye out as they sat sipping. Not espying her immediately, he feared he'd lost her and moreover feared Lucrezia's wrath when she discovered he'd slipped his lead, however inadvertently. Then he caught a glimpse of Carlotta across the canal; just the merest slip of a shadow on the opposite bank, leaning against the wall with apparent indifference as the crowd surged around her, yet her gaze never once leaving where Enzo and Fiore sat. Enzo never would've noticed her if he hadn't known to look. He couldn't decide whether he felt disturbed or comforted by her watchful presence. Still, she made no move to interfere, and for this he gave silent thanks.

But as to the question Fiore had put to him—"They do not require me."

This was evidently the correct answer, for a sly and handsome smile stole over Fiore's perfect mouth. "Then, perhaps, you will not object to escorting me back to my ship?"

A smile of his own grew beneath Enzo's mask. "No objection whatsoever."

Fiore grinned. "Splendid."

The journey back to the *Kingfisher* could not have taken above half an hour. To Enzo it passed in the blink of an eye. Every moment spent with his arm entwined in Fiore's seemed precious. Scarlet sash or no, he felt honored to stride alongside him. It would have been privilege enough to escort him to the ship, bid him good-night, and thank him for a splendid afternoon.

Yet it delighted Enzo still further when Fiore paused in the midst of mounting the rope-ladder and, with a careless tilt of his head that sent his dark curls tumbling across his brow, invited Enzo to follow him.

Enzo wasn't a fool. Or at least not so much of one as Lucrezia believed. He knew this was merely Fiore's trade. The coy flattery and kind attentions were well-honed skills used as needed to procure payment. Doubtless Fiore invited him up only because he knew from their last encounter how deep Enzo's purse ran.

Still, Enzo felt a joyful little thrill run through his veins as he followed Fiore into the ship.

He expected to find the courtesan's bedchamber dim by daylight. Instead it glowed with sunshine—and not from the porthole window, whose scarlet curtain remained demurely shut. The light offered a far better view of the sketches adorning the walls, just as charming as Enzo remembered. Something of his confusion must have shown in his aspect despite his mask, for he turned to catch a knowing look in Fiore's eye. Fiore pointed up to the ceiling, where a glass crystal embedded in the wooden planks cast clear blue light throughout the room.

"Deck prism," said Fiore. "Original to the ship, if you'll believe it."

Enzo saw no reason to doubt him.

"Now, then," Fiore continued, shutting the door gently behind them and striding to brace himself with one hand on the prow of his half-a-boat bed. "How shall we amuse ourselves?"

"I'm content to watch you again," Enzo lied.

Fiore smiled. "Which is most flattering. But it would be easier for me if I had something to admire."

Enzo swallowed hard. "What do you typically admire?"

Fiore's gaze took a lackadaisical journey up and down Enzo's frame. He met Enzo's gaze again with raised brows. An expression which spoke as loud as words; *I've shown you all of mine. Will you not show me some of yours?*

Enzo wracked his mind for what he could safely reveal. He wanted to reveal all, to tear off his clothes and lay himself bare for Fiore to devour as he wilt. But that wasn't the wise choice, and he needed to prove himself wise if ever he wished to regain what he'd lost.

Removing his mask was out of the question. No matter how badly he wanted to kiss those perfect lips or pay tribute to the most magnificent cock he'd seen in longer than he cared to recall. He could probably show off his chest without any danger, though he doubted it would inspire Fiore's performance. And as for his trousers... He could not remove them altogether, of course. But he might slip them down just enough.

Fiore's eyes widened with a gleam of intrigue as Enzo's hands fell to the fall-front of his breeches. He watched with undisguised hunger as Enzo undid the buttons, untied the drawers beneath, and drew up his shirt-front to reveal the trail of dark hair from his navel on down to the forest surrounding the root of his prick. This foliage disguised most of his particular peculiarity. Still, he folded the waistband of his drawers down just to the root of his stem and no farther. It stood proud regardless of his own humility, half-hard from Fiore's suggestions alone and stiffening to full mast beneath the hungry gaze of those beautiful dark eyes.

"Admirable, indeed," Fiore purred.

Enzo knew it was just the sort of flattery required of one in Fiore's trade. Still, that knowledge didn't preclude the warm flush that spread through his chest and flowed down to make his prick pulse with pleasure.

A pleasure which became astonished and eager anticipation as Fiore knelt before him.

The dark lashes swept upward in a glance which enquired after permission. Enzo granted it with a nod. Fiore raised his delicate palm and wrapped his elegant fingers around Enzo's cock.

Enzo bit back a groan. It had been far too long since someone besides himself had taken him in hand.

A self-satisfied smile stole across Fiore's handsome features. He slid his hand along Enzo's length like a sword-smith appreciating the hone of a blade. It sent a shiver over Enzo's skin. Then Fiore's fist closed tight around it for a satisfying stroke. His soft hands belied a strong grip. It wouldn't take much more to send Enzo spilling through his fingers.

And yet Fiore paused. He shot another enquiring glance up at Enzo from beneath those dark lashes and furthermore caught his full lower lip between his teeth.

Enzo's breath caught. He nodded again.

Fiore's smile became a grin. It flashed for but a moment before he bent forward and took Enzo into his mouth.

Enzo gasped. Nigh-on a year of self-deprivation culminated in the all-consuming sensation of slipping into the soft wet heat between Fiore's perfect lips. A velvet tongue lathed his cock-head, delving beneath the foreskin to encircle the sensitive ridge with a delicate tenacity that threatened to buckle Enzo's knees. Then it withdrew—an act both merciful and merciless—only to trace the vein along the underside, following it to the very root as Fiore's throat opened to swallow him down altogether.

And all the while those dark eyes gazed up at him. Enzo felt as if he would fall into their depths and drown.

Instinct bid him take hold of Fiore. Tangle his gloved fingers in his ebony curls, perhaps, or lay his hands upon his shoulders. But as they'd not discussed it beforehand, Enzo restrained himself to grasping the boat's gunwales to haul upright and keep afloat on the storm-tossed seas of Fiore's tongue.

It occurred to Enzo as another gasp escaped him that, from this angle, Fiore could see up into the open underside of the bauta mask. Perhaps that was his cunning plan all along. Enzo thought he well deserved the spoils of it. Even so, the most he could glean would be chin and jaw. Hardly enough to recognize Enzo out of costume. Certainly not enough to describe to another and have them know Enzo for who he truly was. And likely no more than he'd seen already, given the disparity in their heights.

Which was as much coherent thought as Enzo could string together before a mellifluous moan reverberated through his cock from Fiore's throat.

A downward glance showed that Fiore had taken himself in hand. The thought of Fiore deriving his own pleasure from drawing him up to the heights of quivering ecstasy sent a shudder through Enzo's whole frame. He fervently wished he could take Fiore into his own mouth in turn. What tribute his tongue would pay to that splendid prick. Another time, perhaps. Now, however, Enzo clenched the gunwales with a grip that threatened to splinter the wood, as if he'd tumbled into storm-tossed waves and the whaleboat alone could spare him drowning.

Another moan from Fiore shook Enzo to his core. Another coy and knowing glance from beneath those dark lashes stole what little breath remained. Fiore's sharp cheeks hollowed, his tongue lavished Enzo's cock, and all too soon it pulsed with ecstasy that left Enzo barely able to hold himself upright against the boat. He trembled like a sail cut loose in a high wind. The whole room spun before his eyes.

And all the while, Fiore swallowed every drop of his overwhelming tide.

Enzo returned to his senses—still standing, by some miracle—he knew not how many moments after. His ragged gasps rang in his ears. He cast his gaze down at the man who'd brought him beyond the brink.

Fiore knelt back on his heels, still stroking his own cock—idly now, no longer frantic efforts to keep up with Enzo's pleasure. He watched Enzo with the same beautiful self-satisfied smile that had burned itself into Enzo's memory the last night of Saturnalia.

Enzo sank to the floor before him, his thighs enfolding Fiore's own between them. He raised his left glove beneath his mask and tore it off with his teeth. He cast it aside, then moved his bare hand tentatively towards Fiore's cock. "May I?"

Fiore's eyes had flown wide. His smile had drawn even wider. He bit his lip and nodded, an eager gleam in his dark gaze.

Enzo took him in hand. The heft and delicate curve of his cock weighed perfectly in his palm like a well-balanced rapier hilt. The thrill of its velveteen soft skin against his bare fingertips sent a shiver of illicit pleasure through him. He gave it a long slow stroke to test its length. The foreskin rolled over the head and back again, leaving a pearl of seed in its wake. He smeared it over the cock-head with the pad of his thumb.

A moan of pleasure escaped Fiore. Enzo glanced up to find him biting his lip through his smile.

"Like that?" Enzo murmured.

Fiore nodded again and, ever so gently, thrust his hips up into Enzo's hand.

Enzo might not have had all of a courtesan's considerable skill, but he possessed a prick of his own and had lain with many other men besides. He hoped experience would suffice. Indeed, it seemed to, as Fiore's breath quickened, and he thrust to meet Enzo's strokes. A touch here, a twist of the wrist there, a tightened grip and rapid arm—not so different from the delicate manipulation of a sword-hilt to bend the blade to his will, and still more satisfying to hold in his palm. Even so, Enzo imagined the greater pleasures that could be his if he ever got Fiore's cock properly inside him.

Then Fiore released Enzo from his grasp and bent backward, leaning until his shoulders touched the floorboards, his arms tossed over his head and his whole frame rhythmically writhing as he thrust into Enzo's fist—until, with a shudder and a gasp, head thrown back, mouth agape, his cock pulsed in Enzo's fingers and strings of liquid pearls erupted thrice-over to fall across his own bronzed chest.

For several moments the only sound in the chamber was ragged breaths; Fiore's and Enzo's both. If anything could inspire Enzo to a second stand so soon after his own spend, it might have been the sight of Fiore sprawled naked and gasping in the wake, his head lolling and his eyes falling shut, his chest heaving and stomach rippling with the trembling after-shocks of what had seemed a tidal wave that wrecked them both upon an unfamiliar yet welcoming shore. Enzo knew not how many minutes passed as he stared in silent awe.

SEBASTIAN NOTHWELL

Then those beautiful eyes opened and fixed upon him with a slow and lackadaisical smile.

"Forgive me," Fiore murmured. "I didn't want to make a mess of your waistcoat."

Enzo would gladly have forgiven him of far worse. And as for the mess... Instinct brought his hand beneath his mask to his mouth to suck the pearls of Fiore's seed from his knuckles. He tasted of sea-salt and summer sunshine. If it weren't for the damned mask, Enzo bitterly considered, he could have swallowed down Fiore in turn and perhaps have sated his ravenous hunger.

Fiore watched him in open fascination—which only increased as Enzo dared to draw his thumb through the strings of liquid pearls shimmering across Fiore's chest and stomach and devour those as well.

Enzo, having consumed all the mask would allow him, swallowed hard. The afternoon must draw to an end, despite his wishes. "I don't wish to keep you from your business..."

Fiore's smile made Enzo's heart stutter in his chest. "How conscientious of you."

Enzo cleared his throat. "May we meet again? Perhaps you could show me more of the city."

Fiore's smile broadened into a grin. "I should like that very much."

Enzo forgot how to breathe.

"Perhaps mèrcore?" Fiore seemed accustomed to talking around gentlemen he'd stunned into silence. "We could meet in Bellenos Piazza, by the fountain. At mid-day—I'm afraid I'm not often up before then."

Enzo would've heartily agreed to whichever terms Fiore cared to set. As speech still proved beyond him, he assented with a nod.

The encounter ought to have descended into an awkward state as both men stood and redressed themselves. Yet Fiore arose with the liquid grace of a dancer and donned his garb with enough confidence and poise to make it seem as much an art as disrobing. It almost overshadowed Enzo's own shameful shove of his cock back into his drawers. This done, he had only to leave his zecchini on the nightstand and show himself out.

And still he lingered.

Stray curls fell across Fiore's forehead in the wake of pulling on his shirt. A careless toss of his head did not suffice to send them back to their proper place.

So Enzo found himself reaching out to smooth them back for him.

Fiore stilled beneath his touch. Enzo feared he'd over-stepped. But Fiore didn't withdraw from him—indeed, his dark gaze gleamed with intrigue, and the slight smile that had played about his perfect lips in the wake of his orgasmic haze stole over them entirely as his notice fixed upon Enzo in turn.

All Enzo wanted was to whip off his mask and embrace him.

Instead, he took Fiore's hand in his own and brought it beneath the mask's broad beak to press its knuckles against his lips in reverence.

Fiore's grin appeared like a beam of sunlight breaking through the clouds after a storm. "Such a gentleman."

And for once, Enzo didn't feel ashamed to claim the title.

# CHAPTER THREE

The temple to Bellenos stood proud in the center of Halcyon. Its magnificent dome, as pale and perfect as the moon, arose far above any other edifice on the island—save perhaps the towers of the princely palazzo, which lay just a stone's throw beyond it.

In theory, Lucrezia could be standing in one of those towers even now and watching as Enzo strode into the piazza to meet his courtesan. In practice, she likely had far more important matters to concern herself with and had settled for trusting in Carlotta to keep close on Enzo's heels.

Enzo hadn't yet spotted Carlotta this morning on his jaunt through the city. He knew she followed him regardless.

The fountain in front of the temple was likewise enormous. Marble nereides, dolphins, and serpents frolicked amidst at least a dozen spouts in the scallop-shaped basin. Above them all arose a sculpted wave bearing the god Bellenos in androgynous mortal guise. The nude contrapposto pose, with one arm gently curled around a vicious barnacled trident, displayed to full advantage the lithe arms, slender waist, supple thighs, and a peculiarity not unlike Enzo's own.

"Admirable, isn't it?" said a voice at Enzo's elbow.

Enzo turned to find Fiore at his side, leaning back with his arms propped up against the rim of the fountain as if he'd always been there.

"A masterpiece," Enzo agreed, smiling beneath his mask. He gestured towards the benches ringing the fountain. "Shall we sit?"

The shadow of a grimace flickered across Fiore's perfect face—just for a moment. "We might stroll, if you're not already winded from the journey here."

"Not at all," Enzo replied. He held out his arm to Fiore.

Fiore pushed off from the fountain with a wince. He put a smile over it quick enough and twined his arm through Enzo's own. But still, on his first step, he'd winced.

Enzo drew upon the hints and reached a conclusion. "Rough night?"

Fiore gave him a startled glance. It melted into a smile not of pageantry but of genuine relief. "Something like."

"Should we do something more restful?" Enzo asked.

Fiore shook his head. "I've had worse."

Enzo didn't find that particularly comforting. But Fiore laid his head against his shoulder, and when he stepped forward, Enzo felt compelled to follow. Fiore could lead him into a dark alley to rob and murder him for all he cared. It felt worth it to spend but a moment at his side.

Fiore did not lead him down a dark alley. Rather, he led him around the rim of the fountain to admire the back view of the strong-yet-supple Bellenos.

"Have you learnt the trick to the city's fountains?" Fiore asked Enzo. "How to tell which are seawater and which are fresh?"

For Enzo, the trick had been to follow Vittorio's lead on their morning ambles. The hound had a better nose than he for which fountains to drink from and which to spurn. But for those who didn't have a faithful hound at their side, Enzo knew not how they could tell one from the other, and so he shook his head.

Fiore seemed more eager than otherwise for the opportunity to explain. "Well, for one, the fresh-water ones are smaller. Nothing like—" Fiore gestured up at the grandiose sculptural marvel before them. "They only ever have just the one spout. And it's always a human mouth. Or a god in mortal guise," he added. "Silvanus. Faunus. Bacchus. That sort of thing. What's good for them to drink is good for you."

"What's good for the gods is good for the gander?" Enzo suggested with a smile.

Despite being unable to see the smile beneath Enzo's mask, Fiore returned it. "Precisely. Their ambrosia is our fresh-water. There is another hint, however. Have you a guess?"

Enzo shook his head.

Fiore's fingertips trailed through the air before them to trace the distant curve of a particular spouting dolphin. "The seawater fountains depict the creatures that dwell in it. Porpoises, serpents, shells, nereides... and, of course, Neptune himself. Whereas the fresh-water fountains, on the rare occasion when they're more than a mere face embedded in a wall, depict greenery. Mostly foliate heads."

"Foliate heads?" Enzo echoed.

"A face formed from leaves. Sometimes disgorging them as well, alongside the fresh-water. Further proof of its nourishing qualities."

Enzo knew Fiore had dwelled in the city for far longer than himself. Therefore it didn't surprise him that he knew which fountains to drink from. But the depth and reasoning behind the knowledge seemed to bespeak something more than the mere practicality of a casual resident. Which prompted him to enquire, "How came you to be such a local historian?"

Fiore laughed. "I'm not. But one of my gentlemen was. A librarian for a noble household," he added in response to Enzo's curious glance. "Gnaeus—or so he told me to call him. City histories were his pillow-talk."

"Were?"

Fiore's smile transformed into something more wistful. "He's not visited me since he married. Which is a shame, for he paid well, but his wife loves him more than I ever could, so I may content myself with his contentment." He turned from the fountain to the temple behind. "You've already seen the interior, I assume. Mosaics, murals, dragon bones, and all?"

Enzo had. No aristocratic family in the city could escape participation in the pageantry of all the holy festivals on the calendar. Supposedly he could trace his own ancestry to those very dragon bones. In reply to Fiore's enquiry, however, he simply nodded.

"Then," said Fiore, "we may dispense with the tourist's route. Where else do your interests lie? Drinks? Dancing? Not opera and not bathhouses," he added with a sly glance up at Enzo. "That much I remember."

Enzo found himself returning the smile even though Fiore couldn't see it. "You did promise to show me which sights you thought most beautiful."

Fiore blinked as if surprised Enzo had remembered. Still, he smiled on. "So I did. Very well. Art it is. Come along."

Enzo trailed happily in Fiore's shadow.

The artisan districts lay in the south-west quarter of the city. Each guild had its own island; that much Enzo recalled from his childhood lessons in governance. He'd never yet had occasion to visit them himself. His solitary wanderings had not taken him so far.

Fiore, however, took him direct through the bustling Merceria—still far more hushed than the market square of the university town, though a hundredfold more active—and over the sole bridge crossing the Grand Canal, then down side-streets and back-ways and cutting through many a corti to reach another bridge, its destination made apparent by its decoration.

For one, the bridge was made of stone rather than mere wood. For another, every inch of it was slathered in bas-relief. The carved pod of frolicking dolphins along the underside of the arch bore a green tint in their deepest furrows from the algae rising with the tide. Their stone spouts supported Neptune himself on either side of the arch's peak, flanked by nereides.

And if the bridge itself had somehow left the traveler in any doubt of whence they'd arrived, the aedicula that met them upon alighting from said bridge removed all trace of ambiguity. Within its four pillars arose a marble sculpture of Bellenos posed with hammer and chisel in hand, carving himself out of the stone. Everything below the waist remained rough and unhewn. In this aspect, at least, it rendered the god's peculiarity a sacred mystery. The votive oil lamp before him burned bright even by day, bespeaking the district's wealth.

"Admirable, isn't he?"

Enzo turned to find Fiore gazing on the god with undisguised appreciation. He supposed this boded well for when, or if, he chose to trust Fiore with his peculiarity. Aloud, he merely murmured his agreement.

This sufficed to send Fiore along to their next landmark. He chose one particular studio—at random, as far as Enzo could tell—and steered them both inside. The tall windows provided ample light; if they'd proved insufficient, the multitude of deck prisms set into the roof would've seen to the lack. It left the workshop aglow with soft golden sunshine that gave the cold white marble a rosy hue. Several erect slabs drew Enzo's initial notice. They stood in various states of completion; from a complex multitude of geometric charcoal measurements on untouched stone showing where the first chisel-blows ought to fall, to a feminine figure whose smooth limbs were on the brink of emerging from her angular marble chrysalis.

Fiore, however, passed these by in favor of drawing Enzo deeper into the studio. He halted in the center.

Where another Fiore lay before him.

Enzo recognized him at once. The sculptor's skill made the resemblance so lifelike as to be unmistakable. Doubtless Fiore had modelled for it.

Even without his own deep partiality for the model, however, Enzo thought the sculpture would have enraptured him.

The marble Fiore lay supine against a rocky beach. The uneven ground beneath him forced his back to arch, stretching the belly concave between stark ribs and jutting hip-bones, the dip of the navel the only mark on the smooth flesh. A fishing net slung low beneath the hips and across the tops of his thighs belied the imaginary Fiore's profession and provided what little modesty covered the otherwise nude form. His supple slender legs tangled across each other. The arms, tossed over the head with apparent carelessness, formed an organic frame for the lolling head. The curls tumbled across the brow and through the slender fingers, unmistakable in their resemblance despite their pale ivory hue contrasted against the living Fiore's ebony locks. The face held the same high cheekbones, sharp jaw, aquiline nose, and noble brow as the original flesh, though the dark and compelling eyes remained forever shut. The perfect lips appeared just as soft in marble as in flesh. The desire to kiss flesh and marble both ached in Enzo's heart.

When at last he could tear his gaze away from the masterpiece, he found the real Fiore gracing him with an impish smile.

"Look here," Fiore said, his voice low as he pointed to where the fishing net dangled off the hip.

Folds upon folds of netting draped over each other between the statue's thighs and over the outside of the left hip, as perfectly weighted as if it were truly braided hempen cord and not mere marble. As it folded over, the threads crossed beneath each other between real holes so intricate and delicate that a chisel no broader than a needle must have carved them out.

More astonishing than the net—which was already astonishment itself—was what it held. Trapped within the marble marvel were two fish so lifelike in both form and detail, the sculptor having carved out each individual scale on their twisting bodies, that it seemed as if they truly writhed for their release.

And Enzo, enthralled by the human figure, had almost missed them altogether.

As he glanced up to meet Fiore's eyes again, he found him smirking, as if he knew just what Enzo had almost missed and why.

"Remarkable," Enzo declared. "I'm astonished it hasn't sold."

"I'm not," said Fiore. "It's the best example of her skills on public display. I doubt she'd ever let it out of her workshop."

There went Enzo's plans for a return visit to the studio. Though perhaps he could persuade the sculptor to make a copy.

"Come to play at Narcissus again?"

Enzo turned to face the unknown speaker. A woman had wandered up behind them, garbed in shirt and breeches not unlike Fiore's own, though without the scarlet sash that marked his trade. Her round cap and smock marked hers—particularly the chisels and hammers tucked into the latter's pockets. She cropped her hair short, just above her jutting chin, and gazed down at Fiore with an arch indulgence that put Enzo in mind of something between Lucrezia and Giovanna.

Fiore seemed not in the least surprised to find himself thus addressed. "It's your own fault for rendering the copy more beautiful than the original."

The sculptor accepted this compliment with a thoughtful hum. Her sly gaze slid to meet Enzo's. She struck out her hand for a clasp. "Artemisia."

Enzo gave her his hand and his nickname in turn. Her grasp was swift and strong.

"Enzo asked me to show him all the most beautiful sights in the city," Fiore explained.

The corner of her lips arose alongside her left brow. "And so you showed him yourself?"

Fiore shrugged with a smile that begged to be kissed. "I wanted to show him the best artwork. The fact that the best artisans have exquisite taste in models? Pure coincidence."

"Of course." Her sly gaze flicked between them both. Then she jerked a ruddy thumb toward the back of the studio. "If you require me further, I'll be over there."

Enzo followed the gesture and found at its terminus the beginnings of a grand creation in clay. Even in its half-formed state Enzo recognized the two sinewy figures as Phaethon and Cycnus. Phaethon had tumbled to earth from the sun's chariot and now lay cradled in mourning Cycnus's arms, swan-feathers already forming on the latter's limbs.

Beside him, Fiore let out a low appreciative whistle. "For yourself or for a patron?"

"For a patron," Artemisia replied. She answered Enzo's enquiring gaze with, "A centerpiece for a garden. This is just a mock-up for their approval before I go to their site to carve the final vision. Clay is easier to reshape than stone."

"And carving on-site easier than transporting the finished piece," Enzo concluded.

Artemisia smiled in what might have been either sincerity or condescension; Enzo couldn't quite read her. "Exactly so."

And with that, she bowed and withdrew to her work-in-progress.

Enzo's gaze followed her for a moment. Another time he might have remained to watch her work; the process of molding the formless clay into something not just recognizable but startlingly lifelike fascinated him.

But his true fascination lay in his companion, and so his eye returned as it ever did to Fiore.

He found, to his surprise, that Fiore had become quite industrious in the scant few moments Enzo had let him out of his sight. A zibaldone had emerged for him to scribble in with devoted passion.

When Enzo's enquiring glance caught his eye, he smiled and, after a few more strokes of his red chalk, ceased. Then he turned the zibaldone around so Enzo could survey its pages. He beheld a rough sketch of Artemisia's work-in-progress—though to call it "rough" did it no justice. In but a few shakes of a sail Fiore had succeeded in capturing the essence of not just the half-formed sculpture but also its creator, rendering her posture and expression in such a way as to give one the feeling of her quizzical presence.

"Remarkable," Enzo heard himself say again.

Fiore snapped the zibaldone shut and pocketed it with a careless shrug. "Hardly."

Enzo supposed they could let the argument rest there for the time being. He'd caught the ghost of a secretive smile on Fiore's perfect lips which he thought meant the compliment had pleased him despite his modesty.

Fiore bid his friend good-day and led Enzo out of her studio. After a brief pause on the threshold of a woodcarver in the midst of chiseling a unicorn for a ship's figure-head, he led Enzo off the sculptor's island altogether.

They crossed a bridge over a narrow canal to reach the island of painters. A mural aedicula marked this entrance, ensconced in protective pillars and a roof to defend both the painting and its illuminating oil lamp from winter sleet. It depicted Bellenos arising from the seafoam whilst painting the ocean into being around him. Despite existing on a flat plane as opposed to the tactile dimensions of sculpture, the artist had layered the elements to create the illusion of incredible depth, so that the realm behind Bellenos seemed to stretch on as infinite as the actual sea.

Fiore led him onward. Past workshops marked with murals advertising quite plainly the talent of the painters toiling within. Past clusters of artists gawking and scribbling. Past other aristocrats wandering side-by-side in masks identical to his own, save they shone white where his remained shadowed black, bending their pale false faces together to whisper as they went by. Yet Fiore heeded them not, and so Enzo followed his example.

"Here we are," Fiore announced.

Enzo, startled out of his silent admiration, realized they'd arrived at a painter's studio. Fiore trotted in as if he lived there. Enzo ducked in after him.

Rather than figural works or portraiture, Enzo found himself surrounded by landscapes. Not, however, the city- and seascapes of Halcyon. Rather, they represented scenery never found within the lagoon or its islands. A series of pastoral capricci; fantastical landscapes whose exact counterparts did not exist in nature, yet evoked the natural realm all the same, creating something that sang more true to the spirit than mere reality.

Fiore glanced about the studio and tossed a careless wave at a man standing before an easel in the corner—the creator of all this work. The painter returned the gesture along with a puzzled glance at Enzo. Enzo touched the brim of his hat with a nod. This seemed to free the painter from whatever social obligation he might have felt and allowed him to return to his trade. His apprentice, on the other hand, ceased sweeping altogether to stare wide-eyed at the black bauta and his capricious companion. Fiore, of course, took no notice of any attention he attracted and instead fervently gestured for Enzo to join him in admiring a particular painting.

The first capriccio Fiore selected for Enzo's perusal depicted a picnic in a sylvan glade beside a babbling brook. Two gentlemen in roguish garb sat with two nude and voluptuous women. The women cast adoring looks at the gentlemen, but the gentlemen, laughing with ample conviviality, looked only at each other.

"Men of our sort, I should think," Fiore observed.

A low laugh escaped Enzo's throat.

The rest of the studio's gallery offered up similar scenes. Fiore led Enzo through them, pausing now and again with a cheeky half-smile to point out smaller details. Then he halted his dancing gait in front of a particular painting. He clasped his hands behind his back and trained his eye in reverent silence.

Enzo, following him, recognized the inspiration for this piece in the

wooded hills and vales surrounding his sister's hunting lodge. The artist
had added in a crumbling ruin with a half-tumbled tower whose arches
and staircase led to nowhere, overgrown not just with moss, ferns, and
ivy, but with a stout oak growing within its torn walls, its roots and
branches alike breaking through the stone. Rather than standard human
staffage, the artist had inserted capering fauns amongst the foliage and
ruin. And indeed, the fauns looked very familiar to Enzo.

"Did you model for these, as well?" he asked, turning to Fiore with a
smile.

He expected to find Fiore's knowing smirk turned upon him once
again. But instead, he found Fiore still staring at the capriccio.

Fiore had modelled for the fauns—Enzo felt sure of it—and perhaps
that was why he had such an attachment to his particular piece. But if so,
Enzo knew not why the marble fisherman hadn't likewise held him in its
thrall.

Indeed, Enzo observed as he indulged in the liberty of gazing upon
Fiore's beautiful face whilst he remained distracted, Fiore's eyes were not
fixed on the fauns, but rather trailed upward to the mists overhanging
the thickly wooded valley in the far distance of the scene.

Enzo dared not speak, for Fiore seemed captivated by the pieces as
much or moreso as the marble Fiore had captivated Enzo himself.

And as the sight of the flesh-and-blood Fiore, enraptured by a
pastoral daydream with a soft smile playing about his perfect lips and a
queer sort of longing sorrow in his dark eyes, captivated Enzo now.

That is, until those dark eyes glanced sideways towards Enzo—and
glanced again when they caught him staring.

Enzo quickly turned his attention to the capriccio. "It's beautiful."

The sweet little half-smile tugged at the corner of Fiore's lips once
again. "I suppose so. Shall we get on?"

Enzo wondered at Fiore's eagerness to leave. Perhaps he feared he'd
revealed too much of himself in his open admiration of the art.
Regardless, Enzo followed him out of the studio—tipping his hat to the
artist as Fiore passed along his own careless wave—and rejoined him in
the street, where Fiore twined their arms together once again.

"Forgive me," Enzo said. "What was the painter's name?"

"Tiziano," Fiore replied without looking at him. The name dropt from his tongue with a casual air that bordered on disinterest. Enzo suspected it was feigned. This suspicion seemed to prove true when Fiore cast a sidelong glance at him and added, "Why d'you ask? Something catch your eye?"

*You*, Enzo didn't say. Aloud, he answered, "It seems to have caught yours."

Fiore's steps slowed but did not cease. He glanced away from Enzo again, off down the street ahead. A silence grew between them.

Enzo gathered all his considerable courage. "Would you accept it as a gift?"

Fiore worked his jaw. For a moment, Enzo feared he'd overstepped and offended. But the cast of Fiore's brows bespoke deeper thought than anger.

"I don't want to own it now," Fiore explained. "I want to live the sort of life where owning such things might prove less absurd."

Enzo furrowed his brow.

Fiore gave him a wistful smile. "You must admit it would look rather silly hanging in my quarters as they are."

"It would pale in comparison to your own works," Enzo conceded. "But if you admire it, then it gains my approval as well."

Fiore laughed—a breathless little sound, like orange blossoms tumbling from their branches. "I will own it someday. But that day is a long way off."

"It might be tomorrow."

Fiore shot him a startled glance.

The words had come from Enzo's heart rather than his head. Yet he did not regret them. "You might live somewhere full of beautiful things. You need only speak the word."

Fiore stared at him in disbelief for a moment longer before bashful smile graced his perfect lips. "You're very kind."

A refusal as plain as a flat "no," all the more painful for the tenderness of its delivery. Enzo felt very glad for his mask. He knew not what contortions his face went through.

"But," Fiore continued, "there are practical considerations which prevent my accepting your offer."

A gentleman with more self-respect or poise would have accepted this with, at most, a nod. Enzo instead heard himself ask, "What sort of considerations?"

"You are a young man."

Enzo, confused, replied, "So are you."

"For now," Fiore admitted. "But what would you do with me when I'm old and flabby and wrinkled?"

Enzo smiled. "With any luck, I shall likewise become old and flabby and wrinkled by then, and we would make a well-matched set."

Another wistful smile graced Fiore's perfect lips. "Perhaps. But if I accept the offer of a man older than myself—perhaps much older—then he will slip his mortal coil before I pass the bloom of youth, and thus I shall not know the pain that would come when he tired of me and sought another younger blossom."

Enzo stared at him.

Fiore's smile faltered. "Too truthful?"

"No," Enzo assured him, even as his mind continued to whirl with what he'd heard. "Never."

Fiore reached for his mask.

Enzo froze.

Yet the gentle hand did not touch the ties or seek to pull it down. Instead the fingertips slipped beneath the protruding beak to trace the bristled line of Enzo's jaw. A shiver of illicit pleasure ran across his skin.

"I do like you," said Fiore. "Very much."

Enzo felt the same and more besides. He would have said so, but Fiore spoke on.

"I'm content to remain with you for as long as you'll have me," Fiore continued. "But I have to plan ahead. I don't want to end up a bitter dried-up hag with nothing to my name and no one to look after me."

"You won't," Enzo assured him.

Fiore smirked. "I know."

That hadn't been at all what Enzo meant. But Fiore seemed determined not to hear him.

# CHAPTER FOUR

**M**any gentlemen had promised Fiore many things throughout the years. Money, obviously. Myriad luxuries and delicacies. Silks, jewels, horses, houses, ships. Even when Fiore knew damn well they didn't have it. And even when they did, he knew damn well they'd never waste it on him.

None had delivered on their promises. Fiore had always known better than to press the issue.

Enzo's offer, however, had a different ring about it.

He'd spoken not in the throes of passion. Nor in the afterglow. Nor even in an attempt at seduction whilst they negotiated their encounter. Instead he'd made his offer out of the clear blue, a soft and gentle thunderclap that nonetheless rang in Fiore's ears, whilst they'd wandered arm-in-arm through the city as casual as anything. Perhaps it was the tender timbre of Enzo's voice, like one who'd stumbled across some wondrous creature in the wilderness and feared his words would startle it. Or perhaps it was the pleading in his dark eyes, the only part of his face Fiore could see and yet which contrived to speak more than the whole of most men. Despite Fiore's better sense, despite all his experience, the offer sounded unaccountably genuine.

And entirely too tempting.

It was, after all, everything Fiore had sought ever since he realized his own inevitable mortality. No more trying to catch the eye of a dozen fresh strangers each night. No more waiting and wondering when his looks would fade at last and rob him of the only stable career he'd ever known. No more submitting to the whims of those who cared not a whit for him. No more feigning desire when he felt none.

Which, frankly, sounded like a foolish dream.

A return to familiar ground would set his mind to rights. And so he turned to his companion and enquired, "Shall we retire to the *Kingfisher*?"

Enzo served him an astonished blink—whether because Fiore had caught him deep in thought or because he hadn't expected the afternoon to go in that direction, Fiore couldn't say. At last he replied, "Only if you're feeling up to it."

Which threw Fiore into an astonishment of his own. Few men seemed to even hear him when he expressed discomfort. It'd been surprising enough that Enzo noticed his wince at the beginning of their stroll. To have it remembered some hours and adventures afterward... Well. Fiore certainly appreciated it. But his profession demanded a certain response. "I'm game for anything."

A smile warmed those masked eyes as Enzo replied, "Then lead on."

Fiore did so with a sure step despite the frantic spinning of his mind's wheels. He had perhaps overplayed his hand in showing Enzo the capricci. Vanity had informed his motive, true enough. But the capricci contained his own desires as well as a means to gauge Enzo's. His memories of verdant valleys remained dim and distant, as indistinct as the sfumato haze hanging over the painted forest. While he had no singular distinct recollection, a sort of satiety overcame him whenever he encountered something similar, and the fashionable capricci produced in Halcyon sufficed to send his mind wandering off down bucolic pathways of never-was and never-were.

And then Enzo had beheld him thus wandering. Which was at best humiliating and at worst dangerous. Though Enzo didn't seem to mind it. That was something. What, Fiore didn't exactly know, but it was something.

He ought to have shown Enzo the mask-makers or lace-weavers or glass-blowers. The latter Fiore found a fascinating science, though the island itself had clogged with sight-seers in the centuries since the glass-blowers were permitted to come and go freely rather than remain their whole lives in their quarter lest the secrets of their art escape. Enzo would've probably liked it, as well. But then there was Fiore's vanity and his eagerness to show off Enzo to his friends as much as to show off his friends' work to Enzo, and then Enzo's offer and his promise. Now, when Fiore ought to have changed the subject by introducing new sights, his flagging courage instead forced him to retreat to his ship with his tail between his legs and his would-be paramour in tow.

Over and through the myriad bridges and back-alleys, Enzo seemed content to stride alongside Fiore in blissful silence.

Then it broke.

"Were you trained as an artist?" Enzo asked.

Fiore tensed. He forced his shoulders back down into place the very instant they hunched, but still he feared Enzo had noticed, even beneath his mask. He willed his voice to remain even-keeled as he replied, "Never formally. Though I did trade favors for lessons on occasion." He let a smile slip through. "And nothing will prevent Artemisia from critiquing a sketch."

"Have you ever wanted formal training?"

The enquiries, like Enzo himself, were entirely innocent. They sent Fiore's heart into his throat regardless. Still, he kept it from leaking into his voice—his training had granted him that much command, at least. "Even if I did, I'm far too old for an apprenticeship now. Can you imagine me sweeping pencil-shavings?"

Enzo didn't laugh at this image. "And before now?"

"In my youth, you mean? Then I had no family to pay for an apprenticeship. And I've acquired no family since," he added with another smile, hoping the jest would cover up the honesty slipping through the cracks in his answers.

Enzo considered the matter. Or seemed to. The mask made his reactions far more difficult to read than Fiore would've wished.

By then the mizzenmast of the *Kingfisher* had mercifully come within sight. Fiore put on his most charming smile and quickened his step. With any luck, Enzo would mistake his nerves for mere eagerness to get inside and enjoy a private moment or two.

To Fiore's relief, Enzo left off questioning him as they approached the ship. He remained silent as they climbed aboard and slipped belowdecks. The silence held a contemplative rather than a strained quality. Fiore hoped it might hold out throughout their encounter as he shut the door behind them.

But rather than slip off his hat or cloak, Enzo laid a hand on the bed's prow and tapped his gloved fingers. He didn't look at Fiore. Fiore, not knowing what he was about, hesitated to press the issue.

At length, Enzo turned to regard him, and in a voice not in the least bit unkind, asked, "Do you enjoy your present career?"

The most dangerous question of all. The obvious and correct answer was, "Yes." But Fiore had begun to doubt whether Enzo would take that at face value. Again the specter of honesty loomed in his mind. It possessed him to open his mouth.

"It's not my first choice," Fiore admitted. "But then again, few have the luxury of choice at all."

It was certainly better than the path the conservatorio had laid out for him.

Enzo cocked his head. "Would art have been your first choice?"

Again, a question few men had bothered asking him. When Fiore had recovered from the surprise, he smiled. "Rather. Though the stories I hear from Artemisia about her patrons aren't much different from my own."

"How so?" asked Enzo.

Fiore caught his tongue, realizing too late he'd already revealed too much. "Nothing sordid, only—doing as the patron decrees rather than following your own desires."

More than ever, Fiore wished he could see Enzo's face and have just a hint of how he felt about that particular revelation. What little he gleaned from the masked eyes seemed concerned.

With some hesitation, Enzo enquired, "You do desire men, do you not?"

"I do," Fiore quickly and truthfully assured him. But before he could stop himself, he added, "Just… not always in the way they desire me."

"And how do you desire them?"

Fiore's answer stuck in his throat. *I desire to bend you over my bed and fuck you within an inch of your life* was not a proclamation which tended to go over well. In the absence of this, an uncomfortable silence arose.

"Perhaps," Enzo added, "I ought to put it another way. Which do you prefer? To enter another or to have another enter you?"

It wasn't the first time Fiore had heard the question. In his experience, it was never genuine. And so he replied, "I prefer to be paid."

Enzo chuckled. "And if payment is assured regardless of preference?"

Which, again, in Fiore's experience, was never the case.

Except now, however, the dark eyes beneath the mask shone with a sincerity that Fiore had never yet encountered in his profession. An honest desire which demanded an honest answer. The truth had taken them this far together, even with the mask between them. Perhaps Fiore might try the truth again. "I prefer to fuck rather than get fucked."

Fiore waited for the confusion, disappointment, disbelief, or disgust which tended to follow this particular confession.

Instead, Enzo's broad shoulders relaxed in what seemed very much like relief. "Then would you be so kind as to fuck me?"

Fiore blinked up at him. He found a smile stealing over his lips as he replied, again with uncommon honesty, "Gladly."

Enzo's eyes gleamed. Then, to Fiore's further amazement, he raised his hands to the brim of his tricorn hat and swept it from his head—taking the zendale hood along with it. He set both aside on Fiore's chair. A shrug of his shoulders and a deft flick of his wrist sent his cloak to the same end.

And Fiore beheld more of Enzo than he ever had before.

Most bauta masks were held in place by the hat-brim of the wearer. Enzo's had the further security of leather cord tied around the back of his head, which meant Fiore still had no glimpse of his face. But he saw long dark hair tied in a queue at the nape of his neck and falling down between his shoulder blades.

Fiore couldn't resist catching that queue in his hand and running his fingers through the dark locks. Nor could he prevent himself, now that he had them in sight at last, from tracing the delicate seashell curves of Enzo's ears with his fingertips. Enzo shivered under his touch. The eyes beneath the mask fell shut. Fiore would've given anything to tear it off his face and kiss him properly.

Instead, he settled for Enzo's waistcoat buttons.

Years of experience made quick work of the dozens of black pearls between him and Enzo's shirt. Enzo helped him along with the final few and shrugged the waistcoat off his shoulders. He made no move to prevent Fiore from moving on down to Enzo's breeches. The fall-front fell away. His fingertips lingered on the buttons securing the knee-plackets, sliding up the stockinged calves to delve beneath the breeches' cuffs, each button coming undone as one-by-one they succumbed to his delicate ministrations.

The loss of breeches was to Enzo's great advantage, in Fiore's opinion, for it revealed that the fullness at the back was not altogether an illusion of the tailor's craft. It likewise revealed a pair of linen drawers. Fiore didn't wear drawers himself—his shirttails did the trick—though he had seen them on gentlemen prior to Enzo.

But before Fiore could strip them, Enzo grasped the hem of his shirt and drew it off over his head.

His chest, once bared, exceeded all Fiore's expectation. Musculature to rival a gondolier rippled beneath a virile pelt of dark hair. Fiore raised an enquiring hand. Upon receiving an affirmative inclination of the masked head, he ventured to run his fingers through the dark hair. A gasp shuddered through Enzo's ribcage at his touch.

And still, the mask remained.

Fiore had lain with many masked gentlemen before—but they tended to remove their masks once his chamber door had shut. Unless they wished to retain their mask for a particular purpose that tended to involve more of the accoutrement Fiore kept in his sea-chest. Enzo hadn't asked after the sea-chest yet or mentioned anything in line with its contents. Fiore wondered if he ought to offer them up or if they'd frighten him off. However, if he required a mask to lie with Fiore, then he might be more inclined towards them than Fiore had previously supposed.

Regardless, Fiore knew better than to remark upon the mask just now. Instead, with another enquiring glance and answering nod, he dropt his hands to Enzo's stockings.

SEBASTIAN NOTHWELL

Fiore and almost everyone else in the city wore stockings as a matter of course. But he'd never yet encountered silk stockings outside of rumor. He found he quite admired the deliciously soft and smooth texture of Enzo's. They provided both ample excuse and thrilling reward for running his fingertips over the sculptural chiseled curves of Enzo's calves. On reflection he decided to leave them as they were.

But when Fiore's fingers arose to dispense with Enzo's drawers, Enzo halted him with a gentle clasp on his wrist.

Fiore of course withdrew his hands at once. He watched with undisguised curiosity as Enzo untied the drawers and began to slide them down over his hips. The root of his prick emerged, nestled amidst dark hair. A sight Fiore had seen before, true enough, but to see it again gave him no less delight now.

Enzo dragged his drawers down an inch or two further; enough for him to reach in and withdraw his half-hard cock altogether. Then he ran his fingertips beneath the waistband of his drawers and slid them down in back just enough to expose his ass. The band rested beneath the globes in such a way as to enhance their already impressive girth.

And there his drawers remained.

Fiore stared even whilst he did his best to conceal his confusion. He certainly wasn't disappointed. Indeed, he could hardly wait to get his hands on the whole of it. But between the drawers and the mask he remained bewildered by what Enzo chose to conceal and for what possible purpose. A dueling wound sprang to mind—he'd heard tell of those who sought to humiliate as well as kill their opponents by striking between the legs before attempting any mortal blow. Perhaps Enzo bore scars similar to his own. Whatever wound may or may not have existed there, it didn't prevent Enzo's prick from arising into a beautiful upward curve.

As Fiore glanced up to meet Enzo's eyes, however, he found a shy hesitance that only a heart of stone could answer with anything less than a reassuring smile.

A breath of relief escaped Enzo.

Fiore encircled his waist with one arm and took him in hand with the other. Keeping both mask and drawers on was a bit odd. He'd have liked to be kissing Enzo by now. But the rest of him more than sufficed to inspire admiration—particularly the garters and hose, which gave Fiore more of a thrill than otherwise.

A few strokes had Enzo hard as iron in his palm. The slightest touch sent him willingly tumbling into the bed, where he knelt and braced himself with a hand on either side of the boat's bow.

The fluidity with which he assumed the posture gave Fiore pause. "Have you done this before?"

It was a pertinent rather than prurient question. Fellows who already knew how to take a cock were less likely to injure themselves in either enthusiasm or hesitation. Fiore would take the same care either way, but he still liked to know what he was getting himself into. Perhaps the modesty which drove Enzo to disguise himself from head to foot had likewise prevented him from engaging in this sort of intimacy.

"Often," Enzo replied with ease.

"Oh." The surprised syllable slipped out of Fiore's lips unbidden.

Enzo merely chuckled.

Between the caresses and the inspiring sights, Fiore had already achieved a full stand. Disrobing was the work of mere moments. He slathered his cock with as much oil as he wished most fellows would use on him, then poured some into the crack between Enzo's globes for good measure. Enzo shivered as it trickled down. Fiore found he enjoyed the sight and resolved to draw further shivers from him in short order. He lined up his cock-head with Enzo's hole, settled his hands onto those sinewy hips, and began.

At the first breach, a deep groan of satisfaction erupted from Enzo's throat, as if Fiore had unlocked the door to a forgotten mausoleum and its hinges sang out in sheer relief at their long-awaited release.

For his part, Fiore had to take a breath to steady himself. Enzo's hole felt as tight as the eye of a needle even as it drew him in. A grip like an iron vise in a silken sheath. And the heat of it—all fellows were warmer within than without, in Fiore's experience, but Enzo had a bonfire blazing within him. A quick thrust wouldn't do the trick. Fiore had to slip inside by fractions of an inch, a drawn-out impalement, steady and delicate work.

Enzo's breath hitched when the head of Fiore's prick grazed the firm knot within him.

"Too much?" Fiore asked, his own words coming ragged.

Enzo shook his head between his arms. "More. Please."

Fiore obliged him. Another inch was gained. He withdrew, adding ample oil, and plunged forth again, sheathing himself halfway up the blade.

Enzo moaned and rocked back against him. Another withdrawal and thrust seemed to please him still more, his back arching, knuckles clenched against the boat's gunwales. Back and forth, steady as the tides, and all the while Fiore fought not to lose himself beneath the surging foam.

The mausoleum groan resounded again as Fiore sank in to the hilt.

Fiore laid himself over Enzo's back like a second skin—both of them already beaded with sweat—and basked in the satisfaction. How he loved to lose himself inside another man. His chest clasped flush against Enzo's spine, his heartbeat thudding through them both, thrumming in and out of time with the throbbing pulse within Enzo. He pressed a kiss to the nape of Enzo's neck and felt his breath catch beneath him.

"Tell me when you wish me to move," Fiore murmured. He combed his idle fingers through Enzo's locks as he waited.

"Now," Enzo said—but before Fiore could obey him, he added with some hesitation, "You might pull my hair."

Fiore blinked down at him. His stunned expression remained hidden from Enzo's gaze. He did his best to keep his shock out of his voice and instead revealed his genuine wonder with a low purr. "Might I?"

Enzo nodded brisk without turning to look at him.

Lightly, gingerly, and ever so slowly, Fiore reached for the black ribbon securing Enzo's queue. Untying it released a river of tresses that poured through Fiore's fingers. He wrapped them around his fist and gave an experimental tug.

A soft gasp escaped Enzo as he bucked his hips back against Fiore's cock.

A grin stole over Fiore's lips. He'd never sat astride a horse, but there remained something instinctive as he settled into the saddle of Enzo's ass and, with one hand firmly clenched in the reins of his hair, began to ride.

Enzo mumbled something.

Fiore slowed at once. "What is it?"

Enzo drew in a shuddering breath and growled out, *"Harder."*

The low command reverberated through Fiore's own ribcage and shot straight down to his cock, which pulsed within Enzo. If this kept up, he knew not how long he could withhold himself. He drew out his prick until the head brushed against the tight entrance. Then he slammed it in to the hilt again in one swift thrust.

Enzo gasped. "Yes—more—please—"

At each exclamation, Fiore obliged him with another draw and thrust. And with every draw and thrust, Enzo rutted back against him. True to his word, he took a cock like one who'd taken many and still hungered for more. Every low syllable that dropped from Enzo's lips made Fiore's cock throb. But it was the pleas that threatened to overwhelm him.

There were many rules Fiore followed in his career. The ritual of making sure Corelli saw him—and more importantly, who he was with —whenever he took a man belowdecks. Accepting the drinks men offered him without taking more than a sip or two. Laying out his laws plainly beforehand to forestall any confusion or complaint if they should receive something other than what they'd expected.

One particular rule he found difficult to follow now.

The whore must come last—if at all.

The concern went beyond the mere practical concerns of the difficulty of continuing to fuck a man after one had already spent within him. In Fiore's experience, if he spent first, the gentlemen tended to take it as an invitation to try and fuck him in turn. He'd never enjoyed that. And despite his preferences, he'd nonetheless endured more than his fair share of it. Worse still were those who saw how their fucking him had made his prick wilt and concluded he'd gone soft because he'd spent rather than because he took no pleasure in the act.

Sometimes he could convince them to let him go below instead. This he far preferred. He derived a great deal of enjoyment from sucking cock. Seeing firsthand the reaction gleaned from his efforts inspired his own pleasure. A sharp contrast to lying on his stomach getting pounded like a cod-skull beneath a fisher's bat. Besides, having his teeth so near to something so tender gave him a well-appreciated sense of control. Should things go sour he had the upper hand.

At present, however, his cock was buried up to its hilt in Enzo's body, and Enzo himself was making it rather difficult for Fiore to restrain his own spend. Between his deep ecstatic moans, the way his breath caught as Fiore wrapped his hair in his fist, his long lean frame shuddering and writhing beneath his grasp, and how the hot sheath of his body clenched tight around Fiore's blade, it was a wonder Fiore hadn't spilled his seed a hundred times over already.

When Fiore could stand it no longer, he dropt his hand from Enzo's hip to find his cock. It had a long, thick, satisfying heft, warm velvet wrapped tight over a steel blade. Enzo's heartbeat throbbed through the vein. A few swift strokes made Enzo moan in pleasure. A few more sufficed to send him spilling over Fiore's fingers. His whole frame shuddered as his prick pulsed in Fiore's palm. Likewise his hole clenched around Fiore's own cock.

With all this, Fiore felt powerless to restrain himself from following Enzo over the brink.

Fiore bit his lip hard enough to break the skin. With a few final rapid thrusts, he lost all semblance of control. He clasped Enzo close to him, his ribs flush against his spine, and poured a torrent of seed deep within him. Sheer relief stung his eyes. He gasped, breathless, his room fading into darkness as he lost himself in Enzo—and beneath his body feeling Enzo take pleasure in forming a vessel for Fiore's ecstasy in turn, as Enzo breathed a gratified sigh whilst Fiore's cock pulsed inside him.

They basked together in their entwined bliss for far longer than Fiore oft allowed. He found his fingers combing through Enzo's locks of their own accord, playing with the silken strands as he soaked in the warmth of his body clasped so tight against his own. He kissed the nape of his neck and tasted the salt of honest sweat on his skin. The sound of his breaths, felt as much as heard, steady as the tides, low and deep and utterly contented, could've soothed them both down into sleep. Something about this moment seemed to slake a thirst Fiore hadn't even realized he possessed.

Yet no good thing could last forever. All too soon, by Fiore's reckoning, the delightful languid haze dissipated. And though he would've gladly remained all evening with Enzo entangled in his arms,

Enzo himself stirred with a determination to rise—so, with no small reluctance, Fiore released him.

Enzo slid his drawers back up to their proper place. He sat up with his back to Fiore. His hands reached towards the back of his head, and for one wild moment Fiore thought he meant to untie his mask—but no, he merely gathered his hair back into its queue at the nape of his neck, then glanced 'round in search of something.

Fiore held up the ribbon with a smile.

An answering smile lit up Enzo's eyes beneath his mask. He reached to pluck the ribbon from Fiore's fingertips as delicately as if it were a blossom. Then he tied up his hair and stood.

"Not disappointed, I hope?" Fiore heard himself ask. He'd meant to catch the words before they ever left his tongue, but they'd escaped him, and now he had to suppress a wince at how needful they sounded. He'd kept up his lackadaisical tone, at least. With any luck Enzo would take it as a mere jest.

And to his relief, Enzo laughed, low and soft and deep, rumbling up from the depths of his chest to resound through Fiore's own ribs. "Not in the least."

Yet Enzo was leaving him. Fiore fixed his own features into a tranquil mask over his unaccountable nerves. The departure of a gentleman caller was a good thing. It gave him a moment to himself between jobs. Some time to collect himself whilst the music started up on deck and the dancing began to echo down through his ceiling before he tumbled up and sought out his next conquest. Watching Enzo garb himself again oughtn't have inspired even half so much dread as Fiore felt.

"Forgive my hasty departure," Enzo said, startling Fiore out of his secret turmoil. "My sister expects me for dinner. And I expect," he added with another smile glinting in his masked eyes, "you have more pressing business to attend to."

"Hardly," Fiore drawled before he could stop himself.

Enzo seemed to take it in stride. Indeed, he seemed rather too preoccupied with his own nerves to notice Fiore's. "When may I see you again?"

"Whenever you like," Fiore purred. Despite the theatrics applied to his standard reply, for once he meant it. Easier to hide his sincerity behind smoke and mirrors rather than bare it for the ridicule of all the world.

Though Enzo hardly seemed the sort to ridicule him. And, indeed, sounded quite earnest as he enquired, "Would mèrcore be too soon?"

A mere three days hence. Fiore smiled. "Not at all."

# CHAPTER FIVE

The sheer satisfaction of Enzo's encounter with Fiore left him feeling more invigorated than he had in months. It lingered on long after he'd departed the *Kingfisher*—and what strength of will it'd required for him to leave Fiore behind—throughout the evening, threatening to rob him of his sleep until he at last relented and dropped his hand to his cock still throbbing at the memory of what Fiore had done to him. The following morning he awoke to a delicious ache in his ass and another cock-stand to match it. Fiore's name tumbled from his lips as he thrust his hips into his own hand and spilled his seed over his knuckles.

Even more potent than the eroticism, however, were the smaller moments which had led up to it. As he quaffed his coffee he thought of the more luxuriant sips he'd shared with Fiore at the Crooked Anchor, where he'd enjoyed a splendid view of every coy smile on those perfect lips and every flirtatious glance of those dark doe eyes. As he took his customary morning run up the three-story spiral staircase on the northwest corner of Ca' Scaevola, he kept his head held high all the while with the recollection of Fiore hailing him from the ship's deck, inviting him to climb up and aboard. As he scraped and bathed afterward, the steam arising recalled the fog hanging over the forested valley in the capriccio which had so captivated Fiore, and Enzo found himself captivated again in turn by the memory of the sweet longing that began in those enormous dark eyes and carried through the whole of his dancer's stance until it seemed as if he would step into the painting and dissolve himself to join its fantasy. Enzo's mind sparked with what little hints he'd gleaned from their conversation, like shards falling away from a gemstone as it was cut, revealing a glimpse here and there of the beauty gleaming beneath—a man who desired nothing so much as art and yet made his living in love.

Mèrcore couldn't come soon enough.

Since leaving university, Enzo had little with which to distract himself. The library of Ca' Scaevola was well-stocked with fantastical tales and fascinating historical and scientific volumes alike, if he could only convince his mind to settle down and fix upon them. But the fantastical tales reminded him of all the adventures he couldn't have, and the sciences and histories seemed to taunt him with his lost university hopes. The alchemical workshop gave him a sort of wistful relief, though his experimentation accomplished little. His lonesome masked wanderings throughout the city conjured the illusion of society with none of the substance of friendship. It'd taken months for Lucrezia to relent and permit him to return to practicing fencing—in private, rather than in any school or club, under the supervision of a singular tutor, to whom he'd quickly grown attached for exercise and companionship alike, despite the professional distance between them. Maestra Rovigatti had become his sole friend in all his limited world.

Then Giovanna had handed him a puppy.

According to her, the round furry wriggling lump was the runt of the litter. The master of hounds had told her it wouldn't grow fit enough to join the hunting pack and ought to be drowned. But perhaps Enzo, as a medical mind, had a differing opinion?

Enzo had taken the hint. It felt better to have a task to focus on, however contrived, after so many months bereft of the course charted for him by university. And so he set about making sure the wriggling black lump not only survived, but thrived.

As it so happened, when one devoted one's self wholly to rearing up a creature, giving it the choicest cuts from one's own plate (for while, on the rare occasion when he could bring himself to attempt to eat, any bite turned to ash on Enzo's tongue, the puppy eagerly had devoured all), making it a soft bed before the fire in one's own bed-chamber (and sometimes allowing it up onto his own bed), finding some small relief in burying one's fingertips in the thick ruff around its neck whilst it napped in one's lap, allowing it to literally dog one's heels as one wandered like a shade through the halls of one's ancestral home, and occupying one's idle mind in teaching it as wide a variety of commands as its wee blinking head could hold—the creature did indeed thrive, growing in the span of a year to a greater height and breadth than any of its supposed superior siblings and becoming wholly devoted to Enzo in turn.

Enzo had named the pup Vittorio. While not quite fully grown, according to the master of hounds, Vittorio did stand with his shoulders almost at the height of Enzo's waist, a barrel-chest as broad as any man's, and his paws as large as Enzo's own fists. Hunting demanded cropped ears and tail, but Enzo found he hadn't the heart for it and so enjoyed the sight of a wagging whip as the hound wriggled with joy to see him and ears which flopped inside-out when the hound cocked its head in confusion.

Despite or perhaps because of his immense size, Vittorio proved more lazy than ferocious. He eagerly followed Enzo out of bed every morning, but after a few game attempts he couldn't be persuaded to accompany him on his daily run up the spiral stairs, instead waiting patiently at the foot for his master's return. He enjoyed a short stroll through the streets immediately surrounding Ca' Scaevola but wearied of the long and meandering walks Enzo had wandered on since his return to the city. His jaws clanged shut on any stick Enzo tossed his way and crushed the bones given him by the cook but never so much as nipped at Giovanna's children, who played with his ears and face and tail and paws as if they were clay and indeed feared the hound far less than they feared Enzo.

While Vittorio didn't oft participate in his own exercise, he did enjoy supervising Enzo's. Teaching the hound that Maestra Rovigatti was a friend and their duels in the Ca' Scaevola garden were mere play took some doing. Enzo began when Vittorio was small enough to hold in the crook of his arm. By the time he'd grown up into almost-a-horse, he proved content to sit by the garden-bench and watch the swordplay like a tennis match—assuming he didn't fall asleep outright.

On this particular day the hound had begun snoring well before their sparring concluded. Enzo, stripped to the waist and streaming sweat, bowed to Maestra Rovigatti and sheathed his blade. He lost most bouts to her and learnt a great deal in the bargain. Today, however, his mind whirled not with parries and counter-parries but with quite another problem altogether.

"Maestra," Enzo said when he got his breath back at last. "Have you ever been in love?"

Maestra Rovigatti, in the midst of reaching for the silver goblets and ewer of water laid out for them beforehand on the garden-bench, raised her brows. "Why d'you ask?"

"I think I may have fallen for someone."

Maestra Rovigatti's eyes widened. It was the most surprise or alarm Enzo had ever seen her express and far more than he thought his words warranted.

As she recovered her poise, she replied, "I'm flattered, my lord, but my heart is already spoken for."

"Oh!" Enzo hastened to explain himself. "No, it's not you—not that you're not very—but rather—"

Maestra Rovigatti continued to watch him flounder with mixed astonishment and amusement writ on her features.

Enzo cleared his throat and tried again. "I've taken up with someone and found myself rather more attached to him than I've felt for anyone in some time."

"Ah." Maestra Rovigatti relaxed her shoulders. "Then I am happy for you."

Enzo wished he could feel the same. "He is, I fear, not so attached to me."

Maestra Rovigatti gave a sage murmur. "Is he at all interested?"

"Very, I should think. We have been intimate—many times—and he is always happy to see me, but whenever I try to offer him anything more, he denies me."

"Define 'anything more.'"

"Gifts," Enzo explained. "He will take food and drink, if I consume the same, but clothing, jewelry, books, art, ornament—he spurns it all."

"Does he have other lovers?"

"Yes." Enzo hesitated. "It is rather his profession."

"Ah," Maestra Rovigatti said again. "So he does take something from you."

"As much as he takes from any other. He will accept no more."

"You have offered more?"

"Of course."

"How much more?"

"Enough so he need never work again."

Maestra Rovigatti blinked. "And he has refused this."

"Yes."

"Then it would seem he desires something more from you than what money may buy."

Enzo knew not what else he had to offer.

"He may have money, and whatever money may procure, from anyone," Maestra Rovigatti continued. "Consider giving him something which could come from you alone."

The things that had come from Enzo thus far in his life—death, dishonor, disappointment, disgrace—were nothing he thought anyone else would want. Certainly nothing good enough for Fiore. Beyond wealth he had little to offer. A bizarre gangling figure and an unremarkable face. Half a medical degree and a disturbing interest in alchemy. He could play the lute well enough, but none so well that he'd dare play before others or assume his playing would prove a blessing rather than a curse to their ears. He could sketch, but none so well as Fiore, and a gift of any art from his own fingertips could only be an embarrassment to them both. What skill he had in embroidery produced nothing worth admiring. Certainly nothing anyone would want to trim their garments with—although he'd oft fancied hemming his own garments with the same chirurgical stitches that would tie together skin and sinew. But he couldn't imagine anyone else, or Fiore in particular, shared his peculiar tastes.

Enzo wanted to give him everything. Yet Fiore would accept nothing.

All told, he remained at a loss.

~

It began with a twinge.

Not quite a pang. Not even an ache. Just a point of queasiness low in Fiore's gut from the moment of waking.

Fiore blamed it on last night's wine and thought no more of it, though it did prevent him from breaking his fast.

Nor did he take anything at mid-day. He spent the hours sketching and waiting for the queasy feeling to subside. It did not. Instead, it grew into a pain that ebbed and flowed, sometimes spreading across everything between his ribs and hips, sometimes diminishing to that singular point low in his gut where it had begun. He supposed he had something within him that would work its way out on its own. He could wait it out.

By evening, the pain had ebbed again, and he had hopes it might vanish altogether by the following dawn. He felt confident enough to go up on deck to the tavern. There he found a gentleman interested in what he had to offer and brought him down to his room.

While Fiore didn't feel up to much, he thought he could make do with his mouth. The gentleman was neither particularly large nor particularly rough. Fiore had many years' experience swallowing others just like him.

Yet when the head of the prick touched the back of Fiore's tongue, he gagged.

Even that he could usually work past. But tonight when he tried to swallow, his gorge arose, and he had to whip the gentleman from his mouth and turn his head to avoid spewing all over him. He'd eaten nothing; most of what came up was acid and bile. Still, it was enough to kill the mood, and the gentleman excused himself without paying.

Fiore remained kneeling on the floor for some time. When the nausea ebbed, he staggered upright to fetch bucket and rag. He managed to clean the mess without adding to it, which he felt a feat worth celebrating, then groped his way to his bed. He crawled beneath the bedclothes and lay clutching his stomach in darkness for he knew not how long before sleep claimed him.

He awoke to a gentle tapping at his door.

Fiore opened his eyes none too willingly. Sunlight poured in through the window. He'd slept through the night, at least, and supposed that was something. His guts still ached and lurched within him as he dragged himself out of bed and shrugged on a robe to answer the knock. He opened the door and found perhaps the only person he could feel genuinely happy to see even in the midst of his discomfort.

Fiore smiled despite his stomach. "Thought you weren't coming until mèrcore."

Enzo blinked beneath the mask. "It is mèrcore."

Fiore's stomach did a queer plunge. "Oh."

"Is everything all right?" Enzo asked.

"I've overslept," Fiore admitted. He did not, however, divulge that he'd overslept by an entire day. That felt a touch too disconcerting.

And yet not quite so disconcerting as the way the whole room slid down to the left as if the *Kingfisher* had slipped back out to sea.

Fiore staggered. His vision blurred. Strong hands clasped his shoulders and held him steady. When the room ceased spinning, he knew not how long after, he found Enzo's masked eyes staring keenly into his own.

"You ought to sit down," said Enzo.

Fiore rather agreed. He let Enzo steer him back towards his bed and sat on the edge of it. Enzo sat beside him and laid the back of his hand against Fiore's brow. His knuckles felt queerly cold.

"Don't," Fiore protested. "I don't know if it's catching."

Enzo heeded him not. "I've already had the plague. That's why I'm mother's favorite."

Fiore didn't have the strength to argue. Still, he groaned through gritted teeth, "So have I."

This seemed to give Enzo pause. He dropt his hand from Fiore's brow and instead began rubbing circles onto Fiore's back, which felt comforting, despite all. At last he spoke again, this time with more hesitation. "I've heard that, in your line of work, there may occur certain interior tears or bruising. Is this perhaps...?"

"Already done as well," Fiore said, biting back another groan. "It's not that, either."

Enzo fell silent again. Fiore knew he ought to send him off. But his touch—and his presence, Fiore had to admit—soothed him and made the sickness feel more bearable.

"May I try something?" Enzo asked.

Fiore nodded.

Enzo ceased rubbing his back, much to Fiore's disappointment. He moved to stand in front of Fiore. His hands reached for his breech-buttons.

"I can't," Fiore began.

"I'm not," Enzo replied.

Fiore hesitated, then nodded his assent.

Enzo unbuttoned him. Rather than pull his breeches down, however, he merely folded the waist-band over and drew his shirttail out of it and held it up above his ribs to reveal the crests of his hip-bones.

"Tell me how this pains you," said Enzo.

Nothing good ever started that way. Still, the gentle tone and tender gaze bespoke a desire to do no harm, and so Fiore nodded again.

Enzo took two fingertips and tapped them against Fiore's belly, just above his left hip-bone.

Fiore winced. It didn't feel good, certainly, but it hurt no worse than the rest of him.

Enzo tapped again, this time just beneath his navel.

It didn't feel much better than the first.

Enzo tapped a third time, above his right hip-bone.

Fiore doubled over with a bitten-off scream.

Enzo caught him by the shoulders again. "I thought so."

"Thought what?" Fiore gasped.

"Appendicitis."

This answered nothing.

Fiore expected Enzo to sit down beside him. Perhaps hold him again. Yet Enzo remained standing.

"You need a chirurgeon," said Enzo.

Panic chased the pain from Fiore's body. "No I don't."

"Yes," said Enzo. "You do."

"I'm fine," Fiore lied.

"You're dying."

Fiore jerked his head up to meet those masked eyes. Enzo met his glance unerringly.

"Let me send for a chirurgeon," Enzo said, his dark gaze softened by something Fiore couldn't quite recognize. "Please."

"Chirurgeons need to be paid." Fiore's protest sounded weak to his own ears.

"The cost is nothing to me."

Fiore had known as much already.

"Something inside of you has festered," Enzo continued. "It must come out, or you will die. No one less than a chirurgeon may do it. Please let me send for one. Do not force me to let you perish when you could be saved."

If he weren't so sick, Fiore could have run.

As matters stood, he found himself nodding his assent.

Enzo slipped out into the corridor. A conversation with someone ensued, too low for Fiore to discern the words. But he returned shortly, which was all Fiore wanted in that moment.

Fiore caught him by the hand and drew him down to sit beside him. Enzo put an arm around him; Fiore leaned his head against Enzo's shoulder, and Enzo smoothed his curls across his scalp in soft, soothing strokes, which almost sufficed to lull Fiore into sleep despite the stabbing pain in his gut.

All feelings of comfort vanished with a knock on the chamber door.

Enzo arose to answer it. Fiore resisted the urge to seize him by the wrist and hold him back. He stared in mute dread as Enzo opened the door and ushered a looming figure over the threshold.

A long leather beak obscured the whole face. Green glass lenses gleamed in place of eyes. A flat broad-brimmed hat covered the head. One gloved hand gripped a leather case; the other, a long silver-capped cane. Any further detail remained hidden beneath the formless waxed-canvas robe, the same black shade as mask, hat, gloves, bag, and cane. The stench of vinegar wafted off the whole. It stood not so tall as Fiore recalled from his childhood, but then again, he was no longer a child. Still, the past ten years had not sufficed to rob the sight of its horror.

Enzo welcomed the chirurgeon in with a smile.

Fiore's fists tangled in the bedclothes as he fought the impulse to bolt for the window.

The chirurgeon approached his bedside. They doffed their hat, which revealed just the hood of their robe and the dome of their mask. A muffled voice emerged from the beak. "Signor Fiore, I presume."

Fiore forced himself to nod.

The chirurgeon took up the post Enzo had vacated and set their bag on the nightstand. From this they withdrew stetoscopio and termometro.

"Hold this under your tongue," they instructed, holding the termometro before Fiore. "If you would."

Fiore supposed he'd already taken more questionable things into his mouth. He pried his lips apart and accepted the cold glass tube.

The chirurgeon brought up their stetoscopio. "If I may."

It didn't quite carry the tone of a question. Still, Fiore nodded. Panic seized him as the chirurgeon raised their hands toward his throat. He fumbled open his own shirt-ties to pull down his collar so they needn't touch him any further than absolutely necessary.

The stetoscopio's brass bell felt colder than ice against his fevered chest and sent a shiver over his skin. Fiore didn't think the chirurgeon needed the instrument to hear his heart flinging itself against its ribcage with the frantic ferocity of a trapped bird. Whatever they thought of his pounding pulse, he could read nothing of it in the blank glass eyes of the beaked mask.

Enzo, meanwhile, had gone 'round to the opposite side of the bed. He perched on it with a tentative delicacy that belied his enormous frame and laid his gentle hand over Fiore's fist tangled in the bedclothes. His touch alone dissolved the Gordian knot of Fiore's knuckles.

The chirurgeon withdrew the stetoscopio and termometro without commenting on the results of either, though they did examine the latter closely. They set their instruments aside and reached for Fiore's waistband before halting.

"Shall you draw it up, or shall I?" they asked him.

Fiore hastened to tear his shirt free from the waist of his breeches, holding it up out of the way above his navel. Then he steeled his nerve and unbuttoned the fall-front.

Much like Enzo had done before them, the chirurgeon took two fingers and tapped just above the crest of Fiore's left hip-bone, then below his navel, then over on the right-hand side. It felt worse than before. Fiore's scream threatened to tear his throat apart as he choked it back.

"Appendicitis," the chirurgeon confirmed. "We must have it out at once."

Fiore had expected nothing less. He still didn't like to hear it.

The chirurgeon picked up their leather case and took it off with them further down towards the bow of the bed. Enzo deftly maneuvered around them to return to his place at Fiore's bedside.

Before he'd even sat down again, Fiore caught him by the elbow.

"Don't let them maim me," he hissed, knowing all the while how ludicrous he must sound.

Enzo replied with solemnity, "I won't."

"Can you undress yourself?" the chirurgeon asked, heedless of their conversation. "Or do you require aid?"

"Must I?" Fiore despised the rising pitch of his own voice.

Not an ounce of pity entered the chirurgeon's tone. "Any lint in the wound will worsen the infection."

Fiore looked to Enzo, who might at least care whether he lived or died. He fought back his desperation even as he begged. "Let me keep my breeches on, at least."

Enzo hesitated, then turned to the chirurgeon. "May he?"

"He may," the chirurgeon conceded. "To a point."

Fiore dreaded that point. Still, he didn't fight back as Enzo's hands descended to slide his breeches down from his waist to rest just beneath the crests of his jutting hip-bones. He submitted more willingly when it came to his shirt, raising his arms as Enzo drew it up over his head.

"Can you give him something for the pain?" Enzo asked as he folded Fiore's shirt and set it aside.

"No." Fiore would have shouted if he had the strength for it. As such, he put everything he had left behind the word. He had to stay awake, He couldn't have his head muddled. He knew what they would do to him if he fell unconscious.

Enzo stared at him. For an instant, Fiore feared he'd seize him, hold him down, and pour opium down his throat or strangle him into sleep. Death would prove preferable.

But when Enzo moved, it was to drop his hands to his own waist, and after a moment, bring forth his own belt. He doubled it over in his fist and held it up to Fiore's lips. "Bite this."

The black leather, richly tooled with intricate scales of twining serpents, must have cost more than everything Fiore owned and his rent besides. After this, it would be ruined.

Fiore opened his mouth. The belt slipped over his tongue. He bit down. An intoxicating scent—one he typically loved, though he found it difficult to delight in at the moment—filled his lungs. The leather gave way easily between his jaws. His teeth destroyed the tooling. Yet the belt held out for now. Enzo didn't seem to give it a second thought.

"Secure his legs," said the chirurgeon.

"What?" Fiore blurted.

"If you insist on remaining awake, we must prevent you from moving," said the chirurgeon in the same pitiless tone.

Fiore gave Enzo a pleading look. Beneath the mask, Enzo's eyes gave him a sympathetic glance in return.

Yet when the chirurgeon withdrew leather straps from his bag, Enzo accepted them with an open hand. And when Enzo began to belt Fiore's ankles to the boat's prow, Fiore did not resist him.

This done, Enzo returned to his seat at Fiore's side and took Fiore's left hand in his own.

"Shall we begin?" said the chirurgeon. Sunlight glinted off the silver blade of their upraised scalpel.

Enzo looked to Fiore.

Against every instinct, Fiore nodded.

Enzo passed the nod along to the chirurgeon.

The scalpel descended. The silver blade bit into his skin. Crimson spilled out. The scalpel drew a line across his belly, as wide as his palm. His flesh split beneath it, a scarlet maw yawning wide even as Fiore clenched his own jaw tight.

A hand touched his cheek.

"Look at me," said Enzo.

Fiore shook his head.

The scalpel lifted from him only to plunge in again, drawing another line to cross the first, more agonizing than the last. Pain bid him swoon. Fear forced him awake.

Enzo did not relent. "It'll be easier if you don't watch."

Fiore shook his head again. He might've told Enzo why, if it weren't for the belt clenched in his teeth and the scream erupting from his throat as the scalpel sawed through gristle and muscle to reach his purpling guts and something jaundiced bubbled up from the fresh wound. The moment he glanced away, the knife would descend below his belt, and then—

Still, Enzo tried anew. "I will tell you all they do. Just look at me. Please."

A pair of long silver instruments entered him. The pain of the invasion screwed his eyes shut. The sickening sliding sensation turned his stomach. His head lolled. It came to rest facing Enzo. His eyes opened.

Enzo's gaze held all of Fiore's pain and fear. Yet his voice remained steady. "They are cutting out the source of the infection. It will be done soon."

Something tore within him. Something deep. Far too deep. His heart hammered in his throat. His breath came in shallow and left him in screams forced out through his teeth. Tears blurred his sight.

But he kept his gaze locked on those masked eyes.

"They have it in hand," Enzo said. "They've cut it free. They're withdrawing it now."

The sensation of the wretched thing slipping out through a hole that shouldn't have existed thrust Fiore's gorge into his throat alongside his heart. He gagged against the belt, but kept it down. Something dropped into the porcelain basin with a hollow clink.

"It is out," said Enzo. "Now they will clean the wound, and then they will sew it shut. Soon they'll be done."

A bottle uncorked with a slick popping sound. The scent of vinegar filled the room as the chirurgeon poured it into the wound he'd made. It stung, which was at least a novel sort of pain beyond everything else Fiore had endured that day.

The chirurgeon mopped up the mess with clean linen. Then, after more clinking from their bag, a bizarre hissing noise arose and a burning mist struck Fiore's ruined flesh. A high-pitched keen escaped him.

Enzo stroked his cheek. "They're taking up needle and thread."

The piercing of his flesh felt more insult than injury. The drawing of the thread through it had the same horrible sliding sensation as the removal of the infection's source. Fiore didn't have anything left within him to protest against it. His throat, raw from screaming, now held only ragged gasps. His right hand had fisted in the bedclothes and tangled to the wrist. His left hand clenched around Enzo's fingers hard enough to hurt his own knuckles.

Yet Enzo did not flinch. "The knots are tied off. The threads are cut. It is over."

Fiore didn't dare hope far enough to believe him.

Enzo smoothed back the sweat-soaked locks plastered to Fiore's feverish brow. The tenderness of his touch made Fiore want to cry. His cheeks were already wet, and cold, as if from rain. Rain seemed to cover all his flesh in a cold damp.

"Will you take something for the pain now?" Enzo asked, his voice low and pleading.

Against his better judgment, Fiore nodded.

Enzo reached for the belt. With an effort, Fiore unclenched his jaw. A shameful whimper escaped him. He saw light through the leather where his teeth had torn it. Enzo merely tossed it aside.

"Morphine, I think," said the chirurgeon. "It's too much for laudanum. And too late for chloroform."

Enzo hesitated and turned to Fiore. "Would you prefer something in drink or in a needle?"

Fiore recalled all too well the taste of poppies in wine. "Needle."

"Told you," said the chirurgeon.

Enzo rolled his eyes into a glare at the chirurgeon. They didn't seem to notice.

Something pricked the inside of Fiore's elbow. His pained whimper became a long, low sigh as the cold fluid spilled into his veins and a floating relief washed over him.

Enzo stroked his hair with a soft and gentle hand. "Better?"

Fiore nodded more slowly than he intended.

A wan smile reached Enzo's eyes.

# CHAPTER SIX

Against all odds, Fiore awoke feeling far better than he had immediately prior to the chirurgy.

He didn't feel well by any means, but the churning nausea had gone, and the throbbing agony throughout his entrails had reduced to a single particular point just above his right hip—and even this seemed dulled in comparison.

It also helped a great deal that he opened his eyes and turned his head to find Enzo seated at his bedside.

The instant their gazes met, the dark eyes beneath the bauta mask brightened in a soft and gentle smile. A hand arose to caress his cheek.

"Good morning," Enzo murmured. "How d'you feel?"

"Better," Fiore admitted, though he couldn't do so without a wince.

Concern clouded the affectionate gaze Enzo cast down upon him. "Can you stand?"

Fiore stared at him.

"You ought to walk around the room a little," Enzo replied. For what it was worth, he at least sounded apologetic. "Not very far. Just a quick turn and straight back to bed."

"What for?" Fiore asked, no less bewildered.

Enzo fixed him with a solemn look. "To keep your blood from clotting in your veins."

"Oh." Fiore supposed that was a sound enough reason. He struggled to raise himself up on his trembling arms.

No sooner had he begun than Enzo's strong arm slipped beneath his shoulders and gently eased him upright.

"Steady," he said as he lifted Fiore, his voice low and soft and sonorous. Fiore's heart sang at the sound. Under the influence of such a voice he thought he could do anything.

Which was fortunate, because at that moment standing up and walking around felt almost impossible.

The brawn of Enzo's arm at least kept his upper half vertical. Then he swung his legs out of the bed—or rather, Enzo delicately moved them so —and, with a bruising grip on Enzo's shoulders, dared to stand. His thighs trembled. His knees threatened to buckle. But he was up and by leaning heavily against Enzo's warm bulk, remained so.

Enzo took a step. Fiore hobbled alongside. One stride became two, then three, and while Fiore's legs did little more than drag themselves into place, still Enzo seemed pleased. Soon, just as promised, they had gone in a circle 'round the room to the portal window—which Fiore could hardly glance out of without feeling light-headed—and back again to bed. There Enzo laid him down again as gently as a feather falling into a nest.

Fiore's ease proved short-lived, as Enzo's next words were, "The chirurgeon would like to see you." Something must have contorted in Fiore's features at this announcement, for Enzo hastened to add, "Just for a moment. They want to listen to your heart and see that your fever no longer rages."

"My fever?" Fiore echoed stupidly.

"You've been pyretic for the last day and a half."

No wonder his very bones ached. A thought struck him. "Have you remained here all the while?"

Enzo hesitated. "You don't mind, do you?"

"Not in the least," Fiore replied, honest but no less astonished.

His fingertips, of their own accord, made the barest reach towards

Enzo. No sooner had they moved than Enzo's hand clasped his own—a warm and secure grip which sent a balm over Fiore's fluttering heart.

A wan smile reached Enzo's eyes. "I'll send for them, then. I'll only be a moment," he added, for Fiore's hand twisted in the bedclothes the instant he released his hold.

Fiore forced himself to nod and smile.

Enzo seemed to understand his pain nonetheless and cast a sympathetic look back at him even as he went on to the door. He opened it the merest sliver. Fiore braced himself for the sight of a chirurgeon's helm cast in shadow with its horrible glass eyes glinting. Instead he glimpsed the slender form of a woman clad in black livery; a more practical version of Enzo's own garb, with the silks and satins replaced by wools and the silver filigree restrained to a single embroidered crest over her heart. Enzo muttered a few words to her. She gave a sharp nod and retreated into the shadows to vanish from sight altogether. Enzo shut the door.

"Who was that?" Fiore croaked as Enzo returned to him.

"Carlotta," Enzo replied. When it became apparent this held no meaning for Fiore, he added, "My manservant."

Fiore had suspected, or rather known, that Enzo held a certain rank. Still, it struck him to encounter one of his staff in the flesh and find proof of his status.

"The chirurgeon hasn't wandered far," Enzo continued. "It shouldn't take her long to find them."

Fiore knew he ought to take comfort in that. Instead his heart filled with dread at the thought of the chirurgeon's return.

Enzo returned to his seat at Fiore's bedside. "You should have something for the pain."

Fiore braced himself for another injection. But instead of needle or bottle, Enzo brought out a small paper packet. He tipped it out and a small round white tablet fell into his hand. This he held up between thumb and forefinger for Fiore's inspection.

"It's much the same as what you got from the needle," Enzo explained. "Distilled, dried, powdered, and compressed by an apothecary. It must be swallowed whole," he added as he laid it in Fiore's outstretched palm.

A simple enough task, Fiore thought as he examined the small round tablet. He tossed it into his mouth, ignored the chalky texture rolling across his tongue, and swallowed it down in a single gulp.

Enzo, who'd gone to pour a glass of water, turned back just in time to witness this feat. He stared in stunned silence.

Fiore held out his hand for the glass with a grin.

After a moment, Enzo gave it over. "Generally, the water is washed down *with* the tablet. Not after."

Fiore supposed that would make things go more smoothly. "Good to know."

The tablet's effect proved not so instantaneous as the needle. Nevertheless the pain did ebb. It helped a great deal to have Enzo beside him. Still more to have his warm, strong hands enveloping Fiore's own. And still more to hear that low murmur that seemed to reverberate within his own ribs. His frantic pulse steadied as Enzo stroked his hand and continued murmuring words of comfort. The words themselves didn't matter so much as the sounds, for it was these that soothed Fiore down into something like sleep.

Only to bolt awake again when a knock resounded against his door.

"Enter," said Enzo with the air of one accustomed to giving orders.

The door opened. Even though Fiore knew it could be no other than the chirurgeon, still the sight of the hideous waxed-leather helm with its grotesque beak and enormous inhuman glass eyes sent his heart flinging itself against his ribcage as if it wished to escape. He clenched Enzo's hand in a fist. His breath came quick and shallow. This didn't improve as the chirurgeon approached his bedside.

"If I may, signore," echoed a voice from within the cavernous leather beak.

Against his better judgment, Fiore nodded. Even then, he couldn't quite suppress a flinch as the chirurgeon pulled down the bedclothes to expose his chest. The shock of the stetoscopio's cold brass bell against his flesh forced a gasp that hissed out between his clenched teeth.

"Careful," said Enzo.

The word came out not in the soothing tone Fiore had grown accustomed to hearing from Enzo's lips, but rather with the hard edge of a warning. It took Fiore a moment to realize Enzo had spoken not to him but to the chirurgeon.

It was impossible to tell how the chirurgeon took to the correction beneath their mask. They said nothing. The brass watch in their other hand ticked loud as thunderbolts. Fiore's heart threw itself against his ribcage in its futile efforts to escape the chirurgeon's clutches. Only Enzo's hand in his own kept him from bolting.

"The pulse is a touch more rapid than I'd prefer," declared the chirurgeon.

Even behind the bauta mask, Enzo's resulting glare communicated caustic disdain for the intelligence of that particular remark.

"Though," the chirurgeon added, sounding somewhat chastened, "there may be other factors complicating the pulse at the present moment."

"Indeed," said Enzo.

The chirurgeon set aside the stetoscopio and took up the termometro in its place. At the chirurgeon's bidding, Fiore opened his mouth and held it beneath his tongue. Silence reigned for several moments whilst the chirurgeon examined their silver watch. Fiore's pulse pounded in his ears. Then the chirurgeon snapped the watch shut and withdrew the termometro.

"Fever greatly reduced," the chirurgeon announced. "Though still a touch elevated. Would you keep an eye on it, my lord? You know well enough how to read the signs."

The queer mixture of reverence and familiarity baffled Fiore.

Enzo merely nodded.

The chirurgeon stood. "Do inform me if he should take a turn for the worse. I'll not be far off."

And with that, they departed, leaving stetoscopio and termometro both on Fiore's nightstand.

Fiore rolled his head across his pillow to fix Enzo with a considering look. "You know something of medicine. Yet you're not a chirurgeon yourself."

"I do," Enzo admitted. "And I am not."

Fiore waited for him to explain.

Enzo remained silent.

While Fiore had nothing but gratitude for all Enzo had done for him in the past two days, he realized more than ever before as he stared at the blank visage of the black bauta mask how little he knew of Enzo and how much Enzo knew of him. Scores of men had seen Fiore in the throes of ecstasy. Few had beheld him in the throes of agony. And none moreso than Enzo. The balance, or lack thereof, hadn't particularly bothered him until now. Now, with his entrails laid bare beneath the gaze of a man who refused to let Fiore know anything of him beyond his prick, his ass, and his eyes...

"Has the pain ebbed at all?" Enzo asked.

Fiore blinked at him. It took him a moment to recall the anodyne Enzo had dosed him with but a few moments ago. He took stock of the throbbing ache beneath the bandages. "It's dulled a little."

Enzo held his gaze. "Something else troubles you."

Not just his body but his soul laid bare to Enzo's eyes, apparently. Fiore swallowed hard and settled on telling a different truth. "My mouth tastes awful."

Enzo laughed, much to Fiore's relief. Then he arose to fetch pitcher, basin, brush, and tooth-powder from the wash-stand.

Fiore did indeed feel much improved after scrubbing the remnants of stale effluvia from his teeth and tongue. Enzo not only poured fresh water for multiple rinses but held the basin for him to spit into. Few men of any rank would suffer such an indignity. Yet Enzo, who could be no less than a patrizio, volunteered for the position. Likewise, when Fiore had done brushing his teeth, Enzo put every article back into its proper place, rinsing the basin for good measure.

"Are you hungry at all?" Enzo asked as he returned to Fiore's bedside.

Fiore furrowed his brow as he considered the question. He supposed some of the ache in his guts might be hunger. "Perhaps."

"There's brioche left over from breakfast—I had Carlotta bring some extra in case you awoke earlier. Or I could send for something else, if you'd prefer. Pastissada de caval is perfectly healthful for an invalid."

Fiore stared at Enzo whilst the cogs of his mind scraped together to perform slow and labored calculations. Horse stew—or any stew, really —took hours to prepare. Which meant Enzo must have thought ahead and ordered it well beforehand. What had probably been second-nature to Enzo nonetheless struck something in Fiore's heart. To have a delicacy prepared on behalf of his invalid appetite...

And yet, it wasn't what he hungered for.

Enzo furrowed his brow at Fiore's continued silence. "Is there something else?"

Perpetually. And it seemed as though its shadow would haunt Fiore until he summoned all his courage and thrust his sword straight into its heart. He drew in a shuddering breath. "You've seen all of me, outside and in. May I not see your face?"

A tense silence fell between them.

That was it then, Fiore thought. He'd tested all boundaries and found one which would not budge. Guts and gore were all well and good. But the bauta balked at revealing his face. Now Enzo would turn his back and leave Fiore behind forevermore—fit punishment for foolish Orpheus demanding to gaze upon his Eurydice.

But then, to Fiore's great astonishment, Enzo brought his hands up to the ties holding the bauta mask in place. He bowed his head as his fingertips worked against the knot. The ties fell free. His fingers slipped beneath the jutting jawline and, after a moment's hesitation and a sharp inhale, Enzo pulled the mask off altogether.

Fiore beheld a long and lean face not much older than his own, though it had seen far more injury. A scar divided it, running from above the left brow over the broken aquiline nose to split the full lips just before the corner of the perfect mouth. It trailed off at the keen edge of a jaw whose strength rivalled the bauta mask that had hidden it from Fiore's view for so long. Whatever blade had dealt the blow had cut deep and split wide. Not long healed, either, by Fiore's reckoning. An older and shallower wound scored a line over the left cheek which did nothing to mar the structure of the sharp bone beneath. The eyes appeared much the same—their dark depths both haunting and haunted—though, now that he could see how the heavy brows knit above them, he found their gaze softer and more gentle than ever before. They fixed him now with a look of hesitation as Enzo waited, Fiore presumed, to see what Fiore thought of him.

Fiore reached out his hand to him.

Enzo didn't flinch.

Fiore laid his palm against that keen-edged jaw and stroked the sharp cheekbone with his thumb.

Enzo shut his eyes and leaned into the caress. Then he turned his head, just enough to press a tender kiss to the inside of Fiore's wrist.

Fiore cupped Enzo's face in his hand to draw him down. Enzo followed where he led, until not a hair's breadth lay between their lips. Fiore shut his eyes.

The kiss Enzo bestowed upon him held every unspoken tenderness that had passed between them. Everything Fiore had ever wondered at. Everything he could have ever wanted. Enzo kissed like one half-afraid of his own desires, yet desperate to sate the yearning hunger within him.

And Fiore wanted nothing more than to give him all he hungered for.

Still, the need for breath demanded they break off long before Fiore felt satisfied.

Enzo gazed down at him with something like wonder in his dark eyes, as if he couldn't quite believe his own good fortune. Softly, like one who feared to break a spell, he asked, "Not half-bad, then?"

Fiore stared. How Enzo could find this face reflected back at him in the mirror every morning and not know it for one of the most beautiful faces in all the world, he couldn't fathom. He opened his mouth to tell him so. Instead, he replied, "If I had any strength in me, I would fuck you until you had none."

Enzo raised his brows. Then a low, soft, sonorous laugh rumbled up from deep within his chest.

And, to Fiore's immense satisfaction, he bent to kiss him again.

～

The remainder of the afternoon passed in a delightful dreamlike haze. In Fiore's estimation, they had a great deal of kissing to make up for. He did his able best to supply the lack, in between dozing off and tending to his infirmity.

At Enzo's urging he finally ate—pastissada de caval, as promised, and delivered whilst he slept from he knew not where. Perhaps the kitchens of

Enzo's own noble house. It arrived in a stoneware crock carried in a black hamper. Enzo himself fed it to Fiore, placing the spoon—silver, emblazoned with a dragon crest—into Fiore's hand and enfolding his own fingers over Fiore's fist to guide the stew between his lips. The rich and savory meat fell apart on his tongue. Though he managed but half the portion Enzo had dished out for him, its warmth suffused and soothed his aching stomach. And it remained there, to his equal astonishment and relief.

As sunset settled over the city, Enzo supplied him with another dose of anodyne. Then he left Fiore's side and began spreading his cloak out on the floorboards.

"What're you doing?" Fiore asked.

Enzo gave him a blank look. "Going to sleep."

Fiore stared at him. "Not there, surely."

Enzo hesitated. "Would you prefer I go?"

"No," Fiore managed to say without hinting at the fear that had seized his heart at the suggestion of Enzo leaving his side. "I want you here."

And he patted the mattress beside him, lest there remain any doubt.

Too late, as a silence stretched out between them, Fiore realized that perhaps Enzo didn't wish to share a bed with an invalid courtesan who'd serviced uncounted men before on that very same mattress.

But then that same soft smile of good fortune and disbelief stole across Enzo's handsome features once more. He swept up his cloak and laid it over Fiore's chair for safe-keeping. Then he stripped himself of waistcoat, breeches, drawers, and hose, leaving just his shirt to cover him, which meant the elegant form of his legs from mid-thigh on down remained bare for Fiore's appreciation.

Better still, he slipped into the bed beside Fiore.

To fit his long lean frame into the curved hull of the boat required Enzo to curl his body around Fiore's smaller form—much to Fiore's delight. Fiore insinuated himself nearer still, his head settling into the crook of Enzo's collar as if they were molded for each other. He stared up at Enzo's face, revealed to him at last. The noble profile, the bristled jaw, the perfect lips, scars and all.

The gaze Enzo cast down at him in turn appeared to echo some of his own admiration, though with an air of confusion, which eventually found its way out in speech. "What are you looking at?"

Fiore reached up to trace one of the knife-sharp cheekbones with his thumb. He felt as much as heard Enzo's suppressed gasp at this once-forbidden touch. "You."

A shy smile Fiore had ever-loved to glimpse in those dark eyes now touched the perfect lips as well. "What for?"

"You've hidden from me for so long," Fiore replied. "I've a great deal of looking to make up for."

Enzo had an exceedingly handsome blush. "You'll weary of it soon enough."

"Never," Fiore declared and kissed him to seal his promise.

Enzo returned the kiss with the same tentative hunger that bespoke eons of repressed desires. Fiore felt his own hunger might never be sated. Still, he endeavored to devour Enzo nonetheless.

But anodyne and exhaustion alike conspired to drag them apart. The fading light robbed Enzo's beautiful face from his sight, as if the night itself wished to mask him again. Even so, Fiore remained reluctant to close his eyes. The faint hint of Enzo's striking profile silhouetted by silvery moonlight served to feed and tantalize him all at once.

And it was Enzo's gentle caress that, eventually, soothed him down into true sleep.

～

With the removal of his mask, Enzo's heart seemed to take flight. His pulse had pounded in his ears as he untied the knot securing it to his skull. Mounting anxiety made his fingertips tremble as he lifted the molded leather from his face. What Fiore would make of what lay beneath, he knew not.

But as the mask fell away altogether, he beheld neither disappointment nor derision in Fiore's gaze. Rather, a wondrous delight stole over his beautiful features and lit up those enormous dark eyes.

Terror and relief had entangled together in Enzo's chest to form exhilaration. He could hardly breathe.

And then Fiore had reached for him.

It was the first time anyone besides himself had touched—much less caressed—his face since university. Astonishment held him still as Fiore's gentle palm alighted on his jaw. A shiver ran through him as Fiore's thumb stroked his cheek. His eyes fluttered shut. Without thinking, he leaned into the caress. On instinct alone he turned to press his lips to Fiore's inner wrist. The skin there felt as soft and tender as his own heart brimming over with everything he'd withheld throughout their acquaintance. The warmth of it shocked him—he'd forgotten how warm a man's flesh could feel against his lips, even as he'd lost himself in the heat of Fiore's throat, after so long spent satisfying himself with the touch of mere hands. Fiore's pulse fluttered against his mouth whilst his own heartbeat pounded in his ears.

Then Fiore had drawn him down, so near that their breath mingled, only to close his eyes and wait.

And—somehow—Enzo found courage enough to kiss him.

Enzo had yearned to kiss him from the very moment of their first meeting. To have those soft lips pressed against his own at last exceeded all expectation. To his further surprise, Fiore seemed almost as starved as himself. And as hungry as his kisses were, the looks he cast over Enzo's features in between them proved hungrier still.

All this exhilaration felt a far cry from the horror of opening Fiore's door to find him on the brink of death. Revealing his face to him—as he'd longed to all the while—was the least Enzo could do to reward Fiore for surviving.

And afterward, the sheer relief of watching him fall into a peaceful sleep loosed the tension in Enzo's own body. To see by moonlight how the pained furrows vanished from his perfect brow and to hear his agonized hiss replaced by soft, steady slumbering breaths would've contented Enzo forevermore. To lie curled around him in his boat felt a thousandfold more comfortable than drowning alone in his own massive four-post bed. And thus, even as he drank in the sight of his beloved beside him, Enzo found his eyes falling shut as he descended to join him in dreams.

Dawn arrived and cast its rays across Enzo's bare face. He opened his eyes to find the same light and warmth playing over Fiore's still-sleeping features.

And with his own mouth uncovered, he could hardly resist smoothing the slumber-tossed curls back from Fiore's forehead and pressing his lips to that beautiful brow.

After all, he told himself, the lips were the part of the skin most sensitive to heat and chill, and to check for a fever by this method would disturb Fiore far less than the termometro. To Enzo's sweet relief he found the fever had indeed abated.

A soft and satisfied mumble escaped Fiore's throat as Enzo withdrew, and a dreamy smile played across those perfect lips. Enzo resisted the urge for further kisses and set about making himself ready for another day of tending his most beloved invalid.

Whilst he plied Fiore's razor to his own face at the wash-stand, his mind wandered. His thoughts never once strayed far from Fiore. Instead they drifted backward to the horrors he'd endured; not just the pain of the chirurgy itself but the all-consuming fear that'd seized Fiore and almost precluded his survival. Enzo knew well what most folk thought of chirurgeons. Giovanna's children fled from the sight of him based on tales from their nursemaids. But they were mere children. And Fiore's terror seemed to outstrip even theirs. He wondered what had happened to make Fiore more afraid of chirurgeons than of death. To witness the agonies of his mind and body alike had proved almost more than Enzo's own heart could bear. He could only hope in some small way he'd helped Fiore through the worst of it.

Carlotta arrived shortly after Enzo had finished dressing. A few whispered words through the cracked-open door sufficed to arrange for such nourishments as befit an invalid in Fiore's condition. She accepted these orders with a nod and departed still more silently than she'd arrived.

Taking charge of something even so small as meals made Enzo feel a touch better. True relief would arrive only when Fiore woke up. Enzo spent the interim perched on the bed's gunwales with his fingertips laid against the inside of Fiore's wrist where his hand had curled beside his head against the pillow. The pulse was neither so weak nor so frantic as he feared. Just a low steady throb of vitality as reassuringly eternal as waves lapping against the shore.

Carlotta returned with breakfast. She remained just long enough to surrender the basket into Enzo's hands before she vanished again. Unwrapping the brioche from their napkin released a plume of fragrant steam. The coffee proved still more aromatic, its scent a welcome change from the iron tang of blood and gore that had seeped into the sickroom. Indeed, they'd used coffee grounds for just such a purpose at university to banish the stench of putrefaction from the dissection hall.

And at present, the smell of coffee as Enzo poured out two cups seemed to banish sleep as well as miasma, for Fiore began at last to stir.

A soft hum escaped his perfect lips as his head lolled across the pillow, tousling curls in its wake. Then his agile limbs stretched languid beyond the boundaries of his blanket. His unconscious movements held all the casual grace Enzo imagined might attend a faun blooming into wakefulness when touched by dawn's first light. At last, the dark eyes opened, blinked, and fixed upon Enzo.

Enzo set the coffee cups aside. "Good morning."

Fiore stared at him in silence. Then his hand shot up, seized Enzo by his shirt-front, and dragged him down for a kiss. All concerns vanished from Enzo's mind as he lost himself altogether in Fiore's soft embrace. That is, until Fiore broke off with a pained groan and fell back against the pillows.

"More anodyne," Enzo prescribed.

"And coffee?"

Enzo felt only too glad to grant him both.

Fiore drank his without assistance, which Enzo took as a good sign, and the sight of which sent his heart soaring disproportionately. After coffee came brioche—Fiore had a good appetite, an even better sign.

After the brioche, Fiore's gaze lingered on Enzo's mouth, flicking up to meet his eyes and back down. Enzo took the hint and bent to kiss him again. His hunger for affection seemed to equal if not outstrip his hunger for actual nourishment. Enzo, for his part, felt no less ravenous. For all they kissed now, he thought he might never feel satisfied. They had not just the past few weeks to make up for but also the years and years in which they'd never yet known each other. So many kisses that they could never make up the debt, much less experience a surfeit. Kisses upon the mouth, along the jaw, and on down the throat to grace the collarbone with a bruise.

Only then did Enzo realize just how far he'd allowed his passions to drive him.

Fiore caught his panicked gaze with a slow and satisfied smile. "You can mark me, if you'd like."

Enzo's pulse stuttered.

Fiore's tongue darted out to grace his swollen lip. "I don't think I'll be seeing anyone else for a while yet."

Enzo's pulse throbbed in places he had no use for it just now. He cleared his throat. "We ought to abstain for a fortnight at the very least."

Fiore raised his brows. "If you insist."

Enzo didn't have the heart to insist upon anything. Still, "It would be medically inadvisable to do otherwise."

Fiore looked as though he didn't have a very high opinion of such medical advice. He smoothed his hand over the beard-shadow on his jaw and throat. "I look a mess, don't I?"

"Hardly," Enzo protested.

Nonetheless he supported Fiore in rising and brought him to his wash-stand. Fiore plied tooth-powder and brush, bracing one hand against the stand itself to remain upright. Enzo hovered within arm's reach all the while. A collapse seemed unlikely, given the promising improvements in his patient's condition, but the possibility yet haunted him. And furthermore...

Fiore reached for something on the wash-stand, hesitated, looked puzzled, then after glancing over it all found what he was after—his razor, which Enzo had replaced somewhere other than its usual position.

Enzo felt an urge to apologize for making himself rather too at home. But he had more pressing matters to consider if Fiore insisted on shaving. Standing for a moment or two was well enough. Standing for anything approaching the quarter-hour mark, however... "Might you sit down?"

Fiore served him a shrewd glance. "Would that be medically advisable?"

Enzo had a feeling he'd hear a lot of that phrase from Fiore over the next few days. "It would be, yes. Lest your entrails tear through your stitches and spill out."

Fiore blinked at him. "Very well."

Enzo fetched his chair.

Unfortunately from his seated posture Fiore could no longer reach the basin or anything else up on the stand. Fiore considered this for a while, doubtless a longer while than usual thanks to the anodyne thrumming through his veins, before looking up to Enzo again.

Enzo held out his hand for the razor. "If I may...?"

A smile crept across Fiore's perfect lips. He handed it over.

Enzo had a decade's worth of experience shaving himself. He'd never employed a valet and had looked after his own needs at university. While he had considerably less experience shaving others, he possessed steady hands and had grown accustomed to manipulating sharp blades with precision.

Even so, the absolute trust in him that Fiore displayed by handing over the razor and baring his throat was certainly something remarkable. Enzo wanted nothing more than to rise to the occasion, however menial. Such trust deserved ample reward.

Fiore waited with perfect stillness as Enzo stropped the blade, lathered up the brush and plied it to his skin. No part of him so much as twitched whilst Enzo slid the razor across his face—save his eyes, which fixed upon Enzo's face and followed him with the smile that couldn't grace his lips. For his part, Enzo didn't breathe easy until he'd washed the lather away and found no nicks beneath.

"Wonderful," Fiore declared as he ran his knuckles down his newly-smooth cheeks. "If you ever tire of a life of leisure, you might make an excellent barber."

Enzo accepted the compliment with a smile.

"Now then," said Fiore. "If we're to live under medically-advisable abstinence, however shall we pass the time?"

"Reading, perhaps," Enzo suggested. "What books do you have?"

Fiore raised his brows.

Belatedly, Enzo realized he'd never seen a book in all his visits to this very room. He supposed such luxuries lay rather above Fiore's touch. Few could claim the privilege of an ancestral library stocked full of tomes. A flame ignited in his cheeks as he tried to amend for his solecism. "Or maybe a gazetta?"

A wry smile wound its way up Fiore's cheek. "More likely. I'm afraid I don't keep much around that doesn't get drawn over."

Enzo followed his gaze to the wall, where indeed more than one of the sketches pinned up thereupon bore the printed lines of a gossip rag beneath the red-chalk form of a muscular masculine nude.

"One of Artemisia's other models," Fiore explained. As if half to himself, he mused on. "I should bring you to the book-binders district when we go out on the town again. We might find something more to your liking there. Or to mine," he added with another languid smile.

Enzo made a mental note to have Carlotta bring over some novels from Ca' Scaevola's library. "What sort of stories are to your liking?"

"Oh, you know," Fiore scoffed in that tone Enzo had begun to suspect meant he didn't want his words to sound quite so earnest as they truly were. "Adventures. Sword-fights. Revenge. Gentlemen of our predilections." This with a knowing glance at Enzo that sent his heart into a temporary arrhythmia. "And yourself?"

Before Enzo could reply, a knock fell on the chamber door.

All the pliability the anodyne had brought to Fiore's form left it in an instant as he lurched upright and whipped his head toward the door. In a voice whose indolent calm belied his evident anxiety, he called out, "Who goes there?"

"Dr. Malvestio," came the muffled reply.

"Enter," Enzo said without thinking.

He realized his error all too late, as Fiore's face drained of blood.

# CHAPTER SEVEN

F iore tried to swallow his fear and bitterness in the same breath. It almost worked.

Of course Enzo could bid whoever he liked to enter Fiore's room. He was, at the very least, a patrizio. The chirurgeon had come here at his behest. Fiore's wishes in this regard mattered not.

But as Fiore forced a smile and turned it upon Enzo, he beheld his scarred features harrowed by remorse, and no sooner did he see the sorrowful cast of those dark brows than his heart forgave him.

The chirurgeon, meanwhile, had no such human feeling. They offered a perfunctory greeting before announcing the hour had arrived to change Fiore's wound-dressings. Fiore submitted to this indignity with a clenched jaw. The anodyne reduced what would otherwise have been a painful episode to mere aches and twinges. It helped to have Enzo's hand in his own, soft fingertips kneading his knuckles and scarred lips murmuring low words of encouragement. The distraction kept Fiore's eyes off the horrible glass lenses and his mind off of remembrances that didn't bear dwelling upon. The old dressings were cast off, the fresh linen sewn in place, and the chirurgeon withdrew—not a moment too soon, by Fiore's reckoning. No noise could've possibly sounded more welcome than the door thudding shut on the chirurgeon's departure.

And then Enzo, who'd sat beside Fiore all the while, dropt to his knees before him.

"Forgive me," Enzo said while Fiore blinked down at him in astonishment. "I should never have bid him enter without your leave. I quite forgot my place."

"Nothing to forgive," Fiore lied.

Enzo gazed off into the middle distance, worried his scarred lip, and at last, spoke. "May I know something more of you?"

All calm and comfort fled from Fiore's veins. He worked to keep his smile in place and his voice level as he replied, "Depends what you wish to know."

"Why are you afraid of chirurgeons?"

Fiore's smile died on his face.

A long silence ensued.

"You've seen my scars," Fiore said at last.

Enzo furrowed his brow in confusion.

"Below the belt," Fiore elaborated.

"Oh. Yes." Despite this, Enzo still looked confounded. "In truth, I hardly noticed them."

Fiore doubted that—although, when contrasted against Enzo's face, he supposed his own scars appeared minimal. And yet, they remained ever at the forefront of his mind. It seemed almost impossible to believe they didn't loom in the thoughts of another, particularly one who'd glimpsed them so oft of late. "I suppose it won't make much sense piecemeal. I may as well tell you the whole."

"If you're willing to speak," said Enzo, "then I'm eager to listen."

Even so, Fiore hardly knew where to begin. At the beginning, he supposed. He drew a deep breath that tugged against his throbbing stitches. "I was born in the countryside. My mother and father tended a flock. If the plague hadn't taken them from me, I'd probably have grown up to become a handsome goatherd. Instead I became an orphaned ward of the temple. They made us all sing in the choir. I sang better than most. A visiting pontifex heard us perform and picked out my voice from amidst the throng. He took me back to the city with him and brought me to the conservatorio. There began my education. Mostly singing and lute-playing. Some literacy. Not drawing," he added with a smile. "They whipped me for scrawling in the margins of my sheet music."

Enzo did not return the smile.

Fiore supposed it was the sort of funny where one had to be there. "And for several years it all went rather well. I learnt quick. I had a roof over my head, clothes on my back, food in my belly. And..." He hesitated; having kept this part of himself silent for so many years, it felt sacrilege to speak it aloud now. Still, Enzo had asked. And Fiore realized he'd do almost anything if Enzo asked. "I found a friend."

A glance at Enzo's face showed he knew precisely what Fiore meant by that word.

"His name was Eliodoro." Fiore hadn't spoken it aloud since... well. "It was he who comforted me after the whippings. He was the better singer by far, but as sweet as his voice sounded, his nature proved even sweeter. We doted on each other. Nothing came to either of us that wasn't shared with the other. We split many an orange stolen from the kitchens, and more besides."

Fiore would've liked to dwell in those memories. He didn't oft let himself wander back so far. Even the sweetest memory of his Elio led to the same end. And it was that very end which he was forced to divulge to Enzo now. He swallowed down the soreness in his throat and forced himself to speak on.

"You're aware of how musici are made."

The sentence hung in the air for a long and horrible moment before Enzo at last served him a solemn nod.

"Both Elio and I were destined for that fate." It felt easier to say his name a second time, though Fiore's heart hurt nonetheless. "The singing maestro liked our voices and wanted to preserve them for the stage. Elio, being the sweeter singer and thus risking the greater loss if they delayed too long, was chosen for the operation first." Fiore's heart beat in his throat. He choked it down. "They had a barber do it. Easier to find than a chirurgeon willing to overlook matters." The words came faster and faster, spilling over his lips like blood, as if it would hurt less if he got it over with quick. "I wasn't there for the mutilation itself. They tried to keep our fates secret from us, lest they lose their investment. We were as cloistered as the figlie di coro and easy to keep in ignorance. One day just like any other they simply declared Elio was sick and required treatment. He went away with the barber and the singing maestro as quietly as a lamb. And to no less bloody a slaughter." Fiore halted. Visions he'd long suppressed roiled up from the deepest pits of his mind. He drew a steadying breath as he told himself to just get through it, get the words out and get it over with. "As I said, I didn't witness the act. But I beheld the aftermath. He fell into a fever. Cried out for parents he'd never known. In his more lucid moments, he cried out for me but could neither see me beside him nor recognize my hand clasping his own. He faltered between sleeping and waking. In the end he awoke only to sob. He breathed his last in my arms."

A silence fell. Fiore's throat ached. From talking so much for so long, or so he told himself. That didn't explain the burning in his eyes or the pulsing behind them or how his own breath resounded ragged in his ears. He dared a glance up to see what Enzo made of his narrative.

Enzo looked about as horrified as Fiore had wished anyone besides himself had felt all those years ago. Worse still, he looked on the verge of speaking.

Fiore hastened to avert his gaze and clear his throat. "Then it was my turn."

Something nudged his knuckles knotted in the bedclothes. Against his better judgment Fiore flicked his gaze toward it. He found Enzo's hand beside his own, palm-up, a quiet and patient invitation.

Fiore forced his fist to unclench so he might entangle his fingers in Enzo's own. Though he grasped Enzo's hand perhaps a touch too tight, he felt nothing but a firm-yet-gentle clasp in return. He swallowed hard and continued his tale.

"They had a proper chirurgeon this time. Mask and all. Because this wasn't just some poor family pinning their hopes of clawing their way out of poverty on the mutilation of a younger son. This was the conservatorio proper. They'd spent years training me to sing already. They'd lost one just like me in the past month. They couldn't afford to lose another. So they wanted the maiming done properly, and got a proper chirurgeon to do it. I didn't know exactly what they'd done to Elio. Just that it'd killed him. I think they hoped I'd assume whatever sickness they pretended he had did the mischief. Regardless, they knew better than to try the same trick on me. They didn't bother pretending I was ill or injured. They just gave me opium in wine and then pounced."

The taste of it seemed to cling to his tongue even now. Bitter. Cloying. A drink that seemed to wrap his head in cotton even as they gagged him with a belt and tied him hand and foot with another.

"I wanted to struggle," Fiore heard himself say as if from a distance. "But my limbs wouldn't move with any strength. It's like all those nightmares where you need to run but can't. I used to think I was the only one who had those and that they stemmed from this."

Enzo squeezed his hand. As if this gesture imbued him with vitality, Fiore found his voice again, amidst breaths which had no reason to ring so ragged in his own ears.

"My vision became a haze," Fiore went on. "The only thing I saw with any clarity was that damned mask looming over me. They brought the knife in. When the blade bit into me—something about the pain seemed to cut through my stupor."

"Adrenaline," Enzo intoned.

"It's a known phenomenon, then?"

Enzo nodded.

"Very well," said Fiore. "Then I suppose it was that which let me twist my stick-limbs out of joint and wrestle free. It took them all by surprise. Doubtless that's the only reason I succeeded. The blade went— well. You've seen the scars. You know. It flew quite out of the chirurgeon's gloves. As did I out of everyone else's."

"Everyone else?" Enzo echoed in enquiry.

"The singing maestro," Fiore answered him. "And a particularly burly ballerino—they're absurdly strong, they have to be, hoisting each other up and flinging themselves about—more than enough to hold down a mere boy, or so they all thought. None were fleet or flexible enough to catch me. I was smaller and swifter than the lot. Slipped out through a gap in a window none but an alley-cat would've attempted. Stole a pair of breeches off a laundry line. I still had my shirt and hose, at least. Then spent the following years dodging the city guard and avoiding the orphanages."

"Why avoid the orphanages?"

Fiore didn't resent the questions in the least. Enzo finding his voice again meant Fiore had a trail to follow, linking his own history up to match the thread laid out by the enquiries. No longer did all depend on his own force of will. "Because they all train up their charges musically. Just like the conservatorio. How was I to know they wouldn't want to mutilate me just the same?"

There was more, of course. Much more. Between the conservatorio and the *Kingfisher* lay years that didn't bear remembering. Certainly nothing Fiore could bear to reexamine beneath Enzo's gaze. He attempted to leap over the gap and land on the other side so perfectly that Enzo wouldn't notice it. "After a while I fell into the line of work you find me in now. And then a few years back I found a place here. My condition has improved steadily since. I've a good reputation for good work. Captains make port specifically to see me. To say nothing of the gentlemen already in town."

Fiore pulled his face into a smile and forced himself to raise it towards Enzo.

The look he found on Enzo's face—brow furrowed, lips thinned, eyes whose depths contained all the darkness Fiore didn't wish to dwell on—spoke plainly that Enzo had, indeed, noticed the gap. Yet he made no mention of it, nor any further enquiry, for which Fiore withheld a sigh of relief.

"I stopped singing," Fiore went on. "Even though my voice is unrecognizable these days, I don't want to risk it. So I draw instead." A queer smile twitched across Fiore's lips. "There's no one to whip me for it now."

Enzo didn't return the smile.

Fiore continued. "The work I do now is much the same as what most of the castrati do, anyways. Opera-goers will pay handsomely to fuck the hero of their favorite piece. But in my case, I didn't have to suffer mutilation for the privilege, and the *Kingfisher* takes a far smaller cut of the profits than any opera house. And the *Kingfisher* is far safer than working on the street. I'm not tall enough to be a gondolier. Not that they'd let me into the guild, anyway."

Still, Enzo said nothing. His brow remained furrowed. Fiore supposed that was understandable; he'd dumped rather a lot of unfamiliar and uncomfortable truths on his head all at once.

"I'm happy for those who've met with success," Fiore went on, unable to stop himself now that the dam he'd spent a decade building had burst. "But I don't know if any amount of fame or fortune could repay what they've sacrificed. And those who've found neither, despite the sacrifice forced upon them, are too numerous to name. Not every castrato gets an opera career," he added, as Enzo's brow furrowed in confusion. "There's a surplus of geldings for every one that makes it onto the stage. The rest end up as music teachers if they're lucky. Most just perish in obscure poverty."

A soft and startled, "Oh," escaped Enzo.

Fiore didn't begrudge him it. How was he to know, when he never attended an opera if he could avoid it, what became of those who never appeared in front of the curtain. "So, that's why I'm not over-fond of the opera." Which wasn't the question Enzo had asked, and Fiore had already said more than he ought, far more than anyone cared to hear, and yet he couldn't halt his tongue. "It's not just the sight of the house, although that's bad enough. It's the sound of it. The music in general and the castrati in particular. They all sound like him, and I..." His eyes burned. "I can't abide the memory."

Enzo tightened his clasp on Fiore's hand. This alone prevented him from falling into the howling void within his own heart.

Fiore forced more words out; the alternative was to let the lump in his throat grow large enough to choke him. "Some of my gentlemen callers wish to take me out on the town. To the opera, specifically. Whether to show off or because they think it'll amuse me I know not. Regardless, I took one of them up on the offer. Once." The memory alone seized his chest in a tight grip that threatened to preclude breath. "I didn't even make it to the end of the first act. I slipped out and ran."

"And the gentleman?" Enzo asked, his low voice soft as lambskin.

"Never returned. Which is a shame," Fiore added. "For he was almost as rich as he was old."

Enzo didn't laugh.

Fiore couldn't bear the silence. His rambling thoughts fell from his tongue. "Sometimes I wonder if I ought to have let them finish maiming me after all. I'm not the breeding kind anyway. And some gentlemen prefer their paramours without stones and are disappointed to discover I still have even just the one remaining." How fortunate Fiore had felt to discover Enzo was not of that sort. "And yet... I know I'm happier as I am. Even if I don't fulfill the purpose society expects of me."

"Society," Enzo intoned with enough venom to make Fiore flinch, "can go and choke to death on its expectations of you."

Some might have felt cowed. Fiore found himself emboldened to hear his own unfounded rage echoed in Enzo's deep commanding tone. To have such a power raised on his behalf... well, that was certainly something. Something which stirred his heart to quicken its pace and bid his mind consider depths which he hadn't dared fathom in years. He did his best to shove these feelings back down where they belonged. While Enzo had shown him more empathy than most, he needn't debase himself in return.

Fiore forced a smile over his turbulent thoughts. "I suppose the shorter version of it is, I fear chirurgeons because I'm a coward."

"Hardly," Enzo scoffed.

"No? I fled the gelding table without a backward glance and have been left hiding ever since. What d'you call that but cowardice?"

Still, Enzo shook his head. "Can't say as I blame you. I'd've run, too."

"No you wouldn't," Fiore insisted. "You'd have skewered the chirurgeon with his own scalpel."

Enzo chuckled. "Aye—and then run."

Fiore wished he could share his mirth.

"Your courage in the face of adversity," Enzo began.

"Is nothing," Fiore hastened to cut him off. And, when those beautiful, scarred lips remained parted as if to argue, he further added, "Pray don't speak of it."

To Fiore's astonishment, alongside some other emotions which were best left unexamined, Enzo's mouth closed at his command.

Fiore cast around for something—anything—to change the subject. "Your manservant brought you some books, did she not?"

Once again, Enzo took the hint immediately. He leapt up to retrieve the threefold stack from atop Fiore's desk.

"Whichever one is your favorite," Fiore said after Enzo parted his lips but before he could actually ask.

As it so happened, Enzo's favorite was the legend of a fae knight carving his way out of a treacherous realm of spider-silk. The tale was well-crafted and in another place and time Fiore would've heard it with rapt attention. But on this particular afternoon with his wound scourging his body and his memories scourging his mind and the anodyne battling both, he hadn't the strength of will to follow all the finer details. He did retain an appreciation for the smooth sonorous bass of Enzo's voice. The mellifluous flow of words from his tongue soothed Fiore down into sleep.

# CHAPTER EIGHT

"Should we consider this a second residence?" Carlotta enquired the following morning. She'd just arrived with the day's provisions from the kitchen of Ca' Scaevola.

Enzo, who'd met her at the door to Fiore's quarters, balked. "I don't think so. Why d'you ask?" A chill ran through his blood as a horrible suspicion took root. "Did Lucrezia…?"

Carlotta shook her head. "The tavern-keeper gave me a gentle reminder that there's an additional fee for double-occupancy."

"Oh." Enzo's bated breath left him in a sigh of relief. "I suppose it's rather up to her, then, whether my presence here counts as an occupancy."

"From what she said, I gather it depends upon the duration of your stay."

Some of Fiore's other gentlemen must have stayed overnight before. Perhaps even several nights. But likely none so long as Enzo intended to remain—if Fiore would indulge him in a continuous visit. He'd have liked to stay until Fiore had recovered enough to return to business as usual. Which could be as soon as a mere fortnight. Yet even this prognosis gave Enzo pause. He'd never met any of Fiore's other paramours, and he didn't trust them to be sufficiently gentle with him during his convalescence. Instinct bid him glance over his shoulder at Fiore, still abed and asleep. His condition had improved, certainly, but still... "Let's say a month."

Carlotta raised her brows but made no further comment. With a bow, she departed.

Enzo shut the door behind her and brought in the basket she'd carried. Unpacking it released tempting aromas. These sufficed to rouse Fiore from his slumbers.

Fiore had slept well, so far as Enzo could tell. Pain hadn't awoken him in the night and he'd remained asleep for some hours after Enzo got up at sunrise. This offered Enzo some small reassurance. His patient's recovery had proceeded smoothly thus far and showed no sign of relapse. So it was with just the background hum of concern rather than overwhelming worry that he'd spent the early morning with his fingertips laid against the inside of Fiore's wrist and counted his breaths as he'd slept.

Even as Fiore had fallen asleep curled up alongside him whilst he read to him the evening prior, Enzo had half-expected him to bolt awake with the nightmare. As for himself, all Fiore had confided in him whirled in his mind well after waking.

Enzo had possessed a dim awareness of what the opera required to create the unique sound of its heroes. While he'd never encountered a castrato himself, certain professors and colleagues at university had treated them as patients. And as one with a physical peculiarity of his own, he'd read up on the available literature concerning the medical symptoms occurring after castration. He knew how the larynx of a castrato was even shorter than that of an adult female, creating a unique tone that couldn't be achieved by any other kind of performer. He knew how the loss of the testes impeded the growth of beard and body hair. And he knew how the castrati could never sire children, unless their castration proved incomplete like Fiore's. But he had not known, until now, what was felt by those who underwent the chirurgy. And though by his own admission Fiore didn't speak for all, still Enzo had remorse for his own total lack of consideration for their condition.

For Fiore in particular Enzo felt still more. The suffering he'd endured as a mere child had borne out on his body as an adult. The loss of only one stone had nonetheless shown itself in his diminished stature and comparative lack of body hair. The scar left behind was painful enough to look upon; Enzo could scarce imagine what agony and terror had seized him as a boy. And the self-same fear had followed him throughout the years until he'd preferred almost certain death to confronting a chirurgeon's mask again. Enzo had wondered at Fiore's desperate plea not to let the chirurgeon maim him. Now that he knew the reasoning behind it, it would echo in his mind for years to come.

And he wondered what Fiore would think if he knew just how close Enzo had been to becoming a chirurgeon himself.

Enzo's sorrow at Fiore's suffering was matched only by his determination that Fiore should never suffer so again. It had cost Fiore a great deal to confide in him. Enzo would safeguard his trust with his life.

At present, however, Fiore stirred. And while he turned over with furrowed brow, it dissolved with a smile the moment his half-open eyes settled upon Enzo. A glance sufficed to draw Enzo to his side. No sooner had he ventured within reach than Fiore drew him down for a kiss.

So Enzo set his pondering aside for the time being.

~

Fiore had never told anyone about Elio or his true origins before. Not even Artemisia. He'd dreaded the danger of discovery. And, even if by some miracle the tale didn't carry back to the conservatorio, he had no expectation of receiving anything like sympathy in return. In revealing his past to Enzo he'd braced for blame. Or criticism, at the very least; outlining all the ways he'd failed and the hundred methods by which a better man would've succeeded in his place.

Enzo had offered neither. Instead, he'd simply listened. Which frankly no one had done for Fiore since Elio's death.

And even after learning of Fiore's weakness, Enzo didn't abandon him.

At least, not yet. Fiore had fallen asleep half-expecting Enzo to be gone in the morning. Better men had been driven off by tales of less woe. But he'd awoken to find Enzo still in his quarters, bringing him coffee and brioche just as he had the day before and seemingly as happy to see Fiore as ever.

Fiore remained wary. Divulging his secrets had unburdened him, true enough, but it also left him feeling hollowed out and harrowed. Breakfast filled some of the lack. To have Enzo close beside him, his warm bulk nestled snug against him in the bed, filled still more. If anything Enzo seemed more attached to him for all his frailties. And against his better judgment, Fiore found himself more attached to Enzo in turn.

There was a certain charm in how Enzo doted on him; bringing him breakfast, checking his pulse and listening to his entrails, helping him shave and wash and dress. Few men of any rank would do so much for Fiore. Much less an aristocrat.

Assuming, of course, that Enzo *was* a genuine aristocrat and not just a wildly accomplished impostor.

Fiore liked him very well—quite possibly too well—but the more he considered the matter the more he realized how little he truly knew of him. Enzo had enough medical knowledge to diagnose a life-threatening infection and seemed on exceedingly familiar terms with at least one chirurgeon. He could either afford or had gone into enough debt to wear an exquisite costume. He thought nothing of offering Fiore a retirement to ease and comfort for the rest of his days. He had at least one servant to his name and through some means had acquired the silverware of some noble house. (Which house in particular, Fiore knew not. He could recognize all the ships whose captains graced his bed, but when it came to the crests of noble houses his repertoire fell far short.) Beyond this, the mysterious, newly unmasked man who graced Fiore's chamber had asked Fiore to call him Enzo—which, again, could be short for at least a half-dozen names or could simply be a preferred alias with no relation to his actual name whatsoever.

It wasn't necessarily unusual for a gentleman caller to keep Fiore in the dark regarding his true identity. Many preferred anonymity, particularly if they resided in the city rather than merely making port like the bo'suns and sea captains and sundry sailors in between. Fiore didn't bother speculating on most of them beyond wondering idly for his own amusement. Enzo, however, had begun as idle curiosity and grown into something rather more. What, exactly, Fiore hardly knew.

The following fortnight passed in idleness. Enzo scarcely left Fiore's side for the first se'en-night. At the end of it he admitted, with evidently sincere regret, that his family required his presence in the ancestral halls for evening dinners at the very least. Would Fiore get on well enough without him for those few hours?

Fiore smiled and assured him he would survive. To himself, he wondered at how Enzo hadn't wearied of his presence earlier. He certainly hadn't been a very interesting or adventurous companion. Sedate and quiet walks could only entertain a gentleman for so long. And ceaseless evenings spent reading aloud to an invalid could prove nothing short of tiresome. Yet Enzo had never once complained. Nor had he given even the slightest hint of anything like annoyance. Fiore marveled at his strength of will.

Enzo didn't ask that Fiore refrain from working whilst he was gone. Fiore didn't return to work regardless. While sheer boredom certainly tempted him, his body remained too weak even if he'd had the conviction to follow through. He had strength enough to read to himself —Enzo had brought several more novels beyond the original three and left them all behind for his perusal—and to draw as the light permitted. This kept him occupied overnight for another week. It certainly helped that every morning he could count on Enzo's arrival bright and early with coffee, brioche, and a comforting presence.

By the end of the fortnight, however, Fiore found his patience for convalescence waning.

Enzo had deigned to kiss him even after seeing him in so truly disgusting a state as his illness and even as his body continued to leech blood and worse. He cared not for the bandages. Nor had he turned up his nose at assisting Fiore in washing and dressing. No gentleman was loved by his valet, to paraphrase the more popular saying, but Enzo seemed fond of Fiore even while valeting for him.

Even so, kissing was all he would do with Fiore since the chirurgy. And while Fiore didn't feel quite up to entertaining strangers, he would've very much liked to entertain Enzo. His quiet care and reassuring strength throughout the past fortnight had transformed him from a charming mystery into an admirable beau. Every gentle caress made Fiore yearn for more. To say nothing of what lay beneath his mask. Now that he could see just how a shy smile stole over those handsome scarred lips, all he wanted was to know how those chiseled features looked in the throes of ecstasy. If he could but see Enzo's face as he spent... His imaginings drove him to satisfy himself in his hand when Enzo departed for the evening. But said satisfaction no longer satisfied.

So when Enzo returned the following day and Fiore coaxed him down into another kiss, his patience had reached its breaking point.

"You could do more than kiss me," Fiore murmured against his mouth. "If you'd like."

Judging by the hard length against his thigh, Enzo would very much have liked. Yet still he hesitated. "I don't want to do anything that would hurt you."

Fiore studied him. Enzo seemed genuine in his refusal—and, in equal measure, genuinely sorry to have to refuse. Which granted Fiore just enough courage to go beyond mere flirtation into the terrifying realm of plain speech. "I'd like you to do more than kiss me."

Enzo's eyes widened.

Fiore held his breath.

Then a smile tugged at the corner of Enzo's scarred mouth, half wonder and half disbelief, and he bent to kiss Fiore again.

Which wasn't what Fiore had asked for, and he meant to say so the moment they parted again, but then Enzo's hands, which 'til now had cradled his jaw, descended below his waist to work at the fall-front of his breeches, and Fiore had no further complaints.

Enzo took him in hand. Instinct sent Fiore's hips bucking up into the tight grip of his fist—which provoked a wince and a hiss as his still-healing waist protested. A gentle palm laid over the crest of his jutting hip-bone stilled him. Enzo broke off their kiss.

"May I use my mouth?" he enquired, his whisper warm on Fiore's lips.

A grin stole over Fiore's face. He nodded.

Enzo required no further prompting to delve.

Other men had paid to swallow Fiore before—with varying degrees of skill. Fiore had few expectations for Enzo's attempt. He resolved to take it in good humor. If nothing else, the request showed a desire to bring him pleasure, which Fiore took as a sign of continued affection, all the more remarkable given how hideous he'd felt throughout his convalescence.

But he found it quite another thing altogether to see Enzo unmasked before him. To meet that dark gaze as it glanced up for his approval. To behold those beautifully scarred lips parting to embrace his prick.

And to feel that marvelous mouth wrap around his cock-head proved beyond all expectation.

Enzo swallowed Fiore down as if this act alone could nourish him. His already-chiseled cheeks grew all the sharper as they hollowed around Fiore's cock. Then he drew back, his tongue tracing the lightning-strike scar up the side. Fiore shivered, wondering if this was how Enzo felt when he'd drawn his fingertips across his slashed face over and again; yet Fiore had caressed him with reverence, and this, too, felt an echo of the same, bringing pleasure to what had once been a mark of agony. Where it split the foreskin, Enzo delved beneath to encircle the cock-head and pay tribute to the slit—all without breaking his dark gaze locked with Fiore's—before devouring him whole again, taking him deep enough to enter his throat.

Damn the mask for hiding this revelation for so long. The distant throb of pain in Fiore's waist couldn't prevent him from rolling his hips to fuck Enzo's willing throat.

In Fiore's experience, the act was less about performing particular actions—although Enzo performed remarkably well—and more about responding to what the particular receiver enjoyed. Enzo proved very responsive indeed. He attuned to every twitch and gasp, every shudder and moan, every shiver over Fiore's skin and hitch in his breath.

Without thought, Fiore tangled both hands in Enzo's locks. And when his fists clenched, an answering moan arose from deep within Enzo's chest to reverberate through Fiore's cock in his throat.

*Fuck*, Fiore thought. He'd not last long like this.

And nor would Enzo, whose hips had begun to grind however slowly and subtly into the mattress beneath, and whose hands continually drifted down to his own waist before he caught himself and replaced them on Fiore's thighs.

Fiore gave his hair a sharp tug to halt his suckling and turn his gaze upward to meet his own.

"You can touch yourself," Fiore murmured. "If you'd like."

The desire that ever-smoldered in Enzo's dark eyes blazed forth. A hard swallow travelled down his shadowed throat—teasing the tip of Fiore's cock as it did so. Without ever breaking their locked gaze, Enzo fumbled with the fall-front of his breeches. From this angle Fiore couldn't see his cock freed, but he beheld it in the way Enzo's eyes fluttered shut and felt it in the renewed moans that echoed up from the deep as Enzo swallowed him down again.

The knowledge that Enzo took his own gratification in bringing Fiore pleasure heightened all sensation. Whatever restraint Fiore had was lost in the dark locks tangled in his fists, the reverberating moans, the sight of Enzo's furious arm and his thrusting hips, the tongue lathing the vein beneath and the throat swallowing him down, down, down—until, with an exultant cry that he but half-caught in the palm clutched hastily against his lips, he spilled a roaring tide of seed into Enzo's all-devouring mouth.

For a few moments, the whole world fell away. He knew only ecstasy, only decadence, only Enzo. Then it ebbed, gradually, gently, but did not disappear altogether. The lovely languid feeling that had washed over him in the torrent of his spend left him in a delightful haze. He opened his eyes again to find Enzo staring up at him. His softening cock had dropt from his mouth, scattering a few glistening pearls across those scarred lips in its wake.

"Did you...?" Fiore asked breathlessly.

Enzo caught his lip between his teeth before admitting in his bashful way, "Not just yet."

As if his hips yet rolling into the mattress between Fiore's calves hadn't already told so. Fiore blamed his failed perception on the sensuality yet clouding his mind. His fingertips delved into Enzo's hair again, drawing him up even as he softly demanded, "Come here."

Enzo obeyed—at once, without question, as he always did, and as Fiore never failed to marvel at. His long frame loomed over Fiore, propped up on sinewy forearms that bracketed Fiore's head on either side whilst he straddled his hips. The breeches and all remained on, as ever, but his cock was yet free, and Fiore clasped it in his fist and slid along its magnificent curving heft whilst dragging Enzo down for a devouring kiss so he might taste himself on his lover's tongue.

Enzo's final moan escaped into Fiore's mouth and resounded in his own throat as Enzo spent across his chest with a shudder. He collapsed beside him, his taller frame curving around his smaller one like a crescent moon.

Fiore dragged his thumb up through the string of liquid pearls and sucked it off for good measure.

"Where else have you plied this talent?" Fiore asked.

Even after all they'd done, Enzo still cast a shy look upon him. "Amongst friends."

A huff of laughter escaped Fiore. "How fortunate these friends."

The grin that crept across Enzo's dashing features begged to be kissed —and so Fiore did.

# CHAPTER NINE

"Why d'you wear a mask?" asked Fiore.

The question startled Enzo. They sat together in Fiore's quarters aboard the *Kingfisher* just as they had every morning since the appendectomy. Fiore arose far later in the day than Enzo—nearer to noon than to sunrise—which left Enzo time to walk Vittorio, run up the stairs, bathe, break his own fast, and practice with Maestra Rovigatti before he brought coffee and brioche to Fiore. Nonetheless he would've gladly cast all this aside if Fiore required him one moment earlier.

Enzo ought to have felt at ease. Fiore had almost wholly recovered. His chirurgical wound had closed over; bandages were now necessary only for bracing during labor, and as Fiore was not a bricklayer or fisher or gondolier, his labor hours were short indeed.

But Enzo had arrived at the *Kingfisher* that morning already on edge. He carried with him tidings which weighed upon his own heart—and this question off-put him further.

"I know why you wear it to see me of course," Fiore explained into the silence Enzo had let settle between them. "But you were already wearing it at the opera as well. Am I correct in supposing you're not oft without it?"

Enzo, still staggering in the wake of the "of course" that had dropt so casually from Fiore's lips—as if he assumed Enzo considered him something to be ashamed of, and worse yet, believed it himself—took another moment to reply. "You are correct."

Fiore cocked his head at him with a look of one who awaited further explanation.

Enzo wanted to tell him everything. But he knew he'd already revealed far more than he ought. His face alone told too much. If Fiore had likewise glimpsed the Scaevola crest on either the silverware or Carlotta's livery...

Gently—far more gently than Enzo deserved—Fiore asked, "Is it because of your scars?"

"To a point," Enzo admitted. They certainly formed some of the reasons.

Fiore looked unaccountably disturbed by this answer. He held Enzo's gaze for a moment with furrowed brow. Then he raised his tender hand to trace the scar that ran across Enzo's face, from brow to chin, his fingertips lingering where it crossed Enzo's lips.

"I think," Fiore said, his voice softer than silk as he ran his thumb over the scar on Enzo's cheekbone, "they look rather dashing."

The sympathetic compliment, as superfluous as it might have been, nonetheless drew a smile out of Enzo. Though he wondered how Fiore would feel about them if he knew under what shameful circumstances he'd acquired them. Still, "They don't vex me."

Fiore raised his brows with a smile. "I'm glad to hear so. Though then I must wonder again why you go about masked everywhere."

"For the sake of my family," Enzo confessed. It seemed safe enough to tell Fiore so. He needn't divulge which family in particular.

And, to Enzo's relief, Fiore didn't ask. He simply gave him a sage nod. Enzo supposed many others amongst his gentlemen had preferred to keep their liaisons separate and secret from their own families.

Which only made it far more urgent for Enzo to disabuse Fiore of the notion that he considered their affair a shameful secret. "And—because it is a relief to not have everyone looking at me."

A far truer reason than he had yet divulged to anyone else in the world.

Fiore cocked his head again; somehow, not unkindly. "Folk don't stare at a black bauta?"

"They gawk at the mask," Enzo explained. "At the cape and hood and costume. Not at me."

Fiore's furrowed brow suggested he did not yet comprehend him.

Enzo plucked up the article in question from the seat of Fiore's chair; his cloak lay folded over the back. The black leather felt familiar in his fingertips. He rubbed them over where the interior suede had worn smooth from daily friction against his brow.

"Perhaps," he ventured, hardly daring to look Fiore in the eye as he did so, "you might understand better if you wore it yourself?"

Silence met his proposal. Enzo forced his gaze up from the mask at last and found Fiore with brows raised. Still, the smile curling up one cheek bespoke intrigue rather than dismissal, and so Enzo relinquished the mask into Fiore's outstretched hand.

To see someone else don his mask was more disconcerting than he'd anticipated. To be robbed of the sight of Fiore's face in particular sent a queer sort of muted panic through his heart.

Fiore, however, appeared perfectly comfortable as he tied the cord 'round the back of his skull. When he raised his head to meet Enzo's gaze again, his dark eyes—the sole recognizable feature remaining in the mask's blank void—gleamed.

"Rather comfortable," Fiore declared.

Enzo certainly found it so.

Fiore turned his head this way and that, stroking down the beak's length with his hand as another man might stroke a bearded chin in thought. He caught Enzo's gaze again with smiling eyes. "You needn't look so concerned. Unless it really doesn't suit me at all. I'll have to trust you for that—I haven't a mirror."

Enzo made a note to provide him with one at the earliest opportunity. Aloud he replied with honesty, "It suits you."

For once Enzo made his peace with the absence of all Fiore's other charming features, he found the mask heightened the expressive powers of the eyes, which captivated him even more now than they had before. The fluttering lash and the flickering glance could consume him if Fiore willed it.

All too late, Enzo understood the implications of declaring a man looked better with a mask on than without.

Fiore, who'd watched him keenly all the while, burst out with a laugh as this realization dawned across Enzo's own naked features.

"I'm only teasing," Fiore said, raising his hand to cup Enzo's scarred cheek.

Enzo leaned into his palm. Every touch of his bare face still sent a shiver of illicit pleasure through him.

"I see what you mean, though," Fiore continued. "About the mask shielding one from notice even as it courts it. A domino teases the idea of anonymity. A bauta teases the barest hint of identity. One may be perceived without being perceived."

Just as Enzo had concluded for himself. There remained, however, one singular exception. For even with the mask on, Enzo had felt more seen by Fiore than he had by anyone since he'd first donned it.

Which made leaving Fiore behind all the more difficult.

"I'm afraid I must leave you," Enzo forced out. He'd dallied long enough. The moment had arrived to speak his piece, however painful.

Indeed, Fiore flinched and shot him a startled look from beneath the mask.

"Temporarily," Enzo hastened to add. His own heart relaxed alongside Fiore's shoulders. "My family enacts a ritual to Diana in the countryside each spring. My attendance is required."

Fiore fixed him with a sardonic gaze worthy of a satyr. "The gods must have their blood."

Enzo smiled despite himself. "I intend to return as soon as possible—within days, if I may—but I fear filial obligation will detain me for a fortnight at the very least. But, gods willing, I shall not be gone above a month."

Fiore absorbed this rambling explanation in silence. With the mask on, Enzo couldn't see how he took it—except that, unless Enzo very much mistook him, there appeared a sort of grief in his dark and beautiful eyes.

This vanished as Fiore whipped the bauta off over his head to kiss him.

The kiss, for Enzo, was equal parts astonishment and serenity. The startled stiffness of his body melted into an easy embrace as Fiore wrapped his arms 'round him and devoured his scarred mouth in those perfect lips. A kiss very like the multitude Fiore had bestowed upon him since the moment the mask had first left his face—a kiss he would ever hunger for no matter how oft he indulged in it.

Yet part they must. And when they did, Fiore breathed against Enzo's lips, "Just so long as you promise to return."

Enzo resolved above all else to do so.

~

The day after Enzo's departure dawned with rain. This sufficed to keep most of the populace bundled up snug indoors, venturing out only if they must. Fiore, awaking alone and having spent the better part of the last month-and-a-half convalescing in his quarters, felt nothing short of a hailstorm could prevent him from disembarking his ship for the rain-slicked streets. He tried not to let his mind linger on Enzo's absence, the lack of a warm body beside his own, arising without the scent of coffee filling his quarters. He had his hooded cloak and a pocket to keep his zibaldone dry, and that would suffice alongside a dim inkling of a destination. He might try a bathhouse, perhaps; his chirurgical wound had closed over at last, and Enzo had recommended swimming to restrengthen his weakened muscles. There were certainly enough bathhouses to go around in the crimson sash district, and he knew which ones would actually let a fellow take a plunge undisturbed.

But before he'd trod even half the distance between the *Kingfisher* and the bathhouse he had in mind, he encountered another solitary figure in a hooded cloak rather like his own, though they stood a touch taller than him. Something about their gait seemed familiar as well. And when they took note of him in turn, their pace quickened into a run—a dangerous thing over the rain-slicked masegni—which brought them near enough for Fiore to recognize.

"Artemisia?" he called out as she drew up to him. "Aren't you supposed to be sculpting Cygnus in the countryside?"

"I was," she admitted. The gaze she fixed upon him held an unaccountable bewilderment. "I returned just this morning."

"Then," Fiore concluded with a smirk, "there must be some romance to call you here from your studio in miserable weather. Who is it, then? Anyone I know?"

Artemisia stared at him. "I came here because I thought you were dead."

"Oh." Now it was Fiore's turn for bewilderment. "Really? Why?"

Artemisia gave him a look which told him without words she thought him unfathomably stupid. "The city is swirling with rumors. An unknown masked figure visits the *Kingfisher*'s male courtesan with a chirurgeon in tow. The courtesan is not seen again for weeks. What conclusion ought I have formed?"

"Corelli saw me," Fiore pointed out. "And her sons. And Serafina."

Artemisia snorted. "None of them saw fit to inform me. I had to come find out for myself."

Fiore smiled. "And are you satisfied in what you've found?"

"To a point. What truly occurred? Or is it purely rumor, and nothing at all happened to you in my absence?"

Fiore hesitated. The rain showed no sign of letting up, and despite bandages and anodyne a twinge made itself known in his gut. Enzo's warnings as he'd left, delivered in pleading rather than condemnatory tones, echoed in his mind. "I'll tell you all. Only I'm not supposed to stand in one place over-long. Shall we continue on together? To the Crooked Anchor, perhaps?"

The coffeehouse lay farther off from the *Kingfisher* than Fiore had yet ventured since his chirurgy. Despite his efforts not to dwell on Enzo's absence, he nonetheless found himself wondering whether Enzo would approve. Enzo had asked him—begged him, more like—to send for the chirurgeon if anything went awry. And while Fiore felt extremely reluctant to do so, he thought he might be willing, for Enzo's sake.

As if she could read his thoughts, Artemisia arched her brows and asked, "Should you walk so far?"

"Walking is good for me," Fiore insisted—which was true, according to Enzo. "I've a prescription for it."

This at last provoked a snort of laughter from her. She turned and led the way.

Between the crimson sash district and the coffeehouse she divulged more details of her commission in the countryside. She'd acquired the marble and her patron had arranged for its transport to his villa's garden. However, her patron didn't want his garden disheveled for the summer, so he put off any further work until autumn. Sensible enough, by Fiore's reckoning, as he'd never heard of a statue on the proposed scale taking any less than seven months to carve. This postponement left Artemisia at leisure to return to Halcyon—whereupon she heard the rumors regarding her favorite model and hastened off to find out for herself.

"I've made good progress with his head gardener, at least," she concluded just as the coffeehouse drew in sight. "Very sensible woman. She's assured I'll damage neither the flora nor the symmetry."

Rain drew crowds to the Crooked Anchor. The collective heat of the artistic swarm meant one could keep warm even without huddling 'round the hearth-fire or snuggling up in a wrapping-gown—not that this made Fiore any less jealous of those who swathed themselves in yards of bright silk velvet patterned with brilliant birds or radiant butterflies. By some miracle Artemisia found them a table with room enough for two tucked away into a corner.

"So," she began, setting the coffee cups onto the table with decisive precision. "What actually became of you whilst I was away?"

"Appendicitis." Fiore wondered if the word would mean anything to her. It'd meant nothing to him until he'd fallen ill with it, but then again he was less inclined to seek out knowledge in the medical vein than most.

Artemisia by contrast sought to know something of everything, and indeed when he pronounced the diagnosis now she paired her raised brows with a sage nod rather than a bewildered glance.

"Beyond that," Fiore continued, "it resembles the rumors. I fall ill. I am visited by a masked figure and a chirurgeon. However, contrary to rumor, my condition improves under their care. And now I am well enough to sit before you and tell you all."

"So it would seem," Artemisia conceded. "Would this be the same masked figure you brought to my studio?"

"The very one." Fiore smiled. "So you see, I'm hardly at the mercy of an *unknown* masked figure."

"What do you know of him?"

The question oughtn't have set Fiore back on his heels quite so much as it did. And while he kept his smile on, he had the disconcerting feeling that Artemisia could see through it. Still his voice remained airy and unconcerned as he replied, "I know his face."

She arched her left brow. "Do you, now."

His smile grew into a sincere grin. "He's very handsome. Distinguished dueling scars."

Her right brow joined her left. "Do tell."

So Fiore told. He'd already divulged a great deal to her in the course of his modelling sessions with her twice a week—how he'd met an intriguing stranger on the final night of Saturnalia; how said stranger had teased Fiore with glimpses of what lay beneath the bauta costume; and how, just after Fiore had slyly introduced him to his most constant friend in the whole city, said stranger had offered to keep him in ease and comfort for all his days. Now Fiore could add how, after he'd fallen ill, this same mysterious figure had not only come to his rescue by diagnosing his illness and bringing a chirurgeon to cure it, but also remained by his side throughout his frankly disgusting convalescence—and dropt the bauta mask at long last. The only details he omitted were those relating to his own past. He trusted Artemisia with his naked body and his sordid exploits, true enough, but self-preservation demanded he keep his conservatorio origins close to the vest.

"He only left me just yesterday," Fiore concluded, having finished his first coffee and begun another in the course of his talk. "His family performs a ritual hunt for Diana each spring-tide. But he's promised to return the moment he can slip away."

Truth told, Fiore had expected as much. Most aristocratic families departed in the spring to enjoy summertime in the countryside.

Artemisia had remained almost completely silent throughout Fiore's recounting. This by no means indicated disinterest on her part. Like Fiore, she knew one could glean a great deal more by listening than by talking. Still, it left Fiore in unbearable suspense as she traced the rims of her own empty coffee cups.

"So?" Fiore asked when he could stand her silence no longer—

though it meant he lost the game of patience between them. "What do you think of him?"

A sly smile tugged at the corner of her mouth. "I hardly suppose it matters what I think of him. But," she added as a huff of frustration escaped Fiore, "it seems he treats you well, at least."

"And you've already formed a hundred suspicions as to his true identity," Fiore concluded.

She shrugged. "I've narrowed it down to a few dozen. Assuming he's truly an aristocrat. The dueling scars are certainly a strong hint in that vein."

Fiore hesitated. As a rule he didn't speculate on the identities of his anonymous gentlemen callers—though he let Artemisia draw whatever conclusions she pleased. But he found himself more interested in Enzo than in any of the others. And Enzo already knew all of him, with Fiore having divulged more to him than he had even to Artemisia.

And she, taking more interest in the inner workings of the city than himself, might have a better idea as to who his bauta paramour truly was.

Fiore didn't concern himself with politics beyond keeping up in conversation with Artemisia—and even then just barely. From her he knew the city council was populated half by elected citizens and half by nobles who inherited and held their positions through their family name. Regardless of by what means they acquired their post, when a vote was called, all who cast their ballot were required to wear identical plain rough wool robes and blank paper masks. According to Artemisia, the election of Prince Lucrezia was controversial because at the time she was considered rather young for a lifetime appointment at only twenty-eight years of age. But that was some years hence now.

And now, Fiore wished to know something more than he ought.

"Do you know," he ventured, knowing even as he dropt his gaze and fiddled with his empty coffee cup that he'd failed to sound casual enough to fool her, "which noble house's crest has a dragon?"

The question twisted his already-aching entrails. What he ought to do was ask Enzo himself. But that would risk driving Enzo away. He only just glimpsed his face. How dare he presume to ask for his family name? And again, that assumed the crest on the silverware he brought to Fiore's quarters belonged to his own house. Even if it weren't stolen, it might have been pawned or seized in a bankruptcy settlement. Yet still it turned Fiore's stomach to ask behind Enzo's back.

Artemisia served him a blank look. "Many. The city was founded by a dragon. All who wish to conjure the illusion of antiquity have woven it into their heraldry."

This was not so helpful an answer as Fiore might have wished. He tried again. "Any who favor a black dragon?"

"Sable," she corrected him. "And again—several."

Fiore sipped his second cup of coffee.

Artemisia studied him all the while. At length, she continued. "The number of young gentlemen belonging to aristocratic houses and bearing dueling scars as you describe is narrowed further if their family crest includes a sable dragon. But it does not yet dwindle to one."

Fiore supposed that'd been rather too much to hope for.

# CHAPTER TEN

"I t's refreshing, isn't it?" Giovanna asked. She rode beside Enzo in the hunt, both of them having ventured a little off the beaten track together whilst keeping the rest of the party—hounds, horses, and hunters alike, including Giovanna's husband and her personal retinue numbering a full score—within sight between the trees. "Getting out into the wilderness and away from the city."

In any other year, Enzo might have easily agreed with his sister. The vernal hunt in Diana's honor was perhaps his favorite of the ancient rites his family enacted. They rode through the darkest hollows of the forest surrounding the mountainside estate on the trail of the mightiest stag the season had to offer. He sat astride his favorite steed, Fabio, and his faithful Vittorio trotted along beside him. To say nothing of the human company, which included the sister who remained fond of him rather than furious.

This year, however, he'd found one particular charm in the city which the countryside lacked.

"It's nice," he told Giovanna, because it would be rude not to reply, and frankly she deserved better given all she'd put up with from him since he'd left university.

And it was nice, after all. He liked riding and missed it when he dwelled in the city. He liked the mountainous forest and all its greenery and creatures. Gazing upon it now, however, he saw only the inspirations for the capricci Fiore had admired in the painter's studio. How he longed to return that capering faun to his natural habitat and show Fiore the breathtaking reality responsible for his fantasy.

But Giovanna wasn't letting him off so easily today. With the same sweet smile as she ever cast upon him, she continued. "Will you be joining us at Bluecliffe for the summer? Or will you linger here?"

By here, she meant Wolf's Head—the family's ancestral hunting lodge from whence the ritual hunt always commenced. The implication that she and by extension Lucrezia might permit him to remain and live alone for a few weeks or perhaps even months boded well. Some of their trust in him had returned at last.

And yet, to linger at Wolf's Head was not his desire. Gods willing, their trust might extend a little further.

Enzo drew in a steadying breath and replied, "I thought I might remain in the city."

A marked pause ensued. Enzo didn't dare look to Giovanna to see how she took his suggestion. He kept his eyes on the path ahead, the silence broken only by their horses' hooves thudding steadily through the undergrowth.

At length, she ventured, "For what purpose?"

She'd kept her voice light, indicating curiosity rather than suspicion. Enzo appreciated the difference.

Still, he couldn't quite meet her gaze as he answered her. "I've made a friend."

Another pause ensued. Giovanna doubtless waited for him to say more. He waited for her to ask again and won out.

"Is this," Giovanna enquired, more teasing than accusatory, and even then hardly teasing, "the same 'friend' for whom you left me at the opera?"

"…Yes," Enzo admitted. His glance met hers at last.

Giovanna didn't appear in the least slighted. Instead, a gleam of intrigue lit her eyes. Enzo wasn't sure if that was better or worse.

"And is this," she continued, "the same 'friend' with whom you've spent the last month and a half?"

Now they trod upon dangerous territory. Carlotta reported to Lucrezia, not Giovanna. So Giovanna hadn't heard the exact particulars of his liaisons from that quarter. But sharing Ca' Scaevola with him as she did, she could hardly escape noticing his absence from the family halls, even with allowances for his solitary habits. The fortnight of missed fencing lessons, if nothing else, must have attracted her attention.

He knew not how she'd react to Fiore. She had a romantic streak, as evidenced by her passion for her husband. But while Antonio had worked as her mere steward before their marriage elevated him to the title of duke-consort, as a viscount he'd still ranked above any courtesan.

And yet Enzo could answer his sister with nothing less than honesty. So he replied with reluctance, "Yes."

A reluctance which she, of course, noted. With a smile alongside her raised brows, but noted nonetheless.

Enzo cleared his throat. "He was injured." Partly true; chirurgy was a form of controlled wounding. He didn't want to say *illness*, for that implied contagion, which, while not at all possible in Fiore's particular case, would require a great deal more explanation than Enzo wished to give her at present and would give her a great deal more worry than the situation warranted. "His wounds required tending, and as his friend I could do no less than keep him company in his convalescence."

Giovanna's smile lost its mischief. Her brows had knit in concern at the mention of injury, though her overall expression remained fond. In gentler tones than she had yet used, she enquired, "Him, you say?"

Even in his circumlocution Enzo had revealed far more than he'd intended. And again, he could do no less than respond with, "Yes."

He consoled himself with the reminder that she'd known of his romantic preferences long before now. He only hoped she'd forgotten how they played into his departure from university.

Giovanna gave a thoughtful nod. "And wounded, as well. How unfortunate. On the mend, I hope?"

From another quarter these words would've been mere politeness. Enzo knew Giovanna well enough to tell her courtesies from her sincere sympathies. And her comments now, to his heart's great relief, were the latter. Even if Fiore remained an anonymous stranger to her, it eased Enzo's burdens to know she shared in his sufferings.

"On the mend," Enzo echoed in affirmation.

Giovanna's smile widened, dimpling her cheek. "Else you never would've agreed to return to the countryside, however briefly."

Fabio's ears flicked backward. Enzo forced his hands to unclench their grip on the reins. He likewise forced himself to confirm his sister's suspicions with an honest nod.

Mercifully, she accepted this with a knowing glance and a gracious reply of, "We'll speak more on this after the hunt."

Enzo expressed his overwhelming gratitude with a brisk nod. He took the opportunity she'd granted him to urge Fabio into a trot which carried him onward and away. Vittorio kept pace with him like a shadow.

As he left his sister and the rest of the hunting party behind, the forest seemed to consume him. He hardly minded being so devoured. Enzo liked hunting well enough. The chance to prove his strength and cunning against the wild brutality of nature. And, on this particular venture, the opportunity to please the gods as well.

But it was the aesthetics of the hunt which drew his admiration as much as the act itself, if not moreso. The sylvan surroundings put all of Fiore's capricci to shame. Verdant growth erupted from every corner, with trees bearing trunks broader than three men standing abreast and slathered with moss. Ferns and fallen leaves carpeted the ground amidst the ancient gnarled roots, turning the forest floor into a mosaic of brilliant-hued fractals. Boulders gilded with lichen jutted out from paths carved by wandering creatures following trails laid by their ancestors centuries ago. Brooks and streams crossed and joined together in splendid waterfalls leading ever on down towards the distant mighty river. All combined to create a lush tranquility which Enzo felt he could taste as the forest's breath filled his own lungs. Whatever claims the city had upon serenity, the forest far exceeded. The only thing it lacked was a particular faun with horns of dark curls frolicking between the shadows and shafts of sunlight breaking through the canopy. If he could but have Fiore here beside him, Enzo couldn't imagine himself more content.

Vittorio drew Enzo out of his mind's wanderings with a sudden halt. The hound, who'd trotted alongside the horse and rider all the while, now froze in place, nose upturned. Then he dropt low, snuffling through the underbrush with renewed purpose. Enzo brought Fabio to a halt as well and waited for Vittorio to either find what he sought or lose interest. Fabio flicked his ears.

Then Vittorio bolted upright.

And bounded off into the forest.

A mere nudge of Enzo's knees sufficed to send Fabio galloping after him.

Whatever scent Vittorio had caught drew him deep into the wood. Fabio leapt nimbly over rocks and streams and fallen trees whilst Enzo ducked beneath branches. Even so, Vittorio proved nimbler still.

All too soon Enzo lost sight of him altogether.

Another few hoof-beats passed. Vittorio failed to reappear. Enzo cursed beneath his breath and called out for his hound aloud.

No answering bark resounded through the wood. Nor did a familiar black shadow bound out of the underbrush to greet him.

Enzo drew Fabio up to a halt. Without the hound in sight, every horse-stride likely took them further away from him rather than catching him up. He called again. His voice echoed away into the eternal silence of the forest.

No sign of Vittorio emerged.

Enzo tried to ignore his growing unease. There was no call to worry. The master of hounds knew well how to retrieve a lost cur; go to where they were last witnessed and leave an old shirt so they had a familiar place and familiar scent to return to. And this course of action would only prove necessary if Vittorio failed to return on his own by morning.

Still, Enzo didn't like having his faithful hound out of sight.

And Vittorio, loyal as he was, ought to have responded to his master's call by now.

Unless, as the fearful voice in the back of Enzo's mind insisted, something had happened to him.

As if in answer to Enzo's fears, a noise arose at last from the depths of the wood. Vittorio was not a baying sort of hound. But Enzo had heard him whimper now and again, usually when he wasn't permitted to accompany Enzo somewhere. He heard the whimper again now, raised amidst yelps, barks, and growls.

Enzo dug his knees into Fabio's flanks. The horse plunged into the wood anew.

The distressed cries didn't cease. Enzo ignored his heart's pangs and told himself the sounds were a good sign. If Vittorio could cry out, that meant he yet lived. And each cry resounding through the wood told Enzo where he lay and drew him ever nearer to his rescue.

And then, with a final leap from Fabio over a fallen log into a glade where a bending brook had carved out a bowl in the earth, Enzo found his quarry.

It seemed Vittorio had cornered the stag. The stag, however, had turned matters around on the hound and now had him backed against the muddy bank. Hooves like knives lashed out against Vittorio's gleaming fangs. The hound's jaws thudded shut on air as they tried and failed to latch on to the fleet beast twice his own size. Its slender limbs belied the bulk of its body, and the thick ruff around its neck protected the mighty sinews that even now sought to plunge its sixteen-pointed antlers into Vittorio.

Vittorio was swift. The stag was swifter. It caught him up on its tines and flung him against an ancient oak. A hideous crack broke the forest's tranquil silence. A few scraps of bark fell down alongside Vittorio's limp form. The stag surged in to trample him.

All this within the three shakes of a sail it took for Enzo to arrive and perceive how matters stood.

Enzo drew Fabio up short. Then he braced his palms against Fabio's withers and swung himself out of the saddle in a singular leap. He rolled as he landed and came up with his knife unsheathed.

And a good thing, too, for no sooner had he stood than the stag rounded on him.

Better him than Vittorio, he thought.

He didn't have time to do more than think before the stag charged.

Behind him, Fabio shrieked and bolted. Understandable. Arguably wiser than Enzo's own action, which was to brace, crouch, and seize the stag by the antlers.

It mostly worked. With his left hand wielding his knife, he could only seize the stag's left antler in his own right hand.

Which meant the right antler, with a quick twist of the stag's sinewy neck, remained free to plunge through his ribs just beneath his heart.

The pain was not entirely unlike anything he'd felt before. Still, it knocked the breath out of him. And what breath he tried to draw afterward leaked into his punctured lung as much from the wound as from his throat. Blood bubbled up around the antler to ooze down his front. His black waistcoat disguised most of the crimson stain. He felt it nonetheless, a cold damp soaking through the linen shirt beneath.

The force of the blow drove them both to the ground. The stag tried to wrench itself free. Enzo's fist clenched tighter around the antler he'd caught. The one stuck within him twisted. He tried not to imagine it splintering as it sent ripples of agony from the sucking wound. The stag's legs scrambled against the tree roots beneath them, scattering whatever dead leaves of autumn had survived winter's snows over the fresh-grown moss of spring. Its eyes rolled wildly in the skull lashed by bone to Enzo's own chest.

Well within range of his knife.

If he'd still had it.

His left arm trembled. The antler hadn't struck his pectoral, but the pain nevertheless radiated up to his shoulder and out through his fingertips. It'd forced his fist to splay in a convulsive jerk. The knife had dropt to the ground. He couldn't see it now—could hardly see anything past the stag's chaotic bulk. Nonetheless he grit his teeth through the pain and forced his shaking arm to grope across the tree roots in search of a familiar handle.

A rough bark rent the air. Something thudded against the stag, driving it hard into Enzo again and forcing out what little breath he'd regathered. The stag itself kicked wildly and screamed. Enzo had heard a deer's scream before, but never so near to his ears as this. And small wonder it screamed and kicked, for Vittorio had scrambled up to leap onto its back and latch his mighty jaws on the nape of its maned neck.

And still Enzo kept up his blind search. His fingertips went numb before they brushed against something smooth. The blade rather than the handle, but the knife nonetheless. His scrambling fingers snatched it up, flipped it over, and held it firm. He summoned all his remaining strength to drive the blade down through the stag's eye.

With a final shriek and a shudder that sent lightning-forks of agony sparking from the wound throughout Enzo's body, the stag perished. It gave a few final futile kicks of its legs. Then it lay still. Its dead weight pinned him to the ground. Even if he weren't wounded, he could never have hoped to move. He struggled in vain. His strength ebbed with every throb of his heart forcing blood out from the wound. His eyes shut against his will.

A low whimpering rang in his ears. Something wet grazed his cheek. He forced his eyes open to find Vittorio had limped over to where he lay and now nuzzled his face, trying in his own simple bestial way to assist.

"Good boy," Enzo said. Blood left his lips alongside his words.

Vittorio whined.

Enzo supposed he ought to feel victorious. While the stag had proved no Ceryneian hind, it'd certainly put up a fury of a fight, and to have the honor of slaying it showed he held Diana's favor.

But all he could think of was how, even if he survived the rising tide of blood filling his left lung, he couldn't possibly sail back to Halcyon tomorrow. He'd have to wait at least a fortnight until he could gaze again into Fiore's soft dark eyes. To hear the sweet music of a voice that refused to sing whispering low in his ear. To feel a tender and well-practiced caress remove his mask and grace his cheek with the touch he yearned for. He thought of Fiore, still recovering from his own infirmity, waiting in vain for his return.

Distantly Enzo heard the cacophonous approach of hounds and hooves. The remainder of the hunting party would arrive soon.

But they did not arrive before the flock of ravens clouding his vision overtook him altogether and sent him spiraling down into darkness.

# CHAPTER ELEVEN

The knock on his door in the early afternoon didn't strike Fiore as unusual.

The sight of a woman on the threshold when he opened it, however, was rather unusual indeed.

After an astonished blink, he realized he recognized her. He'd had but a glimpse of her before, a mere shadow through a sliver of a cracked-open door, but her black woolen livery, severe countenance, and long hair tied back in a simple queue struck his memory nonetheless. This, then, was Enzo's manservant.

Unfortunately, Fiore could not recall her name. But before he could apologies or even greet her, she spoke.

"A missive from my mistress," she said briskly, proffering a sealed letter as she did so.

Fiore, no less bewildered, accepted it from her. The black wax bore a noble coat of arms depicting a dragon segreant. He broke it and unfolded the letter to read.

*Fiore of the Kingfisher in Halcyon is hereby summoned to appear at*
*Wolf's Head at his earliest convenience by order of the Duke of Bluecliffe.*

Fiore blinked at the parchment. "And why am I thus summoned?"

"You have some familiarity with my master."

Fiore recalled no familiarity with any person of ducal rank. However, as Enzo had named her as his manservant... "Is this to do with Enzo?"

The manservant blinked at him. "There are some who call him that, yes."

Fiore counted himself among a lucky few. "And where is Wolf's Head? Not in the city, surely."

"I'd advise packing whatever personal effects you may require for at least a fortnight." She paused. "I know not how long his grace may require you."

His grace. Whether she meant the Duke of Bluecliffe or Enzo or one and the same, Fiore knew not. He knew whom he considered his own grace.

Fiore owned little. His personal effects—zibaldone and pencils, shaving kit, spare shirts, his only other pair of breeches—fit easily into his leather satchel. He left the manservant waiting in the hall for a mere five minutes at most whilst he packed. She expressed no surprise, nor any other emotion, as he announced himself ready.

"Where're you off to?" asked Corelli when he emerged on deck with the manservant in tow.

"Wolf's Head," Fiore replied with confidence, as though he hadn't just heard the name for the first time not a quarter-hour past. "On the mainland."

Corelli raised her brows. "For how long?"

"A fortnight, perhaps." Fiore grinned. "Ciào!"

And with that, he went over the side and down the rope-ladder to the narrow fondamenta between the ship's hull and the canal.

A private gondola awaited them there—all in black, much like Enzo's own garb, his manservant's livery, and that of the gondolier. The gondolier drew himself upright at the sight of the manservant and served Fiore a brisk nod, which he returned. The manservant opened the door for Fiore to enter the hooded felze and followed him in afterward. The moment Fiore had settled himself against the black leather seat within, she gave a brisk knock to the wooden ribs overhead, and the gondola slid smoothly on its way. Fiore had a fair a view of the city outside through the elaborate black caning over the windows. But truth told, he found matters within the felze far more interesting.

The manservant did not make much conversation. Fiore hadn't expected her to. She was a respectable and trusted member of an aristocratic household. What could she possibly have to say to a mere courtesan? Or perhaps, if he gave her a more generous motive for her silence, she considered it her duty to interfere as little as possible— ideally, not at all—in either the conversation or quiet contemplation of her charge.

Which made it all the more astonishing when she broke her silence to enquire, "Do you ride?"

Fiore blinked. He'd dwelled in Halcyon for most of his life, and the city had banned horses centuries ago to keep the streets and canals clean. Even those slaughtered for meat were relegated to the butcher barges. As such, he could return her no answer other than, "I do not." He paused, then added, "Will that be a problem?"

"No," she replied. "I ask because the overland part of the journey would go faster by horseback than by carriage. But a carriage will go fast enough for our purposes."

"Speed is a necessity, then?" Fiore concluded.

The manservant shot him a sidelong glance. "To a point."

"Very well." Perhaps Enzo wanted him for a certain event, then, like a hunt or a ball. Or perhaps Enzo simply couldn't bear to remain parted with him for so long as he'd promised. Either way, Fiore supposed he'd find out when he arrived. He hesitated, not wanting to irritate the manservant when they still had a journey together ahead of them. "Forgive me—I wasn't quite myself when last we met—what ought I to call you?"

She arched an eyebrow. "You may call me Carlotta."

"A pleasure to make your acquaintance, Carlotta." He knew better than to offer her his hand. "I'm called Fiore, though you probably already knew that."

"I did," she conceded with the ghost of a smile.

Fiore returned it. Then, as she seemed to prefer silence to conversation, he resumed his visual study of the felze interior's intricate scale-patterned serpentine carvings, with occasional glances out the latticed window.

The gondola continued winding on through the canals until, quite all of a sudden, it left them behind altogether for the open lagoon.

Fiore had travelled widely and freely throughout Halcyon ever since his arrival more than a decade hence. But he had never yet departed it. A queer dread he hadn't anticipated crept up the nape of his neck now. Instinct bid him look over his shoulder at the city vanishing into the mist in the reverse of how it had appeared as if by magic out of the aether the first time he'd ever beheld it.

Yet, as he sat facing the gondola's aft, with Carlotta in the reverse seat facing him, he reined in this instinct to a mere twitch he could brush off as a slight chill. He didn't want her to see him looking back. He must seem worthy of her master and not like a coward or rustic.

Carlotta, meanwhile, appeared to take no notice of his inner struggle and instead cast her own mild-verging-on-disinterested gaze out across the lagoon.

Fiore likewise didn't look back when the gondola reached a dock on the mainland. If a departure was an arrival in reverse, then he couldn't imagine the city from this distance would look any differently than it had over a decade earlier; nothing but a cluster of fog clouds, assuming he could even perceive anything at all this far out.

A carriage awaited them at the dock. Shellacked black, fully enclosed, with the dragon crest carved in bas-relief on the doors, four wheels, and four horses to draw it.

Fiore hadn't seen a horse since he'd left his ancestral home behind. He'd quite forgotten how tall they were.

Carlotta ushered him into the carriage. Like the felze, it was done up all in black, though with velvet upholstery rather than leather. As she'd done in the gondola, Carlotta took the seat opposite him, with her back to the horses. A folded furred blanket and velvet pillow lay on the seat beside him. A picnic hamper sat on the floor.

"We won't be stopping for dinner," she said when his curious gaze lingered on the hamper. "Straight on through the night. With any luck we'll arrive before mid-day tomorrow."

That explained the pillow and blanket as well, then.

Carlotta rapped the roof of the carriage just as she'd done for the gondola. It lurched off with far less grace and ran along far less smoothly. The rattle of wheels and rumbling of hooves resounded. Fiore braced himself against the velvet cushion and took in the swaying scenery through the carriage window. The seaside became pastoral countryside not unlike Tiziano's capricci, minus the fantastical creatures and epic ruins. Then trees and hills arose around them as they entered a wooded valley. The sun sank to the west.

When the sky turned a particular shade of purple, the carriage stopped. Carlotta broke open the hamper and proffered wine, bread, and cheese for Fiore's perusal, which he eagerly accepted. This done, they both got out, at Carlotta's suggestion, to stretch their legs. The ride resumed within the quarter-hour. Night fell, leaving only the lanterns suspended from the carriage itself to aid the full moon in illuminating their journey forward. Against all odds, Fiore fell asleep.

He awoke to find the pale blue light of dawn peeking through the curtains. Yet this hadn't roused him. Rather, the carriage had halted. Carlotta remained seated before him in exactly the same posture as she'd held the previous evening. Fiore wondered if she, too, had slept or sat up like a gargoyle all night.

"Wolf's Head?" Fiore asked.

"Not quite," Carlotta replied. "We're changing the horses."

Fiore supposed fresh steeds would go faster and further than those who'd dragged the carriage through the night.

Carlotta opened the carriage door to reveal an inn surrounded by pines. Fog rolled across the ground, colder than what drifted through the canals and alleys of Halcyon. Fiore stepped out and beheld the carriage-driver strapping black horses into their harnesses—different black horses, if he took Carlotta's word for it. Within the inn itself they had just enough time to gulp down coffee whilst the innkeeper pretended she was too worldly to stare at her strange guests who'd arrived in a ducal carriage. Then back into the carriage they went and lurched off again, deeper into the mountains.

The dark forest looming ever-higher all around them ought to have disturbed him, but Fiore found himself more intrigued than otherwise by his new surroundings. A narrow path led them higher and higher until a

particular curve let the window pass by a break in the trees to reveal a
castle perched on a peak.

"Is that...?" Fiore asked before he could stop himself from sounding
like such a rube.

"Yes," Carlotta replied in her matter-of-fact manner.

Fiore stared until the forest shifted to block the castle from his sight
again. Its image lingered in his mind long after, appearing like a shade
before the dark shadows of the trees. What had once been a medieval
fortress built around an ancient temple had since grown into a pleasure
palace of exquisite modern architecture with high towers flung out in
all directions on spiraling columns. Its enormity overshadowed any
edifice Fiore had ever seen within the bounds of the city, save for
perhaps the temple to Belenos. He glimpsed it again and again through
gaps in the trees as the road wound back and forth up the steep hill,
until at last they reached the bridge leading through wrought-iron gates
as tall as the *Kingfisher*'s mast into the palace courtyard itself. A
towering hedge encircled the carriage drive, thick as any stone wall. A
draconic fountain in the center proved the sole decoration. The austerity
forced one to appreciate the smaller details of carved scales and sinewy
form. But as the carriage halted, Fiore just felt trapped between the high
pointed arch of the hunting lodge's enormous doubled doors and the
shriek of the wrought-iron gates clattering shut across the path behind
them.

It didn't help that, contrary to his expectations of a grand party, their
carriage remained alone in the drive.

What struck Fiore most as he stepped down from the carriage onto
the gravel was the silence. The carriage—with its creaking springs,
rattling wheels, clinking harness, shuffling horses—and its occupants
seemed to make the only sounds in the courtyard aside from the
intermittent wind whistling through the trees.

One might attribute the curious quietude to the natural stillness of
the countryside compared to the bustling city. Even so, Fiore would have
expected to find the human presence within and without the castle itself
in the midst of the inherent chaos of a hunting party or ball—or at the
very least, the chaos of arranging some sort of celebratory entertainment.

And yet the hush prevailed with an almost sepulchral quality as the doors groaned inward to allow him entrance into a vast and echoing foyer.

For the first time since his unexpected journey began, Fiore considered the possibility that he might not have been summoned for festive purposes.

Nevertheless, Carlotta led on, and Fiore saw no path forward but to follow her.

The dark and moody interior reminded Fiore of Enzo's customary garb—minus the brightening warmth of Enzo's smiling eyes. Carlotta showed him up a vast spiraling staircase carved of black marble, its banister yet another coiling serpent. Fiore glimpsed what he thought might be the shadows of servants scuttling out of sight as he passed through the floors. Then Carlotta broke away from the stairs to take him down a corridor lined with suits of armor toward a particular door carved with the same noble crest that adorned her own livery.

The door opened into a quaint antechamber about twice the size of Fiore's own quarters. A handsome balcony overlooked the garden courtyard. Another identical door stood on the opposing side. Since the antechamber had no other apparent egress, Fiore assumed this must lead him nearer to his Enzo, whom he felt more desperate to see now than ever before.

Between Fiore and this door, however, stood a lady.

Her gown alone marked her out as such. Her bearing confirmed it. For, even though it was evident Fiore and Carlotta's entrance had interrupted her in the midst of pacing, she turned toward them with remarkable poise, her shoulders back, head held high, and chin upraised in silent enquiry.

Fiore knew not how to answer her.

The lady's gaze searched Fiore's face, then fell to the scarlet sash tied 'round his waist to mark his trade. She looked to Carlotta with a raised eyebrow.

"This," said Carlotta with a slight bowing of her head, "is Fiore."

"Oh!" The lady spun to regard him. Her voluminous skirts billowed with grandeur to equal any sweeping cloak. "So *you're* Fiore!"

Fiore admitted as much.

She declared it a pleasure to make his acquaintance, adding, "We were wondering why our dear Enzo kept saying half his own name. Particularly when no one calls him that. We thought the brain-fever had taken him. It's quite a relief to find you're a real person. Is yours short for Fiorenzo, too?"

"Not to my knowledge," Fiore replied, his mind whirling. Then again, the people who'd named him that had died before he might've grown out of any childish nicknames and taken the longer version with them to their graves.

Reflections of an unhappy past were overshadowed by an alarming present, for the lady had revealed disturbing details. As gratifying as it might have felt under other circumstances to learn how oft Enzo mentioned his name, the remark of a possible brain-fever, in particular, painted a portrait which gave Fiore considerable unease.

"Simply Fiore, then," the lady declared with an approving nod. "Enzo will be delighted to see you, or so I'm told," she added, glancing at Carlotta. "The chirurgeon is with him now. You may go in once they're done."

Fiore's whirling confusion ceased as her words struck him with dread. "Has something happened to him?"

The lady blinked. "Has no one told you?"

Fiore shook his head.

"Oh, you poor dear," she continued, her astonishment and concern apparently genuine. "Yes, a little something, I'm afraid. A hunting accident. Too dreadful for me to speak of more, forgive me, but he has pulled through, and the chirurgeon declared him out of danger and on the mend. You may go in just as soon as they're done."

What Fiore might do in the meantime, he knew not. The thought of harm befalling Enzo had sent his mind reeling. He stood stupidly clutching the shoulder-strap of his satchel in some strange and grand estate with very little idea of where he was and still less idea of his purpose here. He hadn't felt so small since he'd first arrived at the conservatorio. His glance flicked to Carlotta, the sole point of familiarity in these unknown surroundings despite their scant few hours of acquaintance.

And for the first time in those scant hours, he saw a hint of something besides stoicism in her features. A slight downward twitch at the corner of her mouth. Or perhaps it lived in the hairs-breadth descent of her brows. Regret, maybe. More likely it was pity.

"His Grace the Duke forbade me to speak on what befell him," Carlotta said. After a slight pause, she added with the faintest hint of warmth, "He didn't wish to cast a pall over your journey."

Fiore didn't think the shock felt much better.

The lady's reassuring smile waned. Fiore realized the silence between them had stretched far too long. He knew not what to say to make up for it.

"You've come all the way from Halcyon, haven't you?" the lady said, startling him. "And in the span of a single day! You must be exhausted after such a journey."

"Really, it's nothing," Fiore said—half because it was the polite response in these situations and half because thinking on his own mere discomforts seemed selfish beyond words when Enzo lay in the hands of a chirurgeon and possibly suffering a brain fever alongside whatever wounds he'd sustained.

"Nonsense," declared the lady. "You must take some refreshment at the very least. Belladonna," she called, turning toward one of the many shadowed alcoves the corridor contained.

A young woman in a stark black gown—the skirted version of Carlotta's own garb—emerged from the dim corner with a curtsey.

"Bring up some limonata for our guest," the lady continued, adding with a glance at Fiore, "If that will suit?"

"Yes, thank you," Fiore replied, glad at last to feel certain of the correct response.

The lady beamed at him and sent her handmaiden on her way with a nod. No sooner had the door shut on said handmaiden than the lady swept across the antechamber to the card table and chairs set up along the balcony. There she sat and with a gracious wave of her bejeweled hand invited Fiore to join her.

Fiore could do little else. He perched on the edge of his seat. His fingers refused to unclench their hold on the strap of his bag across his shoulder. He glanced out from the balcony to the courtyard. It held another draconic fountain, this one surrounded by benches. Rhododendrons and hydrangeas filled the remainder.

"Have you dwelled in Halcyon long?"

Fiore snapped his gaze back to the lady, who seemed altogether unperturbed by his rude behavior. He swallowed hard and endeavored to answer her in a conversational tone. "Most of my life, yes."

"Do you get out to the countryside often?" Her words remained light, balanced on the knife's-edge between friendly and indifferent, but Fiore couldn't help suspecting an ulterior motive behind her interrogation.

Still, he could hardly do otherwise than answer honestly, "Not often, no."

The limonata arrived far quicker than Fiore had anticipated, interrupting whatever subsequent enquiry the lady might have for him. If Enzo dwelled here then he certainly enjoyed excellent service. And the bright tart-sweet of the limonata itself cut through even the heavy fog of Fiore's anxiety.

"Refreshing," he said, setting the glass down again after his initial sip.

The lady's smile showed his compliment had landed precisely as he'd hoped. She seemed nice enough, or at least had the grace to act so. That didn't stop Fiore from wondering exactly who the fuck she was.

The far door creaked open.

Fiore whirled towards the sound, half-hoping to see Enzo emerging through it. Instead he beheld a figure in a black-waxed gown—though, mercifully, he wore a plain paper mask over his nose and mouth rather than the traditional hideous glass-eyed beaked mask of the trade.

The chirurgeon paid no attention to Fiore's stare. He approached the lady, who stood to speak with him. Their voices remained too low for Fiore to catch more than a few snips of phrases. The words "resting comfortably" eased his nerves a fraction. He kept his gaze on his limonata to disguise his eavesdropping.

"You may see him now."

A marked silence ensued. Fiore glanced up to find both lady and chirurgeon gazing down upon him. Belatedly, he realized the chirurgeon had intended that particular remark not for the lady but for himself.

Fiore set down his glass and arose. With what dregs remained of his dignity, he bowed to the chirurgeon and lady both.

Then strode past them to the door the chirurgeon had left ajar.

Enzo's bedchamber appeared at first as dark and solemn as the rest of the hunting lodge. The mural covering the walls depicted a forest so startlingly lifelike that for an instant Fiore thought he'd stepped if not into the wild wood then at least into an arboretum. The skins of slain beasts served as rugs across the wide walnut floorboards. The coffered ceiling loomed above him at twice his own height. The enormity of the cavernous interior made the bed within seem small—all the more ludicrous, for as Fiore approached it he realized it rivalled the size of his own entire bedchamber. No mere half-a-whaleboat this. Green silk curtains, hand-painted with myriad ferns, hung from four black-walnut posts carved with scaled coiling serpents whose enormous claws, at the base of each, clutched eggs the size of Fiore's skull.

And in the enormity of such a bed, a gentleman whose towering frame Fiore knew well appeared very small, indeed.

Enzo lay with the bedclothes drawn up under his arms, leaving his throat and shoulders bared. His hair spilled across his pillows like the rays of a dark sun. A gigantic black hound lay across his feet, but even this monstrous presence left plenty of room for whoever cared to join them. And while the hound appeared ferocious, it seemed no moreso than Enzo himself, whom Fiore knew to be sweet and gentle.

The hound raised its head at Fiore's approach. This alerted Enzo, who lolled his head across the pillow toward the door. His face held the pale hue of candle-wax, with his sharp cheeks sunken and his dark eyes hollowed by fever.

And yet Fiore couldn't help but find him handsome, for when this ghastly visage turned toward him, it greeted him with a smile.

Fiore closed the distance between them in a dash which bordered on leaping. His hand found Enzo's amidst the bedclothes and clasped it tight—far too tight, yet he couldn't will his fingers to loose their hold.

"Fiore," Enzo said softly, his deep voice no less affectionate for its hoarse tinge.

"Fiorenzo," said Fiore.

Enzo blinked in alarm.

"You don't like it, then," Fiore observed.

"I like it well enough," said Enzo. "Though I don't hear it often. Where did you...?"

"From a lady pacing outside your chambers."

"Giovanna," Enzo groaned. At Fiore's confused glance, he added by way of explanation, "My sister. The Duke of Bluecliffe."

No wonder she hadn't bothered to introduce herself to Fiore. "Which makes you...?"

"Fiorenzo Scaevola, Duke of Drakehaven, brother to Prince Lucrezia, Serenissima of Halcyon."

Fiore blinked.

"Just call me Enzo," he added—pleaded, more like.

Fiore felt only too happy to indulge him, though he couldn't suppress a smirk as he replied, "Enzo."

Enzo clasped his hand with a contented smile.

"The duke told me you were out of danger," Fiore confessed. "Do you feel so?"

"Better than I was, certainly." Enzo's throaty chuckle became a cough. Not a hacking one, and the attack didn't last very long. Still, it was enough to unnerve Fiore.

"Don't let me overtire you," he began, but Enzo waved him off.

"What tires me is boredom," Enzo croaked. "You're the best cure I could hope for."

Fiore had been called many prettier and more flattering things in the past. Yet this simple proclamation nonetheless fluttered pleasantly in his heart. "What happened? The duke said something about a hunting accident."

Enzo nodded, stifling another cough. "My own hubris. A stag went after Vittorio. So I leapt between them and, well..." He moved to draw back his bedclothes. "Would you care to see?"

Fiore, never before permitted to see more than scraps of Enzo's nude form and eager to behold anything further Enzo deigned to show him, nodded.

With Fiore's assistance, Enzo drew the bedclothes down to his waist, revealing a swathe of clean white linen pulled tight 'round his ribcage and secured over the left shoulder. Nothing seemed to have bled through, at least not that Fiore could see, which he took as a good sign.

"There." Enzo pressed two fingers against a particular point on his chest with a wince. "The antler gored me between the ribs."

To Fiore's untrained eye it seemed as though it'd missed his heart by mere inches, if that. Fiore's own heart shot into his throat. He swallowed it down and tried all the while not to appear even half so unnerved as he felt.

"So the lung is punctured." Enzo let the bedclothes fall back into place with a weary sigh. "And it collapses. And no sooner is it restored than pneumonia sets in—an infection," he added in response to Fiore's bewildered gaze. "So I'm left in a fever for what they tell me was three days. Finally I come out of it, and Giovanna suddenly wants to know who 'Fiore' is."

Fiore smiled to hear it, though now that he knew the full extent of Enzo's injuries, he couldn't keep from asking, "Should you be talking quite so much?"

Enzo rolled his eyes to meet his gaze. "Are you sick of the sound of my voice?"

"Never," Fiore declared—and in all honesty, for once. "Only I fear I might never hear it again if you injure yourself further by it."

A self-depreciating smile wound its way up Enzo's cheek. "Would that pain you so?"

"Terribly." Fiore wished he could make it sound as sincere as he meant it. "It seems Vittorio owes you his life. Where is he?"

For indeed, he had proved himself a very poor friend by Fiore's estimation if he couldn't even attend Enzo's sickbed.

Enzo gestured to the foot of his bed where the hound lay.

Fiore glanced to the hound, then back to Enzo, confused.

"Vittorio," said Enzo.

The hound raised his head and thumped his tail against the bedclothes.

"Ah," said Fiore.

"You think me foolish," said Enzo.

"Not at all. I think you loyal, and courageous besides."

A huff of laughter escaped Enzo—and another cough besides—but his soft smile appeared nonetheless pleased. "I'm not keeping you from any pressing business, am I?"

"You are my most pressing business," Fiore laughed, adding, "And my pleasure."

Too late he realized how the jest might come across. Fortunately, Enzo took it in just the sort of humor Fiore had intended. Unfortunately, his chuckle turned into a hacking cough. He recovered quick enough, as before, but it gave Fiore no less alarm.

"Perhaps I ought to go and let you catch some rest," Fiore offered, if half-heartedly. He would tear himself from the bedside for Enzo's sake, though he did not wish to let him out of his sight.

"Perhaps," Enzo echoed, sounding about as reluctant as Fiore felt. "There are guest chambers not far distant from this suite. Unless…"

Fiore dared not hang all his hopes on a single word. "Unless?"

Enzo swallowed hard. With a glance far more bashful than anything Fiore had seen from him in some time, he replied, "Unless you wouldn't mind remaining here with me."

Fiore couldn't restrain his grin. "The bed's certainly big enough."

Enzo's answering smile appeared as much relief as good humor. "There's books if you wish to pass the time reading. And a tarot pack in the card-table drawer if you don't mind playing solitaire. Vittorio is too lazy for much, but his favorite chewing rope is by the hearth if you want to coax him into action."

"Never fear." Fiore tapped the bag which held his zibaldone. "I can amuse myself for as long as you require."

Enzo chuckled again. This time, at least, it didn't become a cough, for which Fiore gave silent thanks to whichever gods felt like listening.

Fiore circled around the enormous bed to the other side, where there remained ample room for him and at least three others like him to stretch themselves out. Instead, however, he laid himself down beside Enzo— atop the bedclothes, for once, but nonetheless as close to him as he could well cleave.

"Will this do?" Fiore asked, turning his gaze up to meet Enzo's.

Enzo nodded in reply. Fiore hardly saw it, for the soft warmth in the unmistakably fond look Enzo cast down upon him quite drove all other thoughts from his head.

And, despite declaring his intention to amuse himself otherwise, Fiore's hands found their natural place in stroking through Enzo's hair until he fell asleep.

# CHAPTER TWELVE

E nzo awoke to the soft strains of a lute.
The sound had entered his dreams as he'd slept, and thus upon waking he assumed some of his dream had lingered. It'd proved a pleasant dream, one in which he lay much as he did now, but with his beloved Fiore come to tend his bedside with sweetness and good humor.

As he opened his eyes, however, the music didn't fade away. He lolled his head across his pillow towards it and discovered Fiore himself perched at the foot of his bed, strumming his lute with a contented Vittorio stretched out beside him and looking very real indeed.

"Fiore?" Enzo muttered, confused. The effort of drawing in air and then forcing it out again to create speech pulled at the wound in his chest. He supposed the morphine tablets had worn off somewhat as he'd slept, for every breath throbbed with distant pain.

Yet as Fiore whipped his head up to regard him and he met the gaze of those soft dark eyes flown wide first with wonder and then delight when he realized Enzo had awoken at last, it seemed to Enzo as if he could feel no pain at all.

Fiore set the lute aside to bestow a kiss on Enzo's lips.

"Sorry to wake you," Fiore murmured against his mouth as he

withdrew. He waved a careless hand towards the lute. "I figured you wouldn't mind."

"Not at all," Enzo replied. "Play on."

An impish smile stole over Fiore's handsome features. He sat up beside Enzo and took the lute into his lap again. Yet even as he began to pluck its strings, he said in a mock-chiding tone, "You didn't tell me you played."

"I don't," Enzo replied with honesty. "At least, not well. Giovanna procured it for me after I left university. She thought I needed something to occupy my hours with less violence than fencing."

A wry half-smile tugged at Fiore's perfect lips. "But it didn't suit you."

"It suits me to hear you play it." A thought occurred to Enzo amidst the fog of receding anodyne. "You don't have your own."

"No," Fiore admitted, sounding almost reluctant to say so.

"Why not?"

Fiore raised his brows. "The expense, for one. Though I suppose I could find a luthier to fuck if I felt so inclined."

Enzo's chuckle ended in a cough. When it subsided, he said, "But you're not so inclined."

"No," Fiore said again. "I don't want to draw the notice of musical circles in the city. If folk hear me playing, they'll want to know where I learnt, and as I am unwilling to answer, it would make matters awkward at best. At worst..."

Enzo need not hear the sentence finished. He knew Fiore feared rediscovery by the conservatorio.

"But," Fiore continued, a smile plucking at his mouth just as he plucked at the strings, "a forgotten lute in a hunting lodge in the wilderness is fair game. With your permission," he added.

Enzo granted it with a nod. "You may have it for your own, if you wish."

Fiore raised his brows. "I accept—on one condition."

"Name it."

"You look after it for me here."

"Done," Enzo declared with a laugh that turned into a repressed cough.

Fiore set the lute aside again and laid the back of his hand against Enzo's brow.

"I'm not feverish," Enzo told him.

Fiore withdrew his hand, which Enzo regretted, until those same fingers trailed down from his brow to caress his cheek. "Probably ought to let the chirurgeon have a look at you anyway."

Enzo's agreement stilled on his tongue. While the suggestion itself was sound enough, to hear it from Fiore's lips puzzled him. He who dreaded their life-saving presence hardly seemed the one to call for their return.

And yet as he searched Fiore's dark and beautiful eyes, Enzo beheld a shadow of concern behind their smiling gaze. It seemed Fiore's fear of chirurgeons had been surpassed by his fears for Enzo's health.

"If you wouldn't mind," Enzo said at last, apologetically.

Fiore shrugged. "Why should I mind?"

If Fiore wished to pretend, then Enzo saw no reason to confront him over it. He reached over to the nightstand and rang the silver hand-bell to summon Dr. Zoccarato. Fiore remained by him, lounging on his side propped up by the piled pillows and smoothing away stray locks of hair from Enzo's brow.

But when the antechamber door's creak and thud echoed through to them, Fiore slipped away and wandered off to the window, taking the lute with him. No sooner had he settled onto the window seat than the bedchamber door opened to reveal the chirurgeon.

While Dr. Zoccarato listened to his heart and took his temperature, Enzo watched Fiore. Fiore had assumed a rather convincing pose of a musician preoccupied with his instrument, though Enzo noted he didn't continue to play. Tension lingered in his posture even as he lounged against the marble frame. The surreptitious glances Fiore cast back at him were not the annoyed looks of an impatient concubine but rather, he realized, the watchful gaze of a lover ready to leap to his beloved's defense should anything go awry. What weapon Fiore had to hand, Enzo knew not. As an alley cat required nothing save its own claws to rend its opponent, so too did Fiore look ready to tear asunder with his bare hands any who would dare lay a finger on Enzo—chirurgeon included.

When it came time to change the wound-dressing, Dr. Zoccarato sent

Vittorio from the bedchamber. Or rather, he attempted to. Vittorio looked to Enzo to confirm it. Only at his nod did the hound slip off the bed and slink out of the room.

Enzo glanced back to Fiore and found a fire in his eyes that swore under no circumstances would he suffer being sent away. The moment their gazes met, Fiore smiled. This did nothing to lessen the blaze.

The smile cracked as Dr. Zoccarato brought out the silver scissors.

Fiore glanced back and forth between the gleaming blades and Enzo's face. His countenance enquired louder than actual speech; ought he to approach?

Enzo stayed him with a slight gesture of the hand and endeavored to reassure him with a smile. He'd endured the change of dressings more than a dozen times over before Fiore had ever arrived. To merely have Fiore in the same room as him sufficed to balm his heart. He needn't force Fiore to suffer the fear that would ensue if he must move but an inch closer to the chirurgeon.

Still, Enzo couldn't quite suppress every wince or grunt as Dr. Zoccarato peeled away the soiled bandages and wrapped him in fresh linen, and with each of these Fiore tensed like a cat ready to leap into a fray. He relaxed his posture only when Dr. Zoccarato finished sewing the new dressings in place and withdrew altogether.

"Walk as far and as frequently as you feel able," Dr. Zoccarato instructed him as he packed up his bag. "Breathe deep, and don't hesitate to cough."

Enzo, who'd heard the same instruction on every visit since he'd come out of his fevered fog, and who recalled well from university the proper treatment for pneumonia, nevertheless thanked Dr. Zoccarato and bid him good morning.

Dr. Zoccarato bowed and, with a final wary glance in Fiore's direction, departed.

The instant the door shut on the chirurgeon, Fiore leapt up from the window-seat and flew back to Enzo's side all smiles. He set the lute aside and devoted both hands to cradling Enzo's jaw as he kissed him.

Which might have turned into something more, if a light rapping on the door hadn't interrupted them.

Fiore, half-atop Enzo, froze in place. He gave the door a wary look as keen as any hawk.

Enzo didn't blame him—who knew when a chirurgeon might return —but he recognized the particular pattern of the knock. "Enter."

And, just as he'd expected, Carlotta slipped through the door.

Fiore, who'd gone rigid in Enzo's arms, relaxed at once. He slipped away with a smile to recline beside Enzo.

Carlotta appeared not in the least bit surprised or affronted to find her charge in bed with a courtesan. "Breakfast is on the card table, m'lord."

Enzo thanked her. She gave a brisk nod and withdrew, leaving the door ajar behind her. Her bootheels clicked away across the antechamber floor. The outer door creaked open and thudded shut to announce her departure.

Fiore slipped out of the bed and reached back to draw Enzo out alongside him. Then he picked up Enzo's wrapping-gown from where it lay over the back of the chair at his bedside. He shook it out—revealing yards upon yards of black silk embroidered with serpentine coils in black thread—and held it up for Enzo to slip into. Or rather, he tried. For he seemed to quickly realize the disparity in their heights would make the posture awkward even if Enzo were at his full acrobatic strength. He made another attempt, holding the garment up with his arms fully extended over his head and hiding himself altogether from view behind it. This lasted for but an instant before a muffled scoff resounded from the other side of the silk and, to Enzo's amazement, Fiore leapt up to stand on the seat of the chair. He shook out the gown again and smiled to see it at the appropriate height at last.

The same smile crept over Enzo's own face as he turned to slide his arms into the sleeves and shrug the gown over his shoulders— withholding a wince as said shrug pulled against his wound.

Fiore leapt down from the chair with the same acrobatic ease and slipped around to stand in front of Enzo.

"You look rather dashing," Fiore said, idly smoothing the gown's lapel between his fingertips. "Very artistic."

Enzo smiled in mild surprise. "Artistic?"

"Oh, yes." Fiore tugged the shoulder seam into its proper place on

Enzo's frame. "It's highly fashionable to wear these out-of-doors as proof of one's creative bent. Every painter has one. And most sculptors. If you go down to the Crooked Anchor early enough—or late enough—you'll see quite a few. I'm surprised you didn't glimpse any when last we visited."

"My gaze was elsewhere."

Fiore shot an astonished glance up at him. Then a smile—small and slight and sweet to behold—tugged at the corner of his perfect lips. It remained as he cast his eyes down at the wrapping-gown again and continued running his fingertips along the cuffs. Enzo's own heart warmed to see the transformation from surprised to bashful to pleased across his handsome features.

"Do you have one?" Enzo asked before he could think better of it.

Fiore paused in his tactile admiration of the gown. His eyes remained downcast. Something flickered across his features for just a moment— long enough for Enzo to realize that of course Fiore didn't own one, else Enzo would have seen it himself on more than one occasion by now, and how cruel of him to remind Fiore of what he didn't have when he so obviously admired it—only to be replaced by a serene smile as Fiore tilted his head up to meet Enzo's gaze.

"No," Fiore replied, his voice smooth and sweet. "I'm not a real artist, after all."

Enzo heartily disagreed. But before he could do so aloud, Fiore took him by the hand and led him out of the bedroom and into the antechamber.

There the breakfast tray awaited them on the card table, just as Carlotta had prophesied. A wisp of steam coiled up from the spout of the coffee pot set out beside two cups and a matching silver dome.

Vittorio had curled up under the card table to wait out his exile. His tail thumped against the floor as Enzo and Fiore entered. Out of habit, Enzo dropt a hand to scratch him behind his ears and winced again as the gesture twinged his wound.

Fiore's hand graced his shoulder as if it belonged there.

The touch—soft, brief, equal parts comforting and comfortable— suffused Enzo's whole body with warmth. He glanced up sharp.

And found Fiore simply smiling and sitting down as if he'd done nothing out of the ordinary at all.

Whilst Enzo continued staring, Fiore poured both cups. He set one in front of Enzo. Then he raised the dome to reveal a tray of a half-dozen brioche.

Giovanna's cook had a tendency towards over-providing, in Enzo's opinion. Still, this was a bit much even for her. And as he considered the coffee cups, one for him and one for Fiore, he reached a belated-by-anodyne conclusion; this was a meal for two men.

Instead of anything sensible, however, he heard himself say, "You haven't broken your fast yet? You must be starving."

Fiore laughed. "One meal missed is hardly starvation."

Enzo paused. It held the off-hand cadence of a jest, and yet there seemed an undercurrent of something darker. As if Fiore knew full well what true starvation felt like.

But Fiore smiled on, to the point where Enzo thought it would be gauche to mention it, and so he said nothing.

Enzo satisfied himself with the sight of Fiore devouring his share of their breakfast. To see Fiore take nourishment sated his own hunger as much or moreso than actually eating. Yet as Enzo nibbled on his brioche, his mind returned to what Fiore had told him of his history at the conservatorio and the significant gap between that and the *Kingfisher*. Perhaps Fiore's knowledge of true hunger lay somewhere in there.

"How shall we amuse ourselves today?"

Enzo, startled out of his grim musings, glanced up to find Fiore smiling at him over the rim of his coffee cup.

"However you like," Enzo replied with a shrug, wincing again. He ought to have learnt by now not to do that. Still, the gesture twinged his wound less and less every day, which marked some improvement.

Fiore's hand alighted on his shoulder gentle as a moth's wing and a hundredfold more soothing. Though his smile remained, concern shadowed his gaze. "Something restful, perhaps?"

Enzo marveled at how attentive Fiore was to his comfort—particularly when Fiore himself was still a convalescent, though his wounds were of an elder vintage. "I'm supposed to get up and about as much as I can well stand. Keep my lungs breathing deep and my blood flowing. Chirurgeon's orders."

Fiore didn't look altogether convinced but relented with a shrug. "You'd know better than I."

"Perhaps," Enzo ventured, a spark of inspiration striking his brain, "I might give you a tour of the lodge?"

Fiore raised his brows with a grin. "You might very well, indeed."

~

Fiore would've gladly doted on Enzo in his convalescence.

If only Enzo would let him.

Even in the midst of his infirmity, Enzo remained self-sufficient—or as much so as anyone of his rank could be. He didn't require a flock of servants to dress or to dine. Fiore's own proffered assistance in the former had proved a courtesy rather than a necessity. And his attendance at the breakfast table was that of a guest rather than a nursemaid, Enzo being more than capable of raising his own coffee cup to his lips and consuming his share of the brioche. Fiore ignored the wretched little voice in the back of his mind telling him his presence here was, at best, superfluous and focused instead on remaining alert to any need of Enzo's which might arise.

When Enzo stood, Fiore leapt up and rounded the table to reach his side. Enzo raised his brows at this but smiled as Fiore entwined their arms together. Fiore found even more satisfaction in the weight of Enzo leaning upon him, however slightly, as they returned to the bedchamber.

Fiore would've gladly helped Enzo shave. But the intermittent coughing fits precluded any attempt, however benevolent, to press a blade to his throat. And so the admittedly handsome shadow of a beard must remain on his features. Fiore settled for kneeling before Enzo to fasten his garters and hose. Breeches and shirt required no assistance; Enzo precluded Fiore's offering by merely slipping them on swift and sure as if he hadn't almost had his heart gored out by a wild beast not a fortnight past. The merest wince told upon him. Fiore leapt up to kiss it from his lips and restore his smile. Then Fiore mounted the chair again to slip the wrapping-gown back up over Enzo's shoulders—an unnecessary gesture, perhaps, but one which brought another smile equal parts amusement and gratitude to Enzo's face, and for that Fiore would've done anything.

And with the both of them washed and dressed at last, nothing remained to prevent them from sauntering forth arm-in-arm into the as-of-yet unexplored corners of the hunting lodge, with Vittorio trotting along at their heels.

On his initial entrance to the lodge, Fiore had felt far too exhausted from his journey and far too nervous about the somber state of its halls to properly notice his surroundings. They felt far less sepulchral now with his arm entwined with Enzo's and his warm weight staggering along beside him. It remained dark; both in the ancient hardwoods forming its pillars and beams and in the tall slender windows coming to pointed arches, designed to keep out the cold whilst allowing slivers of sunlight to penetrate the interior. Enzo led him down a particular hallway with walls covered in antlers from centuries of successful hunts. Then, as they continued on, the antlers gave way to full heads—some stags, others wolves or boars or bears—and then the hallway met with a circular chamber where whatever adorned the walls paled in comparison to the entire beasts mounted in lifelike scenes against actual trees. Against the gnarled trunk of one particular oak, a wolf braced its fore-paws and howled at the leopard snarling from the branches, whilst squirrels and ermines raced up and down in serpentine configuration to match the walnut columns that appeared throughout the lodge.

Fiore would've gladly remained there for some time, if only for the opportunity to sketch all the animals. To have them preserved in stillness made for far more cooperative models than living specimens. His own hasty scribbles of the city's alley cats and wandering dogs proved that all too well.

But as Fiore peered in wonder at the sculptural bestiary laid out before him, he noticed something darting into shadow down the hall. Too short for a servant, he thought. Even a page must come above his waist. But undeniably human in shape.

"My sister's children," Enzo murmured.

His voice drew Fiore's notice away from the shadows and towards his face, which appeared distinctly ill at ease.

Enzo cleared his throat. "Would you care to see the garden? It's rather small but includes some interesting specimens."

Fiore put on his most reassuring smile and allowed Enzo to lead him out of the chamber, pretending to forget the dancing shadows behind him. He didn't need to ask why no introduction would be forthcoming. A common courtesan could hardly expect to be presented, formally or otherwise, to any noble family, much less that of the reigning prince. His encounter with the Duke of Bluecliffe could only have happened by mere chance—as it had.

Still, it stung more than Fiore wanted to admit.

Enzo's discomfort remained writ on his scarred face even as they passed from the sepulchral darkness of the hunting lodge into the dappled sunlight of its enclosed garden. Fiore began to worry it stemmed from his injury and illness rather than a mere awkward almost-encounter. Enzo said nothing of it but merely led Fiore deeper into the greenery until it obscured all hint of the household.

"Forgive my retreat," Enzo said, startling Fiore out of his concerns. "The children's curiosity is at odds with their fear of me. Any approach on our part would only send them scattering."

Fiore blinked up at him. If this was a mere excuse to spare his feelings, it had taken a bizarre form. "Why should they fear their uncle?"

Enzo grimaced. "Because their uncle departed for university before they were old enough to know him."

"Their parents don't encourage this fear, surely."

"No," Enzo admitted. "But I think it a cruelty to force children into an acquaintance with a stranger they're already frightened of."

Fiore found he quite agreed. "So you avoid them as much as they avoid you."

Enzo nodded, looking no less abashed for his confession.

In the interest of turning the poor fellow's mind towards something more pleasant, Fiore glanced about them. Enzo had led him into a grove of gnarled trees whose greenery grew together overhead to enclose them in verdant shadow. Despite the darkness it felt not even half so sepulchral as the interior of the lodge. From this vantage point one could easily forget the surrounding edifice existed. If Enzo considered this garden "small," Fiore wondered at what he compared it to.

And yet, lacking in botanical knowledge, all Fiore himself could find to say about it was, "What are these trees called?"

Which was just about the stupidest sentence that had ever dropt from his lips.

Enzo, however, didn't seem to think so. The smile he cast down at Fiore grew softer. "Hornbeam."

"They're marvelous," Fiore declared.

Out of sheer habit he withdrew his zibaldone and pencil from his breeches pocket, only realizing what he'd done when he looked up from the blank open pages to find Enzo watching him with undisguised interest.

Fiore hesitated with his pencil poised over the page. "May I?"

"By all means," Enzo replied and sounded remarkably as though he meant it.

The sketch didn't take long, just a quick impression of their surroundings, the shafts of light falling into the deep shadows. Fiore didn't want to linger lest he bore his host.

But when he shut his zibaldone, he glanced up to find Enzo didn't appear in the least bit bored. On the contrary, his dark eyes held a delighted gleam.

"I'm afraid only the periwinkle is blooming this early," Enzo said. "If you would consent to return later in the season, we'll have some resplendent flowers for you to see—and draw, if you'd like."

Fiore blinked at him. To have been invited here at all was extraordinary. To be invited to return... well. He smiled. "I think I'd like that."

Enzo beamed.

Fiore offered him his arm again. Enzo accepted it with evident pleasure and led him on through the supposedly "small" garden. Beyond the hornbeam grove lay the periwinkle, blooming just as Enzo had promised and carpeting the edges of the white gravel pathway with a brilliant blue-purple. They continued on to another particular tree.

"Dragon's blood," Enzo said as they halted to admire the singular specimen. "So called for its sap. Bright red," he added in response to Fiore's inquisitive glance. "Supposedly the first of its kind sprouted up where the blood of a true dragon spilled onto the ground."

"Bellenos?" Fiore guessed.

"That's one of the prevailing theories," Enzo answered. "They don't grow naturally in Halcyon itself, but the land surrounding the lagoon is rife with them. It's possible Bellenos seeded the first saplings with his own blood as he wandered through the region before crafting the islands."

Fiore couldn't halt his tongue before he heard it ask, "Just his blood?"

Enzo blinked down at him—then turned aside and muffled his throaty laugh in his hand, not meeting Fiore's gaze again until he'd regained his composure. Good humor brightened his dark eyes. Or at least Fiore hoped it was humor and not the return of a fever. It made his face still more handsome regardless.

"Possibly more than blood," Enzo conceded with a smile. "The sap itself is certainly more than blood. It dyes wool, varnishes violins, quenches steel... to say nothing of its medicinal properties. It's both stimulant and coagulant—it halts the flow of blood," he added at Fiore's raised eyebrow.

Fiore bit back a grin. Enzo's features were so well-formed as to never appear anything less than handsome. But as he divulged the tree's secrets, his passion lit up his whole face with a delightful spark that would leave even the most hardened heart enraptured by his countenance. He revealed the breadth of his knowledge not with the didactic boredom of an aged tutor but as a friend who found the world wondrous and wished to share this wonder with another. Fiore, meanwhile, wondered how Enzo had come to possess all this expertise. What manner of education had he sought to learn so much of chirurgy and botany?

Between his silent enquiries and his admiration of Enzo, Fiore feared he took in very little of what Enzo tried to impart. He'd simply have to ask him about it again later. It would make a charming opportunity for further conversation.

"And then, of course," Enzo ran on, "there are its alchemical uses, which—"

Whatever the alchemical uses of dragon's blood might have been, they were cut off as a coughing fit seized Enzo and threatened to choke the life from him.

Fiore froze.

The hound—whose presence Fiore had almost forgotten, for he followed them as dark and silent and close as a shadow—leapt to alarm. Yet while more attentive, there seemed just as little for him to do. He stood beside Enzo in alert posture, ears pricked, head cocked. Even this proved more useful than anything Fiore failed to attempt.

Enzo muffled his coughs in his voluminous sleeve and braced his free hand against the dragon's blood tree. Each cough came like a thunderclap, a veritable hurricane of ceaseless bolts, one atop the other in a cacophonous cascade.

Fiore found it possible to move at last and rushed all-too-late to Enzo's side. He half-expected the hound to warn him off. But Vittorio simply stared up at them both with sorrowful concern. Fiore slipped a hand around Enzo's back to rub between his shoulder blades. The hacking downpour drew off at last, little by little, until there was space enough for both of them to breathe between the outbursts. At length Enzo dropt his arm from his mouth to reveal a wan smile. He fumbled his hand into a pocket of his wrapping-gown and withdrew a handkerchief. This he spat into with more delicacy than most. Despite his grace under the circumstances, he looked deeply ashamed to have done so—though still not even half so ashamed as Fiore felt for failing to do anything to assist him.

"Your pardon," Enzo croaked.

Fiore, who had all the pardon in the world to beg for, could force nothing past his lips.

Enzo folded the soiled handkerchief and slipped it back into his pocket. His hand emerged again clutching a flask.

"Medicine?" Fiore asked before he could stop himself from demanding answers of one who could hardly draw breath.

Enzo shook his head and creaked out, "Water."

"Oh," said Fiore.

Enzo fumbled with the flask. His frame trembled as he withdrew from the tree's support to set both hands to the stopper.

Fiore—equal parts eager and relieved to do something for him at last —gently plucked it from his grasp and opened it.

Enzo gave him a pale yet courageous smile of thanks as he accepted it back from him. The water seemed to help. He breathed a little easier afterward. The faintest hint of color returned to his hollow cheeks.

"Ought we to turn back?" Fiore suggested, keeping his voice low lest his words wound Enzo's pride.

Enzo shook his head.

"Coughing is good," he insisted in a voice barely more than a wheeze.

Fiore didn't bother trying to look as though he believed him.

Enzo cleared his throat and took another draught from his flask. When he spoke again he sounded almost hale. "I'd like to show you the stables at the very least—if you'll indulge me," he added with another self-deprecating smile.

Fiore would indulge him in anything if it would keep him breathing. He offered Enzo his arm. To his great relief, Enzo accepted it with a smile. The ever-so-slight weight of a fraction of Enzo's bulk leaning against his shoulder eased Fiore's nerves further still.

The stables, as it so happened, lay on the opposite side of the garden. They passed a great deal of greenery on the way. Fiore could see how Enzo bit his tongue to keep from divulging all he knew of the plants and provoking another coughing fit. He made a note to ask after all of it when Enzo had regained his strength. Assuming the duke let him remain that long.

The brief acquaintance with the horses that drew the carriage through the woods had not prepared Fiore for the sight of a herd some two-dozen strong gallivanting about a fenced meadow. All wore coats of gleaming jet black. A few looked small enough for a child to ride. Most were enormous, ranging from lithe elegance to brute strength in build, but all standing taller than Fiore at their shoulders. He'd seen horses before in paintings and sculpture—Artemisia had a full equine skeleton she'd bought whole from a butcher and wired up so she might articulate it for reference—but all artistic representation belied their true size.

Enzo approached the wooden fence—painted as black as the horses— and leant against it with an ease that defied the monstrous enormity of the creatures penned within it. Fiore endeavored to match his poise in appearance if not in spirit. He didn't wish to look half so awestruck as he felt, lest Enzo know him for a charlatan.

They'd not paused there long before one particular horse approached them. Fiore fought the urge to back away as it drew nearer, for with every thudding step of its anvil hooves it loomed larger in his vision. Its shoulders stood taller than Enzo himself by a full head—and its head ran as long as Enzo's torso. Enzo himself remained unmoved, a serene smile gracing his scarred lips. The horse stuck its head over the fence and bent its sinewy neck to nudge its nose against Enzo's shoulder. Enzo scratched its brow as easily as he would've patted Vittorio's head.

"This is Fabio," Enzo told Fiore as if he were introducing a human acquaintance. "My steed in the hunt."

The gentle waves of its midnight mane tumbled down in an echo of Enzo's own. This, combined with its black coat in imitation of Enzo's bauta costume and its long, lean frame capped off by a long, lean face reminiscent of its master's, made Fiore think rider and steed peculiarly well-matched. Furthermore, as he glanced upon Enzo's countenance to find only unsuspecting serenity, he inferred this was all an unconscious coincidence on Enzo's part—which made it all the more amusing. He bit back his smile lest he give offense. "I suppose I ought to thank him for bearing you safely home."

Enzo hesitated. "He didn't do that, exactly…"

"He abandoned you?" Fiore asked before he could think better of it.

Fortunately Enzo seemed to take no offense. "I abandoned him first by swinging out of the saddle. And in bolting back to his herd—that is, the remainder of the hunting party—his riderless state alerted them to my peril and allowed them to rescue me all the sooner."

In light of that, Fiore supposed he could forgive the horse.

"We might go riding, if you'd like," Enzo said apropos of nothing. In response to Fiore's startled glance, he continued, "Not today, I'm afraid, but Dr. Zoccarato says I might return to the saddle in as little as a fortnight if all goes well. That is," he added as a rosy tint bloomed beneath his high cheekbones, "if I could persuade you to stay so long."

Fiore would've gladly remained for years if Enzo would permit him. Still, he couldn't help pointing out with a smile, "I should have to learn to ride first."

Enzo blinked down at him in surprise.

Fiore didn't see why. No one rode horses within the city bounds of

Halcyon, and Fiore was hardly of a class who could afford to withdraw to the countryside and ride for pleasure—until now.

But before Fiore could say anything further to banish the threat of awkward silence, Enzo spoke on. "I'd be delighted to teach you."

Fiore knew he ought to feel some form of gratitude. Enzo's offer entailed not just his horses but likewise his time and patience. A generous proposal by any reckoning. Yet as he gazed out over the paddock at the mighty muscled beasts within, he felt more than a twinge of apprehension.

"They're all... rather large," he heard himself say before his mind could catch his tongue.

Enzo looked from Fiore to Fabio and back again as if the disparity in their size had only just occurred to him. Despite this, he proclaimed, "You needn't fear them."

Easy enough for a man of Enzo's frame to say. But Fiore kept that thought to himself.

Enzo continued. "The largest horses are often the gentlest. It's the same with hounds," he added, gesturing to Vittorio, who had sat silent behind them all the while and merely wagged his tail when he gained his master's notice. "Creatures that are confident in their own size and strength can go forth without the fear that might elsewise cause them to shy and snap at shadows."

Fiore supposed he could accept that theory. A sly smile drew across his lips. "It would seem this rule holds true for certain people as well."

For Enzo was both the tallest and the gentlest man of his acquaintance.

And as the rosy blush bloomed again over Enzo's sharp features, it seemed Enzo had likewise arrived at Fiore's conclusion.

The ideal moment had obviously arrived for a kiss. Fiore drew nearer and reached for him.

Enzo recoiled as another hacking cough bent him double and wrenched him out of Fiore's grip altogether.

Again, Fiore froze. Fabio did not. The horse reared and bolted back to its herd, none of whom seemed pleased with the sudden eruption of noise. Vittorio leapt to his feet but stood his ground, glancing between

Fiore and Enzo, his pathetic whine just audible above the sound of Enzo's coughs.

Enzo braced against the fence with both hands. He leant down to do so, which brought his shoulders within Fiore's reach. This freed Fiore from his paralysis—he could do something at last, though his palm kneading slow and soothing circles between Enzo's shoulder blades hardly seemed enough. Still, the coughs grew quieter, less frequent, less violent, until at last they'd diminished to the point where Enzo could draw himself upright and accept the water flask Fiore again uncorked for him.

"Forgive me," Enzo wheezed. "My own folly."

Fiore could only hope Enzo forgave him for his impotent efforts to help him in turn. He swallowed down the howling void of his own inadequacies with a smile he hoped appeared sympathetic. "Perhaps we might withdraw from the field?"

Enzo nodded, though with evident sorrow writ on his handsome features. Fiore, having just escaped a long indoor convalescence himself, could well understand his reluctance.

"I could read to you," Fiore blurted before he could halt his ungoverned tongue. "Or play the lute, if you'd rather."

He just barely escaped voicing the truth—that he'd do anything, absolutely anything at all, if it could ease Enzo's misery by one jot.

Despite what paltry offerings of entertainment Fiore had laid out for him, Enzo smiled.

Fiore didn't question his luck—though he knew his failings didn't deserve a smile of sincere gratitude, and certainly not one so hopeful and handsome as Enzo had granted him.

The disparity in their heights made Fiore almost the perfect size to act as a living crutch for Enzo. Fiore felt queerly comforted to have Enzo's bulk for his burden as they entered the lodge. On their way they passed the shadowy specter of the manservant Carlotta, who spared them a blank glance before disappearing on her own unknown venture. Fiore didn't have the presence of mind to question it before he and Enzo had returned to the self-same bedchamber where their adventure had begun. There he could at last assist Enzo in shrugging off his wrapping-gown and slipping off his shoes.

SEBASTIAN NOTHWELL

A knock fell on the chamber door.

"Enter," said Enzo. His voice rang out clear and strong without a trace of the reedy weakness from the field. Fiore's heart sang to hear it.

The door opened to reveal the chirurgeon.

Every muscle in Fiore's body tensed to run and drag away Enzo alongside him. As the chirurgeon approached the bedside, these instincts turned toward seizing the pitcher of water on the nightstand and smashing it against the chirurgeon's face to keep him back—but Fiore resisted those as well. Instead he fixed a close-lipped smiled over his clenched teeth and forced himself to remain rooted in his place at Enzo's side. If nothing else, at least Enzo wouldn't have to face the chirurgeon alone.

Not that Enzo seemed particularly bothered by facing the chirurgeon. A sincere if wan smile graced his handsome scarred features as he greeted the chirurgeon like an old friend. Vittorio, who had followed them into the chamber and now lay sprawled on the floor by the bed, likewise took no alarm at the chirurgeon's entrance. By comparison Fiore made a poor guardian, unable to recognize friend from foe and snarling at all who ventured near his Enzo.

The chirurgeon plied termometro and stetoscopio. Enzo's pulse remained strong and steady; the fever had not returned. Their tour of the lodge grounds had not been a bad idea necessarily, according to the chirurgeon, but retiring indoors nonetheless had proved the correct course regardless. A little rest, and then Enzo might venture out of his chambers again. Perhaps even so far as the library. Such a declaration ought to have cheered Fiore. But his tension eased only when the chirurgeon withdrew altogether and shut the door behind him.

Then Enzo turned his scarred smile upon him, and the sight of his handsome and contented features banished the remainder of Fiore's chirurgical anxieties.

Fiore, desperate to do something to aid Enzo, snatched up the lute again from where he'd set it aside just that morning.

"I did promise you some music, after all," Fiore said, trying to make his smile match Enzo's.

Enzo leaned back against his pillows and settled in to listen—the very picture of perfect contentment.

Even with lute in hand, Fiore remained painfully aware that he could do nothing of any real use to assist in Enzo's recovery. His presence in the lodge was at best superfluous. Amidst doctors, servants, and family, a courtesan had very little to offer a duke—particularly when the duke in question wasn't well enough to even consider carnal pleasures. Fiore didn't mind spending a quiet afternoon with Enzo. Indeed, he found he liked it rather more than he probably ought. But it made him nervous all the same.

As his fingertips found their familiar places on the strings and neck of the lute, he let his thoughts fall away into the music and tried to appreciate the moment for what it was rather than vexing himself over what he felt it ought to be.

Yet no music could soothe the snarling beast within him even half so well as the sight of Enzo's dark eyes falling shut and his bandaged chest steadily rising and falling in serene slumber.

# CHAPTER THIRTEEN

Enzo knew not what Fiore made of the hunting lodge.

He'd never been particularly gifted with reading people outside of his own family. Fiore presented a particular challenge. His very career demanded he feign enthusiasm when he felt none. In consequence, Enzo doubted his own ability to pick up on the difference between polite cheer and genuine joy.

Even so, he dared to think he might have begun to catch on. He'd had a glimpse of genuine emotion when Fiore gazed upon the capriccio. And he thought he saw an echo of that as they wandered aimless through the lodge and its grounds. The hunting trophies, gardens, and stables all seemed to meet with Fiore's approval. Still, Enzo noted how an uncharacteristically somber expression overtook Fiore's fine features whenever he didn't notice Enzo had glanced his way. A graver one appeared when the infection attempted to seize hold of Enzo's lungs once more. Despite Fiore's disguised distress, Enzo took comfort in the warm, slender weight of him tucked up under his arm.

Enzo didn't permit his weakened state to prevent him from studying Fiore throughout their return to his chambers and afterward. The visit from Dr. Zoccarato did nothing to improve Fiore's mood—though the chirurgeon's departure brightened his aspect considerably. Enough so that he reached for Enzo's lute and began to play. The soft strains seemed to echo Fiore's return to a happier state, which lightened Enzo's concerns likewise. He supposed it wouldn't hurt to take his ease for a while. He let his eyes fall shut so he might focus on the beautiful sound—though the sight of Fiore cradling the lute in his arms and gently smiling over its strings proved no less beautiful.

When his eyes opened again to a silent room with shadows tilting in the opposite direction, he realized to his alarm that he'd taken entirely too much ease and fallen asleep altogether. His nerves eased as his gaze alighted on Fiore—lounging beside him atop the bedclothes, the lute set aside in favor of his zibaldone, his brow furrowed with the intensity of his sketching, his pencil scratching over the page—but the sight of his devoted lover did nothing to ease his growing guilt.

Enzo drew breath to apologize for drifting off during Fiore's performance. But instead of words he produced a coughing fit. This at least caught Fiore's notice, though with more distress than Enzo had wished to evoke. Fiore startled up and dropt his zibaldone to pour a glass of water and tilt it to Enzo's lips. His embrace around Enzo's shoulders and his palm working between his shoulder blades did as much or more to alleviate his discomfort as the water.

"Your pardon," Enzo croaked out at last.

Fiore tsk'd and insisted Enzo required no pardon whatsoever. "Besides, you needed a rest. The chirurgeon said so."

Enzo had a feeling Fiore had cited the chirurgeon's prescription only for the sake of bolstering his own argument rather than out of any trust in the medical opinion. He appreciated it regardless. Likewise he appreciated Fiore's hand in his own, Fiore's fingers combing through his hair, Fiore folding a cool compress against his brow or bathing his face in rosewater or proffering a fresh handkerchief for Enzo to discreetly dispose of what his coughing fit wrought. A thousand small gestures for which Enzo thought he might never express sufficient gratitude, for whenever a creaky thanks escaped his blistered lips, Fiore simply smiled and shrugged and declared his work nothing.

Enzo knew not how to make Fiore understand—for while he hadn't strictly-speaking *invited* Fiore to the hunting lodge, to awaken and find him at his side overjoyed him all the same. Despite the chirurgeon and staff and his own family surrounding him, Enzo had felt wholly alone until Fiore arrived. The brilliance of his smile banished all gloom from the shadowy corners of the ancestral halls. The sweet sound of his voice sent Enzo's heart soaring. His gentle touch eased all pains. And the gaze of those enormous dark eyes compelled him wherever they might lead.

A sharp contrast to his own grim appearance. How Fiore could smile to see him, Enzo knew not. But he felt glad of it all the same.

Likewise Fiore impressed him by choosing to remain by his side despite the ugliness of his wound and subsequent illness. Most without a medical background would shy from such gory details. Enzo supposed Giovanna would say he hardly had a choice—though Enzo hoped Fiore realized he didn't need anyone's permission to leave. Saying as much aloud got him only a raised eyebrow and a smiling assurance from Fiore that he felt content by his side. Which, if it was a mere polite lie, was one well-told regardless.

On an intellectual level, Enzo understood his recovery from his wound had thus far gone very well, and at present he enjoyed greater strength and chance of survival than most would in his circumstances. On all other possible levels, his frustration with his infirmity grew with every passing moment. Touring a mere fraction of the lodge and its grounds had utterly exhausted him. All he had desired in the hunt was to bring Fiore into the wilderness with him and show him everything he'd craved in the capriccio. And now here Fiore was, beside him, in the wilderness—trapped indoors with an invalid. The irony tormented him. He could only begin to imagine how bored Fiore must feel. What tenfold frustrations endured by one condemned to stagnate in the ancestral hall of his convalescent lover.

And yet, while Enzo yearned to grow strong again for Fiore's sake, Fiore didn't seem to mind him weak. Though Enzo noted how Fiore worried his perfect lip between his teeth as he glanced over the bandages swathing his chest.

"Ought we to call the chirurgeon back?" Fiore asked, much to Enzo's astonishment.

How great Fiore's fears for him must have grown if he would suffer a chirurgeon's return. Enzo knew not whether he felt more gladness for his own sake or pain for Fiore's. "Not just yet."

All tension vanished from Fiore's frame like a bow unstrung. With a smile he replied, "Then it falls upon me to amuse you."

Enzo felt quite the reverse. He was the host, after all. It was his responsibility to see to the cares and wants of his guest—if he could get Fiore to admit to any. "What were you drawing?"

Fiore plucked up his zibaldone and handed it over to Enzo for his perusal.

Enzo beheld a sketch of Vittorio as he now lay sprawled across the foot of the bed. Fiore's rendering, however, showed more truth than the mere reality of the image. It showed the enormity of the hound's form filling the whole of the page, the cross-hatches depicting not just the grain of the fur but somehow also the sheer weight and strength of the muscles rippling beneath—a mighty creature in perfect repose that nonetheless left no doubt as to his power should he choose to wield it.

"He's an excellent model," Fiore mused aloud. "Very patient. And fantastic at holding a pose."

Enzo glanced up to find Fiore stretched across the bed to scratch the hound behind his floppy ears. Vittorio thumped his tail against the bedclothes.

"Remarkable," Enzo declared. He wished he knew a better word, one that fitted Fiore's wondrous ability to conjure images out of the aether.

Fiore scoffed. "Hardly. Though I hope you'll forgive me."

"What for?"

"I ought to have asked permission. He's your hound, after all."

This did nothing to dispel Enzo's bewilderment. Nor did it change his answer. "You may draw whatever you like."

Fiore smiled in a way which said quite plainly that he didn't believe him. Whilst Enzo wracked his brains to think of what he might say to prove he'd meant every word, Fiore caught his lip between his teeth again and looked very much like he might ask for permission to draw something in particular. Those teeth upon that lip held Enzo suspended upon a precipice; anything Fiore asked for, Enzo would grant him at once.

But when Fiore opened his mouth at last, before any words could escape, there emerged a growl—from his stomach rather than his lungs.

Fiore clapped his hand over his mouth. This did little to muffle the startled laugh that followed the growl. And there remained nothing to stifle Enzo's own chuckle beyond his coughing.

"Dinner?" Enzo proposed when they'd both recovered.

Fiore concurred with a grin.

Dinner was rabbit cacciatore. One of Enzo's favorites, though he hadn't asked for it. Giovanna had acquired the habit of asking the cooks at Ca' Scaevola, the villa, and the hunting lodge alike to serve his favorite dishes by default whenever he was in attendance. He suspected this had been her effort to combat his near-total lack of appetite when he'd first returned from university. As the months passed and his condition improved, so had the offerings of the kitchens changed to a more equitable rotation of things everyone enjoyed. But now—spurred on by his injury, he supposed—she had reverted to ordering what she considered the choicest morsels for Enzo's particular palate.

Which was all very well for him, but as he sat down to it at the card table with Fiore, he worried whether or not it would suit Fiore's palate as well.

"Have you any objection to rabbit?" Enzo enquired, doing his able best to sound conversational rather than concerned.

Fiore raised his brows. "None at all."

A sigh of relief escaped Enzo alongside his smile, the latter of which was echoed in Fiore's own handsome features.

And Fiore did seem to like the rabbit, judging by the way he polished off his plate. Still, Enzo hoped he didn't do so out of a sense of obligation.

"If there's anything else you'd particularly like," Enzo said, working hard to keep his tone bright rather than desperate, "you need only ask."

Fiore raised his brows again and assured him with another smile that he'd have no hesitation in asking.

The delight of dinner was dampened by the return of Dr. Zoccarato. Again Fiore retreated to the window. The sun had set and a splendid moon had arisen over the mountain peaks. But while Fiore faced these natural wonders, his dark gaze cast continual sidelong glances towards the doctor performing his examination. Enzo endeavored to reassure him with a smile. It seemed to work.

At last, Dr. Zoccarato declared Enzo quite recovered from his earlier exertions and predicted a good night's sleep and a stronger day ahead.

"Good evening, your grace," Dr. Zoccarato concluded before departing with a bow.

Fiore waited until the door had firmly shut upon the chirurgeon before he leapt to rejoin Enzo abed.

"Good evening, your grace," Fiore echoed with a grin.

This was all the warning Enzo received before he devoured him in a kiss. Enzo certainly didn't mind. But his injury forced him to break off for breath far sooner than he wished. Fiore sat back astride him and gazed down with a curious expression.

"Fiorenzo Scaevola," Fiore murmured in a thoughtful air, as if half to himself. "Duke of Drakehaven, brother to Prince Lucrezia, Serenissima of Halcyon."

Enzo regarded him warily. Whatever reason Fiore had for recalling his full title now, Enzo couldn't imagine anything good.

"Does this," Fiore ventured, "make you the dueling duke of legend?"

Enzo had dreaded this moment ever since his return to Halcyon. Whispers of "the dueling duke" had preceded his arrival. Enzo considered that particular appellation unfounded. He was far from the only duke to have ever fought a duel.

The dread had taken on a particular pall after meeting Fiore. Before he'd braced himself for the scandal and scorn of mere strangers. The stakes sharply increased for any one individual—particularly when that individual held Enzo's heart in thrall as Fiore did.

But Fiore didn't seem scandalized or scornful. Just curious. As he was ever curious, in his impish, capering way, like any faun in the forest observing the mannerisms of mortals. Even now his head tilted whilst a soft smile played about his lips and teased the return of the dimple in his left cheek.

After a long pause, Enzo admitted, "I have dueled."

Fiore ran his fingertips through Enzo's hair strewn across the pillows. "I've not paid much mind to the whispered tales. I'd like to hear your truth of it—if you're willing to tell."

The second silence between them stretched even farther than the first.

Fiore's smile waned. "Or if you'd rather not—"

"I will," said Enzo. He wearied of dodging this fate. And Fiore had already divulged the dreadful history of his own worst fears. The least Enzo could do was reciprocate. He just had to find where to begin.

Fiore settled in to listen. He did so by insinuating himself between Enzo's arm and chest on his good side, slipping down snug as if Enzo's body were molded to hold him. His slender weight brought with it more comfort than others might have expected to gaze upon his insubstantial form. To Enzo, his warmth and softness became a most welcome anchor. And the gaze he cast up at Enzo as he laid his head against his shoulder —the enormous dark eyes holding a promise of solemn patience—would have drawn a confession from a man of bronze, to say nothing of Enzo's own mortal flesh.

Enzo endeavored not to disappoint him.

"Lucrezia's hand governs the realm," he began.

If the non-sequitur confused Fiore, he didn't show it.

Enzo continued. "Giovanna's fields feed it. Our mother's fleet enriches it. Which leaves very little left over for me to do." His fingertips worried the bedclothes as he fought against the anodyne to connect his disparate thoughts. "My father perished in the plague when I was small. I sickened but recovered. My mother removed me from the city to our vineyards for the remainder of my youth."

A coughing fit seized him. As if the mention of his father had summoned his ghost to choke his surviving son. While Enzo had inherited his father's deep bass voice, his pneumonia coughs didn't sound quite like the horrible, withered, wet hacking of his father's final hours.

A concerned furrow marked Fiore's perfect brow. "Perhaps this story might be better saved for another time."

Enzo shook his head. In a wheeze, he explained, "Coughing is good. It breaks up the mucus and expels the infection from my lungs. Keeps it from taking root."

He wouldn't have blamed Fiore for feeling disgusted at that description. Most would, outside of the medical profession. Yet Fiore didn't flinch. Instead he plucked his handkerchief from his pocket and offered it to Enzo. The moment Enzo accepted it from him, Fiore leapt up to pour a glass of water from the pitcher on the nightstand and held it patiently whilst Enzo hacked up whatever dregs his speech had dislodged. When Enzo could breathe free again, Fiore handed him the glass. He drank deep and gasped out his thanks as he came up for air. Fiore simply smiled and stroked his hair.

Yet even this couldn't ease all of Enzo's nerves when it came to divulging his history.

Enzo plunged on. "The fact of my recovery in contrast to my father's death perplexed and vexed me. My guardians told me the answer lay in the field of medicine."

He paused to see how Fiore took it—if he realized where this story must inevitably lead.

But Fiore simply served him an encouraging smile. And from it, Enzo drew courage enough to continue.

"As I grew older I knew nothing I learned in that vein could save my father now, but I thought perhaps if I studied something more of disease I could spare others from my father's fate. Furthermore, I had a certain interest in anatomy, even as a youth." The reason poised on the tip of his tongue, ready to fall into Fiore's waiting ears. And yet he checked himself, as he always did, or as he always had until... "This grew into an interest in medicine, and so, when I passed the age of private tutelage and my family agreed I might be sent to university, I convinced them to allow me to pursue that particular interest."

Fiore regarded him curiously for a long moment. When he spoke at last, his voice emerged low and steady—Enzo could glean nothing of his thoughts from it.

"To become a physician," Fiore asked, "or a chirurgeon?"

Enzo swallowed hard. "A chirurgeon."

This, of all his myriad secrets, was the one he'd most dreaded revealing. He'd kept silent on the precise subject of his education only partly for his family's sake. The truth of Fiore's past, and all he'd suffered under the guise of chirurgical necessity, drove Enzo's own truth deeper down into the darkest pits of his heart. Now that heart leapt up into his throat, its pulse pounding in his ears with anxiety. Bad enough that his sister's children feared him. If Fiore should flee from him—and with tenfold good reason—then he knew not what he'd do.

Fiore continued to regard him with an expression he couldn't quite read. Then the ghost of that familiar handsome smile flickered at the corners of his perfect lips. "Well. That certainly explains how you knew enough to save my life."

Relief flooded Enzo's veins. Fiore didn't hate him. Fiore would not abandon him. He knew not how to even begin expressing his infinite gratitude.

"But you were saying," Fiore murmured.

And Enzo realized the best way he could thank him now was to finish giving him the full account he'd asked for.

"Chirurgy is not a trade fit for a duke to practice," Enzo went on, echoing his own mother's words. "But I thought perhaps by learning something in that vein I might write a treatise or make an experiment or devise something that might, in some small way, contribute to the field and therefore assist in healing the city."

Fiore appeared to think far better of this plan than his own family had. His soft smile encouraged Enzo to speak on.

"Whilst at university," Enzo said, forcing his way through the urge to hesitate, "I made a friend."

A glance showed Fiore understood the full meaning of that fateful word.

"His name was Orazio," Enzo continued. "A baron engaged in the study of ancient literature. We met through the fencing society and together joined the secret dueling club within it." Even as he spoke he could hear the inadequacies in his own description. The bare facts of the case didn't suffice to show Fiore or anyone else who Orazio had been to him. Enzo tried again. "He came from the north. Golden eyes." Words didn't suffice. How to explain how softly those strong arms had enfolded him—how those eyes had flashed whenever they caught Enzo's gaze—how oft he'd made Enzo laugh, and how Enzo cherished the few moments when he could make Orazio laugh in turn, when no one else seemed to understand him. He hadn't Orazio's lyrical gift. Yet still he kept trying. "He used to whisper poetry to me as we lay together, both ancient verses and those composed by his own hand for my ears alone."

The tightening of his throat at the memory set off another coughing fit. Fiore's hand clenched in his. The other stroked his hair and smoothed its way down through the strands to rest its warm palm against Enzo's chest, bracing, steadying him. When Enzo's eyes ceased watering, he blinked them open to meet Fiore's somber gaze fixed on his own face, infinite solace in the dark depths of his eyes and the ghost of a wistful smile on his perfect lips.

"We got on very well for two years," Enzo continued, his voice hoarse for reasons beyond his infirmity. "Through our academic work and the fencing society we made a wide circle of acquaintance. We likewise made a few rivals. One in particular, a viscount of the Delfin bloodline, disliked how quickly I disarmed him in a sparring match. His ire was not doused by the mocking verse Orazio penned in commemoration of the event."

Fiore chuckled. Enzo suppressed his own answering laugh, lest he cough again. Still he smiled despite the turn his story must now take.

"Orazio had likewise begun work on his thesis—a body of writing," Enzo added as Fiore's eyebrow raised in silent enquiry. "To prove all one has learnt at university and to argue a point that adds to the collective body of knowledge. It's a requirement for taking a degree and grueling work, subject to rigorous examination and ruthless critique. Orazio had several dozen pages of which his professors and advisors had finally approved. Then it vanished. Disappeared from his own chambers somewhere between dusk and dawn. And, as he'd yet to copy out the final drafts for the committee to review—"

Another coughing fit seized Enzo. Fiore clasped his shoulders and rubbed circles over his hunched back. Despite Enzo's inability to speak, Fiore seemed to gather the gist of what had occurred.

"He'd spent that fateful night in my chambers." The pang of guilt, like a knife in Enzo's chest, almost provoked his cough again. If only they'd retired to Orazio's rooms instead... "His own were locked; he thought them secure. But he returned to find the lock picked, the door ajar, everything thrown into disarray. And what'd become of his thesis remained a mystery only until he ran down to the common room. The dormitory hearth-fire crackled and blazed almost beyond the bounds of its moon-horns. A mere scrap of parchment had escaped—but this held enough for him to recognize his loss."

Enzo felt Fiore's sympathetic wince against his own body.

"That's when the taunts began," Enzo continued. "Subtle, of course.

Smirks. Knowing glances. Casual enquiries on the progress of his thesis from those who'd never cared before. All friends of the Delfin heir. The heir himself restrained his gloating to a certain smug air. There was no proof of who had done the deed. All physical evidence had gone up in smoke. The only possible witnesses were the culprit's own allies. There was no recourse within the bounds of the university's justice. Which left a duel as the only answer. And so Orazio challenged the Delfin heir. To the death."

Fiore tensed in Enzo's embrace. But when Enzo glanced down to see what he thought of it, he found no fear in his dark gaze. Rather, he beheld determination paired with an anticipatory gleam. It emboldened him to continue his tale.

"The Delfin heir accepted the challenge. At the same time, he made no denial of the crime. Orazio took this as proof positive he had the true culprit in hand. To my mind no one else had the motive—though I suppose my affection blinded me to any of Orazio's faults and made it impossible for me to imagine his enemies. As Orazio formed the better half of my heart, I could do no less than offer myself up as his second. He accepted. I arranged matters with the Delfin heir's second. The four of us, along with a mutual acquaintance in the medical college to tend whatever non-mortal wounds might result, would meet at dawn the following day in the depths of the dueling club—a sunken arena in the bowels of the gymnasium," Enzo added as Fiore's brows furrowed in bewilderment. "The club was both figuratively and literally underground."

"Convenient," Fiore remarked, the ghost of a smirk playing on his perfect lips.

Enzo wished his tale were not so grim as to prevent him returning it. "On the morning of the duel I awoke to find Orazio vanished from my bed." Enzo swallowed down the panic invoked even now by the mere memory of that wretched moment. "I assumed he'd gone to the appointed spot to meet his fate. I hastened to follow him there. When I arrived, I found the Delfin heir and many of the dueling club gathered. But no sign of my Orazio. Nor of the Delfin heir's own second."

The fear Enzo had felt upon awakening alone had only compounded when he couldn't find Orazio in the dueling pit. It'd turned swift enough to rage.

"I asked the Delfin heir where Orazio was," Enzo went on. "He said I'd know better than he. I asked him where his second had gone. Again, he claimed ignorance."

More than a year had elapsed since that fateful day. And yet the mere memory of the Delfin heir's smirk sufficed to send Enzo's fingers into clenched fists. No sooner had they tangled in his bedclothes, however, then Fiore's own soft warm and gentle hand closed over his white knuckles.

Enzo forced his rigid jaw open to continue his tale. "In Orazio's absence, I could do no less than defend his honor."

Enzo expected mockery for this. Disdain at the very least, as Lucrezia had shown him when he tried to explain why he'd gone to such lengths. But Fiore's stalwart gaze bespoke a harmony with Enzo's own choice.

"The duel began. I received this," Enzo gestured vaguely at the scarred slash across his face, "in short order. If we were only going to first blood, the Delfin heir would've won. But as matters stood I served him far worse thrice over. Backed him into a corner. Struck his rapier from his hand. For an instant, the tip of my blade rested in the hollow of his throat. I had but to put my weight behind the blade, and Orazio would be avenged. But then—"

A coughing fit overtook him. He wheezed, as desperate now to gather air and finish his tale as he'd felt then to finish the Delfin heir off. Fiore swept his hair out of his face and rubbed his shoulder. If only Enzo had received any such support then.

"The city guard arrived," Enzo croaked out. "Alongside the Delfin heir's second. Whether he'd informed the authorities on the Delfin heir's orders or of his own accord, I know not. The result is the same. Guards poured into the dueling pit. Chaos ensued. The blade was knocked from my hand, and we were dragged apart."

Fiore spoke up, startling Enzo. "I'm surprised they dared touch you. Being a duke and all."

It'd never occurred to Enzo to think of himself as untouchable. Still, "The wrath of a duke is nothing to the wrath of a prince. If they hadn't stopped the duel, Lucrezia would've..." Truth told, he'd no idea what she would've done and didn't like to think on it. "Well. She certainly wouldn't have been pleased with them."

Fiore searched Enzo's face. "She doesn't approve of dueling?"

A huff of bitter laughter escaped Enzo—which turned into another cough. When he'd recovered, he replied, "She doesn't approve of her brother dueling. Particularly not against the heir to another aristocratic bloodline."

"Ah," said Fiore.

"So much so," Enzo continued with a sigh, "that she withdrew me from university altogether. Oh, the university didn't mind," he responded to Fiore's raised eyebrow. "And the law didn't care. Never found out if the Delfini cared—probably, but I've not heard a word from their quarter since. Lucrezia, however..."

"Cared enough to banish you on the university's behalf," Fiore concluded.

Enzo conceded with a nod. "The Delfin heir is still working towards his degree, to the best of my knowledge. And he still enjoys the privilege of the sword. Whilst my own folly lost me both my hopes of an education and the right to carry a blade in one fell swoop."

Fiore stared up at him with more disbelief than Enzo thought the situation warranted. "You cannot have a sword?"

"Not outside the bounds of our family's holdings, no," Enzo admitted with no small amount of shame. "Lest my actions continue to tarnish our name."

"Hardly," Fiore protested.

Enzo shook his head. While Fiore might hold him in favor, he could know nothing of Enzo's family or his place in it—a fact for which, again, Enzo had only himself to blame. "The only good thing I've ever done for my family is survive the plague that carried off my father." Enzo paused. "And even then, I wonder if they might not be happier had he survived in my stead. He certainly wouldn't have disgraced them with a duel."

A silence fell. His fingers remained entwined with Fiore's—despite all Enzo had confessed, Fiore hadn't shied from his touch. On the contrary, Fiore's free hand laid over both their clasped ones to seal this bond. The warmth of his palm alone soothed more of Enzo's hurts than he could've ever anticipated.

"I never knew your father," Fiore said, his voice low and gentle. "Nor can I speak for your family. But I, for one, am very glad you survived."

For the first time in a very long while, Enzo thought he might feel the same way.

"And what of Orazio?" Fiore asked.

Enzo supposed he ought to have expected that question. Still it struck his heart like a blade. He swallowed down the pain to speak. "I know not."

Fiore stared at him. "You've not seen him since?"

"Nor heard from him," Enzo forced himself to utter the agonizing truth. "Nor heard tell of anyone else encountering him since. Whether he is alive or dead—I presume alive, for if the Delfini had him kidnapped or killed then his family would have done something to avenge him by now."

"But he needs not remain hidden," Fiore pointed out. "He's done nothing wrong. Unless his own shame has driven him into hiding."

"No," Enzo admitted. "He needn't remain hidden."

The unspoken truth hung in the air between them. The same truth that had haunted Enzo ever since that fateful day. The truth he wanted to ignore and yet loomed ever larger with every post that didn't contain some note, some hint, some mere scrap from his Orazio. If Orazio hadn't contacted Enzo by now, either something prevented him—something too horrible to consider—or he did not wish to.

"Have you tried to find him yourself?" Fiore asked, jolting Enzo from his melancholy musings. "Or would your family not permit it?"

"They've not forbidden me." Enzo felt some small gratitude to Lucrezia for that. Of everything she'd denied him, she'd at least not denied him this.

Fiore gazed up at him in expectation. When the silence grew again, he broke it with a gentle enquiry. "And...?"

Enzo tamped down the bitter self-reproach mingling with shame that threatened to choke him. "I have written. He has not replied."

Another silence fell, broken by Fiore's soft voice. "I'm sorry to hear so."

Enzo cleared his throat, which had tightened as if his own heart meant to strangle him. "You must think me beyond foolish."

Fiore grimaced. "Hardly."

"Vicious, then," Enzo concluded. For only an unquenchable thirst for blood could explain how he chose a duel to the death over fleeing the fighting pit to find his lost Orazio.

"Impossible," Fiore declared. His hard stare brooked no argument.

Enzo felt astonished enough that Fiore hadn't recoiled from the revelation of his chirurgical ambitions. If Fiore thought no less of him for that—and for the duel besides—then perhaps he could trust him further still. Perhaps to the extent he'd trusted Orazio. He opened his mouth to speak on the peculiarity he'd hidden throughout their all-too-brief acquaintance.

Fiore met his parted lips with a kiss. Soft and gentle at first; then, as Enzo embraced him in turn, it deepened into something lingering and languid that drove all thought from his mind.

"You are an honorable man," Fiore murmured against his lips when they withdrew for breath. "And better still, you are kind."

Enzo did not consider that judgment entirely sound. Still it balmed his heart to hear Fiore say so. And he resolved with all his heart to live up to it.

# CHAPTER FOURTEEN

The true tale of the dueling duke confirmed most of what Fiore had already supposed. He had not yet connected the city's swirling rumors to Enzo specifically, but he knew the bare sketch of the tale—a betrayal of honor at university and subsequent banishment. The details filled in by Enzo's telling of it, however, created an altogether more haunting picture. One which tore at the heart-strings Fiore thought had snapped long ago. None of the gossips had told how the disgraced duke had lost a love he'd felt worth dying for.

The matter of Enzo's education likewise served to make sense of all Fiore had wondered at. If someone had told him a year ago that he could bed a chirurgeon without remorse, he would never have believed it. Then again, he'd never known a chirurgeon capable of Enzo's depth of empathy. He'd certainly received Fiore's near-constant disdain for the medical profession with far more grace and charity than Fiore himself might have done if their positions were reversed. It left Fiore feeling rather stupid and a bit churlish besides. It was a wonder Enzo hadn't abandoned him.

But if anything, it was Enzo who seemed to fear Fiore would abandon him in light of these revelations. Enzo, who despite his immense height and strength, somehow appeared so small and lost in the vast bed of the hunting lodge—particularly when his soft dark gaze met Fiore's with a mournful cast to his scarred brow.

Which made Fiore all the more determined to prove he would stay.

Knowing full well just how little words meant when it came to fealty, loyalty, and everlasting affections, he preferred to express this intention through acts. He began by returning to the lute. It seemed to please Enzo's ear, but any fool could play a lute, by Fiore's reckoning, if music was all that was wanted.

As night fell, Fiore set the lute aside in favor of kisses and caresses. But while Enzo gladly welcomed him into his bed and slept contented entangled in his arms, he would not let caresses go further than kissing. When Fiore's hand drifted down below their waists, Enzo caught it by the wrist and gently laid it against his scarred cheek instead. Which Fiore felt more than happy to oblige him in. Though he did still wonder at it. He concluded Enzo's wounds must yet pain him too great to allow for any more athletic amusements. And while Fiore knew several ways to please them both without Enzo having to lift a finger, he didn't want to press the issue. So instead he fell asleep smoothing his fingers through Enzo's tresses.

When a run tore through Enzo's stocking the following morning, Fiore thought he'd found an opportunity to be useful at last. But before he could offer to repair it, Enzo produced his own sewing kit and had already begun darning.

"It's a stitch I learnt at university," Enzo explained when he caught Fiore staring in disbelief. "For closing wounds, though it works as well for cloth as for skin."

Fiore supposed he ought to feel disturbed. Instead he found his eye admiring the thread's pattern. Before he could think better of it, he heard himself say, "Looks a bit like sailor's fancywork."

To his great relief, Enzo didn't appear offended. If anything he looked pleased, judging by the bashful smile that graced his scarred lips. "I suppose it does, doesn't it? Perhaps I've found a hobby Mother might approve of at last."

"She doesn't approve of fencing?" Fiore wished he could cut out his traitorous tongue.

The reminder of his dueling folly dimmed Enzo's beatific aspect. "She admires swordplay, but I don't think she'll like the use I've put it to."

"She hasn't heard, then."

"She went to sea concurrent with my enrollment at university. Perhaps some word of it has reached her—though I shudder to think my infamy has flown so far beyond the realm of Halcyon."

And, to hear Enzo tell it, she hadn't approved of chirurgy, either. Fiore tried to give the conversation a lighter turn. "But she enjoys fancywork?"

"She doesn't disapprove of embroidery," Enzo admitted. "She's fond of any sailor's craft—so," he added, hoisting his completed darning aloft, "if this resembles an artful repair of a sail, so much the better."

Fiore wasted no time in assuring him it did. He ought to know, having received several such examples as keepsake tokens from certain sailors and ship- captains who bid him remember them when next they came ashore. Too late he recalled perhaps he oughtn't remind Enzo of his other admirers. But Enzo didn't appear in the least bit jealous. On the contrary—he simply looked happy to hear Fiore was appreciated.

"You're not bored, are you?" asked Enzo, the question's earnest nature surprising Fiore just as much as the non sequitur. "I know you have your drawing and reading and the lute and all, but... I'm not the best company of late."

Fiore protested vehemently.

Enzo only smiled. "Even when I spend the daylight hours sleeping? It's bad enough I'm trapped in here. It's not fair to imprison you as well."

Fiore hardly felt imprisoned. He wondered what had provoked all this. He had the disturbing notion that something of his discontent at not proving more useful to Enzo had leaked out, and Enzo, not knowing its cause, had perceived only Fiore's unhappiness and sought to repair it.

"What about the hunting trophies?" Enzo suggested, oblivious to Fiore's conjecture. "You said you'd like to draw them."

Fiore had to admit the notion appealed to him. But, "I don't want to go poking about where I don't belong."

Enzo appeared far more bewildered than Fiore thought his words warranted. "There's nowhere you don't belong."

Fiore raised his brows.

"Well—barring the private apartments," Enzo admitted. "But beyond that, you're free to roam the halls as you wilt."

Fiore considered the matter. "You'll be all right without me?"

"Vittorio will look after me. Your return will give me something to look forward to. That and the drawings."

If it would give Enzo gladness, Fiore felt most willing to do so.

Enzo returned to bed. Fiore waited until his chest rose and fell with the steadiness of sleep. Then he crept out with his zibaldone to the trophy hall.

A hundred beasts frozen in death snarled around him. He chose a stag with a wildcat leaping onto its back and began to sketch. The familiarity of drawing dispelled his lingering concerns over his own worth and whatever nerves he'd picked up along the way wandering down long dark corridors whose every shadow proclaimed him a stranger.

Until he became aware of a particular shadow by his side.

Fiore turned to find a boy standing at his elbow and staring at his zibaldone with mouth agape. What age, Fiore couldn't tell—anywhere between five and ten, so far as he knew. He hadn't lived amongst children since his flight from the conservatorio. The boy's gold-trimmed blue velvet doublet looked far too fine to belong to a page or any other servant. Fiore concluded this must be Enzo's nephew. Or one of them. He realized he wasn't entirely sure how many children Enzo's sister had.

"Did you draw that?" the boy asked.

Fiore, jolted out of his rapid calculations, replied, "Yes."

"How?"

"Practice."

The boy didn't look as though he believed him. He also didn't look as though he'd wander off on his own anytime soon.

Fiore, not knowing the proper court etiquette for telling a lordling to go back from whence he'd come, tried to steer the conversation into another current. "Do you like to draw?"

The boy nodded vigorously.

That was something at least, Fiore thought. "Have you a zibaldone and pencils?"

"I have pencils!" the boy blurted.

But not paper, Fiore concluded. At least not here. He looked back at his zibaldone, turned to a blank page, and feathered its corner between his fingertips as he thought over the problem. There really was only one thing for it. He looked down at the boy again and forced a friendly smile. "Would you like to borrow mine?"

Another vigorous nod—with even wider eyes, if possible.

Fiore steadied himself with a deep breath and tore out the blank page in a single swift decisive gesture. After a moment's hesitation, he tore out two more for good measure.

The boy accepted them with reverence.

"Why don't you pick out your favorite animal to draw?" Fiore suggested.

Keeping the child occupied would forestall further awkward questions. Or so he hoped.

The boy considered all the creatures in the hall before sitting down in front of a snarling wolf. Fiore turned to a fresh page and began to draw the same. As he'd hoped, drawing kept the boy quiet. At least, until—

"I've finished!" the boy declared.

"May I see?" Fiore said when he'd recovered his composure. Art required audience, after all.

The boy handed over his work.

Fiore didn't have any experience judging the ventures of children. Even so, he thought the boy had some skill. The wolf had turned out recognizable at the very least. "Well done."

Silence met the compliment.

Fiore glanced down. The boy didn't look happy to hear it. A deep furrow had appeared between his brows and his lip trembled. His gaze fixed on his drawing in Fiore's hand—and Fiore's own sketch beside it.

Fiore's heart plummeted as he realized his error. Still he forced his tone to remain light. "What's wrong?"

The boy drew a courageous breath and replied, "It doesn't look how it did in my head."

"Oh." Fiore smiled—a real smile, at last. Drawing, as it so oft did, had quieted his nerves somewhat. "Mine neither."

The boy stared in frank disbelief at Fiore, then at his zibaldone, then at the wolf, and back to Fiore.

"All artists feel that way," Fiore assured him, for it was true. "Nothing we draw ever quite matches up to our vision. But," he hastened to add, as the boy had begun to look even more discouraged than before, "it does come closer to your vision with practice. And your audience will never know the difference. They don't know what it looks like in your head. All they see is what's on the page. They don't have the vision of perfection to compare it to. They can appreciate it for what it is. Which is delightful," he concluded, gesturing to the boy's valiant effort as he returned it to him.

The boy furrowed his brow at his drawing but kept silent. Fiore wondered if he'd spoken rather over the child's head. At least he wasn't crying. His lip had even stopped trembling.

"Andrea?"

Fiore whirled towards the strange voice.

A gentleman not far older than Fiore himself approached them. He wore garb as rich as Enzo's, though with a touch more color—midnight blue rather than black, with saffron embroidery throughout. His beatific gaze fixed on the boy. "There you are! What have you been up to?"

"Drawing," said the boy.

The gentleman halted before them and addressed Fiore. "Forgive me —I haven't introduced myself. Lord Antonio Scaevola, Duke Consort, at your service."

Fiore suppressed the jolt of alarm that ran up his spine into a single startled blink. He'd accounted for a confrontation with a nurse or some other servant; had in fact rather counted on them being too relieved not to be scolded for losing their charge to question his own conduct in introducing his unworthy self to a lordling.

But no. He stood before the boy's own father. The duke consort himself.

Fiore wondered how swiftly and surreptitiously he could leap out of the window. He suppressed the urge and bowed instead. The duke consort didn't seem upset to find his son in Fiore's company. Perhaps he didn't yet realize who Fiore was, and Fiore might still escape unscathed.

"You must be Signor Fiore," said the duke consort.

Fiore reconsidered the window.

The duke consort turned to his son. "Did you introduce yourself?"

The lordling, who had ducked behind his father in the meantime, said nothing.

"Signor Fiore," said the duke consort. "This is Lord Andrea Scaevola, Count of Havenscry."

Fiore bowed deeply and informed the lordling it was a pleasure to make his acquaintance.

"Andrea," the duke consort continued, "this is Signor Fiore—Uncle Enzo's friend."

Again that poor little word held more meaning than it could very well bear. Fiore continued smiling.

The lordling seemed to take it all very well until Enzo's name dropt from his father's lips. Then his eyes flew very wide. He stared up at Fiore with something between awe and terror.

"What a ferocious wolf you've drawn," the duke consort told his son, relieving Fiore of having to break the awkward silence and distracting his son from his fears in one fell swoop. "What do we say to repay Signor Fiore for his hospitality in keeping you company?"

This, at last, was a line the lordling had evidently studied for. "Thank you, Signor Fiore."

Fiore truthfully informed him it was nothing.

"Pray excuse us," said the duke consort. "His lordship has skipped his geography lesson and has much to catch up."

With more relief than he dared express, Fiore bowed and allowed the duke consort and his noble son to withdraw. He waited until their footsteps had echoed away altogether before he fled back to Enzo.

The bedchamber door opened to reveal Enzo still abed but awake with a book in hand. He glanced up with an expectant smile that froze as he beheld Fiore's face. "Are you all right?"

"Possibly," said Fiore. At Enzo's bewildered look, he added, "I think I just met your nephew."

"Andrea?"

Fiore nodded.

Enzo seemed a touch surprised but not even half as panicked as Fiore felt. "Oh. How did it go?"

"I don't know. I met his father as well."

"Antonio?"

"There was a lot more to his name when he introduced himself."

A huff of laughter escaped Enzo, mercifully not followed by a cough. "I'm afraid that runs in the family. Won't you sit down?"

Fiore, who'd stood in the doorway all the while, found the wherewithal to join Enzo on the bed. His pulse had ceased pounding. He wished he could smile. "Will they be vexed, d'you think? The duke and her consort?"

"Why should they be?"

*Because a common courtesan thought himself worthy of speaking with their impressionable heirs.* "I don't know."

"They might be vexed with Andrea for wandering off. I'm assuming that's how you met him."

Fiore nodded. "He found me in the trophy hall. I leant him some paper so he might draw alongside me."

Enzo blinked. "Sounds like an amiable afternoon."

Fiore tried to imitate Enzo's calm. "So... you're not worried?"

"I'm a little surprised, I suppose," Enzo admitted after some consideration. "From what Giovanna has told me Andrea is rather shy. All the moreso around me."

"I've not made a bad impression, then?" Fiore asked before he could stop himself.

"Quite the reverse, I should think. Giovanna and Antonio adore their children above all else. If you've kept Andrea amused and safe from harm, then they're likely overjoyed."

That was something, Fiore supposed. Still, he resolved not to venture forth again without Enzo's escort.

～

The pneumonia dissipated by the close of the first se'en-night. And by the end of the second, the chirurgeon declared Enzo's wound well on its way to closing up.

Fiore ought to have felt happy. In many ways, he did. Once the initial shock of Enzo's condition had waned and said condition had improved, he found himself relaxing into the quietude of country life. The view from every sharp-peaked window showed him a dark green expanse to rival the lagoon he'd left behind. No raucous revelers rang out overhead whilst he slept. No forced smiles for gentlemen who didn't deserve them.

The gentleman who most deserved Fiore's attentions at present, however, didn't seem to want them.

There were gentlemen—more oft than many suspected—who wanted Fiore's quiet companionship as much or more than they wanted his body. Some tired themselves out dancing with him on the crowded deck for hours before they dared venture with him below. Some seemed to occupy his bed for the simple privilege of conversing on his pillow afterward. Some of them Fiore even liked.

And while he found he very much liked the quiet companionship he enjoyed with Enzo in the hunting lodge—a pleasant extension of the queer sort of household they'd set up in his own quarters whilst he'd recovered from his appendectomy—he nonetheless remained unaccountably disconcerted at Enzo's apparent lack of desire for him.

Fiore had beheld more of Enzo's body than ever before since arriving at the lodge. He'd touched a great deal of it besides, assisting Enzo in almost every facet of dressing save drawers and ablutions. But he'd not been touched in return.

Enzo hadn't even invited him to the hunting lodge. Not really. His name had dropt from Enzo's lips in a fever and his sister—the duke— had mistaken it for the name of someone worthy to grace their ancestral halls. What must she have thought when Fiore arrived with his scarlet sash and no idea of his place. And now he was here with no hint as to his purpose or what he might do to prove his worth. If Enzo didn't want him for carnal purposes he had no idea why he'd not been sent on his way.

While Fiore pondered this in the wake of the chirurgeon's visit, Enzo ran a hand through his hair and grimaced.

Fiore supposed his wound pained him. "More anodyne?"

"No, it's just..." Enzo twined a lock of hair between his fingers, looking abashed. "Overdue for a wash."

"Oh." Fiore supposed it must prove difficult for Enzo to wash his own hair when his wound precluded raising his arms over his head. A spark of inspiration struck. "May I?"

Enzo hesitated.

"You did as much for me when I was convalescing," Fiore pointed out.

"It was nothing."

"It was everything," Fiore insisted. "Please. Allow me?"

Enzo relented with a smile.

A quarter-hour saw the kettle over the fire, the wash-stand dragged before the hearth, a towel draped over a chair, and Enzo there seated, leaning his head back into the basin of warm water whilst Fiore worked a lather through the floating ebony tendrils. With Fiore's assistance he'd removed his shirt; the drawers remained. Lest he catch a chill, Fiore supposed. Fiore, meanwhile, delighted in feeling Enzo relax beneath his ministrations. How satisfied his sigh sounded as Fiore poured warm water over his hair. How he bit his lip as Fiore worked his fingertips over his scalp. How patiently he sat as Fiore untangled the soaked strands and combed them dry before the fire. To see Enzo so happy by his hand gratified everything Fiore had wanted these long nights.

And yet, as Fiore stood back to admire his handiwork, he found he craved more. "I could do below the neck as well, if you'd like."

Again, Enzo hesitated.

"Not that I think you need it," Fiore hastened to add. "It's only—I meant, if you wanted—"

A soft chuckle escaped Enzo. "I know."

The rekindling of hope softened the blow to Fiore's dignity. "Then, perhaps…?"

Enzo bit his lip. "There's something you ought to see first."

Fiore knew not what remained for Enzo to reveal to him. Still, "If you wish to show me something, I'm all eagerness to see."

Enzo stood. He set aside the towel Fiore had draped over his shoulders.

Then he untied his drawer-strings and stepped out of them.

And Fiore beheld more of Enzo's bare form than he'd ever seen before.

All the disparate details he'd glimpsed now came together in a cohesive whole that proved far more than the sum of its parts. Fiore's hungry eye swept him up and down, lingering on the lean musculature of the well-formed limbs, the sinews in the thighs and the distinct curve of the calves, the striking Adonis belt leading the eye down to the perfect cock at rest. The body's beauty reignited the spark of Fiore's desire.

Enzo sat down again with thighs splayed wide and took his cock in hand. But rather than stroke it to full mast as Fiore expected, he simply lifted it out of the way of what dwelled beneath. Where one might expect to find a purse of stones—or even a half-full purse like Fiore's own—there instead lay a soft nest of dark curls. Fiore hardly had time to wonder at it before Enzo's fingers parted it to reveal a pair of dusky rose-petals, the narrow chasm between them gleaming wet as if with seed. Curious, unexpected, yet undeniably…

"Marvelous," Fiore breathed.

Enzo's slight sigh of relief nonetheless resounded in the near-silence of the forest's evening.

"I'd like to take you inside me," Enzo said, drawing Fiore's rapt attention from what lay between his thighs. "By a different road, but to the same end."

Fiore knew he ought to say something more to dispel the disguised-yet-evident anxiety writ in Enzo's brows and the worrying of his scarred lip. Instead, he heard himself ask, "Have you done this before?"

"Often." A shy smile flickered across Enzo's face. "Though it's been some time. And you?"

Fiore hesitated. He'd lain with a man who had a cunt before; a particular bo'sun, one who'd paid handsomely and treated Fiore well. But the bo'sun hadn't wished Fiore to enter him by that or any other means. Rather, he liked to have Fiore's mouth upon his cock—a cock far smaller than most men's, perhaps, but undeniably the same flesh, and Fiore had delighted to wrap the whole of it in his tongue and taste its sea-salt spend. Enzo's situation, while it bore some superficial similarities, seemed another thing altogether. A thing which called to mind certain stories Fiore had dismissed all his life as mere sailors' tales.

"I haven't had the opportunity, myself," Fiore said at last. "Though I've heard the legends."

Enzo raised an eyebrow. The corner of his mouth went up alongside it. "Legends of cunts?"

"Most men do sing their praises, or so I'm told," Fiore admitted.

"Though not most of the men who lie with me. But no, I mean the legends of dragons. And the... particulars of their anatomy."

Enzo's left brow arose to meet his right. "You've heard the rumors of my bloodline, then."

"Something more than rumor, it would seem," said Fiore.

Enzo gave a soft laugh like a vernal breeze ghosting across a field of wildflowers. "If I am a dragon myself, or the descendant thereof, I know not. While I'll admit to some self-interested research in the history of the matter, I can speak with confidence only on the particulars of my own body."

Particulars which Fiore found himself eager to learn. "What ought I to call it? A cunt, you said?"

Enzo shrugged. "I've called it so ever since I learnt the word."

Fiore supposed it would suffice. If it were a cunt, however, that raised an important question.

"Will you..." Fiore searched his mind in vain for the correct euphemism, not wanting to give offense. "Is there any danger of...?"

"You cannot get me with child," said Enzo.

"Are you certain? Because from all I've heard, this is exactly how it happens. I still have a stone to my name," Fiore reminded him.

"Even so," Enzo insisted. "I have plumbed its depths and found no womb at its terminus."

Fiore raised his brows.

A faint tint arose in Enzo's face. "My hypothesis is that it is a vestigial vent, or cloaca, left over from when my ancestors transformed themselves from mythic monsters into mortal guise. From the physical changes to my voice and body during adolescence I must conclude that I possess internal testes—again like a reptile or bird. Of course, I can make no experiment to prove it, nor have I found any conclusive evidence for or against. So my hypothesis must remain a mere hypothesis. Nevertheless, for all my experience I remain barren. And those in the family history like myself produced no issue. It seems dragons require something more to beget other dragons."

Fiore supposed that confirmation enough. Still, "Thought you said you weren't a dragon."

Enzo smiled. "I said I didn't know."

"And when you say you plumbed its depths…?"

"I did discover pleasure, yes. Which I should like to share with you. If you'll indulge me." Enzo hesitated. "We might use a lambskin sheath, if that would make you feel more comfortable."

Fiore shook his head. He trusted Enzo's judgment in this. It was his body, after all. "I'll take your word."

Enzo's smile faded. "Or if you would prefer to abstain altogether…"

All too late, Fiore realized how his hesitance had come across. He tried to mask his dawning horror. If Enzo mistook him—if he supposed, even for the merest moment, that any part of him repulsed Fiore—it would prove more than Fiore could well bear.

"Forgive me," Fiore begged, his words tumbling over his tongue in his haste. "I'm eager. It's just—I want to ensure I give you pleasure rather than pain."

Enzo balked. Then his shy smile returned and made Fiore's heart flutter. In a voice as soft as lambskin, he replied, "Trust me to know the difference?"

Fiore dared approach him. For once it was he who bent so they might kiss. Enzo tilted his face up and met him with eagerness.

Better still, he allowed Fiore to draw him back down into the bed.

"Have you any oil?" Fiore asked when they broke off for breath.

Enzo smiled. "You won't need it."

Fiore sincerely doubted it. But he likewise doubted his own doubts. "I don't want to hurt you."

"You won't," Enzo assured him.

Fiore remained unconvinced. "Isn't it rather a…" He trailed off. Years of experience in these matters had nonetheless left him almost totally ignorant in this particular arena. He had only rumor to depend on. "A delicate flower?"

A marked pause ensued. Enzo blinked at him. Fiore feared he'd stumbled into the realm of insult.

Then Enzo chuckled. "Not in the least."

A relieved smile tugged Fiore's lips.

Enzo arranged himself beneath Fiore—face-to-face. A posture not altogether unknown to Fiore, though it typically required the gentleman to throw his knees over Fiore's shoulders. Enzo, however, merely spread his thighs apart. Kisses or perhaps mere anticipation had raised his cock to full mast and revealed his glistening cunt. Fiore stood no less ready. He slipped his hand between them both and aligned his sword with Enzo's secret sheath. His cock-head slid against the innermost petals, already wet with something like seed. Their warmth sent a sensual shiver through his frame. He bent to capture Enzo's lips in another kiss. Then, at his nod, Fiore dared to enter him.

It required a slightly different approach than what Fiore had practiced for so many years. An unfamiliar angle but nevertheless a familiar sensation. His first thrust revealed a far more yielding entrance than he'd expected. He slipped in further than intended, losing the whole of his cock-head within Enzo before his panicked halt. A gasp shuddered up from deep within Enzo's ribs and sent Fiore's own heart into his throat for fear he'd done harm. But an upward glance revealed a bitten-back smile gracing Enzo's scarred lips; the gasp had expressed pleasure rather than pain, and Enzo's arms clasped 'round his shoulders drew him in for an embrace. One hand drifted down to palm the globe of his ass, not-so-subtly hinting he ought to press on. Under such encouragement Fiore could hardly do elsewise save slowly sink inside.

Enzo's head rolled back. The jewel in his throat pulsed beneath his beard-shadow. The sight threatened to send Fiore spiraling off into realms he'd never recover from. He buried his own face in Enzo's collar and kissed a bruise there. Yet he could not deny himself for long. He drew back, hungry for the sight of Enzo—how his noble brow had furrowed, how his dark eyes had fluttered shut, how he caught his scarred lip between his teeth. Fiore had never before beheld Enzo's face whilst inside him. Now he felt as if he could never bear to look away. The mere entrance of his cock sent shuddering waves of sensation throughout Enzo's body clasped in his embrace.

Fiore's own pleasure felt no less so. Having sheathed himself to the hilt, he basked in the hot, wet, tight paradise. He took Enzo's own blade in hand; a few experimental strokes sent Enzo shivering beneath him, around him, through him. To hear Enzo's breath catch at his touch was one thing; to see it flicker across his scarred and handsome features was quite another. Both together were more than Fiore thought he could well stand.

When he could bear to keep still no longer, Fiore dared at last to roll his hips. He rocked as gentle as the lapping of the lagoon against a ship's hull, the barest inch of him sliding in and out of Enzo's cunt. Enzo's cock throbbed in his palm in time with his pulse. Pearls of seed leaked from its tip even as Fiore's own cock was drenched in the slickness of his cunt. Enzo's hips thrust up to meet his ceaseless tide. His hand tangled in Fiore's hair 'til Fiore took the hint and kissed him.

"Harder," Enzo gasped when they broke off for breath. His hips jerked against Fiore in evident desperation. *"Please."*

Fiore could hardly deny him when he asked so prettily. Even less so when his own desires matched Enzo's. He drew himself out 'til just the tip remained, then thrust forth, plunging into depths hitherto unknown to him.

Enzo arched his spine beneath him. His nails drew furrows into Fiore's back. His broken moan bid Fiore on, again and again, and Fiore lost himself in the ceaseless fury. He knew not if he were the storm splintering a ship or the ship itself swallowed up in the storm, torn between stealing Enzo's breath in kisses and gasps and drawing back to behold the splendor of Enzo's face caught in the same tempest, until—

Enzo's cock and cunt pulsed in tandem, spend erupting over Fiore's fist from one and cascading over his cock from the other.

Fiore had felt Enzo come before. He'd tasted his spend, wrapped his cock in his shuddering frame, seen how the mere sight of Fiore could send him into transports—but always beneath a mask.

Until now.

Now, Fiore saw how the gasp overcame him, how his dark eyes rolled back, how his jaw fell open and locked in ecstasy, how the furrow in his brow released at long last.

He was resplendent. Better than Fiore had ever imagined.

And this—combined with how Enzo's cunt clenched 'round him, rippling in rhythm with his spend—sent Fiore following him over the same precipice mere moments after. With a few final thrusts he shuddered to a halt, spilling his seed deep within Enzo, his own groan of satisfaction echoing from Enzo's throat. He collapsed atop him, inside him, tangled in their embrace, one which grew only tighter as Enzo's mouth found his and he lost himself in their kiss.

# CHAPTER FIFTEEN

Fiore returned to himself to find Enzo's face beside him on the pillow, enormous dark eyes gazing into his own with fathomless depths of affection and Enzo's skillful hand stroking his hair as gentle as a summer zephyr. He could respond with no less than a kiss, which Enzo melted into. And when he broke it, he couldn't help but marvel at how the sickly pallor seemed cast aside and youthful vigor returned to those scarred and handsome features. Even so, Enzo's revelations had given him a great deal to ponder.

"So," Fiore ventured before he could halt his tongue. "Dragons."

"Dragons," Enzo affirmed with a brisk nod as though Fiore had said something sensible.

Tales of Halcyon's founding god had whirled through Fiore's mind since the first moment Enzo had revealed himself. He supposed he could put his wonderings off no longer and summoned all his courage to enquire, "Have you ever transformed into an enormous bat-winged scaly beast?"

To Fiore's great good fortune Enzo took his impudence with a smile. "I have not."

"Have you ever tried?"

A marked pause ensued, punctuated at long last by a very low and quiet, "Maybe."

Fiore repressed a smile—for Enzo wore the self-conscious look of one who expected teasing, and Fiore had no desire to shame him. Quite the reverse. "Is that what drew you to the study of alchemy?"

A sigh of relief escaped Enzo as his stiffened frame relaxed in Fiore's embrace. The shy smile returned at last to his lips. "You must think me beyond foolish."

"Not at all," Fiore replied with complete honesty. "I think you a daring and clever fellow. What did you discover?"

"Nothing definitive," Enzo admitted. "One of my ancestors—an aunt some three centuries ago—was situated similarly to myself."

Despite himself, Fiore balked. "You mean... with both a cunt and...?"

Enzo appeared nonplussed by what was undoubtedly one of Fiore's least-respectful enquiries and answered it with a succinct nod.

"Ah," said Fiore. He supposed he ought to have expected as much. Such a condition couldn't befall men alone.

"Her lifelong research into our shared peculiarity has proved the cornerstone of my own studies."

"Did she succeed in transforming into a winged creature?"

"If she did, she didn't write it down." Enzo hesitated. "Though she did vanish without explanation."

Fiore stared at him.

Enzo continued as if he'd said nothing out of the ordinary. "My last serious attempt at a transformation occurred just before I left for university. I've neglected the study since then."

"There's nothing to learn of dragons at university?"

Enzo smiled. "My research there was of a more practical nature."

An answering grin crept across Fiore's own lips. "Well. I've certainly no objection to further practical research."

A rosy tint softened the sharp edges of Enzo's features. Fiore could reward his handsome blush with nothing less than a kiss.

Enzo accepted it with warmth. But he parted with a question on his lips.

"What do you intend to do," Enzo asked, "when you find your elderly patron?"

Fiore had never received that sort of enquiry in afterglow before. It felt rather like Enzo had tipped him out of bed and into the canal. Nevertheless he had a ready answer. "Make him happy 'til the end of his days."

"And after that?"

Fiore shrugged.

"You must have given some thought to what you would do with your share of the gentleman's fortune," Enzo said with a smile. "Would you become a man of leisure? How would you fill your days—drawing? Music?"

"You're a man of leisure," Fiore retorted. "How do you fill your days?"

"With you."

Fiore paused. "I can't very well follow in your footsteps then, lest I become full of myself."

Enzo laughed. "Very true. Would you return to your trade? Set up your own house?"

"I like my trade well enough," Fiore admitted. A thought struck him. "Would you wish for me to return to it?"

Enzo's smile shifted into something more wistful. "It would rather give me something to look forward to."

Fiore ignored the pang provoked by that smile. "You'll have moved on by then."

Enzo did not look as though he agreed with him but knew better than to argue. "If you don't return to your trade after your patron's demise… might I try my suit again regardless?"

"You'll have moved on by then," Fiore repeated, though he believed it less with every passing moment. Particularly as Enzo gazed down at him with those fond and gentle eyes.

And as he realized that he might not have moved on by then, either.

∾

It was not the first time Enzo had revealed his peculiarity to a lover.

It was, however, the first time he had revealed it to Fiore—which rather upped the stakes in his estimation.

188

The strain of suspense had fallen away into relief as Fiore took the revelation in stride. Orazio had likewise taken it well, which Enzo recalled with a pang. Others hadn't. Still others had expressed disgust with the very idea before ever knowing it applied to Enzo in particular. Most of these were anonymous bathhouse encounters and left Enzo with minor disappointment rather than angst. Fiore, however, evidently had more experience with the wider world of possibilities in this particular arena and thus a more open mind, for which Enzo felt very grateful.

Likewise he felt grateful for the speed of his own recovery. He'd enjoyed general good health all his life. Even the plague had seen him come through it far less scathed than most. Still he never took for granted how near his most recent brush with death had proved.

Nor did he take for granted Fiore's determination to remain by his side. No doubt Fiore felt anxious to return to Halcyon. Unlike Enzo he had a wide circle of acquaintance and no shortage of appointments between his work aboard the ship and modelling for artisans and practicing his own craft—though admittedly he could do two out of three at the lodge. Given all of this, Enzo expected Fiore to make his excuses and depart any day.

Yet Fiore remained.

Perhaps it was merely his mistrust of chirurgeons that kept him perched at the window whenever Dr. Zoccarato came to examine Enzo. But the tender nature of his caresses when they were at last alone seemed to speak otherwise—as did his nimble fingers racing to pleat, smooth, tie up, or tug on every piece of Enzo's garb before he could so much as blink, or his skillful hand washing and combing through Enzo's long tresses without his asking.

Finally, a fortnight after Enzo divulged his peculiarity to Fiore, Dr. Zoccarato declared him fit to travel.

Fiore would depart ahead of him, at Enzo's insistence, for Fiore had far more pressing business within the city, and Enzo didn't wish to delay him another moment with his convalescent pace. He soothed his loss with the thought that they would reunite within mere days.

Giovanna, meanwhile, made preparations to retire to Bluecliffe for the season. The fields required the oversight of herself and her devoted Antonio in the spring. They intended to embark within a few days of

Fiore's departure—a circumstance Enzo told himself was mere coincidence.

It seemed far less coincidental when, the very morning after Fiore set out for Halcyon, Giovanna joined Enzo for breakfast unannounced, arriving at his chambers almost simultaneous with the coffee and brioche.

"Dr. Zoccarato tells me you're well enough to travel," she said.

Enzo confirmed this was so.

"Do you still intend to return to Halcyon?" she asked.

Enzo confirmed this as well.

Giovanna gave him a knowing look. "Because of Fiore."

Enzo said nothing. Though he felt the heat arising in his face keenly.

"I did say we'd discuss it after the hunt," Giovanna pointed out. "And we have arrived, at last, at 'after the hunt.' Though I'd intended to do so rather sooner than now."

Enzo acknowledged this with a nod. He tried not to betray his anxiety even as he asked, "What do you think of him?"

Giovanna took rather longer to answer than Enzo felt comfortable with.

"He seems quite fond of you," she said at last in a tone which suggested this was not necessarily a virtue.

And yet Enzo couldn't prevent himself from replying, "No less fond than I am of him."

Giovanna tilted her head to serve him a studious gaze. "What are your intentions towards him?"

Enzo hadn't the first idea what she meant. He understood the words, of course, but what she wished to glean beneath the surface remained beyond him. He endeavored to answer her question at face value. "To make him happy for as long as he'll permit me."

Giovanna furrowed her brow, which Enzo thought unwarranted. "Why shouldn't he permit you?"

Enzo could sense a trap forming around him but knew no way out except through. "He has other plans."

Giovanna's brows arose. "What sort of plans?"

Against his better judgment, Enzo replied, "Plans to find a wealthy gentleman who will support his retirement."

"That sounds rather like making him happy," Giovanna observed.

Enzo shrugged.

Giovanna's gaze grew, if possible, even more pointed. "You are a wealthy gentleman."

Enzo admitted as much.

"Do you intend to support his retirement?"

A dangerous question. Enzo attempted a sideways answer. "He will not permit me."

"You have offered, then."

Enzo, thoroughly ensnared, could only nod.

A slight sigh escaped Giovanna. Wistful, Enzo hoped, rather than disapproving. "And he has refused you."

Enzo nodded again.

"On what grounds?" Giovanna mused. Her gentle tone belied her pointed enquiries. "Does he believe your fortune insufficient to support him—even after all he's seen here?"

Her words were light and teasing, but not outright dismissive, which was better than Enzo had hoped for. "He would prefer the support of an older gentleman."

"Whatever for?"

"So that his patron may predecease him rather than abandoning him for another."

Giovanna stared at him for a long and silent moment.

Enzo knew not how to answer her look save with another shrug.

"And," Giovanna said at last, "how is this plan unfolding so far?"

Enzo didn't like the realization that he didn't have an answer. He ought to have asked. Someone who cared for Fiore doubtless would've done so. Someone better than Enzo. Someone who actually deserved Fiore.

Giovanna understood the answer in his silence. "Are you certain this remains his plan?"

Enzo found it more difficult to meet his sister's gaze with every passing moment.

"I only enquire," Giovanna continued, gentle as ever, "because it seems to me his continued association with you may prevent him from achieving this particular end."

Enzo looked up sharp. "How so?"

Giovanna raised her brows. "Who would dare proposition the consort of the notorious dueling duke?"

Her use of the sordid sobriquet came as a slap in the face. It left Enzo altogether stunned. It was quite unlike Giovanna to be so cruel—at least deliberately.

Giovanna simply smiled. "Your Fiore is an intelligent young man, no? He must realize this. Yet he continues to dally with you. One can only conclude he considers remaining by your side to be worth throwing away his plans. It bespeaks a certain depth of feeling."

Enzo doubted this. For another suitor, perhaps, Fiore would be willing to toss aside all he strived for. But for himself, who'd accomplished nothing save infamy in all his days, Enzo couldn't imagine anyone sacrificing anything—much less Fiore, who had not just a comely face but a quick wit and a deep wellspring of empathy, everything to offer to someone worthy of his affections.

Giovanna took his silence to mean she'd made her point. She smiled, patted his hand, and withdrew.

Which left Enzo with a great deal to consider.

He felt foolish beyond words not to have realized how his reputation stood in the way of Fiore's goals. Nonetheless, having understood his role at last, he resolved to correct his error.

Enzo would do all in his power to assist Fiore in finding his ideal patron.

# CHAPTER SIXTEEN

E nzo arrived at Ca' Scaevola to find a dragon's hoard of post awaiting him.

While he didn't have even half so wide a social circle as Giovanna, he did subscribe to a number of periodicals. A few gazettes, to keep up with Lucrezia and her ilk. More shipping lists, to try and track his mother's passage from port to port. And for himself alone, the medical journals. He hadn't received a letter from anyone outside of his own family since his withdrawal from university. The flickering candle-flame of hope for any word from Orazio dwindled with each passing day.

Invitations, however, he received en masse.

From the very morning his return to the city from university became public knowledge, every household with even the faintest claim to rub shoulders with high society had peppered him with invitations to theatre boxes, private concerts, pleasure-boat outings, banquets, hunts, masquerades, and above all else, balls. None could claim any prior acquaintance with him. They invited him not as a friend but rather because if a host could promise the attendance of the legendary dueling duke, their event would quickly become the most popular of the season —if only so the resulting horde of influential guests could gawk at the city's most infamous recluse.

Lucrezia had not expressly forbidden Enzo from accepting any of these invitations. Nevertheless he felt disinclined to entertain them. Even before his infamy he'd derived no particular enjoyment from crowds of strangers.

Now, however, as he sat at his desk in the alchemy workshop and methodically flicked through the stack, he found himself giving the invitations serious consideration. He might have no use for any new acquaintance amongst the gentry, true enough.

Fiore, on the other hand…

Giovanna's conclusions rang in Enzo's ears even in her absence. If Fiore continued to sacrifice seeking other opportunities for the sake of remaining with Enzo, then his plans of retiring in a wealthy elderly gentleman's estate would never come to fruition. Thus, if Enzo's presence in Fiore's life prevented others from approaching Fiore with opportunities, Enzo must then, as a good and true friend, take it upon himself to bring those opportunities to Fiore.

To that end he selected one invitation in particular. The Grimaldi were not a family of particular influence or long-standing, but they were wealthy enough to host a ball, and a masquerade weighed strongly in Enzo's favor. He set it aside to pen a short missive of his own. This he sealed with the signet ring he carried on a chain around his throat before handing it off to one of the footmen to deliver.

Between anticipation of his scheme and anxiety over the answer to his enquiry he found it difficult to wait. But to his surprise, he received a terse response before dinner. Better still, it was in the affirmative. Prince Lucrezia, Serenissima of Halcyon, had no objection to her brother attending a party hosted by a noble bloodline of inconsequential renown.

Which alleviated only half his concerns. For the rest, he donned his mask, slipped the invitation into his pocket, and set out into the evening to deliver it himself.

It was, after all, Fiore's profession. And one couldn't begrudge an artisan their profession.

∽

Corelli had seemed shocked at Fiore's return from his sojourn into the wilderness. Or as shocked as she ever seemed; a mere elevation of her brows was equal to anyone else's staggering gasp. Fiore didn't see why. He'd told her plain enough where he was going and how long he expected to be gone. He supposed he ought to feel grateful she didn't sell off everything in his quarters and rent it out to someone else in his absence.

Settling in was the work of an afternoon. He returned to his routine by that very evening. The gentlemen he brought belowdecks were all well enough. But none were Enzo. And the lack of Enzo made his lonesome sleep afterward more disturbed than it ought to have been. He wondered as he stared up into the darkness if he could persuade Enzo to sleep beside him if neither of them were wounded. Asking outright would tilt his own hand a touch too far in his estimation.

The following morning dawned without word from Enzo. The three days afterward passed likewise. Fiore began to worry that somehow Enzo had fallen prey to yet another accident when, in the evening just before Corelli's sons drew down the gangplank to open the tavern, he heard the click of familiar footfalls in the hall belowdecks and a knock upon his chamber door.

The knock sent Fiore's pulse fluttering. He leapt to the door. Opening it to see the looming form of his beloved bauta sent his heart soaring even further. He didn't bother to disguise the joy that flashed across his face in a grin. Even beneath the mask, Enzo appeared likewise delighted at their reunion.

Two shakes of a sail saw Enzo dragged within. No sooner had the door shut upon him than he whipped off mask, hat, and hood to give Fiore the kiss he'd so dearly missed these past few days. Only when desperation to breathe outweighed desperation to touch did they part.

"What's this?" Fiore asked as Enzo handed him a thrice-folded page of thick paper. The wax seal was already broken.

"An invitation," Enzo answered him. "To a masquerade."

Fiore, having just unfolded it, saw so for himself. He vaguely recognized the name of the host. As for the recipient, he'd presupposed it would be Enzo, though it still looked odd to have his full name and title written out.

"There will be dancing," said Enzo. "And a banquet."

Fiore smirked. "A banquet of chestnuts?"

Enzo chuckled. "If only we might be so lucky."

Fiore's heartbeat stuttered. He doubted he'd heard Enzo aright. Still he kept his good humor as he echoed, "'We?'"

Enzo served him the shy, handsome smile he'd grown to love so well. "If you'll do me the honor of accompanying me there."

Fiore's pulse continued fluttering. To attend an aristocratic ball was enticing enough. To do so on Enzo's arm was more wonderful than he'd dared hope.

Only when Enzo spoke on did Fiore realize he'd let himself fall silent for far too long.

"That is to say," Enzo continued, a becoming blush arising in his sharp cheeks, "if you would indulge me, then there will be at least one person there whose company I genuinely enjoy."

Fiore felt a matching and unaccountable heat flaring in his own face. He bit back the grin that threatened to steal over it. With concerted effort to sound less earnest than he felt, he replied, "Well, if it would spare you an evening of loneliness, it would be monstrous of me not to accept."

The joy Fiore suppressed in his own features was writ broad upon Enzo's.

"And besides," Enzo added, "it will give you an opportunity to find a patron."

Fiore stared up at him as an icy pall crept over his heart.

Enzo was right, of course. This party would prove a splendid opportunity to make acquaintances he could never hope to attain otherwise. Acquaintances which with any luck would lead all his plans to fruition. By all rights he ought to feel at least as happy as Enzo evidently felt to invite him.

Yet the realization that Enzo could smile so even as he spoke of his intentions to give Fiore away to another didn't sit well in Fiore's chest.

He forced a smile over it anyway. He ought to feel happy. And so he would make himself so until it stuck.

"There is some formality expected in the costume of those attending," Enzo went on, heedless of Fiore's inner turmoil. "And some artistry as well."

"Ah," said Fiore. Enzo had hinted delicately enough but the implication rang in Fiore's head regardless. Nothing in his current wardrobe would suffice to attend a ball of this distinction.

"If it wouldn't be too much of an imposition," Enzo continued, "would you care to accompany me to visit my tailor?"

If nothing else, Fiore would get a new suit out of the bargain. And it was sweet of Enzo to offer—even as Fiore told himself that Enzo could do little else if he didn't want Fiore's garb to shame him. Despite this practical reminder, his smile grew more sincere. "No imposition whatsoever."

Enzo's smile outshone his own.

~

The edifice of the tailor's shop, with its enormous columns flanking broad windows to display a tasteful selection of what the discerning client might expect of its offerings, looked like the sort of establishment which would see Fiore's scarlet sash and block him from entering.

When Enzo had asked him to meet here at the appointed day and hour, Fiore had readily agreed. Now that he stood before it in the broad light of said day, however, he found his courage flagging.

The opera houses and theatres considered courtesans a necessary evil. The more exclusive establishments, in Fiore's experience, had a far less charitable opinion.

The building itself was as ancient as anything could be in the city on the sea. Despite the centuries since its construction, someone had decorated it in the latest fashion—ornate furled gilding adorning every corner, and what wasn't already pale marble painted up in a similar hue. The old and the new combined to lend it a dashing air above its foundation of respectability. Perhaps it had once been one of the early palazzi, sold once its noble family grew impoverished. Or maybe said impoverished noble family had turned to the hands-on trade of tailoring. Either way Fiore admired the impressive result. His librarian friend would've known the building's entire true history at a glance—but Gnaeus could never have afforded to patronize such an establishment on his own behalf, much less on behalf of a mere courtesan.

Enzo arrived in short order. Fiore glimpsed him before Enzo found him in turn. He could hardly do elsewise, given how the combined prow of his tricorn hat and bauta beak sailed a full head above most of the crowd, who gave his billowing cloak a wide berth. Fiore's own scarlet sash seemed demure by comparison.

More striking still was the relief that washed over Fiore at the sight of him. He told himself it was just the intimidating edifice contrasted with the arrival of one who could see him through its doors. But that didn't quite account for the flutter in his heart as his eyes fell upon Enzo's familiar frame.

Fiore gave a cheerful wave, which caught Enzo's eye at last and turned the latter's casual stroll into an eager trot towards him.

"Not waiting long, I hope?" Enzo asked when he reached Fiore's side, breathless.

"Not at all," Fiore replied with an easy smile. It was only a little lie. He wound his arm through the one Enzo proffered him and together they sauntered up the marble steps.

Even with Enzo's escort, Fiore still half-expected to be turned away at the door. But the attendant who arrived in the entryway at the ringing of the bell merely swept his glance over them both and, after Enzo confirmed his identity with a nod, escorted them back through the shop to an exquisite parlor.

The interior of the shop continued the fashionable themes of cream walls accented with gilded scroll-work. The parlor proved the peak of this particular artistic choice. At their escort's bidding, Fiore and Enzo seated themselves on the cream-upholstered, cabriole-legged sofa—Enzo guiding Fiore to it with a sweeping gesture of his immense cloak that felt rather like a curtain drawing across a stage, and ensuring Fiore had made himself comfortable before he descended himself, his brawny arm taking up the whole of the sofa's back and laying across Fiore's shoulders like a mantle molded for them alone. The attendant laid out a tray of coffee and zaletti, then withdrew to fetch his master. The parlor's tall windows gave a splendid view of the courtyard garden—and, Fiore supposed, let in ample sunlight for a tailor to work by besides.

To Fiore's surprise, someone arrived to see them in short order. Two gentlemen of middling age, one walking slightly behind the other with memorandum-book and pencil at the ready, both garbed in suits of exquisite tight-woven wool cut into impeccable fit, because of course how better to advertise their trade than on their own bodies. The quality of the material as much as the sheer quiet confidence of the foremost man told Fiore that no less than the owner of the establishment had arrived to wait upon them. He supposed he oughtn't feel surprised, considering Enzo's rank and familial connexions.

The master tailor had the grace to but glance at Fiore's scarlet sash before continuing his conversation as he would with any other client—or at least, any other client of Enzo's rank. His assistant, however, seemed torn between gawking and turning up his nose. Fiore resolved to ignore the latter and focus on the former.

"I expect," Enzo began after the customary greetings were exchanged, "you've heard by now of the Grimaldi's masquerade ball."

The master tailor confirmed he had and furthermore assured Enzo that he'd enjoyed a great deal of trade as a direct result.

"If you're not already overtaxed with commissions for that particular event," Enzo continued, "we would be most grateful if you could make something suitable for my friend."

The master tailor adeptly disguised any surprise he may have felt to hear Enzo intended to bring a common courtesan to a society soiree. His assistant's brows, however, flew towards his hairline.

"It would be our pleasure," said the master tailor. He turned to Fiore. "If the gentleman would be so kind as to stand."

Fiore arose. Well-accustomed to disrobing before an audience, his hands fell to unwinding the scarlet sash from around his waist. He put a touch less performance into it than usual; while he wasn't trying to seduce the tailors, he did want to put on a bit of a show for Enzo.

And indeed, as Fiore turned to hand the sash off to the latter, he found the eyes behind Enzo's mask smouldering with desire.

Enzo accepted the sash from Fiore with as much reverence as if Fiore were handing him the golden fleece. The intensity of his masked gaze bespoke a hunger the likes of which sent delightful shivers down Fiore's spine.

The master tailor cleared his throat—so subtly Fiore almost didn't hear him. "If the gentleman will join us behind the screen."

Fiore followed the slight gesture of the tailor's chin to the standing screen in the far corner of the room. Upon reflection, he supposed most of the shop's clientele were probably a touch more modest than himself.

The screen, as Fiore discovered upon slipping behind it alongside the tailor and his assistant, was not mere paper but rather extraordinarily fine silk of an ivory shade that allowed sunlight through as easily as if it were a window of frosted glass. He wondered if Enzo minded being deprived of the view and resolved to make it up to him afterward.

Fiore had stripped for a tailor before. Though not for one who worked in so fine a shop as this. The tailor in question had originally visited Fiore at the *Kingfisher* for another purpose—the usual purpose. Eventually, however, said tailor had persuaded Fiore to take some of his fee in goods and labor instead of in coin, and so Fiore had disrobed for intimate measuring rather than more straightforward intimacy.

The master tailor at present lingered far less over Fiore's finer features. Yet he wasn't precisely perfunctory, either. He showed his trade the care and consideration it well deserved, and by extension, showed Fiore far more respect than he'd braced for. Fiore supposed this was due more to Enzo's consequence than to any particular regard for a low-born courtesan—even one so handsome as himself.

The assistant's gaze, however, seemed to catch on a few particular points of Fiore's anatomy, and a faint tint arose in his cheeks.

Fiore suppressed a smug smile. In another circumstance he might have courted the man's obvious interest. But the patronage of a tailor's assistant felt redundant after he'd arrived on the arm of a duke.

The master tailor read out the measurements as he took them. The assistant jotted them down. All told, the work passed in but a few minutes. Then Fiore redressed himself and stepped out from behind the curtain.

To find Enzo with his scarlet sash wrapped tight in his fists.

A smile spread across Fiore's lips. He returned to Enzo's side and held out his hand for the sash.

Enzo gave it over without hesitation—but not before he'd delicately unwrapped it from his clenched fingers, smoothed out its wrinkles, and folded it up for him with the same tender reverence.

Fiore felt prouder than he had in some time to tie it about his waist again.

The tailors, meanwhile, had put their heads together in low and earnest discussion marked by the swift scrape of colored chalk across the master tailor's zibaldone. The sheer number of colors drew Fiore's notice —and, if he were honest with himself, his jealousy.

"Perhaps," said the master tailor, "something like this would suit?"

He turned his zibaldone around for Enzo and Fiore's inspection as he spoke. The human figures on the page remained little more than pale shadows in the vague shape of men. The clothes, however, were rendered with enviable precision. It showed several possible versions of a full court suit in the latest fashion; long-skirted waistcoat, still-longer-skirted coat, breeches, hose, high-heeled shoes, and tricorn hat—a similar cut and style to Enzo's own, which made sense, given it came from the hand of the same tailor.

Fiore had never yet worn such garments, donning a cloak or cape rather than a coat and with his own waistcoat not running half so long as Enzo's or boasting near so many buttons. Nor did he own breeches or hose in silk or satin, as indicated by the sheen in the illustration created by the skillful absence of color in a slashing streak across the fabric on the pale page. Like a true artist, the master tailor evidently knew when the negative space would speak more than any mark he could make.

One of the proposed suits appeared in the soft warm fade of a pink-and-orange sunset. Another in black, presumably to match Enzo's own garb. But the one which arrested Fiore's attention was the seafoam green the precise shade of the lagoon in full sunlight, with gilding unfurling at the hems like golden fern fronds.

"Which do you prefer?"

Fiore blinked, Enzo's sotto voce enquiry interrupting his mesmerized admiration. He threw a shroud over his heart's desires with a hard swallow. Enzo was the one bringing him to the ball and paying for his garb. The final decision rested with him. Fiore turned to him with a smile. "Which do you like best?"

Throughout their acquaintance Fiore had learnt how to read Enzo's expressions in his eyes even beneath the mask. And at present, those eyes held a curious mixture of confusion and disappointment. Both vanished with a blink as Enzo turned from Fiore to the master tailor.

"May we see the fabrics?" Enzo asked.

"Of course," the master tailor assured him. He laid the sketches out on the table beside the coffee and zaletti.

The assistant, meanwhile, vanished deeper into the shop. He returned rapidly in the company of some half-dozen of his fellows. While they did carry yards upon yards of fabric between them, Fiore nevertheless had the impression more of them had volunteered for the task than were strictly necessary. He didn't wonder at it; anyone would leap for a first-hand glimpse of the legendary dueling duke and his courtesan. Even with the mask there could be no doubt of Enzo's identity amongst the shop staff, for he must have made the appointment under his full title.

The vibrant colors and variety of the cloth brought out for inspection put any box of oil pastels to shame. Even the master tailor's admittedly beautiful sketches had not quite done them justice. Plush purple velvet silk, a shimmering peach satin fading into plum in imitation of a sunset, another in saffron gold like butter made of sunshine, still another in peacock blue that somehow attained the same iridescence as the natural feather. A veritable feast for the eyes; Fiore devoured them with his gaze accordingly.

Yet the one that compelled Fiore to touch it was not velvet, silk, or satin, but a seafoam green wool of so fine a weave as to rival the satin in its smoothness—"a cool hand," as his erstwhile tailor friend would've called it. It perfectly echoed the delicious color of the lagoon with the sun at its zenith. Fiore had oft admired the color, and when he could afford the pigments he poured it into his art, but he'd never had the chance to garb himself in it. His own waistcoats and breeches were a perpetual shade of chestnut; partly because it was an affordable fabric, partly because it helped disguise the red chalk smudges from his drawing, and partly because it went well with the one color the law demanded he wear.

Fiore withheld a wistful sigh as he let the seafoam wool fall from his fingertips. "It'll clash with the scarlet."

"You needn't wear the scarlet."

Both Fiore and all the tailors turned startled glances upon Enzo.

Enzo appeared unmoved—though who could tell beneath the mask. "It's a private entertainment. You may wear whatever you like."

His words rang with the confidence of one who knew no one would dare to contradict him. A confidence such as Fiore had never heard from him before. He wondered at it long enough that a marked silence fell over the parlor, and he realized far too late that all—the master tailor, the assistants, the apprentices, and Enzo—were awaiting his answer with bated breath.

"Well," said Fiore, slipping a smile over his fluttering pulse. "If that is so, then I simply must have the green."

Never before had a proclamation from Fiore's lips spurred so many bodies into action at once. The fabric bolts were whisked away. Amidst the chaos the master tailor drew in again for closer conference with Fiore and Enzo, making small enquiries as to the particulars of the design and dashing off notes and adjustments on his sketches in reply. These were passed along to his assistants who scurried to bring them deeper into the shop where work might begin in earnest. The hat and shoes would be the purview of the cobbler and haberdasher rather than the tailor, but from how Enzo and the master tailor spoke of the matter between them, Fiore received the distinct impression that Enzo had his own favorites amongst those professions as well, and the tailor had collaborated with them on similar projects before. Not a word was said as to the cost. Fiore felt some relief at that. He didn't think he could keep up his aloof pretense if he knew exactly how many zecchini would tumble from Enzo's coffers in his name.

As the tailor's shop bustled around them, Fiore also noted how Enzo retained his command over the controlled chaos. He made all the necessary arrangements with an absolute ease. Not at all the bashful fellow Fiore had come to know these past few months. Fiore wondered what had granted him this sudden confidence. Perhaps it was the return to the familiar ground of the tailor's shop, which he had evidently patronized many times before.

Or perhaps, Fiore realized, it was not that Enzo had suddenly become a more confident and commanding figure, but rather that Fiore himself put Enzo on his hind foot.

A realization which seemed confirmed by how, when Enzo had concluded their business with the master tailor himself, he turned to Fiore with a familiar shy smile lighting up his eyes.

Then Enzo arose from the sofa and turned to proffer his arm to Fiore. "Shall we be off?"

Unlike his conversation with the tailor, the deep bass of Enzo's natural voice emerged in a soft and earnest tone that hardly dared to enquire and awaited the answer with bated breath. Fiore knew it well. He could perfectly picture Enzo biting his scarred lip beneath his mask.

Fiore accepted his arm with a grin. "Let's."

# CHAPTER SEVENTEEN

On the following day, Enzo had Fiore meet him at the haberdashery.

Much like the tailor, it resided in a beautiful old edifice done up in fresh trim. And much like the tailor, Fiore didn't feel altogether welcome entering without Enzo.

This time, however, Fiore arrived to find Enzo already awaiting him at the entrance—despite the hovering presence of those employed within the shop, visible through the gilded front windows and very obviously nervous to leave an aristocrat waiting outside rather than serving him within.

If Enzo took any notice of them, it vanished when his eyes met Fiore's. His arm shot up in a cheerful wave, evidently before he realized what he was doing, for it halted halfway over his head and withered into something shy that nonetheless struck a chord in Fiore's heart.

Fiore trotted to meet him with a grin.

The nervous energy of the shop staff didn't dissipate with Enzo's entrance. Indeed, the whole haberdashery—as had the tailor's—seemed on tenterhooks at his arrival. Apprentices peered around corners to catch a glimpse before ducking back into the shadows just as soon as Fiore caught them in the corner of his eye.

Once inside the parlor done up in pink and white with gold trim, matters progressed much as they had at the tailor's. Though this time Fiore kept his clothes on. Measuring for a hat went far more swiftly than measuring for a full suit, as there was but one body part to keep in proportion. Then there were enquiries regarding what Fiore wanted the hat to look like. Or rather, enquiries the haberdasher made to Enzo, who then turned to Fiore for the answer and did so in an increasingly pointed fashion with every repetition, until at last the haberdasher took the hint and lowered herself to speak directly to a scarlet-sashed courtesan.

Fiore accepted all this with a bland pasted-on smile. In truth he had few opinions on how the thing ought to look. He didn't oft bother with a hat, and when he did he wore a round cap not unlike Artemisia's, as much to play into his own wistful artistic daydreams as to keep warm. He'd certainly never attempted a tricorn, much less one done up with feathers and trim like Enzo's. But he delighted in the opportunity to dress up for an enchanted occasion, and a tricorn would suit best to blend into a crowd of aristocrats. Beyond that he merely wanted it to match his suit. Which ought to prove easy enough, as Enzo had arrived with a leather portfolio provided by the tailor and filled with copies of his sketches and swatches of the suit fabric and trim. This they left with the haberdasher, who promised to delight them with her work within the fortnight.

"Are they always so anxious to please?" Fiore asked Enzo as they departed the shop arm-in-arm. He kept his tone light and teasing though his curiosity remained genuine.

Enzo took rather longer to answer him than Fiore thought the question warranted. When at last he spoke, he did so in a bashful manner. "They're always deferential. But I think I may have put them on edge today."

Fiore's heart plummeted. Of course. Enzo had never brought a courtesan into their shop before. And the haberdasher, unable to reveal to the duke himself how this had insulted her, had covered over her indignation with an excess of flattery. Fiore worked to keep his tone light and airy even as he asked a question he already knew the answer to. "How so?"

Enzo inclined his head. "I've never met them in the shop before. Usually they come to Ca' Scaevola."

"Oh." Fiore's relief mingled with self-deprecation. He'd been an idiot to not realize that, of course, one of Enzo's rank would never stoop to wait upon an artisan; they must go to him. He caught himself before he asked why they hadn't met him at Ca' Scaevola today. The secluded hunting lodge in the wilderness had been quite another thing. And he hadn't even been invited there on purpose. Obviously a courtesan wasn't worthy to enter the ancestral palazzo of one of the most powerful noble bloodlines in the whole city.

A shy smile glimmered in Enzo's eyes beneath the mask. He knew nothing of Fiore's inner turmoil, for which Fiore withheld a sigh of relief. He endeavored to match that glimpse of a handsome and heartwarming expression with a broad smile of his own.

From there Enzo and Fiore proceeded to the cobbler. Again, Fiore encountered a familiar process made unfamiliar by the presence of a withdrawing room for clients. Under normal circumstances he merely stood in the midst of the workshop for measuring or just knew his size and asked for the respective prefabricated pair plucked off the shelf behind a counter. To say nothing of the attentive behavior of the staff. The cobbler didn't fawn quite so hard as haberdasher, but she did grant Fiore a degree of respect that he didn't think he'd have received if he hadn't arrived on the arm of a duke.

The cost of a typical pair of shoes—for Fiore, at least—came about equal to the daily wage of a journeyman. The cost of the pair proposed by Enzo's cobbler was never spoken aloud. Enzo simply left her with an identical portfolio to the one he'd given the haberdasher. Then he wound his arm through Fiore's own and they went on their merry way with the cobbler's promise to have the shoes ready within the fortnight.

Still, as they strode down the street together arm-in-arm, something about the shoes raised the faintest hint of a concern in Fiore's otherwise untroubled mind.

"I've never worn a heel before," he confessed after a few minutes had passed.

Enzo glanced down in surprise but didn't halt his stride. "No?"

Fiore confirmed this with a shake of his head. He supposed the notion must seem astonishing to an aristocrat. Even Enzo, at his already incredible natural height, had an inch or two more of assistance from his modest black heel. "Not for lack of desire. I'd be delighted to stand a touch taller."

What he didn't say was that heeled shoes were an aristocrat's purview for good reason. A highly impractical choice that served only to enhance the wearer's appearance whilst hobbling their ability to move or perform any sort of manual labor. An artisan with a heeled shoe would rapidly become a figure of ridicule in their circle.

And yet, Fiore had found it more elating than otherwise to have a pair ordered for him. While the scant inch the cobbler had proposed would bring him nowhere near Enzo's towering height, it would be something, and would mark him out as one worthy to attend an aristocratic entertainment. There remained just one problem.

"But I don't know how to walk in them," Fiore concluded. "Much less dance."

The few clomping steps he'd taken with the mocked-up pair in the cobbler's shop had proved humiliating enough.

Enzo's gaze turned thoughtful. "We might practice. At your convenience," he added. "I don't wish to keep you from your work."

Fiore chose not to remind him that, technically, Enzo *was* his work. Instead he smiled up at him and replied, "I'd like that."

~

The following afternoon, Enzo arrived belowdecks at the *Kingfisher* with a brown paper package.

Fiore accepted it from him with a cocked eyebrow and a curious half-smile. He hadn't the first idea what it might contain. Nothing they'd commissioned in the past few days could possibly be finished already.

And yet, when he untied the twine and peeled back the paper, what did he find but the self-same pair of plain brown mock-up shoes that the cobbler had built for him just yesterday. Or, no, Fiore realized as he examined them in disbelief; rather, a second mock-up pair, for the cobbler required the originals to make the final fancy shoes Fiore would wear to the ball. Enzo must have commissioned these specifically for practice.

Enzo, meanwhile, swept off his hat with one hand and his mask with the other, leaving his beautiful face bare for Fiore to admire when he glanced up in astonished elation.

Fiore sat on the edge of his bed to slip the shoes on. No sooner had he done so than Enzo knelt before him.

"If I may?" Enzo murmured, glancing up for permission with a hopeful gleam in his haunting dark eyes.

Fiore, stunned by his submissive posture as much as by his gaze, could only nod.

He ought to be used to this by now. Plenty of men had knelt before him for one purpose or another.

But somehow, when Enzo dropped to his knees and gently took Fiore's heel in hand to slip off his flat shoes and slide his foot instead into the unfamiliar aristocratic garb, Fiore found his heart fluttering in his throat.

The mock-up shoes fit as perfectly as they had yesterday. Enzo took Fiore's hands in his own and drew him upright. Then he released him and withdrew with an encouraging smile. Fiore could only hope he wouldn't disappoint him.

These hopes were dashed within his first few experimental steps. The ball of his foot clomped against the floorboards—far less graceful even than the thudding hooves of the horses that had carried him to the hunting lodge and back again.

Fiore turned to find Enzo looking thoughtful rather than disappointed, which he tried to take as a good sign.

"Step down heel first," Enzo suggested. In hasty reply to Fiore's skeptical eyebrow, he added, "The heel will bear your weight, I promise. Don't be afraid to come down hard on it."

Fiore had once beheld an aristocrat break off a heel in the street and hobble away amidst the laughter of their supposed friends. At least Enzo wouldn't laugh at him. Probably.

Against his better instincts he took a few strides as instructed. He wavered but did not fall. The heels held up beneath him. Most importantly, he didn't clomp. Instead his footfalls resounded with the same light click-click-click of Enzo's own steps.

"Better," Enzo said with a genuine smile when Fiore looked to him for approval.

Fiore took another turn about the room. It took more steps than he remembered; the heels had shortened his stride. Instinct bid him lean forward. He fought it and rolled his shoulders back, keeping his head high as if he had no doubts to his own prowess. From the door to the window, past an openly-appreciative Enzo, turn and return. Back and forth, back and forth, until—

Fiore set down all his weight on his left heel. It slid out from beneath him with a sharp hiss. His limbs windmilled. He fell.

But rather than striking the floorboards, his body landed in the grasp of two strong arms.

Fiore, suspended between wood and air, blinked up into Enzo's fearful face. His own heart beat double. He told himself it was from the shock of almost falling. Yet even now, in Enzo's firm-yet-gentle hold, his pulse refused to return to normal.

"I should have foreseen this," Enzo muttered with a *tsk*.

"My lack of grace?" Fiore guessed.

Enzo seemed far more alarmed than Fiore thought warranted at what had been a casual self-deprecating jest. "What? No, not in the least. I mean only—this is a known hazard with new heels. If I may…?"

At Fiore's nod, Enzo steered him to the bed and sat him down. Only then did Fiore realize he'd missed the opportune moment to kiss him. He cursed himself bitterly.

Enzo, meanwhile, knelt before him again and slipped the shoes from his feet. He turned one over to expose its sole. Then, to Fiore's astonishment, he whipped a pen-knife out of his waistcoat pocket and began slicing away at ball and heel. A tight pattern of scored cross-hatches appeared beneath the blade. Fiore couldn't help noting that the confidence and speed with which Enzo wielded the knife resembled nothing sort of chirurgical precision.

"New heels are smooth," Enzo explained when he glanced up just in time to catch Fiore's raised eyebrow. "So they slide about. But if you give them a touch of rough, then…"

Fiore wondered if Enzo realized just how badly he wanted to give him a touch of rough. He couldn't quite withhold his smile as he replied, "Then they won't slip."

"Precisely."

"Slip and score," Fiore murmured.

It was Enzo's turn to look puzzled.

"Pottery," Fiore clarified. "It's how you attach one piece of clay to another. A handle to a pot or something like. You score the surfaces that need to connect, and smear them with slip—a mixture of clay and water, to make a sort of glue. But here," he added with another smile, "we're scoring not to slip."

Enzo answered him with the same shy little smile Fiore had come to love so well in the last few months. "Indeed."

To have Enzo bend to slip the shoes on for him a second time proved no less thrilling than the first. Likewise his pulse fluttered anew to let Enzo take him by the hands and gently bear him up to stand. Under Enzo's watchful and appreciative gaze he resumed pacing. His gait grew surer with every stride. And yet Fiore couldn't help feeling a touch disappointed that his heel didn't slip out from under him again, if only to give Enzo another opportunity to catch him.

Furthermore, while his quarters served well enough for strolling back and forth, they hardly had room to do anything else. Fiore had had some dance lessons in the conservatorio. He'd also done a great deal of dancing on deck in his years aboard the *Kingfisher*—particularly with sailors on leave. Still, he certainly didn't object to practice. Especially with Enzo.

"If you do intend to teach me to dance," Fiore ventured, "we ought to begin before the evening crowds arrive."

Enzo's face lit up to rival Phoebus.

Which made Fiore all the more melancholy to see him hide his handsome features behind his mask and beneath his hood before traipsing up on deck. Still it was something to have Enzo's arm entwined within his own.

No revelers had arrived as of yet. Corelli and her sons comprised a disinterested audience, for which Fiore gave silent thanks.

Dancing, however, required music. This necessity led Fiore to a dreadful conclusion.

He excused himself from Enzo's arm, dipped below-decks, and knocked on Serafina's door.

Upon opening it and espying him, her gaze lost none of its annoyance but did gain a great deal of bewilderment.

Fiore tried for a convincing smile. "Might I hire your services for the evening?"

Serafina raised her brows. "One of your gentlemen desires mixed company? Or—not on your own behalf, surely," she added, her eyes going wider still.

"To a point," Fiore admitted. "I'm taking dance lessons on deck and we require musical accompaniment."

Serafina's brows remained aloft. "Since when do you require dance lessons?"

"Since these." Fiore gestured to his heels.

Serafina stared for a long moment. Then she reeled back with a peal of laughter and had to hide herself behind her door for several more moments while she recovered her composure.

"Very well," she declared when she reappeared. "You know my rates. I'll see you above shortly."

"Thank you," Fiore said—sincerely, for once.

She nodded and withdrew. No sooner had she shut the door than another peal of laughter resounded from behind it.

Fiore supposed he deserved the mockery as much as she deserved the amusement and went up on deck to await her. This would allow him at least a few moments to familiarize himself with the steps before she beheld his wobbling folly.

The steps as Enzo explained them without musical accompaniment were not quite so different from those he indulged in any given evening at the *Kingfisher*. A touch more formal in their sequence, perhaps, but the basic gestures remained the same.

Aristocrats of all genders, as Enzo explained, learnt both the leading and following moves of a dance.

"To know only one or the other is considered deficient," he said as he gently arranged Fiore's arms in an embrace around his own torso.

"A true dancing maestro can dance equally well forward and backward."

The warmth of Enzo's flesh blazed through his shirt and waistcoat beneath Fiore's palms. Fiore had touched his bare skin before—had been *inside* him, for fuck's sake—and yet to hold him from even this distance sent his pulse stuttering.

"However," Enzo continued, heedless of Fiore's distraction. "If you'll indulge me, perhaps we might focus on making you a leader rather than a follower."

"Because it's easier to dance forwards?" Fiore guessed, smiling.

No blush could be seen thanks to the mask, but it could be heard in Enzo's voice as he replied, "That—and I myself feel more comfortable following."

Of course. Fiore's smile became a grin. "Then by all means, allow me to indulge you."

Before they could do so, however, something over Fiore's shoulder caught Enzo's eye. Fiore turned to follow his gaze and found Serafina had emerged. She'd changed into her wrapping-gown over her finest dress. Evidently she wanted to make a good impression on Fiore's illustrious client. Fiore supposed she did so for her own benefit but appreciated the effort nonetheless. At the very least she was finally taking his work as seriously as her own. And better still, she carried her violin.

"Anything in particular?" she enquired, tucking the instrument beneath her chin.

Fiore looked to Enzo.

"Perhaps a furlana?" Enzo asked her with as much deference as if he addressed a lady of equal rank.

Serafina nodded and set her bow to the strings. She played well—as she ought, when she claimed to have graduated from the figlie di coro.

Enzo listened for a measure or two with his masked head cocked at an attentive angle. Then he stepped backward on the beat, withdrawing as naturally as the ebbing tide.

Fiore stepped forward into his wake.

And fell against Enzo's chest.

It took a few moments' worth of bewildered clinging for him to piece together what had happened. Coming down on the heightened heel had pulled his stride up short. He'd leant forward to compensate, and without a counterbalance—

"Forgive me." The deep bass of Enzo's voice rumbling up from his ribcage resonated through Fiore's skull pressed against it. "I ought to have mentioned. While one comes down on the heel in walking, in dancing one ought to balance on the balls of one's feet."

Fiore righted himself—with Enzo's assistance—and forced a smile over his humiliation. Again he reflected how this would be a wonderful opportunity for a kiss were it not for Enzo's mask and their judgmental audience. Serafina's music had ceased. He expected her laughter to fill the silence. Yet, somehow, she withheld what must have been overwhelming glee at his folly. Perhaps she didn't wish to anger the duke.

"If we may continue?" Enzo enquired of Serafina over Fiore's head.

Fiore didn't dare look at her.

The music resumed. Fiore took a tentative step, balancing on the balls of his feet as Enzo had instructed. He did not fall.

Again Enzo retreated. Again Fiore advanced. But as he swept in to fill the lack, only for Enzo to withdraw, Fiore realized it was no such thing. Enzo did not flee from him. Rather, Enzo made way for him, inviting him to occupy the space he once held but a moment ago, continually welcoming him into his arms as he'd so oft welcomed him into his body, showing Fiore over and over how eager he felt to draw him into his life. And he drew very near indeed—near enough to feel the warmth of Enzo's heaving chest; near enough for their stockinged calves to brush against each other as they tangled and untangled like they had so oft before amidst the bedclothes; near enough to behold the smiling gleam in his tender gaze beneath the bauta mask. They twirled across the deck in the tentative embrace demanded by the dance. The music seemed to bear them up and swirl them 'round in its irresistible current.

Only when the song ended did Fiore recall they had an audience.

The spell broke. Their steps halted. Before he could prevent himself from revealing his hand, Fiore's head whipped 'round to regard those who surrounded them. He couldn't quite read Corelli or her sons beyond how their faces bore no trace of the ridicule he'd expected. And a glance at Serafina showed, to his astonishment, that she smiled without the glint of mockery in her gaze. He returned to Enzo to find his dark smiling gaze cast down to meet his own.

"Another?" Enzo asked, his voice as gentle as his touch.

Fiore couldn't keep the grin from growing across his face as he replied, "Of course."

Yet Enzo hesitated. "If you feel up to it, I had thought we might try something more."

Fiore raised his brows.

"A lift," Enzo explained. "It's become quite fashionable in ballroom circles."

"No doubt taken from the taverns," Fiore mused aloud. The dance steps Enzo had taught him thus far felt familiar for a reason; fashion travelled upwards as well as down, all the moreso when it came to music.

This seemed to surprise Enzo. "You've done it before, then?"

"Now and again," Fiore confessed with an easy smile.

"You shouldn't even attempt to lift me now," Enzo replied, more adamant than Fiore had ever heard him before.

Fiore wondered if he ought to feel offended that Enzo presumed him so weak—even as his rational mind pieced together his own recent injuries and the stark disparity in the size of his and Enzo's respective frames.

"For another year, at least," Enzo continued. "Lest your abdominal wall rupture and your entrails hernia beneath the skin."

Fiore understood him to mean an errant lift might burst his guts. If that were the case, however... "What of *your* wound?"

"There are bones as well as muscle holding the lungs and heart in place. At worst I would suffer a minor tear. Given the lift is performed with the leg moreso than the arm, I think it unlikely."

Fiore supposed Enzo knew his own body better. And had his medical education besides.

"Traditionally it is the leader rather than the follower who performs the lift," Enzo admitted. "But I think we might bend the rule between us, if you're willing."

215

Despite his bruised pride, the notion sent a thrill through Fiore's heartstrings. "I'd be delighted."

Enzo raised his head to regard Serafina beyond. "Another furlana, an' it so please you?"

She nodded with a poorly-suppressed smile and set bow to string again.

Their dance resumed. Again Enzo drew him in to a whirling embrace, his body flowing where'er Fiore led, every step in perfect harmony. But faster now, and the frantic controlled chaos of Serafina's bow brought them nearer with every slash to the crescendo of the piece. First the leaps —one, two, three, all landing with precision despite Fiore's new heels, for which he thought he deserved some manner of applause—and then a final capriole by Fiore alone, where at the crest of his wave he felt Enzo's thigh arise beneath him to meet his own, drawing him up and spinning him 'round in Enzo's grasp with such grace he felt as if he flew. For three quarters of a turn he hung suspended like the kingfisher coasting over the lagoon. Then came the descent, his feet alighting on the deck with an ease that belied the recent vintage of his heels. Enzo's arms caught him in the most willing snare. Together they twirled out the remainder of their momentum. As they slowed to a natural halt, so too did Fiore's eyes find their natural rest meeting Enzo's masked gaze, shining down upon him with infinite admiration in its dark depths.

Fiore had landed safe and sound in Enzo's embrace.

His heart, however, never came down.

# CHAPTER EIGHTEEN

"Were you ever a sailor?" asked Enzo.

Fiore served him a blank look. They stood on the waterfront, braced against a pile of crates freshly unloaded from one of the ships. Fiore had idly wondered as they'd set themselves up there whether they'd get scolded or crushed for interfering with the work. Enzo hadn't seemed worried about it. Fiore had supposed he could do worse than follow his lead. Perhaps he or someone in his family line owned the cargo or the ship or both. Regardless, it gave Fiore a splendid view of the ships to sketch. And had doubtless inspired Enzo's question.

"Never a sailor," Fiore admitted. "And you?"

As ever, Enzo seemed bewildered to have his enquiries turned back upon him. "Alas, no. Much to Mother's chagrin."

Hence her sailing off with her own fleet the very minute her youngest child entered university, Fiore supposed.

"Was your sea-chest a gift, then?" Enzo ventured with the same bashful caution he used whenever he pried into Fiore's past. "From another sailor?"

"From one of my nautical gentleman, you mean," Fiore replied with a smile. "And yes—a gift from a captain upon his retirement."

Which hadn't been quite the offer Fiore had hoped for from a

gentleman of Captain Scordato's age and standing, but one he
appreciated regardless. It was a splendid piece, worked over for some
five decades, replete with intricate carvings of hippocampi and serpents
and kraken tentacles curled tight around anchors and sailor's knots,
inlaid with seashells and mother-of-pearl. And practical, as well.

With every question asked, Enzo seemed to retreat further into
himself. As such, his subsequent enquiry emerged almost too low for
Fiore to catch.

"What do you keep in it?"

Fiore was only surprised Enzo hadn't asked sooner. Particularly
when he considered their cohabitation in his quarters during his
convalescence.

"Slops and go-ashores," Fiore replied. In response to Enzo's
bewildered glance, he added, "Clothes, mostly. Slops are for day-to-day.
Go-ashores are for special occasions."

Dawning comprehension lit up Enzo's dark gaze beneath the mask.
"Such as going ashore."

Fiore grinned. "Precisely. And then, beneath the clothes…"

Just as Fiore had hoped, Enzo leaned in to the suspense.

Fiore closed the distance between them to whisper into Enzo's ear.
"Shall I show you when we return?"

A hard swallow travelled down Enzo's throat. He nodded.

Fiore withdrew with a smile and returned to his drawing.

Enzo didn't ask again. Not even when the minutes turned to hours
and the light changed and Fiore moved them to another spot for
different sketches. Not even over the moeche they devoured for dinner
on their way back to the *Kingfisher*.

How Enzo survived so many hours without an answer, Fiore couldn't
fathom. He already knew what he kept in his sea-chest and even he
could hardly stand the suspense. Yet Enzo remained patient and demure.
Obedient, even. It seemed he had absolute trust in Fiore to provide a
satisfactory answer at the promised moment.

Which made Fiore think he would like the sea-chest's contents more
than otherwise.

They arrived at the *Kingfisher* just as the sun began to kiss the sea.
Enzo's patience continued as they withdrew belowdecks. His hat, hood,

cloak, and mask were all cast aside without a word of enquiry regarding the sea-chest, though it sat in plain view as it always had. Only a wayward glance of those dark eyes belied his curiosity.

Fiore indulged in a self-satisfied smile. He caught Enzo's gaze and gestured to the sea-chest with a careless flick of his wrist.

"Go on," he said. "You may open it, if you like."

It seemed a just reward for Enzo's forbearance.

Enzo looked as though he could hardly believe his good fortune—but would accept the charge with gravity nonetheless. He knelt on the floorboards (as he had so many times before for Fiore) and eased the chest's lid open with reverence. There lay the clothes Fiore had spoken of; Enzo didn't seem disappointed to see them and furthermore removed them with even more care than if they were his own, setting them aside until he reached the apparent bottom of the chest—mere bare wooden boards, unspeakably plain. Only then did he look to Fiore again with a furrow of confusion between his brows.

Fiore suppressed a grin and bent to poke out the knot in one of the boards. Enzo's eyes flew wide as it fell into darkness, for the chest ran deeper still. Fiore hooked his finger through the resulting hole and tugged. All the boards came up together, being nailed to each other to create a solid panel, and revealed the chest's true depths. He took the false bottom with him as he withdrew to better let Enzo drink in the hidden treasures.

Enzo's eyes had flown very wide. Fiore didn't blame him. But nor, as Fiore carefully examined his face, did he appear in the least bit perturbed. With an enquiring glance, which Fiore answered in a nod, Enzo reached into the secret depths and withdrew a riding crop. Fiore felt rather proud of it. It'd been no mean feat to acquire one in a city bereft of horses. But a gentleman had asked it of him, and he'd risen to the occasion. And several other occasions since.

Enzo gave the crop an experimental swish and glanced to Fiore again. "Thought you said you didn't ride?"

"Well…" Fiore bit back a grin and shrugged. "Not horses."

A bark of laughter escaped Enzo. He set the crop aside and continued delving. Some gentlemen might look askance at the blindfold or the coiled hemp or the cat-o'-nine-tails, but Enzo seemed more intrigued with every item he uncovered. Only the fids and belaying pins gave him pause. These he didn't touch, but merely gave Fiore an enquiring glance.

"The fids are just for knot-work," Fiore assured him. Certain past gentlemen had asked him to do otherwise, but Fiore knew better than to stick a long tapered wooden stake into any hole without a means of retrieving it.

Enzo appeared relieved. "And the pins?"

"A parting gift, alongside the chest. To the best of my knowledge these ones haven't been used for anything besides belaying."

Enzo hesitated. "Are there others?"

"If gentlemen wish to use them, I make them supply their own." The belaying pins, after all, had a flared base—and a handle besides.

Enzo didn't look averse to this idea, either. "How did you stumble onto these notions in the first place?"

"I worked with one particular sea captain," Fiore explained, "with very particular tastes. After a while I acquired a reputation for a deft hand at that sort of work." He indulged himself in a smile. "And the sailors came pouring in."

"Fair enough," Enzo replied. His hand fell to the riding crop again and he began rolling its handle idly between his fingers.

"And you?" Fiore asked.

"There were a multitude of societies and conclaves at university. Some more secret than others."

"Were you a member?"

A very fetching rosy tint bloomed over Enzo's sharp cheekbones. "Of some."

Throughout the discovery and subsequent conversation, they had retained their respective positions; Enzo kneeling before the sea-chest and Fiore standing over him with watchful eye. Now Fiore bent to pluck the crop from Enzo's fingers. Enzo relinquished it without even a hint of resistance. Fiore turned it over in his hands, noting how Enzo's dark gaze followed it all the while. Then, ever so gently, he laid the end beneath Enzo's chin and tilted his face upward to look him full in the eye. Enzo's breath caught. A hard swallow travelled down his throat. And those dark eyes grew darker still as the pupils flew wide.

"Do tell," Fiore murmured.

Enzo drew in a ragged breath. "What do you wish to know?"

Fiore let the leather loop trail down Enzo's throat to rest in the hollow. "Your part in it."

The scarred lip caught between his teeth. "Not quite so involved as I would've liked."

"Why not?"

"My peculiarity," Enzo said, to Fiore's surprise. "I don't like revealing it to strangers—or near-strangers. It's... hard to tell how it might be received. And while the society itself might've been secret, we all knew each other through the university. I didn't need every fellow student knowing the whole of me."

"Fair enough," Fiore replied, though the words hardly sufficed. "How did you involve yourself?"

That enquiry brought the most welcome return of a scarred smile. "I found the knot-work intriguing."

As the conversation had continued, Enzo had folded his hands behind his back. He now knelt in a posture of perfect obedience. Fiore wondered if he even realized he'd done it, or if it came so naturally to him that he could hardly do elsewise once Fiore had taken the crop from him.

Aloud, however, Fiore asked, "Because of the nautical connexion?"

A soft breath of laughter escaped Enzo. "At first. I found a way to involve myself there, however small, in assisting my classmates in restraining each other and themselves. Most assumed my expertise came from erotic experience and gave me respect accordingly. In truth..." He shrugged. "I could never have done my family proud if I didn't know my way around a ship's lines. But really—I just liked to make myself useful. And to witness the result."

"Which was?"

Enzo hesitated. "Surrender. And then—ecstasy. There is... something of a relief, in relinquishing command."

Fiore couldn't relate. But he'd seen enough of other men to know there were some who truly craved such a thing. And he delighted in granting it to them. "Did you enjoy watching for its own sake?"

"Yes," Enzo admitted—which was more honesty than most men

would give Fiore and which he greatly appreciated. "It was a beautiful thing."

Fiore quite agreed. There was something intoxicating in the idea of a dozen-odd strapping university students tying each other up in a secret orgy.

Enzo's tongue emerged to trace the scar that split his lower lip. "And... I carried the sight back with me to my solitary quarters. I spent many nights imagining myself bound in their stead."

Fiore found the idea of Enzo bound rather inspiring himself. The rosy glow of those sharp cheeks, the eager sheen in his dark gaze, and the ragged rhythm of his breath in just the mere anticipation of submission would tempt anyone to indulge him. "Did you never have the opportunity to turn the fantasy into reality?"

"Well..." Enzo bit his lip again. An entirely unwitting gesture, and therefore all the more captivating. "Orazio did indulge me, now and then, once we'd found each other."

Fiore hadn't meant to dredge up anything that might remind Enzo of his loss. He attempted to banish any lingering melancholy with a gentle smile. "How very generous of him."

Just as Fiore had hoped, Enzo echoed his good humor. "Very generous indeed."

And a very good thing, too, that Enzo could now reminisce fondly rather than dwelling on regrets. Fiore didn't flatter himself far enough to believe he bore sole responsibility for this change. But it pleased him to see it regardless. He felt not a drop of jealousy for remembrances past—only eagerness to make Enzo feel so again.

Fiore let the crop descend. It trailed from beneath Enzo's chin, tracing the jewel in his throat that pulsed at its touch, flicking each individual button of his waistcoat, down to where even the fall-front of his breeches couldn't entirely disguise his growing interest in their conversation.

Enzo's breath caught.

The echoes of a hundred voices begging Fiore to tame them rose up in his ears. Now he would turn all he'd learnt towards Enzo's pleasure.

"How shall I have you?" Fiore asked.

Enzo's breath grew shallow. "However you like."

An intoxicating notion. But not the answer Fiore required to give

Enzo what he wanted. He tried again. "How did you imagine yourself on all those lonesome nights? Bound behind your back or over your head?"

The reply came in a fevered gasp. "Over my head."

Fiore grinned. "Then strip."

As much as Fiore liked to put on a show for his gentlemen, there was certainly some satisfaction in leaning back with his hands braced against the gunwales of his bed to watch as Enzo's trembling fingertips fumbled with his waistcoat buttons. Enzo hesitated when it came to his breeches. His eyes flew to Fiore's, seeking permission, and only at Fiore's nod did he stand to divest himself below the waist. The loss of his drawers revealed his cock at full mast, lightly pulsing with the force of his heartbeat, and his inner thighs gleaming wet in anticipation.

But when his hands descended to the garters of his silk stockings, Fiore flicked his wrist, and the crop halted just short of striking Enzo's knuckles. Enzo ceased even without actually receiving the blow. His eyes flicked up to Fiore's face, pupils flown wide, lip caught between teeth, the whole of him shivering in eagerness.

"Those remain," Fiore told him. *For my own pleasure* went unsaid.

Enzo agreed with a fervent nod.

Fiore trailed the crop up from Enzo's calf over the inside of his thigh. It halted just before it reached his cunt. Enzo ceased to breathe.

Then Fiore flicked it back to his own side. "On the bed. Back to the wall. Kneel."

Enzo obeyed with as much grace as haste. Impressive in a man of his immense stature. Fiore intended to reward him well for it. He paused just long enough to select a suitable length of hemp from the sea-chest. Then he set both rope and crop aside on the nightstand—not failing to notice how Enzo's eye fixed on those instruments—to disrobe himself before joining Enzo in the bed.

"Give me your hands," Fiore said, taking up the rope again.

Enzo surrendered them at once.

Fiore drew the rope over his wrists—lightly, teasingly, with particular attention to the blue veins—before binding them in deft knots, ensuring there remained room enough for him to pass two fingers between the hemp and Enzo's arm. Then he took them by the knot and raised them overhead. Enzo offered no resistance, only an eager gleam in his dark eyes as he watched and waited with perfect trust for whatever Fiore chose to do with him.

An iron hook as big as a man's fist protruded from the wall above Fiore's bed. Like almost everything else in the room it'd originally served a purpose aboard ship; now it secured the same hempen lines for entirely different ends. Few noticed it unless they looked for it. Those who found it tended to be those who desired its use.

And now, Fiore hung from it the knot that bound Enzo's wrists.

It left a little slack, with Enzo on his knees, just enough to account for a slight bend of his arms.

Fiore sat back to admire his work. "Like this?"

Enzo nodded. It seemed the sheer force of his desire robbed him of speech. Or perhaps he considered his own silence another aspect of his obedience. Either way, Fiore appreciated both his restraint and his continued communication. To say nothing of how he looked now; face flushed, prick no less so, a single pearl of seed rolling from its tip and still more between his thighs from his cunt.

"Aren't you a handsome sight," Fiore purred.

Enzo blushed further still.

Fiore took up the crop again—to Enzo's evident delight, judging by the way the jewel in his throat pulsed in another hard swallow. He tapped its leather tongue against the insides of Enzo's knees. They slid further apart at his silent command, making room enough for Fiore to slip between them. But he did not do so just yet.

First the crop trailed up the inside of Enzo's thigh, the skin shivering in its wake, to the root of his prick, which stood as rigid-yet-supple as the crop itself. The leather tongue traced the throbbing vein on the underside all the way to the tip. Another pearl of seed rewarded his teasing efforts. Then down again, past the root to his cunt, where the leather came away glistening. A bitten-off moan escaped Enzo at its loss.

Fiore leaned into the space Enzo had made for him. The breath came shallow and ragged. The eyes had fluttered shut. Yet it took just the barest touch of Fiore's fingertips against that strong jaw for the whole immense frame to go taut with a gasp and for the eyes to snap open and fix their enormous darkness on Fiore.

"Can you tell me what you want?" Fiore murmured gently.

Enzo worried his scarred lip between his teeth. Fiore wondered if speech were beyond him. Some men lost their words altogether when they entered such a state as this.

But then a hoarse whisper emerged, so low Fiore had to almost press his cheek to Enzo's to hear.

"Fuck me," Enzo begged. "Please."

Fiore felt as if he'd waited all his life to hear him ask. He tucked the crop away for the moment by threading it through Enzo's arms and behind his head, which provoked another strangled sound of pleasure from the depths of Enzo's throat.

Then he slipped forward and brought his rigid prick to bear with Enzo's cunt.

Despite his own desperate desire to lose himself within Enzo, he restrained his instincts and instead caressed the slick petals with his cock-head. Enzo's hips bucked. Fiore seized them in his hands and held them still.

"Patience," Fiore purred.

Enzo bit his lip hard, but obeyed.

Fiore rewarded him by letting just his cock-head slide into his cunt. There he paused again—as much to master himself as to tease Enzo— before slowly, by the barest fractions of an inch, sheathing his blade within him. The tight, wet heat consumed him and threatened to overpower his resolve. He vented a fraction of this by devouring Enzo's mouth in a kiss.

Enzo's hips remained still throughout. His hands, however, as Fiore beheld when he broke off for breath, clenched and unclenched, his wrists straining against their bonds in his efforts to honor Fiore's command.

Fiore released his waist and let his fingertips trail down over the tops of Enzo's trembling thighs. Enzo shuddered in his wake. Fiore, feeling just as tormented by restraint, if not moreso, rolled his hips at last, slowly rocking in and out of Enzo's tight wet sheath. A broken moan escaped Enzo's scarred lips.

"Is this what you wanted?" Fiore whispered. "All those hours spent binding your fellow students, watching their lovers bring them to ecstasy, and none to give you what you wished in return? Imagine if they had. How many were gathered—a dozen? A score? How many would it take to satisfy you? You would serve them all so well. So obedient. So obliging. You would've taken such good care of them all—if only they would do the same for you."

And between every measured thrust of cock and words alike, Enzo answered him with a hushed and frantic, "Yes."

Enzo's cock lay trapped beneath them, smearing its leaking seed over them both. Fiore took it in hand. Enzo shuddered.

"Too much?" Fiore murmured against his ear.

He felt rather than saw Enzo shake his head in reply. "More. Please."

It was the *pleases* that would prove his undoing, Fiore thought. Each one that dropt from Enzo's scarred lips made Fiore's cock pulse. Enzo's cunt clenched 'round him in turn. He didn't know how much longer he could last. He rolled into Enzo as he rolled his foreskin over his cock-head. Enzo's deep moan reverberated through Fiore's own ribcage.

"Did the ropes and crops mark your fellows?" Fiore asked. At Enzo's fervent nod, he continued. "Did you envy them? Did you covet their reminders of all the pains and pleasures they'd endured?"

"Yes," Enzo hissed.

Fiore grinned. "Do you want your own now?"

Enzo's answer was almost a sob. "Please."

Fiore indulged him, bending to kiss a bruise onto his collarbone. While Enzo wandered the city cloaked head to foot, old habits died hard, and he'd long ago learnt not to mark his gentlemen anywhere a shirt wouldn't cover. He concluded his kiss with a nip. Enzo writhed with pleasure in his embrace.

"You like that, don't you," Fiore observed—having to swallow down his own moan of pleasure to do so. "Yet still you want more."

Enzo nodded. His trembling thighs clenched around Fiore's waist. Shivers chased each other across his flesh. "Please."

"What more do you want?" Fiore asked, though he knew well the answer.

And still it thrilled him to hear Enzo beg. "Fuck me harder."

Fiore withdrew his cock 'til just the head remained within Enzo's cunt. Then he abandoned all denial—his own and Enzo's alike—and plunged in to the hilt.

Enzo threw his head back with a groan of relief. His hips thrust to meet Fiore's every blow. Fiore no longer prevented him. He'd restrained himself long enough; let him enjoy his just reward at last. And let Fiore take everything Enzo had offered. There was a certain thrill in giving a gentleman exactly what he wanted whilst remaining completely in control. And a certain further thrill when that particular gentleman was Enzo. He rode him hard as any steed. Together they raced towards ecstasy. Fiore held back just long enough, 'til Enzo's cunt clenched him tight and his cock spilled over his knuckles. Then he bit down hard into the meat of Enzo's shoulder to mute his own cry as he shuddered to a halt and poured his essence deep within Enzo's welcoming vessel. He clasped Enzo tight in his arms even as Enzo clasped him tighter still within his flesh. Only the bonds around Enzo's wrists held them both upright. Tremulous gasps escaped between desperate kisses. Fiore thought he might sleep forever content if he could but remain cleaved this close to his Enzo.

But his work was not yet complete. One couldn't leave hands bound overhead over-long. Not if one wished to retain said hands, at any rate.

Fiore roused Enzo from his splendid stupor with a long and languid kiss. He waited until Enzo's eyes focused on his own.

"I'm going to untie you now," he told him

Only after Enzo nodded his assent did he raise his hands to the hook. A little lift, then down, and he had Enzo's bound hands between them. The knots untied with a few deft tugs. The rope fell away. Fiore kept Enzo's hands in his own. Beneath Enzo's watchful gaze, he gently kneaded the raw scarlet marks the rope had left behind. Then the knuckles, 'til the grasp became soft as rose-petals, and on down the sinewed forearms to tend each joint up to the shoulder. By then Enzo had regained some power over his constrained limbs and used it to return Fiore's embrace. Fiore rewarded him with a kiss.

"As good as your fantasies?" Fiore teased him when they parted.

Rather than a mere nod, Enzo replied with his voice—hoarse from disuse but no less deep and sonorous. "Better."

# CHAPTER NINETEEN

The tailor's preliminary sketches had not done the final suit justice.

With just a week to go before the ball, the whole ensemble was assembled at last. A vision in seafoam green head to foot, a match which Fiore well knew was no small feat. Hard enough to mix the same color twice, much less make it bind the same to two textiles of divers materials. Yet one would be hard-pressed to find the hair's-breadth of difference between the cool-handed wool coat and the gleaming satin breeches and waistcoat. More remarkable still was how the leather of both the hat and shoes came to hold the same soft lagoon-green shade. The skillfully-applied gilding of the hat's trim and the shoes' heels likewise matched the gold filigree edging the hems of the wool coat. The leather itself was so smooth as to appear molded of porcelain, sleek to the touch on the outside and suede smooth as butter within.

All together, they looked, in a word…

"Perfect," Fiore declared.

A soft sigh cut through the stark silence of the tailor's parlor. Fiore tore his gaze away from the masterpiece to regard the cluster of men who'd held their collective breath whilst awaiting his opinion. Several assistants and twice as many apprentices had gathered behind the master tailor himself, who stood beside Enzo with his hands clasped behind his back. What Enzo thought of Fiore's new ensemble remained hidden beneath his bauta mask—for the moment, at least.

The master tailor retained more poise than his assistants or apprentices. He smiled and gestured to the folding screen in the back corner of the parlor. "If you'd care to try it on, signore...?"

Fiore very much desired to do so, indeed. He'd had regular fittings as the tailor's work had progressed. But never before had he held the whole ensemble complete in his grasp. The work of a moment saw it all folded up in his arms and secreted away with him behind the folding screen. Then he turned his focus to divesting himself of his everyday garments.

No sooner had he untied his scarlet sash, however, than he heard the master tailor's voice again from the other side of the screen.

"If you require assistance, signore, my apprentices would be happy to guide you."

Fiore paused with his sash suspended between his hands. The master tailor's tone had retained its well-practiced deference throughout the offer. And yet it rang in Fiore's ears with a timbre that seemed determined to strike his pride. While he had some hesitance about handling finery, he thought he'd hidden it from his audience; the conservatorio had trained him well for that, if nothing else. Furthermore, even if he hadn't already undergone several fittings in this very shop prior to this moment, the plain shape of the garments—shirt, waistcoat, breeches, stockings—were precisely like his own everyday garb. He obviously knew how to dress himself.

Which gave the tailor's offer a distinct undercurrent of something Fiore didn't like.

Regardless if the tailor proved sincere or false, Fiore's answer remained the same. He didn't bother to disguise his self-satisfied smile as he poked his head out from behind the screen. The master tailor and all his assistants and apprentices watched him with bated breath. But Fiore had eyes for Enzo alone.

"Would you mind helping me?" Fiore asked when his gaze locked with Enzo's beneath the mask.

The collective surprise of the tailor's apprentices sang in Fiore's blood like wine. The assistants kept their poise a little better. The master tailor, if he realized his misstep at all, showed not a hint of it in his face.

And as for Enzo himself, he simply perked up and strode to join Fiore behind the screen.

The duke's consent to act as valet to a mere courtesan did not go unnoticed in the shop. Fiore drank in as much of his audience's astonishment as he could—guzzled it, really—before he withdrew with Enzo.

The spark of desire his request had ignited in Enzo's masked eyes proved even more intoxicating. Fiore bit back a grin as he handed over his scarlet sash and watched Enzo wrap it tight 'round his fists. Really he required nothing from Enzo in the way of actual help, but he still delighted in those dark eyes fixed upon him as he unbuttoned his waistcoat and slipped off his breeches.

Parts of the formal suit remained new to him. He didn't oft wear drawers; hadn't at all, actually, until it came time for his first fitting at the tailor and Enzo had arrived to pick him up from the *Kingfisher* with a pair of fresh linen sewn to the specifications of his own most intimate flesh. His shirttails sufficed to keep his everyday woolen breeches clean. But the sea-green satin required a touch more to shield it from his sweat. And the shirt the tailor provided him with was far more than a mere undergarment.

Fiore had never worn lace before; had only touched it when peeling it off of Enzo. Now, with his own new shirt in hand, he found its lace cuffs as light and ebullient and delicate as seafoam. He knew well the hundreds of hours that went into tatting something so effervescent. He held too much respect for the lace-maker's craft to treat the resulting garment with anything less than reverence.

The silk stockings were likewise a hitherto-unknown luxury. He wore his own woolen stockings, true enough, and had beheld and felt the silk variety on Enzo's beautifully-turned calves. But never before had they graced his own flesh. His anticipation, eager though it was, didn't begin to equal the thrill he felt when Enzo knelt in front of him and held out the stocking for him to step into. And it seemed Enzo had a thrill of his own, given his lingering caress as he smoothed the silk over Fiore's calves. To say nothing of how tenderly his fingertips tied the garters over Fiore's knees. The tailor had provided seafoam green silk ribbons embroidered with golden scales to match the ensemble, which Fiore greatly admired, but he couldn't help wondering at how it might feel to wear an intimate garment embroidered in Enzo's own peculiar chirurgical stitch.

The thrill continued as Enzo tightened the laces on the back of his drawers and again after he slipped on the satin breeches, which required not just the tightening of laces behind but also the fastening of buttons at the knee, and for that Enzo knelt once more, making Fiore's heart flutter to new heights. It increased as Enzo kissed the crown of his silk-clad foot, as a commoner would kiss the knuckles of a prince, before slipping on his heels.

Then there was the waistcoat—with tenfold the buttons of Fiore's everyday garment and whereupon Enzo wielded the buttonhook with all the dexterity expected of a chirurgeon—and the coat proper. Enzo slipped and smoothed it onto Fiore's shoulders in a gesture as intimate as any embrace. No less so was the way he tied the pristine cravat around Fiore's throat.

At last Enzo withdrew, presumably to admire his handiwork. What wonder he found there shone in his masked gaze. He stepped aside, out of the path between Fiore and the standing mirror behind the screen.

And Fiore beheld a masterpiece.

However beautiful it'd been to imagine his suit—however more beautiful to behold the finished work—it proved still more beautiful to see it displayed on the very body it'd been molded for and to feel against his own skin all its deliciously indulgent weaves. He'd never seen himself so handsome. The hand-mirror he kept in his quarters aboard the *Kingfisher* hardly sufficed to show him his own face. The luxury of standing before a full-length mirror alone was worth the tailor's price.

The shop did not have the luxury of privacy, however, which Fiore thought a shame. He could feel Enzo's desire for him even at arm's length. More than ever before Fiore wished Enzo needn't wear the bauta mask. He wanted to know precisely how Enzo felt about the results of his investment. But with the mask concealing all save Enzo's eyes, there remained only one way for him to know.

"Well?" Fiore asked him. "How do I look?"

～

Enzo could hardly speak.

Fiore always looked impossibly handsome. Now, however, in the bright warmth of the tailor's shop, scarcely hidden behind a sheer paper screen, he looked resplendent.

Not because his clothes matched his natural beauty. None ever could. His daily garb was made gorgeous by his presence in it, and even his new attire—however skillfully made and of however fine material—was outshone by his smile alone.

But that very smile now shining on Fiore's handsome, sun-kissed features showed just how well he loved the suit. And his happiness made him look more magnificent than any other gentleman, from courtier to king, could possibly appear in any finery. His sheer radiance made the suit brilliant. Enzo knew not how to begin to explain it aloud.

And all the while Fiore gazed up at him with those perfect lips spread in the most beautiful smile in all the world. He had asked such a simple question. Enzo could hardly refuse him an answer. Mindful of the master tailor and the half-dozen assistants and apprentices besides just beyond the sheer screen, he stepped in to deliver it, near enough to enfold Fiore in his arms as he so dearly wished but hardly dared.

"To think," Enzo murmured. "All this trouble to put it on you... and now all I wish to do is tear it off."

It was not at all what Enzo had intended to say. But it was true regardless. Flames engulfed his face beneath his mask.

Fiore grinned.

Then he spun—the skirts of his coat unfurling like a blossoming rose —and stepped out from behind the screen to bow to the master tailor. Enzo hastened to follow him.

"It's magnificent," Fiore declared. "Better than I might have dreamed. I cannot thank you enough."

From another's mouth the words could hardly have sounded so sincere. Yet Fiore made them ring with truth.

Enzo's heart warmed to think on the small part he'd played in realizing Fiore's wildest dreams. His own thanks to the tailors proved softer and more succinct but no less sincere.

The master tailor at least seemed to realize this. The infinitesimally small smile that appeared on his face was more than Enzo had ever seen from him in all their long acquaintance. Still his appraising eye swept Fiore up and down.

"A few adjustments, if you will permit, signore," he said.

Fiore granted him this with evident gladness. Even an artist's dissatisfaction with his masterpiece could not dull his shine.

Enzo forced himself to sit in still and silent patience on the settee whilst he watched the master tailor flit over Fiore with pins and tape. The attention of all present fixed on Fiore. Which was just as well, because the flames that had sparked in Enzo's face had since spread throughout his entire body. If the tailor dallied much longer they would consume him altogether.

Even when the tailor declared himself satisfied at last, Enzo found no relief—for that meant Fiore must divest himself of his finery, and again he asked for Enzo's particular assistance. As beautiful as the raiments appeared on Fiore's form, they looked still more beautiful as they were stripped away. Enzo's hands had never trembled with a scalpel in their grasp, yet they shivered to slip the silk and satin from Fiore's skin. He could do nothing about it, nor about the coy glances and bitten-back smiles Fiore continually tossed his way. While the tailors couldn't see anything behind the screen, they could certainly hear everything and absolutely knew that both Enzo and Fiore were there. Doubtless so many of them had gathered specifically with the hope of seeing or overhearing something salacious between the duke and his courtesan. Tantalus himself could suffer no more than Enzo did now with Fiore beneath his fingertips yet out of his reach. The rote recitation of alchemical formulae in his mind kept Enzo's breeches presentable but only just. And Fiore himself, as Enzo could well perceive when green satin was swapped out for chestnut wool, felt no less inspired by their present predicament.

Finally they returned Fiore to decency and re-emerged from behind the screen. Enzo fell back on formal etiquette to finalize matters with the tailor—all-too-aware of Fiore waiting in the corner of his eye, the perfect portrait of patient innocence. Somehow they kept their thwarted desires contained long enough to depart the shop with some semblance of dignity remaining.

"A brisk walk back to the *Kingfisher*?" Fiore suggested the moment the door shut behind them. His tone conveyed light indifference but the breathless nature of the words themselves belied his own desperation.

Enzo felt he might die if they waited another moment, never mind the minutes it would take to return to Fiore's quarters. However, unlike Fiore, he hadn't arrived at the tailor's shop on foot.

"I've a gondola waiting," Enzo said, trying and failing to sound casual. "If you'd care to join me?"

Fiore's handsome features lit up with an eager grin.

～

Fiore hadn't ridden in a gondola since Carlotta had whisked him away to Wolf's Head. While Carlotta had proved an adept traveling companion, he found he much preferred to have Enzo join him in the secluded confines of the felze.

The feel of silk against his intimate flesh had invigorated him. Even now with the silks and satins folded up on the seat beside him and his own body garbed in everyday wools, his desire for Enzo still raged. The brief sojourn from shop door to gondola had failed to quench the flame.

And the single brush of their hands together as Enzo followed him into the felze sufficed to reignite the flame into a raging bonfire.

Enzo settled onto the seat and shut the door behind them whilst Fiore simmered with feverish anticipation. No sooner had he whipped off hat, hood, and mask than Fiore was upon him.

"Steady," Enzo whispered even as he returned his frantic embrace.

Indeed, with the gondola rocking beneath them, Fiore supposed he'd better not endanger the gondolier standing on it. His mind whirled with the question of how to satisfy them both under such constraints. He supposed they might make do with mouths and hands. However, even whilst he thought, Enzo extracted himself from their embrace and divested himself of his breeches and drawers with remarkable ease— particularly considering their confined setting.

Which led Fiore to one singular conclusion. "You've done this before."

Enzo grinned. "Maybe."

Fiore made a note to demand full details later. At present he hastened to release his own cock from his breeches. It had been at half-mast when he first entered the felze. Now it stood proud as Enzo's.

And the moment it came free, Enzo straddled him and sank down.

Fiore's breath caught as he slipped once more into that hot, tight, wet sheath. As matters stood now, however—with him sitting on the cushioned bench in the felze, Enzo's weight atop him, and hardly daring to move lest he pitch the whole gondola over—he had precious little leverage to draw them both to completion.

Which left him entirely at Enzo's mercy.

Still, Enzo sought his permission with a glance. Fiore granted it with a nod. And only then did Enzo begin to move.

Enzo's hips rolled in rhythm with the lapping waves; steady, unceasing, relentless, grinding over and again that particular part within him that made his cock pulse in Fiore's fist with every pass. Barely half an inch of Fiore's prick slid in and out of him. Yet even that exquisite torment sufficed to send Fiore perilously near to the brink after all he'd withheld behind the tailor's screen.

Fiore gave Enzo swift strokes in turn, feeling his sheath clench 'round him in time with the pulsing of his cock in his fist, gasping into each other's mouths between frantic kisses, devouring Enzo above whilst Enzo consumed him below, a hair's-breadth of willpower keeping his own crisis at bay, until—

A kiss muted Enzo's broken moan. He shuddered in Fiore's arms. The rhythmic clenching of his cunt reverberated through Fiore's own core. Seed spilled over Fiore's knuckles and cock alike.

Then and only then did Fiore allow his hand to descend, seize Enzo's ample ass, and in a few daring thrusts find his own release. Ecstasy overwhelmed him as he poured himself into Enzo. His pearls mingled with Enzo's salty tide within his cunt. A few glistening drops leaked through its tight embrace.

Fiore fell back senseless against the leather interior. Only Enzo's embrace tethered him to the shores of reality. And it was Enzo's kiss that revived him.

"Will you serve me so well after the ball?" Fiore asked when they parted.

Enzo grinned and gasped out his promise. "Better."

~

"Oh," said Artemisia. "You're alive."

Fiore, who'd just crossed the threshold of her workshop, grinned. "Wonderful to see you again, as well."

Artemisia wiped her dusty hands on her smock and stepped away from her work-in-progress—a fountainhead well on its way to becoming a dolphin's beak. For years now Fiore had modelled for her every luni and zobia afternoon, barring festivals and, more recently, the unexpected circumstances of his and Enzo's concurrent convalescences. Even if she didn't need him for a specific commission she insisted on having him for gestural practice. She appreciated his ability to hold a pose; he in turn appreciated her appreciation, and particularly how it took the form of cold hard coin with no attempts at bartering.

Today she dismissed her apprentices and assistants with a wave of her hand. They all vanished deeper into the workshop or out of it altogether. Her sessions with Fiore were always private. This had inspired countless rumors. Artemisia never gave any such tattle a second thought. Fiore himself just laughed at them. Let the gossip-mongers think her one of his precious few female patrons. All the better for his reputation if his seductive prowess surpassed all genders. Particularly when the list of Artemisia's romantic conquests rivalled his own.

Over the course of their last few sessions Fiore had divulged to her almost all the details of his hunting lodge adventure and the upcoming ball masque. The truth of Enzo's draconic ancestry and how it bore out on his body remained the sole and solemn secret. Fiore had sworn to himself, if not to Enzo, to take it to his grave.

Even so, all Fiore had told her almost sufficed to mollify her disturbance at his second sudden disappearance within the space of a single year. From an outside perspective, as she explained to him, the *Kingfisher*'s male courtesan had been whisked away by strangers garbed in Scaevola livery to no-one-knew-where and remained vanished for the better part of another month. His homecoming was almost as unexpected as a return from the grave. Hence Artemisia's now-customary greeting to him as he entered her workshop twice every week.

From a medical perspective, Enzo still advised Fiore against holding a standing pose. If he moved from pose to pose every few minutes, however, alternating sitting and standing, then Enzo had no objection whatsoever. And a reclining pose held no danger at all. Which gave Artemisia more than enough to work with.

They began with what Artemisia called "gestural" poses. Standing with limbs sprawled and contorted in all directions, each held for no more than a few minutes, most for mere moments. Artemisia sketched them out with rapidity, a few lines slashed across her page to represent Fiore's entire body. When she thought she'd warmed up enough to settle in to a longer session, she likewise allowed Fiore to settle in to her studio chair piled high with pillows and blankets. Only then did either of them have breath enough to spare for conversation. Fiore unleashed his tongue to prattle on about the party, the tailor, the cobbler, the haberdasher, the dance lessons, and all else he'd done to prepare for what would be his finest performance yet. In between all of these he shifted his posture several times over, at one point ending up with his left knee flung over the back of the chair and his hair brushing the floorboards. Artemisia took it all in stride. She asked but one question, and that was mere permission to sketch him in all his finery after the ball, which he eagerly granted.

After he had spent all he had to say, he made an enquiry of her in turn. "Anyone interesting come in whilst I was away?"

This was the usual phrase between him and Artemisia to ask after any potential wealthy patrons who might take a shine to a handsome young man.

Which made it all the more odd when she furrowed her brow as if confused. "Thought you'd already found someone interesting."

Fiore didn't insult her by asking who she meant. "I find him very interesting, indeed. But that doesn't mean I'm not still looking."

Artemisia stared at him. "He's a duke. Brother to the prince. His meagre portion of the family fortune is greater than any sum you or I could hope to see in our entire lives. Or have you set your sights on something higher?"

Fiore, uncomfortable with the path their talk had wandered down, cleared his throat. "His rank is no concern to me. Nor is his fortune."

"You don't like him, then," Artemisia concluded.

Fiore hesitated. He'd acquired the skill of spinning convincing half-truths to almost anyone in the course of his career. But more often than not he found Artemisia saw straight through them. If he wished to conceal something from her, he did better to keep silent on the subject in question and steer their conversation into a more obliging current.

Yet the way she fixed her gaze upon him now told him she would abide neither silence nor steering on this particular point.

And so to her and her alone Fiore confessed, "I like him very well. Too much, in fact."

He tried his able best to sound casual, worldly, or at the very least satirical enough to laugh it off altogether. But he heard the horrible note of honesty leak through his words regardless.

Artemisia, to her credit, replied without a trace of mockery. "Then why look elsewhere?"

Fiore swallowed his heart down from where it had unaccountably crawled into his throat. The mere thought of Enzo inspired feelings he'd not experienced since half his soul was torn out, mutilated, and murdered in front of him. The possibility that such might happen again left him with terror that ripped asunder even the softest and most serene recollections of Enzo's smile, his voice, his touch. Fiore could imagine every blissful moment of their life together.

He likewise knew full well how it would inevitably end.

Perhaps they'd have an enormous fight. Perhaps they'd have a series of small arguments that built up into insurmountable resentments. Perhaps Enzo would simply get bored of him and his eye would wander away towards someone new. Perhaps, as the both of them aged in tandem, Enzo would try to recapture his own lost youth, like so many men did, by seeking another, younger partner.

Or perhaps it would be no fault of Enzo or Fiore, but family obligation would demand Enzo marry. Whether he could produce children or not, an alliance of noble houses through marriage would enrich them both. And Fiore knew of no wife who would suffer her husband to keep a whore. More likely still, Enzo's sympathetic heart wouldn't allow him to put his betrothed through the indignity and humiliation of Fiore's discovery, and he would break it off with Fiore the moment the engagement contracts were signed.

Regardless, Fiore intended to side-step the whole of it.

"When whatever wealthy patron I find casts me aside," he said, "I intend to feel nothing save the weight of my purse."

"You keep saying 'when,'" Artemisia noted.

"Because it always happens," Fiore insisted. "Remember when Serafina bid us all goodbye forever because her patron was taking her away to a private villa all her own in the countryside where she would live in ease and comfort until the end of her days? And how not two days later she was back crying her heart out because his wife had discovered all and her patron—who'd sworn her everlasting fealty—had chosen his marriage over her?"

Artemisia snorted. "I remember."

"At best she was pitiful. At worst she was a laughingstock. And still she's better off than Venanzio. You remember him, as well?" Fiore asked with perhaps more bite than warranted.

That particular tale cleaved closer to his own experience. Too close. Venanzio, a castrato who'd failed to make his mark upon the stage, had instead become the kept creature of a particular pontifex, until he fell prey to the pox and well-regretted surviving it, for it left his face so pitted the pontifex cast him out, and he wandered as a drunken, heartbroken, penniless wretch until the gondoliers found him floating face-down in the Grand Canal one foggy morning.

This time, no trace of humor appeared in Artemisia's features. "I remember."

Fiore felt he might have made his point at last. "And they're hardly alone in the profession. I'm not stupid enough to believe I'm an exception."

Artemisia looked as if she had her own opinion of Fiore's stupidity. "He nursed you through one of the more disgusting infections I've ever heard of, and you're still convinced he'll leave you?"

"Yes, well—ugly as it was, it left no mark on my face. The ravages of time, however..." Fiore gestured towards his still-sharp cheeks, his as-of-yet unwrinkled brow, his undoubled chin, and the jawline which hadn't yet grown over with jowls.

Artemisia didn't appear convinced.

"My bauta, as you call him, cannot discard me if he never has me," Fiore insisted. He didn't add, at least not aloud, *And I can never lose him if I never had him.* "Which is why I seek an elderly patron. Or at least middling-aged. I need never know the indignity of being thrown away if he drops off before I grow too old for his taste."

"So you object to your bauta as your patron merely because he is too young for you."

"Yes," Fiore sighed, half-irritation and half-relief. He tried not to think on what Enzo had said about plying his suit again. "You understand at last."

"Of course," Artemisia replied in her cavaliere tone. "You're so determined not to let him break your heart that you've decided to break it yourself."

Fiore's intended retort died on his tongue.

# CHAPTER TWENTY

"Fiorenzo Scaevola, Duke of Drakehaven," the herald declared. He paused and shot a glance at Fiore that swept him up and down with a faint hint of confusion and a dash of suspicion, before he continued, "And consort."

Fiore supposed the title fit him well enough. It leant an air of mystery to his entrance on Enzo's arm, which he appreciated. Particularly as scores of aristocratic heads whirled towards them at the sound of Enzo's title. Fans fluttered up to cover mouths feverishly whispering to each other.

Enzo laid a reassuring hand on Fiore's arm linked with his own and strode forward. The crowd gathered in the formal entryway of Ca' Grimaldi parted before them like the waves before a ship's prow.

The gondola ride from the *Kingfisher* to the palazzo had calmed Fiore's nerves somewhat. Or rather, having Enzo all to himself within the felze had. The firm clasp of their entwined arms seemed to imbue Fiore with some of Enzo's strength. But all that calm had vanished as they neared the palazzo itself and Fiore saw through the lattice just how many other vessels had gathered in tightly-controlled chaos to jostle for entry to the portico.

Now that they'd entered Ca' Grimaldi proper at last, Fiore's heart had crawled fully into his throat. He'd tried to tell himself no one would notice him amongst the throng—much less single him out as an impostor. Unfortunately all eyes had settled upon him and Enzo. Fiore could only imagine how his death-grip discomfited Enzo's arm.

"Are these sort of things always so crowded?" Fiore murmured into Enzo's ear.

"I suspect," Enzo whispered back, "that the guest list grew considerably once the hosts secured the notorious dueling duke's attendance."

Fiore's fixed smile became a true one despite himself. He beheld it reflected in Enzo's masked eyes.

It became difficult to tell, as they moved through the crowd, whether he or Enzo caught the more notice. This was, after all, the first instance of the dueling duke appearing in society since he gained his notoriety. But then again, if the gazes lingering on Fiore were any indication, whatever rumors had surrounded the dueling duke in shadowy intrigue had evidently not included a consort. Or at least not one of Fiore's particular make.

And yet Enzo didn't seem to feel the eyes as Fiore did.

Fiore recalled the experience of donning Enzo's bauta mask for himself—to be perceived without being perceived. Even so, he felt as though he could perceive Enzo as if the mask weren't even there. He wished he'd gone for the bauta himself rather than a mere domino, but he'd wanted his mouth to be seen by potential suitors so they might yearn to kiss it. If they could see only his lips then said lips would linger in their thoughts long after the whole of him had vanished back into the crowd.

The entryway proved but a fraction of the ball's splendor as Enzo led Fiore into the banquet hall. Provisions enough to satisfy the whole of Halcyon's navy were laid out across a vast round table. Oysters encircled the mighty centerpiece; a life-sized hippocampus sculpted from butter by a hand almost as skillful as Artemisia's.

Nerves had precluded Fiore's breakfast. He hardly noticed hunger pangs amidst the butterflies fluttering in his stomach. Only his wish not to make a fool of himself by wolfing down food at the ball's banquet could persuade him to nibble at dinner aboard the *Kingfisher*. Even so it hadn't settled.

Wine, however, he thought might do the trick. The banquet had many on offer, in every shade from reds deeper and darker than the blood in his own veins to vivacious sparkling whites that glittered to rival the resplendent crystal chandeliers overhead. The latter suited his palate. He didn't have to ask; a glance sufficed to send Enzo to retrieve a glass on his behalf. Fiore determined not to let his gallantry go unrewarded and told him so with another look—though how he took it one could hardly tell beneath the mask. Yet even amidst the ball's splendor Fiore had to admire the hollow-stemmed goblet, which he fancied would feel altogether weightless in his fingers were it not for the wine. The first sip began with the brightness of limonata and lingered with sweet almond. It sufficed to settle Fiore's nerves. He nodded to Enzo, and together they pressed on.

Scores of attendees had lingered in the entryway and the banquet hall. The ballroom seemed to hold hundreds more. Fiore, determined not to gawk at the city's richest splendors like the son-of-shepherds he was, forced himself not to crane his neck upwards to stare at the gilded domed ceiling or its magnificent fresco depicting youthful Achilles astride Chiron's back.

Instead he looked out over the crowd. He skillfully avoided any one person's gaze using the old performer's trick of fixing his own on a point on the wall over everyone's heads so each individual in the crowd felt he was but a glance away from meeting their eye. He'd learnt to do so in the conservatorio to combat stage fright—and this was after all a kind of performance.

In a surreptitious gesture that would've done any pickpocket proud, Enzo slipped Fiore an embossed card. It was not a script but rather a cast, with *Signor Fiore* printed across the top and a dozen titled gentlemen's names handwritten beneath. It took him a second glance to recognize what he'd only heard of in gossip columns and stories and never held in his hand until now; a dance card.

"How is it you've already compiled a list?" Fiore wondered. Enzo had hardly left his side, save for the mere moments required to procure the wine, and if he'd filled out a dance card in so brief a span as that then he was nothing short of a magician.

"I asked our host to assist me beforehand," Enzo answered, his masked smile evident in his voice.

"And what did you tell her?"

"The truth." Enzo shrugged. "That I had a particular friend I wished to introduce into the wider society of eligible gentlemen."

Fiore supposed that safe enough. "Anything for the duke's happiness."

Enzo made a queer humming noise that Fiore had come to understand meant he demurred. "Hardly an imposition for her, as she possessed a full list of her guests and knew which might be interested in making an offer to a handsome and talented man."

"If you insist." Fiore worked to keep his voice indifferent as he replied. He'd received similar compliments before, but to hear them fall from Enzo's lips gave his heart a small thrill regardless. He examined his dance card as much for distraction as for genuine curiosity. "It seems my first is with Lord Vazzoler?"

"Twelfth in line for the dukedom thanks to his eldest sister's grandchildren, but a viscount nonetheless—and rich enough for our purposes, I should think," Enzo added with a knowing smile glinting in his masked eyes.

Fiore endeavored to match it. "Then by all means, introduce us."

They found Lord Vazzoler awaiting them at the outskirts of the dance floor in the company of his friends. Or at least, Fiore presumed them so. They formed an intimidating coterie of glittering splendor in gowns and court suits alike. Many whispered behind fluttering fans at Fiore and Enzo's approach.

Enzo pointed Lord Vazzoler out to Fiore several yards before he ever espied them in turn. The viscount stood a hand's-breadth shorter than Enzo, though who could tell when all wore heels. Crow's feet had just begun to gather at the corners of his eyes. Streaks of grey at his temples shot like lightning bolts through the dark storm-clouds of his hair slicked back as if by rain. Fiore considered these all very handsome features but ones which marked the viscount as not quite old enough for his purpose. Still, he supposed it wouldn't hurt to give him a chance.

Lord Vazzoler stepped forward with a brisk bow. "Your grace."

Enzo returned the gesture and presented Fiore, who did his best to imitate them both. Several of Lord Vazzoler's companions, once they understood Fiore's purpose there, looked him up and down with appreciation and shot approving glances at the viscount. Fiore caught these out of the corner of his eye, for he kept his own gaze fixed on Lord Vazzoler. Let him feel as though, to Fiore, he were the only person in the whole ballroom. Judging by how the viscount's notice flicked to the bitten-back smile on Fiore's unmasked lips before meeting his gaze again, the stratagem was working.

The viscount held out his hand for Fiore's. "Shall we?"

Fiore delicately placed his left hand in Lord Vazzoler's waiting palm. With the other he passed his wineglass off to Enzo. All the while he never took his gaze off the viscount.

Lord Vazzoler's eyes flew wide for the barest instant. Then an appreciative smile caught at the corner of his mouth. Behind him, his friends' fans fluttered afresh with whispers. Fiore supposed few courtesans could boast a duke for a cup-bearer.

In truth Fiore would rather have had Enzo and Lord Vazzoler switch places. But he'd promised to give the viscount a chance, and so he allowed Lord Vazzoler to lead him out onto the dance floor proper. Leaving Enzo behind betrayed all his instincts. He kept his smile fixed on Lord Vazzoler regardless. Foolish Orpheus had lost his Eurydice by daring a backward glance. Fiore would not make the same mistake.

No sooner had they assumed their post amidst their fellow dancers than the viscount settled his hand onto Fiore's waist. Without a word of enquiry regarding Fiore's preference, the viscount stepped forward. Evidently the viscount intended to lead and didn't consider or didn't care if Fiore had other ideas. Fiore supposed he ought to have expected as much. Not every aristocrat could be as thoughtful as his Enzo.

He had some confidence in his ability to dance backwards, having practiced a little of it with Enzo; though it wasn't to either of their liking, it was nonetheless a valuable skill and one which proved its worth at present as the viscount advanced and Fiore withdrew.

Fiore could still feel the eyes of the entire ballroom upon him. But now he was performing. And, be it an audience of one or an audience of one hundred, he could feel how he had them in the palm of his hand. Since he didn't intend to accept the viscount's offer, there were no stakes beyond his own pride. This lifted a great deal of pressure from his performance. There were none who would not feel swept away by the sight of his grace. Already over the viscount's shoulder he caught the glances of a few who looked eager to have him for themselves.

He did not, however, catch Enzo's glance.

And he found he sorely missed it.

The music ceased. Fiore ended his step perfectly on the final note—despite having to do so backwards. The viscount bent to kiss his hand. Fiore smothered his irritation with a smile.

"Shall we find some refreshment?" the viscount asked as he arose, his arm already insinuating itself through Fiore's.

But they'd not gone two steps past the ring of revelers bordering the dance floor before a dark and welcome shadow swept over them.

"Your pardon," Enzo said to the viscount, coolly, as a duke had every right to do to his inferiors. He still held Fiore's wineglass safe in his delicate grasp.

The viscount released Fiore at once. He bowed to them both—far deeper than he had before the dance—and vanished into the crowd. Fans fluttered in his wake.

Fiore accepted his wineglass back from Enzo with a smile.

"All right?" Enzo murmured, laying a feather-gentle hand on Fiore's arm.

The hundreds of bodies crowded into the ballroom had made the air quite warm. Enzo's touch, even through his woolen coat and linen shirt-sleeve both, felt warmer still. It set Fiore's blood deliciously aflame.

As much as Fiore would've liked to indulge that heat, however, he had more pertinent business at hand. And so to Enzo he admitted, "The viscount is a touch too young for my purposes, I think."

Enzo nodded sagely.

Fiore sipped his wine and studied his dance card. "Del Cavallo?"

"A mere cavaliere," Enzo explained with an apologetic tone. "But wealthier than the viscount."

Fiore asked the most pertinent question. "How old?"

"If he is not yet in his sixties then his valet has done him a great disservice."

A snort of laughter escaped Fiore before he could hide the lower half of his face behind his dance card. Enzo's answering smile sparkled in his masked eyes.

"A point greatly in his favor," Fiore said when he'd recovered his composure. "Please show me to him."

They found the cavaliere in the company of several ladies his own age. Evidently they were all passing the time in the ageless tradition of gossip, for their fans ceased fluttering and a hush overcame them at Enzo and Fiore's approach—which Fiore chalked up to Enzo's intimidating shadowy presence rather than his own splendor.

The cavaliere wore his years well, with his wrinkles borne of smiles rather than scowls. Their lines deepened in delight as Enzo introduced him to Fiore. Fiore matched his smile in turn and bowed lower than he had for the viscount.

"A dance, Del Cavallo?" one of the ladies enquired dryly from behind her fan.

Rosy shades tinted the cavaliere's cheeks. He addressed his answer to Fiore rather than to his lady companion. "A slow rather than a spirited one, I'm afraid. If the gentleman will have me...?"

Fiore's smile grew into a grin. He stepped forward and boldly insinuated his arm into the crook of the cavaliere's.

"By all means," he declared, and had the satisfaction of seeing the cavaliere turn a shade pinker.

The cavaliere led him toward the dance floor. By the time they arrived the music had slowed, so they needn't wait long to begin a step in measure with the cavaliere's years. But the cavaliere unaccountably paused on the edge of the dance floor and, after a moment's hesitation, turned to Fiore with a question.

"Would you mind taking the lead?"

"If that is your preference," said Fiore, somewhat surprised but by no means adverse.

The cavaliere smiled. "Indeed, I prefer to be led by a handsome youth —if he is willing."

Fiore mirrored his smile. "Well, I may not be handsome, but for youth, I suppose I'll do."

The cavaliere's eyes widened and he began to stammer something about how he never meant to imply—but Fiore's laugh escaped him and revealed the jest. The cavaliere blinked and then joined him in a hearty chuckle.

Fiore bowed and offered the cavaliere his hand. He could almost see the fluttering of the cavaliere's heart in his awestruck gaze as he accepted. Fiore simply smiled and led him to join the dance.

Indeed, the cavaliere proved quite malleable. Like clay in Fiore's grasp, bending and remaking himself wherever Fiore willed. If this should extend to the bedroom, then it'd be more than Fiore dared hope for. He'd resigned himself to a life of getting fucked and feigning enthusiasm until his elderly patron passed on. This, by contrast, seemed perfect.

Which made it all the more confusing when it didn't feel perfect.

Fiore kept his serene smile pasted onto his face whilst his mind whirled for an explanation. He wouldn't have minded spending an evening with the cavaliere. Or several evenings. Or even multiple evenings a week for a number of years. Yet the thought of tying himself down to this particular gentleman didn't inspire feelings of ease or comfort. Rather, when he considered the matter, he found his heart pounded with the terror of a trapped beast. This was precisely what he'd searched for—the only thing good for him—the best he could possibly hope for—

And yet.

Again his gaze wandered away from his dance partner's face and glanced over the crowd in search of a particular mask. He didn't find it amongst the other dancing couples. Fiore didn't think Enzo could possibly be so hard to spot, no matter how vast the throng. His height alone marked him out. To say nothing of the wide berth his reputation afforded. Fiore could only conclude that Enzo wasn't dancing. Which seemed no less absurd than his disappearance. There couldn't possibly be a dearth of willing partners. Fiore might have only just debuted in society himself, but he knew enough of it to suppose Enzo's title and family connexions would encourage suitors. Even if Enzo were anonymous, his tall and striking figure moving through the crowd with remarkable grace must attract admirers. Perhaps, Fiore considered, he had an unfair advantage in knowing just how handsome the face beneath the mask truly was. But even in a mask, Enzo's calves alone were more than handsome enough to make up for an unknown face. Perhaps Enzo's fearsome reputation precluded finding a willing partner. Or perhaps he didn't wish to dance at all.

Or perhaps he wished to dance with someone in particular who'd yet to ask him.

The thought crossed Fiore's mind for but a fleeting moment. The burning brand it left behind felt as if it would last forever. He pushed it down into the darkest corners of his heart and forced himself to look into the cavaliere's face—as he was supposed to—and mirror the smile he found there. Wizened, but no less handsome for it. Verging on infatuated. Unable to even glance away from Fiore. He did his best to pretend he felt the same.

Whilst his mind returned again to the eternal question of Enzo.

There was a queer part of Fiore that felt some relief in not espying Enzo amongst the dancers. Upon reflection he hadn't thought of what might happen if Enzo danced with someone else. Which was an incredible oversight on his part—it was, after all, a ball, and he knew from their own practice sessions that Enzo was an accomplished dancer. Any one of their fellow guests would be privileged to have him on their arm for his grace alone. To say nothing of how desirable his family and rank must make him. And yet, as Fiore began to consider the matter, the thought of someone else dancing with Enzo sparked a slow simmer in his blood. He didn't know if he could handle the sight of Enzo dancing with anyone else. Which was absurd, because most of the people who fell into his bed had someone else awaiting them back home—and none of them had proved foolish enough to expect exclusivity without paying enough to provide him for life. It was particularly absurd in Enzo's case, when Fiore had already cast aside his offer.

Still, Fiore found himself wondering how Enzo could bear the sight of him in the cavaliere's arms. He dared another glance away from the besotted cavaliere. This time he searched through the crowd rather than amongst his fellow dancers. A hundred masked faces gazed back at him, none of them the one he wanted, until—there, just when he'd despaired of ever finding him again, a dark shadow loomed above the throng.

Fiore's heart leapt as it always did at the merest glimpse of Enzo. But in the lightning flash he had of Enzo's masked face now, he beheld something which gave him pause. From crown to heel Enzo remained covered. Save his eyes. And even from this distance, even in so brief a glance, Fiore beheld a look quite unlike the beatific ease with which Enzo had gazed down at him since they entered Ca' Grimaldi. Now, he saw only a wistful echo of a smile, overwhelmed by the unmistakable look of someone swallowing down their own heartache to make their beloved happy.

A look, Fiore realized, that Enzo wore only when he thought Fiore couldn't see him.

Fiore beheld him for but a heartbeat before the dance whirled him away. But the haunting gaze of those dark eyes lingered in his mind.

The dance came to its natural end. Fiore bowed and, in a stroke of inspiration he hoped might work some sympathetic magic, kissed the cavaliere's bejeweled rings. A delighted gasp escaped the cavaliere, almost too soft to hear above the general murmur of the crowd.

Whatever the cavaliere wished to express beyond that was silenced by the sudden arrival of a billowing shadow.

Enzo bowed to them both. "Your pardon."

The cavaliere granted it at once and withdrew.

Fiore twined his arm into the crook of Enzo's before he quite realized what he was doing. Enzo glanced down in surprise but seemed by no means displeased by this. Fiore smiled up at him and pretended it was his intention rather than mere instinct.

"What did you think of him?" Enzo asked in a low tone as he led Fiore away from the dance.

"Charming enough," Fiore admitted. "In his own way."

It didn't sound anywhere near convincing.

If Enzo noticed, he had the grace to pretend otherwise. "Shall I find you another?"

Fiore hesitated. His heart threw itself against his ribs. He'd always sought whatever he wanted with ease and assurance. Now, however, the thought of possible failure in this venture brought his anxiety to a hitherto unforeseen peak. And yet if he didn't ask, he would know himself as the worst sort of coward to ever grace Halcyon's canals. So he swallowed his heart down out of his throat and replied, "I think I have one in mind already."

"Oh?" Again, Enzo seemed astonished but not unpleasantly so.

Before Enzo could offer to escort him to his intended partner or anything else, Fiore summoned all his remaining courage and slipped his arm out of Enzo's grasp to make way for an elegant bow.

"May I have this dance?" Fiore asked, reining in his flailing nerves to keep his voice level.

Just to prove to himself that one dance was the same as all the others. To show beyond a doubt that all gentlemen were alike. To give himself a taste of what he thought he wanted so he could know that it wasn't half so good as he supposed it would be.

Enzo gave an astonished blink.

Fiore forced his smile not to tremble.

Another silent moment passed between them, in which all Fiore's hopes hung suspended. Then Enzo returned his bow.

"As you wish," Enzo murmured in the tone of one who hardly believed in his own good fortune.

Fiore could barely believe it himself.

It seemed as though they floated rather than strode onto the dance floor. Enzo laid his palm on Fiore's shoulder, relinquishing the other to Fiore's grasp. His hands felt warm, despite the layers of linen and satin between their flesh, warmer even than the incredible heat of the ballroom. Wherever Enzo touched him seemed to vibrate like a plucked lute string. His very blood sang.

The real music began. Enzo withdrew, inviting Fiore into his rightful place.

And Fiore dared to join him.

The whole ballroom fell away. It was just the two of them, now—just as it'd been when they'd practiced aboard the *Kingfisher*. Fiore relearned the intricacies of Enzo's body, just as he'd done on deck and below as well, in his own quarters, and again further back at Wolf's Head when Enzo had first fully revealed himself, and when Fiore had first beheld Enzo's face in the throes of ecstasy, and then further back still, to the barest glimpses he'd had of a form he'd grown far too fond of, when the mask had first fallen from his face whilst Fiore lay in his sickbed, and before that, the very first night, when Fiore knew only a dark shadow whose grace belied his size and strength. And now, despite looming over him, Fiore could lead Enzo through his paces as easily as a docile steed, as eager to please as any hound, and the utterly besotted look in his dark eyes was but the mirror image of Fiore's own feeling. Fiore hadn't truly enjoyed a single dance this evening. Not like this. And then—

The lift.

Enzo's thigh slid beneath his own. Raised him up. Fiore leapt to meet it. They spun together. His heart flew up beyond his body to join the divine frescoes overhead.

And again, it never seemed to come down.

He alighted on the floor with a grace that belied his new heels. Enzo's masked gaze smiled down at him. His pulse fluttered in his throat.

Fiore could deny his heart no longer.

And yet the thought of indulging it terrified him.

The music ceased all too soon. Enzo twined their arms together. They withdrew from the dance floor, withdrew from the ballroom entirely, all the way to the banquet hall and its fountains of wine. Enzo plucked up another sparkling goblet and offered it to him. Fiore shook his head. He didn't want Enzo to see how his fingers trembled.

"Another dance from your card?" Enzo suggested.

Fiore wondered at how he could even think of the card after a dance like that. But the smile in Enzo's voice didn't reach his eyes. And in those eyes Fiore saw something like what he'd glimpsed whilst dancing with the cavaliere. It sobered him enough to speak. "I've already made my choice."

Enzo restrained his astonishment to a single blink, which Fiore appreciated. "Whomst?"

Despite his nerves, a smile tugged at Fiore's mouth at the thought of the wonderful surprise he was about to give him, and how Enzo would appreciate it. Years of happiness spread out before them both—decades, if they were lucky. He had but to speak the word. His lips parted to set it free.

And his eyes fell upon a figure over Enzo's shoulder.

A shadow none so tall as Enzo, though it wore a similar tabarro cloak, conversed with a lady in a sapphire velvet gown. The red domino mask did little to disguise the features of the middling-aged gentleman who wore it. Nothing particularly remarkable in them; a small nose, a severe mouth, a smooth jaw, and eyes which shone for music alone.

Features which perpetually flashed through Fiore's nightmares.

It couldn't be him. It mustn't. And it was with this desperate hope that Fiore forced his heart out of his throat long enough to croak, "Who is that?"

Enzo turned to follow his line of sight. "The fellow in the red domino?"

"Yes," said Fiore, hardly able to gather breath enough for the word. "Him."

"Nascimbene," Enzo replied, returning to face Fiore. "Impresario of Teatro Novissimo."

Fiore couldn't leave off staring long enough to meet Enzo's gaze. From conservatorio singing instructor to lord over the city's premiere opera house. Nascimbene had certainly risen far in a mere decade.

"I don't know if he has any interest in beautiful young men," Enzo continued regardless of the wheels in Fiore's mind whirling so rapidly they felt as though they'd burst into flame. "But I might ask—"

"No," Fiore hissed. "It's not that, it's—"

Enzo stared down at him in utter bewilderment as Fiore struggled to force words out past the weight of what he must tell.

Over Enzo's shoulder, Nascimbene concluded his conversation with the lady with an elegant bow. He turned—away from Enzo and Fiore, Bellenos be praised—and strode off toward the banquet.

His retreat ought to have eased Fiore's fears. Instead, with the monster out of sight, he found himself imagining him behind every pillar, around every corner, lurking in every shadow.

Fiore twined his fingers through Enzo's hair. He retained his pasted-on smile even as he drew Enzo down so he might whisper in his ear.

"He killed Eliodoro."

# CHAPTER TWENTY-ONE

Enzo's first instinct bid him challenge the impresario to a duel.
He reined in the idea the instant it arose. As satisfying as it
might prove to plunge his blade through the monster's heart, to do so
now would hardly aid Fiore in this moment. At present the thing to do
was whatever Fiore asked of him.

But Fiore seemed hardly able to ask anything.

Enzo had glimpsed Fiore's fear before. In the throes of infection, with
more dread of the chirurgeon than the disease. And again at the hunting
lodge, whenever the chirurgeon came to tend Enzo's wounds—but then
it was fear tinged with a sort of protective rage, a bestial thing which
made Fiore as fearsome as his foes and far more beautiful. It'd taken a
more gentle form when they were again alone together and Enzo's
coughing fits overtook him. Then it'd shown itself in a glance Fiore
quickly hid behind a smile, but said smile had never quite reached his
eyes.

And now, while Fiore's beautiful bare lips smiled up at Enzo, his
domino-masked eyes were frantic.

Renewed determination seized Enzo's heart. He would make Fiore
safe again, whatever the cost. He mirrored Fiore's casual tone and
replied, "Shall we be off?"

But Fiore shook his head. The infinitesimal tremble hardly tousled a single curl, with smile still firmly fixed in place. "It wouldn't do to leave now. People might notice—draw conclusions—talk—" He gasped in a steadying breath and forced it out in a laugh; a sound no doubt charming to the ears of a stranger but horrific to Enzo's hearing. "We have to stay just a little while longer. One more dance at least. Then we may go."

Enzo didn't quite follow his logic but resolved to obey it nonetheless. Fiore's hand had clenched tight in his, a desperate grasp that begged him without words to understand.

"Another dance with me?" Enzo suggested.

A touch of sincerity approached Fiore's smile. "If you would be so kind."

Enzo took in the pallor cast over Fiore's face, his panicked gasps, the faint shiver of his arm in Enzo's own. "*Can* you dance?"

Fiore hesitated.

"Perhaps," Enzo suggested, keeping his voice low and gentle—for Fiore resembled nothing so much as a persecuted creature ready to bolt — "we might sit a spell on the balcony. You could refresh yourself in the cool night air. Catch your breath."

Fiore stared up at him as he spoke. At first his eyes flicked between Enzo's own. Then they settled, meeting his gaze and matching his steadiness. With every word from Enzo's lips his breath slowed, until at last, when Enzo had finished, he seemed almost approaching ease.

"Yes," Fiore replied. His smile had softened into something more genuine. "That would be lovely."

Enzo withdrew his hand from Fiore's rigid clasp and offered him his arm in its place.

Fiore entwined them together again at once in the grip of a drowning man.

They skirted the edges of the ballroom. Enzo indulged a quick dip into the banquet hall for a glass of sparkling wine which he thought might calm Fiore's nerves a little. He'd supposed correctly, judging by the glance of frail gratitude Fiore served him up in reply when he handed him a fresh goblet. Then they slipped away out onto the first balcony Enzo could find.

The first breath of fresh air seemed to do a great deal towards restoring Fiore's balance. Enzo led him to a stone seat beneath the rail overlooking the Grand Canal and the lagoon beyond. The moon had waned to the merest sliver, but the stars shone resplendent regardless.

Fiore looked more resplendent still, even in the midst of his horrors. It eased Enzo's heart to see him relax, inch by inch, moment by moment. After a while his hand ceased trembling and he could accept the wineglass from Enzo's grasp. A few sips restored him further. He broke off staring into the night and shot a pleading glance up at Enzo. Enzo swooped down beside him at once and, at another gesture—the slightest of shivers across Fiore's shoulders—drew his tabarro cloak over them both. Under its shield Fiore's trembling, at last, vanished.

"We can't leave."

The sound of Fiore's voice—smaller and softer than anything Enzo had heard from him in all their acquaintance—startled Enzo like a thunderclap. The words themselves proved no less confounding.

"Whyever not?" Enzo rejoined, keeping his voice low to match Fiore's.

Fiore stared up at him with a gaze that threatened to rend a heart of stone in twain. "Won't the gentlemen on my dance card be insulted?"

Despite himself Enzo scoffed. "Their wounded pride is nothing to your security."

A bitter laugh escaped Fiore. "Flattering their pride *is* my security."

Enzo opened his mouth to argue the point—that of course Fiore's feelings took priority—but before a single syllable dropt from his tongue, his mind flashed. Far from the ball and their present predicament, all the way back to a conversation early in their acquaintance regarding preferences, and the preference to be paid above all else, and how only repeated enquiry drew out what Fiore truly desired. In his mind's eye he saw again Fiore wincing as he pushed off the wall to greet him in the piazza, pushing through evident pain with a smile to accompany Enzo on a stroll, and all that a mere echo of the pain he must have pushed through to accrue such an injury in the first place. What else had Fiore pushed through to make his coin—to survive? He hadn't the fortune or the family connexions Enzo himself enjoyed, and while Enzo had a dim awareness of his own life's advantages, he'd never yet thought of Fiore's lack. How much Fiore must put up with from men like him day after day after day. How could Fiore afford to prioritize his own feelings when, in his own words—

*Flattering their pride* is *my security.*

"Enzo?"

A soft and gentle enquiry. Fiore's voice sounded sweeter than birdsong. It nonetheless fell like another thunderclap upon Enzo's ears and jolted him out of his horrific spiral. For Fiore to think of Enzo's distress now—a mere drop of misery in the howling tempest of Fiore's present predicament, with a monster from his past hunting him and him unable to retreat lest he lose his future hopes—

Aloud, Enzo replied, "To vanish mysteriously before the end of the evening would only serve to increase your intrigue and allure."

Which was true.

Fiore studied him in silence. His dark gaze flicked between Enzo's eyes. He worried his lip between his teeth. Then his hunched shoulders rolled back in resolve and he drew in a steadying breath. "Then by all means, let us go."

Enzo withheld a sigh of relief. "I'll have Carlotta summon the gondola. Won't take me a moment to find her."

Fiore tensed in his arms. In a voice Enzo now recognized as forced calm, he asked, "May I accompany you?"

"Of course." For, loathe as Enzo felt to drag poor Fiore around the ball whilst he searched for his manservant, he well understood how badly Fiore wished not to be left alone. And while Enzo might not have been a very good man, he was hardly cruel enough to leave Fiore behind now.

Enzo stood and offered Fiore his arm again. Fiore accepted it with a hand that did not tremble. Together they re-entered Ca' Grimaldi.

Their forward progress allowed Enzo to turn his mind to brighter thoughts. Fiore had agreed to leave. They were going together. All he had to do was find Carlotta and—

"Pray forgive my impertinence, your grace."

Enzo knew from his years at university that it was impossible for the flow of blood to reverse its course in one's veins. Yet he felt very much as if it did when the impresario's voice rang in his ears. He turned—a gesture that appeared as though he meant to address the speaker, but which in actuality placed his own body between Nascimbene and Fiore. He didn't speak. Best to let the mask do the talking. It was marvelous how often a stony, silent, stoic stare sufficed to send an unwanted supplicant on their way.

Tonight, however, Fortuna didn't smile on his efforts.

The impresario bowed. "Allow me to introduce myself—Nascimbene, at your service. I am impresario of the Teatro Novissimo. Our host informs me you wish to acquaint your companion with like-minded society. If it would not intrude on your designs, then perhaps..." He turned to Fiore, just visible over Enzo's shoulder. A smile one might mistake for sincere admiration spread across his lips. "Would you do me the honor of a dance?"

Enzo opened his mouth to inform Nascimbene—politely, but nonetheless firmly—that they were just about to withdraw from the ball and couldn't possibly accommodate his desires.

Fiore got there first. He mirrored Nascimbene's smile.

And to Enzo's horror, replied, "Of course."

~

Fiore's heart throbbed in his throat.

The visage that haunted his nightmares smiled upon him. It didn't help that he could feel Enzo staring down at him in utter confusion.

Fiore willed Enzo to understand. Bad enough if they should run out of the party after merely brushing past the impresario. Far worse if they vanished into the night immediately after he introduced himself. The connexion between Fiore and the impresario could not go unnoticed then. If, however, he indulged Nascimbene in a single dance—gave him a taste of what he wanted without leaving him wanting more—then perhaps they might escape without drawing undue attention.

He feared his resolve would break if he met Enzo's gaze for too long. So with a smile he perched on his toes and whispered directly into Enzo's ear.

"I'll be fine," Fiore said, working double to sound as unconcerned as he needed Enzo to feel. "Go find Carlotta. The dance will be done by the time you return."

It was hard to gauge the effect of his words when he withdrew. The bauta mask covered all. But it couldn't disguise the hesitant gesture before Enzo relented with a bow and swept off.

Leaving Fiore alone with his worst nightmare.

Nascimbene smiled and proffered his arm.

Fiore didn't know whether to feel grateful Enzo had listened or disappointed he hadn't put his heel down and dragged him away from all this. He pasted on his prettiest smile regardless and twined his arm into Nascimbene's snare. From the warmth and refuge of Enzo's company into the icy terror of the impresario's embrace—and he had only himself to blame.

"Shall I lead?" Nascimbene enquired when they reached the dance floor.

Fiore hadn't expected him to bother asking. Still, he knew the correct answer. "As you like."

Nascimbene's hands arranged themselves on Fiore's shoulder and waist.

Fiore thrust his brain forward to an hour when Enzo could carve the lingering sensation of the impresario's touch from his flesh.

The dance began.

On a purely technical level, Nascimbene was a very good dancer. Fiore supposed he ought to have expected as much given the man's profession and the arrangements he'd made to educate Fiore and the other sacrificial bellwethers in that particular art. He wondered if the impresario could recognize him through his dance form. If he did, he gave no sign of it in his face or manner.

They danced in silence for more than half the song, until—

"Are you enjoying the ball?" Nascimbene asked.

"Yes, Maestr—" Fiore cut himself off. Years of referring to Nascimbene as such had overwhelmed his better sense and forced his tongue into rote recitation of the man's title. Over the thunderous peal of his pulse in his ears, he told himself no one would notice the slip. Nascimbene was still a maestro, after all; just over the entire opera now rather than merely the flock of boys training toward their own demise.

Nascimbene smiled. "Please, call me Lotario. And what might I call you?"

Fiore felt an urge to bite out the man's tongue. Nascimbene offering up his own name meant nothing. He'd done it only to demand the same from Fiore, without snatching it from him outright, because reciprocity forced Fiore to give him his own in turn. Or, Fiore thought desperately, give him something else. Not his own name, necessarily. Just enough to keep the conversation flowing. A lie would suffice. If only he could think. The first name which came to mind—Enzo—wouldn't do for obvious reasons. There remained but one other name near enough to his heart for him to recall whilst his mind ran blank.

"Elio," said Fiore.

The resulting silence couldn't have lasted more than a fraction of a single heartbeat. It seemed to stretch on into eternity. Nascimbene blinked. For a moment, Fiore thought he might recognize the name. Recognize the reminder of his own sins. Recognize the name of the boy he may as well have murdered with his own bare hands.

But then Nascimbene smiled again. "A pleasure to make your acquaintance, Elio. You've probably heard so a hundred times over. But forgive me—there is something familiar in your face. Have we met before?"

Fiore's heart froze. He couldn't prevent himself from blurting, in a voice no one could mistake for coy flirtation, "No."

Nascimbene raised his brows. "Then it must be just that your face matches what my heart has long desired." He smiled on as he added, "Perhaps I've seen it in my dreams."

"Perhaps," Fiore echoed. Echoing was easy. Particularly with those who resembled Narcissus. Just feed them back a taste of their own reflection and they would delight in the flavor without ever suspecting its hollow core. Everyone had a touch of Narcissus in them.

*Everyone except Enzo,* his mind supplied, as if it were determined to prove as unhelpful as possible when he needed it most.

Nascimbene didn't seem to notice. "I realize my offer must seem audacious. Particularly when you've already dallied with viscounts and cavalieri. To say nothing of the duke himself. But I think I have the means to make a handsome young man very happy."

Fiore smiled and nodded.

"Do you enjoy opera?" Nascimbene enquired.

Fiore resisted the urge to throw him to the ground and stomp on his throat. He kept his smile fixed in place. "I haven't had the pleasure."

"No?" Nascimbene sounded astonished. "We must remedy that at the earliest opportunity."

This did nothing to assuage Fiore's murderous impulses. But, mercifully, the dance came to a close, and the applause rippling through the throng disguised his lack of an answer.

And, still more mercifully, no sooner had their dance halted than a most welcome dark shadow swept over them.

Nascimbene released his hold.

Before Fiore could blink, his arm was enfolded in Enzo's, and Enzo stood between him and the impresario. The bauta mask bent down to meet Fiore's ear.

"Carlotta is dispatched," Enzo murmured. "The gondola will be ready for us by the time we reach the portico."

Fiore had never heard such welcome tidings in all his days.

Enzo straightened and turned to Nascimbene. "Your pardon, signore. Good evening."

Nascimbene bowed and would doubtless have echoed the same parting words if a certain lady had not approached at that very moment.

"Your grace!" she gasped. Her fan fluttered furiously to regather her breath. Whatever her purpose, she had come with haste. "My staff tell me you intend to depart. I do hope our ball has not offended you?"

This, then, must be their host—the Lady Grimaldi herself. Fiore supposed he ought to have guessed from the splendor of her gown.

"Not at all," Enzo told her over Fiore's head. "On the contrary, we've enjoyed a most pleasant evening amongst delightful new acquaintances. Thank you again for indulging us."

Fiore could hear the polite smile in his voice, no matter how impassive the mask remained. He wondered at how Enzo could sound so satisfied. Perhaps he had encouraged his mind to wander back to earlier in the evening to their shared dance. It seemed so distant now. Fiore tried to recall it himself; twirling across the dance floor, Enzo welcoming him with every step, the two of them perfectly in time as if their very hearts beat as one, the sweeping flight of their leap—

Lady Grimaldi beamed. "You gratify us, your grace. Do come again.

The both of you," she added, turning her smile upon Fiore. "It is a pleasure to meet you at last, Signor Fiore, and I'm sure all my distinguished guests would say the same."

Fiore's heart ceased beating.

Before he could catch himself his eyes flicked to Nascimbene. Had he heard the discrepancy? Did he realize Fiore had given him a false name? Hearing Elio's name hadn't seemed to catch his notice, but perhaps the two names combined—did he even remember the names of the failed sacrificial bellwethers, or did they cease to occupy his thoughts the moment they escaped his grasp? Fiore had just time to glimpse a frown line deepening at the corner of the impresario's mouth. Then he mastered himself again, fixed his gaze on their host, and forced a smile.

"Good evening, Lady Grimaldi," Enzo intoned overhead.

Lady Grimaldi curtsied and withdrew from their path.

Which meant there remained no obstacle to prevent Fiore from half-dragging Enzo out of the ballroom and into the night.

# CHAPTER TWENTY-TWO

F iore hardly dared to draw breath again until he and Enzo were secluded and secure within the gondola.

Enzo likewise remained silent. He rapped his knuckles against the ribs of the felze's roof. The gondola slipped away from the portico into the canal proper. The brilliant lights of the party grew dimmer and dimmer through the woven wicker.

And still Fiore couldn't speak.

Enzo tore off his gloves and swept off hat, hood, and mask. An aedicula outside the felze as the gondola glided beneath a bridge threw precious little light on his features. It sufficed to show how his brow furrowed, how his teeth caught his scarred lip between them, and how his dark gaze shone with a mingled torment of deep concern and sincere regret. His bare hands tentatively reached for Fiore's. Fiore snatched them up in his grasp and clenched them tight.

"Are you all right?" Enzo asked. He sounded like the very first person in history to speak the question in sincerity.

Fiore knew not how to answer him. His heart continued pounding in his throat. His breath shuddered alongside the trembling that'd overtaken his limbs somewhere between the portico and wherever they floated now.

Enzo waited for a reply with more patience than Fiore deserved. Only then did he venture, however softly, to ask, "Is there anything I might do?"

Fiore had braced himself for questions. But not these. He'd expected Enzo to demand he account for his choices in the ballroom—why had Fiore stayed? Why dance with the impresario? Why make the hundred stupid decisions he'd somehow crammed into the course of a single evening?

But Enzo demanded nothing from him. As Enzo had never demanded anything of him.

For even in the midst of the ballroom's terrors, Enzo had taken charge without taking away Fiore's choice—seeing to it that Fiore was kept safe and whole and hale and as comfortable as could be considering the circumstances, and doing all in his power to whisk him away from danger, with only Fiore's own demands preventing him from doing more.

Which meant that, despite all the evening's horrors, Fiore had never felt more certain of his choice than in this moment.

Fiore opened his mouth to confess all.

But his voice would not emerge.

Enzo gazed back at him, brow furrowed in concern, still waiting to hear what he might do to alleviate Fiore's suffering. The silence drew out —too long, far too long, and if Fiore let it stretch any further it would snap like a bowstring and slash them both—

So Fiore leapt forward and kissed him.

Enzo gasped into his mouth. The gondola rocked beneath them. Fiore fell into Enzo's lap and Enzo, after going stiff with shock, melted into Fiore's embrace and returned it with a tenderness that made Fiore's heart feel as though it would shatter. He held Enzo all the tighter against it and kissed him again and again until his lungs burned as though he were drowning and then and only then did he dare draw back just enough to breathe.

His heart still flung itself against his ribcage. He was safe now, he reminded himself, safer with every passing moment, the gondola slipped further and further away from Ca' Grimaldi, and here in the seclusion of the felze no one could touch him. Except for Enzo, and Enzo would only touch him if he asked. Which he did now without words, clutching Enzo tight 'round the shoulders and curling himself up to fit into his lap.

Enzo trailed a gentle hand through Fiore's curls—he'd lost his hat somewhere in the gondola's rocking. His strong arms supported Fiore's weight with ease, and yet without trapping him in their grasp. Fiore couldn't see his face, but he could feel his worry in every attentive caress.

Fiore parted his lips again, determined to speak at least a fraction of the truth. But another lie fell out instead. "I'm fine."

Darkness was as good as a mask. Fiore hadn't the faintest inkling whether or not Enzo believed him.

But he felt more keenly than ever before the warmth coursing through Enzo's firm yet gentle hold around him.

They sat entwined together all the way back to the *Kingfisher*. It required considerable force of will for Fiore to disentangle himself from Enzo when they arrived. His pulse had calmed a little. His hands no longer trembled. At the very least he owed Enzo thanks for bringing him to the party and seeing him safely home. He opened his mouth to say all he'd meant to say before Nascimbene had spoilt everything.

"Won't you join me?" he blurted instead.

Silence reigned for one horrible moment that seemed to stretch out for eons.

Then, in a low and resonant murmur that sent calming reverberations throughout Fiore's own ribcage, Enzo replied, "Of course."

It hadn't been at all what Fiore intended to say. But at least he wouldn't have to face the rest of the night alone. He tried to smile as he led Enzo out of the felze, onto the ship, and below decks to his quarters. He failed at holding his hand in anything other than a drowning man's grip.

No sooner had the door shut behind them than Fiore fell upon Enzo. Again Enzo returned his embrace as if he were molded for it. Divesting each other of their suits was the work of mere moments; even so, Enzo did so with deliberate care for Fiore's silks and satins, which Fiore well appreciated. He had only one good suit, after all. Then Fiore had but to give Enzo the barest nudge towards the bed, and Enzo withdrew just as he had in the dance to let Fiore steer him there and lay him down upon it.

Not a word passed between them. More than ever before Fiore felt far more fluent in the language of touch rather than speech. His pulse still thrummed through his veins, sparkling like the wine in the banquet hall. He knew but one way to turn his fear to exhilaration, and mercifully, Enzo granted him this. Slipping inside Enzo's cunt felt as though the very core of him lay cradled safe within Enzo's firm embrace. Every thrust made his name a perpetual murmur on Enzo's scarred lips. Enzo's cock scattered ropes of liquid pearls. His cunt clenched 'round Fiore, and alongside the rising tide of his impending crisis Fiore felt the urge again to confess, to tell Enzo all he was to him, and all he wished they might be together. His lips already brushed against Enzo's ear; he had but to whisper the fated words. But with another thrust his spend was upon him. His breath caught. The words choked back. His opalescent tide spilled within Enzo's cunt. Ecstasy wracked his body and chased all fear from his mind. He thought only of Enzo and his gentle embrace and how deeply he wished they might remain entangled for all eternity, and all this dragged him down into the silent depths of sleep, broken only by the rising and falling of Enzo's chest beneath him, as steady as the waves lapping the lagoon.

"Fiore?"

He opened his eyes to find afternoon sunlight streaming through the porthole and Enzo sitting on the gunwales of his bed with a cup of coffee in each hand. He offered one to Fiore. Fiore dragged himself upright and accepted it with more gratitude than mere words could carry. Instead he expressed his thanks in a kiss. Enzo's gentle hand arose to caress his cheek, and if only Fiore could awaken like this every morning forevermore he might yet die content. When they parted, he drew back with the intent to confess all.

Instead he heard himself ask, "When shall I see you again?"

Because if Fiore told everything and it frightened Enzo away, he might never see him again. And if he clung to Enzo now, delaying his departure and whatever else he might do with his day, he would breed only resentment for his presence in Enzo's heart. This question, however, was perfectly safe and guaranteed Enzo's return.

Despite the commonplace enquiry, Enzo served him a stunned blink before he responded. "Would mèrcore be too soon?"

Not soon enough, by Fiore's reckoning. His heart plunged like an anchor into storm-tossed seas. But he kept his perfect smile fixed in place as he replied, "Not in the least."

By then he'd surely have figured out how to tell Enzo what he must.

Enzo arose and began to don his cloak and mask once more. Fiore resisted the urge to leap up and fling his arms around him to make him stay. He settled for standing and catching the door for him.

"I did have a marvelous time," Fiore assured him. *Despite all* went unsaid.

Enzo almost looked as though he believed him. He caught Fiore's hand in his gentle grasp and brought it beneath the bauta mask to kiss his knuckles with heartbreaking tenderness.

"As did I," Enzo murmured into Fiore's hand. Then, with evident reluctance, he released his hold and departed.

Fiore's fixed smile faded the instant he shut the door on Enzo's retreat. He could've kicked himself for getting distracted and not telling Enzo how he really felt. He'd allowed the ghosts of his past to cloud his future. First Nascimbene had stolen Eliodoro from him, and now…

Now, Fiore knew not what to do.

If it were an insincere confession, Fiore would've known exactly how to proceed. He'd heard (and made) plenty of those over the years. But he knew not how to make himself sound when he meant every word he spoke. How to speak from the heart when his fears blocked up his throat. It was rather like stage fright, only a thousandfold worse, because on the stage he'd stood before strangers. He knew not how soft their smiles appeared in candlelight, how their breath caught in the throes of passion, how their hair tousled across their face in the morning after, and how gentle their touch proved when he required it most. Their opinion mattered nothing. Enzo, however…

Perhaps, Fiore thought, he could solve the problem in a similar way. Actors rehearsed their speeches. Fiore supposed he must do the same. The thought of talking to himself whilst pacing his quarters seemed foolish beyond words. Yet it could feel no more stupid than his half-a-dozen failed attempts thus far.

But before he even reached that point he required a script. To that end, he brought out his zibaldone. The blank page intimidated him more than ever. He comforted himself with the notion that he could always tear out his failures and burn them afterward. He plucked up his pencil alongside his courage and began.

*Enzo—I've decided to accept your offer.*

Far too formal. Fiore struck it out and tried again.

*Enzo—I've chosen you after all.*

Too glib. He struck it out. Another attempt.

*Enzo—If your offer still stands, then*

Then what? Fiore stared down at the words that had emerged from his pencil almost without thought. Enzo had made his offer months ago. Before he'd nursed Fiore through deathly illness. Before he'd invited Fiore to his ancestral hunting lodge so Fiore might perform the same service for him. And while the events of the ball had only strengthened Fiore's resolve, they might well have cooled Enzo's desire. Fiore had allowed himself to show unforgivable cowardice. He wouldn't blame Enzo for losing all possible respect for a man who couldn't even attend a party without falling to pieces.

A knock fell upon his cabin door.

Fiore glanced up sharp. Nothing followed the knock. Which forced him to swallow down his nerves and attempt an even tone as he enquired, "Who goes there?"

Any hopes or fears that Enzo might have returned were dashed at the sound of Serafina's voice. "There's a gentleman at the bar looking for like company."

A distraction. Just the thing he needed. "I'll be up shortly."

Serafina's footsteps echoed away into the depths of the ship.

Fiore tempered his mixed disappointment and relief as he shut his zibaldone and set it aside. He felt glad indeed he'd chosen to compose his magnum opus in writing rather than in rehearsal. The sheer humiliation if Serafina had overheard him...

Even as he stepped up on deck, he retained some small hope that it might be Enzo after all. But as his gaze flicked over the already bustling crowd that'd gathered to while away the evening with drink and dance, he found no familiar black bauta mask, nor even a servant in the black-and-silver Scaevola livery. He supposed either Enzo or his staff would've just come belowdecks themselves rather than ask him to meet them above.

Perhaps, he thought as he wound his way through the throng, his mysterious gentleman caller was an admirer from the ball. If so, Fiore knew not whether to entertain them or send them on their way. If Enzo withdrew his offer—which he had every right to do, in Fiore's mind, given how Fiore had toyed with him these past months—then…

Corelli caught his eye as he approached and jerked her chin towards a particular patron amidst the clamoring crowd at the bar.

The fellow stood quiet, solitary amidst the many, with only his fingertips tapping against the bar betraying his unease. He wore a well-groomed moustache and an artisan's garb. He didn't appear much taller than Fiore himself, though of a slightly stockier build and about a decade older. His dark hair had grown just long enough to tie back in a queue but not nearly as long as Enzo's. Though if Fiore had compared any gentleman against Enzo, he would find them wanting.

This particular fellow turned at Fiore's approach and swept his gaze up and down his frame. "You're the courtesan, then?"

"One of two," Fiore replied, smiling to smooth over the gruff introduction. "Though I'm told you prefer like company."

The fellow swallowed hard. "Can I buy you a drink?"

"You can buy more than that," Fiore told him with another easy smile.

Most gentlemen took the hint at that point. Some took him up on the offer. Others declined and departed.

This fellow, however, seemed indecisive.

Which still wasn't unusual in Fiore's line of work. He'd assisted several gentlemen who felt ill-at-ease with their own desires, and only through patient and gentle coaxing could they be persuaded to ask for what they wanted, much less receive it. To this end, Fiore gave the fellow an encouraging smile.

The fellow did not return it. "Let's start with a drink."

Again, not the first of Fiore's gentlemen to require liquid courage to seize their chance with him. Perhaps it was his first time with a courtesan. Or perhaps his first time with another man. Or perhaps even his first time with anyone. Nothing Fiore hadn't dealt with before. And handily.

The fellow ordered two glasses of wine. Corelli poured them. The fellow took them from her and handed one to Fiore. Not a strictly necessary gesture—they sat at the bar side-by-side, and Corelli had put down the glasses between them both—but perhaps the fellow meant to play the gentleman. Fiore accepted it with his most graceful smile. Which only seemed to throw the fellow off further.

The fellow cleared his throat and raised his glass.

Fiore clinked the rims together and took a sip. It tasted a little off. Not Corelli's best. Perhaps she meant to make the most of the barrel before it turned to vinegar.

Though vinegar ought to taste sour, not bitter.

Too late, Fiore realized his mistake.

He'd already swallowed. His eyes darted from his glass to the fellow. What incredible sleight-of-hand he'd possessed to dose the wine so quickly and without Fiore or Corelli noticing.

Any doubts as to guilt vanished as their eyes met and Fiore found all the fellow's nerves had vanished. He now looked quite satisfied. A smile that otherwise might have appeared handsome grew beneath his moustache.

Corelli was at the opposite end of the bar engrossed in the needs of a half-dozen other customers. Even if Fiore shouted, which he wasn't sure he could do just now with his tongue heavy as an anchor in his mouth, she'd never hear him over all the music and laughter and talk. He set his glass down—hard—far harder than he'd intended to. whatever was in the wine worked fast; he'd already lost a great deal of grace—and tried to raise his arm to alert her.

The fellow's fingers encircled his wrist before he even saw his hand move. "Shall we dance?"

Fiore wanted nothing more than to tear that smile off his face with his teeth. He summoned what little strength remained to him and lurched to his feet. The deck tilted under him as if the ship had sailed out again to sea.

The fellow caught him with one arm about his waist and the other around his shoulders. "Steady, mate."

Fiore despised the fellow's laugh. He tried to tear himself away. All he accomplished was treading on another dancer's toes.

"Forgive my friend," the fellow told the stranger. "Rather deep in his cups. Come on, then," he added to Fiore with that same false smile. "Let's get you somewhere to sleep this off."

The fellow strode into the crowd. Fiore, entangled in his arms and incapable of standing without his support, had no choice but to follow.

A particular figure emerged from the throng. Tall. Dark-garbed. Yet thrice-fold too broad to be his Enzo. The strange giant fell into step beside Fiore, opposite the mustachioed fellow, and clamped a massive hand on Fiore's shoulder. For one fleeting instant he thought he might be rescued.

Then the mustachioed fellow exchanged a speaking, smiling glance with the strange giant.

And Fiore knew he was lost.

The strange giant's great bulk more than sufficed to obscure Fiore from view altogether. Neither Serafina nor Corelli would witness his disappearance. A hundred strangers surged around him. None had noticed anything amiss. A wave of despair joined the rising tide of Fiore's fear. Shadows crept into the corners of his eyes, growing in pulses that matched the throbbing in his skull.

His captors steered him towards the gang-plank leading off the ship. Where they took him from there, he knew not, as the shadows overcame him and he pitched headlong into darkness.

# CHAPTER TWENTY-THREE

"...Enough for proof, at least."

The voice echoed through Fiore's muddled mind as if from underwater. He came up from it by degrees, each breath he drew stronger than the last, and every pulse of his heart cleared some of the fog from his vision, until he had a clear view of where he lay.

And beheld a field of bones.

Thighbones, he realized from their size and straightness; human thighbones stacked atop each other like planks to craft a wall of death that arose into flickering shadow. At the very pitch he could just barely perceive a vaulted ceiling of further bones, ornamented with skulls.

Isola dei Cadaveri, his addled mind supplied as he stared up in horror. The island of corpses, where hundreds of years ago the city had dumped the victims of the first plague. Then just a hundred years afterward, as Gnaeus had detailed to Fiore in his peculiar pillow-talk history of Halcyon, the following prince had demanded them all excavated and rearranged in a more orderly fashion. Thus emerged the ossuary labyrinth of Halcyon's catacombs, each chamber walled off as it filled with what bones wouldn't fit in its walls. Some of these chambers, according to legend, remained accessible only at low tide and had been hollowed out for criminal purposes.

And one of those chambers, Fiore understood with deepening horror, must be where he lay now.

He willed his leaden limbs to move. His arms tangled with each other behind his back, making his shoulders burn. His knees he found bent double and locked in an uncomfortable yet disturbingly familiar position. An attempt to straighten them as he tried to bring his arms around the front revealed the dreaded truth; he was bound together hand-and-foot.

Just as the impresario had ordered for his failed emasculation.

Fiore's heart leapt into his throat even as he willed himself not to panic.

He rolled his head across the stones—just stones, he lied to himself, ordinary paving stones and not the buried skulls of plague victims past —to see where the watery voices stemmed from. They'd continued murmuring amongst themselves throughout his awakening and subsequent brief examination of his circumstance.

His eyes fell first upon a hooded lantern set on the floor to cast its dim light throughout the cramped chamber. Then on the three legs of a simple stool not far off and the scuffed leather boots of the man who sat upon it. He followed these up to behold the self-same bulky brute who'd spirited him away from the *Kingfisher*, hunched over in conversation with his companions. A man who resembled him enough to pass for his brother, if not his twin, sat on a similar stool beside him, supporting his heft with his hands braced against his splayed thighs. The major difference between him and the brute lay in his face; his nose was cocked to the left, as if someone had broken it flat against his cheek and then pulled it out again only halfway. A third identical stool stood abandoned. The man who ought to have occupied it—the very same mustachioed fellow who'd slipped Fiore the drugged drink—paced what few strides he could in their confined setting.

"We don't need him alive for proof-of-life," said broken-nose. "The duke won't know the difference between a live ear and a dead one once it's off."

Both Fiore's ears burned to hear it.

"The duke will know the difference," the mustachioed fellow insisted, to Fiore's relief. "He studied medicine at university. *Actually*

273

studied, mind—not just flitting about to celebrate his own consequence. He'd be a chirurgeon himself by now if it weren't for his dueling. He knows where the blood ought to be in a live-cut limb. He knows how long it takes a body to grow cold. He knows when the stiffness sets in and when it leaves off. Why d'you think the staff are so afraid of him? The duke loves a corpse."

Broken-nose snorted and gestured to Fiore without looking at him. "He certainly loves a corpse now."

"My point being," the mustachioed fellow continued with a note of frustration, "we ought to keep him alive until we have the money in hand."

"Fair enough," broken-nose conceded.

This seemed to appease the mustachioed fellow. "The only question remaining, then, is which part to send as proof."

"Whatever it is," said broken-nose, "we should cut it off while he's still asleep. Less of a struggle."

"He's awake already," said the brute.

Both broken-nose and the mustachioed fellow appeared as surprised as Fiore felt to hear the brute speak. Their astonished glances quickly shifted from their compatriot to Fiore, who could do nothing but stare back at them in horror. The mustachioed fellow's alarmed expression shifted hastily into a veneer of control. Broken-nose, meanwhile, simply let a slow smile creep across his lips—but it never reached his eyes.

"You'll have as much money as you could ever wish for," Fiore blurted. His first words emerged slurred, but by the end of it he had his tongue under his command. "So long as I'm returned alive."

Broken-nose chuckled. "And I suppose you want a say in what we send off to your patron?"

Fiore didn't want to admit the truth of that. He forced himself to nod nonetheless.

The brute spoke up again. "Perhaps we could get proof by finishing what the impresario started."

Fiore's heart ceased beating.

To his credit, the mustachioed fellow appeared disturbed by the suggestion, if the way he whipped his head 'round to stare at the brute proved any indication. Broken-nose didn't seem surprised in the least.

Fiore willed his voice not to tremble as he replied, "If you take that, the duke won't want me returned—alive or otherwise."

A stunned silence fell. Only the dripping and lapping of unseen water remained.

Broken-nose raised an eyebrow. "Is that what the duke values?"

Fiore put on his most nonchalant tone. "You'd be surprised."

"Very well," the mustachioed fellow cut in. "An ear, then. As we discussed before."

"Would the duke know an ear?" the brute wondered aloud.

"Why not?" the mustachioed fellow scoffed.

Broken-nose levelled him a severe look. "Would you know your lover's ear?"

"Which one?" replied the mustachioed fellow. Then, "Oh."

"Something he touches more oft than an ear," the brute mused as if to himself. "Or what touches him. Besides the prick, I mean."

Broken-nose laughed.

Fiore tried to concoct his escape even as he listened with increasing dread to their plans of mutilation. There were three of them to his one. They had him tied hand-and-foot. Even if he somehow rolled past them into the water, he'd only drown. No doubt they'd counted on that when they chose this place to hold him. And even if he dared to scream, none would hear him save the bones. He wasn't blindfolded, though, which he counted as a small victory.

Until he realized that without a blindfold there was nothing to prevent him identifying his kidnappers after they returned him to Enzo's keeping.

Which meant either they were very stupid—Fiore didn't dare hope for that—or they had no intention of letting him live long enough to set Enzo on their trail.

The mustachioed fellow's voice broke through Fiore's trance of mute horror.

"A hand?" he suggested, twirling his own.

Fiore's stomach plummeted into an abyss.

"Surely a courtesan's hands see a great deal of use," the mustachioed fellow continued. "Lingering caresses, long strokes…"

An unanticipated rage flared in Fiore's heart. Even in the midst of his own peril, he found he had nothing but contempt for his captor's musings on what intimate moments had passed between him and Enzo. How dare this wretch speculate on what he could never understand.

"Fingers," broken-nose declared. "Not hands."

The mustachioed fellow cut himself off mid-pace. "Why?"

"Only two hands," broken-nose explained. "Whereas, with ten fingers, we've ten chances at getting our money. Or at least more than two. If it takes beyond three, we may have to reconsider whether the duke is willing to pay at all."

"He's willing," Fiore hastened to assert.

Broken-nose spared him a bemused glance. But even as he looked at Fiore, he spoke to his compatriots. "Get his hand out."

Fiore hardly had time to flinch before the two men fell upon him. With the swiftness of sailors they had him untied and tied again—hauled up onto his knees—his right wrist caught up in the brute's massive paw—a stool dragged before him—his hand slammed onto its seat and forced to splay—the mustachioed fellow with his blade thrust into the hooded lamp's flame—then broken-nose coming around behind him to put another dagger to his throat.

"You won't kill me," Fiore said. "I'm no use to you dead. You said so yourself."

Broken-nose's voice held a cold smile. "When I slit your throat, your heart will still beat long enough to bring blood to your finger. But you're right," he added, to Fiore's surprise. "We may need another one or two from you alive before the duke sees the wisdom in meeting our demands. So if the threat of death won't keep you still, perhaps this will."

And so saying, he lowered the blade from Fiore's throat and slipped it along the inside of his thigh to the root of his prick.

Fiore wished he'd had the foresight to shut up.

The mustachioed fellow drew near. Fiore's arm trembled in the brute's grasp. He shut his eyes—his captors already knew him for a coward, he'd gain nothing by seeing what they did, and if he couldn't keep still a worse fate would befall him.

Fiore tried to turn his mind towards other matters. He wanted to think of Enzo and how glad he'd be to see him again when all this was done and how he could finally tell him he'd chosen him. He delved into his own memories of happier moments; strolling through the artist's studios, dancing at the masked ball, basking in their shared glory after an indulgent afternoon of love-making, the final night of Saturnalia when a mysterious bauta had first wandered into his life, and the moment when, at long last and after guiding him through the worst throes of fever, Enzo had slipped off his mask altogether and Fiore had beheld his beautiful face...

Instead, his mind went further back. The taste of laudanum in wine. Awakening to find himself face-to-face with a horrible, glass-eyed, beaked mask. The singing maestro impatient with the fools he'd hired to hold down the boy and keep him quiet. Tied hand and foot behind his back. Men forcing his knees apart. A hot knife against his tenderest flesh. Knowing this was the moment Eliodoro had warned him of, and he must escape.

And as he screamed, both now and then, Fiore wondered if the singing maestro would find it musical.

∾

A light rapping fell on the alchemy workshop door, followed by Carlotta's indifferent intonation of, "Luncheon, m'lord. And a letter as well."

Enzo set down his book and looked up from his desk. "Enter."

The heavy black-walnut door swung inward to reveal Carlotta bearing a silver salver laden with brioche, coffeepot and cup, and a small package bound up in twine and brown paper. She maneuvered the salver into an empty place on the workbench that ran down the center of the chamber. Then she bowed and withdrew, shutting the door again behind her.

From what seemed the very minute Enzo had returned to Halcyon after his disgraceful departure from university, the alchemical workshop of Ca' Scaevola had felt like his own sanctuary. Mother's interests lay abroad, Lucrezia's interests lay in the prince's palace, and Giovanna's interests lay in the countryside, which left no one in the family to bother with amateur scientific pursuits. And so Enzo had the whole queer cabinet of curiosities to himself. Its decorations—and its peculiar musk, the result of centuries of alchemical residue seeping into every corner of its work-bench—reminded him just enough of the libraries and laboratories he'd left behind to keep him from going mad with missing university. And it allowed him the space and materials to continue certain experiments into peculiar anatomy. The archived journals of his late great-aunt, in particular, proved very fruitful indeed.

Even when not involved in study or experimentation, he found the workshop had a restorative atmosphere. The desiccated crocodile suspended from the ceiling felt like an old friend within the span of a mere fortnight. And just now, freshly bathed and scraped after his morning fencing lesson, he sat without a waistcoat at the cylinder desk between the life-sized charts of zodiac man and wound man reading an adventurous novel entirely for leisure.

Enzo marked his place in his book with a ribbon, then arose and approached the workbench. He'd sated himself with sarde en saor immediately following his fencing lesson, so the brioche held little urgency for him. Coffee proved a more tempting prospect.

But none so intriguing as an unexpected package.

Enzo took it up from the salver and turned it over. It had no wax seal or any other sign to show who had sent it. It was rather small, fitting easily into his palm, yet felt somewhat heavier than he expected. Whatever it contained did not seem uniform in shape. He raised an eyebrow, untied the string, and folded back the brown paper.

A severed human finger lay in his hands.

The digitus secundus, his mind supplied, alias the forefinger. A grown yet youthful specimen, slender and elegant, tapering ever so slightly towards the nail. It oughtn't have shocked him so much as it did. He'd held stranger things before. Many of them also human organs.

But this particular one held a disturbing familiarity. And an instant afterward, he realized why.

He had held it before.

He had kissed it. He had drawn it into his mouth. It had caressed him in turn, its teasing touch lingering on his skin. It had entwined and interlaced with his own over and again. It had torn furrows into his back and silenced his lips and traced the curve of his ear and delved within him and gripped him with as much strength as elegance—

And now, detached from the whole, it appeared curiously delicate and frail.

It was a jest, Enzo told himself. Fiore playing a prank in waxwork with the assistance of his sculptor friend. But no sooner had Enzo conceived this lie than his own well-practiced eyes confronted him with the truth of flesh and blood. Particularly the frayed edges of veins, arteries, ligatures, and nerve-strings spilling out of its ragged end.

And particularly as he dared, at last, to pick it up between his own fingertips and heard his heart sing at the familiar touch even as it plummeted at the awful truth of the matter.

He knew not how many minutes he wasted simply staring at it. Far too long. When at last he could tear his gaze away from it, his eye fell upon the wrapping, which he realized belatedly had a missive of its own inscribed on the interior.

*We have your musico. Leave one hundred zecchini in the fountain of Isola delle Merlettaie by midnight if you want the rest of him.*

A pulse of rage and fear struck him like a thunderbolt through his chest. For some moments it left him unable to think, much less move.

When he recovered himself at last, he found half the note crumpled into his fist. He set it down and smoothed it flat again. Then he rang the bell-pull.

Carlotta arrived within the minute.

"Find whoever accepted this delivery," Enzo commanded. "Bring them here. Now."

Carlotta asked no questions. She simply nodded and vanished back down the corridor from whence she'd arrived.

Which left Enzo alone with his racing thoughts.

His gaze dropt again—as it must—to Fiore's finger. A tooth if knocked out could be preserved in milk for a time until the means were found to put it back in its proper place. The same principle might hold true for a severed limb. Particularly one so small as this.

But as Enzo delicately picked up the finger again for a closer examination, he realized his error. Even if by some miracle Fiore returned to him within the hour, the digit was already cold and the wound itself half-cauterized. The thought of some sadistic wretch thrusting their knife into coals to bring its red-hot blade against Fiore's innocent flesh sent a spike of rage through Enzo's veins. He tempered it with the grim conclusion that the risk of infection would prove too great to attempt a reattachment. Particularly when it had almost no chance of success. He would never toy with Fiore's life so. The finger would have to be preserved as a wet specimen until Fiore himself could decide what was to be done with it. The alchemy workshop was the very place to do so; he had the jars and the means to whip up the alcohol solution within a quarter-hour.

Except Enzo found he could not persuade himself to set the finger down again. As cold as it felt cradled in his palm, some foolish part of him held the hope that he could imbue it with his own vital warmth, so long as he didn't relinquish his hold.

And so he remained standing at the workbench, staring down at all he had left of his heart in his hand, whilst his mind churned with horrors.

As to who had taken Fiore and ordered his mutilation, Enzo knew at once. Such deeds could only be the work of the Delfin family. They had taken their ease in taking their revenge, but all the better for them, waiting until Enzo truly had something to lose.

A mere trifle of one hundred zecchini could not sate them. Lucrezia had already paid them a king's ransom, let alone a courtesan's. They had a taste of what they wished for in maiming Fiore. Enzo doubted anything short of butchery would slake their thirst for blood. The Delfini would not return their hostage even if they received all their demands. If Enzo disfiguring their heir in a duel had earned this much of their ire, then their pride would find satisfaction in nothing less than murder. And what sanguineous delight they would take in dangling the hope of his heart's return before his eyes, only to snatch it from his chest and rend it asunder.

No, mere coin would not see his Fiore safe again.

"You wished to see me, m'lord."

Enzo jerked his head up and whirled toward the voice. He found one of the footmen standing on the threshold, with Carlotta awaiting just behind him.

"Alvise," said Enzo. He picked up the note and, still cradling Fiore's finger in his other hand, approached the footman. He held out the note for his inspection, flipping it over to show its back as well. "Did you receive this package?"

Alvise nodded with furrowed brow.

Enzo showed him Fiore's finger.

Alvise paled, but to his credit, he did not balk.

"Who delivered it?" Enzo enquired. The effort he made not to shout forced his tone into something low and cold.

Alvise likewise limited his expression of alarm in a mere widening of the eyes. "A messenger."

"In what livery?"

"None."

Enzo's patience wore thin. "What did they wear, then? What color? What cut? Their hair, their height, their stance—anything. Now."

Alvise swallowed hard. "He seemed like any other errand-runner. Freelance. Nothing he wore particularly fine or particularly ragged. About middling height."

"Young or old?"

"Middling aged as well, I'd suppose."

Enzo appreciated his efforts regardless of what little fruit they bore. "And his face?"

Alvise winced with a helpless half-shrug. "Forgive me, m'lord. I didn't think anything of the matter at the time..."

Enzo understood despite his disappointment. "Would you know him if you saw him again?"

Alvise nodded almost before Enzo had finished speaking, doubtless eager to do anything to allay Enzo's fabled wrath. While Enzo had never shouted at the staff, much less struck them, the reputation of one who'd dueled a fellow university student nearly to the death proved difficult to overcome.

And so Enzo withheld his considerable frustration. "Thank you. You may go."

An almost-silent sigh of relief escaped Alvise. He bowed and departed.

Carlotta remained.

"I suppose the prince will wish to hear of this," said Enzo, bitterness seeping into his words. "But I have some tasks for you before you inform her."

Carlotta acknowledged this with a deep nod.

"I require one hundred zecchini from the vaults. Send for Dr. Venier and Dr. Malvestio. And summon Zanetta, Ferruzzi, and Canello to me."

Whatever Carlotta thought of the demand for gold, chirurgeons, and three members of the household guard, she kept to herself as she bowed and withdrew.

Enzo shut the door after her. Now was the time to preserve the finger as a wet specimen. To keep it safe and secure. To set it aside at last and turn his mind over to the matter of readying himself to unleash his fury on those who'd dared touch his Fiore.

And still he could not do it.

He continued to stare down at the pale slender fragment of Fiore in his palm. What horrors was he enduring even now? What else had his captors done to him in the precious minutes—or, Bellenos forefend, hours—since they'd mutilated him? Did he know Enzo would come for him, or did he think himself abandoned? Whatever Enzo himself suffered, Fiore's agonies must be a hundredfold.

Enzo's fist closed gently around Fiore's finger. Then, as his instincts bid him, he slipped it into his waistcoat pocket, just over his heart.

～

The throbbing agony in Fiore's hand almost outweighed the burning ache in his joints as he lay curled backward on his side amidst the bones. The hot knife hadn't worked quite like he or his captors had hoped. Blood poured down his hand, swiftly turning cold in the damp darkness. It didn't do much for the chafing of the ropes against his wrist. But it did make his skin more slick, and this, combined with the fact that, like or not, he now had a hand that much smaller and more slender, gave him some distant hope of escape. He tried to lift his mind above the pain to think of a plan.

Fiore knew not how Enzo would react to the demand for ransom. Perhaps he would ignore it, thinking the price too dear for a mere courtesan, when hundreds or thousands of others remained in the city for him to peruse. Or perhaps, the more desperate and romantic corners of Fiore's mind supplied, Enzo might demand to have Fiore brought to the drop-site in the flesh to prove he lived and hand over gold-for-courtesan all in the same transaction. Though, his more practical side argued, he didn't know if that would make matters better or worse for him.

Particularly given how well he knew his captor's faces.

The mustachioed fellow, who'd gone to deliver the demand to Ca' Scaevola, gave no hint upon his return of how Enzo had taken it. Fiore supposed he hadn't met with Enzo face to face. Otherwise he'd never have come back alive.

Broken-nose and the brute had hardly spoken a word between them in all the uncounted minutes Fiore spent alone with them in the dark. With the trio together again, however, conversation sprouted. It seemed the mustachioed fellow couldn't bear a silence. Instead, he bore a pack of tarot cards, to which his cohorts readily assented.

The game began and ran on for what felt like days or hours. His captors drank, ate, laughed, and muttered together in apparent conviviality with little concern for their captive's thirst or hunger. The game ended. Coins passed back and forth. The mustachioed fellow shuffled and dealt again. And again. And again.

Then, as another game ended, the conversation took a turn.

At first Fiore knew not what they said, for they kept their voices far too low for him to discern individual words. He assumed they argued over the game. More than a few duels in the city had been fought over money lost or won at cards. A cleverer or more dexterous hostage might have used their discord to his advantage. Fiore couldn't think of anything clever to say over the constant ache throbbing through his bones, and no matter how he twisted his wrist, he couldn't get even his bloodied hand free of the ropes.

But as his captors' discussion grew more heated, the volume

increased, until the mustachioed fellow arose above the rest to deliver a blistering solo.

"Of course I'm going to pick up the money!" he hissed, incensed. "I'm the one who knows the territory, I'm the one who knows the duke—"

"I think," said broken-nose, "you know too much."

Dripping water sounded loud as any downpour in the resulting silence.

After taking a moment to recover himself, the mustachioed fellow seemed to find his courage. He crossed his arms and lifted his chin so far that he almost looked down his nose at his taller cohort. "You think I shouldn't be the one to go, then?"

"Oh, you're still going," said broken-nose. He jerked his head at the brute. "And he's going with you to keep you honest."

The mustachioed fellow stared at him. In a voice flat with disbelief, he echoed, "Honest."

"You know the duke so well," broken-nose explained, as calm and collected as ever. "Who's to say you won't offer to sell him the criminal scum who stole his musico?"

The mustachioed fellow continued staring.

"Even if you just run off with the bag yourself alone," broken-nose continued, "you've already tripled your pay by not giving us our fair share."

The mustachioed fellow's stare did not abate. Fiore noted how, in saying nothing, he also declined to deny that he would ever do such things. He wondered if this was the sort of honor one might expect amongst thieves. No surprise they'd got themselves in this mess.

"Fine," the mustachioed fellow spat at last. "Let's be off, then."

However long they dithered, once decided, his captors worked quick. Fiore supposed they ought to be commended for it as they swiftly and silently gathered their effects. The brute sank into the water—just barely visible from Fiore's sideways and floor-level perspective—and swam off out of sight, returning within moments towing a black-lacquered sandolo.

As the brute and the mustachioed fellow piled into the sandolo and sailed off into the darkness, Fiore knew he ought to count himself lucky.

After all, being left alone with just the one captor was surely better than being left with two.

Yet as his own nervous glance met broken-nose's cold stare, he wondered how honest his solitary captor would remain, with no one there to keep him so.

# CHAPTER TWENTY-FOUR

E nzo supposed the kidnappers had chosen a moonless night because they believed darkness conferred an advantage.

In that, they had erred.

Perhaps they knew not what he wore. But his typical costume of black upon black upon black, with his black bauta mask, sank into the shadows the moment he went out into the evening. All the moreso tonight, for beneath his tabarro cloak he'd garbed himself in the same woolen uniform as the three household guards he'd chosen to accompany him on this particular mission. Neither he, Zanetta, Ferruzzi, or Canello wore mail or carried swords. The clinking of armor or even the ringing note of a rapier sliding from its sheath would give them away. Arrows and thrown daggers, however, made almost no noise at all. Even a crossbow, though it would make a sound when at last it released its bolt, could be held in total silence for hours. Particularly if loaded well beforehand. As Enzo had, of course, instructed Canello to do. And so while Enzo himself bore nothing save cloak and dagger, he had all 'round him more than enough weaponry to deal with whatever Fiore's kidnappers chose to throw at him.

Furthermore, he had Vittorio—equally dark and equally silent—by his side, hackles raised whilst he waited for his master's command.

They set out at dusk. Enzo left the bulk of the strategy to Zanetta, Ferruzzi, and Canello. They knew best how to conduct their own business; if they weren't experts in their respective fields, then Lucrezia would never have hired them. Enzo had merely told them his goal. The rest they settled amongst themselves and returned to him with a plan. At their direction, upon arriving at the piazza, Enzo insinuated himself into a particular shadow cast by the arched doorway of one of the surrounding houses.

Carlotta had contrived to persuade the owners of the house to let Zanetta sit atop their roof for the night. Enzo knew not what admixture of talk and coin she'd used to produce this result; enough to buy silence without giving cause to wag their tongues at the strange request.

"And if these strangers prove allies to Fiore's tormentors?" Enzo had asked when the guards proposed this course of action. "Perhaps they chose this piazza in particular because they have friends here."

"It's possible," Ferruzzi had admitted. "But unlikely, we think. If they controlled the area to such an extent, they'd have no cause to hide by night. They'd do just as well to have us drop it during the day and mingle amongst the crowd to retrieve it. A midnight drop shows their lack of confidence. They want this done quick, simple, and quiet."

Quiet they might have. Enzo resolved to make it neither quick nor simple for them.

Ferruzzi crouched at his side beneath the arch. Vittorio sat between them. Guard and hound alike awaited in perfect silence as the darkness grew deeper. Enzo fixed his gaze upon the fountain, its pale marble form fading into something indistinct as night crept on. The fountain depicted Bacchus pouring an amphora into the mouth of a grateful satyr. Which, according to Fiore's system, marked it out as freshwater. The memory of that happier day struck Enzo like a knife through his ribs. He took solace in the small piece of Fiore he still carried with him in the breast-pocket of his waistcoat, just over his heart.

Hours passed. What few folk had mingled through the surrounding alleyways and what few boats had slipped by in the canal abutting the piazza vanished altogether. Enzo's legs ached from holding the same stance for so long—yet the pain seemed to come to him from a distance, and his mounting anxiety far exceeded it. Any discomfort he felt at keeping still and silent for so many hours was nothing to what his Fiore must suffer even now.

Then, when bitter despair told Enzo that his guards were wrong, the monsters did have friends here, and those friends must have warned them off, and he would see neither the kidnappers nor Fiore this night, nor perhaps ever again—

A shadow slipped into the canal.

Adrenaline flooded Enzo's veins. He strained his eyes against the darkness. A boat—a sandolo, for it hadn't the bulk of a felze and no vessel of any greater size could possibly fit in the narrow waterway of this particular neighborhood—had just drifted into view between two houses and now halted against the stone steps leading up into the piazza. Whatever sounds its docking made were blotted out by the eternal waterfall of the fountain.

Ferruzzi tensed beside him as vague shadows emerged from the sandolo. The shadows, one far larger than the other, crept towards the fountain. Enzo held his breath as they lingered by it. Unless some incredible coincidence had occurred, these must be Fiore's captors—and yes, they proved themselves so by searching over the fountain until the smaller one delved beneath the waters to produce the small chest that held the promised coin.

And yet they were but two shadows.

No matter how hard Enzo stared, he could not manifest a third. No bound figure staggering between the two captors. No slumped body left behind on the bank of the canal. Not even a hint of a human silhouette in the sleek and slender outline of the sandolo. Even as Enzo's heart sank like a stone, he thought it'd been rather too much to hope for that the kidnappers would've brought Fiore with them to the drop-site.

Unless, the treacherous feathered thing piped up from the back of his mind, Fiore lay out flat in the bed of the sandolo.

Enzo, who'd awaited with bated breath and high-strung anxieties and seething rage all the while, could bear it no longer.

And so he slipped out from beneath the archway.

The fountain's noise would cover his stealthy tread. The weight of the chest would hinder the culprits in their return to their vessel. Enzo kept close to the walls of the surrounding houses, creeping from shadow to shadow, swift and nearly silent, to reach the sandolo before them.

This had not been part of the guards' plan. They had recommended following the culprits from a distance as they returned their ill-gotten gains to their hideout.

But the faint mote of possibility that Fiore lay somehow concealed in the brigands' boat drove Enzo on. He had to know for certain. If there remained any possibility of Fiore's presence, and Enzo gave him up for lost without a hunt—

Enzo unsheathed his blade as he neared the canal. Since he'd lost the privilege of carrying a sword in the city, he'd trained with Maestra Rovigatti in dagger-fencing as well. He had no doubt he could subdue his foes.

Then, just before he reached the sandolo, the all-but-formless shadows returning from the fountain ceased their progress.

And unless he much mistook matters, it seemed as though their barely discernible heads had turned to fix their gaze upon where he hid.

The larger dropped the chest, leaving the smaller staggering from the weight. A matching blade appeared in the larger shadow's hand, visible only by its glinting edge reflecting the lamplight of the aedicula by the canal. It lurched towards Enzo with rapid strides that belied its enormous frame. Enzo braced himself for a fight. Then—

The larger shadow jerked to a sudden halt. A slender shaft erupted from its throat. It staggered another half-step, then slumped forward onto the masegni. A shudder rippled through its massive bulk. Then it lay still.

A shower of hailstones struck the piazza. No, Enzo realized as he whirled towards the tinkling sound audible even above the fountain's burbling—not hailstones, but rather coins, a golden rainstorm scattering over the masegni as the smaller shadow gave up the treasure for lost and dropt the chest to break out in a sprint for the sandolo.

Enzo dashed to intercept it.

Mere yards remained between him and his quarry when a strangled yelp pierced the night air and another slender shaft appeared, this time in the smaller shadow's thigh. It crumpled to the ground.

Enzo kept running. He reached the sandolo. Hauled it in. Peered inside.

Nothing remained in the empty belly of the boat.

Enzo stared into the darkness. His heart plunged like an anchor. Fiore was still gone—still out there somewhere, stolen, suffering—unless they'd already—

A spark shone bright as a star against the gloom of the piazza. Enzo caught it in the corner of his eye and whirled towards it to find Canello holding a hooded lantern aloft. Both he and Ferruzzi had converged over the fallen form of the smaller shadow, which yet whimpered. Ferruzzi had pinned her bootheel against the brigand's chest.

Enzo supposed they were rather past the point of concealment. He hastened to join them.

"Keep back, your grace," Canello called out even as Enzo approached.

Enzo ignored the advice. By the hooded lantern's light he beheld a man of some thirty-odd years bearing a well-waxed moustache. Wide eyes flicked a panicked gaze between Enzo and the two guards.

"Shall we take him alive, your grace?" Ferruzzi asked.

Enzo nodded.

A sigh escaped the brigand. "Thank you, your grace! You shan't regret—"

What further deceptions the brigand wished to spin were silenced as Enzo dropt to his knees and shoved his handkerchief into his lying mouth. By the time they had him trussed up, Zanetta had descended from the rooftop to join them.

"What of the other one?" she asked as she approached.

"Dead," Ferruzzi declared, having knelt to examine the enormous body.

"Shall we bring the corpse back with us as well?" Canello asked. Both his gaze and his crossbow remained fixed on the smaller brigand as he spoke.

Enzo shook his head. Hauling so many pounds of flesh would only slow them down. Fiore needed him quick. "Into the canal."

Zanetta and Ferruzzi shared a speaking glance. But none of the guard questioned the order aloud. Canello kept watch over the smaller brigand as the other two searched the larger's corpse. They found nothing of consequence.

It took the combined strength of Zanetta, Ferruzzi, and Enzo himself to roll the dead weight into the canal. A tribute, Enzo supposed, to Saturn or Neptune or Bellenos himself—whichever god chose to watch over their deeds this night. He hoped it would gratify them to have a true human sacrifice for once rather than a mere effigy.

For Fiore's plight required all the blessings the gods could bestow.

~

Trapped in a sepulchral chthonic prison, Fiore couldn't keep time by the passage of the sun or moon. A cleverer sort might have known the hour by the rising and falling of the tide. Even if Fiore were so clever, pain proved a constant distraction.

Besides, he needed to focus what little wit and artifice remained to him on planning his escape.

He knew he would be slain the very moment the brute and the mustachioed fellow returned with the ransom money. He'd seen all their faces. Once they had the money in hand, they no longer needed him breathing. If he wanted to live, he had to escape before they returned.

And for all he knew, they would return at any moment.

Broken-nose had ignored him since the departure of the mustachioed fellow and the brute. In a fair fight Fiore had no chance against him. And the fight certainly wouldn't be fair. Even if he could somehow slip his bonds, they'd warped him out-of-joint and mangled his hand besides. Fiore took a fight off the table and focused on his remaining options; persuasion, which seemed unlikely to bring success, or distraction.

Fiore wished he knew more of the man. It would give him something to work off of. From his garb—loose slops rather than breeches—he appeared a sailor. Whether common merchant sailor or pirate, Fiore couldn't say. He knew well the tastes of both. Many of his suitors were seamen, seeking familiar delights in a vessel of familiar shape.

This fancied familiarity gave Fiore enough courage to seek still more. He ran his dry tongue over his cracked lips and forced strength into his voice to ask, "What ought I to call you?"

Broken-nose glared at him. "Call me anything and I'll cut out your tongue."

"The duke will miss that as well," Fiore replied before he could stop himself.

Broken-nose didn't seem amused. Fiore hoped he might consider the thought regardless.

"I'm called Fiore," he said. Perhaps offering his own name would encourage reciprocity.

Broken-nose gave him a dull stare. "I know."

Fiore supposed he ought to have expected that. They had, after all, sought him out specifically. He flailed internally for some point of commonality between himself and his captor. "Don't suppose I could interest you in a game of cards?"

Broken-nose remained unmoved. "I don't need your blood on my deck."

Fiore winced at the reminder of his mangled hand. It'd been rather too much to hope for that his kidnapper might untie him for the sake of mere gambling. "Riddles?"

"Not if you wish to keep your tongue."

"Noted." Fiore shut his jaw with a click.

The ensuing silence filled the chamber like a roiling fog, broken only by the steady drip and lap of water throughout, and the occasional scurry of unseen rats. His captor idly polished his knife with a ragged handkerchief. He hardly seemed to notice Fiore was there—though no doubt that would quickly change if Fiore so much as twitched towards freedom.

Minutes passed like hours. Not that Fiore could tell the difference between either with no watch and no sun. He wondered how long his captor would wait for his companions to return. Perhaps they'd both run away with the ransom and cut him out altogether.

"Do you do a lot of kidnapping?" Fiore asked.

"No," said broken-nose, much to Fiore's surprise. "Mostly we just make folk disappear."

"Oh," said Fiore. Then, a moment afterward and far more softly, "*Oh.*"

The ghost of a smirk tugged at the corner of his captor's lips.

Fiore wracked his brains for something, anything, to distract his captor. He struck upon something. He didn't like it. Still, he swallowed down his own disgust and said, "Perhaps you'd like to know for yourself what the duke sees in me?"

Broken-nose blinked. Whether at his hostage's audacity or stupidity, Fiore couldn't tell.

Fiore kept on. "After all, what's good for the duke is good for the gander."

It was barely a pun. Nonetheless, broken-nose laughed. Fiore misliked the sound.

"Thought you said he was fond of your cock," broken-nose noted.

"He is," Fiore quickly agreed—both because it was true and because he didn't want his captor to consider cutting it off again. "But you don't seem that sort. Unless I'm much mistaken."

Broken-nose snorted. "No, indeed."

Fiore threw out one last desperate crumb. "I'm told a hole is a hole."

Broken-nose gave him a considering look.

Fiore tried to look enticing rather than terrified. There was nothing to hand save lamp oil, and he doubted his captor would waste it on his ass. It would hurt—a lot—but if it would keep him alive…

Broken-nose stood up.

Fiore swallowed hard. Bolting wouldn't help. He'd get knifed before he gained three strides. And even if he made it to the water, he didn't like his chances swimming with his hands tied behind his back.

Broken-nose stepped up to him.

Fiore resisted the urge to test his bonds again.

Before Fiore could even blink, broken-nose seized him by the arm, forced him face-down against the stones, and pinned him there with a knee between his shoulder blades. The hemp around his hands and wrists fell free—but he dared not even flinch towards freedom. Broken-nose had his wrists tied up again in a trice anyways, in case any doubt remained that he was at some point a sailor. Fiore's legs splayed limp, his aching knees creaking their screams of equal relief and anguish.

Then broken-nose hauled him up by his bound wrists and slammed him face-first against the wall of bones. Another hostage might have felt terror. Fiore felt a queer sort of elation. His legs were all pins and needles

293

—without his captor's support he could never have stood—but they were free. When opportunity came, he could run. And if he made it to the water, he could at least kick, which was most of swimming. The water would make his bonds slicker even than blood. His newly narrowed hand could make it out, if he only had the chance.

But first he must wait for the opportune moment. And before that... well. Nothing he hadn't done before.

Broken-nose laid the blade of his dagger against Fiore's throat.

Fiore didn't dare breathe.

"If I have you," said broken-nose, "it'll be like this all the while."

Fiore forced his voice into a semblance of bravery. "Wouldn't be the first time."

Which was true enough, even if it wasn't an experience he cared to repeat.

Broken-nose only laughed.

# CHAPTER TWENTY-FIVE

It took more restraint than Enzo thought he possessed to resist skewering the brigand through the heart on the very stones of the piazza.

However, there remained just one thing in all the world he desired more than revenge—to have his Fiore back alive.

And so he checked his seething rage and settled for merely having him bound, gagged, and shoved into the gondola for transport back to Ca' Scaevola.

The journey passed swift and silent. Within the hour the gondola drifted through the archway beneath the palazzo into the cavernous stone chamber that held the dock. Carlotta awaited them at the foot of the stairs leading up into the house proper.

"The chirurgeons have arrived," she told Enzo before he'd even disembarked.

"Good." Indeed, the first favorable report Enzo had received since the ransom note had arrived. Everything would be in place to tend Fiore upon his return. Just as soon as Enzo got him back. Which he would, damn it all. His heart threw itself against the shriven piece of Fiore still in his waistcoat breast-pocket.

Enzo turned back to the gondola and saw the guards had wrestled the brigand out of the felze. He motioned for them to follow and led them into the pianterreno of the palazzo. Down an unremarkable corridor lay a store room packed with crates of raw silk. This left just enough space in the center of the chamber to bring in a kitchen chair for their prisoner—and would dampen his voice besides, once they removed the gag. Enzo ordered this done only after Zanetta and Ferruzzi had bound his ankles to the chair legs.

"I don't know anything!" the brigand spat out alongside the gag. "They just sent me to pick up the loot!"

Enzo stared down at him. Then he unsheathed his dagger from his belt. "If you know nothing, then you are worthless to me."

The brigand's eyes flew wide. "Wait!"

Enzo waited.

"I—I may know a thing or two that could help you," the brigand spluttered. "But I'm just a simple errand-runner—messenger-for-hire— I've nothing to do with—with whatever it is you're angry about."

"Of course you don't," Enzo deadpanned.

"Ask Portia!" the brigand blurted. "She'll vouch for me!"

Enzo turned to Carlotta.

"One of the kitchen-maids," Carlotta supplied.

The thought that one of his own household could have conspired against him to this extent sent another pulse of boiling fury through Enzo's veins. Still, shouting wouldn't help matters. And so, in a voice flat with the effort to keep quiet, he commanded, "Bring her here."

Carlotta departed with a bow.

Enzo turned to the brigand as the door shut behind her. "You said you may know something. What do you know of this?"

And as he spoke, he withdrew Fiore's finger from his waistcoat breast-pocket and held it up before the brigand's gaze.

The brigand's eyes flew wide. He swallowed hard. His gaze flitted from Enzo's face to Fiore's finger and back again. "Friend of yours?"

If Enzo didn't need information, he would've sheathed his dagger in the brigand's throat then and there. "Indeed. Do you know who did this?"

The brigand hesitated.

A horrible suspicion took root in Enzo's mind. "Did *you* do this?"

The brigand shook his head vehemently.

"Your grace," Zanetta spoke up. "We have his blade."

Enzo turned to find her holding out a simple dagger sheathed in brown leather. He tucked Fiore's finger back into the pocket over his heart where it belonged and took the dagger from her. Grasping its cord-wrapped handle and drawing it from its sheath didn't reveal any tell-tale bloodstains. Those would be easy enough to wipe away.

The fire-scale and soot-stains, however, remained.

A cold rage seeped through Enzo's veins. He held the blade up before the brigand's eyes. "Were you hoping this would keep him from bleeding?"

"That's not mine," said the brigand, his words coming staccato and shrill.

If Enzo had any sympathy for the brigand's plight, it fled him the moment that obvious lie left his lips. He turned to Ferruzzi. "Untie his right hand."

The brigand stared up at Enzo. "No—please—!"

Ferruzzi did as Enzo bade her. The brigand struggled and pleaded all the while. Enzo wondered if Fiore had done the same in his place.

"Hold him fast," Enzo ordered. His words echoed in his own ears, as if they came from somewhere far distant, from another version of himself hardly audible over the screams of anguish resounding in his own heart.

Zanetta drew up a stool. Ferruzzi held the brigand's wrist down on it and forced his palm to splay.

"Mercy, m'lord!" the brigand cried.

"What mercy did you show him?" Enzo asked.

The brigand gaped in silence, another lie stuttering on his tongue.

Enzo thrust the blade down. It severed the forefinger in a single blow. Which was better than the brigand had served Fiore.

The brigand howled regardless.

"This was vengeance," Enzo told him when the howls subsided into sobs. "The rest will be fit punishment for every subsequent lie you tell me. Start telling truths. Now."

"Portia, your grace."

Enzo turned to find a young woman still in her kitchen apron standing on the threshold just ahead of Carlotta. Yet she did not look at him in turn. Her gaze fixed on the brigand tied to the chair.

And his bloodied hand held down by the household guards.

It occurred to Enzo as he regarded her horrified face that he may have gone a bit far and a bit fast.

"Arlotto!?" she whispered in evident shock.

"Portia!" the brigand replied, smiling despite the blood flowing from his hand and the bruises blooming across his face.

Portia did not return the smile.

"Portia," said Enzo. "Do you know this man?"

Portia flinched and jerked her head up to face him. Enzo couldn't blame her for feeling unnerved. The knife in his hand dripped blood. Yet to her credit she stood firm and replied without a tremor in her voice, "I thought I did, your grace."

Arlotto rolled his eyes. "Bellenos spare me from the inconstancy of women."

"The inconstancy of *women!?*" Portia snapped. "You fucked my *sister!*"

A marked pause ensued. Arlotto began spluttering. Enzo silenced him with a look.

"Portia," Enzo said, keeping a wary eye on Arlotto. "What would you have me do with him?"

Without even a breath of hesitation, she replied, "Cut his balls off and shove them down his throat."

Enzo had to admit that sounded fairly satisfying. He drank in the wide-eyed terror in Arlotto's glances between himself and Portia.

"What do you think?" Enzo asked him. "Will you tell me where Fiore is? Or shall I hand her a knife?"

Arlotto shot a fearful glance at Portia.

Not an ounce of pity shone behind her eyes.

"Who do you work for?" Enzo demanded. Even if he knew in his heart it was the Delfini, he needed to hear it for himself.

Arlotto flinched. "Nascimbene!"

Enzo balked. "The impresario?"

"Yes," Arlotto replied, the words tumbling from his tongue as his eyes flicked between Portia and Enzo. "He said the musico knew too much of him and needed to be silenced."

Enzo arched his brow.

"We looked into the matter," Arlotto continued. "Trailed the musico. Saw and heard how he had your favor."

"And you supposed you could be paid twice for the same job," Enzo concluded.

At first, Arlotto appeared relieved to be understood. His faint smile faded into fear beneath Enzo's gaze.

"Where is he now?" Enzo asked.

"They're keeping him beneath Isola dei Cadaveri." Arlotto's words fell over each other in his haste to answer a violent duke. "There's only one left to mind him." Inspiration gleamed in his eyes. "I could guide you to them."

The glimmer of hope dimmed into darkness as Enzo replied, "You will."

～

The chirurgeons cleaned, stitched, and bandaged Arlotto's hand. Which no doubt was more than Arlotto had done for Fiore. Enzo didn't stay to supervise their work. Instead he saw to it that Vittorio was fed and a sandolo readied for the journey. Vittorio, Ferruzzi, Zanetta, and Canello would once again accompany them. Carlotta watched him throughout. She would tell Lucrezia all that had passed, of course, but evidently not before Enzo had gone on his way, for which she had his eternal gratitude.

Soon enough, though not half so quick as Enzo would've liked, they were off. The sandolo slipped silently through the city's canals until it left them behind altogether to traverse the open lagoon.

And then Isola dei Cadaveri loomed out of the fog. A hill of bones centuries in the making, with an ossuary temple marking its peak. The sacred flame ever-burning in its dome guided the sandolo towards its banks of bone. But Enzo's heart lay buried far deeper in the island's sepulchral entrails.

Arlotto sat at the bow of the boat, just ahead of Enzo, with his ankles shackled together and his hands bound behind his back with rope. His mouth remained free, which Enzo accepted as a necessary evil. At least he still had his dagger against the brigand's throat.

"There," Arlotto murmured, lifting his chin towards a particular dark hollow amidst the island's shadowed banks.

At Enzo's signal, Zanetta drew back her lantern's hood to shine its light over the island. The low tide revealed the banks tinged green and worn away by the waves. Legend claimed even this part of the island was bones, ground up into a paste for concrete. It had worn away uneven with many nooks and crannies. One of these, however, just visible at low tide's waterline, seemed to hold darker and deeper shadows than the rest. And it was towards this that Canello steered the sandolo, at Arlotto's direction.

They found themselves in a tunnel. The hooded lantern's rays showed pale walls worn smoothest at the waterline and rusticated at the crest of the arch overhead. A second glance showed the rumors were true; they sailed through a cavern built of skeletal remains, with limbs like timber held together with bone-meal mortar.

Enzo, who had examined more than his fair share of human skeletons in his university career, cared not. The dead were dead and would remain so. His Fiore, however, must yet be alive.

And so the sandolo rowed on.

The tunnel did not stay straightforward for long. The lantern's beam revealed a fork ahead. Both paths plunged into identical darkness.

Ferruzzi braced an arm against the skeletal tunnel wall to halt the sandolo. They hung in suspended silence.

"Which way," Enzo growled into Arlotto's ear.

Arlotto hesitated.

Enzo had no patience. "Tell me or lose another finger."

"The right-hand path," Arlotto hissed.

Ferruzzi pushed off from the wall. The sandolo slipped to the right.

"Musico!"

The deep roar of pure rage echoed throughout the cavern of bones—but particularly seemed to come from the passage to the left.

Enzo didn't recognize the voice. The slur, however, he knew well. He turned his glare upon Arlotto.

"Or the left-hand path," Arlotto blurted.

Enzo suppressed the urge to add another cadaver to the pile of bones.

"Stupid—bastard—catamite!" The shouts echoed down the tunnel. "I'll carve your eyes out!"

Enzo tightened his grip on his dagger. If they dared to touch his Fiore again—

The crew corrected the sandolo's course to the left. It slipped through the tunnel in near-silence. No further shouts resounded. Enzo didn't know if that was better or worse.

"Cover the light," Arlotto whispered.

Enzo stared at the back of his head. "What."

"We're getting close," Arlotto hissed. "My partner will know something's amiss if he sees a lantern coming."

"Sounds like something's already amiss," Canello muttered.

Enzo quite agreed. Yet he turned and nodded to Zanetta regardless, and she shut the hood on the lantern. The tunnel plunged into absolute darkness. Enzo held his dagger tighter than ever against Arlotto's throat. To his surprise, Arlotto made no move toward escape.

And in the absence of light from the sandolo, Enzo beheld a faint flickering glow shimmering across the rippling waters ahead.

The tunnel opened up into a cavern. The sandolo paused just before it left the shadowed archway, halted once again by Ferruzzi and Zanetta's hands against the skeletal walls. Peering out over Arlotto's shoulder, Enzo beheld a bone grotto lit by a hooded lantern not unlike his own. Its minuscule light cast a deep gloom over all. What little it revealed—an overturned three-legged stool, a heap of torn rope that glistened crimson, and no glimpse of either Fiore or his pursuer—didn't bode well.

Enzo turned to Arlotto for an explanation.

"Well," said Arlotto in a defensive tone. "This is where I left them."

Enzo levelled a severe look upon him. "You'll forgive me if I don't believe you just now."

"Musico!" The enraged shout echoed throughout the cavern.

Enzo caught Ferruzzi's eye and jerked his chin towards the bone grotto. "Make landfall."

All three of the household guard shot speaking glances between them. Nonetheless, they obeyed. The sandolo slipped through the water and broke its silence only when its hull brushed against the bone banks.

Enzo alighted from the sandolo, dragging Arlotto along with him. Their heels crunched on the ossuary ground. Now that he'd entered the grotto proper, he saw certain spots of hollow darkness he'd taken for shadows were really further tunnels leading deeper into the catacombs. Blood stained not just the torn rope but spattered scarlet across the greying bones. There had been a struggle—even a fool could see that. And, given the broken bonds and the captor's rage, a hope of Fiore's escape kindled in Enzo's chest. Whether the blood belonged to Fiore or his kidnapper, Enzo knew not. But Fiore had been here—was still here, somewhere—not yet beyond Enzo's grasp.

"How would you signal your friend?" Enzo hissed into Arlotto's ear.

Arlotto drew in a shuddering breath against the dagger blade. Then he cried out in a harsh whisper, "The crabs have shed their shells."

A marked pause ensued.

"Arlotto?" called the deep voice that had cursed Fiore's name not moments before. It seemed to come from the left-most shadowed path. "Is that you?"

Arlotto shot a terrified glance over his shoulder at Enzo. Enzo nodded.

"Yes!" Arlotto cried. Whatever efforts he made to keep his voice level didn't suffice; a slight shrill tremor remained. Enzo only hoped it wouldn't give them away.

Another pause ensued. Enzo's heart hung in the balance.

"Do you have the money?" the deep voice enquired at last.

"Yes," Arlotto said again. His voice sounded stronger this time—perhaps because that much at least was true. In what seemed like an attempt at appeasement, he added, "A hundred zecchini, just as we asked."

Footsteps thudded down the left-most tunnel toward the grotto. Not time enough to think. Only to act.

And so Enzo withdrew his blade from Arlotto's throat and slipped into the shadows of another identical passage.

Arlotto shot him a fearful glance which became a wide-eyed stare as Enzo left him behind. Enzo didn't fear his betrayal even without his dagger against his carotid artery. Four-to-one odds—even a fool such as Arlotto could perform so simple a calculation and conclude it best to aid in Fiore's retrieval rather than attempt his own escape.

Besides, Canello had kept his crossbow trained between Arlotto's shoulder blades.

As Enzo went, he gestured for the sandolo to withdraw as well. Canello shot him a look of frank disbelief. Zanetta and Ferruzzi, however, put their oars into action, pushing off just far enough to take the sandolo out of sight. Vittorio flattened his ears against his skull but made no sound.

All this passed within a few beats of Enzo's thundering pulse.

Then, as he peered out of his own sepulchral alcove, he glimpsed a hulking figure emerging from the left-most tunnel. An enormous brute of a man with a nose that had been flattened and poorly pulled out again came just far enough into the hooded lantern's faint flickering glow to address Arlotto.

"Where is Zuan?" asked the broken-nosed brute.

Arlotto hesitated.

And glanced back to Enzo's hiding place for the answer.

If rage alone could've killed the fool, Enzo would have him dead at his feet.

"What're you looking at?" the broken-nosed brute demanded at once —because of course he noticed this exchange of glances; only an idiot would miss it.

"I—" Arlotto began, stumbling back on his heels, to no avail.

Enzo slipped further into the shadows. But not far enough.

A knife glinted in the broken-nosed brute's hand. "You set us up."

And without further ado, he leapt forward with all the grace and silence of a panther and plunged the blade beneath Arlotto's flailing left arm.

Arlotto's shrill cry of pain echoed throughout the cavern of bone like the aria of a castrato resounding off the opera house's gilded walls.

Enzo drew his sword. The shriek became a hideous gurgle in the two strides it took to bring Enzo to the comrades-turned-combatants. Arlotto was beyond saving, but the brute knew where Fiore had fled, and if Enzo could subdue him—

The brute whirled toward Enzo at his first step. The snap of a crossbow firing seemed to come at the very same moment the bolt itself appeared in the brute's thigh. This did nothing to halt his advance. Enzo parried the first stab with ease. The brute drew back for another.

A slight splash was all the warning Enzo received before an enormous black shadow leapt between them. A cry of mingled agony and outrage erupted from the brute. The dagger clattered to the ground —for the arm holding it was dragged down by Vittorio's mighty jaws.

And before Enzo could call him off, Vittorio released his hold on the arm and went for the brute's throat.

"Vittorio!" Enzo commanded. "Yield!"

Vittorio withdrew at once. His fangs gleamed crimson as he turned to regard his master. He looked as though he would bound to him to reassure himself that he'd done well and Enzo was all right. But Enzo waved his hand and closed his fist, and Vittorio backed off and sat down to await with perfect patience for the next order.

Gurgling gasps wheezed from the broken-nosed brute's torn throat. No chirurgeon could save him now. Even if Enzo had felt so inclined.

Enzo knelt beside his head. "Tell me where Fiore is, and I'll give you a quicker end than this."

The eyes rolled to fix him with a cold stare. The words emerged in a choking hiss. "Where is my brother?"

Enzo took in the frame and the features and realized, perhaps too late, the great resemblance between this monster and the corpse he'd rolled into the canal not two hours past. He found he couldn't summon a lie. "Your brother is dead."

The gaze hardened. A grim sort of smile twitched at the corners of the twisted mouth. He drew in a sucking breath and gasped out, "Your musico is in the walls."

And before Enzo could do more than stare down at the brute in disbelief, a final rattling gasp shuddered through his frame and he lay still, his cold gaze fixed on forever.

"Your grace," said Canello.

Only then did Enzo realize his household guard had all gathered 'round him in the interim. He glanced up to find them with weapons drawn and ready to receive his orders.

Enzo stood. "Vittorio."

His hound, who had waited patient and faithful all the while, bounded to meet him.

Enzo willed his hand not to tremble as he reached into the breast-pocket of his waistcoat. If the brigands had immured Fiore, Vittorio could still find him. The finger felt almost alive in his hand, warmed by the heat of his own chest. He grasped it gently and held it out for Vittorio to sniff.

"Find our friend," Enzo commanded.

Vittorio snapped to attention, then turned and began his investigation, his nose brushing across the bones. He paused at the splashes of blood. Enzo's heart crept into his throat.

Then Vittorio looked to the left-most tunnel. He glanced back at Enzo for permission. At Enzo's nod, he trotted off into the darkness.

"Canello, with me," Enzo hissed. "Zanetta and Ferruzzi, keep watch here."

All three guards looked reluctant to play the parts Enzo had laid out for them. Nonetheless, they raised no objection. Canello fell into step behind Enzo like his own shadow as he snatched up the hooded lantern and led the way down the tunnel of bones.

Vittorio hadn't gone far ahead of them before halting and turning to wait for his master. No sooner had the lantern-light found him than he set out again, his claws clicking against the skeletal floor. The lantern likewise illuminated occasional scarlet spattering.

And, when they caught up to Vittorio again, a smeared scarlet handprint on the bone-white wall.

Enzo halted and stared at the mark. It had but three fingers. Instinct bid him reach out and touch them with his own. His hand came away wet. He tried to tell himself this was a good sign. It meant they were close.

Vittorio, meanwhile, hadn't moved any further down the sepulchral corridor. He sniffed intently at the ground. Then pawed at a particular part of the wall and whined.

The words of the broken-nosed brute echoed in Enzo's mind. He shot forward. There, where Vittorio tried in vain to dig, a shadow which Enzo had taken for yet another crenelation in the naturally uneven pile of bones proved itself to be a far deeper crack—just barely wide enough for something, or someone, to slip inside.

And as Enzo cast the hooded lantern's light within it, a pair of eyes glinted back at him whilst ragged breathing rang in his ears.

"Fiore?" Enzo whispered.

The thing in the crevasse scuttled backward, away from the sound of his voice.

More than anything, Enzo wanted to reach for him—wanted to plunge his whole arm into the foreboding passage, and if Fiore tore it off at the shoulder, so be it—but knew full well to venture even mere fingertips toward Fiore in this state would only send him flying further off, perhaps down into some horrible hole from whence Enzo might never retrieve him. He'd had but a glimpse of his face, and that glimpse had shown him the wild, wide-eyed, ghastly pale aspect of primal fear. Terror beyond all reason had seized Fiore; small wonder, given all he'd endured in the few short hours that nonetheless had passed like centuries and frayed Enzo's own nerves to their breaking point. If Enzo wanted him back, he must offer up something in return.

And so Enzo snatched the mask from his face and cast it aside on the bones.

"Fiore," he repeated, keeping his voice low and soft, though his heart pounded in his throat. "It's only me. It's only your Enzo."

And as he spoke, he turned the hooded lantern away from the crevasse and cast its flickering light on his own face.

For a long and horrible moment the only sounds that echoed through the catacombs were the lapping of water against the skeletal remains and the ragged breathing from deep within the crevasse. Enzo, blinded by the lamp, could see nothing amidst the shadows.

Then a hand as pale as the surrounding bones shot out of the darkness and seized him by the wrist.

"Steady," Enzo murmured even as his heart soared. He set the lantern aside and dared to turn his arm in the pale hand's hold so he might grasp the pale arm in turn. He met with no resistance, though the pale arm trembled like a barren branch in a storm.

Enzo slid his free hand up the sleeve to slip beneath the shoulder and draw Fiore further out. More scuttling sounds echoed from deeper within the crevasse, bone cracking and shards clattering against each other in the darkness as Fiore kicked out his legs to assist in his own rescue. A gentle tug saw Fiore's head and shoulders slip out into the lantern's glow. Blood smeared across his face. The sight sent a knife into Enzo's heart, all the moreso for the haunted and panicked look those dark eyes shot up at him from within a countenance as pale as the moon.

"Easy now," Enzo murmured again, for his own sake as well as Fiore's.

Another firm yet ginger pull brought Fiore out to his hips. Enzo, already kneeling, drew him into his lap. Fiore's body felt not half so warm as it ought. His shirt, its pale linen still darker than his skin, bore a deep crimson stain beneath the bone-white hand that clutched his stomach. At first Enzo supposed this came from the missing finger on that hand. But as Fiore endeavored to curl in upon himself like a dying spider, Enzo's instincts told him otherwise. He reached for Fiore's wounded hand. Fiore flinched from his touch.

"It's all right," Enzo lied. "Let me see."

The frantic breaths that hissed through Fiore's clenched teeth and shuddered through his ribcage slowed. His wide-eyed panic fixed on Enzo's face. A hard swallow rippled down his slender throat.

And at last, with evident strain, he withdrew his trembling arm so Enzo might behold what pained him.

Enzo untucked Fiore's shirt from his trouser-waist—which provoked a heartbreaking choked-off cry from Fiore.

"Steady," Enzo echoed. He gathered his courage and drew up Fiore's shirt-front.

There, beneath the crusted crimson smears over bone-white skin, lay two distinct punctures. One just above and to the left of the navel, the other below and to its right. Both spilled over with every frightful breath that escaped Fiore.

Enzo shoved down his rising alarm. He replaced the shirt and Fiore's wounded hand over it.

"Hold on," he bid him, and with a final draw, brought him whole out of the crevasse.

Fiore gave a sharp inhale but did not cry out. Enzo didn't know if that meant the movement hadn't pained him overmuch, or if he no longer had the strength to give voice to his pain. He cradled Fiore in his arms regardless. Fiore curled in on himself, fitting into his grasp as if he were molded for Enzo's embrace.

Enzo stood. Fiore cast his dark and haunted eyes up to meet his gaze. Their depths shone bright with fever. Then they closed with a shuddering sigh as Fiore turned his head and buried his face in Enzo's collar.

# CHAPTER TWENTY-SIX

The near-silent ride out of the catacombs and through the city's canals seemed to last eons. The gentle lapping of water against the sandolo's hull seemed deafening compared to the soft shuddering breaths that emerged from Fiore. Enzo attuned his ears to them as he cradled Fiore in his arms. He'd wrapped his cloak over him to shield him from the cold and imbue him with some of his own warmth, but still Fiore remained icy pale. The dark and beautiful eyes Enzo loved so well hadn't opened since they left the catacombs. Now and again a half-mumbled whimper escaped Fiore's lips, which had gone from a deep and dusky rose to parchment-pale. Each pained sound sent another knife into Enzo's heart.

"Nearly there," Enzo murmured, idly stroking the dark curls which sweat had plastered to Fiore's brow.

Fiore didn't seem to hear him.

Soon afterward—though not nearly soon enough for Enzo's liking—they turned a corner on the Grand Canal and drew within sight of a particular entryway, the lamp suspended from the highest point of its rounded arch casting a warm glow down over the scales carved into its pillars and reflecting shimmering, slithering lines of light off the water against its own domed ceiling. They had arrived at Ca' Scaevola.

The sandolo slipped beneath the arch into the water-story. A corridor of water ran under the palazzo and allowed the sandolo to withdraw into the shelter of the warehouse. Doors to storehouses of merchandise lined either side of the watery corridor. Ahead lay the sweeping cascade of the stair leading up into the house proper. More lamps burned within, casting the same watery reflections up onto the vaulted ceiling. Every splash, no matter how minor, echoed off the surrounding marble; yet still Enzo kept his ears attuned to the weak hiss of Fiore's labored breaths.

Ferruzzi leapt ahead and darted up the steps to alert the household while Canello and Zanetta secured the craft. Noise erupted from every corner, echoing throughout the marble edifice as staff flew through the halls. Enzo disembarked with Fiore and carried him upstairs in silence. His slender weight felt as delicate as a bird in his arms.

Enzo wanted to bear him up to his bedchamber where he might lay in comfort. Instead he brought him to the kitchen, where all but the cook had cleared out, and the bare table in the midst of the room still steamed from the cauldron of scalding-hot water flung over its wooden boards.

Dr. Venier and Dr. Malvestio awaited him there, their instruments already set out on the counter. Enzo returned their greetings with a bare nod and laid Fiore down on the table. The cook passed him a clean towel to cushion Fiore's head. His already small and slight form appeared still more fragile and frail compared to the enormous length of the table. A pang of reluctance struck Enzo's already-bleeding heart as he let his arms slip out from beneath Fiore's body.

"You may leave us," Dr. Venier told him as he straightened.

Enzo served her a blank look. To leave his Fiore's side now was unthinkable.

Dr. Venier stood firm. "The risk of infection is high enough already, given where you dredged him up."

"I can help," Enzo protested. Though he hadn't attained his degree, he'd come near enough to make him a competent nurse at the very least.

Dr. Venier held his gaze with a hard stare. "Can you?"

Enzo knew not what she meant by it. He'd opened his mouth to demand an explanation when a soft whimper resounded like a thunderclap in his ears. He whipped his head 'round to see Fiore still laid out on the bed, pale and trembling, with Dr. Malvestio delicately drawing up his shirt to reveal the two crimson punctures in the scarlet-smeared hollow of his stark-white sunken belly.

Enzo had anatomized at least a dozen corpses by his own hand at university. He'd watched the dissection of a hundred more. In the dueling society, he'd spilled blood from scores of his fellow students.

Yet to see those crimson punctures in Fiore's pale flesh staggered him.

He thought of taking a scalpel to their corners to open the wounds up far enough to repair the damaged organ deeper within. He imagined piercing his entrails with needle and thread over and over to suture the ragged edges back together. He envisioned how Fiore's flesh would recoil from the sting of carbolic acid spray. It sorely tried his nerves—but he'd stuck by Fiore throughout his appendectomy, and even if he couldn't hold the scalpel or needle himself, he could at least do something. He turned to Dr. Venier.

But before he could speak, a maid appeared in the kitchen doorway.

"Begging your pardon, m'lord," she said, her eyes wide at his evident impatience for her interruption. She ducked her head in a curtsey. "The prince would speak with you."

Enzo stared at her in disbelief. "Tell her to wait."

The stunned silence that greeted his command did not dissuade his course. He couldn't read the chirurgeons' faces beneath their masks, but both their beaks turned in his direction. The cook raised her brows, which was more animation than Enzo had seen in her countenance in all his days. And the maid, poor girl, looked frankly terrified. Enzo didn't envy her position—caught between a duke and a prince—but nor did he let it sway him. On another night compassion might have moved him. Tonight he had none to spare and held her gaze until she fled the room.

"He's afraid of chirurgeons," said Enzo, returning to Dr. Venier. "The masks in particular."

"Would he object to paper?" asked Dr. Venier.

The paper masks, unlike the leather beaks, covered only the nose and mouth. The sight of these at least would not remind Fiore of his worst memories. Or so Enzo hoped. "Paper might suit."

Dr. Venier took hold of her beak and pulled the leather mask from her head. Dr. Malvestio took the hint and did the same. Dr. Venier then delved into her leather case and withdrew three masks. One she kept for herself. Another she handed off to Dr. Malvestio. The third she began to hand over to Enzo, but paused with her arm half-outstretched, her attention arrested by something over his shoulder.

"Enzo."

The voice was not unfamiliar to him. And, given his brief exchange with the maid, he supposed he ought to have expected it.

This did nothing to quell his increasing ire as he turned to behold his eldest sister in the kitchen doorway.

Prince Lucrezia Scaevola, Serenissima of Halcyon, stood just a half-head shorter than Enzo. She wore shirt, waistcoat, breeches, and hose similar to his own—or rather, he wore clothes similar to hers, for she'd established her customary garb long before he'd ever dressed himself. They both had the same long dark hair tied back with the same simple black ribbon. And they both had the same striking Scaevola features.

And those features in her face at this particular moment had formed an expression as arch as it was cold.

"I would have words with you," said the prince.

"In a moment," Enzo snapped.

"Now."

Enzo's fists clenched at his sides. At any other moment, he'd go at once wherever she bid. Indeed, in many other moments, he had. At present, he wished he had sword in hand to make his point. His dagger would not suffice.

Before he could retort with words, however, a third voice entered the conversation.

"Your grace," said Dr. Venier. "We don't have time to wait for you to argue."

Enzo stared at her.

She jerked her chin at Fiore's pale body laid out on the table. "*He* hasn't time to wait for you to argue."

All the more reason for Lucrezia to relent, Enzo thought. But as his gaze slid across the room to fall again on Fiore's helpless form—eyes fallen shut, lips barely parted, dark curls cascading across a brow beaded with sweat, shivers trembling across flesh as cold and pale as his marble twin—he lost all will to parry words with his sister. The sooner he and the prince departed, the sooner the chirurgeons could begin their vital work.

And so, with one last reluctant glance backward from the threshold— foolish Orpheus condemning Eurydice—he followed Lucrezia out of the kitchen.

Lucrezia's bootheels clicked sharp against the marble floor of the corridor. Shadows scuttled off into dark doorways ahead of them as curious servants ducked out of sight. Enzo paid them little heed. All his attention fixated on the back of his sister's head whilst she led on in stony silence. The spiral staircase at the end of the hall would take them upstairs to the piano nobile. Fresh dread seized his heart as they neared it; he dared not go so far from Fiore, not now. If Lucrezia pressed the issue he would fight her on it tooth and nail.

But instead, she turned and laid her hand on the unassuming latch of the larder door. It opened to reveal a mere strip of floor left free of jars, baskets, or sacks, for a person to stand upon. More than enough for what Enzo had determined to make a very brief conversation.

Lucrezia, still holding the door open, gestured him within with an impatient toss of her hand. Enzo stepped inside. She followed and shut the door, plunging them both into darkness. He could feel her disapproving gaze burning into him regardless.

"Why do we have guards, Enzo?" she asked. Keeping her voice down did nothing to disguise the cold rage dripping from every word.

"To protect our household," Enzo replied. He didn't think the question deserved any more thought. It was irrelevant in the face of Fiore's suffering.

"Good," said Lucrezia. "You know that we have guards, and you understand their purpose. Tell me, then, why you didn't send them out to retrieve your courtesan and instead went gallivanting around the catacombs yourself?"

"He'd be dead before they found him." Even considering the possibility long enough to force the words from his lips threatened to shatter what little resolve kept Enzo here in the larder and not by his Fiore's side where he belonged.

Lucrezia spoke on regardless. "If you believe our guards

incompetent, you might have told me so before tonight. Yet I believe the fault lies not in our guards but in your patience. Or lack thereof."

"Patience," Enzo echoed in disbelief. As if he didn't demonstrate infinite patience now by suffering through this dressing-down instead of returning to the kitchen-turned-chirurgical-theatre. Fiore's ghastly form loomed before his mind's eye in the darkness. Slashes and gashes would've been bad enough. But punctures—

"Likewise," Lucrezia continued, "this is why we have chirurgeons."

How she always seemed to know where his thoughts had flown, Enzo couldn't fathom. Still, anger brought a retort. "I would be a chirurgeon myself, if you hadn't—!"

"If *you* hadn't attempted murder," Lucrezia said, cutting him off, "then yes, you might have attained your degree."

"It was a *duel!*"

"You may see it that way," said Lucrezia. "The university might have seen it that way. Your opponent might have seen it that way. The law itself may see it that way. I assure you, however, his family would never have seen it as anything short of cold-blooded murder."

Enzo wondered if she would've preferred he commit a hot-blooded murder. He'd done several already tonight. He felt the impetus for another now.

Lucrezia went on without him. "Just as your death in the catacombs would have proved a cold-blooded murder."

Enzo caught his tongue.

"You're adept as a duelist," said Lucrezia. "You've more than proved that. But a duel in the open air by daylight is one thing. Descending into darkness armed only with cloak and dagger to do battle with unknown assailants is quite another."

"I did bring a brace of guards," Enzo pointed out.

"Better armed, but no less ignorant than yourself of what threats lay ahead," Lucrezia retorted. "You had only a criminal's word to trust on how many Nascimbene had hired to dispose of your courtesan."

Enzo's mind and heart were not so far gone that he couldn't feel at least a little touched by his sister's evident concern—the most he'd heard from her in some time. Yet his thoughts stuck on the particular name that had dropped from her lips. "You knew all along?"

"I knew when you embarked for Isola dei Cadaveri," said Lucrezia. "Carlotta had the foresight to send a messenger to myself as well."

"Oh." Enzo supposed he ought to have expected that. Nothing else tonight had met any expectation. But Lucrezia had eyes and ears throughout the city and beyond. "What else have you learnt?"

"Of your affairs? Everything."

"No," Enzo hastened to explain. "Of the impresario. Fiore left his conservatorio over a decade hence. Dozens if not scores of boys have passed through his training since then. Why the deuce would he care enough to track down and kidnap one lost singer whose remaining stone has already dropped?"

"Because the castration of boys for the opera was banned twelve years before Nascimbene botched your courtesan's chirurgy."

Enzo, stunned, stared into the darkness from whence her voice emerged.

"Technically speaking," Lucrezia continued as if she were talking of the weather, "all the musici produced since then are supposed to be the result of unrelated injuries. Usually the chirurgeon is called to attend a boy who has suffered a 'horse-riding accident.' Which is a particularly absurd circumstance in our fair city. But I digress. Your courtesan, if he so chooses, can testify that his failed emasculation and that of the boys trained alongside him was not a medical necessity resulting from even the most implausible excuse. I'm told he has the scars to prove it. Which means he holds the power to destroy Nascimbene and perhaps the whole opera house."

Enzo, amidst all this, hardly had time to wonder where she'd heard of Fiore's scars.

"Doubtless," Lucrezia went on, "the sight of your courtesan at an aristocratic ball in the company of one so powerful and well-connected as Fiorenzo Scaevola, the dueling Duke of Drakehaven, proved rather unnerving to Nascimbene. Better to make his failed musico disappear before certain words dropped into certain ears and Teatro Novissimo crumbled to ruin."

Enzo's tormented heart boiled over and forced him to break his silence. "Then it is my own fault."

"What?"

Before Enzo could answer her incredulous syllable, a scream rent the air. Sharp. Shrill. Piercing. Resounding throughout the halls for one horrible instant before it cut off in sudden silence.

And though Enzo had never heard Fiore cry out in such a way before, he recognized his voice at once.

Faster than even Lucrezia could move to stop him, Enzo threw the larder door open and bolted out into the hall. His bootheels resounded against the marble like thunderclaps. They slowed only when he seized the kitchen doorframe to turn his momentum toward it.

There stood Dr. Venier and Dr. Malvestio—in their mere paper masks, just as promised—over the table, she struggling to hold something at the head of it, and he doing no better at the foot. Between them writhed the bone-white body of his beloved Fiore.

"Release him," Enzo barked.

The chirurgeons shared a speaking glance. Then they withdrew, all but leaping back from their agonized patient.

"He's not stitched up yet," Dr. Venier warned.

"He awoke too soon," Dr. Malvestio explained.

Enzo hardly heard either one of them. He'd already shot forth to reach the table and clasp the pale flailing hand.

Fiore appeared no better than when Enzo had left him. In many ways he looked worse. Though the chirurgeons had washed away the crackling smears of dried blood across his belly, fresh scarlet streams still trickled from the wounds with every panicked breath that hissed between his tight-clenched teeth. His now-opened eyes rolled wildly in their sockets like a spooked stallion. They came to rest only when they caught Enzo's own.

"It's all right," Enzo murmured. "You're all right. It's me. It's your Enzo. I'm here."

At first Enzo didn't think Fiore understood the words themselves; he only hoped the tone of his voice might soothe him. But as he spoke, the frantic fear in Fiore's gaze dimmed, until his eyes no longer flicked between each of Enzo's own and instead fixed him with the steady gaze of comprehension.

"I'll not let them harm you," Enzo promised him. "But they must do their work."

Fiore's jaw unclenched. His lips parted. "Enzo…"

The thin whisper of his voice, as frail as the rest of him, tore through Enzo's heart. Whatever more he'd intended to say was lost forever as a cough seized him.

Blood splattered across Enzo's face. He didn't flinch.

The cough abated, leaving Fiore shuddering in its wake as he struggled to regain his breath. The look he cast up at Enzo was equal parts found and lost.

"They're here to help you," Enzo insisted. "They'll stitch you up and put you back to rights."

Fiore almost looked as though he believed him.

The muffled pop of an uncorking bottle paired with a wafting scent, half flowering citrus and half spoilt wine with an alchemical undercurrent. Enzo recognized it from university. He turned his head just far enough to behold Dr. Venier pouring chloroform onto folded linen. She caught Enzo's eye and held it out to him. He accepted the charge and held it up for Fiore's examination.

"May I?" Enzo asked. Begged, more like.

Fiore's panicked gaze flew from Enzo to the rag and back again.

"I swear," Enzo continued, working to keep his voice low and calm. "I will not let them mutilate you. All you need do is breathe."

Fiore's eyes flicked to the rag again. Then he met Enzo's gaze and, with a hard swallow, nodded.

Enzo laid the rag over Fiore's nose and mouth. His other hand stroked through Fiore's sweat-soaked curls. "It's all right."

Fiore's brow furrowed at his first sniff of the fumes. Enzo couldn't blame him; the alchemical smell threatened to overpower him, too. But Fiore kept breathing it in, his gaze fixed on Enzo all the while.

"I'm here," Enzo murmured. "I'll stay with you while you sleep. I'll be here when you wake. Just breathe."

The shallow panicked breaths grew slower and deeper as each one passed. The eyes burning into Enzo's own took longer and longer blinks, until, at last, they fluttered shut. Enzo wished more than anything to see them open again.

"You're aware of the convulsions."

Dr. Venier's voice, soft as it sounded, nonetheless startled Enzo. He turned to give her a nod. As he'd learnt in university, chloroform granted a sleep almost as deep as death, but the body fought it on the way down.

"Can you hold on through them?" she asked.

Enzo nodded again. He would hold on through a hurricane if Fiore needed him to.

Dr. Venier went to take up her post holding down Fiore's shoulders. In her wake, Enzo caught sight of a figure looming on the kitchen threshold just out of the corner of his eye. He turned his head further, expecting to find the maid or some other servant.

Instead, Lucrezia stood in the doorway.

Enzo stared. He'd forgotten her altogether. How long had she waited and watched? Not all this while, surely.

He could read nothing in her face. But perhaps she saw something in his—how all anger had fled his countenance, with fear surging in to fill the lack—for she regarded him for a moment longer before withdrawing in silence. Only her clicking bootheels told of her passage echoing down the hallway and fading off into nothing.

"Hold him," said Dr. Venier.

Enzo whipped his head 'round again to Fiore. He slipped his free palm beneath his skull. The other remained on the rag over his mouth and throat. He clamped down firmly yet gently.

Just as the convulsions began.

# CHAPTER TWENTY-SEVEN

Fiore didn't recognize the room.

Above him loomed the brocaded canopy and curtains of a four-post bed, its deep peacock-blue folds adorned with seafoam scale embroidery. Beyond it lay a coffered ceiling in the same shade of ebony as the bedframe. Despite the darkness of decorations, broad beams of sunshine brightened the strange space from a wall of windows set in marble archways. Through them he could see the familiar canals, bridges, and edifices of Halcyon from an altogether unfamiliar angle.

The glint of sunlight off the vivid green waves stung his eyes. He lolled his head—which felt uncommonly heavy—away from it.

And found Enzo sitting beside him.

All the light in the room seemed to infuse his own heart at the sight of him. Likewise, Enzo's features underwent a rapid transformation as their gazes met. The somber cast of the furrowed brow and tight-clenched mouth unknit as the soft, dark eyes widened in astonishment before settling with a gentle smile into quiet elation. In a blink he knelt by the bedside and laid his hand over Fiore's—the left one, his dominant hand, still intact. Fiore turned it to interlace their fingers. He had strength enough for that, at least. Enzo's other hand came up to cradle the side of his face that didn't ache.

"How do you feel?" Enzo asked—softly, as if he still feared to wake Fiore, though Fiore had already awoken.

Fiore knew there existed a polite answer to this question. However, it had flown from his head along with all pretty language. Which left him able to say just, "My gut hurts." He paused, for that was the largest pain, two distinct loci on either side of his navel that throbbed in time with his pulse to send out aching waves throughout his flesh. But loud as it was, it was not his only pain, and it didn't quite drown out the others. "And my hand." He'd hoped that one was just a nightmare. The burn at the knuckle and the lack of anything beyond it spoke otherwise. A glance down showed him a mitten of linen wrappings. He didn't want to see more. "And my face." His ankles, knees, hips, shoulders, and back didn't feel much better, but having been through all this before, or something rather like it, he added, "I suppose I have to get up now."

"Not just yet," Enzo said, much to Fiore's surprise. This surprise turned to dread as Enzo added, "The chirurgeon ought to have a look at you first."

"Do they have to?" Fear forced the words from Fiore's lips before he could think better of them. He hated the pitiful whine of his own voice.

But rather than give the inevitable "Yes," that Fiore expected to hear in reply, Enzo paused. At length, he said, "I shall enquire."

And then, to Fiore's silent dismay, he withdrew.

Fiore restrained his instinctive plea before it could leave his tongue. Even though it sent his heart into his throat to watch Enzo stand and depart from his bedside to disappear behind the massive door leading he knew not where. The sunlight continued streaming through the wall of windows, and yet all brightness seemed to vanish from the chamber in Enzo's wake, leaving Fiore alone in a room that loomed far too large all around him. He supposed he ought to give thanks that he was at least above ground in daylight.

The door swung inward. Enzo reappeared. But rather than the dreaded cold glass eyes and long beak, beside him stood a woman of middling age with close-cropped hair. For an instant Fiore wondered who she was and for what purpose Enzo had brought her to this room. Something about her eyes appeared uncannily familiar. Then his gaze fell from her face to her garb—black waxed-canvas robes.

"Good morning, Signor Fiore," said the unmasked chirurgeon.

Fiore stared at her in silence. He knew it was rude. He still couldn't help it.

"May we come in?" asked Enzo.

Fiore managed a nod amidst his continued bewilderment.

"I'm Dr. Venier," the chirurgeon told him as she approached, setting her leather case on the nightstand. "It's a pleasure to meet you properly at last."

Fiore knew he ought to reply in kind. He found he could not.

Dr. Venier seemed to take no offense. She did however take his temperature and pulse and dispensed mold-tincture in return. Then to his bewilderment, she asked, "Please describe your pain."

Fiore stared at her for a moment in disbelief before lolling his head to stare at Enzo.

Enzo gave the chirurgeon a brief recitation of what Fiore had told him moments earlier.

She nodded sagely. "About what we expected. Some anodyne should blunt its edge, but first—can you stand?"

This part was at least familiar. Fiore assented with a nod.

Enzo slipped his arm beneath Fiore's shoulders to raise him to a sitting posture. Once Fiore had his own arms around Enzo's shoulders to hold himself up, Enzo drew back the bedclothes to expose his legs and gently swing them off the side of the bed.

"Slowly," Dr. Venier instructed as Fiore, with the bulk of his weight supported by Enzo, attempted to stand.

His head went curiously light again as he arose. He shut his eyes, leaned his forehead into Enzo's shoulder—easy enough, given the disparity between their heights—and dragged in shuddering breaths.

"Steady," Enzo murmured into Fiore's curls. Over his head he said to the chirurgeon, "Down again?"

"No," Fiore forced out. He raised his head. Against all odds, it remained upright. The room no longer swam before him. Which made his ensuing lie more believable. "I can walk."

"Shall we try to the window and back?" asked Dr. Venier.

Fiore turned his head—slowly—toward the window. Three of Enzo's paces would reach it. He knew not how many of his own it would require. Particularly in his present state. Still, the sea breeze and sunshine called to him. "Let's."

The first step felt the worst. However many hours his captors had left him tied up in a knot hadn't done his joints any favors. Ankles, knees, hips, and spine all protested as he staggered forward and gained but half a foot.

"Well done," Enzo murmured above him. "Another?"

With such gentle enticement, Fiore could hardly refuse him.

It seemed to take hours to reach the window. Judging by the sunbeams shining across the floorboards, however, and more specifically by their lack of movement, Fiore realized no more than a quarter-hour could have possibly passed.

The window's marble frame held a bench long enough for Enzo to stretch his legs out on if he so chose, cushioned with aquamarine velvet. Beyond its tall glass panes lay a splendid view of the lagoon over the roofs of far smaller edifices.

Enzo shifted his stance as if he meant to turn away from it.

Fiore stood firm.

Enzo shot an enquiring look down at him.

Fiore lolled his head back against Enzo's shoulder to stare up into his eyes direct. "May we rest here a moment? Please?"

The last word slipped out unbidden and came cracked besides. Pathetic, Fiore thought, disgusted by his own weakness.

Enzo, however, appeared more concerned than repulsed. He turned to the chirurgeon for approval.

"He may," said Dr. Venier.

Fiore had never before heard anything so agreeable from one of her profession.

Enzo softly lowered him down to the window seat. Fiore leaned back, letting his skull come to rest on the marble pillar. The cool stone soothed his fevered brow. He gazed out over a familiar view from an unfamiliar perspective. The gondole and sandoli slipping up and down the canals and the people wandering through the streets and over the bridges brought him a long-missed sense of normality. Even the simple sight of sunshine glinting off the sea, after hours trapped underground with no assurance that he would ever see the sun again, filled his heart fit to burst. He could've stared for hours more. But a shiver passed over his skin. Another followed it, then another, until he trembled like a leaf in a storm.

Enzo's hand, which had never left his shoulder all the while, clasped him firm. "Back to bed?"

Fiore looked up to find him wearing an encouraging smile.

More than anything, Fiore wanted to mirror it. But his face felt as if carved from marble and seemed like it would move for nothing less than a sculptor's chisel. With an effort, he returned Enzo a solemn nod.

Standing for a second time went much the same as the first. He clutched Enzo's arm like a drowning cat.

"Steady," Enzo murmured, supporting him with no apparent effort. "Nearly there."

Fiore forced his legs to stagger. It seemed an impossible distance, but each clumsy step brought him nearer and nearer, until, at last, Enzo set him down again, then bent to lift his legs up onto the mattress and drew the bedclothes back over them.

Dr. Venier, meanwhile, scrubbed her hands at the washstand. Then she approached, much to Fiore's chagrin, and plied her termometro and stetoscopio again. She did so in a gentle and considerate fashion, but Fiore felt too drained to appreciate it. All he wanted was to be left alone with his Enzo.

Alas, rather than departing, Dr. Venier announced, "The bandages ought to be changed."

Fiore failed to suppress an exhausted groan.

Enzo fell upon him at once, which was almost what Fiore wanted. Strong hands softly brushed through his hair and stroked his cheek. Into his ear Enzo murmured, "Just a little while longer. Then you can rest."

Fiore caught Enzo's hand in his own good one and clasped it tight.

On the surface, the changing of bandages seemed to require very little from Fiore. All he needed to do was sit up in bed. In practice, it felt almost impossible—that is, save for his Enzo sitting beside him and propping him up with his arm beneath his shoulders, whilst Fiore flung both his own arms around Enzo's neck and held on for dear life. Why

Enzo didn't cast off the anchor of Fiore's weight upon him, Fiore couldn't fathom.

They began with the linen swathed 'round his middle. The chirurgeon cut it away with a pair of silver scissors. Enzo told him not to look. Fiore felt he had no choice but to watch. As the linen came free, his stomach seemed to plummet into an abyss, as if without the bandages to support his wounded flesh it threatened to all spill out. The linen itself came away as scarlet as his trade sash. He wondered what had become of his sash and the rest of his clothes besides. What he wore now, he realized, drawn up under his arms and tucked secure in place by Enzo's hands, was a nightgown made for a much larger man's frame, the seams of its broad back continually slipping off his own narrow shoulders. Perhaps one of Enzo's nightgowns. If so, Fiore hoped he hadn't bled on it.

Then he felt a pull on something within himself—too deep, far too deep—and Dr. Venier drew out something that unraveled wet and crimson.

Fiore had no strength to scream. His arm clenched tight around Enzo's shoulders. A strangled sound escaped his throat.

"Halt a moment," Enzo ordered. Belatedly, Fiore realized he spoke to the chirurgeon rather than to him, for when Enzo did turn his face down to meet Fiore's panicked gaze, he spoke on in a far gentler tone. "It's all right."

"What's—" Fiore choked out, the remainder of the question lost in the pounding of his pulse in his ears.

"The wounds are deep," Enzo explained after some hesitation. "There's bandages within as well as without, to keep the outer wounds open whilst the inner ones heal first."

Fiore tried to keep track. His mind took in the tone of Enzo's voice moreso than the words. At last he managed, "This is routine, then?"

Enzo's apologetic smile shone down on him. "I'm afraid so."

If Enzo thought this the best course, Fiore could do worse than go along with it. "All right."

Enzo clasped his shoulder with an affection that suffused Fiore's heart. Then, over Fiore's head, his commanding tone bid the chirurgeon, "Continue."

The second withdrawal felt no better than the first.

Dr. Venier cleaned the two wounds with something that stung stronger than vinegar. Every daub of the soaked cloth felt like a dull echo of being stabbed. She replaced the withdrawn bandages—which felt worse than taking out the old ones, just in a different direction—and wrapped Fiore up in fresh linen, taking up needle and thread to sew it into place. Then, to his equal astonishment and relief, she told him he could at long last lie down.

Enzo let down the hem of the nightgown and laid him back against the pillows. For a moment a queer terror seized Fiore that Enzo would let go altogether and leave him there alone, but Enzo's arm remained around his shoulders even after he'd settled, and Enzo himself reclined beside him, his other hand now free to continue smoothing back his curls from his brow.

Instinct bid Fiore kick when Dr. Venier laid her hands upon the wrappings around his ankles, but he restrained himself. When she'd done with those, she moved on to his wrists.

Enzo drew in a breath as Dr. Venier began unwrapping Fiore's hand. As if he meant, once again, to tell Fiore not to look. Fiore waited to hear him say it. He would ignore it all the same.

But Enzo merely let it out again in a soft sigh and twined his fingers through Fiore's hair.

Fiore fixed his gaze on his hand. This was what he'd dreaded most amidst all the horrors. He hadn't yet truly seen, by the full light of day, what remained after his captors had mangled him.

The first layer of linen remained white. Then a pale yellow stain. Then a rusty orange. Then a crimson blot turned black around the edge. And then there was no more linen at all, but instead a swollen scarlet lump where the chirurgeons had stitched skin up over the remaining knuckle-bone, crusted over with gore. He had but a glimpse before his guts twisted and he turned his face away to bury it in Enzo's collar.

"Easy," Enzo murmured above him, tucking his head under his bristled chin. "It's all right. She's almost done."

Fiore's whole arm trembled as the stinging liquid ran over the wound. It fell limp in Dr. Venier's grasp as she cleaned and re-wrapped it. Then she set it down in his lap and, judging by the muffled clinking sound off to the side, returned to her bag.

"All done, Signor Fiore," she said as she went. "You're doing very well. Just a quick dose of anodyne and then you may rest."

Which was all the warning he received before Enzo's hand laid gently over his forearm and something pricked the crook of it. The cold fluid forced its way into his veins. His hiss of pain dissolved as his mind floated aloft and didn't seem to know or care how to come back down. Dr. Venier's footsteps echoed away. The thud of the door falling shut sounded as if it reached his ear through leagues of seawater.

And finally, blissfully, he and his Enzo were alone again.

All remained quiet at first. Just the steady rise and fall of Enzo's chest and faint rustling of his fingertips through Fiore's hair. Then Fiore, with substantial effort, raised his head and tilted it back to look Enzo in the eye.

Enzo wore no hint of disgust or irritation, but rather met his gaze with a wan yet sincere smile, despite the shadows beneath his eyes. Only when the silent stare between them drew out through several moments did his brow furrow, but his tone remained light as he asked, "Zecchino for your thoughts?"

Fiore felt like he had both too few and too many to give voice. He opened his mouth regardless. "Any sash tied 'round my waist would turn red now."

Enzo's smile faded. Evidently it wasn't as funny as Fiore had thought. Or perhaps it was only the anodyne skewing his perspective.

Fiore tried again to smile. His face didn't hurt anymore, thanks to the anodyne, but the distant echo of discomfort ran down his cheek regardless. The chirurgeon hadn't touched it whilst she tended all his other wounds. Did it have bandages? He raised his good hand to check.

Enzo—ever so gently, else Fiore would never have abided it—caught his forearm against his palm. "Don't touch; it's still healing."

Which raised more questions than it answered. Fiore forced his muddled mind to form distinct words in sequence. "May I have a mirror?"

Enzo hesitated.

Fiore's blood ran cold. Still, he kept his voice even-keeled as he added, "I promise I won't smash it. No matter what it shows me."

"It isn't that," Enzo said quickly. "It's just—all fresh wounds look worse than they truly are. It won't do you any good to worry over them now. In fact it may do you a great deal of ill. Better to let it heal and examine it afterward, if you still wish to."

Fiore didn't remind Enzo that he hadn't asked for his medical opinion. Instead he said, "Give me a mirror."

A long and dreadful pause ensued between them. Fiore's nerves drew out alongside it. Just when it seemed they would fray and snap, Enzo arose and went to the washstand. He returned with a palm-sized hand-mirror.

Fiore held out his hand for it.

After another moment's hesitation, Enzo gave it over.

Fiore drew a bracing breath, clenched his fist tight 'round its pearl-inlaid silver handle, and raised it to his face.

At first glance, Fiore found it difficult to keep his promise regarding not breaking the mirror. Then, as the horrible moment stretched out over minutes, his eyes grew accustomed to the sight, until the discordant image no longer seared his mind to consider it. A long gash ran down his cheek on the right-hand side, from just above his ear down to his chin, sutured shut and smeared with some glistening salve that didn't disguise the gore beneath. He supposed he ought to give thanks he hadn't lost his eye. He let the hand holding the mirror fall to the bed with a soft thud.

"Just as you promised," Fiore muttered. "We've become a matched set."

Enzo didn't seem to find it even the least bit amusing. Fiore supposed that had been rather too much to hope for.

It likewise seemed rather too much to hope that he could return to his trade. A beautiful and unmarked face had set him apart. Now he'd be lucky if Enzo still wanted him. Certainly he'd wanted him enough to retrieve him from the catacombs. But now, seeing what catch had turned up in his net, there remained nothing to convince him not to toss it back into Neptune's embrace. Fiore wouldn't blame him in the least. Still, he had to ask the practical question.

"How long may I remain here?" Fiore enquired.

Enzo's brow furrowed in unaccountable confusion. "As long as you wish."

Fiore had no patience for romanticism. "How long, truly."

Enzo blinked. "Until you're well again, at the very least. Forever, if you'd like."

Fiore scoffed and turned his head away. Empty promises were the last thing he needed to hear right now. If he were lucky, he'd be permitted to stay until he could walk on his own two legs.

Enzo's hand sought his, still clasped around the pearl-handled mirror. Fiore let him have it.

"You need never work again, if you wish." Enzo's soft words cut all the deeper for their apparent sincerity. "I'm just glad you're alive."

"That'll wear off."

A stunned silence ensued, broken at last by Enzo's bewildered, "What?"

Fiore forced himself to draw breath. "You'll wake up a month from now—maybe six or twelve months from now, if I'm particularly lucky—and wonder why you're supporting a bitter, withered husk of an invalid. You'll realize my ugliness can't be healed and cast me off."

A second silence fell. Fiore couldn't bear to turn his head to see whatever realization dawned on Enzo's face.

"If you'd prefer," Enzo began, his tone more restrained but no less soft.

Fiore waited for the blow to fall.

"I'll draw up a contract," said Enzo.

Shock whipped Fiore's head towards him. The dizzying headache that resulted made the room swim before his eyes. When his vision cleared, he beheld Enzo's somber face. Unmistakable hurt shone behind his gaze, but no less affection. The sight broke Fiore's heart.

"Ironclad," Enzo continued. "Signed and witnessed. Establishing a pension that will see you living in comfort for all your days. You'll have your pick of where you'd like to set up a household, with staff to look after you and tend you. You need never see or speak to or think of me ever again if you truly wish it."

If his expression had broken Fiore's heart, then the sound of his voice shattered it—the restrained recital of an aristocrat determined to cloak their true emotion that nonetheless carried the undercurrent of agonies with a glinting hint of hope.

"But," Enzo added, softer still, "I'd prefer to remain by your side, if you would permit it."

Fiore's heart felt as if it would rip itself in twain between warmth and ache. Every joy was weighed down by bitterness. He'd been a fool to say nothing before, and even if he told Enzo the truth now—that he chose him, that he'd always chosen him, that if Enzo would deign to give him forever, then Fiore would hold fast until the end of his days, and only the fear of having it ripped from his grasp had held him back—there was no chance Enzo would ever believe him.

"I don't want a contract," Fiore forced out. The truth felt far too heavy as it left his tongue. His speech seemed to catch in his chest. It would tear through his heart if he let it escape. Yet to not say it would kill him just as well. And so he swallowed hard and admitted, "I want *you*."

He hated the way his voice broke on the final word. The silence that ensued sounded even worse to his ears.

Then, ever so gently, a hand closed over his own fisted in the bedclothes.

Fiore scraped together what little courage he had left and dared to glance up to meet Enzo's gaze.

There he found the same handsome face he knew so well, save now the striking features had twisted—the brow knit, the mouth thinned—in a sorrow almost as deep as what Fiore felt. And yet, as Fiore's gaze met those self-same soft, dark eyes, no longer shadowed by the bauta mask, he beheld the sorrow lightened by what he dared not hope for but which seemed very like a strong and abiding affection. This, despite all that'd happened, despite his own inconstancy and what marks it'd left upon him.

Enzo raised his other hand, palm upturned, seeking permission.

Fiore granted it with a nod.

Enzo reached for his face. His warm palm came to rest against Fiore's unwounded cheek. His elegant fingers delicately cradled his jaw. His thumb caressed his cheekbone, brushing away something wet.

"You have me," Enzo murmured. A wan smile graced his handsome lips. "For as long as you can stand me, you'll have all of me."

For a moment, Fiore simply stared.

Then he summoned all his strength to fling his arm up around Enzo's shoulders and drag him down beside him.

# CHAPTER TWENTY-EIGHT

F iore lived.

Two mere words could hardly contain all the elation and relief Enzo felt to see Fiore's beautiful eyes open again. To hold his hand, their fingers interwoven, and have Fiore awake and aware to clasp his in turn. To hear his voice, though weak and strained, when he thought he might never hear it again. Even when Fiore spoke of heartbreak and despair, just to be able to converse with him at all felt worth all possible pains. Enzo only wished he could take on Fiore's wounds for himself and spare him his agonies. The morphine helped with that—though Fiore went rigid whenever Dr. Venier approached with a needle.

The remainder of the day passed quietly. Fiore drifted in and out of fitful sleep. Whenever he awoke, Enzo endeavored to coax him into taking at least a glass of water. Fiore proved more pliable than Enzo expected. Though his every glance bespoke exhaustion beyond words, he nevertheless dutifully drank from whatever rim Enzo tilted against his lips. He even managed a few spoonfuls of horse broth. His sole complaint came when Dr. Venier listened to his stomach after he ate. Even this wasn't voiced, but rather a pitiful glance at Enzo, asking without words, "Must I?"

Enzo tried to give him an encouraging smile.

Fiore sighed and lolled his head across the pillow towards Enzo—and, more pointedly, away from Dr. Venier. His hand clenched tight in Enzo's whilst Dr. Venier listened. It didn't take long. Better still, it produced promising conclusions. Fiore's digestion had resumed in good order. He could take more broth if he liked. Fiore didn't appear particularly cheered by this proclamation, but he did brighten a little as the chirurgeon withdrew from the bedchamber—leaving both stetoscopio and termometro in Enzo's hands, returning only to dose Fiore with morphine—and when Enzo again offered up spoonfuls in supplication, he accepted a few more.

As afternoon drew on toward evening and the setting sun cast the clouds into soft gold and purple, however, something shifted in Fiore's aspect. His exhaustion became restlessness. His gaze flitted again and again towards the arched windows and the scarlet horizon spreading out across the once-green sea. His hand in Enzo's clenched and unclenched.

"Is it the pain?" Enzo asked him. Not quite an hour had passed since his last morphine dose, and he oughtn't have needed another for some time yet. If, however, something had gone wrong within him to increase his agonies…

But Fiore shook his head, sparing Enzo a mere glance before returning to the windows.

Enzo followed his gaze. Whatever so disturbed Fiore on the horizon, Enzo couldn't perceive it. He tried again. "Shall I close the curtains?"

"No!" Fiore blurted. The strength of the single syllable rivaled that of any speech Enzo had heard from him since his chirurgy. He added in a gasp, as if the force of the word had sapped him, "Don't—please—"

"Easy," Enzo urged him once he'd recovered from the initial shock. "I won't close them. You may look as long as you like."

Though, truth told, it seemed as though Fiore looked out the windows from revolting obligation rather than desire.

Fiore worked his jaw. His lips parted. He hesitated, then, without looking at Enzo, he said, "Where will you sleep tonight?"

Enzo could tell Fiore had endeavored to imbue the question with a casual air. It didn't work. He tried to figure out what answer Fiore wished to hear. He settled on the truth. "Beside you, if you wish it."

For he could hardly bear to be parted from Fiore now.

And, judging by the vise-grip Fiore kept on his hand, he felt much the same.

"Yes," Fiore said, the word clipped, his eyes never leaving the windows. His voice broke as he added, "Please."

Enzo ran his thumb over Fiore's knuckles. "Then I shall."

Fiore's taut frame relaxed just the merest fraction—the sight of which made Enzo's heart overflow with disproportionate joy.

Enzo withdrew to dress for bed. He tried not to notice how Fiore's good hand tangled in the bedclothes when he slipped out of his grasp. Disrobing, however, seemed to at least draw Fiore's notice away from the window. And there seemed a ghost of the appreciative gleam Enzo loved so well as Fiore's eyes trailed up and down his bared flesh.

The nightshirt Enzo drew over his head was a twin to the one Fiore now wore. There'd been no time to fetch any of Fiore's things from the *Kingfisher*, nor any opportunity to ask Fiore's permission to do so. Fiore must have realized by now that he'd been clad in one of Enzo's own nightshirts—indeed, his small frame seemed to drown in it—but he'd made no comment on it. Doubtless his mind had flown far off to other matters. Enzo only hoped he might draw it back in due course. And as Enzo returned to his bedside, Fiore did seem to perk up a little.

"May we have a light?" Fiore asked as Enzo neared.

"Of course," Enzo replied easily.

Fiore hesitated again. "May we keep it burning?"

The threads came together for Enzo in a flash. The setting sun. The descending darkness. The horrible sunless, moonless, starless void Fiore had plunged into and dwelt in when his captors dragged him down to the catacombs and held him there for hours, where he'd suffered wounds and mutilations and fled into the deepest and darkest crevice to escape.

"Of course," Enzo said again, though it hardly felt sufficient. He'd set every lamp, torch, brazier, and candle in the whole palazzo ablaze throughout the night if it meant his Fiore could rest without fear.

But just those two words seemed enough to ease Fiore's woes, as his rigid body relaxed and sank further back into the pillows.

And the simple act of lighting the oil lamp on the nightstand provoked a small and slight yet unmistakable sigh of relief.

Dr. Venier returned for one final round of termometro, stetoscopio, and anodyne before bed. Then she departed for the evening, which seemed to relieve Fiore more than the anodyne itself.

Enzo made his way around the bed to the other side, keenly aware of Fiore's gaze fixed on him all the while. He drew back the blankets and slipped between the bedclothes beside him. At first he'd intended to merely lie alongside, as near as he could without touching him and bringing pain to already wounded flesh, but Fiore's desperate haunting gaze begged him, as did the feeble gestures of his bandaged hand, to draw still nearer, until he found himself on his side curled around Fiore's frail form, with Fiore's wounded hand entangling in his hair. Fiore's good hand reached for him as well, and at its bidding Enzo laid his arm across Fiore's chest to clasp him as tightly as he dared.

"Like this?" Enzo murmured.

Fiore nodded and buried his face in Enzo's collar just as he'd done when Enzo had carried him out of the catacombs. Slowly yet surely his shuddering breaths deepened until, at last, he drifted off into true sleep.

Enzo ought to have dropped off as well. His mind raced on. Half of it ran on elation. Fiore had awoken. Fiore still breathed. Fiore lived, and he had him in his arms again, and no foul monster could tear him from Enzo's grasp.

The other half wallowed in melancholy.

The sight of Fiore's wounded face had pained Enzo only so much as he knew how a blade to the face felt—twice-over—and though it might prove the least of Fiore's agonies, still he would've spared him it.

But to have Fiore demand a mirror, and for Enzo to be weak enough to give it to him, and to watch how his beautiful features, no less beautiful for what they'd endured, crumbled in hopeless misery, was more than Enzo could well stand.

It wasn't vanity, that much Enzo knew. It was the look of an artisan who'd lost his hand—or his finger, Enzo reflected bitterly—and knew he might never ply his craft again. Certainly never to the same acclaim.

And so at last, by force rather than by choice, Fiore had accepted Enzo's offer.

The cruel twist of fate in granting his fondest desire did not escape Enzo. His heart held no blame for Fiore considering him the last resort.

All his bitterness stemmed from wishing Fiore weren't compelled to settle for him and could instead choose as he pleased.

Still, having been chosen, he would do all in his power to ensure Fiore lived a life of ease and comfort for all his days.

And it was this resolve which allowed Enzo to finally shut his eyes and claim some sleep of his own before dawn.

He awoke at daybreak as Dr. Venier came in to perform the morning's examination. Fiore, mercifully, slept through it. He likewise slumbered on through Enzo's breakfast. Enzo forced himself to swallow the coffee but couldn't manage more than a few bites of the brioche. Fiore continued sleeping throughout Enzo's ablutions and dressing.

Pulling on his own fresh hose and drawers made Enzo think on what Fiore had to wear. Since his departure from the *Kingfisher* had been unplanned, nothing of his had found its way to Ca' Scaevola, including clothes. For shirts he could probably borrow Enzo's, as he'd done for the nightshirt, though the sleeves were a touch over-long, and so would be any breeches or hose. Nothing Fiore had worn in the catacombs remained fit to wear again.

Enzo was still puzzling over the matter when Fiore awoke at last just before midday. It began with fitful stirrings, the limbs coming to life again in jerks and starts, the flickering ghost of a grimace passing over the handsome features, the bleary eyes blinking open beneath a furrowed brow, and the body which moments before had fallen soft in languid slumber going tense and rigid with uncertainty and fear, until at last those dark eyes fixed upon Enzo, and the hunched shoulders descended just a hair. The eyes smiled. The lips did not.

Enzo tried to smile enough for both of them. "Good morning."

Fiore's mouth echoed the greeting, though his voice didn't join in. He swallowed hard and raised his hand towards Enzo.

Enzo gently accepted his grasp and slipped his free arm behind his shoulders to help him upright. Fiore stood, trembling like a newborn foal, and leaned heavily against Enzo as they walked to the window. There Fiore paused, as he had yesterday, and so Enzo relented and settled him down onto the window seat rather than putting him back to bed straight off.

A quick ring of the bell summoned a midday repast fit for an invalid.

Neither Enzo nor Dr. Venier nor Dr. Malvestio thought Fiore's pulse strong enough for coffee just yet. Steamed milk and honey must have seemed a poor replacement to him, but he submitted to it without complaint. Enzo just felt glad he drank it all. In just a few short days his already-slender frame had gone gaunt. The milk would put at least a little meat back on the bones now visible through his skin. Enzo's gaze lingered on the curve of his all-too-distinct clavicle laid bare by the over-large nightshirt slipping off his shoulder.

Fiore began to shiver. Enzo laid his hand gently on his arm.

Fiore lolled his head back to look up at him, then rolled his eyes between Enzo and the bed. His voice arose in a soft creak. "Do I have to go back?"

Enzo hesitated. His heart demanded he obey Fiore's whims. However, his mind knew that if he wanted Fiore to survive, certain needs must be met, regardless of the patient's wishes. "You're cold."

"No I'm not." The lie, obvious and childish, sprang from Fiore's lips like a reflex. Both men knew it would never be believed. But for Fiore to have attempted it in the first place bespoke a certain desperation.

Enzo glanced over the room for an alternative solution. His wrapping-gown hung over the back of a chair. A few strides sufficed to retrieve it. Then he had only to help Fiore stand again on his trembling legs so he could slip his arms into the gown's sleeves. Enzo tugged it up over his shoulders; it slipped off at once, Fiore being far narrower in that regard than Enzo himself. Indeed, the garment's dimensions seemed to swallow Fiore up altogether. The hem that hung at Enzo's mid-calf swirled down around Fiore's heels. He looked as though he were drowning in a tide of black silk. But he didn't seem to mind. His shivering trailed off as Enzo bundled him up in it. And as he settled down onto the windowsill again, he buried his face further into the robe's shoulder.

"It smells like you," Fiore mumbled.

Enzo's heart did a curious flutter. Even so, he resolved to have a gown made especially for Fiore. It would be easy enough as the tailor already had Fiore's measurements. He could just tack it on to the same order when he asked for a new set of everyday wear to replace what Fiore had lost to the filth of the catacombs. Such an order, however, would take some time to fulfill. Which meant if Fiore wanted to wear something besides Enzo's own over-sized wardrobe...

"I had thought," Enzo ventured, "we might send Carlotta out to the *Kingfisher* to retrieve some of your clothes. With your permission."

Fiore considered this for a moment and assented with a nod.

His quietude broke Enzo's heart afresh. Enzo cleared his throat. "Is there anything else you'd like her to bring over?"

Fiore shrugged, a gesture which brought his narrow shoulder almost entirely out of the robe's voluminous sleeve. "Clothes, as you said. And my zibaldone. Pretty much what I brought to Wolf's Head, if she recalls."

Enzo felt certain she would. Carlotta seemed to recall every detail, no matter how minute. It was the work of a moment to send her out with this instruction. Then he returned to Fiore's side where he belonged.

Fiore remained quiet. As silent and pale and still as his false twin carved from marble in Artemisia's workshop. Only the eyes hinted at life, casting their dark gaze over the chamber, lingering on the coffered ceiling, the twist-fluted columns, the quatrefoil windows—details Enzo had taken for granted since his return to the city.

"So this is the fabled Ca' Scaevola," Fiore murmured at last.

"Fabled?" Enzo echoed with a note of amusement.

Fiore didn't meet his gaze. "Never thought I'd see the interior."

Whatever reply Enzo thought he might make died on his tongue. Fiore had spoken without a trace of bitterness. Instead his words carried just the barest hint of weary resignation—something his teasing tone might have disguised, if he'd had the heart for teasing. The tone of one who assumed himself unworthy of sights he longed to witness. And the sound of which gave Enzo's heart fresh wounds. For Fiore was more than worthy of Ca' Scaevola. He was worthy of all the world. Any house small or grand which would shut its doors to him deserved to burn.

Instead of saying any of this, however, Enzo instead blurted, "I could give you a tour, if you'd like."

Fiore turned a startled gaze upon him.

"When you're feeling stronger," Enzo added.

Fiore continued to regard him with his unreadable marble-carved expression. Then, ever so softly, he replied, "I'd like that."

Enzo fancied he saw the ghost of his former smile in those dark eyes.

"Is it just you here?" Fiore enquired. "Of your family, I mean."

"For now," Enzo replied. "The house belongs to my mother, properly speaking, but she prefers the seafaring life now that my sisters and I are all grown. Lucrezia dwells in the princely palace, and Giovanna remains in the countryside for the growing season to better manage her fields."

"So you have the full run of the place," Fiore concluded.

"Indeed," Enzo confirmed with a smile.

Fiore did not return the smile. His fingertips worried the wrapping-gown's lapel. "Do your sisters often interfere in your affairs here?"

Enzo furrowed his brow. "Not often, no."

"Is there anything that might provoke them to interfere?"

Enzo didn't understand where this line of enquiry had stemmed from. "Such as?"

Fiore's gaze had dropt to where he fiddled with the gown. "Harboring a broken courtesan in the family home, perhaps."

Enzo spent several heartbeats staring at him. Fiore never looked up.

When Enzo found his voice at last, it emerged hard and cold. "If they have any objection to your presence here, they will have to answer to me."

"Not the reverse?"

Enzo wished Fiore would look at him, wished his self-worth and fear didn't force his gaze downcast, wished he could make him understand his own value. "If they endeavor to remove you, I shall fight them tooth and nail. But," he added, as Fiore tensed, "it will not come to that. Lucrezia has no objection to us."

Fiore's hunched shoulders, all too visible amidst the voluminous folds of the gown's sleeves, relaxed a fraction.

The remainder of the afternoon passed quietly. Fiore slept through a great deal of it. And peacefully, as well, much to Enzo's relief. Fiore well deserved a decent rest after all he'd suffered of late. He awoke upon Carlotta's return with his effects. The door creaked as she entered, and this small sound alerted Fiore as Enzo received the folded bundle from her and shut the door on her departure.

Plain linen shirts and stockings alongside a single pair of chestnut woolen breeches mingled with the finery Fiore had worn to the ball. Likewise, fondness mingled with dread in Enzo's heart as he regarded them; for, while he'd loved the look of Fiore in finery and loved still more the joy evident in Fiore's face and form as he wore it, it was at that very ball where Enzo foolishly led Fiore into the very peril he now fought to survive. He glanced to Fiore to see what he thought of it now.

Fiore, however, had fixed his dark gaze not upon the raiments in Enzo's arms but on the zibaldone balanced atop them.

Enzo took the hint. He set the clothes aside and plucked up the zibaldone to give to Fiore. Fiore reached out to accept it from him.

But Fiore's grip—no doubt weakened by his ordeal—had not the strength. The zibaldone tumbled from his fingertips to the floor. A curse fell from his lips alongside it in a pained hiss of frustration.

Enzo dropt to his knees to retrieve the zibaldone at once. It'd landed on the spine, at least. He tried to take heart that the pages hadn't crumpled in the impact. That did, however, mean it'd fallen open.

And while under normal circumstances Enzo would never have been so ill-mannered as to glance into the secrets of another man's zibaldone —least of all Fiore's—his eye couldn't fail to catch the sight of his own name scrawled across the page.

Several times over.

And crossed out.

*Enzo—I've decided to accept your offer.*
*Enzo—I've chosen you after all.*
*Enzo—If your offer still stands, then*

Before his better sense could catch up, Enzo's mind flew on in rapid arithmetic. Fiore had left his zibaldone behind in his quarters when he'd gone to meet his captors on the *Kingfisher*'s deck. Therefore these lines must have been penned not just prior to his rescue but prior to his kidnapping.

A silence had descended in the wake of the tumbling book's thud. Now it began to ring in Enzo's ears. Too late he looked up from the page.

And found Fiore staring at him in undisguised horror.

Rather than an apology or even a reassuring word, Enzo heard his own hushed voice ask, "You chose me?"

Fiore met his eyes with a steady, albeit evidently frantic, gaze. "Yes."

"All this while?"

"Yes."

"Why didn't you say anything?"

"I tried." A hard swallow emphasized the jewel in Fiore's slender throat. "I was too afraid."

Enzo well remembered the tempestuous events of the masked ball. He nodded sagely. "Of Nascimbene."

"No," Fiore said quickly, much to Enzo's surprise. He hesitated before adding, "I was afraid of losing you."

This did nothing to alleviate Enzo's bewilderment. "You didn't want to lose me... so you refused to keep me?"

"If an elderly gentleman I don't particularly care for casts me aside, it's nothing to me. But if you..." Fiore trailed off, as if he couldn't bear to give voice to his worst fear.

Enzo could hardly bear the thought himself. The idea of anyone casting Fiore aside made his blood simmer with righteous anger. But to hear Fiore say he feared Enzo would discard him... Enzo wondered what he'd done to make him think such a thing were possible.

Still, for once, Enzo felt he had the correct answer. "I would never."

Fiore didn't look as though he believed him. Yet he reached for Enzo regardless—and, as Enzo descended to meet him, pulled him into a desperate embrace.

And, however privately, Enzo vowed that nothing should tear him away.

~

Hempen bonds burned through Fiore's wrists as he struggled in vain to break free. Every pull of his arms only scraped away more of his skin and embedded the ropes deeper in his flesh. The knuckle stump of his missing finger throbbed all the while. But all this was nothing in comparison to what would befall him—again—if he should fail to escape.

Bound to the mountaintop, he could see little through the roiling fog. He could hear, though. And soon enough, before he could twist his wrist to get his mangled hand out of the rope's coils, he heard that dreaded sound.

An eagle's shriek.

With an answering echo.

Fiore hardly had time for one last frantic attempt at escape before the raptors fell upon him.

Vicious beaks plunged into his gut. They tore screams from him alongside his entrails. The eagles feasted on him as they had every day before, for as long as he could remember, and as they would every day after, unless he could slip his bonds. But they only grew tighter as he struggled. He couldn't even recall what he'd done to deserve this eternal punishment. Some betrayal, some failure of loyalty, some cowardice had led him here. Unlike Prometheus, there was no Hercules come to set him free.

Or so he thought, until a peculiar sound caught the very edge of his hearing.

Above the cacophony of his own screams and the eagles' triumphant cries, a whisper floated on the wind whistling past his ear.

*Fiore.*

His own name, spoken by a familiar voice, one which had no place in this realm of pain. He clung to it nonetheless. Even the eagles rending his flesh couldn't tear him away from that blessed sound. He tried to answer it, but his screams clogged his throat.

*Fiore.*

The eagles, intent on devouring him, didn't seem to hear the whisper. And yet amidst the stabbing agony in his entrails and the burning pain in his wrists and the dull throbbing ache in his hand, another sensation arose—the ghostly touch of invisible yet gentle hands upon his shoulders.

"Fiore?"

Fiore jolted awake with a choked-off gasp. The oil lamp still burning on the nightstand revealed the curtains and bedposts above him and the coffered ceiling beyond. The ghostly hands on his shoulders coalesced into Enzo's very tangible yet still tender grip, and he turned his head to find Enzo half-upright in the bed beside him. Locks of long, dark hair fell across his knit brow and beside his cheek as he gazed down at Fiore with concern in his warm brown eyes.

The eagles and the mountaintop were merely a dream.

The pain, however, remained excruciatingly real.

"Steady," Enzo murmured as a whimper escaped Fiore's throat.

Half of Fiore's heart regretted that his own weakness had forced Enzo awake beside him. The other half held only gratitude that Enzo had arisen to tend him in his hour of need.

Enzo reached across him towards the silver hand-bell on the nightstand. Its tinkling refrain ought to have brought Fiore relief. Instead he found the sound inspired fresh dread, for it heralded the chirurgeon's return. And all the while the phantom eagles continued their assault on his entrails.

"It's all right," Enzo murmured as another pitiful whine forced its way through Fiore's clenched teeth. He stroked the sweat-slicked curls back off Fiore's forehead. "They'll give you something for the pain."

Fiore wished Enzo trusted himself with the needle. He had almost as much education as Dr. Venier or Dr. Malvestio. Surely enough so that nightmare needn't compound upon nightmare as Fiore's worst fears came to deliver him from the tyranny of his mind's horror.

Enzo, meanwhile, took up the termometro and stetoscopio from the nightstand.

The door creaked open. Fiore flinched from the noise, however slight. Footsteps crossed the room, and soon the face of an unfamiliar man of some threescore years appeared at the bedside, garbed in a black waxed-canvas gown. Presumably this, then, was Dr. Malvestio.

"He's only just awoken," Enzo explained to him as he set up his leather case on the nightstand.

"In pain?" Dr. Malvestio enquired.

Fiore wanted to laugh.

"Yes," Enzo replied.

"How much?" Dr. Malvestio asked.

Enzo looked to Fiore.

Fiore knew only screams would emerge if he opened his mouth.

Enzo stroked his brow again. "Better than before? Or worse?"

Fiore summoned all his strength to restrain his cries as he forced out through clenched jaws, "The same."

"A full dose, then," Dr. Malvestio cut in. "Should carry you through 'til dawn."

Yet Enzo didn't appear relieved to hear this. He gazed down at Fiore, worried his lip between his teeth, then glanced up to the chirurgeon. "Has anything gone wrong, d'you think?"

Dr. Malvestio paused in the midst of withdrawing needle and vial from his case. He turned to Fiore. "Does it feel at all changed? Duller? Sharper? More of an ache or more of a bite?"

Fiore shook his head and hissed again, "The same."

And while he hadn't strength enough to say it aloud, he caught Enzo's gaze and pleaded without voice, *Please don't make him stay any longer. Please just let him dose me and go.*

Enzo seemed to understand him, if his wan yet sympathetic smile were anything to go by.

Dr. Malvestio took in the termometro beneath Fiore's tongue and the stetoscopio in Enzo's ears with a single sweeping glance. "Any change in the pulse?"

"Strong," Enzo reported. "Though rapid."

Dr. Malvestio reached for the termometro—then halted as Fiore recoiled. He raised his brows again. "If I may, signore."

Fiore nodded and forced himself to remain still as the chirurgeon pried the instrument from his mouth.

Dr. Malvestio examined the termometro with a placid air. "No fever. Which makes infection unlikely. And, if the pulse is still strong, it is likewise unlikely anything has torn within. I'd rather you have your rest now and we may reassess in the morning. If it's all the same to you, signore," he added, glancing at Fiore, who realized only belatedly the chirurgeon had spoken to him and not Enzo.

Fiore nodded again. He couldn't watch while Dr. Malvestio filled the needle from the vial, and turned his head altogether as the chirurgeon approached.

Enzo laid his palm over where Fiore had fisted his wounded hand in the bedclothes. Fiore dared a glance up at him and found him wearing that same sympathetic smile.

Before Fiore could do anything about it, the needle jabbed into his arm, and the plunge of cold fluid into his vein sent his mind soaring above his body. It floated back down far too slowly for his liking. While his heart no longer raced with fear, he remained cognizant of its causes, and misliked how vulnerable he was in this altered state. At least the eagles had left off. And the chirurgeon packed up and went with them.

Yet despite the alchemical dose, Fiore only truly relaxed when Enzo, at long last, curled his long frame around his broken body and entwined Fiore in his strong arms.

"Better?" Enzo murmured as he stroked Fiore's curls.

Fiore nodded and buried his face in Enzo's collar. The warm and familiar scent of his masculine musk soothed his muddled mind. Soon he drifted off into a mercifully dreamless sleep.

When next his eyes opened, he beheld the bedchamber bursting with brilliant sunshine. Still more brilliant was the smile Enzo cast down upon him as Fiore lolled his head across the pillow to find him sitting up in bed beside him. A book lay propped up against Enzo's half-cocked thighs, but he seemed more concerned with worrying the corner of a page between his fingertips rather than turning it.

Fiore tried to bid him good morning. Instead, he wondered aloud, "Is this your room?"

Enzo confessed that it was.

Fiore knew he ought to say something more after that. He settled on what felt like the correct polite refrain. "It's nice."

A queer smile stole over Enzo's lips as he murmured his thanks.

"What time is it?" Fiore asked. His words felt reluctant to leave his tongue. A fog had settled over his mind.

"Almost midday."

As that was technically still morning, Fiore counted it as a win.

Enzo turned away from him to reach for something on the opposing nightstand. Fiore hadn't noticed that particular piece of furniture before. He supposed he ought to have suspected a matched set.

The sound of liquid pouring between vessels interrupted his meandering thoughts. It ceased. Enzo returned to him with a glass goblet of water. He gave it to Fiore, keeping his own hand on it as well to help support its weight; insubstantial under any other circumstance, but very heavy indeed in Fiore's weakened state.

"Drink this," Enzo urged when Fiore made no move to bring it to his own lips.

"What's in it?" Fiore asked.

"Only water."

Fiore wanted to believe him. He forced down the unreasonable unbidden fear in the back of his mind and raised the rim of the glass to his mouth. It tasted only of water; no trace of laudanum's bitterness, nor of anything like whatever his kidnappers had dosed him with. It slipped over his tongue and down his throat, cool and refreshing, and awakened a thirst he hadn't realized he possessed. Soon it was drained. Enzo poured him another.

"There's limonata as well, if you'd like," Enzo said as Fiore polished off the second glass.

Fiore had to admit that sounded tempting. But habit bid him enquire, "Coffee?"

"Not for a few more days," Enzo said. At least he sounded apologetic. "But you may have bone broth, if you're feeling up to breakfast."

"How long until I can have something..." The word Fiore wanted evaded his grasp. "More?"

"Solid food will have to wait another fortnight," Enzo replied, looking almost as sorry for it as Fiore felt.

"Didn't have to wait last time," Fiore muttered before he could think better of it.

Enzo hesitated. "Last time it was only appendicitis."

Fiore snorted. "Only."

A wan smile graced Enzo's lips. "And while that was a very serious infection, your entrails were not punctured. Now, however, we must wait until the wounds are fully closed before we risk reopening them with too much substance."

Fiore considered him. "You're saying if I ate baccalà now, it would rend me asunder from within?"

"Very possibly, yes," Enzo said, much to Fiore's alarm. "At the least it would make you extremely uncomfortable."

"Oh," said Fiore.

"It wouldn't be the baccalà itself, necessarily. Rather, the undulations the intestines must perform to digest solid food could result in your entrails tearing their own stitches out."

Fiore didn't really see the difference, but he appreciated Enzo's efforts to explain it all the same. "I don't think I'm hungry just now."

The concerned crease reappeared between Enzo's brows. Still, he smiled down at Fiore and stroked his hair. "Do you feel up to walking?"

Fiore didn't believe it truly mattered whether he felt up to it or not. But he liked to be asked all the same. He nodded.

"May I take your pulse first?" Enzo asked.

While the thought of either chirurgeon doing so remained abhorrent, the thought of Enzo listening to his heartbeat sent an unexpected calm through Fiore's veins. He nodded again.

Enzo retrieved his pocket-watch and the stetoscopio from the nightstand, and the termometro besides. The latter he raised with an enquiring tilt of his head. Fiore nodded a third time and opened his mouth so Enzo might gently slip the instrument beneath his tongue.

A brief smile flickered across Enzo's lips as if in thanks. He vigorously rubbed the brass bell of the stetoscopio against his palm before turning down the bedclothes just enough to expose the left side of Fiore's chest. Imbued with Enzo's warmth, the stetoscopio felt far gentler against his ribs. Fiore found himself drawing slow and steady breaths rather than the panicked gasps he'd known of late. Enzo kept his gaze on his pocket-watch for what felt like a minute or two. Then he snapped it shut, withdrew the prongs from his ears, and looked upon Fiore once again with a smile whose soft sweetness threatened to bring Fiore to ruin.

"Better than before," said Enzo. He raised his hand to the termometro in an enquiring gesture, and only after Fiore nodded did he draw it from his lips with exceeding tenderness. Another smile flickered at the corner of his mouth as his gaze fell on the instrument. "And no worse."

Fiore wondered what he had to do to make the termometro reading better.

Enzo merely smiled and held out his hand.

Even if Fiore weren't weak as cobwebs, he had no choice but to take it.

Enzo slipped his other arm beneath Fiore's shoulders and sat him upright, completing the now-familiar ritual of swinging his legs out of the bed so he might stand. Fiore took in more of the room this time, noting in particular the tapestry embroidered with a scene of a unicorn hunt, which had presumably hung over the enormous blank space on the wall by the door but now had been flung over the full-length mirror beside the wardrobe.

This time when they reached the window Enzo sat down beside him. Fiore felt his gaze upon him as he stared out over the city. He still didn't know quite how to answer it. He knew only how Enzo cradled his hands in his own and anchored his aching heart to the soft and calming lagoon.

All too soon, however, his body wearied from the chore of holding itself upright, even with the velvet cushion beneath him and the support of the window's marble pillars against his back. He turned to Enzo and found his dark gaze soft with something he couldn't quite place.

"Back to bed?" Enzo murmured.

Fiore nodded and allowed Enzo to draw him up and half-carry him there.

Then, of course, intruding once again onto what little harmony Fiore could scrape together since his rescue, there came the chirurgeons. Dr. Venier arrived to slice off and re-stitch the bandages 'round his middle. Fiore submitted to this only because his Enzo remained beside him throughout.

When it came to his hand, wrists, and ankles, however, Enzo took sole charge.

It began with the unwrapping. Enzo peeled away each layer of linen from Fiore's wrists and hand with all the soft patience of nature coaxing rose-petals to unfold from bud to bloom. After a meticulous soapy scrubbing of his own hands in the washbasin, he bathed the rope burns and the ragged stump with a cloth soaked in warm water, then patted them dry. His gentle fingertips salved the wounds, and he redressed them with fresh linens, wrapping Fiore's wrists and knuckle firmly yet gently in the long winding bands. The tenderness of his touch throughout as he cradled Fiore's hands in his own threatened to tear through the tight knot that'd formed in Fiore's chest.

Then, to Fiore's astonishment, Enzo brought Fiore's left hand to his lips and kissed his knuckles with all the reverence of a mortal approaching the divine.

Fiore quite forgot to breathe.

Enzo lowered his hand and glanced up with a shy smile. It vanished the moment his gaze met Fiore's face. "Have I hurt you?"

"No," Fiore forced out; the tight knot in his chest had risen into his throat. "Why?"

Enzo hesitated, then raised his hand to Fiore's unwounded cheek and brushed away something wet with the pad of his thumb.

Shame made Fiore's eyes burn all the more. Another blistering tear trickled down his face.

Enzo withdrew a handkerchief from his breeches pocket and daubed at Fiore's cheek. Then, putting the handkerchief into Fiore's own grasp, he turned away to the nightstand and poured a glass of water from the pitcher. This, too, he gave to Fiore, supporting it as he drank.

When Fiore had polished off his second glass and scrubbed the last of his unwarranted tears from his face, Enzo slipped down the bed to examine his ankles. They had fewer abrasions than his wrists; his hose had shielded them somewhat from the ropes. Still, as Enzo slid his palm beneath Fiore's calf and began to bend the limb, Fiore winced.

Enzo ceased at once. "It pains you?"

Fiore nodded with reluctance. "Not as bad as the rest of it."

"Still," said Enzo. "Where does it hurt, beyond the wounds themselves?"

"Mostly in the joints. And the lower back, as well. You'd think years on my knees would've inured me to it," he added bitterly.

It at least brought a wan smile to Enzo's lips, if only for a moment. His brow furrowed in concentration again as he experimentally slid his hand up over Fiore's knee and the outside of his thigh to the jutting hollow of his hip. "How long did they have you tied? Forgive me," he added quickly. "I hate to ask, but..."

"A chirurgical necessity?" Fiore enquired drily.

348

The wan smile flickered across Enzo's features once more. "I'm afraid so."

Fiore tried to remember. It was harder than it ought to have been. The whole sordid night had played out over and over again in flashes throughout his nightmares and in certain waking moments. But any specific useful detail evaded him. "They took me in the early afternoon. Slipped something into my wine. I don't even remember disembarking from the *Kingfisher*. I suppose they tied me up soon after. Hand-to-foot, behind my back," he added, guessing the specific method might be helpful for Enzo's purposes. "I woke up like that, and I didn't get out of it until..." He paused, silenced by his own shame. "Well, until shortly before you arrived."

Enzo wore the look of one trying very hard not to appear even half so horrified as he felt. It didn't quite work. Still, his voice remained calm and even as he concluded, "Twelve hours, then, at the very least."

Fiore shrugged, then winced at the ache in his shoulders. "You'd know better than I."

A hard swallow travelled a long way down Enzo's throat. "The walking should help matters. It doesn't look as though anything was pulled entirely out of joint, but... if I may?" he added, raising a hand to Fiore's shoulder.

Fiore nodded again. He wanted Enzo's touch more than anything—even if it were only a chirurgical necessity.

Enzo's fingertips gently but firmly plumbed the depths of his aching joints. "Does it hurt when you walk, also?"

"Yes." Fiore furrowed his brow in confusion. "Not so bad as now, but..."

"You're almost due for another dose," Enzo reminded him. "That might be why you're feeling the worst of it now."

Fiore shrugged and winced again. "I wouldn't know."

"There are some exercises to restrengthen your muscles, once you're not so exhausted." Enzo still sounded so hopeful that he would recover. "Those should help as well."

Fiore wished he were better at disguising his exhaustion. He wanted to regain his strength at once. At the same time, he couldn't imagine doing anything more demanding than rolling his head across the pillow to face the window.

Another small smile, painful and sweet, tugged at the corner of Enzo's lips. "Could you eat something, d'you think?"

"Drink it, you mean." The words fell from Fiore's mouth with more bitterness than he felt.

Yet Enzo continued smiling even as he conceded, "For now, yes."

Fiore withheld a sigh and replaced it with a nod.

# CHAPTER TWENTY-NINE

The first few days passed in an anodyne haze.

Enzo remained beside him all the while, for which Fiore rejoiced. Apart from the chirurgeons, however, he saw no one save Enzo. Not even Carlotta, whose shadowy presence Fiore had come to expect as a matter of course. Whatever servants brought his meals remained on the opposite side of the imposing door. Fiore heard nothing but whispers between them and Enzo before Enzo returned to him bearing a well-laden tray.

There was no sign of Enzo's family, either—which gave Fiore some small relief. It was all very well for a man to swear he'd defy his family on behalf of his lover, but in Fiore's experience it rarely came to pass. Recollections of Serafina's humiliation remained ever at the forefront of his mind.

But shortly after waking on the third day he heard more than whispers beyond the door. As Enzo dismissed whoever took away the breakfast tray, Fiore caught another voice altogether; a pitiful whine. And for once not from his own throat.

Fiore bolted upright at the sound—wincing as the sudden movement pulled against his multitude of injuries—and caught a glimpse of a dark shadow through the crack in the door. It slunk at waist-height to Enzo and, unless Fiore much mistook it, had a tail.

Enzo shut the door on servant and shadow alike.

"Is that Vittorio?" Fiore asked.

"Yes," Enzo admitted after a moment's hesitation.

"…Can he come in?" Fiore enquired.

Still Enzo hesitated. "There is the concern of contamination."

"How could I contaminate him?"

A wan smile graced Enzo's scarred lips. "I mean that he might contaminate you. Your wounds are yet open and deep besides."

Fiore appreciated Enzo's evident reluctance to remind him even of this obvious fact. And yet. "He visited you in your sickbed when your own wounds were hardly less so."

Enzo conceded the point with raised brows and a tilt of his head. But something else obviously troubled him. "…He did also just kill a man."

Fiore blinked. Vittorio had jaws fit to shatter bones, true enough, but he'd displayed nothing except gentle patience in Fiore's presence. "Who?"

Enzo worried his lip. "One of your captors."

Fiore stared at him. A queer curiosity sparked in his veins despite the dampening effects of the anodyne. "Did he, indeed?" At Enzo's answering nod, Fiore added, "Which one?"

"The large one," Enzo admitted with unaccountable reluctance. "With the broken nose."

"How?" Fiore demanded. He had a dim awareness that his captors had all perished—Enzo had told him so when his more vivid nightmares demanded reassurance that those who'd harmed him could never touch him again—but he knew not the full account.

And yet Enzo still evaded. "I would spare you the gory details. Your nerves—"

"I don't want to be spared," Fiore insisted. "I want to know."

Perhaps Enzo realized at last that forbearance would only agitate his patient further. He relented with a sigh. "Very well. The brigand attacked me. And Vittorio tore out his throat."

Fiore didn't know quite how he ought to feel. At present he felt a sort of elation, which seemed somewhat wrong, and yet if he could have smiled he knew he would've grinned. Grim satisfaction, he supposed. Of all his tormentors, the broken-nosed brute best deserved the fate Vittorio had dealt him. Regardless... "Then Vittorio has proved himself a very good hound. The least we may do is reward him for his efforts."

A crease had appeared between Enzo's brows. His lips parted—doubtless to argue, however gently, against allowing Vittorio in—but again he hesitated.

And in that moment of hesitation, Vittorio's most pitiful whine arose beyond the door.

Fiore fixed Enzo with a pointed look.

Enzo relented and went to the door. The whining ceased as it opened. This time Enzo flung it wide, enough so that Fiore could see how Vittorio quivered with excitement at the sight of his master and yet remained seated in perfect obedience until Enzo pronounced the command.

"Release."

Then and only then did Vittorio bound up with astonishing agility for a creature of his size and throw paws as large as human hands over Enzo's shoulders—for, on his hind legs, he stood fully as tall as his master.

A rare and welcome smile graced Enzo's scarred lips even as his hound's enthusiasm forced him backward into the room. Only after Enzo vigorously rubbed the hound's ribs did Vittorio jump down again at last. Then he settled for leaping and bowing in circles around his master, knocking his anvil skull against Enzo's body to request further pats.

The sight of the hound at play made Fiore feel the nearest thing to a smile since his kidnapping, though he couldn't quite make his face show it.

Several moments passed before Vittorio even noticed Fiore. His ears pricked as his gaze fell upon the bed. Though evidently reluctant to part from Enzo, nonetheless he took a tentative step towards Fiore.

"Gentle," Enzo admonished him.

Remarkable beast that he was, Vittorio seemed to take the instruction to heart—though his tail wagged as vigorously as ever. Rather than leap up onto the bed, he settled for laying his chin on the mattress by Fiore's good hand. Fiore scratched him behind his ears and dug his fingertips into the velvety-soft fur covering his skull. His heart felt a little lighter. It felt lighter still when Enzo sat on the bed beside him.

"He could support your weight, if you're willing to try standing again," Enzo suggested.

Fiore would've felt content to lay there in his half-waking, half-sleeping state with one arm around the hound and the other around his Enzo. But he supposed it must be that time of day again. He assented with a nod.

This time when Enzo drew him upright, Fiore braced his palm between Vittorio's shoulder blades. The hound stood firm as iron. And when Fiore took a step forward, one arm entwined with Enzo's and the other on Vittorio's back, the latter kept pace—and kept a careful eye cast up at Fiore besides. Vittorio stuck by him even as they reached the window and paused so Fiore might rest. No sooner had Fiore lowered himself into the window seat than Vittorio nudged his head into Fiore's lap and cast his worried bestial gaze balefully up at him.

"Good boy," Fiore murmured as he petted the hound's velvety head.

Vittorio's tail thumped against the floorboards with renewed vigor.

The tail continued its enthusiastic wagging on their slow and steady return voyage to Fiore's sickbed. It thwacked the tapestry that hid Enzo's standing mirror. But rather than a thud or even a crack of breaking glass, it instead produced a curious reverberating twang that struck Fiore's ears as unaccountably musical.

Fiore stumbled to a halt. "What was that?"

Enzo winced. "A lute."

Fiore stared up at him. "But your lute is at Wolf's Head."

"I brought it with me when I returned here."

"Why?"

Enzo hesitated. "I thought you might want to play it again."

Fiore's mutilated hand throbbed. He buried his good hand in the thick ruff around Vittorio's collar. The hound had sat down when he'd halted. His tail still wagged but did not strike the hidden instrument again.

Fiore fancied he could both hear and feel the rusted cogs creak together in his anodyne-addled mind as he tried to think. "Giovanna gave it to you so you might occupy yourself with learning to play."

Enzo's brow furrowed in confusion. "Yes."

"And you did learn," Fiore ventured.

Enzo looked no less confused. "Yes."

"Will you play for me?"

Enzo balked. A tempest of mixed emotions—surprise, sadness, concern—whirled over his scarred features. "I don't play so well as you."

Before he could think better of it, Fiore replied, "You certainly play better than I could now."

The agony in Enzo's eyes echoed the ache in Fiore's wounded hand. He glanced away quickly—toward the tapestry and presumably the lute that lay beneath it. A sharp inhale through his long nose left him in a sigh.

"If you'd like."

Enzo had spoken so quietly and moved his scarred lips so little that at first Fiore thought he'd imagined his reply. But after Enzo tucked him back into bed, he returned to the tapestry and drew back just enough to retrieve his lute from beneath its folds.

Vittorio, meanwhile, had settled his head on the bed beneath Fiore's good hand. He looked as though he wanted to leap onto the bed outright, but yet awaited his master's permission to do so and until he received it would remain obedient where he sat.

Enzo sat beside Fiore and laid the lute in his lap. He took a few moments to tune it. He had a good ear for it, Fiore observed, and soon made it fit for music.

As much as Fiore wished to hear Enzo play, his expectations were not particularly high. An aristocrat learning to play for his own amusement was worlds away from an artist honing their craft. Certainly nothing like the musicians of the conservatorio.

Then Enzo began.

It was a bourrée. Though performed at a far slower tempo than Nascimbene would've tolerated, it kept time with itself and became a sweet if simple tune. Within mere measures Vittorio drifted off to sleep like Cerberus before him. Fiore remained awake, but nonetheless felt the release of tensions he hadn't even realized he still carried. And while it may not have moved the opera's audience to tears, the soft and gentle sound nonetheless touched Fiore's heart.

Enzo ceased playing.

"What's wrong?" Fiore asked.

Enzo reached for him—then hesitated, and only after Fiore's confused nod did he gently wipe a scalding tear from Fiore's unwounded cheek with the pad of his thumb.

Fiore wished his face would stop leaking without his permission. He swallowed down the lump in his throat. "You play rather well."

Enzo shrugged. "Giovanna was kind enough to give it to me. An honest effort to learn is the least I could give her in return."

"But you had other matters to attend," Fiore continued, determined to make his meaning plain. "Fencing. Hunting. Medicine." He hesitated, realizing all of a sudden just how little he knew of aristocratic education. "Other... things..."

Enzo's wan smile sent a flickering warmth through Fiore's heart. "A hundred trifles and distractions."

Fiore idly wondered which one he was—a trifle or a distraction.

"Neither," said Enzo, at which point Fiore realized he'd wondered aloud.

Fiore's face went up in flames.

Enzo set the lute aside. He leaned in toward Fiore. A glance to Fiore's mouth and back again begged silent permission. Fiore granted it with a nod. And, at long last, Enzo bent to kiss him.

"You," Enzo murmured against Fiore's lips as they broke off for breath, "are a devotion."

Against all his better sense, Fiore almost believed him.

∼

"Did you ever have to do this at university?" Fiore asked one afternoon as Enzo rewrapped his wounded knuckle. A se'en-night had passed since his rescue, and his doses of anodyne reduced to a point where his mind could connect several thoughts together in sequence, allowing him the luxury of asking slightly more intelligent questions than before.

Enzo paused in the midst of tying off the bandage. After a moment's hesitation, he replied, "I did, yes."

"Under different circumstances, I suppose," Fiore supplied when

Enzo fell silent again. He assumed most university students didn't fall victim to kidnapping. But perhaps Enzo's account would prove him wrong.

A weak chuckle escape Enzo, which Fiore took as a good sign. "Indeed. It's a common injury amongst woodworkers and cabinet-makers. And sometimes particularly unfortunate sculptors if the chisel slips against the marble."

"Then I'm in good company as well as good hands," Fiore concluded.

A wan but no less handsome smile flickered across Enzo's lips. Then they parted as if for speech, only to close again more firmly than before.

Fiore cocked his head at him. "Zecchino for your thoughts?"

After a moment, Enzo ventured, "You draw with your left hand, do you not?"

"Most of the time," Fiore admitted. "The conservatorio tried to turn me right-handed. Most instruments are designed to be played so. But they didn't want me drawing anyway, so I always drew with the left. And then when I started copying actual artists—Artemisia, mostly—I learnt to draw with the right hand for gestural sketches and put finer details in with the left. The dominant hand is better saved for precision."

"Saved from what?"

Fiore shrugged. "Pain, mostly. The same small motion for so many hours will cramp you up, and you can either cease drawing until the pain passes—which may be days, if not weeks—or you can switch hands. Artemisia has practiced so long you can hardly tell her left from her right in her sketches, though to her the difference appears astronomical, and ware her wrath if you suggest her right is as good as her left."

Fiore expected another chuckle in reply. Yet Enzo remained in pensive silence for another moment, a knot appearing between his brows, before he answered with solemnity.

"I've no wish to tell you how you ought to feel about it," Enzo began. "But from a medical perspective, if one must lose a finger, the forefinger is the one to discard."

Fiore stared at him. "Explain."

Enzo couldn't seem to look him in the eye. Yet the gaze he cast down on Fiore's wounded hand held all the tenderness of Flora coaxing roses into bloom. "Most folk would choose to cast off the smallest finger. But it's the smallest finger which contributes the most to the strength of the hand's grip. And while the middle finger can pick up most of what the forefinger would do, the fore, middle, and leech finger combined can't bear the weight of what the smallest finger would hold secure."

Fiore absorbed all this with rapt attention. There seemed something to say in it about size and strength and expectations, but the opium-fog kept it just beyond his mind's reach. Instead of anything literary, he heard himself reply, "And what of the lute?"

Enzo said nothing. A hard swallow travelled down his slender throat.

"Only jesting," Fiore hastened to add. His smile wouldn't stay on his lips.

Enzo's own wan smile did much to balm Fiore's heart as he glanced up to meet his gaze at last. His strong hands enclosed Fiore's wounded one in a gentle shielding grasp. His thumb idly stroked the knuckle of Fiore's. Fiore clasped his palm in turn, and indeed, it seemed as though his remaining fingers still held the strength to do so.

"Where is it now?" Fiore asked.

Enzo's brow furrowed.

"The missing one, I mean," Fiore explained. "They sent it to you, did they not?"

"They did," Enzo admitted, after a silent moment wherein his countenance underwent a rapid transformation; alarm, despair, and anger chased each other across his features like storm clouds whirling through zephyrs above, until stoic resolution settled over all.

"Do you have it still?" Fiore asked, half-afraid of the answer. If Enzo had tossed it into the canal—or thrown it to his hounds—or cast it into the hearth-fire—

"I do," Enzo replied.

Because of course he did, and Fiore felt foolish beyond words to have doubted him for even a moment.

With some hesitation, Enzo continued. "I ought to have told you earlier, but... I thought it might disturb you to hear of it."

Fiore couldn't honestly say the thought of his missing finger didn't disturb him. But to know it remained safe in Enzo's hands eased some of his concerns.

"It cannot be reattached," Enzo said with no small amount of evident chagrin.

Fiore shrugged. "I'd figured as much. May I see it?"

Enzo balked.

Fiore, who didn't think his desire quite so odd, held his gaze.

"You may," Enzo replied at last with no small hesitation. "It's in the alchemy workshop downstairs. Do you feel up to venturing there? Or shall I bring it to you?"

A certain thrill had shot through Fiore's heart at the mention of alchemy. "I'd like to see the workshop as well, if it's all the same to you."

The shy smile Enzo gave him in reply proved no less thrilling.

～

Fiore smelt the alchemy workshop before he saw it. Not an unpleasant scent, but one which nonetheless wafted down the corridor as Enzo led him toward it, their arms entwined, and grew stronger as they approached. It had a curious musk, spiced and strange and somewhat sweet. And somehow familiar. Fiore wrinkled his nose as he considered the matter.

Enzo halted before a particular paneled black-walnut door. He withdrew a silver key from within his waistcoat pocket and slid it into a lock which appeared less ornate than Fiore had expected.

Only when the door opened did Fiore recognize the alchemical scent as the peculiar note he'd long detected in Enzo's own masculine musk.

Given this familiarity, he didn't find the contents of the workshop quite so disturbing as perhaps he ought.

The object which asserted itself first and foremost to his sight was the desiccated crocodile suspended from the vaulted ceiling. It ran some twelve feet long—which covered little more than half the breadth of the chamber—and bared its teeth towards the entrance. Beside it hung a heron and a bat, both with wings outstretched, and the membrane of the bat-wing appearing particularly delicate. Beneath their watchful gaze lay a horde of curiosities. A glass case stood in either far corner; one holding a set of brass orbs suspended on geared arms, the other a diverse collection of living ferns. Stars within stars were inscribed on the slate floor; pentagrams, hexagrams, heptagrams, octagrams, all in perfect geometric harmony with the faint remnants of thousands of chalk marks between their deeply grooved lines. The clouded glass of the singular windowed wall faced the interior courtyard. No prying eyes outside could glimpse even a fraction of this alchemical sanctum. Sunshine lit the room through this and the likewise clouded skylights overhead. The hefty spyglass set on a tripod in the corner, combined with the brass model of the planets, made Fiore think this feature proved useful by night as well as by day. A long workbench ran along the wall beneath the windows, filled with glass-work tubes, beakers, and bottles, interspersed with intricate bits and bobs of silver and brass beyond Fiore's powers of identification. Floor-to-ceiling barrister bookshelves occupied the entirety of the far wall opposite the door. Behind the glass fronts and alongside a multitude of leather volumes, some of which looked quite ancient, gleamed further silver and brass instruments amidst jars of powders and potions. The door, which drew Fiore's notice as Enzo shut it behind them with a gentle yet resounding thud, was flanked by two charts as tall as Enzo himself. Each depicted a nude man; one surrounded by the zodiac beasts arranged according to which bodily aspects they supposedly governed, the other suffering every possible wound from every possible weapon whilst still standing defiantly alive. A menacing system of hooks, pulleys, and chains hung down from the rafters beside him.

"To set a dislocated limb," Enzo said in answer to Fiore's unspoken question.

Fiore, startled out of staring at his unfamiliar yet fascinating surroundings, glanced to Enzo and found him wearing the tentative and anxious look of an artist who'd just revealed the work closest to their heart.

"This is your sanctum, then?" Fiore asked.

Enzo nodded, looking no less bashful than before.

Fiore couldn't make the smile in his heart reach his face. Still, he managed to put some of it into his voice as he declared, "It's marvelous."

Enzo's shy smile spoke for them both.

Emboldened, Fiore stepped further into the workshop. The desk along the wall opposite the windows drew his notice. It resembled the captain's desks he'd seen come up for auction now and again when a ship and all her fixtures were sold off in port. Though rather than jointed shutters, it closed with a singular cylinder of solid wood inlaid with the Scaevola family crest of the sable dragon segreant. The throne-like, shield-backed chair bore a similar design carved in deep relief. More striking than any of these details, however, were the two trinkets balanced on either side of the desk's top-most pigeonhole shelves; a human skull and an egg of almost the same size.

Fiore gestured to the skull. "Friend of yours?"

"An ancestor," Enzo explained. As Fiore's gaze drifted naturally to the egg opposite, he added before Fiore could ask, "Not a dragon egg. An ostrich."

Fiore knew not what an ostrich was but trusted he would find out in due time.

Enzo guided Fiore toward the chair at the desk and drew it out for him. Only after he saw Fiore safely seated—and had clasped and kissed his hand besides—did he leave him for even the mere moment it took to lock the door behind them both.

Fiore cast his gaze over the workshop, both in search of and dreading to find his missing finger. His eye fell upon a spiraling ivory horn, longer than he was tall, affixed lengthwise to the wall just between the molding bordering the ceiling and the arched peaks of the clouded windows. He caught Enzo's notice and pointed to it. "Unicorn?"

"Narwhal," Enzo corrected him, adding in response to Fiore's evident confusion, "A porpoise of the northern seas. Unicorns are smaller."

"Ah," said Fiore.

Enzo approached the desk. Another key from the ring in his waistcoat pocket slipped into the lock on the front. The cylindrical front —either carved from a single block of burlwood or so cunningly crafted as to appear so—rolled smoothly up to vanish within the desk in a hidden crevice above the myriad drawers revealed by its departure. A pair of decorative columns adorned with the house's customary scaled carving of spiraling serpents flanked the pigeon-holes. Enzo reached for the one on the left. With a delicate touch, he slowly spun it.

In the same instant, a slight scraping sound resounded further along the wall.

Fiore turned toward the noise and beheld one of the panels in the wall opposite the windows sliding aside. Behind it lay a scaled bronze door. A bas-relief dragon curled 'round the keyhole in its center.

This likewise had its match in yet another key from Enzo's ring, as he demonstrated by arising to turn its lock. This, at last, opened into a vault. Within it, a glass jar filled with a translucent blue liquid in which curled something small and pale and disturbingly familiar.

Enzo removed the jar from the hidden cabinet as delicately as if he feared it would shatter in his hands. He set it gently down on the desk in front of Fiore.

And for the first time since its violent separation, Fiore beheld his missing finger.

His mind slid away from the notion at the initial glance. It wasn't real. It wasn't there. It was some other fool's appendage. It was a mockery molded out of wax.

Yet the more he stared—for he could by no means tear his gaze away from the sight equal parts horrific and familiar—the more his thoughts settled into truth. His hand throbbed. His stomach felt as if he'd slipped off a precipice. And there his finger remained. Bloodless. Curled. Shriveling. He tried not to look at the stringy matter emerging from the wound at its base.

The weight of a fallen leaf brushed against his shoulder. Fiore recoiled. His eyes shot to Enzo just in time to see him kneeling beside him.

"Forgive me," Enzo murmured. "I didn't mean to affright you."

Fiore had already forgiven him in his heart before a single word had left his lips. He rearranged himself into a more normal pose, dropping his shoulder to replace his good hand on the chair's other arm and clasping Enzo's hand already there. Enzo squeezed his in turn with a wan yet hopeful smile.

With Enzo's grip entwined in his own, Fiore looked back to the jar and found he could gaze upon it without his mind falling into its terrible void. Despite his throbbing hand, he had a marked appreciation for the care Enzo had taken in its preservation and safe-keeping. He could think of no better place for it, besides its original one.

"What will you do with it?" he heard himself ask.

After a moment, Enzo replied, "I leave it to your discretion."

Fiore hadn't the least idea what to make of it. Reattachment was, as Enzo had said, out of the question. There his desires ended. He tried his enquiry again. "What would you do if it were your own?"

A thoughtful silence ensued.

"I'd reduce it to bone—wet specimens don't last," Enzo added with haste as Fiore's eyes flew wide to meet his.

"And then?" Fiore demanded.

"I'd commission a master silversmith to armor it in filigree. Something jointed, so it might still move as before. A chain could replace the tendons."

Fiore knew he ought to feel horrified. Instead he found himself fascinated. The mention of a chain sparked something in his own imagination. "Would you, perhaps, wear it as an ornament?"

"Not where unworthy eyes might see it," Enzo replied. "But... yes."

If they had ever been speaking of Enzo's own hypothetical finger, they certainly weren't now.

Fiore stared at the thing in the jar. It'd been his once. But it couldn't last like this. And he had a queer eagerness to see it transformed from a repulsive reminder of his own pain into something beautiful. Something that someone could cherish instead of cast aside. A part of him kept safe in the hands of the only person in the world he'd trust with such a burden. "In that case... I think you ought to keep it."

Another silence descended upon them. Fiore dared to lift his gaze from the jar to meet Enzo's glance.

Soft dark eyes glistened down at him. Enzo bent his head. He caught Fiore's wounded hand in his ever-gentle grasp and raised it to his lips to bestow a kiss on those much-abused knuckles.

And Fiore knew he'd chosen right.

# CHAPTER THIRTY

E nzo could not begin to measure his relief.

He'd never revealed the alchemy workshop—his haven in a gilded cage of misery—to anyone outside the household since his return from university. He'd braced himself for revulsion, repugnance, rejection. Fiore, however, had looked on it all with curiosity verging on genuine admiration. Enzo hadn't even dared to hope for so much.

And as for the finger—Fiore seemed to take its loss well. Far better than many others in his unfortunate position. Enzo resolved to look after it as though it were his own. He knew not yet how to resolve his own guilt over the loss of said finger, but his own feelings mattered not, so long as he did right by his Fiore.

But above all else, Enzo was glad that Fiore felt well enough to wander the halls beyond the bedchamber. Though he had to lean heavily on Enzo to do so, it was still a far further distance than he'd yet travelled since his rescue, and he'd managed it with little to no evident discomfort, which boded well for the success of his recovery.

The finger's fate decided, Fiore looked away from it in a rather deliberate fashion. Enzo took the hint and tucked it back into the secret vault.

"Have you any experiments underway at present?" Fiore asked, his eye trailing over the workshop.

"Yes," Enzo replied honestly, though with some hesitation.

Fiore's dark gaze flicked towards him and gleamed with more vigor than Enzo had seen in him in some time. It spurred him to further honesty.

"I'd intended to make it a surprise," Enzo explained. "But if you'd like, I can show you what I've accomplished thus far…?"

"By all means." Though no smile touched Fiore's lips, an echo of it shone in his eyes.

Enzo drew the thick, black woolen curtains over the windowed wall. When he took up the hooked pole to do the same to the skylights, however, a strangled sound from Fiore stopped him. He turned to find Fiore glancing nervously from him to the skylights and back again.

"We will not be plunged into darkness," Enzo promised him.

He wouldn't at all have blamed Fiore for doubting this proclamation. But Fiore met his gaze and gave his assent with a small, sharp nod.

Enzo drew the curtains over the skylights. Sunlight was banished from the workshop.

And in its absence there came a soft blue-green glow from one of the glass terrariums.

Fiore whipped his head towards the glow the moment it appeared. He stared in wonderment.

Enzo suppressed a smile and went to the case. He withdrew the glowing object and brought it to Fiore.

"Foxfire," he explained, holding it out for him to take if he so wished. "A luminescent fungus. It feeds on dead wood."

Indeed, the sample he had grew on a chunk of an olive tree taken from his villa's groves.

Fiore accepted it from him with an enraptured expression. The myriad fins of emerald green reflected in the dark pools of his eyes.

"Brighter than a candle," Fiore observed.

Enzo nodded eagerly. "Bright enough to read by. I had thought to make a lantern of it for our chambers."

Fiore tore his eyes away from the foxfire to meet Enzo's gaze with furrowed brow. "Our chambers?"

"Instead of a candle or brazier," Enzo explained. "Something to light the room by night without an open flame."

Still Fiore stared at him. "But they're *your* chambers, surely."

Enzo realized his error. "They were. But they're ours now. Unless—if you'd prefer your own?" Many happily-married couples kept separate suites. And if Enzo had the alchemy workshop as his sanctuary, it seemed only fair that Fiore ought to have a space of his own as well. "It will take some time to create it, but there are plenty of guest rooms lying fallow, and you may have your pick—"

Fiore laid a finger on Enzo's lips.

Enzo fell into confused silence.

The secret smile shone again in Fiore's eyes. "I'm happy with our chambers."

Enzo's own half-smile caught him by surprise. He supposed it would have to suffice for both of them for now. Though he did wish to return to the matter of Fiore's sanctuary in the future. He deserved a studio, at the very least.

A knock fell on the workshop door.

Fiore flinched. Enzo, who recognized Carlotta's distinctive knuckle-rap, laid a hand on his shoulder. It seemed to steady him.

"Enter," Enzo commanded.

Carlotta did so. "Pardon the interruption, your grace. The Duke of Bluecliffe has arrived."

Enzo stared at her. Her words made no sense. There was no reason for Giovanna to return to the city now. Unless... "Is she in her own chambers?"

"For the moment," Carlotta replied.

That would make things a touch easier for him. "Ask her to meet me in the library once she's settled."

Carlotta bowed and withdrew.

The very instant the door shut on her, Fiore spoke.

"What does she want?" he demanded, looking frantic.

"I don't know," Enzo answered honestly. Then, realizing from Fiore's even more horrified expression that would not suffice to calm him, he added, "I will find out in the library."

Fiore still didn't look soothed. "Where should I go?"

While Enzo would've felt perfectly comfortable if left to his own devices in the workshop for hours on end, he didn't think the same would hold true for Fiore. "I will accompany you back to our chambers. You may wait there, if you like. You'll have Vittorio with you." They'd left the hound behind asleep. Enzo tried not to dwell on how similar he sounded to his childhood nursemaids when they wished to distract a small boy from his father's imminent demise. "And I won't be gone long. I'll return to you just as soon as I've figured out what she wants."

"And if she wants me gone?" Fiore asked.

Enzo set his jaw. "Then she will have to cast me out alongside you."

This, at last, seemed to calm at least a few of Fiore's nerves.

Enzo led Fiore back to the bedchamber by a route that circumvented the library and Giovanna's quarters alike. He settled Fiore into the window seat and bid Vittorio stay and guard.

Then, against all his wishes, he left Fiore behind and continued on to meet his sister.

She could have come for but one purpose. Lucrezia had wearied of Enzo keeping Fiore in the family house and, rather than deliver her verdict herself, had persuaded Giovanna to pass it along in more congenial terms. The result would be the same regardless. Enzo would carry Fiore elsewhere. Perhaps back to his quarters aboard the *Kingfisher*. Or, if that would not placate Lucrezia, to Enzo's own holdings on land. Either the villa or the hunting lodge would suffice. Or, if Lucrezia forbade even this, then Enzo would hire a ship and carry his Fiore so far away that none could ever find or separate them.

He arrived at the library to find Giovanna awaiting him. She whirled toward the door as he opened it. Then rushed at him with open arms.

"Oh, Enzo! You poor boy. I came as soon as I heard."

All this, while she crushed him in an embrace. It was not the welcome Enzo had expected in this particular circumstance. But it was not entirely out of the ordinary for her.

Enzo let her have a moment or two. Then he extracted himself to ask, "Is Antonio with you?"

"No, no, he's looking after the villa."

"And the children?" Enzo asked warily.

"Oh, never fret," Giovanna assured him. "They're home with Antonio. I daresay they'll hardly miss me."

That had not been Enzo's primary concern.

"Quirina is preoccupied with her fencing," Giovanna went on. "You've made quite the impression on her. And Andrea is just the same with his drawing. He's all eagerness to show Fiore how he's improved. But speaking on Fiore—how is he? The poor dear. May I see him?"

Enzo balked. Before he could restrain his tongue, he heard himself reply, "No."

"Oh." Giovanna blinked. Then her face fell. "Oh no, is he—he's not—?"

"He is convalescing."

"Oh!" Giovanna said, this time relieved. "Don't frighten me like that. Bad enough the poor thing has suffered so. But—he is on the mend?"

Enzo nodded.

"Very glad tidings indeed," said Giovanna. "But not well enough for visitors?"

Enzo thought he'd already made that plain. "He's really not in any condition for new acquaintances just now. And," he added, lest she take offense, "while your presence is comforting to me, I fear the presence of a stranger would not prove so to him."

"We are already acquaintances, surely. I met and conversed with him at Wolf's Head, and he did the same with my husband and my son."

Enzo tried again. A touch more honest this time. "He is afraid of you."

Giovanna stared up at him. "Afraid of me?"

Perhaps, Enzo thought, he'd been too honest. "He's afraid you or Lucrezia will throw him out of the house altogether." He did not add, *And so am I.*

"Then a visit from me is all the more vital," Giovanna countered. "I must reassure him that I've no intention of throwing him out. And that if Lucrezia says otherwise she will have to answer to me."

While surprised by this, Enzo could truthfully reply, "I'm glad to hear it. But—forgive me—why have you come, if not to cast him out?"

Giovanna blinked. "My only brother's beloved has been grievously wounded. I came to lend whatever support I might."

Enzo felt more than a touch of guilt for misjudging her. And yet. "How did you hear of it?"

"Lucrezia told me."

"So she did send you," Enzo concluded. Just as he'd suspected.

"She did not *send* me," Giovanna protested. "She merely informed me that your Fiore had been cruelly used and that you'd taken him into the house to look after him."

Enzo thought he knew pretty well Lucrezia's motives for telling Giovanna all she knew. Though if Lucrezia wanted a pair of loyal eyes and ears within the palazzo, she already had Carlotta and every other servant besides. Perhaps she thought he'd reveal more to his own flesh and blood. There wasn't much more to reveal in any case. Still he misliked the business.

"May I not see him?" Giovanna asked, interrupting his bitter musings.

Enzo considered her. "I will inform him you've arrived."

~

According to the shadows lengthening across the bedchamber floor, hardly a quarter of an hour could've possibly passed. Nonetheless Fiore had all but tied his fingers into knots in Vittorio's ruff by the time Enzo returned.

"What does she want?" Fiore blurted the moment the door shut behind him.

"To see you," Enzo replied.

This did nothing to allay Fiore's concerns.

"You don't have to see her if you don't wish to," Enzo added quickly. He sat on the edge of the bed beside Fiore. "I've told her already that you're in a delicate stage of convalescence. There's every chirurgical excuse for you not to see her. But she does wish for you to know that she's here for a good reason rather than an unpleasant one."

"Is she?" Fiore wondered aloud before he could think better of making his doubts known.

"Yes," Enzo said. "She heard you were unwell and wishes to see you're all right."

Fiore wished his unwellness weren't public knowledge. He didn't know whether or not to trust the duke's stated motives. Though Enzo probably knew his own sister better than most. Probably. "How much does she know?"

Enzo appeared reluctant to recount it—whether because it troubled him to think on Fiore's suffering or because he didn't wish to divulge, Fiore knew not. "She knows you were kidnapped. And that you were grievously wounded and returned by the skin of your teeth. Beyond that she knows nothing specific. No one does, save myself and the chirurgeons."

And even Enzo didn't know all he'd suffered, Fiore mused uneasily. He wondered if Enzo or his sister would like him half so well if they knew the whole. Aloud, he said, "Am I fit to be seen, d'you think?"

Enzo balked. "You don't have to see her."

"But if I wished to see her," Fiore insisted. "Might I, then? Or would I just make an even worse impression?"

Enzo appeared at a loss.

"I want her to like me," Fiore explained. "I don't want to offend her by refusing. But," he added, as Enzo opened his mouth, presumably to repeat his earlier claim, "I also don't want to offend her by appearing… informal."

Which was a kind euphemism for "corpse-like," Fiore thought.

Enzo studied him for a long moment. "You really don't have to see her. But if you wish to, you may. You needn't fear offending her in either case. She is determined to like you."

Fiore tried to feel relieved.

"I would recommend an abbreviated visit regardless," Enzo went on. "Less strain on your nerves."

Fiore quite agreed. He wished he had his own clothes. While Enzo's wrapping-gown was beautiful and perfectly appropriate for the Crooked Anchor, it and the nightshirt beneath were obviously too large for Fiore's frame even if he weren't withered. But there was nothing to be done for that on such short notice. At the very least Fiore wished he might not meet the duke abed. "Is there somewhere else in the house we might meet? Some kind of sitting room, or…?"

He trailed off, struggling to imagine the interior of Ca' Scaevola beyond what precious little he'd already glimpsed. He doubted the duke would enjoy the alchemy workshop.

Enzo picked up where he'd left off. "The library is not terribly far from here. There's a particular sofa which I think might prove suitably comfortable for an invalid."

Fiore wished he had the strength to make the smile on his lips match the smile in his heart. "Lead on."

The library might have left more of an impression on Fiore had the impending interview with the duke not preoccupied his thoughts. He had a dim impression that the collection, while smaller than the library at Wolf's Head, would nonetheless prove far beyond even Gnaeus's wildest hopes. But the library's splendor only made Fiore feel all the more unworthy to occupy it in his diminished state.

Enzo settled him onto a velvet sofa. Fiore, bereft even of slippers, tucked his bare feet out of sight in the voluminous folds of Enzo's wrapping-gown. He hoped the duke wouldn't take offense at his poor dress. Beautiful as the wrapping-gown might appear, Fiore doubted anyone else had dared to meet her in so little.

This feeling of inadequacy did not dissipate when the duke herself entered the library swathed in a magnificent brocade satin gown.

Her gaze fell on him. For an instant her eyes flew wide in unmistakable alarm. But her self-command returned in force alongside an indulgent smile.

"Signor Fiore," she said. "How wonderful to see you again—though I'd hoped we might meet under happier circumstances."

As she approached, Fiore had a sickening feeling he ought to arise and bow to her. But before he could do more than shift in that general direction, Enzo stayed him with a hand laid feather-gentle on his arm and a soft smile besides.

The duke outstretched her hand to him. For a moment he thought she intended for him to kiss it, until he realized her upraised palm meant a clasp. He hesitated before offering her his unwounded left hand. She grasped it warmly and settled into the armchair adjoining the sofa.

Enzo sat down on the sofa itself, on Fiore's opposing side. Fiore had rather hoped Enzo might put himself between Fiore and his sister as a sort of shield. It felt too transparent to even hint at such a wish now.

Not wanting to make another poor impression on the duke, Fiore managed a tremulous smile. He was not well-practiced in making himself pleasing to women in general—or in making himself pleasing in the sense of friendship rather than more amorous pursuits. But he did know that the one thing gentlemen liked to discuss most was themselves, and he suspected this might prove true across genders. To that end he asked the duke, "Your husband and children are all well, I hope?"

A smile as delighted as it was surprised sparkled across her features. Then she was off, divulging everything Fiore could possibly wish to know about a subject most pleasing to her. He learnt the name of Enzo's niece—Quirina—and how she sought to imitate her uncle's skill with a blade. He discovered to his alarm that the boy, Andrea, not only remembered his impromptu drawing lesson fondly but also wanted to continue his education in that vein. The duke-consort, meanwhile, divided his time between his children and looking after the estates during the duke's however-brief absence.

"Forgive my impudence," Fiore broke in when she paused for breath. "But pray tell me of your affairs in the countryside. Enzo has hinted at precious little."

Which gave both the delightful reward of watching Enzo's sister playfully scold him for failing to inform Fiore and also a rapid and very informative lecture on points of agriculture he'd never even considered before. The duke seemed most pleased to have a willing audience for her interests. Fiore dared to hope he might earn her approval yet.

"But enough about me," she concluded, to Fiore's astonishment. "Do you find Ca' Scaevola to your liking?"

Fiore stared at her in stunned silence.

"Or rather," she continued, adeptly making up for his lack of conversational fortitude, "has Enzo made you comfortable? Is the house too hot or too cold? Is there enough to amuse you in your convalescence? Are there any particular foods you might prefer?"

For a duke to ask a common-born courtesan even once for his opinion on a palazzo was unheard of. For said duke to continue peppering him with enquiries on whether or not the hospitality he'd received within said palazzo sufficed... Fiore couldn't keep up, much less respond.

But the last question in particular rang in his ears.

Food had become something of a sensitive subject since his rescue. To tell the duke that he remained restricted to liquid fare for at least another se'en-night would reveal rather more to her than he wished about the specifics of his injuries. Despite his best efforts not to appear so lost as he felt, he found his gaze flick tellingly towards the safe harbor of Enzo.

And Enzo, ever gallant, told the duke, "He is on an invalid's diet, I'm afraid."

"Oh, you poor thing," she said to Fiore. "Is there nothing you might have to your taste?"

This, at least, he could answer with honesty. "I've enjoyed the sanguinaccio dolce."

"Have you?" The duke seemed genuinely delighted. "Oh, wonderful —it's Bettin's particular talent. Our cook," she added in response to Fiore's ill-disguised confusion. "When you feel well enough to eat as you wish, do make your tastes known to her."

Fiore vowed to do so.

"And do forgive me for exhausting you with conversation," she added, to his further surprise. "I'm very glad to hear you feel welcome in our home. Pray don't hesitate to call upon me if you require even the least thing to make you more comfortable. I'm afraid I won't tarry in the city long, but you may always send me a note—unless…?" Her gaze fell to his bandaged hand.

"I'm not prevented from writing," Fiore assured her. She didn't need to know he'd learnt to write in a conservatorio. He wished only he could feel more certain his injury had inspired her doubts rather than his class.

The storm-clouds gathering on Enzo's brow didn't bode well in either case.

The duke smiled. "Then I look forward to your correspondence, Signor Fiore."

～

With that, she arose. By then Enzo had contrived to pin a tight smile over his stormy features. He escorted his sister from the room.

"Do send for me if there's anything we might do for him," she stressed again on the library threshold.

Enzo managed a firm nod.

And at long last, Giovanna mercifully went on her way.

Enzo shut the door on her retreat and hastened back to his Fiore, who reached out to catch his hand in his own as he drew near.

"Please don't say anything to her," Fiore begged sotto voce. "It's not worth it."

Enzo heartily disagreed. "I won't take her to task, but I'd still like to have a quiet word with her about assumptions."

"I don't want her to see me as an obstacle," Fiore insisted, to Enzo's surprise. "It's bad enough that I'm here at all. It'll be far worse for me if she thinks I'm coming between you and your family."

Enzo recalled earlier conversations about what Fiore wanted versus what Fiore permitted himself to ask for. The thousand insufferable behaviors he nonetheless suffered to survive. Fiore had only just entered the aristocratic circle and already he'd understood its rules far better than Enzo had divined in the course of twenty-odd years.

"And besides," Fiore added, drawing Enzo out of his bitter musings. "She does mean well. As you've said."

"She does," Enzo conceded. His mind ran on. He'd failed to protect Fiore from Nascimbene. Now he'd failed to shield him from the intrusive —if well-meant—demands of Giovanna. An invalid already exhausted by his ordeal shouldn't have had to endure the further strain of entertaining a duke. Enzo ought to have considered it before it ever arose. He would make matters clear to his sister later. For the moment, he knew of no other way to begin righting his wrongs than by saying, "I'm sorry."

~

Fiore stared at him. "Whatever for?"

"Everything," Enzo replied.

Fiore's encounter with the duke had exhausted all powers of polite conversation. He hadn't the wit or the patience left to decipher riddles.

"You're going to have to be far more specific if you wish me to understand you."

"I should never have brought you to the ball."

Fiore knew not what he could mean by this besides the obvious. "Because you're ashamed of me."

"What?" Genuine horror struck Enzo's features. "No, no, never that. I meant only—I exposed you to terrible danger."

Now Fiore began to see what he was driving at. "Did you know Nascimbene would be there?"

The name grew easier and easier for Fiore to say with repetition—less of a haunting, unspeakable presence and more of a solvable problem.

Enzo didn't feel the same way, judging by how he flinched from the sound. "I should have thought to ask."

"How could you when I never told you his name?"

"I should've thought to ask that as well."

Fiore scoffed. "Ridiculous."

"I should've stayed with you at the very least."

"You stayed the whole night."

"I should've brought you back here with me afterward." In reply to Fiore's cocked eyebrow, Enzo added, "Or offered to."

Fiore knew full well why Enzo hadn't. The reminder stung nonetheless. A mere courtesan was obviously unworthy to grace the ancestral halls of Halcyon's reigning prince. Enzo's self-flagellation now would never change that, and frankly Fiore didn't think he possessed the patience to listen to it.

Yet Enzo spoke on. "I shouldn't have let my own distaste for these halls prevent me from offering you sanctuary within them."

Fiore balked at the sudden turn. "Your what for what?"

Enzo grimaced. "I returned here after I was banished from university. I remained within its walls until... well, until shortly before I met you. The memories in between are by no means pleasant. I began to resent this house. I couldn't imagine anyone feeling otherwise. Bringing the source of all my joys to visit the site of all my miseries... It repulsed me. I didn't want to show you what I could only suppose you, too, would despise."

Fiore stared at him.

"But," Enzo added, a wan smile ghosting across his scarred lips. "Your presence here has greatly increased my tolerance for it."

Fiore wanted to take the compliment in its intended spirit. "So... it's not because I'm a courtesan that you didn't invite me before?"

"What?" Enzo seemed genuinely astonished by the possibility. "No, of course not."

"Then it's doubly not your fault." Fiore doubted any student of debate would follow his trail of logic. That mattered not to him now. He wanted only to dissuade Enzo from any sense of guilt.

All the while knowing how much worse it would be if Enzo knew the truth of all that had happened in the crypt.

"I've failed to protect you at every peril," Enzo said, drawing Fiore out of his dire spiral.

"You've done more than enough," Fiore protested, the words spilling from his heart rather than his head. "You rescued me from the catacombs—"

"It was my fault you were—"

"Few other gentlemen would bother to retrieve a captive courtesan, I assure you. Even *if* the courtesan's captivity were their own fault."

Enzo fell silent.

Fiore pressed his advantage. "And setting that aside—though I'm loathe to do so, for it's no small thing—if it weren't for you, I'd have died of infection in my quarters aboard the *Kingfisher* months ago."

Enzo had no argument. A hard swallow travelled down his throat. His haunted gaze searched Fiore's own.

"I owe you my life twice over," Fiore insisted. The nearest thing to a smile since the night of the ball stole over his lips. "And I cannot imagine anyone I'd rather be indebted to."

A pale echo of Fiore's own wan smile graced Enzo's handsome features.

Fiore had never been a word-smith. But there remained one language in which he felt not just fluent but eloquent. His gaze flicked to Enzo's mouth and back again into the dark depths of his eyes. He tilted his head ever so slightly.

And, just as he'd hoped, Enzo bent down to meet his lips in a kiss.

Fiore had but to open his mouth to entice Enzo to devour him.

Fingertips trailing along his jaw sufficed to drag Enzo down onto the sofa beside him. A hand on his thigh coaxed Enzo into straddling his waist. Fiore wished he had the strength to do all he desired. Kissing would have to sate him for now. They hadn't kissed nearly often enough for his taste since his rescue.

Yet even as Fiore received almost everything he'd longed for, he knew one incontrovertible truth.

It wasn't fair for Enzo to continue on in ignorance.

And so Fiore pulled away.

To Enzo's evident confusion and concern, given his furrowed brow. "What's wrong?"

"Before we…" Fiore trailed off, his courage failing him. He cleared his throat and tried again. "There's something you ought to know."

"About what?"

"About what happened." Fiore drew in a tremulous breath. "Down in the catacombs."

Enzo's eyes flared wide for the barest instant. But he mastered himself quickly. He set his jaw and nodded for Fiore to continue.

There was no point dancing around the issue. To dissemble would only draw out his own torment. Fiore drew in a sharp breath and spoke. "One of them had me."

A horrible silence fell.

"You mean…" The suggestion seemed to pain Enzo almost as much as the memory haunted Fiore. "He took you by force."

Fiore hastened to correct him. "He didn't have to force me. I offered."

Enzo's brow furrowed. "Of your own volition?"

"I offered," Fiore insisted.

Enzo appeared no less perplexed.

Fiore endeavored to explain. He owed him that, at the very least. "I knew they meant to kill me from the start. They never bagged or blindfolded me. I saw their faces all the while. So I knew I'd be disposed of as soon as they received the ransom. I had to escape before then. When they…" His hand throbbed at the memory. Worse still were the recollections that echoed further back to his escape from the conservatorio. "When they acquired their proof, the blood made the ropes slick, and one less finger made my hand smaller. I had to slip my bonds—but I needed a distraction, and—"

Enzo raised his hands and looked as though he meant to say something.

Fiore's tongue ran on, the flood of words erupting from him, unable to stop himself. "The one they left behind didn't like me talking—he didn't want to play at cards or riddles—and so I offered him all I had left —what everyone wants of me—and—"

"Fiore," said Enzo.

"There was a moment afterward—there's always a moment afterward—he was weak, disoriented—I knew I had to slip free in that instant—and I did—"

"Fiore," Enzo said again, reaching for his hands.

Fiore snatched them from his grasp. "That's when he stabbed me. And I ran."

And when Enzo had arrived, at long last, to rescue his traitorous concubine.

Enzo stared at him in the ensuing silence.

Fiore knew not how to break it.

"I defer to your expertise," said Enzo at last. "But from your description, it doesn't sound as though your offer was sincere."

Fiore winced.

"Forgive me," Enzo added quickly. "A poor word for it. I didn't mean to imply... What I meant is, to offer something—anything—in exchange for your own life... You realize the difference, don't you?"

"There's always an exchange," Fiore replied, his bitter tone surprising even himself.

Enzo fell silent.

Fiore drew in a steadying breath. "I understand if you wish me to leave."

Enzo's already-furrowed brow twisted further in confusion. "Why the deuce would I ask you to leave now?"

"Because I'm soiled. Or because I'm disloyal." Fiore shrugged. "Pick one."

Enzo stared at him. "You're neither."

Fiore scoffed.

Yet Enzo wasn't daunted. "You offered up what you had to survive."

"Out of cowardice," Fiore spat. "Because I feared death more than…"

Enzo took up where he trailed off. "You could never have escaped without courage. Only a monster would condemn you for it."

"Then I must be a monster."

Another silence fell.

The pain in Enzo's eyes was unbearable.

Fiore looked away. The library loomed all around him. Vast. Historied. Beyond anything he deserved to witness, let alone dwell within.

"May I?"

Fiore glanced up sharp to find Enzo offering his hand, palm upraised.

Against all his better instincts and in service to all his most foolish desires, Fiore grasped it.

Enzo caught and held his gaze in return. A silent enquiry shone in his eyes. Only after Fiore answered it with a nod did Enzo raise his hand to his lips and kiss his knuckles. Then, when Fiore could not halt his hand from caressing Enzo's cheek, Enzo pressed another kiss to the inside of his wrist. He met Fiore's gaze again as he broke away to speak.

"Nothing you've said has altered your place in my heart by even one drop."

An intelligent fellow would accept those words at face value. Fiore couldn't stop himself from replying. "Yet you're angry."

Enzo shook his head. "I'm only angry with myself for not arriving sooner."

Fiore had anticipated anger, but not like this. He'd anticipated blame and jealousy and rage and spite and perhaps if he was very lucky, forgiveness. He hadn't dared dream of anything like this.

Instead of any of that, he heard himself say, "I'm just glad you arrived at all."

Fiore hadn't intended for his voice to break. But it'd broken all the same, and the sorrowful cast in Enzo's eyes dispelled any hope that it'd escaped his notice.

Fiore's gaze flicked to Enzo's mouth and back again.

And to his infinite relief, Enzo indulged him with another kiss.

# CHAPTER THIRTY-ONE

The following fortnight of Fiore's convalescence passed quietly.

While Fiore had enjoyed the pastissada de caval, sanguinaccio dolce, and many flavors of gelato served up by Ca' Scaevola's cook, he felt beyond ready to sample solid food at long last—even if it wasn't the sarde in saor he wished for. (Enzo had vetoed that, saying the onions, raisins, and pine nuts would do his entrails no favors at this point in his recovery.) Instead he had eggs and ham cooked in butter, the latter a luxury he'd never even witnessed apart from the sculpture at the ball, much less tasted. It certainly felt rich on his tongue. Enzo insisted he required hearty fare to keep up his strength, and Fiore certainly wasn't about to argue if it meant he could eat like a king. Better still, he sat upright at a table by the window rather than being forced to recline abed with a tray across his lap. How long he could stay upright remained to be seen, but for the moment, anodyne kept the pain at bay and his bandages kept his entrails in place. Likewise it was a delight to actually share a meal with Enzo rather than just have Enzo spoon-feeding him. Not that Fiore didn't appreciate the spoon-feeding, but this was a wonderful relief for his dignity.

It was as they concluded this long-awaited meal that a distinctive knock fell on the bedchamber door.

"Carlotta," Enzo said in reply to Fiore's enquiring glance and went to answer her.

Carlotta herself did not enter the bedchamber. Instead her hands alone emerged, bearing two flat stacked boxes and a package tied up in brown paper. Her voice echoed in from the antechamber. "From the tailor, your grace."

Enzo accepted them with thanks. She withdrew in total silence and vanished not unlike a ghost.

Fiore's mind whirled with curiosity as Enzo shut the door on her departure and returned to the table. His bewilderment only increased when Enzo laid the packages out in front of him.

"For me?" Fiore asked. The words sounded stupid the moment they left his lips but he couldn't catch them before they fell.

Enzo nodded with his shy and handsome smile—as if he were abashed to offer Fiore something paltry.

What Fiore found beneath the paper wrapping proved far from paltry. Slipping off the string and lifting just one corner of the first package revealed pearl-white gleaming silk. It unfolded into a pair of stockings, one of three, the other two wool knit almost as smooth as the silk. In the box beneath them lay three linen shirts—sewn to his own proportions rather than Enzo's, whose shirt he now drowned in beneath a similarly voluminous wrapping-gown—and a pair of chestnut wool breeches almost identical to those lost to the filth of the catacombs, save their superior cut and cool-handed weave.

"This is just the beginning," Enzo broke in with an apologetic tone. "I wasn't sure what you might want for waistcoats. Or what other colors for breeches."

Fiore knew he must say something. But in his weakened state the gift left him too stunned to speak. He hardly dared open the second box. His hands trembled as he raised its lid. Within lay two pairs of shoes; one identical to those he'd lost, the other a less-ornamented but no less beautifully-crafted match to his heels.

Gratitude overwhelmed him. With it came a creeping dread that told him he wasn't worthy of such things. And amidst all the replacements for everything he'd lost, he noted no sash—scarlet or otherwise. Fiore supposed he wouldn't have cause to wear the scarlet sash again. He felt odd without it. He anticipated it would feel odder still when the bandages came off for good and removed any illusion of the sash's familiar sensation. What would he wear over his waistcoat in its place? A belt? A sash in another color? Or would these seem an uncouth reminder of what he'd once been?

"And, if you'd like," Enzo continued, heedless of Fiore's inner turmoil, "another evening suit in whatever shade strikes your fancy."

Fiore, dragged out of his mind's whirlpools by those words, heard a very stupid question fall from his own lips in reply. "Where would I wear it?"

Enzo shrugged. "Another ball?"

Fiore wondered at Enzo's willingness to bring him to another party after how badly he'd botched the last one. And besides... "Could I not wear my green one?"

Enzo stared at him.

"Unless..." Fiore hesitated. "Is it not the done thing, to wear the same suit twice?"

Enzo blinked. "Have you ever seen me wear something different?"

Fiore had to admit he hadn't. But if Enzo could wear an identical suit everywhere he went, then... "Is there some reason I shouldn't wear my green suit?"

"Forgive me," said Enzo, to Fiore's surprise. "I never meant to imply you shouldn't. It's only—I thought it might remind you of things you'd rather forget."

"It does," Fiore admitted. "But I love it nonetheless. Isn't it beautiful?"

"You make it so," Enzo agreed.

Fiore had to smile at that. "I love it for its beauty. For how it feels to wear it. And because you procured it for me. As I loved attending the ball before Nascimbene appeared."

Enzo winced at the impresario's name.

Fiore refused to flinch. "I don't want my only memories of a ball to be tainted by his presence. And I don't want a beautiful suit given to me by a beloved hand to be ruined by association. So I'd like to wear it again, to another ball, and form new memories with you by my side. If you're willing?"

"More than willing," Enzo said with the shy smile Fiore loved so well.

Fiore kissed him for it.

"If you do want another suit," Enzo said as they parted, "just say the word and I'll summon the tailor."

"Here?" Fiore blurted stupidly.

"Of course," Enzo replied as if it were the most natural thing in the world.

Fiore recalled Enzo's assurance that only his own distaste for Ca' Scaevola—and not for Fiore's low origins—had prevented him from inviting Fiore to his ancestral home sooner. Only now did he realize that this was also likely why, when it came time to procure Fiore's suit for the ill-fated ball, Enzo had met him at the tailor's shop rather than summoning both Fiore and the tailor to Ca' Scaevola. And now that Fiore had taken up residence in Ca' Scaevola, there remained no barrier to recalling the tailor to wait upon him there. That was the reason Enzo didn't want to take Fiore out to the tailor's shop, and not because... "Are you ashamed to be seen out with me?"

After all, even if Fiore weren't a courtesan anymore, he likewise wasn't the immaculate beauty he'd once been.

Enzo stared at him. "Hardly."

Fiore nodded and mustered an insufficient, "Good. I mean," he added hastily, "I'm glad you don't mind how I—" He broke off and gestured vaguely to the whole of his fallen form.

To Fiore's great relief, Enzo didn't appear in any way offended by his odd speech. He did however look concerned, which wasn't good either.

"We can go to the tailor's shop if you prefer," said Enzo—far more patient and gentle than Fiore deserved. "I only thought you might feel more comfortable remaining here. At least, until your wounds are better healed."

Fiore well remembered the flock of assistants and apprentices. While he did enjoy showing off, his body at present was not what it once was. Scars and starvation had taken their toll. He found he didn't really want to strip in public just now. "You're right. I should remain here."

Enzo didn't look altogether convinced. "If you really prefer—"

"I don't." Fiore winced. His voice had come out too sharp by half and cut off Enzo besides. "I'm sorry, I'm not making sense. But truly—I don't wish to go out as I am just now. I'd like to stay here until I feel more myself. If I may…?"

"Of course," Enzo assured him. "Shall I summon the tailor, then?"

Still, Fiore hesitated. "After my wounds are healed, perhaps."

The tailor would, after all, have to see him in some dishabille. Fiore didn't like the notion of being measured around his bandages. Better to wait until he was at least whole—or as whole as he might ever be—if not hale.

Enzo looked a little confused at this. Fiore could hardly blame him. But nonetheless Enzo nodded.

"Whenever you're ready," he said.

Fiore couldn't find the words to express all the grateful relief in his heart. Instead he reached for Enzo's hand.

Enzo clasped his at once.

Fiore almost felt he could smile as he drew Enzo down to kiss him.

～

Three fortnights passed before all Fiore's wounds closed.

The slice on his cheek healed first. While it would never fully vanish, Fiore took some comfort in how Enzo's own cheek scar appeared more faded than the slash through his whole face. He found greater comfort in how handsome and dashing Enzo's scars looked. While Fiore would never enjoy Enzo's dueling infamy, there remained some hope that those who gazed upon him might assume he'd earned his slash under more courageous circumstances. At any rate he finally had unfettered access to the hand-mirror and furthermore convinced Enzo to remove the tapestry covering the full-length looking-glass. With concerted effort Fiore could glance into both without flinching.

His hand healed second. While Enzo had tried not to show it, Fiore could nonetheless tell this wound in particular had worried him. Something about the way the brigands had cut the finger off—they hadn't left enough flesh behind to close the wound as Enzo would've preferred. Fiore didn't know the difference. When the bandages came off for good at last, what he beheld looked no better or worse than he'd expected. His eyes flicked away from it of their own accord. But as they came to rest on Enzo's face, he saw Enzo looked more relieved than otherwise at the result, and this eased some of the tightness in his chest.

The wounds around his navel took the longest to heal. Long after Fiore had wearied of chirurgical visits and dressing changes and the stinging silver nitrate. (He still didn't know what exactly a nitrate was, but he'd heard the word murmured over him oft enough to know that was the spray that burned his flesh to cleanse it, and he was familiar enough with silver to suppose that whatever property prevented tarnish on fish-forks would likewise prevent infection in his wounds.) Eventually the holes in his entrails healed. Then the muscle over them. And, at long last, Dr. Venier withdrew the bandages to reveal the skin had healed over all.

Fiore stared down at himself while she spoke to Enzo over his head. Two scarlet punctures sunk in on either side of his navel, with a red ribbon curving around it to tie them together; the original stab wounds tangled with the chirurgical incision to repair them. He tried very hard not to let his mind fly back to the smooth, unblemished skin that had once held taut across his stomach. The hair between his legs hid the scars over his missing stone. Perhaps the trail up over his navel would disguise these.

And, Fortuna willing, Enzo would still find him desirable.

"Well done, Signor Fiore."

Dr. Venier's voice startled Fiore out of maelstrom thoughts. He glanced up to find her smiling gently. Enzo beside her fairly beamed with joy.

Fiore tried to make his face reflect at least a fraction of it. He thanked her for her troubles. She took her leave.

Enzo's smile became a grin the moment the door shut behind her. It faded somewhat as it became apparent that Fiore couldn't match it. "Zecchino for your thoughts?"

Fiore tried to think of something to say other than the truth. But before he could, what fell out of his mouth was, "I used to go to the bathhouse thrice a week."

The non-sequitur provoked a confused furrow in Enzo's brow.

"To entice gentlemen," Fiore explained. Enzo had both witnessed and assisted in his daily stand-up wash back at the *Kingfisher*; the bathhouse probably seemed superfluous to him. Fiore dropped his gaze to his fresh scars. He traced the scarlet ribbon with a hesitant fingertip. "Don't know who'd be enticed now."

Quiet fell. Fiore didn't dare look up to see how Enzo took it.

Enzo's soft voice shattered the silence. "Do you mind my scars?"

Fiore snapped his head up. "Hardly!"

Enzo held his gaze. "Then why should anyone mind yours?"

Because Fiore's delicate frame couldn't carry off distinguished marks half so well, in his own estimation. And besides— "Yours were acquired under far more noble circumstances."

"Hardly," Enzo echoed. In more insistent tones, he added, "Anyone who would call your scars ugly doesn't deserve to speak."

Fiore knew there wasn't any real logic behind Enzo's argument. Still, it warmed his heart to hear it.

"But," Enzo continued, his words gentle again, "if you would prefer a private bathhouse…"

"You would arrange for one to be emptied?" Fiore guessed, a half-smile tugging at his lips despite himself.

"That, yes," Enzo admitted. "But there's also a bath here."

Fiore stared at him. "In this house, you mean."

Enzo nodded.

Fiore knew he'd explored a mere fraction of the palazzo in the course of his convalescence. Even so, he'd never dreamed so far as this. On reflection, however, he recalled Enzo's reluctance to enter a public bathhouse on account of his peculiarity. He'd assumed this meant Enzo had resigned himself to stand-up washes and hip-baths. But of course a duke must have more amenities.

"Shall I show you?" Enzo asked, drawing Fiore out of his bewildered musings.

"Please," Fiore said—perhaps a bit too eagerly, but a month and a half without a proper bath had worn him down in ways he hadn't realized until the prospect dangled before him once more.

Enzo proved no less eager. He beamed all the way out of the bedchamber and down the myriad corridors to a door hitherto unseen by Fiore's eyes. Fiore, swathed in Enzo's wrapping-gown, felt a touch queer walking about without the support of bandages against his abdomen. The support of Enzo's arm twined with his own, however, certainly helped matters.

The door—broader than the full span of Fiore's own arms, thicker than the breadth of his palm, carved up in bas-relief serpentine scales, like all the other doors in Ca' Scaevola—opened into a paradise.

Ample sunshine beamed down through the vaulted ceiling of frosted glass panes and shone over the soft hues of the marble walls and floor. Pink and gold stone accented the soft white that made up the bulk of the chamber, far brighter than the rest of Ca' Scaevola. The marble floor, Fiore noted even through his shoes, held heat just like the caldarium of the public baths. A plunge pool, miniature compared to the public baths Fiore was used to but enormous when contrasted against any other private residence, sunk into the floor in the room's center. An artificial waterfall kept it filled and perpetually flowing. A smaller pool—one which could fit perhaps two people, or three, Fiore thought, if they proved particularly determined—tucked away into a corner, guarded by a white marble statue of Bellenos in mortal guise emerging from a carved cloud of seafoam. Bronze dolphins poised to spew water into the smaller bath; Fiore had seen porpoises leaping in the lagoon and knew full well they looked nothing like the scaled and beaked creatures here, but heraldic tradition prevailed, he supposed. A bronze tray laid across a marble bench held folded towels, olive oil, soap, and strigil.

As Fiore took in the sights, Enzo explained how, somewhere within the palazzo, a glass prism magnified the sun's power and concentrated it on a particular point to boil the water drawn in from the lagoon at high tide, which, becoming steam, then condensed on its journey through the pipes and came down from the spouts as pure, distilled freshwater.

Fiore hadn't even remotely asked but appreciated the explanation regardless; all the moreso for Enzo's evident joy in divulging it.

"Furthermore," Enzo concluded, "swimming is the ideal invalid exercise. The body may regain its strength gradually without the burden of supporting its own weight."

Fiore didn't know enough anatomy or medicine to confirm or deny that off-hand. He was, however, more than willing to experiment.

Enzo led him to the smaller bath. Steam arose as the bronze dolphins gushed forth. Beneath Bellenos's eternal gaze, Fiore shrugged the wrapping-gown off into Enzo's hands and slipped into the water.

In all aspects of Fiore's care, Enzo had proved meticulous and attentive. From the moment Fiore had first complained of pain, Enzo had massaged and gently manipulated the joints that had twisted out of place in the twelve-odd hours Fiore had spent tied up. Thus far it'd helped a great deal.

The hot bath improved matters further still. Slipping beneath the waters released tension in muscles whose pain Fiore had taken for granted. His eyes fell shut and a satisfied groan escaped him as he leaned back against the marble rim.

"Good?" Enzo asked.

Words had escaped Fiore, but he mustered up some affirmative noises as he nodded.

Fiore knew not how long he lay simply soaking in the restorative waters. A slight splash prompted him to open his eyes, whereupon he found Enzo stripped to the waist and in the midst of filling a bronze ewer from the bath.

Enzo set the full ewer down and held up a bar of soap embedded with rose petals. Catching Fiore's gaze, he enquired, "If I may...?"

A lackadaisical grin spread across Fiore's lips. He held out his arm for Enzo to lather.

Enzo hadn't shied away from touching Fiore after his rescue—much to Fiore's relief—but his touch had remained... chirurgical, for lack of a better word. It became affectionate only when Fiore insinuated himself into Enzo's grasp. And even then, while comforting, it remained chaste.

Now, however, with the warm water and the rose-scented soap and Enzo's hands lovingly burnishing filth and pain alike away from his flesh, Fiore thought he might persuade Enzo into something more.

"The plunge pool?" Fiore suggested when Enzo had scrubbed and sluiced the whole of him.

Enzo brightened. "If you're feeling up to it."

Fiore would arise to any occasion if it meant he could have Enzo alongside him. And indeed, Enzo wrapped him up in linen towels—lest he catch cold whilst crossing the room, Fiore assumed—and led him arm-in-arm to the plunge pool.

The pool proved cool and refreshing after the hot bath. Fiore sat down on the steps leading into deeper waters and let the gentle waves lap at his waist. He glanced back at Enzo with the words to entice him to join poised on his tongue.

At the very moment Enzo finished stripping off his drawers and dove in.

Fiore grinned even as he flung up an arm to ward off the splash. There was little enough of that—Enzo dove beautifully. Neptune himself couldn't ask for better.

While Fiore's body had been on display for Enzo and chirurgeons alike over and over again for the past month-and-a-half, he hadn't had a chance to drink in the sight of Enzo's nude form for a good long while. To have Enzo bare before him now, lithe and lean and as graceful beneath the water as above it, his dark locks pouring down from his crown like ink as he arose to meet Fiore again.

"Do you feel up to underwater exercises?" Enzo asked him.

Fiore, poised to embrace his long-awaited Nerites, balked. He knew whatever exercises Enzo had in mind weren't anywhere near his own erotic hopes.

But Enzo seemed so happy to have found another way to bring Fiore nearer to health that Fiore could hardly do less than acquiesce to his scheme.

Fiore supposed he could wait just a little longer for his own satisfaction.

And besides, even purely healthful exercises involved Enzo swimming closer to him and catching him up in his arms.

With Enzo's support, Fiore entered deeper waters. The underwater exercises proved less draining than those Enzo and the chirurgeons made him perform on land. They swam together, playful as porpoises, with Fiore slipping in and out of Enzo's grasp and Enzo perpetually welcoming him into his arms. His body floated all but weightless, and what little weight remained was borne up by Enzo's strength.

The weight returned in force, however, when it came time to haul himself up out of the water. After toweling Fiore off and wrapping him up in his own gown just as if he were his valet, Enzo half-carried him back upstairs to their bedchamber.

The servants had changed bedclothes whilst he and Enzo were out. Fiore wondered if he'd ever get used to that.

In addition to his leaden limbs, Fiore felt hungry—as he always did after a swim, but moreso now he felt a very particular sort of ravenous that only Enzo could satisfy.

Yet though Enzo laid him down on the bed, he did not join him in it.

Fiore thought he might draw him down with a kiss. A glance from Enzo's eyes to lips and back again sufficed to hint at what he wanted. But while Enzo did bend to kiss him, the rest of him did not follow. Not even when they broke off for breath and Fiore's fingers remained tangled in his hair.

"What's wrong?" Fiore asked, working double to keep his tone light. If Enzo thought him soiled by what had occurred in the catacombs, Fiore knew not what to do. He'd never get cleaner than he was at this very moment. If this didn't suffice, then—

Or, worse still, his scars—which would never wash away. Perhaps they reminded Enzo of the craven circumstances that had caused them. Though he'd said he didn't hold it against Fiore, that was whilst the hideous wounds remained concealed beneath clean white linen. Now, fresh and scarlet as his former sash, they felt like a brand that emblazoned Fiore's cowardice. No wonder the sight of them failed to inspire Enzo's passions.

Enzo, meanwhile, stared at him in alarm. "Nothing's wrong."

An obvious falsehood. If nothing were wrong, they'd be fucking right now instead of talking. Fiore pressed on. "Is it the scars? Or what happened in the crypt?"

"Neither," Enzo insisted, his eyes flying wide.

A wiser courtesan would accept defeat and preserve what precious little dignity remained to them. Fiore instead heard himself ask, "Then why don't you want me?"

Enzo blinked. "I do want you."

Fiore stared at him in total incomprehension.

"But your wounds," Enzo continued as the gears in Fiore's mind tangled together and caught fire. "I didn't want to risk imperiling your recovery."

"My wounds are closed now." Fiore's voice sounded dull and pathetic even to his own ears.

"They are," Enzo conceded.

"Then why—?"

"I didn't want to press you. To make you uncomfortable. After all that's happened—after all you've unjustly suffered—I don't want you to feel obligated to return my affections."

Fiore felt nothing of the kind. He did feel as though he'd waited forever to regain strength enough to enjoy intimacy with Enzo again. The knowledge that even now his Enzo wanted him and had only held himself back to protect him threatened to overwhelm him. The terror in his heart turned to joy and brimmed over. His eyes burned with tears he couldn't let gather, much less fall, lest Enzo mistake them for sorrow.

"I want you," Fiore blurted. "Desperately. But," he quickly added, horrified at how much had slipped past his lips already, "if you don't desire me now—if you just feel guilty or obligated or—I understand entirely, and I don't hold it against—" He was rambling, spiraling, and with an effort silenced himself. But not soon enough.

Enzo didn't look half so horrified as Fiore felt to hear his own words. Instead he took Fiore's hand in his own and brought it gently to his lips to press a soft kiss against his knuckles.

Fiore's traitorous tongue stilled at last.

"So we're agreed," Enzo concluded. "We both want this, and we both want the other to do this because they want to and not because they feel obligated."

"Well," said Fiore, "when you put it that way, we sound foolish beyond all measure for not realizing it sooner."

Again, Fiore wished he could snatch his words back out of the aether the moment he'd spoken them.

But Enzo didn't seem sorry to hear them. Quite the reverse. A soft huff of laughter escaped through his shy, bitten-back smile.

And for that, Fiore had to reward him with a kiss.

This time Enzo followed him down onto the bed.

Tumbling Enzo down beside him proved easy enough. Divesting him of his wrapping-gown easier still. The tease of their aquatic adventure left him at half-mast, and brushing his cock against Enzo's revealed him similarly eager.

However, when the moment came for Fiore to rise up atop Enzo and drive his sword into his willing sheath, he found his strength wanting.

His arms trembled under his own slender weight. His stomach lurched without bandage or sash to brace it. After a month-and-a-half of celibacy, after all his shameful begging and pleading, after he finally had his Enzo back in his arms and willing to fuck him—now he could hardly hold himself up, much less move. Fiore supposed he ought to count himself lucky his cock still stood, even if the rest of him could not.

Enzo didn't seem disgusted or impatient or anything else Fiore felt. He took in Fiore's infirmities with a glance and said, "Would you be willing to lie back and let me do the work?"

Fiore stared down at him. "Straddle me, y'mean?"

Enzo nodded with a shy and hopeful smile.

Fiore devoured that smile in a kiss.

Ever so gently, and with tenfold strength, Enzo laid Fiore down and arose. He sat astride Fiore's hips with all the confidence of a man who could afford to ride horses. Their cocks slid against each other in Enzo's fist, and Fiore bit back an unseemly sound at the welcome return of a delicious sensation. Enzo's cunt followed in his cock's wake, up to the tip of Fiore's blade; then he canted his hips and sank down onto it, all the way to the hilt.

And *fuck*, Fiore had missed this.

The tight, wet heat of Enzo's cunt held both the fiery passion of the forge and the perfect fit of the sheath. All this before he'd even begun to move. When he rolled his hips at last, Fiore had to seize his waist and hold on lest he come undone. Pleasure rippled through the walls of Enzo's cunt and reverberated through Fiore's prick. He dared to take Enzo's cock in hand in turn and was threefold rewarded with an ecstatic shudder through Enzo's frame, a broken moan escaping his throat, and the biting of his scarred lip. Fiore only wished he were near enough to kiss it. He settled for stroking Enzo's cock and delighting in how Enzo thrust to meet his hand. The other reached up and caught a few tendrils of Enzo's hair still wet from the bath. He twined them 'round his fingers. A gentle tug sufficed to bring Enzo down to kiss him—needfully grinding his cock into him all the while. Fiore devoured him, just as ravenous as Enzo. Then breath demanded they break off and Enzo rose up once more, and Fiore drank in the view of Enzo towering over him, gleaming, triumphant, his lip caught between his teeth again, his head thrown back, hair cascading down his shoulders as spend cascaded from his cunt, heaving, writhing, riding him with equal parts gallantry and desperation. Fiore gave him another swift stroke, running his thumb over the cock-head beading with pearls—and with a shudder like sails in a storm, Enzo stuttered to a halt, his cunt clenching around Fiore in rhythm with his cock pulsing in Fiore's fist, spilling liquid pearls over his knuckles. Fiore seized his ass and thrust into him from below, hard, fast, deep, another shudder from Enzo bent over him, another clench of his cunt, and Fiore followed him over the precipice to pour his own sea-salt spend into the tide flowing from Enzo's cunt.

Enzo collapsed, retaining the presence of mind to support himself on his forearms braced on either side of Fiore's head rather than crushing Fiore beneath him. Fiore threw his arms around him and dragged him down into his embrace. A kiss followed every gasp and a gasp followed every kiss until, sated at last, they settled for twining their limbs together and breathing as one.

"How d'you feel?" Enzo murmured against his lips.

"Wonderful," Fiore told him—truthfully. The sheer relief of having Enzo in his arms again mingled with the raw ecstasy of fucking and the aching comfort of knowing Enzo still wanted him, Enzo didn't despise his weakness, Enzo believed him worthy of desire and protection alike.

Enzo, not privy to any of this, pressed on. "Are you certain? Nothing pulled or twinged or—?"

Fiore caught his lips in a kiss.

"I'm fine," Fiore insisted when they broke off for breath. But his secret satisfaction to have Enzo fussing over him belied itself in his bitten-back smile.

And, better still, Enzo gave him a bashful smile in return.

～

So many things Enzo hadn't dared hope for.

SEBASTIAN NOTHWELL

For Fiore to survive. For Fiore to choose him. For Fiore to recover enough for intimacy—and, more importantly, to *want* to be intimate with him again.

And now Enzo had all these things quite literally wrapped up in his arms.

The sheer satisfaction of sating those desires Fiore had kindled in him paired with sentiment. He'd longed for Fiore to fuck him again, not just to fulfill his own erotic needs—and by the gods, how Fiore filled him— but in hopes that Fiore might for one brief moment feel pleasure rather than pain. He'd yearned to take Fiore's most vulnerable flesh within his own body to shield him from the slings and arrows of the world, as a sheath would protect a blade. Still he'd kept his distance, all too aware of the toll Fiore's ordeal had taken on his mind and body alike and not wanting to rob him of any more choice than he'd already lost.

So to have Fiore willingly, enthusiastically, and deliberately demand the affection Enzo had so desired to give him—well. Enzo knew not how to express his delight in granting both their fondest desires other than by riding him to their united finish and basking with him afterward in tender bliss.

Eventually Fiore's hungry kisses gave way to softer caresses. His breaths slowed. His eyes fluttered shut. And, at last, he fell into the sweet sleep of Endymion.

Enzo remained awake a few moments more. Just long enough to run his fingers through Fiore's soft curls and note how Fiore insinuated himself into his collar in return. Joy and relief mingled in his chest. He gave thanks to all the gods that his Fiore felt well again.

And vowed to wreak absolute vengeance on those who'd tried to destroy him.

# CHAPTER THIRTY-TWO

"There's a woman in the canal," Enzo remarked the following afternoon.

Fiore sat with him in the Ca' Scaevola library. They'd just finished a novel about a vengeful duelist who rescued her beloved from becoming a sacrifice to a sea monster—a story which Enzo had hesitated to read, given its parallels to Fiore's freshly-escaped predicament, but Fiore had insisted and, indeed, found it rather more cathartic than otherwise. Enzo had arisen to replace the book on its shelf by the window, where he'd glanced out at the canal below and relayed what he saw.

Fiore balked. "A woman in the canal?"

"Forgive me," Enzo added with haste. "I mean—she is in a sandolo."

Fiore had assumed as much.

"Here, come look." Enzo gently supported Fiore in approaching the window. "Her boat has stopped."

Fiore could see as much now, leaning half on Enzo's arm and half on the windowsill. There, in the canal beneath Ca' Scaevola, drifted a sandolo bearing two passengers. One, with the oar in hand, Fiore didn't recognize. The other stood upright in the middle of the vessel and shaded her eyes with her hand as she gazed up at the palazzo. Though this gesture hid much of her face from view, Fiore nonetheless recognized her round cap, cropped hair, and smock. But even if she'd changed her garb, he'd have known her bearing anywhere.

"Artemisia?" he wondered aloud.

"Your sculptor friend?" said Enzo.

Fiore nodded absently. He waved down at her, though the anodyne made him feel as though his arm-bones had filled with lead.

A jolt seemed to run through her figure. She waved back. The sandolo rocked beneath her, but her upright posture never wavered.

Fiore wondered why she'd come and how long she'd waited there. Surely if she had business with him she could've simply knocked on the palazzo door. He drew breath to shout down to her—but even just his inhale sparked enough pain to give him second thoughts. He turned to Enzo instead, who had hung back from the window all the while, tucked against the wall beside it. Fiore couldn't fathom why, until he realized that Enzo lacked his bauta mask, and indeed Fiore hadn't seen him don it since he'd awoken within Ca' Scaevola's walls. Even within his own home, Enzo didn't wish the outside world to perceive his bare face.

"Can we ask her how long she's been down there?" Fiore asked him.

"We may ask her anything you like," Enzo replied. "Shall we invite her in?"

The notion hadn't occurred to Fiore. While an artisan might enter a palazzo on matters of business, it was unheard of for social calls. He'd hardly expected the privilege of inviting his friends to join him within the hallowed halls of Ca' Scaevola.

Despite his astonishment, he managed a nod, which sufficed to set Enzo to rapid work. Within minutes a passing servant was hailed, a messenger dispatched, something in the portico drew Artemisia's notice and subsequently her vessel, and another servant arrived in the library with a tray of coffee and zaletti and still another quick on their heels to announce Maestra Artemisia Zuccato.

Artemisia entered. Enzo bowed to her. Fiore, tucked into the corner of a settee, hoped she would find his wave sufficient.

"Forgive me if I don't stand," he said, pasting a smile over his fears of her taking offense. "I'm a convalescent, you see."

"Yes, so I've heard," she replied.

Fiore wished he'd thought to ask for a comb and mirror in the hectic meantime. Even without the mirror he could recall the bruises beneath his eyes and the crimson scar on his cheek, but there was nothing to be done for them. Other than that, he felt perfectly fit to be seen. Enzo had helped him wash and shave that very morning. And while Enzo's wrapping-gown thrown over his nightshirt might not pass ballroom muster, he knew he'd be the envy of the Crooked Anchor if he only had the strength to go out. Artemisia had seen him plenty handsome in far less.

Yet her gaze now lingered on his scarred cheek and missing finger.

"How did you find me?" Fiore asked, hoping to change the subject. He tried to keep his voice bright.

Artemisia flicked her gaze almost imperceptibly toward Enzo before she answered. "Corelli said a servant in Scaevola livery had arrived to collect your effects."

Belatedly, Fiore realized this was the first time Artemisia had met Enzo without his mask. While Fiore had described his face to her, no doubt his words had not done justice to the strikingly handsome features. "And you went to the *Kingfisher* because you missed me as a model. Forgive me—I ought to have written to tell you what'd become of me."

Artemisia shrugged. "One makes allowances for convalescents."

"Won't you sit down?" Enzo said with his shy and handsome smile.

Only then did Fiore realize Artemisia had remained standing since her entrance.

Artemisia unaccountably hesitated before she did so. Enzo poured her coffee. Again she hesitated before she accepted it. Fiore supposed she was unused to having a duke perform small services for her. Even so, she'd dealt frequently enough with the aristocracy in her work. There was no call for her to seem as nervous as she did—though Fiore doubted anyone besides himself would recognize her behavior as nervous rather than arch. Perhaps the sheer enormity of Enzo's specific rank balked her.

Artemisia sipped her coffee. "You have a beautiful house, your grace."

Enzo demurred.

A tense silence settled over the library.

Artemisia set down her cup and turned to Fiore. "Pray forgive the intrusion, but I had wondered, in light of your absence from my studio, if I might sketch you today?"

A return to business was at least a return to the normalcy Fiore had greatly missed. Still, he had misgivings about his invalid appearance. He looked to Enzo. "Would it be chirurgically advisable?"

"Reclining poses ought to be safe," said Enzo. "I'd caution against standing over-long. Or contorting."

Much the same as the instructions Fiore had received after his appendectomy. To Artemisia, Fiore said, "How will you have me, then?"

"As you are now will do." Artemisia cast a wary glance at Enzo. "If your grace has no objection?"

Enzo blinked. "None whatsoever."

Artemisia produced her zibaldone from her satchel.

Enzo gave it a thoughtful glance and turned to Fiore. "Would you like to draw as well? I could fetch yours."

Fiore felt as touched by the gesture as he did delighted in Artemisia's evident if suppressed astonishment. To have a duke not only at his beck and call but also anticipating his needs was certainly a feather in his cap.

At his nod, Enzo left the library.

Fiore thought in Enzo's absence Artemisia might behave more like herself. She did begin to draw. But even her sketching didn't proceed as normal. Artemisia typically began her sketches with broad sweeping gestures to block in the angles. (Fiore did much the same when he drew, for it was she who'd taught him.) Today, however, she made a series of small scratches in the middle of the page, hunched over it all the while as though jealously guarding some secret.

Before he could question her on the point, she ceased sketching, straightened out, and turned the zibaldone to face him.

"What d'you think?" she asked.

The whole of the page was blank save for a single scrawled line across its dead center. In letters so small Fiore had to squint to read them, she had written the following.

*If he is holding you against your will, tell me this sketch is beautiful.*

"Hideous," Fiore declared without hesitation. "Your worst one yet."

She raised her brows. "If you insist."

Despite himself, Fiore felt genuinely touched. "Your concern is appreciated."

Artemisia shrugged with nonchalance, but a smile tugged at the corner of her mouth. "Just thought I'd ask."

She might have liked to pretend her heart was as much stone as the marble beneath her chisel. Fiore might have even believed her once. But he knew better now, and to know it made him smile, if softly.

"You have to admit," she went on, having turned her zibaldone 'round again, flicked to a blank page, and begun sketching in true earnest, "it all looks rather concerning from the outside. You attend the ball on the duke's arm, only to vanish immediately afterward. Then the duke's staff arrive to remove personal effects from your quarters. And the only hint of your survival is a pale figure sometimes spotted in the highest windows of Ca' Scaevola."

Fiore conceded the point.

"He's looking after you well, then?" Artemisia asked, glancing up from her sketch to meet his gaze with raised brows.

"Exceedingly well," Fiore assured her. Then, because he couldn't resist needling, "Were you planning to mount a rescue if you found otherwise?"

Artemisia shrugged. "Maybe."

If it weren't for the ache in his wounded cheek, Fiore might've grinned. "What else have I missed in town?"

"Not much. Most of the gossip is about you. Though that might die out soon. Evidently Lady Zampieri's latest novel is just Lord De Laurentiis's marriage woes with the names changed. Tagliabue did the engravings. Supposedly based on Bissacco's portraits of the not-so-happy couple—at the author's instruction."

"Far more interesting than a duke's courtesan going missing," Fiore declared with more hope than confidence.

Artemisia hummed doubtfully.

The click of Enzo's heels echoing down the hall announced his return. He appeared on the library threshold shortly thereafter. Fiore expected Artemisia to grow nervous again, but she sketched on in absolute ease, as if she were in her own studio rather than a duke's palazzo. He realized, belatedly, that it was not Enzo's rank or wealth that had unsettled her, but rather his own uncertain fate.

"Pardon," Enzo said as he approached. "I don't mean to intrude..."

"It's no intrusion, your grace," Artemisia assured him without looking up from her sketching.

Thus permitted, Enzo handed Fiore his zibaldone with the shy, handsome smile Fiore loved so well.

Once he had his zibaldone in hand, however, Fiore found he hardly knew what to do with it. He hadn't possessed the strength or focus required to draw since his rescue. Ca' Scaevola held plenty of beautiful compositions for him to capture—the architecture alone would suffice to fill several volumes—yet as he flipped through the leaves to reach a blank page, he found the last one he'd scrawled over. His rough draft begging Enzo for another chance. Heat flooded his face in echo of the humiliation he'd felt when Enzo discovered it, tempered by his own good fortune that Enzo had taken the lines in their intended spirit and, against all odds, realized the simple truth of how desperately Fiore wanted him.

And now, all Fiore wished to draw was—

"Does it meet with your approval, your grace?"

Artemisia's voice jolted Fiore out of his lovesick musings. He glanced up from his zibaldone to find her presenting her sketch for Enzo's examination.

Enzo's soft smile and the wondrous gleam in his eye bespoke approval. "Resplendent."

Fiore wouldn't have praised it quite so high. Though he admitted Artemisia had a very skillful hand, and when rendered by her pencil his emaciated frame seemed not altogether so corpse-like as he'd feared. Perhaps there remained something for Enzo to desire after all.

And no doubt Artemisia knew as well as Fiore that so long as she kept him as her model she would have an eager patron for whatever works she created in his image.

Artemisia accepted her zibaldone back from Enzo, tucked it back into her satchel, and stood, thanking the duke for his hospitality and Fiore for his time. Having accomplished what she came to do—both overtly and covertly—she seemed disinclined to overstay her welcome.

"When shall we meet again?" Fiore inquired. "You did ask to sketch me in my ballroom suit."

"You're most welcome to return," Enzo told her. He looked to Fiore. "Or if you'd prefer...?"

The implicit reminder sufficed to send a thrill through Fiore's heart. He grinned at Artemisia. "I'm very nearly well enough to wander the city again, if you'll suffer my return to your studio."

A wry half-smile wound its way up her cheek. "Either would delight me. What should I tell Corelli?"

Fiore raised his brows. "That I'm alive and well?"

"About your quarters, I mean," said Artemisia with more patience than he deserved. "And your plans therein."

Fiore knew not how to answer her. While he didn't intend to return there to dwell, he had left behind all his worldly belongings, only a fraction of which Carlotta had brought to Ca' Scaevola. And he owed rent at the very least. He looked to Enzo. "When could I visit, d'you think? From a chirurgical perspective."

Enzo shrugged. "Tomorrow, if you felt up to it."

The thought of going outside so soon sent an unexpected thrill through Fiore's veins. He turned to Artemisia with a grin. "Then you may tell her she will see me on the morrow."

She replied with a smile and took her leave of them.

Now that Fiore no longer felt the need to preserve his posture or composition for her sketching, he caught Enzo's eye and made a slight gesture of his hand. This sufficed to draw Enzo to him, like winding a thread, and soon Fiore had him snug beside him on the sofa just as he'd wished.

"It's nice to know I've not been forgotten by the outside world," Fiore observed.

Enzo looked more disturbed by this than Fiore thought warranted. "Who could forget you?"

"You'd be surprised," Fiore mused. Though he supposed he wouldn't know either way if those who'd abandoned his bed recalled him whilst wrapped in the arms of their lawful spouses. He worried the corner of his zibaldone's page between his fingertips. Then, realizing that it remained open to the page of his failed script, and that Enzo couldn't help but look over his shoulder from their present position, he hastily turned it to a blank.

"What do you wish to draw?" asked Enzo.

Perhaps Artemisia's visit had emboldened him. Or perhaps the anodyne meandering through his veins dulled his better senses. Regardless, when Fiore intended only to shrug, he instead heard himself reply, "I dare not say."

Enzo furrowed his brow. "Why not?"

"Because it's not my place. And because you'd only grant it out of pity or desperation to make me happy."

Enzo remained silent so long Fiore feared he'd insulted him. When he spoke at last, however, his words emerged soft and gentle as ever before. "I cannot deny it delights me to make you happy. But pity has never once entered into it."

Fiore wanted so badly to believe him. And perhaps that drove him to reply with more honesty than he might have otherwise done. "I wish to draw you."

Enzo didn't look offended—as he had every right to be, when a mere courtesan asked him to play artist's model. Instead his furrowed brow bespoke only confusion. "Me? Why?"

"Because you have a strikingly handsome aspect. And because I'd like to have your image to look at whenever you're not before me."

Enzo appeared no less bewildered by this. "Then why hesitate?"

"I know you don't like to be perceived."

"I like to be perceived by you."

This assertion, so gentle and unassuming yet undeniably honest, left Fiore in stunned silence for some moments. For he realized even amidst all his own artifice that the same held true for him as well.

Still, it wouldn't do to let Enzo continue on against his best interests, no matter how appealing that course felt to Fiore. And so he forced his tongue to say, reminding himself as much as Enzo, "If I preserve your likeness in my zibaldone, then anyone who gazes upon it may perceive you."

No small thing to ask of a man who never left his house without a mask.

Yet Enzo didn't balk at the prospect. Instead, the shy smile Fiore loved so well plucked at his scarred and handsome mouth. "You preserve things as you perceive them. And the way you perceive me is how I'd like others to perceive me. So really I wouldn't mind at all."

In the face of this sincerity, Fiore could deny his desires no longer. He indulged them first with a kiss, lingering on Enzo's lips until breath demanded he break off.

Then he curled into the corner of the sofa with his zibaldone propped against his knees and, at long last, laid down the decisive pencil strokes to capture the features burned indelibly on his heart.

~

The gondola journey from Ca' Scaevola to the *Kingfisher* went smoothly. Fiore encountered difficulty only with embarking and disembarking, and Enzo's assistance made both far easier.

The fresh air was well worth the trouble in Fiore's opinion. After a fortnight indoors, even the vast halls of Ca' Scaevola had begun to feel closed in. Now, as he alighted from the gondola onto the street flanking the ship, he breathed in deep and delighted in the myriad incidental sounds of the serene city. He tucked his arm into Enzo's and strode up the gangplank—Carlotta had arranged for its rolling out in daylight hours beforehand.

Corelli and her sons greeted them with a wave as they passed. Serafina was not out; it was only midmorning, and like Fiore, she didn't oft arise before midday. Fiore tried not to think about when last he'd trod this very deck. He plastered on his best effort at a smile—close-lipped, thin, hardly tugging at the scar on his cheek—and went below.

His quarters looked almost precisely as he'd left them. Minus all the sundries Carlotta had retrieved for his use at Ca' Scaevola. Only furniture and decoration remained, alongside his sea-chest.

Enzo removed his mask, cloak, hood, and hat, just as he'd done hundreds of times before when crossing Fiore's threshold. "Where shall we begin?"

Fiore knew not where. An unaccountable melancholy had crept over him. The sunlight drew his gaze, sparkling down through the deck-prisms overhead and streaming into the porthole window. Despite

Enzo's nautical ancestry there were no porthole windows in Ca' Scaevola. At least not so far as Fiore had seen. Nor had he beheld a single deck prism. It was a stupid thing to fixate on, and yet he found himself seized with a desire to carve the prisms out of the ceiling and shove them into his sea-chest like stolen treasure for transport back to the palazzo.

Forcing his gaze away from the light did nothing to improve his mood. He'd covered a whole wall in his sketches—and for what? What pride he'd foolishly placed in mere scribblings on scrap paper from an amateur hand. Any one of the paintings hanging in Ca' Scaevola's galleries outshone the lot.

The furnishings looked even more ridiculous. His stupid half-a-whaleboat bed could barely hold one man, let alone two, let alone the hundreds if not thousands who'd graced its timbers in the half-decade Fiore had spent here. The sea-chest he could at least tuck away out of sight, but—

"Fiore?"

A jolt ran through Fiore despite Enzo's soft tone.

"Here." Enzo gently led him to his old chair—one of a set, bought third-hand from a sale of effects, its shield-back carved with fish scales, yet even if he had the whole set it would not equal one-tenth of a single stick of furniture from Ca' Scaevola. "Sit down."

Fiore sat. His eyes burned. He'd spent years curating and decorating his quarters, and now it all looked so stupid. He should never have come back.

"Why not?" asked Enzo.

Fiore realized, far too late, that his last thought had left his lips. He swallowed hard to master his voice. "It's ridiculous."

Enzo's brow furrowed. "What is?"

"All of it." Fiore threw his arm aloft at his drawings. "How stupid would these look on your walls?"

Enzo glanced to the drawings and back to Fiore. "Not at all."

Fiore scoffed. He thought of the capriccio Enzo had offered him, so long ago it seemed, and how then he'd feared it would seem silly in his own quarters. How foolish he'd been then. He flung out his hand toward the bed. "How absurd would that be in your bedchamber?"

"Our bedchamber," said Enzo.

Fiore rolled his eyes so hard they ached.

He regretted it at once. Not for the pain in his skull, but for the silence that fell in its wake and the way Enzo worried his scarred lip between his teeth.

Fiore's own lips parted for he knew not what. No apology could suffice, not after he'd thrown everything Enzo had done for him back in his face, but—

"We still haven't created your chambers at Ca' Scaevola," Enzo said. "Perhaps you might like a nautical design? One which would suit what you have here?"

Fiore stared at him. No mere words could begin to express all his regret for his own behavior and all his gratitude for Enzo's continued efforts to understand his wild moods.

"Or," Enzo continued, "if not here in the city, then we might construct new quarters for you in the countryside. There's more room to expand out there. We could build an addition to the villa, all your own design."

Fiore knew not what to say. His mouth opened regardless. "You have a villa?"

"Yes." Enzo blinked at him. "Didn't I mention...?"

Fiore shook his head.

"Oh," said Enzo. "Forgive me, I ought to have said something."

Another wave of regret washed over Fiore's heart. For Enzo to apologize when it was Fiore who'd wronged him—

"It's near to Giovanna's," Enzo explained. "But it's all my own. So you needn't worry about my family interfering—not that they would, but I know you're concerned, so—"

Fiore caught Enzo by the hand.

Enzo fell silent.

"I don't need my own room at your villa," Fiore explained. "Or at Ca' Scaevola. I just..." He trailed off. He knew not what he needed. At the moment all he wanted was for Enzo to hold him.

And as if Enzo could hear words he hadn't spoken, he raised Fiore's hand to his lips and kissed his knuckles. He kept that hand cradled between his own as he knelt before him.

"You don't have to decide what to keep just now," Enzo said. "Or where to put it all. We can store everything at Ca' Scaevola until you know what you want to do with it."

What he ought to do, Fiore knew, was turn his back on the lot and let Corelli sell or toss or burn whatever she saw fit. But the thought of leaving behind everything he'd poured his heart into, carving out a small slice of the city to make his own and fill with whatever brought him comfort, filled him with stupid, short-sighted, unbearable melancholy. Everything he held dear here would hardly take up even a corner of Enzo's bedchamber. Still, he realized even as he scolded himself, that meant it wouldn't burden Enzo to tuck it way somewhere in the enormous palazzo for a little while. At least until he could think properly.

"I'd like to keep the frame," Fiore heard himself say as he gazed on his whaleboat bed. "Not the bedding. That's due for a change anyway. But the frame…"

Enzo glanced over it. "Agreed. And the hook as well?"

Fiore hadn't dared consider the hook worth keeping.

A handsome rosy tint bloomed over Enzo's sharp cheeks. "I do have some fond memories here."

Fiore's mouth twitched in something like a smile. Still close-lipped and thin but far more sincere than what he'd worn on deck just moments ago. He leaned in and gave Enzo a kiss.

"The hook as well," Fiore said when they parted.

The strength of Enzo's arm and his ingenuity sufficed to extract the hook from the wall. More care was taken with Fiore's drawings—more care than Fiore thought they deserved, anyway, but Enzo insisted on treating them thus. All were laid into Fiore's sea-chest atop its own treasures and what shirts and sundries had been locked away inside it when Carlotta came for his clothes. Then Enzo donned his mask again, swung the sea-chest over his shoulder, and carried it up on deck.

Where Corelli, her sons, and now Serafina awaited them.

Serafina raised her brow at the sight of a duke bearing Fiore's sea-chest. Whatever doubts she had about it she kept to herself, which was the greatest gift she could give Fiore in parting.

"Farewell for now," Fiore told them all. "I'll be back to drink and dance as soon as the chirurgeons allow."

Corelli accepted this with a nod and struck out her hand for him to grasp. Fiore shook it. But rather than release him afterward, she instead used their hand-clasp to draw him into a rough and hearty embrace.

"You're always welcome back," she said, too low for anyone but him to hear.

"Thanks," Fiore managed, stunned. He supposed she meant as a visitor rather than as a returning tenant. Even so, he appreciated her offer. The recollections of Serafina's misfortune with her own wealthy patron weighed heavily in the air.

Corelli released him.

Fiore entwined his arm with Enzo's once more.

And together, they left the *Kingfisher* behind.

# CHAPTER THIRTY-THREE

Fiore expected Enzo would hand the sea-chest over to a trusted servant once they arrived at Ca' Scaevola.

This did not come to pass.

Instead, Enzo insisted—in his quiet and deferential way, but insisted nonetheless—on transporting it himself. He hoisted it out of the felze, carried it up the staircases and down the corridors, and did not set it down again until it reached its final resting place in his bedchamber. Or rather, their bedchamber, Fiore reminded himself.

Fiore felt as astonished as he did pleased that Enzo took personal charge of the sea-chest. While the chest itself remained locked and the false bottom concealed all Fiore would want concealed, nonetheless he wouldn't have fully trusted it in anyone else's hands. He well appreciated the deliberate effort Enzo made to show respect to even his meagre belongings.

Once Enzo set the sea-chest down at the foot of the bed, however, Fiore couldn't help but notice how stark it stood out against everything else in the room.

"What do you think of it?" Fiore asked Enzo.

Enzo glanced between him and the sea-chest. "How do you mean?"

"Don't you think it looks a bit..." Fiore bit back his own first impressions. Ludicrously small when set before the vast breadth of Enzo's bed. Quaintly carved and garishly painted when compared to the dark and grandiose decoration of the surrounding room. Downright cheap amidst the splendor of Ca' Scaevola. "Like it doesn't belong?"

Like Fiore himself didn't belong.

Enzo furrowed his brow. "Not at all. But," he added, "if you'd like, you might decorate your own rooms along similar lines."

"Sounds like you're eager to get me out of your bedchamber." Fiore had intended to sound teasing. He wasn't sure he'd accomplished it.

Nevertheless, Enzo insisted, "Our bedchamber."

Fiore supposed he could let the matter rest there for now. He dropt to one knee in front of his sea-chest—somewhat more awkwardly than he had in days past, with an unpleasant twinge in his stomach—and took out his drawings. As the sea-chest's decoration paled in comparison to Ca' Scaevola, so too did his artwork. He tried to put it from his mind and think instead how Enzo appreciated them even if he himself couldn't. Indeed, when he handed them over to Enzo he noted the quiet and handsome smile that lit up his dark eyes at the mere sight of them.

Likewise, as Fiore got his clothes out to air them, his old raiments seemed not worth the bother when contrasted against what he wore now. Still, he liked to have them. Perhaps they might see more use if he ever progressed from drawing to painting.

When he reached the false bottom, he paused. Its contents loomed in his mind's eye. Enzo's remark regarding the hook and happy memories had surprised him. While he also treasured those moments spent in Enzo's willing submission, he'd assumed they'd remain a thing of the past. After all, Enzo could hardly take Fiore seriously as a dominating force, knowing what he did now about his weakness in the catacombs. He was lucky enough that Enzo still wanted to fuck him at all.

And yet Enzo had retrieved the hook specifically. Fiore turned it in his hands as his thoughts tumbled over each other in his mind, until at last he raised his eyes to the four spiraling posts framing the bed's canopy.

"D'you suppose," Fiore asked, forcing his voice into nonchalance, "it could support the weight of a man?"

Enzo followed his gaze. "I see no reason why it shouldn't."

SEBASTIAN NOTHWELL

Fiore's heart fluttered into his throat. He hadn't dared to hope, and yet the thing with feathers had caught him up regardless.

Enzo, meanwhile, took in whatever passed over Fiore's face with some alarm and quickly added. "If you're willing."

Not the answer nor the stipulation Fiore had expected. "Why shouldn't I be willing?"

"I thought you might have..." Enzo trailed off, evidently searching for a kinder way to say what he wished. "Lost your desire for restraint. Given recent events."

*I thought the same of you,* Fiore didn't say. The reference to specifically *recent* events, however, proved Enzo required a reminder. And so he said, as gently as possible, "I was tied up against my will long before we ever met."

Enzo blinked. "Fair point."

"So..." Fiore found he couldn't continue whilst meeting Enzo's gaze. His eyes fell to the hook in his hands. His knuckles clenched around it. "You wouldn't mind taking orders from..." He held back the phrase that sprang to mind—*a crippled coward*—and instead simply asked, "...me?"

Silence reigned. Fiore's heart hung in the balance. He fixed his gaze on the hook.

Then, beneath his own clenched fists, he saw Enzo hold out his hands, their palms upraised.

Fiore lifted his eyes to meet Enzo's.

Though Enzo still stood over him, somehow the way he bowed his head meant his dark and solemn gaze by no means looked down upon Fiore.

"An order from your lips," Enzo declared, his low voice rumbling through Fiore's own ribs, "is both an honor and a privilege to obey."

Fiore's heart stuttered in his chest. Enzo had exceeded all his hopes once again. He wanted to kiss him. And yet... "On your knees."

After all, he knew of no better reward for him than an order.

Enzo sank to the floor—without question, without hesitation, and with absolute devotion in the gaze he cast up at Fiore.

Fiore's heart soared to see it. He forced himself to glance away long enough to open the false bottom and retrieve his riding crop. When he returned to Enzo, he found his beloved's dark gaze fixed on the leather tongue, following its progress in undeniable anticipation.

"Are you willing to experiment?" Fiore asked.

Enzo's pupils blew wide as his eyes flicked to meet Fiore's. He nodded eagerly.

Fiore let slip the smile he'd bitten back. He held out the crop to Enzo. After a moment's confused hesitation, Enzo took it from him.

Fiore's smile widened. "Will you hold that behind your back for me?"

The gleam of understanding lit Enzo's gaze. Within two shakes of a sail his hands were clasped behind him tight around the crop's handle.

"Well done," Fiore purred.

A handsome rosy tint bloomed over Enzo's sharp cheekbones.

Fiore shut his sea-chest and sat down on its lid. His thighs splayed open. He trailed his hand down his shirtfront, undoing waistcoat buttons as he went, until his fingertips landed on the fall-front of his breeches.

Enzo's eyes followed him all the way down. They flicked back up to meet Fiore's gaze when he paused. The hands clenched 'round the riding crop never once loosed their hold.

Fiore grinned. "Would you care to taste me?"

Enzo's scarred lip caught between his teeth. He nodded.

Fiore released his cock from his breeches. The sight of Enzo kneeling before him in perfect obedience had already raised him to a half-stand. Enzo gazed at it with unmistakable hunger.

"Make yourself comfortable," Fiore told him, lest he assume pain was supposed to be part of this particular pleasure.

Enzo arranged himself between Fiore's thighs. His grip on the crop never wavered. Even if Fiore weren't already predisposed to be pleased with him, he had to admit the display impressed him. Many gentlemen who'd offered themselves up to him before couldn't have done half so well. It certainly did a great deal towards raising his mast to full sail.

Fiore leaned back against the bed and draped his arms across the footboard. "You may begin."

Enzo bowed his head. His scarred lips enveloping the head of Fiore's prick felt divine as ever. Soft and gentle even in their barely-restrained hunger. Fiore gasped as the tongue slipped under him, guiding him inside the soft, wet heat of Enzo's throat as he swallowed him down.

Fiore trailed his fingers through Enzo's hair. Enzo shivered with pleasure beneath his touch. Fiore wrapped his fist in the raven locks and gave a gentle tug—reward rather than punishment. A deep moan, desperate for more, resounded from Enzo's throat and through Fiore's cock.

From this vantage point Fiore had an excellent view of Enzo straining against the crop behind his back. Not just the hands—though that would've sufficed for Fiore's purpose—but the arms as well, muscles rippling beneath linen sleeves, shoulders trembling with the force of Enzo's restrained desire, all his brawn pitted against itself.

Nor was it Enzo's sole struggle.

Robbed of any ability to touch himself with his hands, he nonetheless persevered with ingenuity. Whilst his mouth did delightful and unspeakable things to Fiore's cock, Fiore beheld Enzo rolling his own hips to the same rhythm of his bobbing throat, rubbing off inside his breeches with just the friction of the fabric against a cock obviously hard as adamant beneath the fall-front. The mere thought of Enzo ruining his drawers just from sucking his cock—Fiore bit his lip for restraint.

"You could spend without a touch, couldn't you?" Fiore mused aloud once he'd regathered himself. "You wanton thing."

Another choked-off moan reverberated around his cock.

Someday Fiore would've liked to test that theory. Today, however, his own desires proved too great to deny.

"Shall I be merciful?" Fiore asked. "Shall I fuck you at last?"

Enzo's dark gaze shot up to meet his own. Ravenous. Pleading. Desperate. Fiore felt rather than saw his hard swallow.

"You may speak," Fiore told him.

His cock slipped from between Enzo's lips. Enzo regarded it like Tantalus gazing on an apricot plucked out of his reach. Yet when his eyes met Fiore's, the resolve in their depths held firm.

"Fuck me," Enzo begged. His hips jerked, seemingly of their own accord. "*Please.*"

Fiore grinned. "Give me the crop."

Enzo relinquished it at once.

Fiore twirled it in his fingers. "Strip."

Enzo leapt to do so. Fumbling with his waistcoat buttons. Frantic as he tore off his breeches. Shirt and drawers cast off, leaving him standing before Fiore in stockings and garters alone, his thighs gleaming with his cunt's tide, a pearl of seed glistening at his cock's slit.

Fiore likewise couldn't stand another moment's wait. "Straddle me."

Enzo's welcome weight settled onto Fiore's thighs. Their blades crossed—slid against each other—Enzo's cunt following in his cock's wake, up Fiore's length to the very tip—then Enzo's hips rocked back, and he impaled himself on Fiore's sword. A tremulous sigh of satisfaction escaped Enzo's throat as he sank down onto Fiore. Fiore, for his part, buried his unseemly sounds in a bruising kiss to Enzo's collar.

But when Enzo tried to roll his hips again, Fiore halted him with a hand on his waist.

Enzo stilled at once.

Fiore held up the crop. "Hold this."

Enzo's eyes flicked from Fiore to the crop with ravenous gaze. Reverently he accepted his charge and once again clasped it behind his back.

Balance would prove a touch more difficult now—but that was what trust was for, in Fiore's opinion. He laid both palms on Enzo's waist to steady him. "You may move."

Slowly, tentatively, Enzo began fucking himself on Fiore's cock. His pace increased with rapidity, and soon, finding he did not fall, he rode Fiore with reckless abandon.

Fiore, unable to restrain himself any further, embraced him. His arms clasped Enzo as tight as Enzo's cunt gripped him in turn. Bruising kisses followed bites across Enzo's collar. He dared to kiss his throat and felt as well as heard the debauched moan that escaped him in return.

Enzo's cock remained trapped between them. Pearl after pearl emerged from it and smeared across Fiore's abdomen. Fiore, on the brink of losing himself in his cunt, took Enzo's cock in hand. Enzo shuddered in his grasp, his cunt rippling around Fiore.

"You're doing so well," Fiore crooned in his ear. "Come for me. Now."

This, alongside a swift stroke of his wrist, sufficed to send Enzo over the brink. His seed poured over Fiore's knuckles and drenched his blade besides. His cunt clenched in tandem with the pulsing of his cock in

Fiore's fist. Fiore seized an ample handful of his ass and with this leverage thrust hard into his quivering sheath. He spent, filling Enzo with his torrential tide, clasping him in his arms even as his cunt clasped him in turn, both gasping for breath as they drowned in their shared ecstasy.

The storm of pleasure passed, leaving Fiore tranquil in its wake. He tucked his head into Enzo's collar and ran his fingertips down his shivering sides, over his arms, tracing the muscles straining beneath the skin, until he came at last to his hands.

And discovered the crop still clenched in Enzo's convulsive grasp.

Fiore's heart sang out. He raised his head 'til his lips met Enzo's ear. "Well done."

Another shiver of pleasure rippled through Enzo.

Fiore smiled against his ear. "You may release."

Enzo loosed his hold on the crop. It fell into Fiore's waiting palm.

Just as Enzo threw his newly-unfettered arms around Fiore and clasped him tight.

No embrace could've felt more welcome to Fiore in that moment. Enzo wanted him. Even after all that had happened. Enzo still desired him, still sought to please him, still granted him this small control in his otherwise chaotic and disrupted life.

And Fiore could still find it within himself to command.

His heart brimmed over with something he couldn't name. Rather than try to speak it, he tangled his hand in Enzo's hair and drew him up for a ravenous kiss.

"You alright?" Enzo murmured against his lips as they parted.

A natural smile found its way onto Fiore's mouth. "Better than alright. You?"

Enzo, his pupils blown wide, simply nodded and kissed him again.

~

"Maestra Rovigatti wishes to know when you intend to resume your training."

Carlotta delivered this verbal message alongside the morning post over breakfast some two months after Fiore's rescue. Most of the pile was

414

for Enzo, but since Artemisia's visit, Fiore had begun to receive occasional notes from her as well. It felt quaint to take up a correspondence with someone he'd always spoken with in person. Still Fiore couldn't deny it delighted him to have proof that someone outside Ca' Scaevola's walls recalled his existence.

But the message from Maestra Rovigatti, whoever she was, seemed to give Enzo a fraction of the surprise Fiore felt to hear it.

"Tell her she shall have my answer within the day," Enzo said, after a moment's pause and a none-too-subtle glance at Fiore.

Carlotta withdrew as silently as she'd arrived.

"Maestra Rovigatti?" Fiore asked when Carlotta had gone.

"My fencing tutor," Enzo replied.

Fiore had known in a dim and distant way that Enzo had a tutor in swordplay. Enzo had told him of his daily practice. Yet only now did Fiore realize he'd not seen him take up a sword since he arrived at Ca' Scaevola. The training must, he concluded, have remained suspended throughout his convalescence. Not on his behalf, he hoped. Enzo could hardly continue to love him if he kept him from something he held dear.

"And how will you answer her?" Fiore enquired.

Enzo hesitated. Rather like a hound straining at its leash. Or a cat trapped behind a windowpane, its hungry gaze fixed on songbirds hopping along the sill. But all he said was, "I wouldn't want to leave you to fend for yourself."

Fiore doubted much harm could come to him within Ca' Scaevola's walls. Still, he thought he had the answer to sate both his and Enzo's desires. "May I watch?"

After all, watching his beloved perform feats of athleticism whilst stripped to the waist sounded like a delightful way to pass a few hours.

Yet still Enzo hesitated. "I fear I'm rather out of shape."

"Hardly." Fiore swept his gaze over Enzo's handsome form.

Enzo appeared unconvinced. "It's been months since I last ran up the stair."

Confusion robbed Fiore of his flirtatious prowess. "Since you last what the what?"

"The spiral staircase in the northwest tower," Enzo replied as though it were a natural feature in any household. "I used to run up and down it every morning to warm up for my fencing lesson."

Fiore stared at him. He knew Enzo was an early riser, far earlier than himself, but he'd never yet considered what Enzo had done with his time whilst Fiore slept. He supposed this explained Enzo's stamina at the very least. Nevertheless his reply remained the same. "I'm certain you'll impress me regardless."

A skeptical twist marred Enzo's perfect mouth.

Fiore kissed it back into shape.

"There's nothing I find so inspiring as the sight of a gentleman gleaming with honest sweat," Fiore proclaimed in a whisper against Enzo's lips as they parted.

The shy smile Fiore loved so well graced Enzo's handsome features. Then he leapt up from the table and strode from the room to deliver his answer to Carlotta.

~

The lessons resumed the following day.

Not at dawn, as they had before, because Fiore didn't arise until halfway through the morning. He had some regret for delaying them, but Enzo waved off any attempt at apology. Only after Fiore had broken his fast, drunk his coffee, washed, dressed, and announced himself ready did Enzo—who'd done all this well before Fiore had awoken—consent to go downstairs and prepare for his lesson.

"I told Maestra Rovigatti we couldn't meet her before midday," Enzo confessed as he led Fiore arm-in-arm to the courtyard.

Fiore felt torn between guilt at altering Enzo and Maestra Rovigatti's established routine and relief at not needing to arise a minute sooner than he had.

Enzo settled Fiore onto the marble bench, cushioned by furs. Vittorio, who'd followed them down in loyal silence, lay down at his feet.

Then, under Fiore's watchful eye, Enzo took up his rapier and began.

Fiore had come prepared to enjoy a show. Any excuse would've satisfied for the opportunity to see Enzo stripped to the waist and gleaming with sweat.

Even so, Enzo's display surpassed his expectations.

From the moment he raised his blade, Enzo became a conduit of grace. The precision and rapidity of the changes in his posture as the sword slashed through the air reminded Fiore of the ballerini rehearsing for the stage. (Fiore had oft admired the ballerini—at least, before events that didn't bear remembering.) Enzo's long, lean frame had belied his poise. Now Fiore saw where he'd learnt to carry his immense height in elegance. There was a pattern to Enzo's movements now, obvious enough to Fiore's eye, but too rapid for him to discern any specific gestures within or even begin to reckon their purpose. It was a dance, as so many storytellers had asserted in the fairy tales of Fiore's magazines, but only now did he realize the truth in what they'd written.

Then, in the midst of a particular gesture, something caught Enzo's eye. He shot up straight, flung out his sword in a slash to his side, then raised its hilt to his face in salute.

Fiore turned to follow his sight-line and found a woman entering the courtyard from one of its many archways. Middling-height and middling aged, with her whip-cord frame garbed in waistcoat and breeches and carrying a sword at her hip. She wore her hair cropped even shorter than Artemisia's. Indeed, her casual confidence reminded Fiore of his sculptor friend. But while no one would describe Artemisia as clumsy, the sword-bearing woman moved with more perceptible finesse than her or indeed most people.

"Good morning, your grace," she said as she approached.

"Maestra Rovigatti," said Enzo, bowing. "This is Fiore. Fiore, Maestra Rovigatti."

Fiore stood just long enough to bow—despite the ache in his gut and Enzo's alarmed glance. Maestra Rovigatti seemed to appreciate the gesture and returned it. She removed her coat, waistcoat, and sword, laying all aside on the bench beside Fiore and taking up the remaining blunted practice blade in its stead. Then she rejoined Enzo.

Enzo raised his sword. Maestra Rovigatti held out her blade. Enzo tapped it with his own. Both withdrew with their swords before their face and their points skyward. Then a slash to the side, as if to shake blood from the blade. With that, they dropt into the same stance Fiore had seen Enzo assume in his practice.

On some signal unseen to Fiore's eye, they began.

The first bout was over almost too quick for Fiore to realize they'd started. To his understanding, they both burst into motion in the same instant—the ring of steel-on-steel resounded thrice, though Fiore saw only a blur—then, all ceased, with blades crossed and the blunted point of Maestra Rovigatti's sword frozen in the air, poised to pierce Enzo's heart.

Both withdrew. The same salute. The same burst. The same blades whirling too fast for Fiore to parse. The same sudden halt, this time with the maestra's sword ready to skewer his stomach. Another ensued, ending with the blade at Enzo's throat. Then—a longer bout. Back and forth. Ground lost and gained on either side, until Maestra Rovigatti caught Enzo's sword in a clinch that, somehow, allowed her to throw him to the ground.

But no sooner had he fallen than she struck out a hand to draw him up, and he wasted not a single breath in arising to meet her next challenge.

The bouts grew longer. They circled. Dashed forward. Scrambled back. A glancing blow—a true strike—ending, for once, with Enzo's blade in the hollow of the maestra's throat and the faintest hint of a smile flickering across her lips. Then they returned to their marks and began again.

And, though Enzo lost almost every time, each attempt made him appear all the more dashing to Fiore's eyes.

The fluidity of movement from fingertip to hand to wrist to arm to shoulder to waist to leg—the way strands of hair came free from his queue and fell across his face in tandem and defiance alike of the scars already there—the angles of his rear leg outstretched as he lunged forward—each one a divine glimpse of elegant majesty.

Fiore had his zibaldone to hand but dared not glance down long enough to even attempt to capture these fleeting moments, however beautiful. He wondered if he could convince Enzo to pose later and for how long he could hold such handsome postures. Artemisia's talent alone could snatch gesture sketches out of a duel such as this.

He knew not how much time had passed. Only that he would've gladly kept watching long after Maestra Rovigatti's blade touched the hollow of Enzo's throat, and instead of returning to their starting positions, she let her sword fall to her side and declared their practice finished for the day.

Fiore could do nothing even half so impressive as what he'd witnessed. He could, however, slip off the bench to pour the silver ewer of water into two glasses for the combatants. Both accepted with thanks.

"She's certainly put you through your paces," Fiore murmured to Enzo as he drank.

Enzo finished off his glass with a gasp and shook his head. "She's going easy on me. She knows I'm far out of practice. I oughtn't be winded so soon."

Fiore, meanwhile, had envied Enzo's stamina from the perspective of his own convalescence. He'd envied far more than that—the casual ease with which he held a blade and the deft manner in which he wielded it. After feeling so defenseless at the hands of his tormentors, to see Enzo with a weapon in his hand both reassured him and sparked a ravenous hunger. He turned to Maestra Rovigatti.

"A marvelous display of your talents, Maestra," he told her. "Would you ever consider taking on a new pupil?"

Maestra Rovigatti arched her brows. "Depends on who asked."

Fortuna favored the bold. Fiore summoned all his courage. "Will you teach me?"

Both Maestra Rovigatti and Enzo stared at Fiore. The maestra's countenance remained unreadable. Enzo's revealed great alarm on his part.

Fiore's own face grew hot. He ignored it and endeavored to explain himself. "I should like to learn to defend myself. With cloak and dagger at the very least. I know I've no right to carry a sword—"

"You've every right to carry a sword," Enzo declared.

Maestra Rovigatti's raised eyebrows mirrored Fiore's own astonishment. Though Fiore's remained tempered by the fond realization that Enzo had spoken from his heart rather than his head.

And so it was more gently than otherwise that Fiore replied, "Not by the laws of this city, I don't."

"Not yet," Maestra Rovigatti spoke up. "However, if you had the proper training…" Her gaze slid to meet Enzo's.

"Then Lucrezia would be persuaded to make an exception," Enzo concluded.

Fiore envied his confidence. He had no such faith in the Serenissima's mercy. And he knew of no courtesan who wielded the privilege of a sword at their side.

Maestra Rovigatti appeared somewhat less skeptical than himself. Yet there remained a hard glint in her gaze as it fell upon Fiore once more.

"Are you prepared," she asked, "to lose another finger?"

Enzo's head whipped 'round to regard her with undisguised alarm. Fiore felt an echo of the same, though he hoped he hid it better.

Maestra Rovigatti did not relent. Her eyes flicked to Fiore's mutilated hand and back again to meet his bewildered stare. She drew her sword and dropt into a fighting stance as easily as rain dropt into the lagoon.

"You see my hand?" she enquired.

Fiore knew not which she meant. His notice went first and quite naturally to the one which held the sword. Her grip beneath the tangled web of silver strands furling 'round the handle appeared complicated enough to imitate with four fingers, let alone three.

But a sudden movement drew his eye higher. She flicked the wrist of her free hand held up by her face. Her joints remained loose, the whole arm fluid yet poised to leap at any moment. Like a cat lounging in a sunbeam with eyes half-lidded in feigned sleep as it watched songbirds inch ever closer and waited to strike.

"Do you know why I hold it here?" she asked.

"It's a guard," Fiore ventured. He'd gleaned that much of the trade jargon from living in a city filled with would-be duelists.

"Yes," Maestra Rovigatti said with more patience than Fiore probably deserved. "It's a guard. Which means it is ready to block my opponent's blow. Whether that be by seizing their arm or their wrist or their hand… or their blade."

Fiore beheld his own understanding mirrored in Enzo's solemn features.

Maestra Rovigatti continued. "It's better that I should lose a finger or several or my entire hand, than to let my opponent sheathe their sword in my heart or throat or eye. Do you concur?"

Fiore nodded.

She held his gaze. "You are resolved, then? Hesitation will not save you. Quite the reverse."

"I am resolved," Fiore told her—truthfully. He'd made the same bargain before. And even knowing its true cost, he wouldn't hesitate to do so again.

She gave a nod as graceful as any bow. "Then I may teach you."

"Not just yet," Enzo broke in. At Fiore's astonished glance, he added, "Fencing is rigorous exercise—doubly so for one just beginning to practice it. You would risk wound dehiscence. Incisional hernia," he continued in response to Fiore's ongoing bewilderment. He drummed his fingertips against his thigh, evidently searching for the correct term, and landing upon, "Evisceration."

"My insides would become my outsides, you mean," Fiore concluded.

"Precisely so." A smile flickered across his scarred features—which Fiore recognized as joy at being understood at last—fading quickly to reflect the more somber tone of the subject at hand.

Which only made Fiore smile to see it.

# CHAPTER THIRTY-FOUR

T he summons from the princely palazzo arrived at Ca' Scaevola on
an otherwise uneventful morning.

Even Fiore, who'd never seen anything of its like in his life, knew
from the quality of the parchment alone—thick, smooth, crisp—that
something beyond the typical flood of invitations had arrived atop the
pile of Enzo's post. The wax crest Enzo broke through to read it was as
broad as Fiore's palm.

"Glad tidings?" Fiore ventured with more optimism than he felt as
Enzo's eyes ran across the page.

"Routine tidings," Enzo replied. "The Wedding of the Sea is nigh."

Fiore had known that already without requiring a royal summons
to remind him. Every citizen of Halcyon did. On the summer solstice
of every year, the reigning prince commemorated the occasion of
Bellenos seducing Neptune and forming an alliance between his
islands and the sea, sailing the flagship out into the lagoon to renew
the vows spoken by the gods themselves. The whole city turned out
for the ceremony and its accompanying festival; aristocrats vying for
an invitation to the former at sea, and the common folk reveling at the
latter ashore.

"The flagship is filled with the senate and those Lucrezia wishes to reward or impress," Enzo continued. "My attendance is mandatory as the prince's brother."

"May I wear my green suit?" Fiore asked.

Enzo hesitated.

Fiore thought he knew the problem. "Or would it offend the prince to not have a new one made for the occasion?"

Still, Enzo hesitated.

And Fiore at last realized the true issue at hand. "It would offend the prince to have me attend at all."

For while he might be welcomed behind closed doors into the hallowed halls of Ca' Scaevola, it would be quite another thing for the prince's brother to parade a courtesan on his arm on the most sacred date of the city's calendar.

Enzo looked deeply uncomfortable with this unspoken truth. But to his kind-hearted and selfless credit, he said only, "I will ask Lucrezia—"

"Don't," said Fiore. "Please."

Enzo balked. "If you wish to attend then there's no reason—"

"I don't wish to attend," Fiore lied. "Does that settle it?"

Enzo didn't look as though he believed him.

"I've no desire to rock the boat," Fiore insisted. "Figuratively or literally."

While he'd by no means earned Lucrezia's approval, he hadn't yet earned her ire, either. Fiore didn't wish to push his luck by drawing her notice—much less forcing himself on her sphere or being thought to do so by others.

A tense silence drew out between them.

"The ceremony itself is very dull," Enzo said after a lengthy pause. "There's no real celebration to speak of until the flagship returns to the city."

Fiore smiled. "Perfect. Then I shall alleviate your boredom on your return and regale you with tales of the revels conducted in your absence."

The hunch in Enzo's shoulders eased by a hair's-breadth. "Will you be aboard the *Kingfisher*?"

"Very likely. Or with Artemisia at Bellenos's temple. She's concocted something with the puppeteer's guild for the parade." Fiore tried not to think of what had happened to him the last evening he'd spent in a crowded celebration.

And from the furrow in Enzo's brow, the same recollection had occurred to him. But rather than questioning Fiore's judgment or forbidding him outright, Enzo only said, "Artemisia will be with you, then?"

"She will," Fiore promised.

A slight sigh of relief escaped Enzo. Still he hesitated before asking, "Would you like to take some of the household guard with you, as well? They needn't intrude on your celebrations," he hastily added as Fiore blinked in surprise. "Canello or Zanetta could shadow you from a distance, as Carlotta does for me."

Fiore didn't want to admit how much safer he felt at the prospect. Particularly in the wake of a brigand kidnapping him from his own home out from under his landlord's nose. With a lackadaisical smile, he declared, "I'd be delighted for their company."

A shy echo of that same smile plucked at Enzo's scarred lips. "And maybe Vittorio would like to stretch his legs as well?"

Fiore's feigned ease burst into a genuine grin.

～

Enzo had oft fantasized about the wedding night of Bellenos and Neptune. Perhaps he might persuade Fiore to re-enact it when he returned to Ca' Scaevola. For the moment, however, he remained trapped aboard the prince's flagship until the rite concluded.

It was a simple enough ritual. The pomp and circumstance surrounding it, on the other hand, had grown immense over the centuries. Now it required a full day to assemble all the aristocracy into a fleet of their most ostentatious ships and set sail out of the lagoon to the true sea.

As brother to the prince, Enzo had pride of place aboard the flagship. The largest ship, naturally; a sleek thing carved over with serpentine scales and slathered black with tar and lacquer alike. Bellenos in mortal guise formed the ship's figurehead, his outstretched arms transforming into leathery wings, seafoam and scales alike obscuring his peculiarity.

Whilst the other aristocratic guests—the senate, plus a few courtiers hand-selected by Lucrezia based on those who had already proved their loyalty and those she wished to encourage to prove themselves to her—mingled on deck over coffee and chocolate and sumptuous treats, Enzo withdrew to the helm at the stern of the vessel. There he stood atop the hind-castle beside the captain, half-watching the crew go about their work and half-sneaking glances back at the city they'd left behind. He hoped Fiore was enjoying himself. Artemisia would be with him, alongside Vittorio, with Canello and Zanetta keeping guard from a distance. Still, Enzo worried.

They reached the sea at sunset. Then Lucrezia took her position at the prow of the vessel. A hush silence consumed the hundred vessels gathered around the flagship. Only the whistling wind, the rolling waves, and the calling birds remained.

"Desponsamus te, Neptune," Lucrezia intoned, "in signum veri perpetuique dominii."

She reached out her hand and dropt the ring into the sea.

Every year the city's jewelers competed to craft a wedding band worthy of the gods. This year's ring, chosen by Lucrezia from a selection of a mere score hand-picked by the senate, held a simple yet perfect black pearl for its jewel. The ceremony would return the pearl to Neptune's embrace, or so the half-jesting refrain ran throughout the city. A minuscule net of silver threads formed its setting with a trident weaving through them as the band. Like the rings of years before stretching back beyond what Enzo could remember, it would likely set the trend for espousing couples in the following social season.

Enzo wouldn't mind wearing it himself. He'd feel happier still to offer it to Fiore. To murmur those same words into Fiore's ear and slip the ring onto his hand. With the ceremony complete and preparations underway to return to the city, Enzo found his imagination returning to the wedding night of Bellenos and Neptune—this time with Fiore as Neptune, catching Enzo in his net, the prongs of his trident around Enzo's throat as he claimed him, pouring pearls within the salty tide of Enzo's cunt—

Until then, Enzo made a note to enquire if the jeweler who'd crafted this year's wedding band would take on the commission of armor for

Fiore's finger-bones. The delicacy of the silver netting in particular boded well for their meeting such a challenge.

It would take some time for the prince's flagship to reverse course. First the hundred-odd vessels clustered 'round it had to make way. Only after they'd cleared a path could the flagship return to the city where his Fiore awaited.

The prince and her guests passed the hours with a sumptuous banquet. The other guests knew better than to bother trying to start conversation with Enzo. His mind continued to wander, not just towards his fantasies but down more mundane paths, wondering what Fiore would make of the festivities and what commentary he might provide on the guests and their conduct. There must be something, Enzo thought, that he could do to ensure Fiore's attendance next year. He would have to speak with Lucrezia about it.

Tonight, however, he had more pressing business to conduct with her.

Night had fallen by the time they docked in Halcyon again. The brilliant lights of the city's celebrations rivaled the glittering stars above.

The prince disembarked first. Enzo followed close behind; as much a requirement as a privilege of his fraternal position. For once it felt more like the latter, as it allowed him to catch a moment alone with her as they entered the princely palace.

"May I have a word?" Enzo asked.

Lucrezia exhaled sharply through her nose but nonetheless indicated an alcove with a jerk of her head. There they found some modicum of privacy.

No sooner had they arrived than Enzo cut straight to the point. "How ought I to go about bringing a suit against Nascimbene?"

Lucrezia raised her brows.

"The impresario of Teatro Novissimo," Enzo added.

"I know of whom you speak," Lucrezia replied almost before he'd finished, her words clipped. "I wonder only that you wish to pursue him legally rather than with a sword."

"I'm given to understand you disapprove of my dueling. Therefore the law seems a better recourse."

The shadow of a sigh left her nostrils. "It would have been. And I commend you for thinking so."

Dread seized Enzo. "But...?"

"But," she echoed, "it seems all possible witnesses against Nascimbene have somehow perished. We have no evidence to go on save the word of dead criminals. There is nothing to support your case."

"Our staff bore witness—"

"Any jury will assume they've been paid off to testify in your favor. Any suit you bring against Nascimbene now will reek of corruption. You have no case."

Enzo stared at her. "So he is never to answer for his crimes?"

Lucrezia met his eyes with a look that outmatched him in severity. "If that answer disappoints you, perhaps you ought to have thought the matter over before you murdered all three of his criminal contacts without a trial."

It would've stung less had she taken up a cat-o'-nine tails and scourged his actual flesh. As matters stood, the truth of her words struck Enzo like a knife to his heart. It left him quite unable to reply.

Something softened in her gaze. She laid a princely hand on his shoulder. "I do not mean they shouldn't have perished for their crimes. Only, the moment of their execution might have been better chosen." She paused. "I am sorry."

Still Enzo couldn't speak.

Lucrezia clapped his shoulder and departed the alcove. A courtier approached her. Soon she was engaged in conversation, leaving Enzo as far behind as the antipodes.

Enzo continued staring in her direction long after the crowd of courtiers surged in to fill her wake and hide her from his view altogether. Uncounted moments passed before he could force his hands to unclench. He had no one to blame but himself for this injustice.

"Carlotta," Enzo spoke into the aether.

He knew not in which particular shadowy corner she lurked in just now. But he doubted she'd wandered far out of earshot on so auspicious an occasion as this.

And, true to form, she emerged from somewhere in the crowd off to his left within two shakes of a sail.

"The gondola, please," he told her.

She summoned it without question. Hardly a quarter of an hour passed before Enzo was poised to enter it.

"Ca' Scaevola, your grace?" Ippolito asked.

Enzo shook his head. "Teatro Novissimo."

If this directive surprised them, neither Carlotta nor Ippolito questioned it. At least not aloud.

Enzo entered the felze. Carlotta followed swiftly behind. He rapped his knuckles against the roof's ribs. The gondola slid silently through the canal. Glinting lights and festive clamor permeated the woven wicker screen. Enzo thought only of what lay ahead.

He heard the theater district before he saw it. The queer echoes from all the disparate opera houses mingled in the air. All the more haunting now that he knew the horrors endured to create the sound. The gondola drew up to Teatro Novissimo. Enzo disembarked.

"I won't be long," he told Ippolito.

Carlotta followed him into the opera house. Enzo wondered if she suspected his true purpose here. He didn't have his sword on him. He didn't need it. Not yet.

The performance had already begun. Most late-comers would be refused entry. Enzo's family crest opened doors regardless.

"Where may I find Maestro Nascimbene?" Enzo asked the usher.

The usher led him up several grand flights of stairs to a private box at the top of the theatre. There sat Nascimbene, enjoying a brilliant aria amidst several admirers of diverse sexes.

Nascimbene, in Enzo's opinion, was foolish not to leave the city the very moment his murderous scheme failed. Perhaps, like Fiore at the ball, he thought it would appear more suspicious to run. If it in any way alarmed him to see Enzo now, he hid it well.

"What a remarkable surprise!" Nascimbene stood to bow. "Welcome, your grace. Do tell us if there's anything we might do for you."

"Name the time and place of our meeting," said Enzo.

Nascimbene's brow furrowed. "Pardon, your grace?"

Enzo drew back his arm and cracked the back of his hand across Nascimbene's jaw.

# CHAPTER THIRTY-FIVE

Vittorio espied Carlotta long before Fiore ever could. As such, from the pricking of Vittorio's ears and the wagging of his tail, he had warning long before she emerged from the shadows of a ramo on his way back from the *Kingfisher*.

"Good evening," Fiore called to her.

She returned the greeting in kind, adding, "Are you returning to Ca' Scaevola?"

The question should've been casual. Indeed, it sounded so in her clipped and efficient speech. Yet something about it gave Fiore pause. Her very presence boded ill. Carlotta was supposed to accompany Enzo for the evening. If she had left Enzo's trail then something unexpected must have occurred. If the unexpected thing were good, then Enzo would've come to find Fiore and give him the glad tidings himself.

But if Enzo had sent Carlotta to fetch him, then...

Fiore had kept one hand between Vittorio's shoulder blades all afternoon—more to control his own nerves than the hound. Now that same hand clenched in the hound's thick ruff.

"Yes," Fiore answered, endeavoring to match her indifferent tone. "Why?"

"May I accompany you?"

There was no reason Fiore's heart should leap into his throat at that. "Why?"

Carlotta hesitated—which did nothing to allay Fiore's rising and unaccountable panic. "His grace the duke has asked me to do so."

"And again," Fiore said, trying to retain at least the pretense of patience. "I must ask you why."

"His grace would prefer to inform you himself."

Enzo was alive, then, at least. Still Fiore remained wary. "Is he all right?"

"He is unwounded, not imprisoned, and, to the best of my knowledge, free from illness or infection. May I accompany you back to Ca' Scaevola?"

Fiore had to admire her tenacity even in the midst of his frustration. "Something tells me you will do so regardless of my answer."

Her deferential nod in reply held the merest suggestion of an apology.

Fiore supposed he ought to feel grateful she'd bothered to ask even if only as a formality.

"If you prefer," she added, "we may go by gondola rather than by foot."

That would at least be faster. "Lead on."

Carlotta remained tight-lipped throughout their silent journey down the city's crowded canals. Vittorio didn't even so much as whine—which astonished Fiore, who thought a creature of his brute bulk might object to cramming himself into the confines of a felze. But evidently Enzo had trained him up to ride in one just as a person might. Indeed he took up about the same amount of space. Fiore was glad to have him; his arm wrapped snug around the hound's ruff seemed to be the only thing that kept him from drowning in his own anxieties.

They arrived at Ca' Scaevola to find it consumed in a frantic hush. Servants scurried in all directions. They communicated between themselves in occasional hisses and whispers but mostly in wild glances. All their eyes which chanced to meet Fiore's widened in horror at the sight of him. This did nothing to alleviate his concerns.

Carlotta ignored them all and led Fiore straight upstairs to the alchemy workshop. Her distinctive brisk knock fell upon its door.

"Enter," Enzo's solemn intonation resounded beyond it.

Fiore's heart sang at the sound of his voice.

Carlotta opened the door. "Signor Fiore, your grace."

Enzo stood braced against his alchemy bench. His head turned toward the door as it opened. The instant his eyes met Fiore's his stormy aspect brightened. He drew himself upright. Fiore swept his gaze up and down his frame—evidently unwounded, as Carlotta had promised, and by all appearances very well. Even his suit remained as pristine as when he'd departed for the festivities, save for his cravat, crumpled and undone around his beautiful throat.

Fiore endeavored to look as though he felt fine in return.

Enzo's gaze dropt to Fiore's side. There Vittorio stood as he'd done all evening. Fiore supposed his knuckles knotted up in the hound's ruff rather told all as concerned his frantic state.

Mercifully, Enzo made no comment on this. Instead he turned to Carlotta. "Any word of Maestra Rovigatti?"

"None yet, your grace," Carlotta replied as though this were a perfectly normal enquiry. "Allow me to discover what delays her."

Enzo dismissed her with a nod. The door shut behind her.

Then and only then did Fiore release his hold on Vittorio and fling himself into Enzo's embrace. The strength of Enzo's arms around him soothed the bulk of his nerves within moments.

"What's happened?" Fiore asked when he could at last bring himself to draw back, though he kept his hold on Enzo's arms. "Why do you require Maestra Rovigatti at this hour of night?"

Enzo hesitated. "I've challenged Nascimbene to a duel."

Fiore stared. All his anxieties vanished. A grin stole over his face. "Have you, indeed?"

~

Not since Orazio had anyone reacted positively to Enzo's dueling. It left him somewhat stunned. He knew not what to say.

Fortunately Fiore told him. "What happened? How did he reply? When will you meet him?"

"I will meet him at the time and place of his choosing. I gave him no chance to reply; I left directly after."

Fiore stared in unaccountable yet unmistakable admiration. "Why?"

"Because Lucrezia said we have no other recourse."

"She told you to duel him?"

"She told me I couldn't bring any legal suit against him."

Fiore blinked. "Fair enough, then."

Enzo couldn't have asked for a better reception. Still, he hesitated. "May I ask you something about his habits? Forgive me—I know it pains you to think on him."

Yet still Fiore smiled. "To think on his demise pains me not a whit. What do you wish to know?"

"Has he any training with a blade? Or any inclination towards athletic pursuits?"

"Not to my knowledge." Fiore shrugged. "But perhaps he's changed since I left the conservatorio. He's graceful enough. Dance training and all that. Would that make him better with swords?"

"Better than a clumsy fellow, assuredly."

Whatever else Fiore might have told him was interrupted by another knock on the workshop door. Not Carlotta's. Most likely another member of the staff.

"Enter," Enzo commanded.

The door opened to reveal one of the footmen—Ignazio—bearing a letter on a silver salver. Enzo took it and dismissed him. The letter bore a wax seal of Teatro Novissimo's insignia; a comic and tragic mask entwined. Enzo felt a queer satisfaction in breaking it.

*To His Grace, Lord Enzo Scaevola, the Duke of Drakehaven.*
*I shall meet you at dawn a fortnight hence at Isola dell'Anfiteatro. Any*
*further enquiries may be made to my second, Signor Bonato.*
*I have the honor to be your obedient servant,*
*Maestro Lotario Nascimbene*

No sooner had Enzo read the missive than he passed it on to Fiore.

Fiore's dark eyes dashed across the page twice-over. He raised his brows. "Isola dell'Anfiteatro?"

"So it would seem," Enzo replied, for he knew not what else to say. The island had once hosted gladiatorial bouts. Now it mostly held horse races, both recreational and ritual. While in the same lagoon, it lay very technically beyond the city limits and thus remained except from the equestrian ban. It could hold ten thousand spectators, though Enzo doubted so many would attend his duel with the impresario.

"Seems fitting," Fiore said, drawing Enzo out of his musings. "Dying in a duel is the greatest show Nascimbene could possibly put on in his whole career. An amphitheater is ideal. Do duelists typically wait a fortnight?"

Enzo shrugged. "It depends. If the contest is particularly heated, the meeting is often set for the following day. Three days or so gives the opponents time to put their affairs in order. Longer would give both more time to prepare and more time to fret over the result."

"Perhaps he requires a fortnight to learn to fence," said Fiore.

"If he has no training already, I hardly think he can learn to fight in so brief a span."

"Perhaps he's over-confident."

Enzo supposed Fiore would know better than he. "Or he thinks my reputation is overrated."

"Perhaps he's suicidal," Fiore suggested.

Whatever the impresario's motive, the result remained the same. Enzo would see him dead.

Fiore looked over the note again. "I don't recognize the name of his second. Who shall be yours?"

Enzo shrugged again. In his university days he would've had a few names to hand besides Orazio. His circle of acquaintance in the city, however, didn't stretch far beyond his own family. And while Maestra Rovigatti would certainly prove more than capable in the role, Enzo hesitated to thrust it upon her. "It's not strictly necessary to have one."

"Would you object to a volunteer?"

"I cannot imagine who'd offer."

"I would."

Enzo stared in stunned silence.

"I know I'm not yet trained in swordplay," Fiore hastily continued, "but if I begin now I'll know as much as Nascimbene will by the hour of the duel. Unless," he added, hesitating. "If it would shame a duke to have a courtesan as a second—"

"You are the worthiest of seconds." The words erupted from Enzo's heart rather than his head.

Worth it, however, to see Fiore's surprise melt into a smile.

In more measured tones, Enzo added, "It would be an honor to have you at my side."

Fiore's smile became a grin. He drew nearer to Enzo—near enough to slip his arms around his waist.

And to himself, Enzo vowed not to abandon Fiore as Orazio had once abandoned him.

~

Another hour passed before Carlotta found Maestra Rovigatti.

Fiore spent it with his very blood transformed to sparkling wine. The sheer relief of finding Enzo alive and well after Carlotta's dire summons, paired with the satisfaction of knowing vengeance against his life-long tormentor was close at hand, left him elated beyond expression. A mere fortnight would see Nascimbene skewered on Enzo's blade—justice for every boy he'd sacrificed beneath the chirurgeon's knife. Only Maestra Rovigatti's impending arrival prevented him from showing Enzo the full depth and breadth of his gratitude there and then on the alchemy bench. He settled instead for devouring him in kisses—an aperitivo for his intended reward.

Before they could get too carried away, Carlotta's distinctive knock fell on the workshop door.

"Enter," Enzo called, once Fiore had put them both back to rights.

Carlotta did so with Maestra Rovigatti close on her heels.

"Good evening, your grace," said the latter. She didn't seem irritated or even surprised to be dragged away from the festivities at an hour drawing ever nearer to midnight.

Enzo returned the greeting in kind. "Pray forgive the late hour of my summons. I wouldn't call for you now were it not an urgent matter."

"So I've heard," said Maestra Rovigatti. "You're to duel Maestro Nascimbene in a fortnight."

Fiore supposed the whole city must even now be buzzing with rumors.

"From what we've gathered," said Carlotta, "Nascimbene has not taken up fencing either as a sincere vocation or a fashionable hobby."

Fiore noted she made no mention of who she meant by "we."

"Which means if he is trained at all, he will only know what he can learn between the challenge and the duel itself," Enzo concluded.

"Encouraging to hear," said Fiore.

Enzo smiled. "With his inexperience against my practice, it ought to be over quick."

Fiore found Enzo's confidence more thrilling than otherwise. "Have you ever killed before?"

"Not in a duel," Enzo admitted. "But not for lack of trying, either."

"If I may offer an opinion, your grace."

Both Fiore and Enzo turned sharp to Maestra Rovigatti, who had just spoken.

"I would not consider Nascimbene's lack of training as an advantage for you," she continued.

Enzo stared at her. "Your reasoning?"

"You were trained in fighting from the moment you were old enough to hold a sword," said Maestra Rovigatti. "Would I err if I assumed you have always fought either maestri or those of your own rank, trained up in the same way? You've never fought an untrained opponent?"

"You would not err in that assumption," Enzo admitted.

"Nascimbene has not your experience," Maestra Rovigatti continued. "He knows you. He knows your reputation in swordplay. He is already panicking. He will not have ceased panicking by the hour of your appointed meeting. Whatever training they may give him in a mere fortnight, he will forget the moment your blade is in your hand. He will make foolish moves—stupid moves—moves no one else would ever make, moves you cannot possibly predict, and because you cannot predict them, some of them will hit, and one of them may very likely kill you."

Fiore had never considered that. And judging by Enzo's contemplative expression, he hadn't considered that before, either. But he seemed willing to listen to her expertise, which to Fiore's mind put him on better footing than many other more confident men.

"How would you advise me to proceed?" Enzo asked her.

"I would advise you not to proceed at all," Maestra Rovigatti told him. "But in the event you do not follow that advice, I would recommend finding a practice opponent who is equally as unskilled as Nascimbene."

"One without any experience whatsoever," Enzo concluded.

"Or with only a modicum of training," Maestra Rovigatti added.

"Do you know anyone who might suit such a purpose?" Enzo asked.

Maestra Rovigatti's gaze slid over to where Fiore stood.

Enzo's eyes flew wide.

Fiore's heart soared.

"You did profess a desire to learn, signore," Maestra Rovigatti reminded him.

Fiore grinned. "So I did."

Enzo glanced between them with increasing alarm.

"Shall we begin on the morrow?" Maestra Rovigatti enquired, turning to Enzo again.

Enzo gave her a grim nod.

Maestra Rovigatti bid them good-night, bowed, and departed. Carlotta followed her out.

To Fiore's mind, they'd discovered the perfect solution. For once he could prove of use to Enzo. This training would make him worthy of the office of second. And better still, it would improve Enzo's chances against Nascimbene.

The only part that wasn't perfect was the dismay writ across Enzo's handsome features.

Now that Carlotta and Maestra Rovigatti had gone, no one and nothing remained to prevent Fiore from entangling himself with Enzo once again, as he so dearly wished. He began by threading his arms around him, and, when this failed to provoke a smile beneath the scars, raised a hand to caress his cheek as he asked, "What's amiss?"

Enzo cast a sorrowful look down at him. "I don't wish to fight you."

"You won't really be fighting me." Fiore trailed his fingertips up

Enzo's back, and Enzo leaned into him just as he wanted in return. "You'll be teaching me to fight."

Enzo's mouth retained a skeptical twist.

Fiore ran his thumb over Enzo's lip. "I promise I won't hold it against you."

Enzo bit his lip in Fiore's wake.

Fiore stretched up to kiss him. Enzo melted into it and embraced him in turn. Fiore lined up their hips to meet Enzo's evident interest with his own.

"Perhaps," Fiore said when they parted, "you might cross blades with me tonight?"

A low chuckle escaped Enzo's throat. He consented with a kiss.

# CHAPTER THIRTY-SIX

W hen Enzo arose the following morning to perform his daily exercise, Fiore—for the first time in all their acquaintance—got up alongside him.

He didn't join Enzo in running up and down the spiral stair. Instead he spent the quarter-hour or so quaffing coffee in solitude to try and wake himself up several hours earlier than usual. When Enzo returned to him, he could keep his eyes open without effort. A final cup of coffee shared with Enzo—Fiore's third that morning—gave him enough energy to keep up as Enzo led him downstairs to the courtyard, where Maestra Rovigatti awaited them.

Two rapiers lay ready on the marble bench as they had every morning since Enzo resumed his fencing lessons. Today, however, a wooden sword had joined them.

"A waster," Maestra Rovigatti explained as she handed it to Fiore. "Drilled and filled with lead to match the weight of a rapier."

It weighed far more than Fiore would've expected of even a true metal sword.

"We'll move on to blunted steel when you understand the basics," Maestra Rovigatti continued, either oblivious to or more likely politely ignoring his undisguised astonishment at the wooden weapon's heft. "For now, we begin with the grip."

Without further ado, she adjusted his instinctive hold on the handle from a tight fist to a more delicate grasp that included, to his surprise, curling his forefinger and thumb over the cross-guard and around the base of the blade.

"The hilt is like a bird," she explained. "Hold it too softly, and it will escape. Too hard, and you'll crush its hollow bones."

Fiore had already arranged his legs into an imitation of the perpendicular crouch he'd seen Enzo assume so many mornings before. Maestra Rovigatti had a few adjustments here as well before she moved on to his arms. Here she centered his sword-bearing arm in front of him, bent, with his elbow a handsbreadth from his waist.

"The goal," she said as she moved him about not unlike Artemisia oft did, "is to present your opponent with the narrowest possible target."

"Turn sideways and disappear?" said Fiore.

"If you like," Maestra Rovigatti replied in a far more patient tone than his insolence deserved.

The resulting posture felt far less graceful than Maestra Rovigatti or Enzo had looked to Fiore's untrained eye. He felt more keenly than ever before Enzo's eyes upon him. To fail at all was mortifying enough. To fail beneath Enzo's watchful gaze—Fiore wondered how he would survive the humiliation. Yet survive he must, for Enzo needed him. Long hours spent in perfect stillness assuming whatever pose Artemisia devised for him had prepared Fiore somewhat for the rigid-yet-fluid postures of fencing. He could bear up under whatever Maestra Rovigatti threw at him. Somehow.

As she bid him scuttle backward and forward like a crab, Fiore wondered at how Enzo contrived to look so graceful with a sword in his hand. He felt like one of Artemisia's wooden models flailing about with its string-joints cocked at odd angles. Things improved a touch when at last the maestra faced him with blade in hand and showed him the sequence of parries that would block her attacks. The fencing drills reminded him of dance practice at the conservatorio—a set sequence of movements divided into measures. Then she came at him with speed.

Clack—clack—clack—wood against wood, until Fiore couldn't decide whether to bring his sword up or out, and hers halted at his throat.

She stared at him with brows raised. "You understand?"

Fiore, already scolding himself for failing to recall the sequence, nodded.

This seemed to satisfy her. "Again."

And this time, he parried every strike.

Over and again they drilled. Scuttling back and forth. Clack—clack—clack. A glance at the courtyard sundial told Fiore not a quarter of an hour had passed since he took up his wooden blade. The arm holding it burned as if he'd borne its weight for hours. His thighs didn't feel much better. Whatever athleticism he'd once possessed had fled his body over the course of his long convalescence. How pathetic he must appear under Enzo's gaze. He'd witnessed Enzo's strength and stamina before but had never considered how he might've acquired these traits. No wonder Enzo could lift him with ease and fuck for miles if his daily regimen demanded all this of him.

Maestra Rovigatti, meanwhile, had not yet broken a sweat an hour later. Still, she looked Fiore up and down and declared their practice finished for the day.

"When you're ready, your grace," she added, turning to Enzo.

~

Enzo could've happily watched Fiore spar for a century.

Like Fiore, he quite enjoyed the sight of a man with a sword in his hand—even a mere wooden waster. He likewise enjoyed seeing men half-bare and engaged in rigorous exercise. These familiar delights heightened when the man in question was as beloved to him as Fiore; more particularly when for so long Fiore had languished in convalescence and only now began to return to the health he'd enjoyed before his ordeal. All the moreso when the trials Maestra Rovigatti set for him sparked a gleam in his eye that Enzo had long missed.

Furthermore, Fiore had a great deal of natural grace which made him a wonder to watch in any athletic pursuit. While not a sword-fighting prodigy by any means, his fluid poise made even his mistakes beautiful.

So beautiful, in fact, that Enzo could almost forget that soon Maestra Rovigatti would require him to raise his blade against Fiore.

Far sooner than would've sated Enzo, Maestra Rovigatti declared Fiore's training done for the day. Enzo hastened to pour a glass of water for Fiore as he resumed his seat on the bench.

"You're doing very well," Enzo told him.

"Doesn't feel like it," Fiore gasped.

Adrenaline spiked in Enzo's veins. "Have you torn something?"

Fiore shook his head and quaffed the water.

"Where does it hurt?" Enzo pressed.

"Legs, mostly," Fiore replied while Enzo refilled his empty glass. "Arms a bit. Gut least of all—not a rip," he quickly added as Enzo's head shot up in alarm. "Just the same burning as everything else."

That, as Enzo knew well, was normal. Still he would've spared Fiore it. "If that should change—"

"I'll speak up," Fiore promised. An exhausted but no less sincere smile curled up his cheek. "I'm fine. Don't worry."

Fiore might as well have told a dolphin not to swim. But Enzo took him at his word nonetheless and went to meet Maestra Rovigatti, who'd waited with her sword all the while.

Enzo's own sword-fighting lessons always had an audience in Vittorio. But to have Fiore watching him in the months since his lessons had resumed remained an altogether new experience. No one else—save perhaps Orazio—had held such an open admiration for Enzo's dedication to his sport. And even now, exhausted though Fiore was by his first bout with swordplay, still Enzo could feel Fiore's appreciative gaze upon him. It made him all the more eager to excel, to prove himself worthy of his affections, to show what he would do to all who dared threaten his beloved.

Likewise he felt eager to soothe Fiore's physical pains. Enzo had been trained up in swordplay from the moment he could hold a blade. The pose and pace felt natural to him. To Fiore, however—Enzo could but begin to imagine his aches. He looked forward to doing something towards ending Fiore's pain.

As he looked forward to ending Nascimbene.

~

Fiore's legs burned. His gut throbbed. His left arm ached from the weight of his false blade, and his right felt only slightly better after holding itself aloft for an hour, even loosely. He guzzled water as Enzo and Maestra Rovigatti played out the same rapid and elegant dance of blades as they had every morning, and which even now he never tired of watching.

When their sparring came to a close, as all good things must, Fiore's aches had deepened rather than dissipated. He discovered this as he attempted to leap up and return the favor Enzo had done for him. He accomplished only staggering upright with a groan.

Enzo dropt his sword and caught Fiore by his shoulders. "Are you all right?"

"Fine," Fiore said through gritted teeth. "I promise I'm fine. My limbs are just cast-iron, that's all."

Enzo's look of frantic concern melted into wistful sympathy. He guided Fiore back down onto the bench and poured his own water—shameful, ridiculous, Fiore ought to have done it for him, if only he weren't so weak and pathetic—

"Thank you, Maestra," Enzo told her.

Maestra Rovigatti bowed. Belatedly, Fiore echoed the sentiment.

"Now," Enzo said to him with a smile. "Perhaps a bath?"

"Yes, please," Fiore groaned.

Enzo softly chuckled and, despite Fiore's stiffness and no doubt his own aches, drew him upright and led him off.

Soaking in the hot bath felt as glorious as Fiore had predicted. The view proved better still, as he had the perfect vantage point to watch Enzo ply oil and strigil to his sinewy limbs. Enzo had just finished when a servant arrived with a well-laden tray of lardo and porchetta crostini, which left him free to bring it with him to join ravenous Fiore in the bath.

When Fiore's fingertips began to wrinkle, Enzo drew him out of the bath. He could hardly have arisen under his own power. The weight of his own body without water to buoy it felt like an anchor's chains draped over him. He leant heavily on Enzo as he staggered upright.

"How pathetic," Fiore muttered.

Enzo balked. "What?"

"Me, not you," Fiore hastened to explain.

"Hardly," Enzo protested.

Fiore raised his brows. "Of the two of us, who cannot stand under his own power?"

"That's not pathetic," Enzo insisted. "It's perfectly reasonable. You've leapt head-first into rigorous exercise after a lengthy convalescence. Considering the circumstances you're doing remarkably well."

Fiore remained unconvinced. "That's all very sweet, but I doubt Maestra Rovigatti shares your opinion."

"She praised your form."

Fiore scoffed. "Mere flattery, I'm sure."

But Enzo held his gaze. "She doesn't flatter."

"Oh." Upon reflection, Fiore supposed she didn't seem the type.

Enzo smiled and bid him lie down on the marble bench. There his strong hands and clever fingers worked out all the knots softened by the hot bath. Fiore melted beneath his touch. He knew he ought to return the favor—or, as he truly desired, drag Enzo down into a more intimate embrace—but his body begged for slumber, and he could hardly move, much less initiate. He couldn't even shrug on Enzo's wrapping-gown afterward; Enzo had to swathe him in it.

"Shall we retire to the library?" Enzo asked.

Fiore's mind assented. His body protested. Fortunately, Enzo had no objection to half-carrying him from the baths up to the library. There he curled up in a corner of the sofa with his feet in Enzo's lap whilst Enzo read to him. The shadows grew long. His eyelids grew heavy.

"Fiore?"

"I'm listening," Fiore insisted, though his eyes refused to open. "The pirate captain just revealed himself as the lost prince and enlisted the swordsman's aid."

He heard rather than saw Enzo's smile. "You might be more comfortable abed at this hour."

Fiore forced his eyes open. The sun had set. The library sparkled with candlelight. Enzo had set down *The Pirate King* and taken up another volume in its stead, evidently to pass the hours whilst Fiore slept.

"Fair enough," Fiore sighed.

Enzo softly laughed.

~

Fiore had never arisen so early for so many days in a row.

He didn't complain—although his body certainly did—because Enzo did this every day, and furthermore, with the duel's hour set for dawn, he wanted to acclimate himself to it, lest he oversleep on the day itself.

Still, it required about double his typical ration of coffee to get him upright and downstairs with a blade in his hand.

Every morning for a se'en-night he spent drilling with Maestra Rovigatti. Every afternoon he spent watching Enzo do the same. Every evening he spent in spoilt luxury with Enzo, soaking in the bath and devouring delicacies—while he'd never lacked for appetite, the fencing regimen increased it tenfold—and Enzo working out the knots in his muscles and caressing the aches from his flesh. Fiore would've liked to cap off these adventures by showing Enzo just how enticing he found him with a sword in his hand, but inevitably he fell asleep before he could do anything more than dream of it and awoke to do it all over again the following day. While he by no means felt himself anywhere near Enzo's equal, much less Maestra Rovigatti's, he nonetheless noted how with each passing day he could hold out a little longer before his body revolted. Perhaps, he hoped, he might someday feel well enough after practice to put the inspiring sight of half-clad Enzo to good use.

The beginning of the second se'en-night brought a still greater change. When Fiore dragged himself out of bed and quaffed his coffee and tumbled downstairs to the courtyard, instead of handing him his wooden waster, Maestra Rovigatti instead held out a true steel blade.

Fiore accepted it with eager reverence.

He'd never held a real sword before. Like every other child in the city he'd picked up his fair share of sticks or rolled up sheets of paper to play at dueling. But to hold the true thing now, even after a se'en-night of acclimating himself to its weight through leaded wood, was certainly sobering. Blunted, of course, but even so—a sense of power sparked within him. Woe betide anyone who tried to kidnap him with a blade in his hand. He'd not go down without a fight.

The difference proved palpable as Maestra Rovigatti drilled him. The satisfying ring of steel against steel resounded through the courtyard. If this was what Enzo had been raised on, Fiore understood how he'd come to crave the sport.

Then—abruptly, from Fiore's perspective—Maestra Rovigatti declared their practice finished.

Fiore didn't feel even half so winded as he typically did after their lessons. A glance at the sundial showed the truth; Maestra Rovigatti had called him off early. He wondered if he'd done something wrong. Disappointed or offended her. While she remained stoic, he'd thought himself a better judge of people than to completely miss so grave a misstep as would provoke her to dismiss him.

But when he turned to go take his place on the marble bench, she halted him with an upraised hand.

"Remain here," she said, though she herself withdrew. As she did so, she turned to Enzo, who waited as patient as the hound at his feet. "If you would take up your sword, your grace."

~

Throughout the first se'en-night of their training, Enzo expected Lucrezia to intervene.

The whole city knew of the impending duel. Even if it weren't whispered in every corridor and alluded to in every gazzetta, Lucrezia would know of it from Carlotta before anyone else heard. Given her disapproval of his dueling, Enzo had anticipated at the very least a sternly-worded note from her the very evening he made his challenge, if not another scolding visit in the flesh.

Yet even now, halfway to the fated date, he'd received nothing. No missive demanding he call it off. No not-so-subtle suggestions that he ought to depart for the countryside or attempts to make him do so by force. Perhaps, he thought, she meant to manipulate matters from another quarter, and knowing her brother would remain stubborn, she would instead either bribe or threaten Nascimbene into fleeing. But he'd heard nothing of the kind.

A queer hope sprung in his mind, that maybe, just maybe, she realized how her refusal to allow him to proceed through the law had forced his hand down a bloodier route. Even to his own optimistic instincts, such prospect seemed faint.

The sight of Fiore training drove all suspicions from his mind, however temporarily. A curious pride bloomed within him to see Fiore had advanced so far so quickly that Maestra Rovigatti granted him the privilege of a steel blade.

All of which meant Enzo shouldn't have felt even half so surprised as he did when Maestra Rovigatti announced that the hour had arrived for Fiore and Enzo to spar with each other.

Enzo, caught off-guard, staggered upright and clutched at his sword to take up the post Maestra Rovigatti had vacated.

"The most important lesson for you to learn now," Maestra Rovigatti told Enzo, "is one I've endeavored to teach you for some years. And that is..."

She trailed off. Silence reigned in the wake of her words, broken only an unseen lark's call. Enzo waited with bated breath for what she wished to impart. Perhaps she wanted him to know the answer already and supply it—but whatever it was remained beyond him.

Maestra Rovigatti smiled. "Patience."

"Ah," said Enzo.

"That is my advice to you in your duel against Nascimbene," she continued. "An inexperienced opponent will only grow more nervous if you wait to let them make the first strike. You need but continue to parry and retreat until they are exhausted. And then you may strike at your leisure. With tenfold precision, and, ideally, to tenfold success. You follow me?"

Enzo nodded.

Maestra Rovigatti smiled. "To that end—Fiore! Have at him!"

With that, she slipped away, vanishing from between them swift and silent as a shadow to stand off to the side where Vittorio slept.

Enzo stared at Fiore standing in front of him not three strides distant.

Fiore blinked back at him. He raised his blade in salute.

Enzo returned the gesture out of sheer habit. Everything within him, however, cried out at the mere thought of sparring against Fiore. Even with his own mastery—what if he failed to hold his blows? A blunted blade could nevertheless wreak havoc on the frailties of the mortal frame. What if Fiore were hurt? Or worse, what if—?

Fiore, with a gleam in his eye, dropt into the fighting stance.

"I can't do it," Enzo blurted.

Both Fiore and Maestra Rovigatti stared at him.

"I won't strike you," Enzo told Fiore. "I can parry, but—I cannot attack." He turned to Maestra Rovigatti in desperation, willing her to understand.

Maestra Rovigatti shrugged. "Then don't attack him."

Enzo's brow furrowed.

"Practice your defense," Maestra Rovigatti continued. "You already know how to attack. You need only wait for the opportune moment to strike."

A skill which had eluded Enzo up 'til now.

"I trust your courage will not fail you against your true opponent," Maestra Rovigatti concluded.

No, it certainly wouldn't. Enzo had resolved to destroy Nascimbene before he'd challenged him. Only Lucrezia's intervention had prevented him from killing the Delfini heir. Now he would have the chance to redeem himself and punish the monster who'd brought his beloved so much agony. He would not fail his Fiore.

And from the firm gaze Fiore cast upon him now, he knew it without Enzo having to say a word.

Enzo mirrored Fiore's stance.

"Begin," said Maestra Rovigatti.

Enzo followed her advice and waited.

Not for long, either, as Fiore immediately lunged for him.

Enzo saw at once what Maestra Rovigatti had meant about the unpredictability of an untrained fencer. He parried the attack, of course, but it left him off-center and struggling to make sense of it.

And rather than any recognizable or reasonable counter-parry, Fiore just wrenched his sword free and hacked at him again.

Relentless. Absurd. No pattern save bloodthirsty violence. No possible way to anticipate where the following blow might fall.

Openings for counter-attacks abounded, if Enzo could bring himself to make use of them, but as matters stood he was wholly preoccupied with blocking each strike as it occurred. Not just stabs, as the rapier was designed for, but slashes and chops—including one overhead strike wherein Fiore left his whole front open yet Enzo could do nothing about it except stare, aghast, at his sheer audacity, and bring up his own sword almost as an afterthought to block the blade from splitting his skull. Then—

Enzo staggered back as Fiore's point jabbed him in the ribs, just over his heart.

"There," said Maestra Rovigatti. "He has killed you."

Enzo could think of no hand he'd rather die by.

Fiore dropt his sword to his side. Gone was the ferocious fury that'd driven the blow. Now his gaze held only concern. "Are you all right?"

Enzo couldn't answer him straight off. His voice failed him. He'd always enjoyed crossing blades with other gentlemen. He'd fallen for Orazio at the fencing club, after all. But this was something else. Something more. There was true purpose behind Fiore's swordplay. Not mere formality. Not showing off skill. Just pure, raw aggression. The desperate attack of a cornered beast that would not surrender its life without claiming flesh and blood in return. All of Enzo's blood, meanwhile, had flown straight down to pulse betwixt his thighs.

"Enzo?" Fiore closed the stride between them and raised his hand to cradle his face.

The touch drew Enzo out of his daze. He smiled and nodded. All the while his mind whirled. Perhaps once the duel was over and done with —or, if he were lucky, sooner than that—he might persuade Fiore to bring the blade into the bedchamber.

"Again, gentlemen?" said Maestra Rovigatti.

Enzo nodded.

Fiore hesitated. His gaze flicked from Enzo's eyes to the bruise blooming over his heart. Then he leapt up and caught his mouth in a tender kiss.

"Are you sure you're all right?" Fiore whispered against his lips when they parted.

Enzo smiled and nodded again. "You're only making me stronger."

Fiore's anxious, furrowed brow melted away as a beaming grin overtook his face. He spun 'round and returned to his starting position with a capering skip.

Enzo took up his sword and grinned back.

# CHAPTER THIRTY-SEVEN

The crowds packed the opera house to the gills on opening night. Fiore couldn't see them from the stage—the mirrored lights blinded him—but he could hear them, rustling silks, fluttering fans, whispering together in a hideous chorus. He peered into the shadows regardless, desperate for a familiar face. If he could only find Enzo then he would be rescued.

But then the orchestra struck up.

And he knew he must sing.

Fiore drew breath. He opened his mouth. An aria emerged.

His voice cracked.

A gasp rippled through the crowd. Then came the hisses. Whispers raised in anger to speech and then to shouts.

Before Fiore could even attempt to placate them, someone stormed onto the stage from the wings.

Nascimbene.

Fiore stumbled backward. Nascimbene advanced, scolding him for his vocal inferiority. A knife appeared in the maestro's hand.

"We must fix your voice," Nascimbene declared.

Fiore protested—his voice had already changed; mutilating him now wouldn't turn it back; there was nothing to be done—but in vain.

Enraged patrons leapt onto the stage to pin down his limbs. Fiore thrashed in their grasp. Yet he could not loose their hold. If he could but find Enzo amongst them—

He found only the glass-eyed, beak-hooded chirurgeon staring down at him.

Nascimbene's knife pierced his flesh.

Fiore bolted upright with a haggard gasp.

The opera house was gone. The harsh glare of the stage had been replaced by the soft green glow of the foxfire lantern in the darkness. He sat abed in Ca' Scaevola. The ache came not from his groin but the scars in his gut. Every breath pained him so he could hardly catch it. His heart flung itself against his ribcage. The night's silence deafened him. There was no one here save his Enzo asleep beside him.

Fiore had found him at last.

Enzo's chiseled, handsome features looked rapturous in repose. Even the dashing scar that cleaved his face in twain appeared softer in the foxfire's glow. One arm lay thrown over his head. The other had clasped Fiore before the nightmare dragged him out of reach. Even now the whole of Enzo's lean frame still curled towards where Fiore had lain. Luna herself could not find more beauty in her Endymion than Fiore saw in Enzo now.

Fiore drank in the sight of him, more soothing than any anodyne. He knew not how long he spent drawing ragged shuddering gasps. At length the ache in his abdomen ebbed. He supposed he'd aggravated his wounds in sitting up so suddenly. But he could breathe properly again.

Yet he could not quite match the slow and steady rising and falling of Enzo's broad chest.

Nor was he the only one awake. As he slipped out of bed, he found Vittorio poking his head up from where he'd curled up on his fur rug, his black silhouette limned in foxfire green. The hound's ears pricked, and the tail made a few cautious muffled thumps against the rug. Fiore put a finger to his lips lest the noise wake Enzo. The tail ceased, but Vittorio continued to watch with foxfire glow glinting in his eyes as Fiore discarded his nightgown and drew on shirt, hose, breeches, and waistcoat in its place.

Enzo kept their rapiers in the bedroom ever since Fiore had made an off-hand comment one morning after practice that he felt much safer to see a blade in Enzo's hand. It worked; Fiore slept far easier knowing they lay within reach.

Still, merely having them to hand hadn't banished the nightmare this night. And so he took up his sword before he made for the door.

Vittorio watched his progress all the while. As Fiore laid his fingers on the doorknob, the hound cocked his head. He glanced between awake Fiore and sleeping Enzo, seemed to decide something in his bestial brain, and got up to follow Fiore, silent and dark as a shadow. Fiore supposed Vittorio must think him more in need of guarding than Enzo.

The whole palazzo remained quiet as the grave. Fiore passed not a single servant as he made his way down into the central courtyard. Moonlight bathed all in silver. His own footsteps resounded in his ears despite his stealthy tread—as did the ring of steel as he drew his rapier.

Vittorio left Fiore's side to take up his post by the marble bench like he did every morning.

Outside guard. Inside counter-guard. Inside guard. Outside counter-guard. Fiore ran through the fencing drills, over and over, everything he knew and many things he didn't, imagining foes leaping out of the courtyard's dark shadows and striking them all down, until his arm ached with the weight of his blade, until sweat ran in rivulets down his spine, until the twinge returned to his gut beneath his sash, until—

"Fiore?"

Fiore whirled, blade in hand, with a stroke that ought to have slit the throat on whoever dared to sneak up behind him.

The sword slashed through mere aether. Enzo, wiser than most, had called to him from beyond the marble bench, well out of the blade's reach.

Fiore's chest heaved. The sword trembled in his grasp. He dared not let it fall.

Enzo had likewise changed from his nightgown into just shirt and breeches. Moonlight shone resplendent over his powerful form. It limned the black rain of his hair in silver. His pale linen shirt seemed to glow as it clung to his sinewy chest and arms.

And the blade of his rapier glinted as he raised it in salute.

A queer sort of relief washed over Fiore's pyretic heart. He returned the gesture.

Their duel began.

Enzo leapt over the bench with a stag's grace. Fiore braced for his attack. But there Enzo paused, perfectly poised, waiting for Fiore to make the first move.

And so Fiore struck.

He darted forward—a reckless stab. Enzo parried it handily.

Fiore struck again. And again Enzo parried. The ring of steel-on-steel sang in his ears sweeter than any music. The force of one particular lunge sent Fiore flying past Enzo. Enzo simply spun as he parried, committing to it until he faced Fiore again, just in time for Fiore to strike afresh. Thrust after thrust, exhausting all he knew, until his fury drove him to hack away as if he wielded a longsword rather than a rapier, all possible form forgotten.

Enzo parried all. Not once did he counter-attack, even when Fiore repeatedly left himself open to it. He never stepped forward, never advanced on his opponent, only withdrew, perpetually, gliding backward as easily as when they danced, forever making way for Fiore to enter his life again and again, every thrust welcomed as gladly as when Fiore drove his blade into Enzo's sheath in their shared bed.

Then—

Fiore thrust. Enzo parried with a swift circle of his wrist. The blades slid against each other, up from the point, corkscrewing, tangling, until at last the ringing steel clanged together at the hilt, and the swords stuck fast in an upright clinch between the two men, leaving hardly a handsbreadth between their bodies, their faces framed by the crossed blades.

A swift pull might've torn Fiore's sword free. Or he could drop it altogether and retreat.

Fiore's pulse rang in his ears as he fought to catch his breath. Enzo's chest heaved likewise. Beads of sweat glistened in the moonlight like the morning dew that would soon cover the city. The chill night air proved a sharp contrast to the warmth radiating from Enzo's body.

And Enzo's soft dark gaze wordlessly pleaded.

Fiore's eyes flicked to his scarred mouth and back again. Then he darted his head between the blades to seize Enzo's mouth in a kiss.

Enzo dropt his sword to embrace him. Fiore did the same. The kiss held all the passion of their duel despite Fiore's exhaustion. Their recent exertion forced him to break off for breath far sooner than he wished.

"Shall we retire?" Enzo asked in a breathless whisper.

Fiore hesitated.

"We don't have to sleep," Enzo said. "Just rest our eyes for a while."

Fiore's eyes had already fallen shut. He'd thrown his arms around Enzo's shoulders and now clung in desperation. Enzo's arms wrapped snug around him in turn, one for his shoulders and the other for his waist, with a palm trailing down to trace soothing circles in the small of Fiore's back. The embrace seemed the only thing holding Fiore up now. Despite the nightmares, Fiore had to admit Enzo's proposal sounded nice. He let his head fall to Enzo's collar. There, he nodded.

Vittorio seemed most relieved of all to be going back to bed. Fiore couldn't begrudge the lazy fellow. His withers came above Fiore's waist, and by bracing his palm between the hound's shoulder blades, combined with his opposing arm draped across Enzo's back and Enzo's arm encircling his waist in turn, he remained upright.

By the time they reached the bedchamber, Enzo half-carried him. Fiore let Enzo tuck him beneath the bedclothes. When Enzo slipped in beside him, Fiore entangled himself in his embrace once more, his ear pressed to Enzo's chest so he might hear his heartbeat alongside his own pulse.

And thus Fiore slept dreamless at last.

～

Enzo arose before dawn on the day of the duel.

The sleeping form of Fiore beside him bid him linger. As much as Enzo longed for his embrace, he dared not wake him. While Fiore certainly possessed Endymion's beauty, his sleep would not prove eternal.

But, fates willing, it would last long enough for Enzo to slip out unnoticed.

Vittorio raised his head from where he slept curled on his rug on the floor beside the bed.

Before a curious whine could escape the hound, Enzo made two swift signs with his hand—*Silence. Guard.*

Vittorio pricked up his ears and cocked his head.

Enzo trusted the hound would take his charge to heart and shut the door behind him.

In the unlikely event that Nascimbene somehow overpowered him, at least Fiore would remain out of harm's way. Enzo had already drawn up the necessary papers to ensure Fiore would live on in comfort if the worst came to pass. To this end he left Carlotta behind as well to see his will carried out in his absence.

The gondola slipped out of Ca' Scaevola even more silent than Enzo's own tread. Enzo sat alone in the felze with his sword laid across his lap. It'd been too long since he'd carried a blade out-of-doors. He hadn't realized how much he missed it. Now that he had it back, a queer calm settled over his nerves. With blade in hand he could surmount any obstacle. Nascimbene was nothing. And within the hour he would be still less.

The city beyond the woven screen of the felze had hardly awoken. The aristocratic districts through which the gondola now travelled were particularly silent. Anyone who labored before dawn here did so behind closed doors and within high walls.

Then they came to the princely palazzo.

This didn't surprise Enzo. Bellenos's temple, the princely palace, and the piazza that connected them lay in the city's center, between Ca' Scaevola and Isola dell'Anfiteatro. The grand canal was the quickest route through Halcyon and led straight past the palazzo.

But in the shadow of the palazzo, the gondola halted.

Enzo saw no impediment to their progress through the wicker screens. Still, he didn't have so complete a view as a gondolier, and so he waited a few moments before he rapped the roof-ribs with his knuckles.

The gondola didn't move.

Enzo waited another moment before he called out. "Ippolito?"

No reply came.

On another occasion Enzo might have had more patience. Today however he had a most urgent appointment. He could not afford to lose many more minutes.

And so, seeing the gondola had halted within reach a palazzo portico, Enzo opened the door and disembarked.

A half-moon of some dozen princely guards surrounded him.

Enzo remained undaunted. "Where is Ippolito?"

One of the guards jerked their chin at something over Enzo's shoulder.

Enzo turned his head just far enough to catch Ippolito in the corner of his eye—still standing on the gondola's stern, unharmed.

Which was when someone tackled Enzo from behind.

Enzo cursed himself for not drawing his sword before he'd left the felze. None of the guards had drawn theirs, or any other weapon, but there were at least two for each of his limbs, and though he thrashed and kicked and sent more than a few away with cracked jaws and bloodied noses, still they bore him to the masegni. He lost his sword and hat. His mask remained. The guards bound his hands behind his back.

Then they hauled him upright and dragged him, still struggling, into the bowels of the palazzo.

Enzo had heard tell of the dungeons beneath the princely palazzo. The whole city knew of them. He'd never yet explored them himself. He found them damp—unsurprising, as they lay below sea-level—and dark, lit solely by the hooded lantern of the guard who led the pack. He passed no other prisoners. All remained silent as the grave.

His journey ended in a circular cell somewhere in the unfathomable labyrinth of corridors. The guards shoved him—again, with significant struggle—into an iron chair. More hempen bonds secured his wrists to the chair's arms and his ankles to its legs.

There they left him alone, though with the hooded lantern on the floor for light and, Enzo supposed, company. And the door, Enzo noted as it slammed and locked upon him, had a grate in it just large enough for a human face. That was something. He continued struggling. His strength couldn't rend the rope asunder, but perhaps if he could contrive to slip a hand free, then—

Bootheels against stone echoed down the corridor towards the cell. A tread familiar to Enzo's ears. And one he'd expected in a place like this.

"Lucrezia," Enzo called out.

His sister's face appeared in the door grate. Her expression remained unreadable. A key scraped in the lock. She entered, shut, and locked the door behind her—bold, Enzo thought, to lock herself in with him when he trembled with rage. A single stride brought her near enough to whip his mask off his face.

"Enzo," said Lucrezia.

Enzo snarled. "Let me go."

Lucrezia continued as if he hadn't spoken. "Do you recall what it cost to convince the Delfini to forgive the injury you did to their son?"

Enzo knew the sum well. It had rung in his ears oft enough in the weeks following the duel, when Lucrezia's wrath had burned bright against his foolishness.

"I've no wish to pay it over again," Lucrezia went on after giving him a moment to consider it. "Nor do I wish to lose my only brother in his second idiotic venture in this vein."

"You will not lose me," Enzo retorted. "I've far more skill with a sword than any impresario can claim."

Lucrezia ignored what Enzo had thought a very good point. "Your insistence in solving problems with a blade—"

"The first duel was not of my own creation," Enzo said, not for the first time. "A friend had been injured and insulted. He sought satisfaction. His cause was just. He named me his second. His courage failed him. I fought in his stead. The duel—"

Lucrezia spoke over him. "As his second, you ought to have convened with that of his opponent and brokered peace between them. And as for your duel today—"

"Wrought by my own hand, yes," Enzo admitted, "and with twelve-score justification! You know what that wretched creature has done to Fiore—twice over—!"

"Then the matter ought to be settled by purchasing the opera house from under him," said Lucrezia. "Or by opening our own and ruining his in the comparison. Or by convincing his lovers to leave him and spread reports of their dissatisfaction with his performance."

"Nothing would suffice," Enzo snarled. "Save blood."

Lucrezia arched her brow. "And it is because of precisely that, dear brother, that you will remain here until all danger of a duel has passed. Good morning."

"Lucrezia!" Enzo cried, struggling against his bonds in vain.

But she had already strode from the chamber.

# CHAPTER THIRTY-EIGHT

Fiore awoke alone.

The barest hint of sunlight had begun to bloom across the lagoon. He supposed Enzo had wanted to let him sleep in, even if only for a few scant minutes. Which, while very sweet in its intent, did leave Fiore with precious little time to prepare himself as Enzo's second. Enzo himself was doubtless off on his morning run up the spiral stair and liable to return at any moment.

Fiore performed a stand-up wash and dressed with haste, all the while doing his able best to ignore the trembling in his fingertips. There was no point in worrying about the duel. Enzo had a rare talent with a blade. His victory was all but assured. The best Fiore could do to assist him was to match his courage.

Still, his nerves strained further with every minute Enzo remained out of his sight.

By the time Fiore had finished his ablutions and dressing, Enzo had not returned. Suspicions began to cloud his thoughts despite his best efforts. In attempt to silence them, Fiore ventured out to find him. He half-expected to run headfirst into him upon moving from the bedchamber to the antechamber. Instead he encountered only the coffee service set out on the card table. Steam still curled from the pot's spout.

Of the two cups sitting beside it, one bore dregs. Evidence of Enzo's recent occupancy soothed Fiore's nerves somewhat. He poured and quaffed the second cup before moving on.

If he hadn't found Enzo in the antechamber, then Fiore thought surely he would meet him in the halls or courtyard between the bedchamber and the spiral stair. But no trace of Enzo appeared in the liminal spaces. Nor, upon reaching the stair itself—the absolute last sensible place left to look—did Fiore find him.

Fiore did not permit himself the luxury of panic. He simply turned on his heel and marched back to the bedchamber. Perhaps he and Enzo had somehow passed each other like ships in the night. And perhaps they might come face-to-face now, if Enzo had gone to the bedchamber himself and doubled back when he found Fiore missing.

In the midst of this maelstrom of speculation and anxiety, Fiore didn't perceive the path ahead quite so clearly as perhaps he ought. Which left him running headlong into the tall shadow that crossed in front of him.

Whatever relief he might have felt proved short-lived. He'd collided not with Enzo, but with one of the footmen.

"Your pardon, Alvise," said Fiore when they'd both recovered from the shock. "Have you seen his grace the duke this morning?"

"I have," Alvise replied with a reverent nod. "He went out not half an hour ago."

Fiore's heart plunged into fathomless depths. Still he tried to sound casual as he enquired, "Out for a stroll?"

"Out in a gondola," Alvise gently corrected him.

Fiore stared. Not a trace of doubt remained. All his worst fears were realized.

Enzo had left for the duel without him.

His first instinct was to bolt. But sprinting on foot would hardly get him to the site of the duel in time. Certainly not if Enzo had a half-hour's head start. He forced his heels to stick in place and plastered a smile over his rising panic. "If it wouldn't be too great an imposition, might I also borrow the services of a gondola?"

Alvise blinked at him.

"Or a sandolo," Fiore hastened to add. "Any watercraft, really."

"You may have either at your pleasure, signore," Alvise replied.

"And quickly?" Fiore asked before his better sense caught up with his tongue.

Alvise raised his brows but nodded nonetheless.

"A sandolo, then," Fiore decided. It was the faster and more maneuverable of the two. "Thank you, Alvise."

Alvise bowed and withdrew.

Fiore diverted his own course just long enough to snatch a true rapier from the armory, then dashed downstairs to the water entrance. If the staff awaiting him there considered it at all out of the ordinary to see him so armed, they said nothing of it aloud—though Fiore thought he caught a speaking glance between Alvise and the woman readying the sandolo. Another speaking glance came when he asked her to set a course for Isola dell'Anfiteatro. But no argument arose, and none emerged from the house to prevent his sailing out into the canal.

∽

Enzo screamed himself hoarse in Lucrezia's wake. For some time—he knew not how long, with neither clocks nor shadows to tell him, though it felt like days—only his own echoes answered him.

Then, as he drew breath for another attempt, he heard what sounded very much like but what he dared not hope were footsteps.

"Lucrezia?"

The footsteps ceased. The door swung inward. The figure silhouetted in the doorway could not be Lucrezia; they weren't tall enough and were garbed in a gown besides.

Giovanna stepped into the cell. She wore a beatific smile. Enzo supposed she meant it to seem reassuring. He was not reassured.

"Where is Fiore?" he demanded.

"Wherever you left him, I suspect," said Giovanna. "Shall we fetch him down? He cannot come in, lest he free you, but you may speak with him through the door. I see no harm in it."

Enzo stared at her. "I left him in my bed. If he is not there, then he has gone to the duel without me."

Giovanna furrowed her brow.

"He is my second," Enzo hastened to explain.

Giovanna's brows took flight.

"If he awakens without me," Enzo hurried on, "he will assume I've gone to meet Nascimbene. He will go to Isola dell'Anfiteatro. And when he doesn't find me there, he will duel Nascimbene himself."

Giovanna pressed her lips into a thin line even as her brow knit in concern.

"He will die." Enzo's voice broke on the last word. He pressed on. "He is a brave man, but his skill with a blade is not up to the task. Giovanna, *please*—"

Giovanna turned and strode to the door she'd left ajar. She exchanged a few words through the gap with someone, her voice too low for Enzo to discern their meaning. Bootheels clicked off down the hall and faded into nothing. Giovanna returned.

"Where—?" Enzo began.

"Carlotta will fetch your Fiore," said Giovanna.

Enzo wished he could share in her faith.

∿

Fiore spent the entire sandolo journey with heart in throat and fist white-knuckled upon the hilt of his rapier. He clenched his jaw against demanding the staff move faster. They well understood the urgency of his mission. There were natural limits to how swiftly a vessel could go through Halcyon's canals. Still, his mind raced on. Enzo had doubtless already reached Isola dell'Anfiteatro. Perhaps the duel had already begun. Perhaps Enzo had already slain Nascimbene. Or perhaps Nascimbene had already—Fiore shook his head. It didn't halt his racing thoughts.

The amphitheater loomed on the northern horizon. To the east the sun climbed slowly yet steadily into the sky. Fiore willed the sandolo to fly faster than Phoebus's chariot. Still he knew nothing approaching relief until the boat's bow knocked against the island's dock. He leaped ashore before the gondolier had finished tying off and ran headlong into the amphitheater itself. His footfalls echoed off the empty stone halls beneath the seats.

Until, at last, he stumbled out into the ring.

The sunlight stung his eyes after the relative darkness of the stone tunnels. The vast field lay empty save for a few indistinct figures silhouetted against the dawn. They came into focus as Fiore staggered toward them.

With a jolt he recognized the beaked masks and glinting glass eyes of two chirurgeons. Which one was Dr. Malvestio and which belonged to Nascimbene he couldn't discern; their garb rendered them identical.

Two figures remained. One was Nascimbene himself. Even when Fiore expected to see him, the sight still gave him a nasty shock, like an icicle driven into his spine. The other figure remained a stranger. Not Enzo.

Which was really the only thing that mattered.

Enzo wasn't here. Or if he was, he wasn't able to stand upright.

All the panic Fiore had held off until this point threatened to overwhelm him. Had they already dueled? Had Enzo lost? Was he wounded—dead?

The gathered four took notice of him at last. One of the chirurgeons approached.

Without thinking, Fiore braced to draw his rapier.

"Is his grace the duke with you?" Dr. Malvestio's voice emerged from beak.

A spark of hope cut through the overwhelming tide of Fiore's panic. "No. Is he not here?"

"No," Dr. Malvestio replied.

The wave of relief that ought to have washed over Fiore only served to buoy his nerves to unforeseen heights. "You've not seen him? They've not dueled?"

"No, and no." Dr. Malvestio hesitated. "Do you know where he is?"

Fiore shook his head.

By this point the stranger had approached as well.

"Forgive my interruption," he said. "Bonato at your service. I am Maestro Nascimbene's second."

He was a tall, well-built man around Fiore's own age. A ballerino, if Fiore had to guess, by his powerful frame and his proximity to Nascimbene. His confidante, perhaps. Maybe even his lover. Or merely whoever stood to inherit the post of impresario in his stead. It mattered not.

"Has his grace the duke sent you to broker peace?" Bonato asked.

Fiore stared. A strangled laugh escaped his throat. He strode past him

Nascimbene and his chirurgeon stood together in close conversation. Fiore wondered if it was the same chirurgeon who'd attempted to castrate him. There was no real way to tell; the chirurgeon then had been masked, just as this chirurgeon was now, and as all chirurgeons were throughout the city. Yet still Fiore wondered. Both ceased talking as Fiore drew up to them.

"Where is the duke?" Fiore demanded.

Nascimbene swept him up and down with white-rimmed eyes. Still his voice emerged arch and cold. "Not here."

Fiore wondered if Nascimbene and his cohorts had somehow overpowered Enzo and hidden him away. But surely Dr. Malvestio would've intervened. And no one would dare attack the prince's brother direct. "How long are you willing to wait for him?"

"If he does not arrive within the hour, then it is forfeit."

Fiore would've gladly waited an eternity if he only knew he would see his Enzo at the end of it. "Very well. I am the duke's second. If he does not arrive, I am prepared to duel you in his stead."

Nascimbene balked. "To the death?"

A gallows grin spread across Fiore's face. "Of course."

Minutes passed like hours in the agony of Enzo's anxiety.

Giovanna appeared unbothered. She stood by the door and waited with the same look of beatific idleness on her features as one might find if she were perched on the balcony of her villa in Bluecliffe and gazing out over her fertile fields. Whatever thoughts the delay inspired in her mind remained her own.

Enzo, meanwhile, stared at the watch chain trailing from her bodice as if he could will the timepiece out of its pocket with sheer desperation alone.

Rapid footsteps echoed down the hall.

Enzo bolted upright at the sound. Giovanna merely gave a casual twirl to face the servant who whispered through the bars. At first her expression remained placid. Then a singular furrow of confusion appeared between her brows.

"What is it?" Enzo asked.

Giovanna hesitated.

"Have they found him?" Enzo heard his voice take on a pleading tone. He would beg her on his knees if he could for just the barest scrap of anything regarding his Fiore.

"They have not," Giovanna admitted.

Enzo slumped in despair. But he could not indulge it for long. Desperation demanded better of him. He strained against his bonds anew. "It is just as I said. He has gone to the duel. He will fight. Let me save him. I won't fight Nascimbene—only let me stop the duel and save Fiore."

Giovanna shook her head.

"Giovanna, please—"

"I cannot. Lucrezia has ordered your confinement. I gave her my word."

"And would you defy her for nothing?" Enzo snapped. "What if your Antonio were about to duel for your honor?"

Giovanna stared at him.

"Would you not go to stop him?" Enzo demanded.

Giovanna continued staring in abject horror.

"His devotion to you is absolute," Enzo continued, pressing his advantage. "He would fight a hundred duels for your sake. Fiore is no less devoted to me, nor I to him. You say keeping me here will save my life. What would your life be without your Antonio? What would be saved if he were—?"

"Stop," Giovanna whispered.

Enzo fell silent.

Giovanna ceased looking at him. Her gaze fell to the floor, brow furrowed, and she crossed her arms with one hand at her chin. She turned away from him altogether and paced the breadth of the chamber with small swift steps. Over and again. Back and forth. Her heels clicked against the pavement like the ticking of an unseen clock.

465

Enzo held his breath.

Then Giovanna rounded on him. "Swear to me you will not fight."

"I swear it." Enzo would swear to anything that might spare his Fiore.

Giovanna held his gaze. "Even if you should arrive to find him killed."

Enzo's heart ceased to beat. How could she ask him that. How could she dare demand such a condition. How could she be so cruel as to give it voice.

Yet there remained but one answer he could give if he wished to save his Fiore.

"I swear," he lied.

Whether Giovanna believed him, he knew not.

But she did stride to him, unsheathe her dagger, and cut his bonds.

# CHAPTER THIRTY-NINE

Nascimbene's chirurgeon consulted their pocket-watch. Their voice emerged in the same muffled echo as Fiore's nightmares. "The hour is nigh."

Fiore had waited out each of the agonizing minutes with his nerves taut and his mind whirling with suppositions. He'd expected Enzo to arrive at any and every moment. Every second that passed without him he spent in agonizing anxiety. He comforted himself, but barely, with the rationale that Nascimbene had not the power to kidnap or otherwise dispose of the prince's brother. And Enzo himself would never abandon a duel—not after what happened with Orazio. Therefore he had to conclude that the prince had done something to prevent his arrival. Probably she wouldn't kill her own brother. Probably. Perhaps Enzo would be waiting for him when he returned to Ca' Scaevola. Wouldn't that be nice?

The announcement of the hour by Nascimbene's chirurgeon freed Fiore from his mind's relentless revolving. He shoved off from the wall where he'd stood waiting beside Dr. Malvestio and strode toward his opponent.

"Ready whenever you are," Fiore declared.

Nascimbene's eyes swept him up and down with a look he couldn't read. His jaw clenched. He gave Fiore a cold nod.

They both stripped to the waist. Nascimbene bore no scars on what flesh Fiore could see. He wondered if the maestro realized he held responsibility for almost all of Fiore's own. The mark on his cheek, the missing finger, the twin punctures bookending his navel and the thin, ragged line that traced their repair, and the one further down that remained beyond Nascimbene's sight yet ever at the forefront of Fiore's mind.

Fiore drew his sword. He kept its handle clutched like a bird in his fist and his off-hand up by his face. He dropt into a fencing stance. His eyes burned into Nascimbene's.

Nascimbene's well-oiled blade glinted in the morning sunlight. To Fiore's astonishment, he raised it in salute. Fiore belatedly returned the gesture. Mere matter of form on Nascimbene's part, no doubt. It oughtn't unnerve him.

Dr. Malvestio stood between them with a handkerchief clutched in his upraised hand. He and Nascimbene's chirurgeon had tossed a coin between them for the privilege.

Nascimbene assumed a posture mirroring Fiore's own—truly mirroring it, as Nascimbene held his sword in his right hand, and Fiore did so in his left. He presented not so thin a line as Enzo had. Fiore stood shorter than Enzo and Nascimbene alike—as he stood shorter than most gentleman. And while this left him with a shorter reach, it likewise meant he presented a smaller target. Being younger than Nascimbene by some thirty-odd years would make him faster and more agile. Or so he hoped.

The moment they'd taken their places, Dr. Malvestio let the handkerchief fall and hastily withdrew from the field.

The duel had begun.

Fiore stood.

And he waited.

Nascimbene's hard stare held for a few moments. Then it softened in confusion. A singular furrow appeared between his brows.

Fiore withheld a smile and continued to wait. He'd delayed his revenge for over a decade. He could hold back just a while longer.

And Nascimbene, just as Maestra Rovigatti had predicted, could not.

The feint came to Fiore's left. It began in Nascimbene's arm. His foot never moved, lest there remain any doubt the strike would prove false.

Fiore didn't bother to even pretend he would parry it.

Nascimbene returned to his stance quickly—yet still far slower than Enzo ever had. His next feint came at Fiore's right. Again, the arm moved first and the foot not at all.

And again, Fiore didn't parry. His pulse thundered in his ears. He hardly felt his rapier's weight on his arm.

Another feint to Fiore's left. Except this time, when the arm led, the foot followed. Not a feint at all, but a true thrust. Nascimbene's poor footwork and form had led Fiore astray.

Fiore realized it almost too late to parry altogether.

A twirl of his wrist. A flash of the blade. The point that would've skewered his heart instead scored a glancing blow across his chest, just below his left shoulder.

The force of the thrust and parry combined sent Nascimbene stumbling past him. Fiore spun and leapt backward—poor form, Maestra Rovigatti wouldn't approve, but it got him away from the impresario, who'd yet to recover. He chanced a glance down at his wound, a mere scratch, just a few garnet beads of blood along a slender crimson cord. It didn't even sting.

Nascimbene regained his footing and bolted upright, whirling to face Fiore again. He glanced between Fiore, the wound, the scarcely-pinked tip of his own sword, and back to Fiore. He made no move to attack again. A strange smile plucked at his lips. It looked almost triumphant. Premature, in Fiore's opinion.

"First blood," Fiore conceded. "But we said to the death, did we not?"

Nascimbene's smile faded.

A grin crept over Fiore's own features. Then he burst into an attack.

First a thrust at the impresario's heart—the mirror image of the point he'd scored on Fiore. Nascimbene parried, stumbling backward. His eyes had flown wide. As if he'd never anticipated a counter-attack.

Fiore supposed he was, after all, the first conservatorio boy to ever strike back.

Another thrust from Fiore, this time at the arm that held the impresario's blade. Parried again, but with a third thrust—this at the eyes—close on its heels. Nascimbene parried it as well and the overhead cut that came after and another thrust at his heart after that. Fiore plunged on. Every possible attack above the waist. Falling into a predictable pattern.

Just in time for Fiore to strike below the belt.

Fiore lunged. For the first time in the fight he felt a pang. A slight tearing sensation behind his navel.

Well worth it to see his blade plunge between Nascimbene's legs amidst a crimson tide.

Enzo might wield a rapier as deftly as a scalpel. Fiore had not his skill. But what he lacked in skill he more than made up for in fervor.

And, to his ears at least, Nascimbene had a most musical scream.

As much as Fiore wished to drive his sword deeper, what little better sense remained to him demanded he retrieve his blade for another strike and withdraw out of his opponent's reach.

Nascimbene dropt to his knees. His howl weakened to mere whimpering. It aroused no pity in Fiore's heart—just as the cries of a thousand innocent boys before him had aroused no pity in Nascimbene.

The impresario's off hand flew to the wound. Blood soaked through his breeches and oozed between his fingers. His sword-arm shook, the weapon trembling in a convulsive grasp at his side, lacking even the pretense of a guard.

A flick of Fiore's wrist crossed their blades. A twirl entangled them. A single sharp heave sufficed to tear Nascimbene's sword from his hand.

Nascimbene glanced up at that. Fear and rage mingled in his gaze. He scrambled backward, flailing for his sword. He turned his head from Fiore to find it.

Fiore leapt between him and his blade. His heel struck Nascimbene's shoulder and sent him sprawling supine. Another wrist-flick saw his sword's tip at the hollow of the impresario's throat.

Now fear alone shone in Nascimbene's eyes.

Fiore hesitated. He'd served Nascimbene the same wound he himself had suffered on the impresario's orders. Elio had died of it. But Fiore had lived with it. As had thousands of boys before him.

And how could Nascimbene understand—truly understand—the

horrors he had inflicted upon them all, unless Fiore allowed him to live with it, too?

But as this thought flashed through Fiore's mind, a counter-argument arose. Even if Fiore let him live now, Nascimbene would never know the true miseries of the castrato. He'd carried his stones into adulthood already. His body had grown and changed as nature bid it. He'd had every opportunity to sire children if he so wished. He would never know the shame of an unbroken voice in a broken body.

Worse yet, he might well continue his monstrous work.

And while Fiore couldn't stop them all—while Nascimbene was by no means the only monster involved in such crimes—he could stop Nascimbene, here and now.

Forever.

With a final thrust, Fiore slid his blade into its mortal sheath.

Nascimbene spluttered—gurgled—gasped—but could not scream. The blade stole his breath. Robbed him of the voice he'd unjustly kept whilst denying the same to every boy who passed through his conservatorio. He drowned on a mere fraction of the blood he himself had spilled.

And Fiore could not summon even a fraction of remorse.

Blood ceased to pour from the wound. The chest beneath it no longer rose and fell. The impresario's eyes stared beyond Fiore into eternity's abyss.

Fiore found a regret at last. Nascimbene had died far too quick.

"Fiore!"

The voice ringing out across the amphitheater sounded sweeter than any aria. Fiore whirled towards it, his bloodied blade still in his grip, freshly torn from the impresario's throat.

And there was his Enzo.

Bereft of mask. Flanked by city guards. Breaking from their ranks to run toward him. Heedless of the bloodied blade still in Fiore's grasp. Never fearing for a moment that Fiore might hurt him.

Fiore spread his arms wide to meet him.

Enzo clasped him tight with enough force to lift him off the ground. The sword dropped from Fiore's hand and clattered to the dirt forgotten. His blood sang with satisfaction. The devouring kiss he bestowed upon

Enzo couldn't begin to express even a fraction of the relief he felt to have him in his embrace again. The fight had left him winded, forcing him to break off sooner than he wished. Over Enzo's shoulder he caught a glimpse of the guards blocking Nascimbene's cohorts from departing the arena. A welcome sight, yet still not so welcome as Enzo's dark eyes gazing down on him, safe at last.

"I'm sorry," said Enzo.

Fiore knew not what for.

"Are you hurt?" Enzo asked.

"Only a scratch," Fiore intended to tell him—except before he could get the words out, a pulse of exhaustion overtook him—like being struck a blow over the head with something soft and suffocating—a wave crashing over him and dragging him down into depths he couldn't kick out of.

Fiore staggered. Enzo caught him. His embrace was all Fiore wanted in that moment. Even so, he tried to stand. But just lifting his head from Enzo's collar felt like dragging an anchor.

Enzo called for the chirurgeon. To Fiore he asked, "Where are you wounded?"

"Nowhere," Fiore insisted—though it felt impossible to gather enough breath to do so. He tried again. "Just a scratch."

Enzo knelt and laid Fiore gently down, his upper half in Enzo's lap. Which, again, was everything Fiore wished. Apollo could not have cradled Hyacinthus even half so tenderly. Gazing up at his Enzo, Fiore wondered if the mortal had felt as contented in the god's arms. He wished only that he could do something to alleviate the fear in Enzo's eyes.

But all strength failed him as he sank down into oblivion.

# CHAPTER FORTY

F iore didn't expect to open his eyes ever again.

Because of this, the sight of the peacock-blue bed-curtains and coffered ceiling of Enzo's chambers in Ca' Scaevola, while familiar, nonetheless surprised him.

All appeared hazy at first, the image growing more distinct by gradual degrees, and with a curious tilting sensation as if he lay aboard a ship that rocked in rhythm with the pulse thudding slow in his ears. He waited with mounting impatience for his vision to clear. When at last the room stilled and no shadows encroached on the corners of his eyes, he dared to loll his head to glimpse what he might of his surroundings.

Enzo sat at his bedside. He didn't look at Fiore. Instead he fixed his dark gaze on the middle distance, hunched over with his elbows propped against his knees. His fingers laced over his mouth in a Gordian knot to match his furrowed brow. Blue shadows hung beneath his eyes. Strands of hair had torn free from the cord at the nape of his neck to fall across his scarred face. He wore no coat, just his waistcoat and breeches, with his shirtsleeves not folded nor rolled but rather shoved up past his forearms.

"Enzo." Fiore's voice left him in a creak hardly above a whisper.

Yet Enzo leapt and whirled as if he'd heard a thunderclap resound

473

from a clear blue sky. His shock dissolved into a disbelieving smile as he met Fiore's gaze. In two shakes of a sail he was upon him, cradling his jaw in his soft palms, smoothing sweat-slicked hair off his brow.

Fiore craved nothing more than Enzo's touch. Yet even just Enzo's fingers gently combing through his hair made his scalp sting and burn. His very bones ached with fever. Down to the teeth. All the joints pulled out of place by his captivity in the catacombs were set aflame. A pained whimper escaped his throat despite his best efforts to suppress it.

Enzo ceased caressing him. Fiore couldn't gather the wit or wherewithal to protest the loss before Enzo had poured a glass of water and ever so gently cupped the back of his skull to tilt his lips to the rim. Fiore drank with a thirst he hadn't realized he'd possessed until the water touched his tongue.

"Coffee?" he croaked as Enzo took the empty glass away.

"Not just yet," Enzo replied with an apologetic wince.

Fiore supposed that'd been rather too much to hope for. Still, "Wine?"

A wan smile graced Enzo's scarred lips. "I'm afraid not yet, either."

Fiore didn't have the strength to conceal his disappointment. "...Limonata?"

"Soon," Enzo promised him. "And chocolate as well, if you'd like."

Something to look forward to at least. More importantly, however... "You saved me."

But Enzo shook his head. "Dr. Leopardi saved you."

Fiore furrowed his brow—which did nothing good for his headache. "Who?"

"Nascimbene's chirurgeon."

This left Fiore no less confused. "Why?"

"Because I told him I would kill him if he failed to give you the antidote."

"Antidote?"

"To the poison on Nascimbene's blade."

Fiore stared at him. His mind was not in any condition to work through this. "From the beginning, please."

"Soon," Enzo promised again.

Fiore was starting to hate that word.

"You're not altogether well," Enzo added with a sympathetic smile.

His hand trailed through Fiore's hair again, a comforting gesture despite the pains it inspired. But then he left off to ring the silver hand-bell on the nightstand. "Dr. Venier ought to have a look at you. I swear I'll tell you everything afterward."

Fiore thought he'd suffered quite enough already without having to submit to yet another chirurgical examination.

Dr. Venier arrived in short order. Fiore kept his complaints to himself for the most part while she plied stetoscopio and termometro, though a few more pathetic whimpers escaped him as she, however gently, probed and prodded. She dosed him with mold tincture and anodyne by mouth, along with a third medicine she didn't explain, nor did Fiore recognize its queer taste. The reveal of bandages around his middle—when Dr. Venier listened to his entrails—came as something of a surprise. Distantly he recalled a sudden pang there during the duel.

"Pulse much stronger," she declared when she'd finished. "And fever reduced."

All good tidings. Fiore wondered why Enzo didn't look happier to hear them. Aloud he said, "I suppose I have to get up now?"

Enzo exchanged an alarmed glance with Dr. Venier.

"We may try," Dr. Venier said.

Fiore wasn't sure he liked the sound of that.

Enzo slipped an arm behind his shoulders. Dr. Venier held out her hands for him to clasp. Between the two of them Fiore attempted to sit up. Every muscle in his body protested. The room spun violently.

"Down, down, down," came Enzo's voice, low and urgent. "Steady now."

Fiore's pulse throbbed in his skull. But the dark fog encroaching on his vision receded with every beat, which was something. Soon he could see clearly Enzo's deeply concerned face above him and realized he was lying down again.

"We'll try again later," Dr. Venier said. "Just keep kneading his limbs in the meantime. But on the whole, Signor Fiore, you're doing very well."

And with that, she mercifully withdrew.

Fiore didn't necessarily feel like he was doing very well. But he was alive, which was frankly more than he'd expected. He turned to Enzo, who'd taken up his hand in Dr. Venier's absence.

"If I have a fever," Fiore protested, "why do I feel so cold?"

Enzo hesitated. "Your heart is weakened."

Fiore didn't see what that had to do with it.

"Your pulse isn't strong enough for your blood to reach your extremities as it ought," Enzo further explained. "It's withdrawing towards your vitals to keep them warm."

Fiore, his head dulled by the throbbing ache that seemed to thrum from within the skull-bone itself, could only reply, "Oh."

A wan yet sanguine smile graced Enzo's lips. "But it grows stronger by the day. And until you're well again, there's rosewater for your fever and braziers and furs for your feet."

Fiore had to admit he liked the sound of that. Still, he thought he had a better idea. "You could keep me warm."

A moment of silent astonishment ensued, during which Enzo blinked down at him with those soft, dark, enormous eyes Fiore loved so well.

Then he withdrew, stripped down to his shirt, and, to Fiore's infinite relief, slipped into bed beside him.

As glad as Fiore had felt to see Enzo's face upon waking, it was nothing compared to his gentle embrace, his arms curling protectively around him. The anodyne dose had banished all but the deepest aches, allowing Fiore the delicious pleasure of insinuating himself snug into Enzo's grasp.

"So," Fiore said. "Tell me how you rescued me."

"I didn't," Enzo insisted again. He gently combed his hand through Fiore's curls as he spoke. "Nascimbene coated his blade in cantarella oil. Either he did so too far ahead of the duel, so a great deal of it evaporated, or whoever procured him the dose lied about its potency. Regardless—a scratch such as he gave you is not oft survived."

"Oh," Fiore said softly.

Enzo held him tight. "Dr. Leopardi—Nascimbene's chirurgeon—"

"I remember," Fiore mumbled.

"He carried the antidote with him to the dueling field."

"In case Nascimbene pricked himself on his own sword?" Fiore guessed.

A bitter huff of laughter escaped Enzo. "Possibly. More likely in case through some freak accident Dr. Leopardi himself was cut with the poisoned blade."

"How did you know he carried the antidote?"

"He'd be a fool not to."

Fiore supposed that sound enough. "So you demanded it from him."

"I told him to surrender it if he wished to live, yes."

Fiore smiled into Enzo's collar. "So you did save me."

If Enzo demurred again, Fiore slipped off to sleep before he heard it.

⌒

Enzo indulged himself as much or more than Fiore when he agreed to lie beside him.

Three days had passed since the duel. Three of the worst days Enzo had lived. Enzo hadn't left Fiore's side since he'd arrived all too late to the dueling field. The only thing that had sustained him throughout was Fiore's fight for survival.

To see Fiore awaken banished all Enzo's frantic fears. To feel his pulse grow stronger beneath his fingertips, to watch those dark and beautiful eyes open again, to hear his perfect voice—Enzo hadn't dared hope for any of it. To have it all at once threatened to overwhelm him. Only the knowledge that Fiore's delicate health required a calm and quiet atmosphere to improve kept Enzo in check.

He'd hardly slept the past three nights. He had lain abed beside Fiore for a few scant hours, hoping his presence might calm him as it had before. Then by some blessed twist of fate Fiore had awoken and demanded Enzo join him. Enzo could do no less than acquiesce.

And then, to watch Fiore fall into a true and peaceful sleep—not the fitful febrile thrashing nightmare nor the cold and deathlike trance he'd alternated between for the last three days—and to feel his frail form relax in his protective embrace... Enzo couldn't have relinquished him even if he'd wished to.

Yet even as Fiore sank into tranquil repose, all the guilt Enzo had shoved down to focus on Fiore's survival now resurfaced. His mind ran through the events of the fateful morning of the duel over and over again, trying to work out where he had failed to outmaneuver Lucrezia and what he might have done differently. His remorse for leaving Fiore to fight in his stead threatened to drown him. He wondered if Orazio had felt the same when—

Carlotta's distinctive knock fell upon the door.

Enzo raised his head. He didn't dare move more, lest he wake Fiore. "Enter."

Carlotta slipped into the room. If the sight of her charge abed with his poisoned lover surprised her, she didn't show any hint of it. "Her grace the prince would see you in the library."

Enzo stared at her. For Lucrezia to leave the princely palazzo required extraordinary circumstance. For her to encroach upon Enzo now when she bore as much blame as himself for Fiore's present suffering required brazen foolishness. Only his unwillingness to disturb Fiore prevented him from storming out to scold her. "You may tell her grace the prince that I do not intend to leave this chamber until Fiore is well."

Carlotta accepted this with a nod and withdrew.

Enzo breathed again only when the door had shut after her. He trailed his hand through Fiore's dark curls and took comfort in his ease. Endymion did not enjoy so serene a repose as Fiore did now. Nor did he look even half so beautiful. Enzo could remain as he now lay content for hours. He might even fall asleep himself at last.

Another knock fell on the door.

The noise sent a spike of anxiety through Enzo like an icicle hammered into his spine. It was not Carlotta's knock. Indeed it wasn't a knock like any servant in the house. It was a knock he hadn't heard since before he'd left for university.

One which demanded answer.

Gently and with great reluctance, Enzo disentangled himself from Fiore. He arose from the bed, slipped on his wrapping-gown, and went to the door. Against all his better instincts, he opened it just the slightest crack. He required no more than that mere glimpse to recognize the shadowy figure in the antechamber.

Lucrezia stood erect, hands clasped behind her back, and one severe brow cocked at her brother.

Enzo supposed he ought to feel grateful that she'd bothered to knock at all.

"Good morning," said Lucrezia. She kept her voice down, at least.

"Farewell," said Enzo, and attempted to shut the door on her.

Her boot on the threshold halted any such efforts. "There are matters I would discuss with you."

"Matters which are nothing to me until he is hale again," Enzo hissed.

"You would do better to listen—"

"And you would do better to leave him well enough alone!" All the fear that'd consumed Enzo throughout the past three days, briefly held back by Fiore's tentative recovery, now surged forth in the guise of rage. He struggled to rein it in, succeeding only in keeping his voice quiet but by no means restrained. "He'd be perfectly well by now if you hadn't kept me from—"

"Enzo?"

Enzo shut his jaw with a click. Slowly and deliberately he moved so as to block any possible view through the slender gap between door and frame. Then he turned over his shoulder and attempted to appear at ease for Fiore's sake.

For it was after all Fiore who'd roused and spoken.

Fiore arose with furrowed brow and dark hollows beneath his eyes. What little sleep he'd caught had already mussed his fever-tangled curls. He raised just his head at first, rubbing his eye with the heel of his hand, but the moment he caught sight of Enzo at the door he shoved himself up onto his elbows and seemed intent on rising further.

Enzo resisted the urge to dash to his side and prevent him from sitting up. He settled for begging. "Go back to sleep. It's nothing."

Fiore did not go back to sleep. Instead he leant over and craned his neck to try and see beyond Enzo. "Who's there?"

"No one of consequence," Enzo insisted.

To Enzo's great dismay, Fiore's eyes widened in alarm. "What's wrong?"

"Nothing," Enzo repeated. His voice cracked as he added, "Please lie down."

Fiore remained upright. His chest heaved. The nightgown hung loose about his collar, the neckline dipping low and revealing his sternum, stark against his skin, so much flesh had fallen away from his form in just a few short days—

Without turning 'round, Enzo shut the door on Lucrezia. He hesitated before turning the key in the lock behind his back. Then he forced himself to take slow and measured steps to Fiore's bedside.

"Who is it?" Fiore demanded as Enzo knelt beside him and laid his hands on his shoulders.

Despite Enzo's gentle efforts, Fiore remained upright. Enzo knew he'd never get him back to rest without an honest answer. "Lucrezia."

Fiore's face, already ghastly pale, somehow drained of further color. In a voice of dull horror he intoned, "What does she want?"

"To speak with me."

Fiore's hunched shoulders relaxed the merest fraction. "Why don't you go to her, then?"

"Because I've no wish to speak with her."

Fiore stared at him. "Why not?"

"Because it's her fault that you're ill."

Fiore's eyes flew wide. "She gave Nascimbene the poison?"

Enzo cursed himself for his amateur speaking error. "No, no—I mean, she prevented me from going to the duel. If it weren't for her you'd have never gone in my place, and…"

Fiore looked thoughtful as Enzo trailed off.

Enzo considered Fiore in turn. He seemed stronger now after his all-too-brief rest. Obviously still in distress, but holding himself upright regardless. Breathing with ease. Clear-headed in the wake of his fever.

None of which prepared him to hear Fiore ask, "May I speak with her?"

Enzo balked. But he could refuse Fiore nothing now. Whatever he wished for he deserved as just reward for sheer survival. And even in the midst of his shock, Enzo had a grim notion of forcing Lucrezia to confront the consequences of her actions. Let her see what her choices had wrought on Fiore's body.

"If you're feeling up to it," Enzo relented. "Just for a few moments."

A queer smile curled up Fiore's scarred cheek. "That will suffice."

Enzo returned to the door. He unlocked and opened it to find

Lucrezia still in the antechamber, adjusting her gloves and gazing on him with marked incredulity.

"Fiore wishes to speak with you," said Enzo.

Somehow this lessened her incredulity. "Very well."

She made as if to step into the sickroom. Enzo halted her with an upraised hand.

"He cannot stand," Enzo warned her. "Not on ceremony or anything else."

"I would hardly expect him to," Lucrezia replied coolly.

And so, against all his better instincts, Enzo allowed Lucrezia in.

Lucrezia's gaze swept over the bedchamber like a hawk. Her efficient stride brought her to Fiore's bedside. She made no move to occupy the chair there. Enzo took it for himself, putting his own body between Fiore and his sister.

For his part, Fiore held himself upright and cast an equally-appraising look up at Lucrezia in turn.

Lucrezia broke the silence. "Signor Fiore, I presume?"

Fiore nodded.

"Prince Lucrezia Scaevola, Serenissima of Halcyon, at your service."

"Fiore of no consequence at yours," Fiore replied.

At another time, Enzo might have laughed.

Lucrezia took it in stride. "My brother tells me you desired an audience."

Fiore nodded again. "Enzo said you're the reason he arrived late to the duel."

Lucrezia cocked her brow at that. Enzo supposed not many folk dared speak to her so boldly. Nonetheless she maintained her arch serenity—which only serve to enrage Enzo further—as she replied, "I am."

"And had you known he stood my second," Enzo demanded before Fiore could continue, "would you still have kept me from the duel?"

Lucrezia stared straight into his eyes, unblinking. "Yes."

Enzo could have killed her.

"Thank you," said Fiore.

Enzo whirled to stare at him.

But Fiore's gaze remained fixed on Lucrezia. "In a single stroke, you've allowed me the personal satisfaction of revenge and kept Enzo safe from harm."

Enzo continued staring at him.

"Masterful, really," Fiore continued, still to Lucrezia.

"I know," said Lucrezia.

Enzo glanced back just in time to find the ghost of a smile playing about her lips.

He couldn't imagine that this was her original intent behind detaining him from the duel. Perhaps she'd wished to keep Enzo safe, fair enough, but she couldn't possibly have cared about Fiore's vengeance.

Lucrezia's voice startled Enzo out of his whirling thoughts.

"May I speak to you in confidence, Signor Fiore?" Lucrezia asked.

Fiore nodded.

Enzo waited for Lucrezia to speak.

Instead, she served him a pointed sidelong look and still more pointed silence.

Enzo knew the look well. She'd worn it throughout their childhood whenever she wanted him to leave a room. Her audacity in casting it on him now, however, made him balk.

A long and silent moment ensued before Lucrezia broke it with a sharp sigh of disappointment. "If you would be so kind as to leave us, Enzo."

Enzo stared at her, aghast.

Her annoyed look softened somewhat. "Only for a moment."

"I'll be all right," Fiore spoke up, startling Enzo.

Enzo glanced between them. Lucrezia, wearily irritated, a mirror of his own feelings without even half his justification. Fiore, harrowed yet smiling, weak as cobwebs and insisting on his own way regardless.

And while Enzo might withstand a thousand blows from his sister, he could not deny his beloved.

Enzo took Fiore's hand in his and brought his knuckles to his lips. He would've done more, far more, but for his sister's presence. What small gesture he permitted himself would suffice to tell her all he wished.

Better still, it sufficed to provoke the ghost of a smile on Fiore's perfect lips.

Enzo stood. To Lucrezia, he said, "If he takes a turn—even by the slightest degree—for the worst, ring for aid."

"As you like," Lucrezia replied, much to his surprise.

Enzo ought to have left her with that warning alone. But as he passed by her on his way out of the bedchamber, he found himself pausing to clap a hand on her shoulder. He leant to her ear and whispered.

"If he dies, I will follow him into the grave."

Then, without waiting to see how she took it, he forced himself to leave Fiore's sick-room.

~

Long afterward, Fiore would blame the anodyne and his receding fever for his boldness in demanding an audience with the prince.

He'd only just awoken. He hadn't even had time to consider the why behind Enzo arriving to Isola dell'Anfiteatro only after the duel was over. Too exhausted by his fight against the poison. Too relieved to have Enzo by his side at last.

And now Enzo had gone.

And only the prince remained.

Only after Enzo had left did Fiore realize just how unprepared he was for this interview. Undressed, abed, not even washed, still bearing the sweat of the fever he'd only just broken. He could not make a worse impression on arguably the most important person in Enzo's life if he'd tried.

The prince held the fate of the whole city in her palms—and more pertinently Fiore's fate. Whether or not Fiore could remain with Enzo was entirely up to her discretion, for while Enzo might intend to defy his family on Fiore's behalf, Fiore would be a poor friend indeed to actually allow him to do so.

That said, their discourse in Enzo's presence seemed to have gone well. She had well earned his respect. He only hoped he hadn't earned her disdain in turn.

The prince took the chair Enzo had abandoned.

"You've heard the rumors of our bloodline," she began. "I assume you and my brother are close enough for you to know the truth of it is borne out in his flesh."

Fiore admitted this with a nod.

The prince continued. "Dragons are fabled for their loyalty. But Enzo's loyalty has at times lain with those who don't deserve it."

"Courtesans, you mean."

The prince's sharp glance told Fiore that either the anodyne or the fever or both had allowed his thoughts to slip past his lips and become speech.

Fiore held his foolish tongue whilst he waited for the prince to pass punishing judgment on his words.

But her hard gaze softened as it fixed on him. Not by much but by a perceptible degree. Marble rather than granite. Stone nonetheless.

And to his further astonishment, she said, "No. I do not mean courtesans."

Fiore found the wherewithal to reply, "Oh."

The prince leaned back. "There are those who would goad my brother into making a challenge on their behalf. Or make their own challenge only to fall back and let him fight their battles for them."

Even through the anodyne haze, Fiore thought he might know whom she meant.

"Few would take up the sword in his stead," the prince went on. "Fewer still would dare to fight their own battles when he didn't stand behind them." The faintest hint of a smile graced her lips. "And still fewer would succeed."

Fiore dared not hope she meant to commend him.

"However." Here the prince gave him a pointed glance. "There is something to be said for discretion when it comes to choosing one's battles."

Fiore understood her perfectly.

The prince continued. "When first I heard Enzo had begun paying particular attention to a particular courtesan, I feared his loyalty was again abused. But the events of the past few months have proved you are a far worthier recipient of all he has to offer."

Fiore didn't know if he would ever feel worthy of Enzo's loyalty. He could hardly believe he even held it. Whatever regard Enzo had for him, he resolved to return tenfold.

The prince fixed him with a hard stare. "May I trust you will continue to guard his best interest?"

It mattered not if a prince or a beggar had asked him; the answer would remain the same. Fiore smiled. "With my life."

~

Enzo paced in the antechamber. No panther had ever stalked circles in its cage with more impatience. When Lucrezia emerged at last, he pounced.

"Is he—?" Enzo began.

"Your Fiore is well and eager to see you again. However," she said, halting his return to the sickroom with an upraised hand, "I've yet to impart what I came here to do."

"Quickly then," Enzo snapped.

"We've found the alchemist who provided cantarella to Nascimbene."

"Most welcome tidings indeed," Enzo admitted after a moment of stunned silence. Certainly far better than anything he'd expected from her. "What's to be done with him?"

"He has been dealt with."

A phrase Enzo had grown familiar with, given his sister's position. Still he found he couldn't rest easy with vagaries. "May I know how?"

"He has sampled his own wares."

Enzo stared at her. Cantarella when decanted properly granted a swift if painful death. The quality of the poison given to Nascimbene, however...

Lucrezia raised her brows. "We can't have someone dealing in something so dangerous without any oversight."

Enzo quite agreed. And as he pondered the end the poison-seller must have met, he found he had no real regret for his suffering but wished only that Nascimbene could've shared in it as well. "It will gladden Fiore to hear of it."

Lucrezia nodded and turned to go. Three swift strides brought her to the door. There she paused, however, with her fingertips on the knob. After a moment's hesitation she turned to Enzo again.

"When your Fiore is well enough to travel," Lucrezia began.

A greater relief than Enzo had expected washed over him. It did his spirits a deal of good to hear someone speak of Fiore's recovery as a certainty rather than an unlikely chance.

"It may behoove you both," Lucrezia continued, "to retire to the countryside for the season."

Enzo knew precisely what she meant. Nevertheless, he heartily agreed.

# CHAPTER FORTY-ONE

I n the prince's wake, Fiore slept.

When next he opened his eyes, he found Enzo pressing a kiss to his forehead.

"Is that all?" Fiore asked when he withdrew.

A rosy tint bloomed over Enzo's sharp cheeks. "The lips are very sensitive to temperature."

"So you only wish to see if my fever's returned," Fiore concluded.

Enzo nodded.

"If you're going to do that," Fiore told him, "then you have to kiss me properly afterwards."

Enzo did so with a fond smile.

Afterward, Fiore suffered through the return of Dr. Venier, whereupon he learnt he had, in fact, torn open his freshly-healed abdomen in his fight with Nascimbene, hence the bandage 'round his middle. Fortunately it was a small tear in the outer layer of muscle rather than anything broader or deeper, but it required chirurgical intervention nonetheless. Dr. Venier declared both his temperature and pulse satisfactory. His second attempt at rising went far better than his first, and while he could by no means have taken a turn around the room without Enzo's assistance, by twining their arms together and leaning the whole of his weight upon him he made it to the window and back again without incident. There Enzo nestled him amidst pillows and tucked him into the bedclothes. The true comfort, however, lay in Enzo's fingers laced with his own. There Dr. Venier left them and promised not to return before evening unless they asked for her.

And then, at last, Fiore heard the full truth of the duel.

Lucrezia had kidnapped Enzo and kept him locked away in the princely palazzo until Giovanna released him. Nascimbene had coated his blade in cantarella so that he need but nick his opponent to ensure his victory—or so he'd thought. The alchemist who'd provided the poison was as dead as the impresario himself. No one else involved had committed any crime. Nascimbene's second presumably returned to the stage and his chirurgeon to his practice. Teatro Novissimo remained open; whatever successor Nascimbene had appointed hadn't yet run it into the ground, though it'd been but a few days. Fiore supposed he'd have longer to wait to see how that worked out. The show must go on and so forth.

Yet Enzo did not seem altogether satisfied with the results of the duel.

"It's all my fault," he concluded, to Fiore's bewilderment. "I should've trusted you."

"How d'you mean?"

"If I hadn't crept out while you were still sleeping, none of this would've happened."

Fiore served him a blank stare. "Then we'd both be imprisoned in the dungeon."

"Temporarily," Enzo added with haste. "And you'd have been far safer there than on the dueling field with Nascimbene."

Fiore disagreed. But that wasn't important now. "The fault lies with Nascimbene and the fool who agreed to poison his blade."

Enzo did not appear altogether convinced.

Before he could argue the point, Fiore cut in with another. "Is your sister the duke still at the princely palazzo?"

Enzo hesitated.

"Is she here?" Fiore hazarded.

Enzo admitted as much with a glum nod.

"May I speak with her?" Fiore asked.

Enzo blinked. "Why?"

"To thank her for freeing you." This particular deed had considerably warmed Fiore's opinion of her.

A queer smile tugged at the corner of Enzo's mouth. "You thank Lucrezia for imprisoning me and Giovanna for freeing me?"

"Both necessary actions, in their own way."

Enzo chuckled softly. "A brief visit shouldn't hurt, if you're feeling up to it. She'll be delighted. She's been asking after you."

When the duke arrived a quarter-hour afterward, Vittorio bounded in alongside her. The hound's excitement to see Fiore exceeded hers—but not by much.

"Oh, Fiore!" she cried as she took the chair by his bedside. "You poor thing! How do you feel?"

"Well enough, all things considered," Fiore managed, unused to anyone looking after him so forcefully.

Vittorio, meanwhile, had obeyed Enzo's gestured commands for gentle silence and limited himself to merely resting his head on the bed and nudging Fiore's hand with his nose, his tail wagging furiously.

Fiore scratched the velvety fur between the hound's ears. To Enzo, he asked, "Can he come up?"

Enzo patted the mattress down by the foot of the bed. Vittorio heaved himself onto it and curled up there, tail thrashing. His warm weight proved a welcome comfort over Fiore's legs.

The duke continued on regardless. "When Enzo told me what that beastly man had done—poison! Of all the cowardly tricks. You certainly put him in his place. Well! We're all very glad to see you awake again. Poor Enzo was frantic. But you've come through all right, and now you're not to worry about a single thing. Just let Enzo and me look after it all."

Fiore still didn't know how to reply, other than, "Thank you, your grace."

"Oh, there's no need for all that," she demurred. "Please, call me Giovanna."

Fiore stared at her.

"After all," she went on, "we're practically family."

And so saying, she took his hand and smiled.

Fiore knew not what to do with a non-romantically-entangled aristocrat who offered first-name familiarity. A glance over her shoulder at Enzo showed a faint rosy tint on his cheeks and an expression that pleaded for Fiore to humor her.

That alone sufficed to provoke a smile on Fiore's lips. To the duke, he said, "As you wish, Giovanna."

Giovanna beamed. "And Enzo tells me you may eat and drink whatever you like—"

"Save wine," Fiore cut in. "Or coffee."

Giovanna looked appropriately horrified. She cast this gaze on her brother.

"Temporarily," Enzo emphasized again. "Just until his pulse steadies."

Giovanna didn't appear altogether convinced but returned to Fiore regardless. "Well! Until then—perhaps Bettin might tempt you with some sanguinaccio dolce?"

Fiore smiled. "She might."

~

To watch Fiore begin to thrive again after languishing on the brink of death was a far better reward than Enzo dared dream of.

On the dueling field, with Fiore cradled in his arms, he'd feared the worst. Then he'd found the antidote close to hand, and Fiore had slipped into mere sleep rather than true death, and still Enzo couldn't bring himself to allow the thing with feathers to carry his heart further than a few scant moments into the unknown future. Then Fiore had awoken, and Enzo felt as if he'd awoken beside him, breathing for the first time since the duel. And that would've been enough, just to see him open his eyes again and hear his voice.

Then, slowly yet surely, Fiore began to improve.

His pulse steadied. His limbs strengthened. He ate heartily. He walked—leaning heavily on Enzo's arm, but walked all the same and smiled and talked and laughed and kissed him and demanded to be kissed in return, and all of Enzo's hopes danced in the light shining in Fiore's eyes. The wound dehiscence in his abdomen, while alarming, was not surprising, given the recent vintage of the original injury, the vigorous exercise building up to the duel and during the duel itself, and cantarella's known-if-little-dwelled-on property of dissolving scar tissue. The fact that it hadn't torn through skin or the entrails themselves was a sure sign of Fortuna's favor.

All told, Fiore had got off extraordinarily lightly. Enzo could not even begin to express his gratitude for it.

And so, after a se'en-night in which Fiore's pulse did not waver, Enzo broached the subject of Lucrezia's suggestion over dinner.

"Would you care to go to Drakehaven?" Enzo asked Fiore.

A light which Enzo had long missed ignited behind Fiore's eyes. A coy half-smile tempered it. "The self-same Drakehaven of which you are the duke?"

Enzo cleared his throat, much to Fiore's evident amusement. It'd been far too long, in Enzo's estimation, since Fiore had felt playful enough to bother teasing him. He'd gladly endure a hundredfold darts at his own expense if it earned him another smile flickering across Fiore's paled lips. For the moment, however, he still had a point to make and an invitation in need of answering. "The orchards and gardens are particularly beautiful this time of year. And the weather very fine."

Fiore's impish look became something more contemplative. "Would the chirurgeons permit it?"

"I did ask them already," Enzo admitted—and then, realizing how presumptuous this might sound, added, "I didn't want to offer you something you couldn't actually accept."

"Oh." Another smile stole over Fiore's features, this one smaller, shyer, more tentative, and yet more hopeful. "They said yes, then?"

"They did," Enzo assured him. "Fresh air is quite healthful."

Fiore laughed. A mere abbreviated breathless huff, but a laugh nonetheless, and one which sufficed to make Enzo's heart rejoice a hundredfold.

"It's three leagues by sea," Enzo explained. "And thirty miles over land afterward. If we keep a leisurely pace it oughtn't take more than three days to reach it."

"And if we don't keep a leisurely pace?"

Enzo hesitated. "One day. But I would strongly advise a leisurely pace."

"As you like," Fiore replied with a smile. "I'm eager to see it nonetheless."

~

They set out from the city not in a gondola but in a proper ship.

Fiore hadn't sailed on a proper ship since his first arrival to Halcyon so many years ago. Many of his sailors and sea-captains had invited him to do so. He'd demurred. None had offered him enough coin to tempt him from his berth.

Carlotta and Dr. Venier accompanied them, as did Giovanna. As it so happened Giovanna's lands adjoined Enzo's, and in her own words she thought she might as well journey with them to Drakehaven on her way home just in case she might prove helpful.

Fiore dashed off a note to Artemisia just prior to their departure, telling her where he was going, inviting her to come visit, and reminding her that—never fret—her last sketch of him remained hideous.

The nautical leg of the journey went by very smoothly. While Fiore had sat with his back to Halcyon on his last departure from the city, this time he had no such pride and instead stood atop the hind-castle with Enzo's arms around him to watch the wistful sight of the islands growing smaller and smaller until the lagoon's fog obscured them altogether, as if they'd faded into the aether.

The party split up when they made landfall. Giovanna went ahead with Carlotta; they could travel far faster without a convalescent in tow and make the villa ready for Enzo and Fiore's arrival. Dr. Venier would remain with her patient.

The overland leg of the journey in a four-horse carriage proved more exhausting than Fiore remembered from his previous adventure to the hunting lodge. The jolting of wheels-over-road did his fever-bruised joints no favors. He grit his teeth through it and gave thanks that at least this time he had Enzo by his side, holding his hand, walking him about when they halted to change horses or eat meals, and conveying him straight to bed when each evening they arrived at whatever inn Carlotta had arranged for them beforehand. He took in very little of the much-vaunted scenery. He supposed that would have to wait for the return trip to the city, when he hoped he might feel more himself.

The third day dawned with the promise of arriving at Enzo's villa before the sun reached its zenith. Even so, Fiore found he awoke drained. He curled up against Enzo's bulk in the carriage and didn't stir to glance out the windows until, at long last, Enzo roused him with the tidings that he could see the villa.

Fiore beheld orchards laid out in perfect ornate symmetry on either side of the road leading up to an edifice that appeared just as tall and twice as broad as Ca' Scaevola. He supposed the countryside afforded more space to expand than the confines of the city's islands.

"Two temples?" Fiore asked, staring out at the identical columnar domes at either end of the villa.

"The western one is a temple to Bellenos," Enzo explained. "The eastern one is the columbarium."

"And the trees?" Fiore added, his curiosity piqued despite his exhaustion.

The ensuing narration on the wide variety of fruits cultivated on Enzo's lands—lemons, peaches, apricots, apples, quinces—gave Fiore a welcome distraction from his pains. Further divulgences on the vineyards, the rabbit warren, and the poison garden carried them all the way up the road to the courtyard. The carriage drew around the fountain depicting a larger-than-life Bellenos in mortal guise buoyed by the spray and came to a halt at the base of the bifurcated stone stairs cascading down from the villa's front doors.

Stairs which looked insurmountable to Fiore as he staggered out of the carriage on Enzo's arm.

Enzo took both Fiore and the stairs in at a glance. He bent his mouth to Fiore's ear. "Would you mind if I carried you?"

Fiore's heart thrilled at the notion. His dignity, however, protested. "I think your arm will suffice."

It did but barely. Fiore reached the foyer in no condition to admire its beauty.

"Perhaps the baths?" Enzo suggested.

Fiore perked up. "Like at Ca' Scaevola?"

"Similar. Fed by a hot-spring."

That sounded divine. Fiore meant to say so, but all that escaped his throat was a needful groan.

Enzo gave him a sympathetic smile. "Shall we head there first?"

With an effort, Fiore found his voice. "Yes, please."

Enzo clasped his hand and led him onward.

They'd not gone three strides when Carlotta appeared before them in a doorway.

"A ship has been sighted approaching the lagoon, your grace," she proclaimed.

Fiore knew not why this mattered. Hundreds of ships approached the lagoon every day. Halcyon could hardly survive without them.

And yet, even through his weary haze, he thought Carlotta looked a hair less serene than usual.

Enzo furrowed his brow. "What ship?"

"The *Swiftsure*," Carlotta replied. "Her grace the Duke of Wolfwater is aboard."

Fiore didn't think he could've recognized the name even if he weren't exhausted by three days of travel and with anodyne coursing through his veins besides. He turned to Enzo. "Who?"

Enzo would not meet his gaze. "My mother."

~

Enzo hadn't seen his mother in almost half a decade.

Her intention—as he understood it upon her departure—was to remain at sea for the span of his university education. That had, of course, ended prematurely. In the back of his mind he'd known this intelligence would reach her. Perhaps not so quick as it'd reached all of Halcyon, but it would reach her all the same. And when it did reach her, there remained the possibility that this intelligence would induce her to end her voyage early and sail home to deal with her disappointing son.

Still, recent events had stolen his focus away from that particular concern.

Now she loomed on the horizon.

And Enzo knew not what to do.

"Enzo?"

Fiore's voice drew him out of his spiraling thoughts. He didn't bother attempting a smile; it would never fool Fiore. Instead he turned to Carlotta.

"Thank you," he told her. Then, returning to Fiore, he said, "I believe we'd set our course for the baths?"

While he couldn't do anything about his mother's imminent arrival, he could do something to alleviate Fiore's evident—if courageously silent—suffering.

Fiore cast a curious look up at him. But he nodded nonetheless.

And so Enzo half-carried him there.

Fiore remained quiet throughout their soak. It ended when he dozed off, at which point Enzo, not wanting to risk his drowning, roused him, dried him off, and this time actually carried him off upstairs to their bedchamber. Fiore was almost asleep again by the time they arrived.

The sun had only just passed its zenith. Enzo tucked Fiore into bed anyway. Three days on the road would sap anyone's strength, and Fiore had suffered more than most.

"Will she come here, d'you think?" Fiore murmured.

"Who?"

"Your mother."

A spike of adrenaline shot through Enzo's veins. Nevertheless he kept his face still and his voice low. "I can't imagine why she would."

"You're her favorite. You said so yourself."

Trust Fiore to recall even the most insignificant words that dropped from his lips. Enzo smiled despite himself. But while he might have been his mother's favorite when she embarked on her voyage, his behavior in the intervening years could hardly have kept him so. "She'll have plenty to occupy her in the city."

Fiore remained silent long enough that Enzo thought he might have drifted off again. But then his voice emerged even smaller than before. "What if she sends me away?"

All of Enzo's own fears coalesced into resolution. "She cannot. We are in our own dukedom."

"Your dukedom."

"*Our* dukedom," Enzo insisted. "You belong here as much as Antonio

495

belongs in Giovanna's realm. This is your home—if you'll have it," he added, suddenly self-conscious. Fiore had hardly seen the place yet. If he turned out not to like it, Enzo didn't want to foist it upon him. "No one has the power to remove you. Not even my mother."

If she tried, she would find her supposed-favorite child a force to be reckoned with.

Fiore fell silent. But his gaze lingered on Enzo's face, flicking down to his lips and back to his eyes.

Enzo took the hint and kissed him.

Within a few more gentle caresses, Fiore had fallen into deep slumber.

Enzo remained wretchedly awake.

For all the reassuring truths he'd told Fiore, his own mind spun on horrible conjectures. He couldn't begin to imagine what his mother would think of the man he'd become. Sent down from university for dueling only to issue another challenge when he got his bearings in the city. Whatever rumors she'd heard at sea of his behavior couldn't have proved flattering. The shadows grew long as he fixed his gaze on his sleeping beloved and his mind flew down pointless pathways. The sun drifted ever lower toward evening. Yet Fiore did not wake, so Enzo did not stir.

In a dim and distant way Enzo knew he ought to go and find Giovanna. Thank her for accompanying them on their journey and for readying the villa ahead of them. Consult with her regarding their mother's return. But he didn't want to leave Fiore alone. While a turn for the worse remained unlikely, it was nonetheless possible, particularly after the stress of a three-day voyage.

A soft pitter-patter of a knock fell on the bedchamber door.

Enzo turned, not entirely certain if he'd heard the sound or merely imagined it. He went to answer it nonetheless.

And found Giovanna on the other side.

Enzo slipped into the antechamber and shut the door behind him lest their voices wake Fiore. "I was just thinking of you."

Giovanna wore a smile. But it was the smile of someone who wished to feel like smiling rather than someone who had the genuine urge to smile. "Mother is here."

Enzo blinked. "You mean her ship has been sighted in the lagoon."

"No," said Giovanna. "I mean she's here."

Enzo stared. "In the villa."

"Yes."

"Why?"

Giovanna's smile grew wistful. "You always were her favorite."

It sounded no less absurd from his sister's lips than it had from his lover's. There had to be a more practical reason. Enzo supposed his mother's decision to divert her course would make it easier to navigate the quarantine. Rather than spending a fortnight aboard her ship on the city's docks, she could spend a fortnight ashore at her son's estate, within Halcyon's territory and thus exempt from the quarantine once she moved on to the city proper.

"She wants to see you," Giovanna said, jolting Enzo out of his feverish logical puzzling.

"Now?" Enzo blurted.

A hint of exasperation leaked into Giovanna's manner. "She hasn't seen you in almost five years."

"Yes, but—still." Enzo glanced back at the door leading into the bedchamber, beyond which Fiore now slumbered. He would probably be fine without Enzo for a few moments. The prospect gnawed at Enzo's nerves regardless. "Let me fetch Dr. Venier first."

"Oh, Carlotta may do that." Giovanna caught him by the arm.

Against all his better instincts, Enzo allowed her to draw him out of the antechamber and downstairs to the southwest withdrawing room.

Were it not for his sister, Enzo might've paused on the threshold. As matters stood she all but thrust him over it.

And there was his mother.

Her sailing uniform, black as the day she'd first donned her widow's weeds. Her dark hair drawn into a low queue with silver streaks at her temples. Her strong jaw—like his own—anchoring her round face—like Giovanna's—and her severe brows—like Lucrezia's. Her gaze swept over him in frank appraisal.

She appeared precisely as he remembered. Which made him all too aware of how he himself had changed. The scars alone must shock her.

And yet she smiled to see him.

Enzo hardly felt brave enough to return it. A ghostly echo tugged at his lips nonetheless.

The lines of wisdom in her face deepened with her evident joy. She held out her arms to him.

Three strides saw him swept up in her embrace.

And over her shoulder he beheld Lucrezia.

# CHAPTER FORTY-TWO

"How?" Enzo demanded, releasing his mother.

Lucrezia didn't even blink. "Mother's vessel was sighted by lighthouses on the lagoon's perimeter the day after you departed. Word reached me within the hour. The moment I realized her course would take her not into the city proper but to your dukedom, I made arrangements for a brief absence and set out to intercept her. I think I've done rather well despite the overland delay."

An intellect like Lucrezia's demanded careful forethought to meet and match. Instead, Enzo blurted, "Why?"

Enzo had done everything she'd asked. He'd left the city for the season and taken Fiore with him. They could create no further scandal whilst sequestered in the countryside. What more she could want from them, Enzo couldn't fathom.

Lucrezia regarded him with arched brows. "May I not visit my own mother?"

Enzo stared at her.

"But yes," Lucrezia added, turning to address the group as a whole. "There is something else. This conversation will not continue past sunset. Officially it is not occurring at all. I am not here."

Enzo expected no less. Giovanna likewise made no argument. And whatever authority the Duke of Wolfwater felt she possessed as their mother, she proved wise enough not to undermine her eldest daughter's princely purview by questioning the terms in front of her other two children.

Still, Enzo did have one question. "May I ask for what purpose you haven't gathered us here?"

Lucrezia shot him a very familiar sidelong glance reserved for younger siblings who made annoying inquiries. "I intend to bring Mother up-to-date on your adventures in her absence."

Giovanna cut in before Enzo had a chance to express his indignance. "I've already told her."

Lucrezia looked only slightly less annoyed at this.

Enzo, meanwhile, panicked.

"You've heard of the duels, then?" Lucrezia asked their mother—in almost the same instant that Enzo blurted at Giovanna, "What did you tell her?"

Giovanna looked to their mother for the answer.

Yet their mother's gaze remained fixed on Enzo. "I know of your duel against the Delfini heir. And of your withdrawal from university. And of the challenge you issued to the impresario."

Enzo knew the human heart could not literally shatter in its cage. Yet his felt just the same. From the moment Lucrezia had withdrawn him from university and through every misadventure since he'd wondered how to explain it to his mother upon her return. Even just in the past day —the hours spent fretting over what impression he would make on her after a half-decade's absence—only for her to arrive and, within minutes, he found himself robbed of the opportunity to make any impression on his own behalf at all. In the wake of this he could but stare aghast.

"Then you've heard tell of Fiore," said Lucrezia.

Enzo, jolted out of his bitter spiral at his beloved's name, cut in. "And everything he's suffered?"

"Most of it, I think," Giovanna replied. Her tone suggested she may have just begun to realize what she'd stolen from him. "All I knew of, at least. Which is what you've told me."

"What I and Lucrezia's spies have told you, you mean," Enzo spat.

Giovanna balked at this rebuke. Lucrezia didn't so much as blink.

"I'm curious to hear what you make of it," Lucrezia told their mother.

"Aren't any of you the least bit curious what I think of the matter?" Enzo demanded.

Lucrezia regarded him archly. "Your actions have made your thoughts quite plain."

Enzo seethed.

Giovanna's voice rang out above the both of them. "I will say, since Fiore's arrival, Enzo is the happiest I've seen him after university."

Lucrezia gave her the sidelong glance she used whenever she considered a matter not worth the energy of rolling her eyes. "Thank you for your contribution. On a more pertinent note—"

"No, you *will* listen!" Giovanna snapped, startling all. "You may have made the choice to withdraw him from university, but it was I who bore witness to the consequences. He wouldn't speak. He wouldn't sleep. He wouldn't eat. In daylight hours he'd lurch from room to room, a silent, miserable, ghoulish shade haunting the halls. By night he simply sat and stared. I tried everything—reading, theatre, music, sport —and nothing provoked more than resigned and perfunctory participation from him. Nothing of his life before would draw him out. Even bringing him back to the city and letting him wander under his own devices barely changed him. His routes were altogether aimless until he stumbled upon Fiore. Just a corpse wandering in search of a soul. Why do you think I fought so hard for him to return to fencing? Because if you put a sword in his hand, he would at least stand upright and *move!*"

Enzo stared at her. He well recalled how miserable he'd felt in those months, true enough. But he'd never suspected anyone else had noticed his suffering.

Their mother and Lucrezia likewise appeared astonished.

Lucrezia recovered first. Rather than address Giovanna direct, she turned to Enzo. "I'm glad to see you've revived since then. You look very well."

A wise man would've accepted this with a silent nod. Enzo instead replied, "Thanks to Fiore."

Lucrezia raised her brows. Giovanna stewed behind her.

"Fiore has had a long and storied career," said Lucrezia. "Nascimbene cannot be the only man who has wronged him. Do you intend to challenge all his worst paramours to duels?"

She could not have struck nearer to Enzo's heart if she held an actual blade in her hand. He swallowed hard. "Recent events have soured my taste for that particular approach."

"I'm delighted to hear so." Lucrezia turned to their mother. "I've encountered Signor Fiore but twice. I very much doubt if he remembers our first meeting. He was insensible for most of it."

Enzo remembered it all too well. Rescuing Fiore from the catacombs —laying his frail bloodied body out on the kitchen table for chirurgy— the frantic fear in his dark eyes when he awoke, however briefly, amidst the gore—how Enzo had pleaded with him to accept the chloroform— and how, against impossible odds, Fiore had trusted Enzo with his life.

Lucrezia's gaze flicked towards Enzo so briefly he thought he might've imagined it. To their mother, she said, "From the evidence of my own eyes and ears on that occasion, I believe Enzo's devotion to Fiore is absolute and cannot be lightly cast off."

Enzo wondered that Lucrezia had any understanding of something so heartfelt as devotion. Perhaps, he supposed, she knew it in a courtly sense, as an aspect of fealty.

"On our second meeting," Lucrezia continued, "I found him bright and well-spoken."

"Despite the poison coursing through his veins," Enzo cut in. "And the fever he'd just thrown off. And the fact that his frail health rendered him in no fit state to entertain any visitors whatsoever."

Lucrezia gave him another look he recognized from their childhood —the one she wore when she was both surprised and disappointed that he'd dared to interrupt her. "Despite all that, I appreciate that Fiore seems to place a higher value on Enzo's life than Enzo himself does."

Enzo wished she'd cease talking about him as if he weren't there.

"On the one hand," Lucrezia continued, "some of the stupider actions Enzo has taken in the past year have been for Fiore's sake. On the other hand," she added as Enzo's temper flared, "Fiore seems to have a good head on his shoulders so far as Enzo's well-being is concerned—going so far as to fight a duel to the death in his stead and, more importantly, not begrudging my efforts to keep Enzo from said duel."

Even in the midst of his stewing rage, Enzo appreciated her tact in not mentioning how Fiore formed the sole reason Enzo had challenged Nascimbene to a duel at all.

"There are additional points in Fiore's favor," Lucrezia continued. "There are no records in the city of any debts in his name. From this we may conclude that his tastes are not expensive—or at least not more expensive than he can afford. Nor does he gamble. His account at the bank is in good standing. That he keeps an account at all would seem to indicate he is more sensible with money than many of greater rank. If he imbibes to excess he must do so behind closed doors for no one has seen him disorderly in public, and—Why do you look surprised?" she said, turning to Enzo.

Enzo stared at her. "How do you know all this?"

"I asked."

"You've spoken to him but the once," Enzo protested. "I was there. You didn't ask him anything about all this. Unless—was this your private conversation, then?"

If she'd demanded to speak alone with Fiore for something so invasive yet inconsequential as this, Enzo knew not what he'd do.

"Of course I didn't ask him," Lucrezia scoffed. "My staff made enquiries throughout the city. The bank has his name down in a ledger and his funds directly beside it. It's all quite simple. What puzzles me is how this surprises you."

Enzo wondered if he and Lucrezia would ever understand each other. "I didn't know any of this."

Lucrezia blinked at him. "You never asked him how his fortunes stood?"

"No." Enzo didn't bother trying not to sound incredulous. "Are you in the habit of asking all your acquaintances how much money they have in the bank?"

"Not personally," Lucrezia replied coolly. "But if I have reason to suspect they may have ulterior motives towards my own fortune, then yes, I do make enquiries."

"Fiore has never given me reason to suspect any such thing." At last, a specific point on which Enzo could reassure her.

Yet she didn't look reassured. Her expression remained arch, with a faint air of disbelief. "Well. I may happily inform you that, despite your lack of interest in divining such things, I have it on good authority that your Fiore lives well within his means."

"I could have told you that myself," Enzo snapped.

Lucrezia proceeded as though she hadn't heard him. "To conclude—apart from his low origins, there is very little to say against him."

Enzo seethed.

"And Enzo would be far from the first duke to keep a courtesan," Lucrezia added. "Provided they both agree to live quietly—" Here she acknowledged Enzo again, however briefly, with a speaking glance. "I have no real objection to Fiore."

"I'm gratified to hear it," Enzo growled.

"With all this in mind," Lucrezia continued, turning to their mother as if Enzo hadn't spoken, "and having already heard Giovanna's thoughts on the matter, I would greatly appreciate your opinion."

Their mother raised her brows. Her gaze slid away from Lucrezia towards Enzo. "I'm very curious as to what you have to say on it."

Relief flooded Enzo's veins. At last, a chance to speak in his—and more importantly, Fiore's—defense. He opened his mouth.

"Enzo?"

Enzo's pulse quickened at the familiar yet unexpected voice behind him. He whirled toward it.

There in the doorway, pale as bone and drowning in the voluminous folds of Enzo's wrapping-gown, stood Fiore.

Whatever instinctive joy flashed through Enzo's heart at the sight of him proved short-lived as his rational mind realized the risk.

Fiore's dark eyes met his. Then they flicked to each of the three women behind Enzo. They flew wide—then rolled back. He collapsed like one whose thread of life the Fates had snipped.

Enzo leapt to catch him.

# CHAPTER FORTY-THREE

F iore had never intended to eavesdrop.

He had, however, awoken to find Enzo gone and arose to wander in search of him. He didn't have to venture far before he heard Enzo's voice—raised in strong feeling, no less. The sound led him to a chamber he'd not yet had the privilege of exploring. The door was already ajar, and Fiore ventured towards it assuming he'd find Enzo conversing with Carlotta or another member of the staff.

So to see instead not just Giovanna and an unknown lady but the prince herself—well. The shock alone would render anybody senseless.

He fell. He didn't remember landing. But he did blink himself awake again to find Enzo's face swimming into view above him.

"Fiore?" Enzo murmured urgently, smoothing his hair back from his brow with one hand whilst the other cradled Fiore's fallen body. "Can you hear me?"

He sounded as if he were underwater at first, but his speech grew clearer with every word, and so Fiore didn't consider it a lie to nod. Though nodding did make his head swim again. "Forgive me, I—"

"There's nothing to forgive," Enzo rushed to reassure him. What more he might have said, Fiore knew not, for something drew his notice behind, and he flung his head over his shoulder with a ferocious hiss. "Keep back!"

"Enzo—" one of the women began. Fiore couldn't tell which. He hadn't realized how shockingly alike Giovanna and the prince sounded. He supposed he'd never encountered them together before.

"Leave him be," Enzo snapped. He turned to Fiore again. In soft speech at sharp contrast to how he addressed his sisters, he asked, "Can you stand?"

If Enzo needed him to, then he would certainly make the attempt. But lifting his head only made the room spin again.

"It's all right," Enzo told him. "Hold on."

And with that, he stood, lifting Fiore into his arms as though he weighed no more than fog.

One of the women said something Fiore couldn't quite discern. Enzo whipped his head toward them.

"This is my house," Enzo insisted. "Therefore it is his home. He has every right to wander where'er he wishes."

Which was all very well and romantic but did nothing to allay Fiore's nerves. If Enzo's family took offense, then—"Please don't shout."

The hard lines of Enzo's knit brow and clenched jaw softened at once as he regarded Fiore. And in a voice softer still he murmured, "Forgive me."

Fiore didn't think it was his place to forgive Enzo this particular outburst.

Enzo turned to his sisters and the unknown woman. In a tone not a shout but which nonetheless brooked no argument, he declared, "We will finish this later."

And without another word nor backwards glance, Enzo strode from the room, Fiore clasped tight in his embrace.

The journey passed in a blur. Before Fiore could blink, it seemed, he found himself back abed. Enzo knelt beside him. He worked feverishly, daubing Fiore's brow with a rosewater-soaked cloth, anointing his wrists with the same as his fingertips searched for his pulse, pouring a glass of water and proffering it to his lips.

"Are you hurt anywhere?" Enzo asked, his voice hushed and urgent.

"No." Fiore felt better already. His breath came easier. His vision had cleared. He supposed lying down had helped.

"Any pain? Where? Sharp or dull?"

"The only thing wounded is my dignity," Fiore insisted.

Enzo didn't quite appear as though he believed him. "Dr. Venier ought to have a look at you all the same."

Fiore didn't have the wherewithal to fight that. His thoughts returned to the room he'd stumbled into and the people there gathered. Giovanna and Lucrezia together was certainly unexpected. And as for the other…

"The third woman," Fiore said, though he had a sinking feeling he already knew the answer. "Who is she?"

Enzo hesitated. "My mother."

Fiore ought to have known. Carlotta had announced her imminent arrival mere days ago. But he had to be sure. And now he was sure. Likewise he was absolutely certain that he'd made the worst possible impression on the most important person in Enzo's life. "Did I offend her?"

"No," Enzo said almost before Fiore had finished speaking. "Not in the least."

Fiore remained unconvinced. "Should I apologize?"

"You've nothing to apologize for."

A horrible suspicion crawled up Fiore's throat like a spider. "You don't want her to see me."

"You're not well," Enzo insisted. "She shouldn't intrude on you now."

"But even if I were well—"

"If you were well and you wished to see her, I would be delighted to introduce you. But you're not—"

"I wish to see her," Fiore declared.

Enzo stared at him. He bit his lip. "The very instant you feel more yourself, I promise, you will see her. But—"

The arrival of Dr. Venier interrupted both Enzo's speech and Fiore's spiraling thoughts. Having his pulse and temperature taken distracted him for a few annoying yet blissful moments.

"Wouldn't hurt to keep a watch on you," she told him. "But from what you've described it seems like just nerves."

Fiore could've told Enzo that before. Instead of bringing it up now, however, he asked Enzo, "What do they want? The prince and the duke and—"

"Nothing," Enzo insisted. "We were only discussing family matters."

Fiore hadn't ever considered himself part of Enzo's family. But he'd never felt like more of an outsider than now.

"It's nothing you need to worry about," Enzo continued. "I promise. Mother's just returned from the sea and Lucrezia came to see her. That's all."

"Why here?"

"Because Giovanna and I were here already. Two out of her three children, leaving only one to travel and join the rest. Mathematically it's the only sound choice."

A wise man would accept that as a perfectly reasonable and logical explanation. Fiore instead replied, "I thought I heard someone say my name."

Enzo hesitated.

A knock fell on the door.

Enzo turned toward it with undisguised impatience. "Who goes there?"

A voice both familiar and unfamiliar replied, "Your mother."

Fiore's heart leapt back into his throat.

Enzo stood.

Fiore seized his arm.

Enzo halted as if compelled.

"Please don't be angry with her," Fiore begged.

Enzo worked his jaw. "Fiore—"

"Please don't shout. Please don't make a scene. Please—"

"Fiore, I—"

*"Do not give her a reason to hate me."*

Enzo balked.

Fiore felt no less offended at his traitorous tongue. Yet it ran on. "Please."

Enzo studied his face. Then he dropt to his knees at Fiore's side and raised a hand to cup his cheek. His thumb wiped away the single boiling hot tear that had spilled from Fiore's burning eyes. In a low voice that rumbled through Fiore's own ribcage, he said, "I promise I won't lose my temper."

Despite himself, the tight knot behind Fiore's breastbone eased.

"You don't have anything to fear," Enzo continued—which Fiore knew full well wasn't true, but he wanted so badly to believe him. "I won't be gone long."

Fiore searched his gaze—then seized a lock of his hair and dragged him down for a desperate kiss.

Enzo returned it tenderly. Then he withdrew just far enough to smooth tumbled curls back from Fiore's brow.

"I won't be gone long," Enzo repeated sotto voce and waited until Fiore nodded before he stood and turned to Dr. Venier, whom Fiore had quite forgotten. "You will remain?"

"Of course, your grace," she replied.

Enzo turned to something on the floor beyond Fiore's line of sight. "Vittorio—stay. Guard."

Vittorio's tail thumped against the floorboards.

And with that, Enzo slipped out the door and was gone.

~

Against all his better instincts, Enzo left Fiore's bedside.

Dr. Venier stayed with him. Vittorio would stand guard over him. Between the two of them Fiore would remain safe and sound for the scant few minutes it would take to inform his mother that now was not the time for whatever it was she wished to discuss with him.

Still, Enzo felt as though he tore himself in twain when he shut the door on the bedchamber behind him.

Where he found his mother standing in the antechamber.

Before she could say anything, Enzo—ever mindful of Fiore a few scant yards away—jerked his chin towards the door behind her. They were less likely to be overheard if they conversed in the hall.

To his infinite relief, she took the hint and led the way out.

Only after the second door had closed upon them did she turn to him and ask, "Is he hurt?"

"No moreso than before," said Enzo.

"May I see him?"

Enzo stared at her.

His mother stood her ground. "If this man is so important to my son, I should very much like to meet him."

"And you shall," Enzo promised her. "Fiore wishes to meet you, as well." Fiore's wishes were the only reason Enzo even considered allowing her anywhere near him, but he didn't think she needed to know that just now. "At present he is far too delicate for any interview."

His mother studied him. "When do you think we might meet?"

"When he's strong enough to walk to the solarium under his own power." Not in the sickroom. Not even in the antechamber. Not anywhere near their private quarters—because this was Enzo's house, and therefore Fiore's house, and Enzo was determined to draw and hold the line he ought to have drawn and held twice-over already, when Giovanna had insisted on seeing Fiore after his kidnapping and when Lucrezia had intruded on Fiore after the duel and both times Enzo had allowed them to encroach on Fiore's peace and comfort, to trespass in what ought to have been his sanctuary. Enzo might have failed him then but he would not fail him now. He would not suffer Fiore's sanctuary to be invaded by anyone. Not even his own mother.

Who now gazed upon him with an expression he couldn't quite read. It reminded him of Lucrezia. Or rather, Lucrezia reminded him of her.

Enzo hesitated. He dared not hope. "You don't disapprove, then?"

"I like to form my own opinion," she admitted. "But from what Giovanna and Lucrezia have said, he seems an amiable fellow."

"He's far more than that," Enzo blurted.

Something like a smile flickered across her lips. "He's a lucky man to have you looking after him."

"I'm a lucky man to have him to look after," Enzo replied.

A truer smile shone on her face now. Wan and wistful, but a smile all the same.

And all at once, Enzo realized that—of course—she alone in his family could understand what torment he now suffered. She, who had secluded herself with her dying husband for the protection of their children. She, who had watched his father wither and perish in three short days, but how long those days must have seemed whilst clutching her beloved's hand and hearing him breathe his last, and herself helpless to prevent it.

"I would still like to hear—in your own words—of all that's happened whilst I've been at sea. When he is well enough to spare you," she added.

Enzo knew not what to say. The sudden and unaccountable lump in his throat precluded all speech. His eyes burned. He took in a tremulous breath.

His mother held out her arms.

Enzo seized her in a crushing embrace and buried his face in her shoulder.

He knew not how long they stood there. He remained conscious only of a comfort he'd missed more than he'd realized over the years. His breath came in shuddering gasps, but tears did not fall.

His mother broke their silence.

"When you have a moment," she said, very softly, "you might consider apologizing to Giovanna."

Enzo said nothing.

"She was only doing what she thought best," his mother continued. "She wanted to spare you from having to make long explanations whilst preoccupied with greater concerns."

Enzo relented with a sigh. "And I suppose you want me to apologize to Lucrezia as well?"

A pause ensued. "If you like."

Despite himself, a huff of laughter escaped Enzo's throat.

∽

Fiore's first words upon Enzo's return were, "What of your mother?"

Enzo balked but told him, "She's eager to meet you. For good reasons," he quickly added as a spike of panic stabbed through Fiore's chest. "Both Giovanna and Lucrezia spoke very highly of you to her."

"Did they?" Fiore said before he could temper his incredulity into something more palatable.

Enzo hesitated. "In their own way."

Fiore supposed he could believe that. If only to make his heart cease trying to batter its way out of his ribcage.

"I've told her she can't see you until you're well again," Enzo continued.

Fiore doubted a duke would have so much patience with a mere courtesan. Privately, he vowed to recover as soon as possible.

He spent the first day almost entirely supine. He took a few turns about the bedroom with Enzo and glimpsed the greater estate outside the copious windows. Enzo professed himself eager to show him more. They said not another word of his mother.

The second day Fiore spent mostly upright. He felt strong enough to sit up under his own power. Enzo walked with him arm-in-arm throughout the master suite. Not only did Enzo point out rooms that remained vacant and convenient to the bedchamber that he thought Fiore might want to claim for himself, but he also brought out architectural diagrams to show him what parts of the property he'd not yet visited.

"In case you'd prefer your sanctuary more distant from our quarters," Enzo explained as Fiore stared bewildered at the plans laid out before him.

Fiore couldn't fathom wanting to be anywhere but by Enzo's side.

"For instance, here," Enzo ran on, tapping a point on the plans to the southeast of the bedchamber where they now sat. "I've never found use for this tower, but at its peak there's a room with windows all around—sunshine at every angle all hours of the day—might it suit for a drawing studio?"

When he put it that way, Fiore could hardly say no.

On the third day Fiore walked to solarium—on Enzo's arm, but upright nonetheless. Enzo tucked him into the corner of the sofa with pillows and blankets. Vittorio slept at their feet whilst Enzo read to him. They passed a pleasant afternoon in warm sunshine.

By the fourth day Fiore felt almost himself again.

"I don't want to keep her waiting any longer," he told Enzo shortly after quaffing the first cup of coffee permitted him in four days.

"She's found plenty to occupy herself in the meantime," Enzo assured him.

"Still," said Fiore, and this, combined with a particular tilt of his head and speaking glance, sufficed.

Fiore insisted on wearing a proper suit rather than just a wrapping-gown over his nightshirt. Enzo hesitated but assisted him in dressing nonetheless.

By then the hour had arrived for coffee in the solarium with Enzo's mother.

Enzo installed Fiore on the sofa first, for which Fiore felt grateful. Far easier to appear strong—or at least, to not appear weak—if he was already settled in when Enzo's mother came in, rather than staggering in to meet her and having her watch as he required Enzo's assistance just to sit down. A maid Fiore hadn't met yet brought in the tray with coffee, brioche, and zaletti before departing in silence. He made note to ask Enzo for her name when he was in a fit state to remember things.

And then a figure loomed in the doorway.

A woman of middling age and regal bearing, garbed in a stark black gown almost devoid of decoration but wondrous in its cut and weave. Her handsome face remained an impassive mask. For a confusing moment she looked eerily familiar. Then Fiore realized—of course—that he recognized her daughters in her. Giovanna's figure. The prince's arch features. He dared not hope he might see something of Enzo in her as well.

"Mother," said Enzo, standing to greet her but keeping a hand on Fiore's shoulder lest he rise as well.

The duke's smile warmed her aspect considerably. Not so much that Fiore dared breathe in her presence, yet enough to make her seem somewhat less carved from marble than her eldest daughter. She sailed in as smooth and swift and silent as a sandolo.

Two chairs perched on either side of the sofa. She chose the one nearest Fiore. This did nothing to improve his nerves.

Enzo's hand clasp, however, helped a great deal.

"Signor Fiore, I presume?" Her voice lay in the perfect mid-point between Giovanna's warmth and the prince's command.

Fiore nodded and wished that, just once, he might meet Enzo's family on his feet.

"My daughters spoke very highly of you," she continued, much to

Fiore's confusion and alarm. "It's a pleasure to meet you at last. And to see you looking so well in your convalescence."

"Likewise, I'm sure," Fiore replied before he could think of anything better.

She smiled not unkindly. "Do you gamble?"

Enzo shot his mother a look that began appalled, became mortified, and flickered into enraged before he evidently mastered himself.

Fortunately, Fiore had a ready and honest answer. "No."

"Why not?" asked the duke.

Fiore shrugged. "I hate losing."

The duke raised her brows and sipped her coffee—a gesture which almost disguised the smile curling at the corners of her mouth. It had smoothed away by the time she set her cup down again. "What are your ambitions?"

Ambition seemed a very far-away thing. Fiore blamed the anodyne. But there remained one hope foremost in his heart. "I want to make Enzo happy."

"And what else?"

Fiore knew not what else she wanted from him. "I also like to draw."

The duke blinked.

"His drawings are beautiful," Enzo cut in.

The duke stared at her son for another moment before a low chuckle overtook her. "Then I should be gratified to see them at your leisure."

Fiore wasn't sure whether that boded well or ill.

"Your journey here must have been very tiresome," the duke continued. "All the way from the city. And as a convalescent."

"The destination is worth a great deal more trouble than I've had," Fiore replied—truthfully. What little he'd glimpsed of the villa thus far was wondrous and made all the moreso by Enzo's company. "And I traveled not even half so far as your grace to reach it. How was your voyage? Forgive me, I'm very curious about nautical matters. I've only just crossed the lagoon—I've never truly been to sea."

The duke cocked an eyebrow at this. Fiore feared he'd given offense. Perhaps she wearied of pedestrian inquiries regarding her seafaring. Or perhaps she merely didn't appreciate his efforts to turn the questions back upon her.

But then, with another enigmatic smile, she began to speak on her own adventures. The trade routes she sailed with her fleet, as it so happened, allowed her to indulge a passion for collecting specimens of marine life; not just fish, whales, and sundry creatures of the deep but also the birds that soared over them.

As she spoke, a warm weight draped across Fiore's shoulders— Enzo's arm, subtly bracing and shielding him, quite literally backing him up.

Fiore dared a glance at Enzo to see if he'd done the right thing in inducing the duke to discuss her own interests.

Enzo met his gaze with an approving and admiring smile.

~

Enzo desperately wanted his mother to like Fiore.

Not because he required her approval. Far from it. But he wanted her to appreciate Fiore as Fiore so richly deserved. And—perhaps more importantly—he was anxious for her not to offend Fiore.

So far all had gone well enough, aside from the gambling question. That had sent a spike of outrage through him. He could trace the trail of her logic; while Lucrezia had already confirmed Fiore's habits in this regard, the inquiry to Fiore direct would give him the opportunity to explain his behavior and further reveal his character to her. But understanding her reasoning did not make Enzo appreciate it.

Even so, Enzo felt tolerably certain his mother didn't dislike Fiore. If she didn't enjoy his conversation, she would not have suffered through it so long.

Enzo was not enough of a rube to actually take out his pocket watch whilst she and Fiore talked. But he did note the shadows growing across the room. Between the three of them they'd drunk all the coffee—twice-over, as the maid had returned with a fresh pot. The brioche and zaletti, however, were hardly touched. Enzo knew Fiore liked both, which led him to conclude that either Fiore didn't feel well enough to eat, or he felt too nervous to eat in front of her grace the Duke of Wolfwater.

This, combined with a subtle tightening of Fiore's smile and a slight tension felt in the shoulders beneath Enzo's arm, induced Enzo to suggest to his mother that perhaps the visit ought to draw to a natural close.

Catching her eye, slightly raising his brows, and flicking his gaze to Fiore and back again sufficed. She took the hint at once and made the appropriate excuses.

Enzo arose to show her out instead of removing Fiore, all too aware of how painful it might prove for Fiore to move just now and of how self-conscious Fiore felt at appearing weak, particularly in front of her. For these same reasons he'd brought Fiore to the solarium first—to show his mother, with decorum but nonetheless inarguably, that this was Fiore's home and she was a guest there, rather than the reverse.

This had the added benefit of allowing Enzo a moment to converse with her alone in the corridor.

"Well?" Enzo inquired sotto voce. "What do you think of him?"

A slight smile curved his mother's lips—which was more than he'd dared hope for. "I think him an amiable young man. I should like to meet him in better health. I trust you will see to that."

# CHAPTER FORTY-FOUR

The following day, Giovanna embarked for her estate with their mother in tow.

"We'll remain there for the rest of the season," Giovanna explained to Enzo. "The children will be so excited to see their grandmother."

Enzo appreciated this not just for their sake but for the very transparent unspoken reason behind Giovanna and their mother's departure; namely, unwillingness to further impose on the household of a convalescent.

"Do visit as soon as you can," Giovanna continued. "Often, if you cannot stay long. Quirina still needs to show you her swordplay. And Andrea has so many drawings awaiting Fiore's approval."

Enzo relayed the invitation to Fiore after her departure and found him not averse.

"Once you've recovered," Enzo amended.

Fiore simply smiled. "Then I must apply myself to recovery."

∼

Recovery came easier than Fiore had expected. Not that it was easy in and of itself; rather, he found recovery from an extraordinarily faint dose of cantarella and a slight tear in his abdominal muscles more straightforward than anything else he'd suffered in the past year.

And having Enzo by his side made everything serene.

For the first few days they kept each other company entirely indoors. Enzo read to him and played his lute. Fiore slept and swam and strode a little further each day. Before the se'en-night was out he could accompany Enzo on short walks into the gardens that bordered the villa. Soon he had strength enough to venture into the hedge-maze, the arboretum, and the grotto on Enzo's arm. Strength enough to bring out his zibaldone and capture every architectural quirk of the villa, every natural caprice of its gardens, and most importantly, every shy smile, every gentle gesture, every guileless glance that Enzo displayed—all of which kindled Fiore's passions.

After a fortnight of settling in and regaining his strength, Fiore found he felt well enough, at long last, to act on his desires.

So when he and Enzo retired to their bedchamber for the evening, Fiore went to his sea-chest.

An eager gleam lit up Enzo's dark gaze the moment he realized Fiore's intention.

Fiore, meanwhile, took a moment to gloat beside the open chest and drink in Enzo's hungry gaze at its treasures revealed.

"The crop?" Fiore suggested.

Enzo nodded.

"And what else?" Fiore continued. "Rope, perhaps?"

Enzo's pupils blew wide. He nodded again.

Fiore indulged in a smile. He drew out the hemp in a lingering lackadaisical gesture, basking in Enzo's fixed gaze on every slithering slip. The crop came out with a swift swish of his wrist. He shut the sea-chest and stood.

"Strip," Fiore commanded.

In a trice, Enzo bared his flesh, leaving just his garters and stockings. Fiore loved how he didn't need to be told to keep them on.

Fiore flicked crop towards the bed. "On your back."

Enzo laid himself out supine. His scarred lip caught between his teeth as he watched Fiore undress with ravenous eyes. He all-but-shivered in eagerness for whatever Fiore had planned for him.

Fiore straddled his waist. "Give me your hands."

Enzo surrendered them at once.

Fiore bound his wrists together with tender care. "Hold them above your head."

Enzo's back arched as he stretched his arms over the pillows above him.

Fiore sat back to drink in the view. Here in the villa, Enzo was master of all they surveyed.

And Fiore was master of Enzo.

A wrist-flick brought the crop's tongue to Enzo's mouth. Fiore traced the scar across his lips and trailed it further down, over the jewel in his throat pulsing with every hard swallow, down the breastbone of his heaving ribcage, following the trail of dark hair over his navel, tracing his cock-stand from root to tip, and coming down again, over the throbbing vein on its underside to the glistening petals of his cunt. He gently bore down, and Enzo's hips jerked in desperation to meet the crop's caress.

Emboldened, Fiore asked, "Do you want it inside you?"

Enzo's breath hitched. He nodded fervently.

Fiore grinned. He drew back the crop, twirled it, and brought the handle to bear against Enzo's cunt.

A shuddering gasp escaped Enzo's throat as the crop's handle slipped between his glistening petals. Fiore allowed him a moment to adjust to the sensation. Then, slowly, relentlessly, like the ceaseless roll of waves lapping the lagoon, he drew it out to the very tip and slid it back inside.

Fiore could but imagine how the braided leather felt against the rippling sheath of Enzo's cunt. From the needful moans escaping Enzo's throat and the way his hips rolled to meet every gesture of Fiore's wrist, he seemed to enjoy it well enough.

So Fiore bent his head to take his cock into his mouth.

Enzo gave a strangled cry as Fiore swallowed him down. Fiore had missed this; the taste of him, the way his cock pulsed against his tongue, how the smallest gesture on his part rippled through Enzo's whole frame and left him begging for more. All the while the crop fed his hungry cunt. Fiore knew the signs better than most. Enzo was close now—so close—another moment longer, and—

Fiore let his cock slip from his lips and withdrew the crop from his cunt.

Enzo's head fell back with a groan. His hips thrust against the air, desperately chasing the lost sensation.

Fiore sat back, propped up on one arm, and waited until Enzo had opened his eyes and met his gaze. Then he drew the crop-handle across his tongue—much to Enzo's wonder, judging by his wide eyes and his mouth agape. Fiore couldn't decide which tasted better; Enzo's cock or his cunt. Fortunate, then, he supposed, that he didn't have to choose.

"You want more, don't you?" Fiore purred.

Enzo found his voice. "Yes—please—"

Fiore twirled the crop in his fingertips. "Please what?"

"Please—fuck me—"

Words Fiore never wearied of hearing.

Fiore swept over Enzo, seizing his bound wrists in one hand—his right hand. Some men might shy from its mangled touch. Enzo leaned into its caress. His left hand, meanwhile, brought the crop to Enzo's mouth.

"Bite down," Fiore commanded.

An ecstatic and wondrous gleam shot through Enzo's dark gaze. His lips parted. Fiore slipped the crop between them lengthwise like a horse's bridle.

And Enzo, ever obedient, bit down.

The sight alone sent a pulse of pleasure through Fiore's cock. He wasted not another moment in slipping it into Enzo's cunt. The familiar sheath welcomed him into its wet, hot, tight embrace—all the way to his hilt. There he shuddered to a halt, biting his lip to master himself. Enzo wasn't the only one desperate for this. He wrapped his left hand around Enzo's cock. It pulsed in his palm, his cunt rippling in the same instant. Fiore rolled into him, and his cunt clenched him in turn. Enzo's thighs trembled around his waist.

Fiore drew himself out 'til just the tip remained. Then he slammed the full length into Enzo's ravenous cunt. Enzo arched his back beneath him, ecstatic gasps and broken moans escaping around the crop clenched in his teeth, every stroke of Fiore's cock paired with a stroke around

Enzo's own, until at last, Enzo shuddered in his grasp and spilled liquid pearls over his knuckles, whilst the same tide rippled through his cunt.

Fiore rode out Enzo's spend. Then he stilled and took hold of the crop. "Release."

Enzo unclenched his jaw.

Tenderly, Fiore withdrew the crop from his mouth. He replaced it with all the kisses he'd so dearly wished to bestow on Enzo since he'd first bit down.

"Please," Enzo begged against his lips when he broke off for breath.

Fiore bit back a smile. "Please what?"

"More," Enzo groaned. His hips rolled around Fiore's cock, still rigid inside him. "Harder."

Fiore released his hold on Enzo's wrists and settled both hands onto his waist. Enzo's arms came down to embrace his shoulders as his thighs around his hips drew him deeper in, begging for more, entangling them both. Overwhelmed with how Enzo welcomed him—wanted him—Fiore held out for but a few thrusts more before ecstasy overtook him and he poured all of himself into Enzo's willing vessel. He collapsed atop Enzo's heaving chest. Enzo's bound arms clasped him tight.

After a few moments of delicious delirium, Fiore forced himself to rise. He slipped out of Enzo's embrace—arms and cunt alike—and untied his wrists. He worked his hands between his own and reverently kissed the scarlet marks the rope had left behind. Glancing up, he found Enzo watching him with adoration.

Fiore, who felt no less, slipped into his embrace once more and was rewarded by Enzo's strong arms holding him tight.

He knew not how many minutes passed. Enough for Enzo to drift off, his chest rising and falling steady beside him.

Fiore remained awake.

Calm had come over him, but it didn't drag him down into slumber beside his Enzo just yet. He ran his hands idly through Enzo's hair and cast his eye over their bedchamber for something to occupy his mind whilst he waited for sleep to claim him. The pile of books on the nightstand might've tempted him if he'd not spent the last few months abed reading. His zibaldone proved a more promising prospect.

But even as he considered it, his gaze fell upon Enzo's lute, propped up against the nightstand from when Enzo had last serenaded him.

Fiore stared at the instrument for a long moment. Then, surrendering to impulse, he reached across the bed to retrieve it. Drawing it into his lap felt as familiar as breathing. He laid his hands across its strings experimentally. He hadn't dared to try since his hand had healed. Now, while he couldn't quite achieve the grip the conservatorio had trained into him, he nonetheless found it less impossible than he'd feared. It was different, certainly. And it required something of a contortion.

But it wasn't altogether beyond him.

～

Enzo awoke to a curious sound.

The soft strains of music echoed through the night. Enzo rolled towards them and beheld Fiore perched on the foot of the bed, limned in the foxfire lantern's mossy glow, bent over Enzo's lute in his lap.

This would've been wondrous enough, given his wounded hand, but something else had caught Enzo's notice. Another sound hovered just beneath the plucked strings. The merest whisper weaving through the melody, beautiful and ethereal, so faint Enzo thought he imagined it. But as he stared he beheld Fiore's mouth, and the movement of his lips left no further doubt.

Fiore was singing.

～

*The End.*

If you enjoyed this story, you may also like the following titles from Sebastian Nothwell.

Oak King Holly King
Tales From Blackthorn Briar
Mr Warren's Profession
Throw His Heart Over
Hold Fast
The Haunting of Heatherhurst Hall

Sebastian Nothwell writes queer romance. When he is not writing, he is counting down the minutes until he is permitted to return to writing. He is absolutely not a ghost and definitely did not die in 1895.

Milton Keynes UK
Ingram Content Group UK Ltd.
UKHW011300100124
435795UK00006B/557